*This trilogy is dedicated to Prince Kamose, one of the most obscure and misunderstood characters in Egyptian history. I hope that in some small way I have contributed to his rehabilitation.*

# THE OASIS

## Lords of the Two Lands
### Volume Two

# Pauline Gedge

VIKING

VIKING

Published by the Penguin Group
Penguin Books Canada Ltd, 10 Alcorn Avenue, Toronto, Ontario,
Canada M4V 3B2
Penguin Books Ltd, 27 Wrights Lane, London W8 5TZ, England
Penguin Putnam Inc., 375 Hudson Street, New York, New York 10014, U.S.A.
Penguin Books Australia Ltd, Ringwood, Victoria, Australia
Penguin Books (NZ) Ltd, cnr Rosedale and Airborne Roads, Albany, Auckland
1310, New Zealand

Penguin Books Ltd, Registered Offices: Harmondsworth, Middlesex, England

First published 1999
1 3 5 7 9 10 8 6 4 2

Typesetting by Laura Brady

Printed and bound in Canada on acid-free paper ∞

CANADIAN CATALOGUING IN PUBLICATION DATA

Gedge, Pauline, 1945–
    The Oasis

(Lords of the two lands; 2)

ISBN 0-670-88671-8

1. Kamose, King of Egypt – Fiction.  2. Egypt – History – To 332 B.C. – Fiction
I. Title.  II. Series: Gedge, Pauline, 1945- . Lords of the two lands; 2.

PS8563.E33027 1999    C813'.54    C99-931270-7
PR9199.3.G415027 1999

Visit Penguin Canada's website at www.penguin.ca

# Acknowledgement

HEARTFELT THANKS TO my researcher, Bernard Ramanauskas, without whose organizational skill and meticulous attention to detail these books could not have been written.

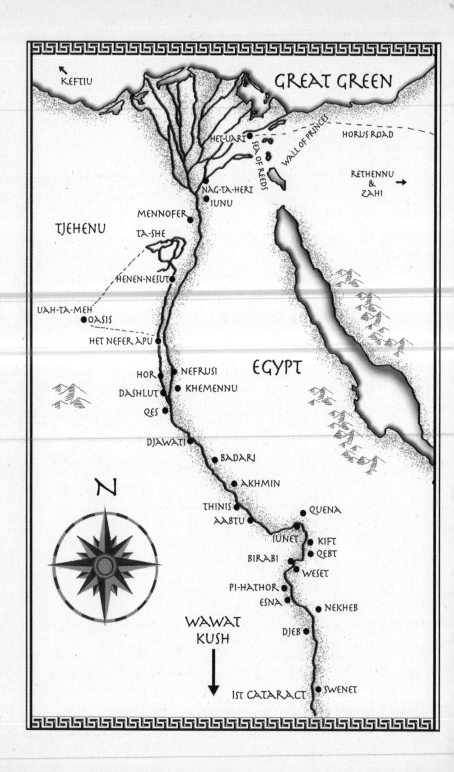

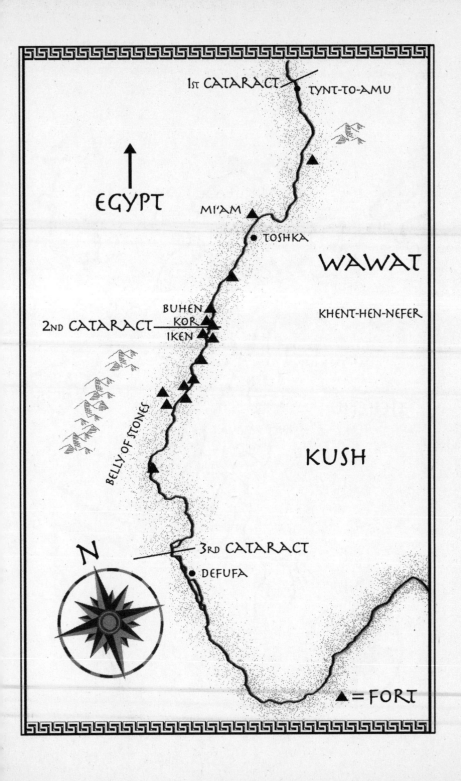

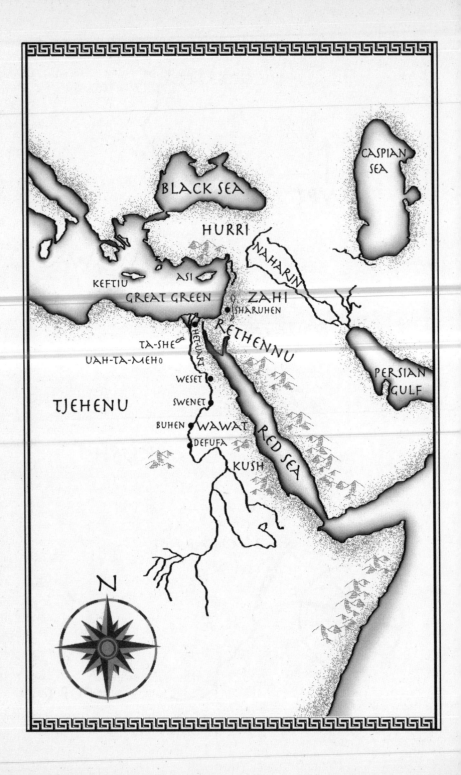

# Character List

### THE FAMILY

Kamose Tao—Prince of Weset
Aahotep—his mother
Tetisheri—his grandmother
Ahmose—his brother
Aahmes-nefertari—his sister and Ahmose's wife
Tani—his second sister
Ahmose-onkh—Aahmes-nefertari's son by her eldest brother and first
    husband, Si-Amun, now deceased
Hent-ta-Hent—daughter to Ahmose and Aahmes-nefertari

### MALE SERVANTS

Akhtoy—the Chief Steward
Kares—Steward to Aahotep
Uni—Steward to Tetisheri
Ipi—the Chief Scribe
Khabekhnet—the Chief Herald

### FEMALE SERVANTS

Isis—Tetisheri's and later Aahotep's body servant
Hetepet—Aahotep's body servant
Heket—Tani's body servant
Raa—Ahmose-onkh's nurse
Senehat—a servant

### RELATIVES AND FRIENDS

Teti—Governor of Khemennu, Inspector of Dykes and Canals, and
    husband of Aahotep's cousin

Nefer-Sakharu—Teti's wife and Aahotep's cousin
Ramose—their son and Tani's betrothed
Amunmose—High Priest of Amun
Turi—Ahmose's childhood companion

### THE PRINCES

Hor-Aha—a native of Wawat and leader of the Medjay
Intef of Qebt
Iasen of Badari
Makhu of Akhmin
Mesehti of Djawati
Ankhmahor of Aabtu
Harkhuf—his son
Sebek-nakht of Mennofer
Meketra of Nefrusi

### OTHER EGYPTIANS

Paheri—Mayor of Nekheb
Het-uy—Mayor of Pi-Hathor
Baba Abana—Guardian of Vessels
Kay Abana—his son
Setnub—Mayor of Dashlut
Sarenput—Assistant Governor of Khemennu

### THE SETIU

Awoserra Aqenenra Apepa—the King
The Hawk-in-the-Nest Apepa—his eldest son
Kypenpen—a younger son
Nehmen—the King's Chief Steward
Yku-didi—his Chief Herald
Itju—his Chief Scribe
Peremuah—the Keeper of the Royal Seal
Sakhetsa—a herald
Yamusa—a herald
Pezedkhu—a General
Kethuna—a General
Hat-Anath—a female courtier

# Foreword

A T THE END OF THE Twelfth Dynasty the Egyptians found themselves in the hands of a foreign power they knew as the Setiu, the Rulers of Uplands. We know them as the Hyksos. They had initially wandered into Egypt from the less fertile eastern country of Rethennu in order to pasture their flocks and herds in the lush Delta region. Once settled, their traders followed them, eager to profit from Egypt's wealth. Skilled in matters of administration, they gradually removed all authority from a weak Egyptian goverment until control was entirely in their hands. It was a mostly bloodless invasion achieved through the subtle means of political and economic coercion. Their kings cared little for the country as a whole, plundering it for their own ends and aping the customs of their Egyptian predecessors in a largely successful effort to lull the people into submission. By the middle of the Seventeenth Dynasty they had been securely entrenched in Egypt for just over two hundred years, ruling from their northern capital, the House of the Leg, Het-Uart.

But one man in southern Egypt claiming descent from the last true King finally rebelled. In the first volume of this trilogy, *The Hippopotamus Marsh*, Seqenenra Tao, goaded and humiliated by the Setiu ruler Apepa, chose revolt rather than obedience. With the knowledge and collusion of his wife, Aahotep, his mother, Tetisheri, and his daughters, Aahmes-nefertari and Tani, he and his sons, Si-Amun, Kamose and Ahmose planned and executed an uprising. It was an act of desperation doomed to failure. Seqenenra was attacked and partially paralyzed by Mersu, Tetisheri's trusted steward, who was also a spy in his household. Despite his injuries he marched north with his small army, only to be killed during a battle against the superior forces of the Setiu King Apepa and his brilliant young General Pezedkhu.

His eldest son, Si-Amun, should have assumed the title of Prince of Weset. But Si-Amun, his loyalty divided between his father's claim to the throne of Egypt and the Setiu King, had been duped into passing information regarding his father's insurrection to Teti of Khemmenu, his mother's relative and a favourite of Apepa, through the spy Mersu. In a fit of remorse he killed Mersu and then himself.

Believing that the hostilities were over, Apepa travelled south to Weset and passed a crushing sentence on the remaining members of the family. He took Seqenenra's younger daughter, Tani, back to Het-Uart with him as a hostage against any further trouble, but Kamose, now Prince of Weset, knew that his choice lay between a continued struggle for Egypt's freedom or the complete impoverishment and separation of the members of his family. He chose freedom.

# Chapter ONE

K AMOSE HAD HIMSELF bathed and dressed
in a mood of conscious calm, standing
in the centre of his denuded bedchamber while his body servant wound a simple white kilt about his waist and set plain
leather sandals on his feet. His tiring boxes lay open and empty,
his clothes having already been stowed aboard his boat. The
small household shrine containing an effigy of Amun now
rested in the cabin. There was a square of dust on the floor
where it had been. His lamps, his favourite cup, his ivory headrest were also waiting for him in their new places. Most of his
jewellery had gone, used to buy supplies, but Kamose took up
the pectoral he had commissioned and set it about his neck.
The cool, impersonal touch of the gold, warming slowly to the
heat of his skin, seemed to cast a cloak of divine protection
around him, and his fingers rose to clasp the god of eternity
nestling just under his breastbone in a gesture that was already
becoming habitual. "Send Uni to me," he ordered the servant
who had finished painting his eyes and was closing the cosmetic box before it too disappeared. "Give me the helmet. I
will put it on myself." The man passed him the headdress and
bowed himself out the door.

Kamose did not need a mirror to set the white leather on his brow. Its wings brushed his shoulders and its rim cut pleasingly and familiarly across his forehead. Sliding his commander's bracelets onto his wrists and buckling the belt from which hung his sword and dagger around his waist were actions he had repeated innumerable times but today, he reflected grimly, it is as though I have never done these things before. Today they are the accoutrements of war, heavy with purpose. He gave Uni a tight smile as the steward entered and bowed. "I am of course taking Akhtoy with me," he told the man. "Therefore you will be the senior steward here. It is up to you to maintain order in the house, Uni, as well as seeing to the needs of my grandmother. You are aware of the instructions I have left with her and my mother regarding the sowing throughout my nome, the watch upon the river, the regular reports that are to follow me. I require reports from you also. No," he said impatiently at the changed expression on Uni's face. "I am not asking for confidential information no steward's loyalty would allow him to divulge. Tell me of the health of the women, their spirits, how they are able to cope with the administrative problems that will inevitably arise. I will miss them," he finished quietly. "Homesickness assails me already. I want to see them through your words." Uni nodded sympathetically.

"I understand, Majesty. I will do as you desire. But if any conflict arises between a thing you wish to know and a thing my mistress wishes kept a secret, I must disobey you."

"Certainly. Tell Tetisheri of my request to you. Thank you." Uni cleared his throat.

"I pray for complete success in your endeavour to continue the fight your blessed father began, and free Egypt from the yoke of our oppressors, Divine One," he offered, "and a speedy return to the peace of this blessed place."

"May it be so." He dismissed the man, following him out into the passage and then parting from him, walking with measured steps across the deserted reception hall towards the new light of the early morning.

They were already waiting for him, standing huddled together on the brink of the watersteps in the shadow cast by the reed boat moored there, his boat, its decks alive with the frenetic activity of purposeful men whose time is short. To right and left along the Nile's banks the other craft rocked gently, their bowels churning with the same furore, the sweet, slightly rank scent of the bundled reeds from which they were constructed hanging thickly in the motionless dawn air. Beyond the family, along the river path, the conscripts were forming ranks in clouds of dust and a tumult of voices that mingled with the screeching of pack asses and the sharp shouts of harried officers. But around the solemn little group lay a pool of silence.

Kamose approached them swiftly and they watched him come, their faces grave, their eyes holding the mixture of awkwardness and gravity he himself felt. Only Ahmose-onkh grumbled fretfully in his nurse's arms, hungry and bored. With a tug at his heart Kamose saw that the women had arrayed themselves as carefully as though they had been bidden to a royal feast. Their gilded, semi-transparent linen, heavy face paint and oiled wigs should have appeared garish and unseemly at that hour, but instead the adornments served to lift them out of the dust and noise, away from the looming hulk of the boat and the still-dark water lapping so close to them, taking them out of this moment and this circumstance and placing them on some other, more mysterious plane. Kamose was unwillingly reminded of their gathering before the joint funeral of his father, Seqenenra, and his twin brother, Si-Amun, both casualties in different ways of this terrible conflict. Seqenenra, who had first been grievously injured by an assassin's vicious attack and then later slain in that intial, abortive battle, and Si-Amun, dying by his own hand after betraying his father's plans to the enemy. The same cloud of mute resignation hung over them now and seemed to enfold him as he came up to them and halted.

For a while they simply looked at him and he regarded them in turn. There was everything and yet nothing to say and whatever word might be ejected into the cool air would inevitably sound trite. Yet the emotions filling each one, love, anxiety, fear, the pain of separation, thickened the space between them and in the end drew their bodies together. Arms around each other, heads lowered, they rocked slowly as if they too were a craft of Egypt, adrift on the bosom of unknown waters. When they broke apart, Aahmes-nefertari's eyes were large with tears and her hennaed mouth quivered. "The High Priest is on his way," she said. "He sent a message. The bull that had been selected for sacrifice this morning died in the night and he did not think that you would want to choose another. It is a terrible omen." Panic knifed through Kamose and he did not fight its sudden sting.

"For Apepa, not for us," he objected firmly. "The usurper took to himself the title of Kings, Mighty Bull of Ma'at, and in slaying a bull today we would have been not only binding Amun to our aid but also making the first move in destroying the Setiu's power. However, it is dying of its own accord. There is no need to slit its throat here on the watersteps. The omen is good, Aahmes-nefertari."

"Nevertheless," Tetisheri broke in tartly, "you must make sure that the soldiers do not hear about it, Kamose. They are too simple to fathom such a sophisticated reason for what they will see as a future disaster. I will inspect the remains of this beast myself when you have gone, and order it burned so that any negative influence its death may have will not linger. Do not forget the hawk, Aahmes-nefertari, and try not to start and tremble at every sign or you will end up seeing portents in the lees of your wine and calamities in the dust whorls under your couch." The harshness of her speech was belied by the rare smile that lit her creased face.

"You all believe that I cannot be strong," the girl said, "but you err. I do not forget the hawk, Grandmother. My husband will be King one day and I shall be Queen. It is for Kamose that I start and tremble, not for Ahmose or for myself, and he knows this. I love him. How could I not then be afraid, and watch for the omens that will tell of victory or defeat? I only say aloud what you all think in your hearts." She turned to Kamose, her chin high.

"I am not a child, dear brother," she said defiantly. "Prove the omen wrong. Wield the sacred power of a King before which all omens of doom melt into nothing." He could not answer either the force of her words or the agony in her face. Bending, he kissed her and turned to his mother. Aahotep was pale under her paint.

"I am a daughter of the moon," she said in a low voice, "and my roots are in Khemennu, the city of Thoth. Teti is my kinsman. You know this, Kamose. If you are wondering what you will do there, if you are afraid of meting out justice because Teti's blood is also mine, do not worry. If the city proves recalcitrant, purge it. If Teti fights you, slaughter him. He corrupted Si-Amun on behalf of his master, Apepa, and deserves to die. But before you move against either, sacrifice to Thoth." A tiny, bitter smile twisted her features. "I do not doubt that the god of my youth waits eagerly for the cleansing your sword will bring. Yet I beg you to show mercy to Ramose if you can, for Tani's sake. He has shown himself loyal to our cause while still attempting to remain obedient to Teti. Such a division within himself must surely have brought him much grief. It was not in his power to prevent Apepa from promising our nome to his father once this family was scattered." The smile became frozen as she tried to control herself. "Word of your insurrection is bound to reach the Delta before long. What it will mean to Tani, imprisoned there as a hostage, we dare not think. But we must hope that Apepa is not fool enough to execute her and that Ramose still loves her and will try to save her if his life is spared."

"I will do everything possible to reason with Teti for your sake," Kamose replied, a lump in his throat. "Yet we both know he cannot be trusted. If I must kill him, then it will be as a last resort. As for Ramose, his testing in this matter is his own affair, but I shrink from any necessity to destroy him. His choice will be hard."

"Thank you, my son." She swung away from him, reaching for her grandson, lifting him into her embrace and holding him tightly, and Kamose felt his grandmother's grip go around his wrist. The old lady's fingers were like pincers.

"You and I understand one another very well," she rasped. "No soft words of parting will disguise the fact that you are going north to bathe this country in blood. Your arm will grow tired and your ka will sicken. Take care that it does not die. You have my blessing, Kamose Tao, King and God. I love you." Yes, he thought as her shrewd, clear gaze met his own. I am your son in spirit, Tetisheri. I share the pride and ruthlessness that stiffen your spine and keep your own blood hot in your veins. He merely nodded at her and she stepped back, satisfied.

There was a stir and then a sudden lull in the din around them as the High Priest came striding into view. The soldiers on the path gave way for him and his acolytes, bowing respectfully before closing in expectantly behind him. Amunmose was clad in his full regalia. The leopard skin of his sacerdotal office lay across his white-clad shoulder and the gold-tipped staff was in his hand. The young priests flanking him held lighted censers and the acrid odour of myrrh suddenly filled the nostrils of the family as they paid him their reverence. Ahmose, who had remained silent throughout but had stood close to his sister-wife, his white-booted feet apart and his eyes grave under the rim of his own helmet, now whispered to Kamose, "He has brought neither blood nor milk to mingle under our feet as we go."

"It is correct," Kamose whispered back. "The bull died and we must not depart with the milk of welcoming hospitality sticking to the soles of our sandals. We need no more than the protecting desire of Amun."

"Kamose, I am afraid," Ahmose muttered. "So much planning and preparing and talking and it all seemed unreal. But the time has come. Today, this morning, under the glare of the sun, we go forth to wrench Egypt from the grasp of foreigners who have occupied us for hentis and thus far I am unable to pull myself out of the dream. I should be hunting in the marshes and working up an appetite for the breaking of my fast, not dressed as a commander and surrounded by an army. Are we mad?"

"If we are, it is the madness of those who answer the call of destiny," Kamose replied under cover of the High Priest's opening prayers. "Sometimes it is not a call, Ahmose. Sometimes it is a harsh imperative that we disregard at our peril. I see us cornered in that hard place and it is no use wishing that we had been born into a safer, less turbulent age. We must justify ourselves before the gods here, now, on this day, in this month. I hate it as much as you."

"Will we be remembered as the saviours of Egypt or will we be defeated and vanish into the obscurity of future ages?" Ahmose murmured, more to himself than to his brother, and they straightened together from their obeisance as Amunmose turned to them, holding out his staff and beginning the chants of blessing and victory. On the ships, on the packed ground, the soldiers knelt quietly while in the east Ra, having freed himself from the clutches of the horizon, poured his golden light over the vast assembly and high above, a dark speck against his molten glory, a hawk balanced on the wind of his breath and watched them.

When the ceremony was over, Kamose thanked the High Priest, reminded him to petition Amun every day on behalf of the army, kissed the members of his family, and with a last look at his house lying sun-drenched and peaceful beyond the vine trellises and the palms he turned to the ramp of his ship, Ahmose behind him. But before he could ascend it, something cold was pressed against his thigh. Looking down, he met Behek's eager gaze. The dog had thrust itself past Ahmose and was waiting for permission to lope ahead onto the deck. With a pang of regret Kamose squatted, taking the great, soft head in his hands and caressing the warm ears. Since Seqenenra's death Behek had transferred all his simple affection onto Kamose, padding after him wherever he went and sleeping at the end of the passage to the men's apartments where Kamose had his quarters. Kamose had understood, and indeed had shared, the animal's loneliness, and a mutual devotion had sprung up between them. Now he met the trust in Behek's brown eyes with a gentle denial. "You cannot come, my friend," he said sadly. "You must stay here and guard the rest of the family. The confines of a boat are not for you." Kissing the dog's broad forehead, he rose and pointed to the watersteps. "Go home, Behek," he ordered, and after a moment's hesitation Behek obeyed dejectedly, his tail dragging. Kamose gained the deck, followed by his brother. His officers bowed and at his gesture Hor-Aha shouted the order to bring in the ramp and cast off. Freed from its tether the craft swung ponderously away from the watersteps. The helmsman grasped the helm in both hands. Kamose and Ahmose moved to stand in the stern, the reeds waist high before them. The other boats had already followed their lead and all were manoeuvring into the middle of the river, their prows pointed north.

Ahmose looked up and pointed, and Kamose, following his gaze, saw the strengthening morning breeze lift the flag fastened to the mast and unfurl it with a crack, revealing the colours of royal Egypt, blue and white. Startled, Kamose turned an enquiring eye on his brother. Ahmose shrugged smiling. "Neither of us gave any thought to such a minor detail," he said. "I am willing to wager that this is Grandmother's work." Kamose's eyes slid to the bank. Already the gap between the deck where he stood and the warm stone where his family huddled had grown wider, filled by the glittering heave of water. They looked so small standing there, so defenceless and vulnerable, and his heart contracted in pity for them, for himself, for the country he was about to plunge into war.

Then he saw Tetisheri step away from the others and raise a clenched fist. Sunlight glinted on her silver bracelets as they slid down her arm and the wind caught her linens and pressed them against her wiry body. The gesture exuded such defiance and arrogance that the feeling of pity fled. Raising both his own fists in response, Kamose began to laugh, and his home slid away behind him and was lost to view.

"I'm hungry," he said to Ahmose. "Let's go into the cabin and eat. It will be an easy journey to Qebt, and we will be sailing through our own nome for most of the way. Hor-Aha! Join us!" It has begun, he thought with something close to exultation. The die is cast. Pulling up the curtain and fastening it open as he entered, he flung himself down on the cushions within the cabin. Akhtoy snapped his fingers at the cook's servant waiting to tell his masters what could be offered. Ahmose was fingering the throwing stick hanging from his belt as he crossed his bare legs and lowered himself beside his brother.

"I had to bring it," he said apologetically at Kamose's surprised glance. "The opportunity for hunting may arise, you never know. But of course it will not be the same without Turi."

"No, it won't," Kamose responded. "You and Turi have fished and hunted together since you were boys. I hope you have forgiven me for sending him and his family south out of harm's way. His father's peculiar skill as a mason specializing in the design and construction of stone forts is rare these days and might be useful to me later on. Such expertise has not been in demand for many hentis, although the knowledge continued to be passed down through Turi's forebears." Ahmose nodded sagely.

"Turi's father has been quite content building watersteps," he assured Kamose. "He has no respect for the Setiu who scorn stone and build their garrison defences out of mud. They do not even have an interest in erecting stone monuments. They are very uncivilized under their veneer of grandeur."

"All the same," Kamose said grimly, "I am told that the walls of the Setiu forts are very high and as unyielding as rock. We shall see. Is there fresh bread?" he asked the patient servant. "And a little cheese? Good. Let us eat."

The flotilla put into Qebt in the early afternoon, and within minutes of its arrival Prince Intef appeared, his officials ranked behind him. Kamose answered his obeisance courteously, hiding the tide of relief that swept over him as Intef bade him come to his house for refreshments. He had been secretly worried that the Princes who had journeyed to Weset at his summons might have been wafted home again on a tide of cautious enthusiasm that would rapidly dissipate in hours of solitary reflection beside their own fishponds, but here was one governor at least who had fulfilled his lord's request.

After greeting Intef's wife and family and drinking a cup of the wine politely offered to him in the Prince's cool reception hall, Kamose sent for his Scribe of Recruits and Scribe of Assemblage and for Hor-Aha, and he, Ahmose and Intef retired to the latter's office to conduct their business. "The division on foot will not catch up to us until late tonight," he said to Intef as they settled themselves around his desk. "Once your additions are tallied, Intef, I want to take a skiff to Kift and worship Min in the temple there. It is only seven miles farther downstream and Min is, of course, a type of Amun and must receive my homage. Have you delegated your authority here? Are you ready to sail with us?" Intef inclined his head.

"As best I can, Majesty," he replied. "This nome will be in the capable hands of my assistant governor at Kift. The sowing has begun. It will be completed by the women." He shifted in his seat. "There has been considerable confusion among the conscripts I have managed to gather," he went on frankly. "It has been very difficult to try to explain to them why they must leave their homes and march against men whom they have regarded as their fellow Egyptians for a long time. Many have been stubborn and my officers have been forced to almost drag them to the river. There has been little time to train them either. You will find them an undisciplined rabble."

"I will distribute them among the men from Weset," Hor-Aha answered him, although Intef's eyes were apologetically on Kamose. "They will quickly learn both discipline and the reasons for it, if they are scattered thus." There was a small, uncomfortable silence. Intef's regard swung to the Medjay and his glance became neutral.

"They may not take well to orders from officers that do not come from the Herui nome," he remarked carefully, and Kamose spoke swiftly into the moment of veiled hostility.

"I am asking a great deal from your peasants as well as from your loyal officers, Intef," he said soothingly. "Your authority will not be usurped. Your commanders will be answerable to you and to no one else, and you will have the dispersal of your troops in battle, but under my direction. Sometimes that direction will come through the mouth of the Prince and General Hor-Aha. I ask your pardon for reminding you that neither you nor your officers, let alone your peasants, have seen any military action for many years, while this General has."

"But the chasing of Kushite tribesmen in that accursed desert land must surely be a far cry from campaigns against civilized cities," Intef retorted coldly, and Kamose sighed inwardly. I was afraid of this, he thought to himself sourly. Are we to wade through these same pettinesses with Iasen and Ankhmahor and the others before we can bully Egyptians into a unified army? Hor-Aha had folded his arms and was leaning back, his head on one side.

"Let us attempt to be honest with one another, Prince," he said calmly. "You do not like me and are loath to trust me. I am a black man and a foreigner. By what right do I command my lord's Egyptians? By what right do I bear the title recently bestowed upon me? But what you think of me is not important. Think only that in denigrating me you show distrust in your King's judgement, for he has seen fit to employ me as General and elevate me to the nobility. He has done this because I am seasoned in those desert skirmishes of which you know nothing, and I have a gift for controlling common men. I will gladly place myself under your command if you are able to demonstrate superior talents in the field and I will relinquish my own authority if my lord desires it. Until then, is it not enough that we fight in a cause that has both our hearts? Can we not work as brothers?" And that is a word Intef will find hard to swallow as he looks at Hor-Aha with his shining black skin and his sooty eyes, Kamose thought again. Yet Hor-Aha was clever to form his comments as questions. Intef must answer.

But before he could, Ahmose broke in. He had been listening

restlessly, shifting his weight on his chair and drumming his fingers noiselessly on the surface of the desk. Now he planted both feet on the floor and leaned forward. "Consider it thus, Intef," he said conversationally. "If we win through to Het-Uart, this Medjay will have performed a service for every noble in Egypt. If, the gods forbid, we lose, then you can blame him for everything because he devised the strategy for Kamose and me. Either way, the yoke of responsibility is on his shoulders. Do you really want it on yours?" This time the silence held stunned disbelief. Intef fixed Ahmose with a stony scrutiny and Kamose almost held his breath. You have gone too far, he said urgently in his mind to his brother. Are you really so simple, dear Ahmose, or do you understand better than I the uses of apparent guilelessness? Hor-Aha was relaxed, his expression unreadable.

All at once Intef burst out laughing. "You are right, Prince," he chuckled, "and I am being stiff-necked and foolish. It is a sensible decision to place the peasants of this nome together with yours, and if you or Your Majesty," here he bowed to Kamose, "had suggested it, I would have applauded such wisdom. But I would like to command them in any pitched battle Apepa may render necessary."

"Agreed." Kamose nodded. Ahmose had gone back to his absent fidgeting and Hor-Aha obviously knew better than to smile. His expression remained non-committal. "How many men have you gathered?" Kamose asked Intef.

"Between Qebt, Kift and the arouras of the nome, twenty-two hundred," Intef answered promptly. "Also I have had the granaries opened for the Scribe of Assemblage but I beg you, Majesty, to take no more than is needed. There must be an Egypt left when all this is over." At that moment Intef's steward interrupted them to announce both scribes and Kamose and Ahmose rose to leave. "I will go on now to the temple at Kift,"

Kamose said. "Hor-Aha, see to the distribution of Intef's men and give Paheri leave to requisition whatever boats are available. The more troops can sail, the faster we may move."

"That could have become a wounding confrontation," Ahmose remarked as the two men left the house and strode out into the blinding afternoon sunshine. "Perhaps it would be wise to restrict the arena of Hor-Aha's authority to the Medjay alone."

"I have no intention of jeopardizing our success in order to pander to the self-importance of a petty Prince!" Kamose snapped back. "Hor-Aha has proved himself time and again as both friend and loyal soldier to our family and thus to Egypt herself. He will remain Supreme Commander under me, Ahmose, and the nobles must get used to that."

"I think you are wrong, Kamose," his brother objected quietly. "Antagonize the nobles and you offend more than just a handful of men. You also lose the trust of the officers under them. The scene just played out will be repeated with Iasen and the others as we go north. Hor-Aha would understand if you curtailed his power, at least until Egypt is secured."

"I will not insult a friend!" Kamose said hotly. He did not know why Ahmose's words had struck a tinder of anger in him. It was not just the fear that his brother might be right, it was something else, dark and obscure. "They have sat idly in their little palaces, drinking their wine and eating the fat of their nomes, content in their anonymity, perhaps even grateful for it, while Apepa taunted our father and worked to destroy us. But Hor-Aha has risked his life for us many times while they sat by and gave thanks that they were not involved. They are fortunate that I do not censure them harshly instead of soothing them!" Ahmose took his arm and brought him to a halt.

"What is wrong with you?" he said urgently. "What has caused you to lose your good sense, Kamose? We desperately need the co-operation of the Princes and the goodwill of their men. This you know. Maintain Hor-Aha in his present position if that is your decision, that can be done with a little tact, a little graciousness on our part. But from whence comes this fume of personal acrimony?" Kamose's shoulders slumped. He squinted up into the deep azure of the sky then smiled wanly at Ahmose.

"Forgive me," he said. "Perhaps I am envious of their lack of true concern when my own need for vengeance burns in me without cease. It is all on my head. Ma'at stands or falls with my decisions and I resent such a heavy load. Let us tread the flagstones of Min's sacred precinct and I will try to leave some of my fury at the god's feet."

With their personal guards in attendance they got into a skiff and were rowed downstream to Kift. The town, larger and busier than Qebt, lay serenely dreaming at the precious hour of the afternoon rest, and the two of them completed their prayers in peace. Returning to Qebt, they found no sign yet of the marching soldiers but the docks were a confusion of dust, milling men and screeching donkeys, in the midst of which Hor-Aha gave them a distant greeting and went on dictating to his harried scribe.

Kamose and Ahmose retreated to the relative sanity of their cabin. Ahmose fell promptly asleep, sprawled on the cushions, but Kamose brooded in the close heat, his chin on his knees and his unseeing eyes fixed on his brother's unconscious form. Two and a half divisions, he thought. That's good. Aabtu is next. I wonder how many men Ankhmahor will have gathered up? He is a more formidable Prince than Intef, touchier with regard to his prerogatives but possessing a keener intellect. I believe that he will not allow any prejudice against Hor-Aha to cloud his cooler judgements.

Unlike you, a small inner voice spoke up. Did you know that

you held within you, like a coiled asp, a contempt for the blue blood of southern Egypt? How many men? he mused determinedly, forcing his mind back to the logistics of the campaign. And how soon must I begin to send scouts ahead? At Badari? Djawati? Tomorrow I will dictate messages for the women. Can I have better rations issued to the troops in the hope that food will be available all along the Nile? Has Hor-Aha given orders that every weapon here at Qebt must be gathered up? His head was beginning to ache. Leaving the cabin to Ahmose's gentle snores, he asked Akhtoy to bring him beer and he retired to the shade cast by the curving prow of the boat to await word of the remainder of his forces.

The army shuffled into Qebt two hours after sunset, the tired men casting themselves down beside the river where they were issued their food and drink. Kamose, Ahmose and Intef had just finished their own meal, seated on a deck across which shafts of soft yellow light fell from the lamps fastened to the railings and hanging from the mast, when Hor-Aha came and bowed. At Kamose's gesture he sank cross-legged onto the planking and accepted a cup of wine from Akhtoy. "They are weary and sore from the march," he said in answer to Ahmose's question. "But by morning they will be refreshed. Our Commander of Recruits is already dividing up the men of this nome and partnering them." He turned to Intef. "He is working with one of your officers, Prince. Thank you for your generosity in this matter." His attention returned to Kamose. "The Instructor of Retainers is anxious that you should permit at least two days of training for them, Majesty. What shall I tell him?" Kamose sighed.

"They must glean what knowledge they can as they march tomorrow," he replied. "If we delay at every stop, we will not reach the Delta by the time Isis cries and the Inundation could spell complete disaster. No, Hor-Aha. I am sorry. We must adhere to our original plan. The Medjay and such soldiers as have found berths on whatever boats Intef has provided will leave for Aabtu at dawn. It is another day's sailing from here to Quena and three to Àabtu. That means many more hours for those on foot." He considered. "What if we put in between Quena and Aabtu, and while I go forward to meet Ankhmahor, the soldiers can catch us up, sleep for a night, and there undergo a rudimentary instruction?"

"It is a nuisance," Intef put in. "We need rafts, Majesty, but we have none."

"We must manage as best we can," Ahmose said. "Speed is less important at the moment than the chance to organize ourselves well. Your idea is a good one, Kamose."

"The army need not be on alert until Djawati," Hor-Aha pointed out. "Although the whole of Egypt is nominally under Apepa's control, yet from Qes south he has never bothered to provide the towns with garrisons. From Djawati to Qes it is only about thirty-three miles. North after Qes is Dashlut and there I think we may meet our first real opposition. Let us relax our pace, my lords, so that the men may be somewhat prepared and we may more easily assimilate the men the other Princes will give us." Kamose nodded his assent, his thoughts drifting to Qes, that accursed place where his father's army had emerged from the cleft between the rocks only to be outflanked, outmanœuvred and decimated.

"Is there any indication that Apepa has had wind of our coming?" he asked in general. "Have any heralds been arrested on the river?" Intef shook his head.

"No. The river traffic has been light. The Delta is still celebrating the Anniversary of Apepa's Appearing and official business has come to a temporary halt. I expect us to be able to approach Khemmenu before any alarm is given." Khemmenu, Kamose thought again. Another name of anxiety. What shall I do there? What will Teti do? His mother's face resolved before his mind's eye, pallid and implacable, and he lifted his wine to his mouth and drank quickly.

They cast off at dawn, leaving a drowsy Qebt to sink below the horizon even as Ra rose above it. The soldiers lining the riverbank were shaking and folding their blankets while the army servants moved among them with the morning's rations. Intef, though given a choice by Kamose, had elected to stay with his peasants so that in the midst of the upheaval they might be reassured. He kept with him most of his officers. "I will catch up with you beyond Quena," he promised, "and by then my men will no longer need to see me. Would that we had chariots, Majesty!" Chariots, horses, more axes and swords and more boats, Kamose thought. He took his leave of the Prince amicably enough and settled back for the day of enforced but uneasy idleness on the water.

Two nights and half a day later the Nile bent west before straightening towards Aabtu and here the boats came to a halt, nudging the east bank. Kift and Quena were behind them, and Kamose surveyed the pocket of sandy isolation before him with satisfaction. Here there was an hiatus in the pattern of green fields, palm-lined canals and small villages that habitually rested the eye of the traveller and the desert rushed to fill it, tumbling in dun waves right to the water's edge. No shade gentled the vista of hot sand and burning sky. No shadow of wandering ox or human moved over it. It would be perfect for a day or two of military drilling. Kamose turned to Hor-Aha, standing silently beside him. "I will leave for Aabtu at once," he said. "I'll take the Followers with me. I should arrive there tomorrow evening. When the land troops arrive, let them rest briefly and then put them to work. Keep them away from the Medjay, Hor-Aha. The last thing we want is the mindless brawling their ignorance might incite."

"You fret needlessly, Majesty," the General commented. "A

few days of battle will serve to show them all, Egyptian and Medjay alike, that they complement one another. I think I will send the Medjay out onto the desert with their officers. They need to feel firm ground beneath their feet for a while. Will you take Prince Ahmose with you?" Kamose hesitated, then nodded, remembering his brother's surprising interjection that had swayed Intef at Qebt, and it came to him that he did not know Ahmose well at all. The young man with the sunny disposition, in love with hunting and swimming and the simple delights of family life, was maturing mysteriously. Turning from the arid view, Kamose began to give his orders.

Aabtu lay on the west bank, and as his craft tacked towards the wide watersteps of the town, Kamose was at first alarmed to see crowds of men milling about in the dusty red air of sunset. His thoughts flew north. Apepa had learned of his intent. These were Setiu soldiers and he and Ahmose would be slaughtered at once. But Ahmose said, "This is a fine sight, Kamose. It looks as though Ankhmahor has assembled an even greater force on our behalf than Intef," and Kamose came to himself with a shaky laugh.

"Thank the gods," he managed. "I was afraid . . ." Ahmose signalled and the ramp was run out.

"Not yet," he said quietly as together they walked onto the bank with the Followers moving to surround them. "We have a little time yet." A pool of silence began to spread out around them as the throng recognized the symbols lying on Kamose's chest. Many went to their knees and many more bowed respectfully. "Aabtu is not quite as provincial as Kift and Qebt," Ahmose went on. "After all, the head of Osiris is buried here and many pilgrims come to the temple and to see the holy dramas enacted every year. Khentiamentiu is worshipped here also. It is a sacred place." They had left the river behind and were striding beside the canal leading to Osiris's temple and

Ankhmahor's dwelling beside it. Beyond the protecting circle of their bodyguard the women and children of the town ran to see them and then hung back shyly. Kamose saw an official pushing his way towards them. At a word from him the Followers let the man through. He bowed profoundly.

"My lord instructed me to watch for your arrival, Majesty," he explained. "We have been in readiness for you for a week now. My lord has just returned to his house from the temple. With your permission I will tell him that you are here."

"I would like to pay my respects to Osiris before meeting the Prince," Kamose replied. "Let him know that I will see him in an hour. There will be no time in the morning," he added to Ahmose as the man bowed again and withdrew. "The sanctuary should still be open."

The High Priest received them gravely. The sanctuary was indeed open and he was about to intone the evening prayers before the god was shut away until the morning. Kamose and Ahmose joined him in the prostrations and Kamose took the few extra steps that led him to the small shrine his ancestor Mentuhotep-neb-hapet-Ra had erected to the glory of the god. With his face pressed to the stone floor, Kamose prayed less to Egypt's most revered deity than to the King whose blood ran in Kamose's own veins and who had built the old palace in the days of Weset's former eminence. His mortuary temple lay hard up against the Cliff of Gurn on the west bank opposite Weset, yet another place where the dreams of the living mingled with the unquiet promptings of the dead. Kamose begged him for his aid, and it seemed to him that there in the deepening gloom, amid the scent of wilting flowers and stale incense, his father's ka came close to him and his royal ancestor's presence hovered briefly, bringing with it a temporary peace.

The two men emerged into the last of the twilight, but the strange sadness of the hour was dissipating under the bright force of cooking fires and flaring torches. The odour of roasting meat filled the air. "I'm hungry," Ahmose said. "I hope the Prince sets a good table." The man who had approached them before had been waiting. Detaching himself from the encroaching shadows of Osiris's outer court, he bowed and bade them follow him.

It was not far to Ankhmahor's estate. The Prince's garden glowed in the light of many lamps and through their radiance Ankhmahor himself came briskly to greet them, smiling and bowing. "Majesty, Highness, I am happy to see you," he said. "The bath house is ready if you wish to refresh yourselves and my steward tells me that a meal will appear shortly. Tell me your pleasure." There was none of Intef's caution in this Prince's demeanour, and not so much deference either, Kamose reflected as he thanked Ankhmahor and asked to be ushered to the bath house. Ankhmahor's domain spoke of more wealth than that of the governor of the Herui nome and it was obvious that the proprieties would be observed. No business, however pressing, would be discussed until bellies had been filled. Such adherence to time-honoured conventions was reassuring, Kamose's thoughts ran on, as the moist, scented air of the bath house surrounded him and servants rushed to disrobe him and Ahmose. But it also spoke of pride and an awareness of high lineage. Oh must you pick apart everything? he scolded himself as he mounted the bathing slab and closed his eyes under the gush of hot water a servant was cascading over him. Accept what is, and do not see traps and dangers where there are none. The real ones are threatening enough.

Later, scrubbed, shaved and oiled, they were bowed into a reception hall redolent with the mingled odours of food, flowers and perfume, and seated before individual tables upon whose gleaming surfaces spring flowers quivered. Ankhmahor's family, his wife, two sons and three daughters, came to offer their obeisances. They were handsome people, slender and dark-eyed, their features alike under the kohl and henna, their jewellery not so much an adornment as a part of what they were, aristocrats to their core. Kamose, relaxing among his own kind, found no lack of general conversation, while Ahmose exchanged views on hunting with Ankhmahor's sons and expressed his regret that he would not be able to take advantage of Aabtu's abundance of ducks and wild game, much of which had found its way, transformed and delectable, onto the succession of dishes placed before him.

Ankhmahor is brave to put all this in jeopardy, Kamose thought. For us it is a matter of survival or destruction, but he could go on enjoying this security for ever. As though the Prince had read his musings, he looked across at Kamose and smiled. "It is perhaps an illusion, is it not, Majesty?" he said. "My Abetch nome is rich and I live well. But always there is the shadow of the future, because I refuse to leave it in the hands of a minor noble and attend Apepa at court in the Delta. When Apepa passed through Aabtu on his way to pass judgement upon your House, he stopped here for a day and a night. I entertained him well, but I do not think he was pleased." He paused to drink, his long throat working delicately against the golden filigreed necklaces he wore. "His eyes missed nothing. The abundant fertility of my arouras in granaries and storehouses, the opulence of my estate, the beauty and grace of my family, and perhaps above all, the contentment of my peasants and servants. I gave him no cause for complaint and yet I sensed distrust in him." Ankhmahor shrugged. "I think without your war I might have looked forward to the same slowly intensifying harassments that drove your father to his desperate measures."

"Apepa does not like to be reminded of his foreign roots," Kamose answered slowly. "He likes to keep the native lords of

Egypt around him in the Delta, for there they may be watched and also there they may be gradually corrupted by Setiu gods and Setiu ways." He glanced at Ankhmahor. "But outside the Delta the hereditary lords do not forget so easily that sheep herders are an abomination to gods and men, nor can they be subtly persuaded to relinquish their hold on the purity of their blood and their memories of true Ma'at. The more hospitable and respectful you were, Ankhmahor, the more you rubbed salt in the wound of his foreignness. Yet you could avert his suspicious eye by sending one of your sons north." Ankhmahor laughed and rose. At once the harpist ceased playing and the servants drew back.

"It would be like opening a wound in my own body and leaving it to fester, Majesty," he said frankly. "No son of mine will be subjected to such corruption as long as I live. My elder son, Harkhuf, will come with us and fight beside me. Now, if Your Majesty pleases, we will retire to the pool and discuss our business."

"I think I will do a little night fishing with these sons of yours, Ankhmahor," Ahmose said as he scrambled to his feet. He met Kamose's eye. You do not need me, was the message Kamose read. This Prince will not trouble us.

"Very well," Kamose said aloud. "But we must leave here at dawn, Ahmose."

"I need this," his brother said simply, and Kamose turned away and followed his host out between the pillars of the hall and into the dim garden.

Cushions had been placed on the verge of the fishpond. A flagon of wine stood ready on the grass, together with fly whisks and cloaks, all illuminated in the flickering orange glow of the single torch that fluttered in the intermittent, lazy gusts of air. Kamose lowered himself to the ground and crossed his legs, shaking his head at the cloak Ankhmahor offered him but

accepting a whisk and a brimming cup of wine. A few mosquitoes hummed nearby, the sound strident and yet somehow reassuring, a natural component of the sweet Egyptian night.
Crickets rasped out their tuneless song. An unseen frog leaped
into the pool with a plop, sending slow ripples across the dark
surface and rocking the lotus pads resting there.

Ankhmahor sank down beside Kamose with a grunt, and for
a moment he glanced across the fragrant serenity of his domain
before his gaze returned to his guest. "I do not like your General
Hor-Aha," he said at last. "I think that his imperturbability
comes from an overconfident estimation of his importance to
you and an overweening belief in his invincibility as a military
strategist. Thus he is not predictable, Majesty. Such excesses
usually have their roots in a secret fear of failure. He may make
a wrong decision and be unable to take the advice of others in
order to change it."

"Yet I am Commander-in-Chief and I am not so much in
his thrall that I would not make such a change if it became
necessary," Kamose objected. He knew that the Prince's words
did not come from the murky well of a prejudice against Hor-
Aha's foreignness and he had no wish to thank Ankhmahor
for the virtue. To do so would have implied that he had
expected less from a member of Egypt's oldest aristocracy.
"Besides, Ankhmahor, our strategy will be plotted together; I,
the Princes and the General working as one. I understand the
Princes' fear that I owe this man a debt that may weaken my
ability to lead with clearsightedness. It is true that I owe him
a great deal, but Hor-Aha knows his place. He will not step
outside it."

"I hope you are right." Ankhmahor pulled a cushion under
him and reclined, his elbow in its soft depths. He sipped his
wine. "There was some grumbling on the part of the others on
our way north from the council," he said frankly. "I grumbled

myself. But let this man prove his worth to us as he has done to you and we will gladly accept his authority in the field."

"I do not anticipate the need for any sophisticated battle plans until we reach the Delta," Kamose said. "It is a matter of sailing from town to town, overcoming any resistance, weeding out any Setiu, and making sure that the mayors and governors we leave behind are fully loyal to us. I think our first problem will come at Dashlut." Ankhmahor nodded.

"Of that I have no doubt, but it is Khemmenu that will try the mastery of the Medjay archers and the obedience of the soldiers. Teti does not love you, Majesty, in spite of his ties with your mother, and of course there is the Setiu garrison a mere nine miles downstream from the city."

"A good testing place," Kamose agreed. "Tell me, Prince, how many men have you gathered here? The number seems large."

"It is." Ankhmahor sat straight. There was a pardonable pride in his movement and in his words. "I have eighteen hundred for you from my own nome and a further eight hundred gleaned from Quena. Two hundred of them are volunteers. That warms my heart. I have also expropriated thirty craft of various kinds, everything from fishing skiffs to a raft for the transportation of granite from Swenet. It was on its way to Het-Uart, heavy with a piece of undressed stone to be used to construct a new statue of Apepa in honour of his forthcoming Jubilee, I believe, when the load shifted and the raft was damaged. Another raft was sent for from Nekheb and the damaged one left here. I have had it repaired."

"Thank you," Kamose said evenly. "I intend to take the professional soldiers from each nome and group them together as Shock Troops. I would like you to command them." Ankhmahor, his cup halfway to his mouth, paused. The cup was lowered.

"Your Majesty is generous," he said in a low voice. "I am

humbled at your trust. But what of Prince Ahmose? Should he not be their commander?"

Kamose gripped his knees. He sighed, looking up at the roof of white stars blazing in their black setting and then closing his eyes. Ahmose should not be placed with men who bear the brunt of any attack, he wanted to say. Ahmose is still in many ways a sunny youth, uncomplicated and innocent, given to flashes of surprising maturity, it is true, but not yet ready to be broken by the harshness and brutality of war. He has killed, but the killing was still somehow a part of that dream in which he lives. It is not time yet for him to awaken. "My brother will be the last surviving male of the House of Tao if I die," he said instead. "Si-Amun left a son but he is still a baby, and Egypt will need a man to continue the fight. Ahmose will not be cosseted into cowardice, but neither do I want him exposed to danger unnecessarily." He stared unseeingly at his fingers that now curled into fists. "My Grandfather Osiris Senakhtenra Glorified left a son and three grandsons. Now only two of us remain."

"Your reasoning is understandable," Ankhmahor commented. "The gamble you take is terrible, Majesty. We Princes will only lose our lands and our lives if you are defeated, but the House of Tao will lose divinity." Kamose glanced at him sharply but read only sympathy under the shadows playing across his face.

"Then let us refuse to consider any such thing." Kamose forced his fingers apart and relaxed, smiling at the man. "Tell me what weapons you have, Ankhmahor, and then I must sleep before an early start in the morning."

They talked desultorily for a further hour while the torch burned low and the wine jug was emptied. Kamose decided to leave Aabtu's men where they were, to be gathered into the rest of the army as it passed through. Ankhmahor's store of weapons, though more comprehensive than that of Intef, was still disappointing. Only the Setiu garrisons of the north would yield what Kamose needed, and only the Medjay archers could so far be relied upon to get it for him.

He thanked the Prince for his hospitality and returned to his skiff through the tranquil night. Falling into an exhausted slumber, he did not hear Ahmose come aboard in the early hours of the morning and did not wake until he felt the craft tremble under him as it left its mooring and the rowers fought to turn it against the current. "I knew Ankhmahor would be more than acquiescent," Ahmose said as, over their meal of freshly grilled fish, salad and bread, Kamose related to him the conversation by the pool. "He has courage and besides, as a scion of one of our most ancient families he can be assured of an important post when you set up your court at Weset. This fish is good, is it not?" He gestured with his knife on the point of which a piece steamed. "I thoroughly enjoyed catching it and I gave the others to Ankhmahor's younger son for the family to eat. He is intelligent, that boy. He wanted to know all about Tani and what you will do with her when you have liberated Het-Uart." He grinned happily across at Kamose's bewildered frown. "Don't worry," he went on with his mouth full. "I explained about Ramose and added that the best way to further one's ambitions in these unpredictable times was on the field of battle. Was Ankhmahor able to furnish us with more than a few blunt swords and a handful of rakes, Kamose?" I love you but I do not know what to make of you, Kamose thought fondly as his brother chattered on. Is your artlessness a studied pose to hide a swiftly building complexity beneath or are you truly guileless? Well, I would trust you with my life as I would trust no other. You are a favourite of the gods and with that I must be content.

They rejoined the army on the evening of the third day and received Hor-Aha's report as soon as they disembarked. The divisions were taking shape, but were still a long way from being the tight fighting units Hor-Aha and Intef envisioned. The peasants' response to commands was slow but increasingly willing. Pride in their cohesiveness was beginning to sprout and the grumbling had diminished. For three days they had drilled and feinted at imaginary enemies. "But no one has told them yet that as well as Setiu those enemies will include their fellow Egyptians," Hor-Aha pointed out as he squatted before Kamose under the shadow of one of the reed boats. "By the time that necessity arises, they must be trained to follow orders without thought. It is a hard lesson to learn." Kamose did not comment.

"There are messages from the Princes of Badari and Djawati," Intef said. "They have finished with the conscription and wish to know when you will arrive. Mesehti reports that the miles below Djawati are quiet. Qes and Dashlut are unaware of us so far."

"Send a runner and a skiff to Badari and Djawati," Kamose ordered Hor-Aha. "Tell them we left here in the morning, for that is what we will do. Aabtu is organized and ready."

"It is the first day of Pakhons tomorrow," Ahmose remarked, and at that they all fell silent. Shemu had begun, the hottest time of the year, when the crops ripened towards the harvest and then Egypt waited breathlessly for the Inundation. Kamose rose abruptly.

"Bring Ipi to me," he said. "I want to dictate a scroll to everyone at Weset." He was seized with an overwhelming need to speak to his women, to be strengthened by his grandmother and reassured by his mother, to touch the roots from which he had sprung. "I will be in the cabin," he added over his shoulder as he walked towards the ramp. "Pass the word to the officers that we march on in a few hours, General."

Once behind the privacy of the cabin's drapery he exhaled, a long gust of frustration and, undoing his sandals, he pulled them off and tossed them beside him. The town of Qes was well back from the river, huddled against the cliffs. Could they perhaps creep past it unnoticed during the night and so not have to expend the energy needed to deal with it before the undoubted hostility of Dashlut? Ipi knocked politely on the lintel of the cabin door and Kamose bade him enter. He did so, greeting his lord and preparing his palette and brushes to receive the dictation. Kamose, watching the scribe's calm face and routine motions, felt himself loosen.

I address my home also, he thought. The vines clinging to the trellises and heavy with dusty grapes, the pool with its scattering of crisp sycamore leaves, the warm curves of the entrance pillars against which I liked to brush my hand before walking into the dim coolness of the reception hall, all of you harken to my voice and remember me, for I love you, and surely the better part of me lingers there, my breath going forth to mingle with the rustle of warm wind in your grasses at morning and my shadow blending with your own as Ra descends behind the western cliffs. He opened his mouth and began to speak.

# Chapter TWO

THREE HOURS AFTER sunset on the eighth day, the fleet was easing quietly past the beaten track that ran west from the river to the invisible town of Qes, its ranks now swelled by a motley collection of craft that held all the professional soldiers the Princes could provide. Behind Kamose came Ankhmahor and two hundred Shock Troops on the raft that had once been used to ferry granite, and behind them the Medjay in their reed boats. The remainder of the flotilla beat ponderously after. Prince Makhu of Akhmin had gathered together four hundred conscripts and Prince Iasen of Badari a further eight hundred. Mesehti of Djawati had driven an astounding three thousand to the river so that the army now numbered almost four divisions, the bulk of which marched three days behind the ships in a slow-moving snake whose tail could not be seen by the leading officers.

In order to preserve his secrecy for as long as possible, Kamose had elected not to wait for them until the Medjay had secured Dashlut. They were in many ways a nuisance, poorly armed or weaponless, barely disciplined and unwieldy, but he knew that they would come into their own in the heavily pop-ulated Delta where arrows shot from the river would no longer be enough. By then, if the gods willed it, the richer settlements would have been plundered of their swords and bows and he could leave his boat and march at the head of men armed and ready for assault.

His conversations with the Princes of Akhmin, Badari and Djawati as he was reunited with each one had followed much the same pattern as his encounters with Intef and to a lesser degree, Ankhmahor. They had greeted him with reverence and shown their willingness to fulfil their pledges of aid and loyalty, but they clearly did not like the prospect of sharing their responsibilities with, or worse, taking orders from, a black Wawat tribesman. Each agreed to reserve judgement. Each insinuated politely and indirectly that they were risking a great deal in supporting Kamose's claim to the Horus Throne while the foreigner faced nothing more than a swift trek through the desert back to where he clearly belonged if they failed.

In vain, and with a mounting impatience that threatened to become rage, Kamose recounted Hor-Aha's faithfulness to Seqenenra, his return to Weset with Apepa's departure when he might have been wiser to stay safely in Wawat, the sealing of his commitment to the House of Tao when he accepted Egyptian citizenship and a title. "He will stay with us until he has amassed enough plunder and then he will disappear," Iasen had said bluntly, before returning to the polite to-ing and fro-ing in which he and Kamose were engaged. "Foreigners are all the same and the barbarians of Wawat are the worst of all." Ahmose had clutched his brother's arm to prevent Kamose from an outburst of frustrated temper, and Kamose had clenched his teeth and made some pacifying reply. He understood their attitude. Egypt was an occupied nation. Foreigners held the power. Setiu or from Wawat, they were all suspect in the eyes of these men.

Hor-Aha himself did not seem much affected by the slights. "I will prove them all wrong," was his response. "Give them time, Majesty. Insults cannot harm a man with confidence in himself and his own abilities." Kamose thought his imperturbability in the face of such insults unnatural but quashed the niggle of doubt regarding his General by reminding himself that Hor-Aha had been spawned by a very different culture, one where perhaps it was not wise to rise to every bait. Iasen had been entirely correct in his assessment of the barbaric temperament. The men of Wawat were primitive in their beliefs and behaviour, their tribal vendettas and the petty squabbling of their chieftains over trifles, but Hor-Aha was different. He could see farther than his fellows. He had been born with the qualities of a leader. His Medjay obeyed him without question in their dumb, pagan way, and their coolness under fire, their awesome skill with the bow, their facility for going without food or water for long periods, spoke of a way of life unknown to the peasants who sweated and stumbled towards the north under the lash of their officers' tongues and dreamed of their peaceful little hovels and the comfort of their tiny arouras.

Well, to Set with them, Kamose thought sourly as he stood beside Ahmose in the prow of his boat, the darkness of night around him and the darkness of water below. The sound of the muffled oars was an almost imperceptible creaking and the occasional whispers of captain to helmsman struck somehow sinister to Kamose's straining ears. He glanced behind him to where the stern reared black against the scarcely lighter background of the sky but could not see beyond it to Ankhmahor's raft or Hor-Aha's boat beyond that. Hor-Aha is my right hand, and they will have to accept him as such. What would they say if they knew that at the first opportunity I intend to have my Egyptian bowmen trained by the Medjay and then placed under Medjay officers as free-wheeling units to harry the enemy's flanks?

On his left the shrouded bank slid past, the end of the path along which the dwellers at Qes led their oxen and donkeys to drink showing briefly as a patch of grey. Ahmose's head also turned towards it and Kamose knew that his brother's thoughts were suddenly entangled in the past, even as his were. At the farther end of that ribbon his father's blood had gushed into the sand and changed their lives forever. Then it was gone, replaced by an irregular row of tall palms, and Ahmose sighed lightly. "All the boats should be safely past Qes within the hour," he said in a low voice. "We have seen nothing and no one, Kamose. I think we may risk some time to sleep before we approach Dashlut. How much farther is it?"

"About eight miles," Kamose responded automatically. "We can put in soon. Besides, I want to send out scouts. I must know if there are any soldiers in the town and how the houses lie. What I ought to do is order one of the ships on past Dashlut to intercept anyone trying to escape and warn Teti at Khemmenu, but as Khemmenu is only a further eight miles north it will not matter. We will be on him before he can crawl from his couch, let alone summon his Setiu from their beds." He made no attempt to disguise the tone of contempt. "Yes, we will rest, Ahmose. And beyond Dashlut I think we will rest again." He must have betrayed the secret thought behind the words, for Ahmose swung to him, peering into his face.

"Kamose, what are you going to do to Dashlut?" he asked urgently. Kamose put a finger at his lips.

"I will rouse the mayor and give him one chance to surrender. If he refuses, I shall destroy the town."

"But why?"

"For two reasons. First because it is Apepa's southernmost outpost. Qes does not really count. Apepa rules all Egypt but his fingers only reach as far as Dashlut. Like the fool he is, he has not bothered to garrison anything farther south, although Esna and Pi-Hathor are actively his and of course he treatied with Teti the Handsome of northern Kush. Thus he presumed that the rest of Egypt was safely enclosed, and with the arrogance of all the Delta dwellers he saw us as crude, provincial and impotent. If I demolish Dashlut, I send a message to the whole country that I am bent on conquest, not talk. Secondly, I must leave fear at my back. There must be no doubt regarding my intention, no temptation on the part of the administrators I leave behind to hope for aid or send for it once my forces have passed by. The Setiu defeated us without one arrow being fired against them, Ahmose," he finished emphatically. "Such complacency must never be allowed again."

"Kamose, there are certainly Setiu in Dashlut," Ahmose said anxiously. "Farmers and artisans. But there are also many Egyptians. Is it wise . . ."

"Wise?" Kamose broke in roughly. "Wise? Don't you understand that if we stop at every village to sift through the populace to determine who is Setiu and who not, who will ally themselves with us and who will say the words only and then stab us in the back, we will never reach the Delta? How will you tell friend from foe, Ahmose? Will the man who smiles be a friend and the ill-favoured a foe?"

"That is not fair," Ahmose protested quietly. "I am not as ingenuous as you suppose. But I shrink from such indiscriminate bloodshed. Why not simply station loyal troops in each town as we go?"

"Because such a strategy would bleed the army dry when every man will be needed at Het-Uart. How many professional soldiers has Apepa got in his capital? A hundred thousand? More? Certainly not less. Besides, when victory is ours, the men will want to take their earnings and go home. They will not wish to stay in northern towns and I cannot blame them. Then, if I were Apepa, if I fled and survived, I would plot a countermove. That must not happen."

"Gods, how long have you been nursing this ruthlessness?" Ahmose muttered.

"What choice do I have?" Kamose whispered. "I hate the necessity, Ahmose. Hate it! I must maim Egypt in order to save her, and I pray every day that in wounding her I do not damn myself. Dashlut must go!"

Ahmose stepped back. "You hope the mayor refuses your offer of surrender, don't you?" he said. "Oh, Kamose, I do know, I do understand. I was not able to reason it all through before. But it is horrible."

Kamose could not reply. He was suddenly cold and the hand that rose to silently grasp his pectoral was shaking. Amun, have pity on me, he begged his totem. It is horrible indeed.

They tethered the boats loosely to the western bank but no ramps were run out. At once Kamose dispatched scouts in the skiffs and then retired to the cabin, but he could not sleep. Neither could Ahmose. They lay side by side in the dimness, each knowing by the speed of the other's breath that unconsciousness was eluding them. There was nothing to say. Kamose thought of the woman of his dreams, escaping briefly into a fantasy he missed and longed for, and he had no doubt that his brother's thoughts were with Aahmes-nefertari, surely lying peacefully asleep on the couch they had shared with such joy in the house whose tranquillity they had forfeited in order to save it.

Yet in the end he must have dozed, for he came to himself at the sound of footsteps crossing the deck. Shaking Ahmose gently by the shoulder, he answered the request to enter, and Akhtoy's head appeared around the curtain, haloed in the light of the lamp he held. "The scouts have returned, Majesty," the man said. "I have ordered a meal to be brought to you."

"Good." Kamose rose, his joints cracking. His sleep had not refreshed him. He felt heavy and slow. "Let them also break their fast, Akhtoy, and while they eat I want to shave and bathe. Tell Hor-Aha to gather the Princes."

"How late is it, Akhtoy?" Ahmose asked. He too was on his feet, tousled and yawning.

"Ra will rise in about five hours, Highness," the steward replied, and placing the lamp on the floor of the cabin, he retired.

"The scouts made good time," Ahmose remarked. "Gods, I am weary! I dreamed that all my teeth were rotten and falling out one by one."

"It is a false vision of impotence, nothing more," Kamose said. "After Dashlut it will not return."

They held a hurried meeting with the General and the Princes on the shrouded bank. Night still hung thick and unrelieved around them as the scouts made the report, laying out for them the plan of the town and the details of the small garrison fronting the Nile. "There can be no more than thirty Setiu soldiers within it," Kamose was told, "and we saw no watch. Dashlut will offer little resistance."

"Very well." Kamose turned to Ankhmahor. "I will not need Shock Troops yet," he said. "Therefore I ask you to fall back and shadow my boat to the east. Hor-Aha, take my western flank with the Medjay craft close around you and have the Followers board my boat at once. Let us go."

He stood in the prow with Ahmose, the royal bodyguard crowding stiffly around and behind them, as Ra moved ponderously and invisibly towards his birth and the miles slipped away, taking with them the last shreds of his fatigue. To his left, the oars of Hor-Aha's boat made rhythmic grey smudges on the dark surface of the water. To his right, he could faintly hear the slap of the current against Ankhmahor's craft, and to his rear he could sense the comforting presence of the remainder of the Medjay, their bows unslung, the black pebbles of their eyes

questing the darkness before them. Mutely he began his morning prayers, and by the time Dashlut slid into view, limned in
the fleeting softness of a pearly dawn, he was ready.

His ramp and the ramps of his flanking boats were run out
and a contingent of Medjay had their arrows trained on the
unsuspecting garrison before anyone in the town was aware of
their presence. But they did not have long to wait. Two young
women appeared, empty water jugs on their heads, chattering
to each other as they made their way towards the river. They
halted, dumbfounded, as the morning shadow of the three great
hulks bristling with armed men fell across them, and the sound
of one of the water jugs smashing on the ground echoed clearly
in the limpid air. One of them screamed. Both of them turned
and ran shrieking into a narrow lane between the squat mud
houses and impassively Kamose watched them go. "No one is to
disembark and no arrow is to be loosed until I give the word,"
he called to Hor-Aha. "Stand to arms."

Dashlut was stirring in the wake of the girls' loud panic.
Anxious faces began to appear, sleepy, puzzled, wary, and a
whispering crowd began to gather, well away from the silent
men on the decks. A few children straggled closer, staring up at
them in wonder until sharp words from the women sent them
scurrying back. Kamose waited.

At last the throng parted and Kamose felt his brother tense
beside him. The mayor of Dashlut was approaching, the confidence of his stride belied by the expression of alarm on his
face. He was accompanied by two distinctly apprehensive
officials. They came to a halt near the foot of Kamose's ramp
and stood for a moment irresolute. Kamose continued to wait.
The mayor inhaled visibly. "I am Setnub, mayor of Dashlut," he
called. "Who are you and what is this force? Do you come from
the Delta?"

"You are addressing King Kamose the First, Beloved of Amun,"

Kamose's herald called back. "Prostrate yourselves." A sigh of mirth passed through the listening crowd and the mayor smiled.

"I believe I am honoured to be speaking to the Prince of Weset," he said, bowing. "Forgive me, but is the King not on his throne in Het-Uart? What passes here?" Kamose stepped forward and looked down.

"He will not be on the throne much longer," he said smoothly. "I am reclaiming my birthright, Setnub, Mayor of Dashlut, and I demand the surrender of this town in the name of Amun." One of the men beside Setnub began to laugh and an answering chorus broke out behind him. The townspeople swayed.

"Highness, you are in the Mahtech nome," the mayor responded promptly. "The governor of this nome is Teti of Khemmenu and his overlord is His Majesty Awoserra Apepa Living-for-Ever. What you are asking makes no sense."

"He has fallen under the special protection of the gods," the other official murmured, and Kamose heard him.

"No, I am not insane," he rebuked the man. "I have five hundred bowmen present and four divisions of foot soldiers marching towards Dashlut to give weight to the clarity of my sanity. Setnub, I ask you once again, will you surrender Dashlut or take the consequences?" The mayor flushed angrily.

"You are a Prince, Highness, and I am nothing but an administrator," he said. "I cannot assume such a responsibility. You must either go home to Weset or sail on and put your request to our governor." The combination of condescension and bluster in his voice caused a wave of muttered indignation among the Followers, but Kamose was unperturbed.

"These are harrowing times, Setnub," he replied evenly. "A man may be compelled to assume many decisions beyond the scope of his authority or ability. This is such a moment. Surrender or be destroyed." The mayor glanced towards the garrison which had disgorged a group of men who were clutching various weapons and looking about with a confusion that was rapidly becoming vigilance.

"Surrender?" the mayor shouted. "You have indeed lost your wits! I would be the laughing stock of every town administrator in Egypt! I would lose my position and perhaps even my freedom!"

"Would you rather lose your freedom or your life?" Kamose said quietly. The mayor whitened.

"Ridiculous," he spluttered. "Remember Qes, Prince Kamose, and go home!"

He does not understand, Kamose thought. He sees but does not see my soldiers. They do not belong to the reality of Dashlut on a warm and sunny morning, therefore they do not exist. Deliberately he held out a hand and the captain of the Followers laid an arrow on his palm. "Kamose . . ." Ahmose whispered but Kamose ignored him. Calmly he fitted the arrow to his bow, lifted the weapon, adjusted his stance, and sighted past his gloved hand to the centre of the mayor's heaving chest. In the name of Amun and for the glory of Ma'at, he breathed and released the arrow, watching it plough deep into the man's breast, seeing his eyes open wide in shock and disbelief before the body slumped to the ground.

"Now, Hor-Aha!" Kamose shouted. "But no women or children!"

He was answered by a triumphant roar from the throats of the Medjay. At the General's signal the air was suddenly thick with missiles and the townspeople unfroze. They had seen their mayor go down in a stunned surprise that lasted until Kamose's voice rang out. Now they scattered, screaming in terror, snatching up their children and fighting to escape. Kamose noted with satisfaction that the Medjay's first volley had been directed at the garrison whose soldiers, to their credit, were trying to take cover and shoot back. But their arrows sank harmlessly into the reed sides of the boats or soared overhead to pierce the Nile, so great was their surprise, and soon they too turned and ran. Kamose nodded across at Hor-Aha who raised an arm and barked a command. The men began to swarm from the boats, some leaving their bows and drawing their axes, some fanning out to encircle the town. After that first mighty upsurge of sound they had fallen silent, a tide of black death moving swiftly and with a chilling efficiency through Dashlut while its inhabitants shrieked and wailed.

Kamose watched. For a while the dusty expanse between the river and the collection of houses was deserted but for the sprawled bodies of the mayor and his hapless companions, while out of sight, in the narrow alleys, behind the mud walls, beyond the town where the fields spread out, the slaughter went on. But before long it was as though the houses, the palms, and the boats themselves formed the outer limits of some strange theatre. The space between began to fill with children who ran to and fro in a mad parody of play before cowering against the walls or kneeling, sobbing, with their faces hidden in the dirt as though by shutting out the hysterical clamour around them they could make it go away. Women emerged from the early shadows, some dazedly pacing, some running uselessly from one group of children to another, some wailing as they staggered about laden with objects they had snatched up instinctively from their homes and clutched to themselves as though the familiar touch of pots and linens could defend them.

One woman came stumbling to the foot of Kamose's ramp and stood looking up at him, tears running down her cheeks, her bare arms glistening red with blood that was obviously not her own. Grasping the neck of her coarse shift in both hands, she struggled to tear it, her breath coming in great gasps. "Why?" she screamed. "Why, why?"

Ahmose groaned.

"I cannot bear this," he muttered. "I will sit in the cabin until it is over." He turned away. The Followers around Kamose stood silent and the woman too eventually closed her mouth. Shaking a soiled and trembling fist she wandered to the nearest tree and flung herself down, curling in on herself and crying. Kamose crooked a finger at the captain of his bodyguard.

"Tell General Hor-Aha to have the bodies collected here and burned," he ordered. "I want a great plume of smoke to go up. I want the stench to sting Apepa's nostrils even as the sound of my father's hippopotamuses offended his ears." He did not trust himself to speak again. The man saluted and strode towards the ramp and Kamose entered the cabin. Ahmose was sitting on one of the camp stools, his arms folded and his shoulders hunched.

"The garrison would have been mostly Setiu," he said. "Though I don't suppose they think of themselves as foreigners any more. The townsmen . . ."

Kamose flinched. "Not now, Ahmose! Please!" Turning his back on his brother, he sank to the floor, a sudden tide of anguish breaking over him, and felt the tears come.

All afternoon the dead were dragged to the edge of the river, and when no more were to be found, Kamose sent Akhtoy and his servants to herd the women and children into the houses. Then he commanded the fire to be lit and the boats readied for departure. At sunset word came to him from his divisions still marching steadily north, and he decided to wait for them four miles on, halfway between the ruin of Dashlut and the challenge of Khemmenu. Akhtoy, having discharged the distasteful duty Kamose had imposed on him, came back on board to see to his master's evening meal, but neither Kamose nor Ahmose wanted to eat. They sat together on the deck with a flagon of wine between them as Dashlut slid away from view, the greasy black smoke from the burning bodies coiling upward in a thick column to stain the peacefully darkening sky.

They tied up a little over an hour later and Kamose fell into a sodden slumber, from which he woke with a start to hear the watch changing on the bank. The night was quiet. No wind was stirring and the river reflected placidly the white clarity of the stars as Kamose left the cabin. At once his body servant rose from his mat but Kamose gestured him down, going softly to the ramp and descending it quickly. He answered the guard's salute and gaining the narrow track that ran beside the water he turned left, instinctively veering away from the faint but still identifiable whiff of kindled flesh, and when the boats with their sleeping cargo were out of sight he waded into the Nile.

The water was cold, making him gasp, but he plunged beneath the surface, pulling towards the bottom and then presently letting himself drift slowly upward until he lay spreadeagled, face down and rocking on his own small swell. When his lungs began to beg for air, he stood, reaching back into the murky depths and bringing up handfuls of sand. Vigorously, almost savagely, he abraded himself, not for a physical cleansing but in an effort to peel the agony of Dashlut from his ka. When his skin was raw and tingling, he regained the bank and, sheltered by some bushes, he stretched out his arms and began to pray. Dashlut is only the first, he said to himself, to his god, and already my ka cries out its danger and its pain. Harden my heart, Great Amun, against the things that I must do so that Egypt may be purified. Let me never forget my father's sacrifice and let it not be wasted. Forgive me the murder of the innocent, for I dare not try to distinguish the innocent from the tainted for fear of the night that would engulf my country if I should fail.

He did not know how long he stayed there, but dawn was a hint of definition in the shrubs around him and a quick puff of breeze, soon over, touched him as he walked back to the boat. The Medjay were stirring, talking in low voices to one another, and on the bank the first tentative flames of the cooking fires were springing up. Akhtoy met him as he stepped onto the deck. "There is a scroll for you from Weset, Majesty," the steward said. "Will you eat before you read it?" Kamose nodded. "Also a scout is waiting to see you."

"Let him come."

Ahmose greeted him soberly as he entered the cabin and he replied in kind, waiting while his body servant brought hot water and fresh linen. He admitted the scout and heard the news while he was being dressed. Survivors from Dashlut had been spotted during the night making their way north on the edge of the fields, and in another day the army would be here. Kamose thanked him, and when he had gone he turned to Ahmose. "Teti will hear of the sack of Dashlut before noon today," he said. "That is very good. I hope he trembles in his jewelled sandals."

"He will send at once to Apepa," Ahmose remarked. "That is both good and bad. Fear will spread through the towns along the river but Apepa will be forewarned." Kamose glanced at his sombre face.

"How is it with you, Ahmose?" he queried gently. "How did you sleep?" Ahmose smiled grimly.

"I am nauseated and ashamed," he said. "But I know that what you told me before is true. We cannot discern friend from foe. I am resigned, Kamose. Yet we will find the way of expiation hard when the time for atonement comes."

"I know." They stared at one another in a moment of mutual understanding. Kamose's body servant lifted the royal pectoral and stood waiting. Kamose took it from him, but instead of setting it about his neck, he laid it on the table. "Not today," he said. "You can go." The man bowed himself out and Ahmose held up the scroll.

"It is from Grandmother," he commented. "It is her seal. I received one from Aahmes-nefertari and I have read it already. They all seem so far away, Kamose. Well." He sighed. "I will eat on the deck this morning. Join me when you wish."

Kamose broke the seal and unrolled the scroll. Tetisheri's scribe had a unique hand. The hieroglyphs were tiny and the words tightly crammed together but surprisingly easy to read. Kamose lowered himself onto the edge of his cot as his grandmother's voice came back to him, loving and yet crisply acerbic. "To His Majesty King Kamose Tao, greetings. I send you the prayers and adoration of your family, dear Kamose, together with our heartfelt concern for your welfare. I went to inspect the entrails of the bull that died, as I promised you I would, and I found the letter 'A' clearly picked out in the fat deposits on its heart. After much deliberation on my part and many prayers to Amun from his High Priest we have decided that the weight of the letter, representing as it does the Great God himself and also the usurper, was too much for the bull to bear. Amun warred with Apepa and the heart gave out. We are all well here. The crops grow apace. My vigilance on the river has brought forth no fruit, so I must presume that Pi-Hathor has chosen to lie quiet for the time being. I have also posted sentries on the edge of the desert. When word reaches us that you have taken Khemmenu, I will call in my soldiers to the perimeter of the estate and rely on scouts for information from the south. Last night I dreamed of your grandfather Osiris Senakhtenra Glorified. 'I miss you, Tetisheri,' he said to me, taking my hand in the way he used to. 'But you cannot join me yet.' When I woke, I made a sacrifice for him, but I was glad my time has not come. I will not die until Egypt is free. See to it,

Kamose." Her name and titles followed, scrawled in her own hand, and Kamose let the scroll roll shut with a rueful smile. I am seeing to it, Grandmother, he answered her in his mind, but I do not think that I will be the one to drive the Setiu from the Nile. "A" also stands for Ahmose.

He had the scroll delivered to Ipi and joined his brother on the deck. His appetite had returned and he ate and drank his fill, feeling the heat of the sun sink into his bones and affirm his own hold on life. Then he sent for Hor-Aha and heard the General's report. No Medjay had been wounded in the battle that was in reality nothing more than a massacre. All weapons stored in the garrison had been removed for distribution among the peasant soldiers due to arrive soon. There was no sickness among the archers, but they did not like to eat so much fish. Kamose laughed at that and as he did so the burden of Dashlut lifted a little. "Fish," Ahmose said hopefully. "I think I will do some fishing this afternoon. I might as well, Kamose. There are no preparations to make for our push to Khemmenu and the scouts are keeping us informed of the progress of the army."

"It will be here early tomorrow, Highness," Hor-Aha assured him.

Ahmose took two soldiers and a skiff and disappeared into the tall, cool reed beds that filled many of the small bays the flow of the water created. Kamose had warned him not to stray too far from the boats, feeling his seniority as he did so, but Ahmose had merely grinned, shot his brother an oblique look, and sauntered off, his throwing stick in one hand and his rod trailing from the other. It is no use worrying about him, Kamose had thought, watching him go. Somehow the gods protect him and I envy him their especial attention. Would that we could change places, he and I!

The afternoon passed uneventfully enough. Kamose debated whether or not to call in his officers but decided that he would council with all of them, including the Princes, in the morning. He drank a little beer, played a board game with Akhtoy, and spent a rather sad hour reminiscing about his father with Hor-Aha. He walked the zone of safety he had ordered established on the west bank beyond the boats and spoke briefly to the sentries, and on his way back to the river he noticed several tiny groups of women and children begging furtively from the Medjay who had gone ashore to dice with each other or simply lie in the cool grass under the trees. He was momentarily annoyed. Dashlut had not been robbed of its stores. Nor had its crops been destroyed. The women had plenty of food both for today and next year but perhaps, he mused as he ran up the ramp of his boat, they beg not so much for food as for a small acknowledgement of what the archers took away from them. What I took away from them, he corrected himself. Bread and the green shoots of new barley are no compensation at all for the lonely nights and empty days that lie ahead for them.

Ahmose did not return until just before sunset. Kamose was beginning to worry about him when his skiff was spotted tacking swiftly from the east bank. Soon he was bounding exuberantly up the ramp, calling for beer and gracing his brother with a wide smile. He lowered himself onto the stool beside Kamose, and taking the wet linen his servant had immediately offered, he mopped his face. "Did you catch many fish?" Kamose enquired, his concern turning to relief. Ahmose looked at him blankly for a moment, then his expression cleared and became sheepish.

"Fish? No, they were not biting, Kamose, so I decided to have a look at Khemmenu instead."

"You did what?" Relief became anger. "How stupid can you be? Supposing you had been recognized and captured, Ahmose? The town is surely on the alert! We have scouts to shoulder that danger!" Ahmose tossed the cloth into the basin the servant held out and took a long swallow from his beer cup.

"Well, no one saw me," he said obstinately. "Really, Kamose, do you take me for a fool? I approached it when every sensible inhabitant was snoring away the afternoon heat. Shemu has begun and it will get hotter. The scouts make good reports, but I wanted to see for myself whether or not Khemmenu had changed since I was there last and if any preparations had been made following the warning the Dashlut survivors have certainly given by now." Kamose did not want to ask him what he had seen. Furiously he wanted to punish his brother for his escapade by refusing to betray any interest at all, but with a great effort he swallowed his ire.

"Please, Ahmose, do not do such a thing again," he managed. "What did you see?"

"Khemmenu has not changed at all," Ahmose replied promptly. "It is still very beautiful. The palms are the biggest in Egypt and cluster together more thickly than anywhere else. Is it the soil do you think, Kamose? The dates are forming nicely." His gaze slid sideways to his brother and he laughed. "Forgive me," he went on. "Sometimes I feel compelled to exaggerate the very traits in myself that you find the most alarming. Or endearing." He drained the beer and set the cup beside him on the deck. "The roofs of the buildings are crowded, mostly with women and a few soldiers, all looking south," he told Kamose. "Word of our coming has definitely reached them. There are even men standing on the walls of Thoth's temple. Many soldiers fill the paths and groves between the river and the town. I think that the story of Dashlut's downfall has grown in the telling."

"It will not matter," Kamose said slowly. "Our army has grown also, and if we cannot defeat Teti's Setiu forces, we should not even be here."

"Agreed." Ahmose sighed. "There was a bevy of ducks just

out of range of my throwing stick," he said wistfully. "They were too close to the town's watersteps for safety so I had to leave them alone." He yawned. "The sun has made me sleepy," he added. "I think I will sleep now before it is time to eat." As he rose, he met Kamose's eyes. "It is all right, Kamose, really it is," he said quietly. "I do not need you for a bodyguard. I have plenty of my own."

Night fell at last, but Kamose, lying on his cot and listening to the regular challenges as the sentries changed and the hours wore away, did not want to sleep. He thought of Khemmenu as he remembered it, the dense fig trees everywhere, the bright whiteness of the painted houses glimpsed through the smooth trunks of many palms, the glory of Thoth's mighty temple where Teti's wife fulfilled her obligations as one of the god's servants. He had shared in the feasting at Teti's sumptuous house, its blue-tiled lake and sycamore groves overshadowed by that other temple, the one Teti's father had built to Set in order to curry favour with the King. He thought of his brother Si-Amun, subtly corrupted amid those trellised grapevines and sun-drenched lawns, and of Ramose, whom he might or might not have to kill. Finally, before unconsciousness claimed him, his mind turned to Tani. Was she still safe? Did she still yearn for Ramose or had the strength of her emotion been nothing more than a puppy love now turned to indifference? Kamose hoped so. He wished he knew.

The army arrived in a cloud of dust and commotion two hours after dawn and Kamose called his council at once. He held it on the bank, for his cabin was too cramped to accommodate them all. They had marched through Dashlut not long before and the faces turned to him as he rose to address them were solemn. "Dashlut was a warning to Apepa and a promise of retribution to the north," he told them. "I do not regret what I did there. I would do it again. But Khemmenu will not

be such an easy massacre. Its population is larger and the proportion of soldiers stationed there much higher. They have
been alerted. They are waiting for us. But they only know
about the infantry by rumour. They will be too confident. I
intend to approach the town from the river with the Medjay
and attempt to parley with Teti. The soldiers there must be put
to the sword, of course, even if Teti surrenders, but I hope to
spare the inhabitants."

"And what of Teti himself?" The sharp question came from
Prince Intef of Qebt. Kamose had not missed his restlessness or
the wary glances he had been giving an imperturbable Hor-
Aha. He is still not resigned to my policies, Kamose thought
with exasperation. He will have to be carefully watched. "Teti
is your kinsman," the Prince was saying. "Moreover, he is a
nobleman. Surely you will not harm him!" The atmosphere
around the table immediately changed at his words. All heads
lifted and turned to Kamose. I know what you are thinking,
Kamose said to them silently. If I can murder a nobleman, then
none of you are immune. Good. Ponder your own insecurity. It
will help to keep you all loyal to me.

"Teti will be executed," he said deliberately. "He is completely committed to Apepa. He seduced my brother Si-
Amun into betraying my father and took an active although
indirect part in the cowardly attack on Seqenenra. These
deceits are unworthy of any nobleman, let alone any honest
peasant, and Teti is an erpa-ha. But if you still have doubts
about his culpability, consider the fact that he was promised
possession of my nomes and my estate once my family had
been separated and scattered. He is indeed my kinsman, but it
is a connection of which I am ashamed." Without looking
from one to the other, he swiftly gauged their responses. Intef
sighed and placed his hands on the table. Makhu and Iasen
appeared to be pondering. Their frowns matched. But Prince

Ankhmahor was nodding, and a faint smile came and went on Mesehti's mouth.

"It is just," Ankhmahor agreed. "We are risking everything we have. The cost of sparing Teti is too high."

"Of course you would have no qualms, Ankhmahor," Iasen objected. "You have been given the honour of commanding the Braves of the King. Why would you jeopardize a position of such trust by arguing against your lord?"

"That is exactly the sort of crooked reasoning that appealed to the baser side of Teti's nature," Mesehti snapped back. "If Ankhmahor commands, it is because our lord has recognized his ability to do so. A little humility is a welcome ingredient in the character of a noble, Iasen. Let us not become mired in this issue, although we agree that it is a painful one."

"I welcome dissent, Iasen," Kamose cut in. "I would not have my nobles and officers hide their thoughts from me for fear of some petty penalty. Yet all ultimate decisions are mine, and I have decided that for the sake of our security as we move north and for the sake of Ma'at, Teti will die for his treason. Does anyone wish to voice a formal dissent?" No one spoke. After a moment in which Kamose saw their faces go blank, he sat down and signalled Akhtoy to have the waiting servants pour wine and offer the sweetmeats they held. "Very well," he continued. "I will now hear reports from each of you on the state of the peasants under you, and I will take your suggestions regarding the dispersal of expertise within the divisions. Dashlut yielded a few more weapons and they must go to those men who have shown a talent for using them."

"There are many chariots and horses in Khemmenu," Ahmose interposed. "We must capture all of them we can. We have no charioteers but we can train some as we go. Ask your officers to keep their ears and eyes open for that particular aptitude in the ranks."

"Charioteers should be officers," Makhu muttered, and Kamose clenched his fists under cover of the table's edge.

"Then we will promote those men who show such promise," he said coolly. "Let us move on to other things."

When the council was over and the Princes had retired to their tents or boats, Kamose took his brother and Hor-Aha and, walking as far away from the din of the army as possible, they stripped and swam for a while. Then they lay in the sun beside the water. "What will you really do at Khemmenu?" Ahmose asked him. "Do you intend to spare the civilians, as you told the Princes you would?"

"I was wondering the same thing," Hor-Aha said. He had loosened his braids and was running his fingers through the waves of his long black hair. "It is a dangerous idea, Majesty. Why decimate Dashlut and spare Khemmenu, a town full of Setiu? Traders, artisans, wealthy merchants, by far the bulk of the town's population is foreign and the remainder have mixed with them happily for many years, taking on the colour of their thoughts and their modes of worship. Khemmenu is as diseased as Het-Uart."

Kamose studied his General. No emotion played across those even, dark features. Water from his thick hair ran down his brawny arm to spatter in the sand between his parted thighs. His brows were drawn together in a frown, but Kamose was sure that the grimace had more to do with Hor-Aha's thoughts than any feeling for the people he wished to see killed.

"I shrink from such a slaughter because of Dashlut," he replied. "It was not easy to do what I did there and another butchery at Khemmenu would be doubly horrible." Hor-Aha shot him a keen glance.

"So my King has had enough already?" he said.

"I do not like your tone, General," Ahmose interposed. "It may be that in Wawat the life of a tribesman is worth no more than an animal but we are not barbarians in Egypt." Hor-Aha eyed him with composure.

"Forgive me my words, Highness," he said evenly. "I meant no offence. But the Setiu are barbarians. They are not people. Only the members of my tribe in Wawat and those born within the borders of my adopted country are people." Ahmose looked nonplussed but Kamose smiled. He knew of the quaint belief held by most primitive tribes that nothing human existed outside the bloodlines of their own communities. But is such a conviction so far removed from the Egyptian suspicion of everyone outside our borders? he mused. Ma'at is our treasure. It belongs nowhere else. Egypt is the blessed land, uniquely favoured by the gods. Once every citizen believed this fervently, but that certainty has dissolved, been diluted in the Setiu's attempt to corrupt our gods and pervert our way of life. Hor-Aha is right. Egypt must be restored to its former purity. Yet his mind filled with the vision of the woman who had stood at the foot of the ramp and screamed up at him. Would she have understood his answer to her agonized question?

"Dashlut shook my nerve," he said to his brother. "But Hor-Aha sees clearly, Ahmose. Why one town and not another? Khemmenu must be razed."

"The Princes will not like it," Ahmose responded.

"The Princes want to go to war soldier to soldier as our ancestors did," Kamose said. "That is the honourable way. But such a philosophy can only be held if one's enemy is as scrupulous as oneself. We do not yet fight a war. At Het-Uart we may, but until then we are disposing of the rats infesting our granaries." Hor-Aha had begun to plait his hair again. He was smiling and nodding at Kamose's words and in that moment Ahmose realized that he did not like the General at all.

In the afternoon Kamose sat under a tree, with Ipi folded beside him, and dictated a letter to his family at Weset, telling them of the events at Dashlut and wishing them well. He was tempted to issue orders to them regarding the care of the estate and the watch on the river but he desisted. They were entirely capable of making those decisions themselves. As he spoke, he watched the barge and the boats swing slowly across the river to the east bank and return, only to repeat the exercise, for Khemmenu had been built to the east and all twenty thousand men had to be ferried from one bank to the other.

They were still embarking and disembarking when targets were set up on the west bank and he and Ahmose spent several hours with the Princes, practising their archery. There was much laughter and good-natured scoffing. Ankhmahor and Ahmose proved themselves the best shots until several of the Medjay officers who had been watching with barely concealed impatience were invited to join in. Their calm skill easily defeated the Egyptians who conceded with good grace, but Kamose privately wondered if allowing the tribesmen to compete had been a good idea. On the one hand the Princes might now see why they were playing a major role in his plans. On the other their jealousy might intensify. Still, it was better to be jealous than dead. Kamose gave the Medjay archers a cow taken from Dashlut to roast, and an extra issue of beer.

In the morning the whole host prepared to move on. Kamose was not yet ready to take to the land. He had placed four of the Princes in charge of the four infantry divisions under Hor-Aha, making it clear that his orders would go to the General first and then to them, but Ankhmahor sailed behind Kamose with the Braves of the King. The Medjay, grumbling at the time they still had to spend on the accursed river, manned the boats and the barge.

Only a little more than four miles lay between Kamose and Khemmenu, and he was tense as the flotilla left its mooring and began to beat its way upstream. He had called in the scouts. For the time being they could tell him nothing new. Khemmenu was waiting. There would be no surprise. He called for a camp chair and with Ahmose beside him, he sat on the deck beneath the huge bundles of reeds that composed the prow. The marching army had already fallen back, its slower progress marked by a smudge of dust against the sky. Kamose found himself missing the comfort of Hor-Aha's presence at his back. Surrounded by his Medjay bodyguard, Hor-Aha now walked with the Princes. His orders were to hold back the foot soldiers until the archers had done their work and then to fall upon the town. There was nothing to say. The two young men sat in silence as the riverbank slid past and Ra mirrored their progress, gaining power as he rolled upward through the heavens.

Their first sight of Khemmenu was a sudden lifting of the horizon to the east where the famous palms reared high, delineating the fields and marking the shady streets of the town. At Kamose's curt order, the boats began to tack towards them and the archers scrambled onto the roofs of the cabins and lined the decks, bows unslung. At the same time, they were spotted. Shouts rang out, not the voices of panic but the measured tones of purpose, and Kamose saw men appear from the trees and the reeds and grasses lining the Nile and congregate quickly between the wide stone watersteps and the palm-choked houses. "This will be easy," Ahmose commented. "Look at them, Kamose. Hardly a bowman among them, and they cannot get at us with their swords or spears." It was true. The bank bristled with a forest of spears whose tips caught the sunlight and flashed ominously but impotently, and the clatter of drawn swords, equally useless, came clearly to the two of them across the water. Kamose grunted.

"How many are there, do you think? Two hundred? Three? At least their officers have not thought to bring out the chariots. Perhaps they do not know about our infantry. Word from

Dashlut was probably garbled. The Medjay will deal with most of them, and if Hor-Aha engages the rest before they can organize the stables, we will have beaten them by sunset."

In a few more minutes, they had come within hailing distance and Kamose gave the order to heave to. The water churned suddenly as the oarsmen brought the boat to a standstill and Kamose rose with Ahmose and went to the side. Kamose gestured at his herald. "Bring me Teti," he said. The herald cleared his throat and his call went echoing against the stiffly swaying palm trees.

"King Kamose the Mighty Bull of Ma'at, Beloved of Amun, desires to parley with the Governor Teti of Khemmenu," he announced. "Let Teti appear." There was a flurry among the men by the watersteps and then a long pause. Finally someone shouldered his way to the forefront, putting a hand up to shield his eyes and staring out at the three boats crowded with archers.

"I am Sarenput, the governor's right hand," he called back. "The governor is not here. When word reached him of your cruel massacre at Dashlut, Prince, he left at once for Nefrusi to confer with Prince Meketra who commands the garrison there."

"Then I will speak with his son Ramose." Sarenput did not reply for a moment. When he did, it was with hesitation.

"The noble Ramose accompanied his father," he said. Kamose laughed.

"So Teti gathered up his family and ran away like the coward he is," he mocked. "Leaving you, Sarenput, to defend Khemmenu. But it cannot be defended. Go back and warn all your women and children to stay within their houses if they wish to live." Relief washed over him. I will not have to kill Teti today, he thought. That necessity has been postponed, thank the gods. He saw Sarenput's gaze traverse the boats with their lethal cargo. The soldiers on the bank were surveying them also, their stance unsure. Then as if some silent signal had passed between them, they turned, weapons still in their hands, and made a rush for the safety of the walls. Kamose raised a hand. At once a hail of arrows from the boats descended on them. Many fell and the rest crouched low, running with their shields above their heads. Again the Medjay fired. Sarenput's figure could be made out, dodging the fallen and falling bodies, making for the shelter of the town.

"I do not think that these soldiers drill very often," Ahmose remarked. "Listen to them yell!"

"They could not have imagined an attack from the Nile," Kamose replied tersely. "We will not pursue the survivors, Ahmose. Not yet. The army will be here at any moment." He was interrupted by a cry from Ankhmahor, and turning he saw the spiral of dust that heralded Hor-Aha's approach. Grimly he watched it spread until the vanguard could be seen, trudging four abreast and bearing down on Khemmenu relentlessly. He had no orders to give. Hor-Aha knew what to do. Now we will see how eager the Princes are to do as a black man will tell them, he thought.

In a few moments the rhythmic thudding of the marchers' feet could be heard, an ominous undercurrent to the sporadic shouts of the officers, and the sudden silence of a cornered animal descended on Khemmenu. The women had vanished from the walls. The roof of Thoth's temple lay naked and shimmering in the sun and Kamose, gazing at it anxiously, remembered all at once that his mother had told him to sacrifice to the god before he attempted to take the town. Now it was too late. The infantry was approaching the walls, spreading out, drawing weapons, and that unnatural silence broke in the roar of impending slaughter. Kamose turned to the soldier behind him. "The Medjay are to sail at once for Nefrusi," he said. "They are to surround the fort, all five thousand of them, and then wait.

See that their officers feed and rest them, but they must remain alert. No one is to escape their net. Remind their commander that there is water to the west of Nefrusi as well as the Nile to the east and it must be watched. That is all." The man saluted and left.

"That lesser branch of the river runs all the way from Dash-lut to Ta-she," Ahmose pointed out. "Nefrusi is rightly called 'Between-the-Banks.' If I were Teti I would bundle my family onto a barge and sail north as fast as possible, avoiding the Nile itself. He may have gone by now, Kamose."

"He may," Kamose nodded. "We know he is a coward. But I think he will pause long enough to assess his chances of a stand at the fort. He is not stupid. If he flees, leaving the defence of Nefrusi to Meketra, and Meketra somehow defeats us, his cred-ibility is destroyed and he will have lost Apepa's patronage. He believes that his means of escape is secure, therefore he can take some time to play the hero."

"What do we know of Nefrusi?" Ahmose asked. "Or of Meketra himself, for that matter? What manner of man is he?"

Kamose shrugged. "I have never been farther north than Khemmenu," he replied. "The scouts tell me that the fort is large and walled, that it lies closer to the main branch of the Nile than to the lesser tributary, and that the gates to the west and the east are wide enough to permit the passage of chari-ots. They estimate the force within at about fifteen hundred men. Teti will feel safe there for a while. As for Meketra..." Kamose hesitated. "He was once the Prince of Khemmenu and now commands at Nefrusi. That is all we know of him. I have done all I can for now, Ahmose. The Medjay will cover the four miles between us and the fort very quickly and by the middle of this afternoon they will be deploying around it. No matter how many Setiu troops huddle inside, they cannot stand for long against us. What worries me is the possibility of a siege, however short. We must not waste time and food on such a paltry undertaking, yet Nefrusi must not be left intact behind us."

His voice had been rising and his last words were almost shouted over the din assaulting them from across the water. A plume of black smoke was coiling into the air from a fire some-where close to the temple, and even as they swung to watch it, they saw the dry leaves of a palm tree burst into orange flames. The strident sounds of panic and violent death beyond the walls fused into an invisible tumult that thundered in their ears and pounded almost physically against their hearts.

By sunset it was over, and the riverbank teemed with soldiers bent on tending small wounds, slaking their thirst, and stowing what booty they had gleaned into their leather satchels. Many of them had plunged into the river to wash off the filth of engagement and were sending showers of sun-fired droplets high into the air as though the blood that had mired their bodies now infused the water. Officers moved among them restoring order, their shouts cheerful, but a darker stream wove between the relieved men. The women and children of Khem-menu were emerging to stand numbly staring at the activity around them. Kamose, who had remained on his feet as the hours went by, noted that in spite of the confusion around them, they were not jostled or taunted. The soldiers were ignor-ing them, and Kamose had the distinct impression that it was respect, not indifference, that was prompting the averted eyes and wide circles around the women's vicinity.

At last Hor-Aha appeared, surrounded by his junior officers. Kamose saw him pause, confer briefly with them, then step into the skiff awaiting him. Before long he was bowing before the brothers, bringing with him the stench of burning and the rank, coppery odour of fresh blood. "There is little left, Majesty," he said in answer to Kamose's curt query. "Most of the males are dead, as you ordered. The fires could not have been avoided, unfortunately. We found the stables, but they were empty and the chariots gone. To Nefrusi, I presume. I have detailed men for the burning of the bodies but it will take a long time. Khemmenu was not Dashlut." He drew a brawny wrist across his cheek, leaving a smear of mud, and Kamose, chilled, did not miss the General's use of the past tense. Khemmenu was.

"Let the surviving male citizens see to the bodies," he said. "We must move on. I have sent the Medjay to Nefrusi. How did you fare with the Princes, Hor-Aha?" The man smiled wearily.

"I gave them no time to debate my orders and afterwards there would have been no point," he said dryly. "They are seeing to the needs of their men."

"Good. Go and see to your own needs, then have the infantry mustered and ferried to the west bank. They must not eat or sleep within sight of what remains of Khemmenu. We do not want to give them time to brood over what has been done, therefore march them out of sight of the town. I intend to sail downstream and tie up close to Nefrusi for the night. Give the army no more than five hours' rest, then bring them. You are dismissed." When the General had left, Kamose took his brother's arm. "I want to pray," he said. "Come with me, Ahmose."

"Pray?" Ahmose repeated. "Where? In the temple? Are you mad?"

"I forgot the promise I made to Aahotep," Kamose said in a low voice. "I need this god's indulgence. I have all but razed his city and I must explain to him why. We will take Ankhmahor and a contingent of Braves. We will be quite safe."

"From spears and daggers, perhaps, but not from the accusing gaze of women and priests," Ahmose retorted gloomily. "I am tired and hungry and sick, Kamose." But he followed Kamose across the deck and descended with him to the skiff that carried them the short distance to the shore.

The sun had already set behind the western hills, but the last of its light washed softly against Khemmenu's white walls and cast a fleeting, kindly glow upon the noisy groups of soldiers pushing to board the barges, the bodies strewn haphazardly in the sand, the knots of women still huddled aimlessly together. Kamose and Ahmose, surrounded by the Braves of the King, approached the gate on a wave of silence as they were recognized and reverenced. Then the babble broke out behind them again and they passed through into the wreck of the city.

Except for the men engaged in dragging bodies to the riverbank, the streets were deserted. No evening candles glowed in the deepening shadows of gaping doorways that had vomited the contents of the rooms beyond onto the packed mud of the thoroughfares. Pots, stained linen, crude ornaments, cooking utensils, wooden toys, everything rifled and then rejected by the soldiers had been flung out. Here and there, the dimness was pierced by garish flames that carried with them the choking smell of burning flesh or blackening wood. Dark pools underfoot that Ahmose took to be donkey urine turned glossy crimson in the intermittent, leaping light and with an exclamation of disgust he veered, only to find himself inches from the wall of a house streaked with the same repulsive substance. Occasionally cries or half-articulated laments came echoing from the increasing darkness and Ahmose was fervently glad of the bodyguard before and behind him.

To Kamose's great relief, the avenue leading to the temple seemed untouched, lined as it was with graceful date palms whose fronds trembled in the night breeze. No soldier had dared to desecrate the precincts. As if by unspoken agreement, he and Ahmose walked faster, passing under Thoth's pylon and entering the wide outer court almost at a run; then they halted abruptly. The vast, pillared space was full of people. Women and children squatted against the walls or sat crowded together with their arms around one another as though for comfort. A few men lay sprawled on blankets, their moaning a pathetic harmony to the quiet sobbing melody of many of the women. Priests were moving from group to group, carrying lamps and food, and Kamose saw at least one physician kneeling beside an ungainly form, his dishes of herbs and pots of unguents beside his busy hands.

Kamose let out a long breath. "There are lamps still burning in the inner court," he said quietly. "Ankhmahor, stand with your men under the pylon until we return."

With his hand on his brother's shoulder, he began to cross the court, and as he did so heads began to turn in their direction, the faces indistinct in the fitful light. There was no mistaking the growing hostility in the air. "Murderers, blasphemers," someone called, but the words were timbreless, almost thoughtful, and the taunt was not taken up by others. Kamose gritted his teeth and tightened his hold on Ahmose's shoulder.

The sound of chanting came floating towards them, gaining in strength as they went. "The priests are singing the evening hymn," Ahmose whispered. "Soon the shrine will be closed." Kamose did not reply. The feeling of peace that had engulfed him as he stepped over Thoth's threshold had fled, leaving him cold and apprehensive. It is too late, he thought with dismay. Thoth will not be appeased. I should have remembered. Why, how did I forget? Mother, forgive me.

Either the newly charged atmosphere in the outer court or that curiously apathetic cry must have alerted the men gathered around the High Priest at the entrance to the sanctuary. The singing faltered and broke off and before the brothers could step through into the inner court they found themselves face to face with Thoth's servants. There was a moment of shocked silence. In the steady flare of the lamps Kamose studied them. Expressionless dark eyes stared back. Then the High Priest shouldered his way through. "I know you, Prince," he said hoarsely. "I remember you from the days of your first youth. You often worshipped here with your family when your mother came to visit her cousin, a priestess of this temple. But now you do not bring your worship, you bring torment and death. Look around you! You are not welcome in this sacred place." Kamose swallowed, his throat suddenly dry.

"I bring a return to Ma'at," he said as evenly as he could, "and Thoth gave Ma'at to Egypt together with his gift of writing. I am not here to argue with you, High Priest. I have come to abase myself before the god and beg his forgiveness for what I have done to his city in the name of that same Ma'at."

"Forgiveness?" the man said sharply. "Are you contrite then, Prince? Would you undo the horror you have caused?"

"No," Kamose replied. "It is not forgiveness for my deed that I seek. I wish to apologize to Thoth for neglecting to bring gifts and explanations to him before I fell upon Khemmenu."

"Do you bring a gift?"

"No." Kamose looked straight into the man's angry face. "It is too late for that. I bring only a plea for his understanding and the promise of a cure for his Egypt."

"It is you who are sick, Prince Kamose, not Egypt." The High Priest's voice trembled. "You have not even washed yourself. There is blood on your sandals. Blood! The blood of Khemmenu clings to your feet and you want to tread this holy ground? The god repudiates you!" Kamose felt his brother tense before speaking, and forestalled him. Jerking his head curtly he spun on his heel and walked away, and after hesitating, Ahmose followed. When they reached the pylon, Ankhmahor and the Braves gathered once more around them and they set off for the river.

Full night had now fallen and Kamose found himself close to panic as they trod the disordered streets whose black shadows were surely swollen with the spirits of the men who had fallen. He felt himself watched. Invisible eyes followed his progress with steady malevolence and he resisted the urge to draw closer to his brother. Thoth will give me no support, he thought, but I will not let it matter. Thoth is a god of peaceful times, of wisdom in prosperity and lawmaking in security. Amun has willed this thing. Amun protects the Princes of Weset and his power is not the gentle power of slow enlightenment. Henceforth I will bow before no other god but Amun. He must have spoken the last words aloud, for Ahmose glanced across at him. "It was the High Priest speaking, not the god, Kamose," he offered. "Thoth will remember the devotion of our mother and her family and will not punish."

"I don't care," Kamose snapped back. "Amun will be our salvation. I must eat something soon, Ahmose, or I will collapse on this accursed ground."

Before they entered the skiff to return to their boat, Kamose wrenched off his blood-soaked sandals and flung them into the river. The acrid smoke from the burnings hung so thickly in the air that he only heard them strike the surface of the water. Ahmose began to cough, but bending, he did the same. "Let us eat while the rowers work to take us away from here, Kamose," he said. "Khemmenu was a dirty business. Nefrusi is a garrison and will give us a clean fight."

# Chapter THREE

NEFRUSI WAS ONLY four miles downriver from Khemmenu and Kamose ordered his captain to find a suitable place to tie up a mile south from the fort. Word was passed to the following craft and one by one they left the ruin of Thoth's city behind. Food was brought. Ahmose ate heartily but Kamose forced down the herbed bread and dishes of vegetables without appetite, knowing that he needed sustenance. He drank his wine sparingly and was overcome with weariness before he had emptied his cup for the second time. Stumbling into the cabin, he flung himself onto his cot and was asleep at once.

It seemed to him that his feet had only just left the floor before a light fell on his face and he heard Akhtoy's voice pierce his dreams. "Majesty, forgive me," the man was saying, "but someone wishes to see you urgently." Kamose fought to unglue his eyelids, and when he had done so, he saw Akhtoy retreating and Hor-Aha's dark visage taking the steward's place.

"Light another lamp, Akhtoy," Ahmose was saying. He was already standing and wrapping a kilt around his waist. Groggily Kamose sat up, and Hor-Aha bowed. He too was clad in nothing but a kilt. His braid had come undone and tendrils of waving black hair trailed across his chest. His expression was grave.

"What is it?" Kamose demanded, now fully alert. The General raised a dismissive hand.

"The army is safely bivouacked and the Medjay have a cordon around the fort," he said. "Don't worry. But Prince Meketra is outside with half a dozen Setiu soldiers. He begs to speak with you."

"Meketra?" Kamose blinked. "Was he captured somehow, Hor-Aha?"

"My archers seized him as he tried to slip through their lines," Hor-Aha explained. "He was coming south, not north, so I presume that he was not trying to get a message to Apepa. It seems that he is anxious to see you."

"Bring him in then, and, Akhtoy, send for Ipi, but find me a clean kilt first."

The man who was ushered in was so tall that he was forced to bend his head to avoid the lintel of the cabin door, and Kamose recognized him immediately. Bald-headed, with bushy eyebrows above heavy-lidded eyes and a prominent adam's apple, he had been on the periphery of Kamose's youthful vision during visits to Teti's estate at Khemmenu. Kamose had never spoken with him. He had simply been one of Teti's innumerable guests, a man of Seqenenra's generation, holding no interest for the children who raced about the gardens and played with Teti's collection of cats and monkeys. The memories surged in Kamose, colourful and sweet, and then receded. Meketra bowed. "You resemble your father, the noble Seqenenra, Prince Kamose," he said. "And you, Prince Ahmose, I am honoured to find myself in your presence."

"These are strange circumstances in which to meet again," Kamose said noncommittally. "You will forgive me if I am blunt, Prince, but what is the Commander of Nefrusi doing on my boat in the middle of the night? Have you come to surrender the fort and throw yourself on my mercy?" His tone was sardonic and Meketra laughed without humour.

"In a way, Highness. How is it with Khemmenu?" Kamose and Ahmose exchanged surprised glances. Ahmose raised an eyebrow.

"You don't know?" he blurted. "No one from Khemmenu escaped to Nefrusi?" At that moment, after a discreet knock on the door, Ipi entered and took up his post at Kamose's feet. Although tousled and obviously still sleepy, he set his palette across his bare knees, laid papyrus on it, and wielded his scraper. The small sound, so strongly linked to business and household affairs, brought an air of normality into the room. Ipi opened his ink, dampened a brush, and looked inquiringly up at Kamose.

"Record this conversation," Kamose ordered him. "Please sit, Meketra. Akhtoy, serve wine to the Prince. Now, my lord, before I answer your question tell me why and how you are here."

"I told Teti that I would take scouts and try to ascertain the state and position of your army," Meketra said, lowering himself onto a stool and crossing his legs. "I lied. My intention was to reach you and that I have done, though not in the way I anticipated." He smiled ruefully. "I did not know that Nefrusi was already surrounded. Your native archers almost shot me. I have come to give you any information you require regarding the fort and the number and disposition of my troops there and I will open the gates for you if you wish."

There was a second of speculative silence during which Kamose regarded the Prince reflectively. He seemed completely at ease, his hands resting loosely together on his thigh, his gaze coolly encompassing all in the cabin. He wants something, Kamose mused. That is why he feels in control of himself and us. He watched the Prince reach for the wine cup, raise it to his mouth, drink delicately, lower it, without a single tremor in his fingers. "Why would you do all that?" Kamose asked at last. Meketra regarded him imperturbably.

"It is very simple, Highness. Many years ago I was the governor of the Mahtech nome and the Prince of Khemmenu. My home was the home your kinsman Teti was already inhabiting when you came there as a boy. Teti had always coveted it and finally Apepa gave it to him, along with the governorship of the nome and authority over the city—for his loyalty and, it must be said, his uncommon talent for spying on his noble neighbours. Teti kept Apepa informed of activities in the south. He was an invaluable tool." Meketra grimaced. "For my loyalty and efficiency as governor I was allowed to command the fort at Nefrusi. I live in the commander's quarters. My family inhabits a modest estate outside. I hate Apepa and loathe your kinsman. I will help you take the fort if you will promise to reinstate me to my former positions. That is why I asked you how Khemmenu has fared." Kamose's heart had begun to race. He dared not look at his brother again.

"And you are telling me that no news has come to you of the sack of Khemmenu?" he said deliberately. "No one in the fort knows anything?" Meketra shook his head.

"Teti and his family arrived with a garbled tale of an army under your command that had destroyed Dashlut and was marching on his city," he said. "Teti requested that the fort stand to arms. I gave that order. Since then we have waited."

"Then I may tell you that Khemmenu has been put to the sword, Nefrusi is surrounded, and I go north with nineteen thousand men to take Egypt away from Apepa," Kamose said. "I agree to your proposition, Meketra; in fact, as soon as Nefrusi falls to me, I will give you the documents you require and you can begin to set Khemmenu to rights." Meketra leaned forward.

"You will kill Teti?" Kamose kept his expression composed,

but something in him recoiled from the naked hatred on the Prince's face. Meketra wanted personal revenge. Well, so do you, he told himself. So do you.

"Teti will be executed for treason," he answered. "Now describe the fort to us." Meketra gestured and, at a nod from Kamose, Ipi handed him a sheet of papyrus and a brush. Swiftly he began to draw Nefrusi.

"Here is the Nile," he said, "and here is its western branch. There are perhaps eight miles between the two. The land is cultivated and well irrigated. Beware the canals. My family lives here." He placed a cross on his map and glanced up at Kamose.

"The order will be given not to molest them," Kamose assured him. "Go on."

"The fort itself is situated close to the Nile. There are two gates, one in the eastern wall, one to the west, both large enough for chariots to pass through. The walls themselves are a mighty defence. They are of thick mud plastered very smooth, vertical on the inside but sloping upwards outside. They cannot be scaled. If the gates are closed and barred, nothing will avail an attacker but a siege. Archers patrol the top of the walls."

"This is the standard Setiu design?" Ahmose interrupted. "Are all Apepa's northern forts like it?"

"Yes. The Setiu like to build such places on hills if they can, but Nefrusi is on flat ground. Some are better fortified, some less, but they resemble each other. Apepa has a string of smaller garrisons that you will encounter as you move north, but none are as mighty as the fort at Nag-ta-Hert where the Delta begins. It protects the heart of Apepa's power."

"We cannot worry about that now," Kamose said. "What is inside Nefrusi?"

"The barracks are here. If you attack at dawn, most of the soldiers will still be performing their ablutions. The armoury here, and the stables behind it. A small shrine to Reshep here," the brush moved swiftly, "and my command barracks here. The main barracks, as you can see, are closer to the western gate than the eastern. If I were you, Highness, I would concentrate my forces at that gate, but confront both gates at once of course."

"Of course," Kamose murmured. "What is the strength?" Meketra sat back, handing Kamose the map.

"Twelve hundred men, one hundred charioteers and two hundred horses. The granaries and storehouses are full, but the supply of water within the fort is limited. This is true of all the forts, I think, with the Nile so close to them. Apepa has never anticipated a full-scale revolt." He rose and bowed. "I must return at once," he said. "I will unbar the gates just after dawn but leave them closed. They open inwards. You will leave my family alone. May the god of Weset give you victory."

"One moment." Kamose stood also. "Ramose came to Nefrusi with his father? How is he?" Meketra looked nonplussed.

"In good health but silent," he said. "In fact Ramose has had little to say about anything."

"Thank you. I will keep your escort here, Prince. Have we understood one another?" Meketra smiled.

"I believe so, Highness." With another short bow that managed to encompass the whole cabin he left them.

Ahmose did not speak until the sound of the Prince's footfalls on the deck had died away, then he drew a gusty breath. "Who would have thought it?" he exclaimed. "We do not know our history well enough, Kamose! Can we trust him?" Kamose shrugged.

"We have little choice," he replied. "But I see the weight of the grudge he is carrying. Apepa is such a fool. Ahmose, take a couple of Braves and find the army. It cannot be more than an hour away. Hor-Aha, we attack just after dawn. Remember that the inhabitants of this estate," he pointed to the map and then handed it to his brother, "must not be harmed. Neither must Teti or Ramose." He turned to his steward. "Akhtoy, we must move north immediately. Tell the captain."

Before long they were beating upriver and Kamose took his accustomed place in the prow, his eyes on the shrouded bank gliding slowly past. The moon was waning and its light was faint. The dull illumination of the stars barely reflected off the tremulous surface of the water. Ankhmahor and a contingent of Braves had come aboard in readiness to protect Kamose during the coming engagement. They stood quietly behind him, Ankhmahor to his left. Even war can become routine, Kamose thought. I have already grooved this habit upon my consciousness. Rise in the dark, wash and eat hastily, then walk out to take up my station in this precise spot on the deck with my senses raised to the same level of alertness they reached yesterday. The command to bring death has not yet become a familiar custom but it will, it will. So also the sight of blood and fire. He stirred and sighed.

Barely an hour later there was movement on the bank and a scout signalled to them. Kamose gave the order to heave to, and waited while the man came on board. "Nefrusi is there," he said in answer to Kamose's permission to speak. "You can perhaps make out the top of its walls, Majesty. The army has arrived. It marched between the fields and the trees. Prince Ahmose requests that he be allowed to remain with the troops. He waits for your word to the Medjay to begin closing in. It lacks an hour to the dawn."

"Very well. He may begin. He must be ready to storm the gates at first light." Other instructions sprang to Kamose's tongue. Target the archers on the walls first. Make sure the men do not bunch up and fall over each other once they are through the gates. Make for the barracks immediately. Keep the horses contained or they will cause confusion. Cordon off the armoury so that the Setiu cannot replenish their weapons. Above all, be careful, Ahmose. He expressed none of them aloud. Dismissing the scout, he watched the skiff return the man to the bank, where he soon melted into the darkness. Ankhmahor sniffed the air. "The night is almost done, Majesty," he remarked. "Ra is about to be born." There were questions in his tone. Kamose turned to the cabin.

"Akhtoy, open my Amun shrine and prepare incense," he called. "We will pray, Ankhmahor, and then we will disembark. It is time."

The sky was almost imperceptibly paler when they emerged from the cabin and entered the skiff, the Braves remaining in the other vessels following suit at Kamose's shout. Gathering on the bank, they set off along the river path, Kamose in the centre of his bodyguards, the two hundred Braves before and behind. Now the roofless height of the fort could be discerned, and even as Kamose scanned it anxiously, a cry rang out. Something formless dropped from the wall and suddenly a dozen such shapes sprang into focus, men crouched above, peering down even as Kamose looked up. Another cry tore through the limpid morning air. Then the Medjay howled, the primitive sound echoed almost at once by an answering clamour off to Kamose's left. The figures on the wall fell one by one. Abruptly the vegetation gave way to naked space, wide watersteps against which two large barges rocked, and Kamose and his men found themselves confronting the full elevation of the fort.

The gate was open and already a seething mass of soldiers mingling with the darker, slighter Medjay were pouring inside. Behind them, filling the area between fort and watersteps, more troops jostled as they joined the flow. The noise was deafening. Kamose made out Prince Iasen and Prince Mesehti with their standard bearers, calmly issuing orders in the midst of what seemed to be chaos. There was no sign of Hor-Aha or Ahmose, and Kamose presumed that they were with the majority of the army as it stormed the western gate.

The light was strengthening rapidly. Long shadows began to resolve and lengthen at the foot of the wall, snaking dark and increasingly sharp towards the river, while the sky flushed with a delicate pink and in the trees the birds burst forth with their morning song. All at once Kamose and the Braves found themselves alone but for the few bodies of the Setiu archers that had fallen and now lay trampled into the sand by the hordes rushing heedlessly over them. Beyond the gate the noise continued unabated, yells and screams, the frightened shrieks of horses, the loud shouts of officers. But no hysterical sobbing, no voices of women raised in terror, Kamose thought. Compared with what else I have done, this is clean. Now all I have to do is wait.

Long before the shadows had foreshortened towards noon, the struggle for Nefrusi was over and Kamose and his men walked through the gate and into a vast compound littered with bodies and debris. Picking his way, he was approached by Ahmose, Hor-Aha and Meketra. Ahmose was drenched in sweat and streaked with blood. The axe at his belt hung crusted and the sword in his hand was befouled to the hilt. "It was no battle, Kamose," he said. "Look around you. It was like trapping frightened rabbits in a small field. I held back a large portion of the army or else we would have been packed elbow to elbow in here. Less than half a division was necessary. Of course, if the gates had not been opened, it would have been a different story." He cast a sidelong glance at Meketra who was standing stolidly beside him.

"We are in your debt, Prince," Kamose said. "Take your family and go to Khemmenu. All Teti's possessions are forfeit to me, and I deed them to you. Go at once." He thought he saw disappointment flare in the man's heavy-lidded eyes. Meketra wants to see Teti die, he realized with distaste. He is willing to endure the mute hostility of the survivors here so that he may glut himself on Teti's death throes. After a slight hesitation Meketra bowed and backed away.

"Every Prince under you could be called traitor by those loyal to Apepa," Ankhmahor said in a low voice. "Why then should Meketra conjure such disgust in me?"

"Because there is something polluted in his ka," Kamose answered immediately. "His cause is just, but there is no honour in him." He turned to his General. "What are our losses, Hor-Aha?"

"None, Majesty," Hor-Aha replied promptly. "A few scratches, nothing more. This small quarrel will go a long way towards inspiring the men with confidence. After this, they will begin to be soldiers." He passed Kamose a scroll that he had been holding. "The man carrying this was caught and killed just after the battle began," he said. "He had no hope of slipping through the Medjay cordon in any case but, of course, Teti did not know that."

Puzzled, Kamose unrolled the papyrus. It was a hastily scrawled, terse message. "To His Majesty Awoserra Aqenenra Apepa, the Mighty Bull of Ma'at, greetings. Know that your ungrateful and traitorous servant Kamose Tao has even now fallen upon your fort here at Nefrusi with a great force of renegade men. Send us help at once or we perish. I am your loyal subject Teti, Governor of Khemmenu and Inspector of your Dykes and Canals." Kamose laughed grimly.

"What did he think? That Apepa would somehow magically receive the scroll within moments and just as magically waft an army southward to rescue his worthless carcase? Let us move on. Hor-Aha, have your officers distribute the weapons in the armoury. Find men who can handle horses and put them in charge of the stables. The chariots must go to the Princes first and then to the commanders. Ahmose, return to the boat and wash. Give this scroll to Ipi for filing and tell him to arrange for the contents of the granaries to be tallied and loaded onto the barges moored here. Hor-Aha, make sure that Meketra and his family have left and then order all the crops around to be fired. I also want you to choose several capable men, promote them to officer rank, and put them in charge of any surviving Setiu. They are to stay here and see to the razing of these walls. I want Nefrusi reduced to nothing but a firmness under the sand. And take Reshep out of his shrine and smash him loudly, in full view of everyone. Where is Teti?"

"He is still in the commander's quarters," Ahmose said. "I set a guard over him but he showed no inclination to come out. Ramose is with him. He is wounded."

"Ramose fought?"

"Yes. Fortunately he was recognized and overpowered before one of the Medjay could run him through. I had no time to speak with him, Kamose." How did a man of such integrity spring from Teti's loins? Kamose wondered. I have looked forward to eating this dish, but now that it has been set before me my gorge rises and I want to flee.

"The sun is hot and the stink around us is becoming overpowering," he said aloud. "Come with me, Ankhmahor. I will confront my kinsman but I will pass no judgement until you return, Ahmose, and the Princes can be gathered together." His head was beginning to ache. He knew that the pain had no physical cause and he ignored it, making his way with an inner shrinking towards the building where Meketra had brooded, nursing the bitterness of his demotion.

The guards on the door of the commander's quarters saluted and gave way, and with a deep breath Kamose went in. The building was merely two rooms, one for sleeping and the larger one, in which Kamose and Hor-Aha now stood, for the administration of the fort. It was functionally bare, containing little more than shelves for the boxes that held the records of Nefrusi's inhabitants, a few stools, and one chair behind a desk. The floor was beaten earth without covering, but out of the corner of his eye Kamose could see the edge of a piece of yellow flax matting in the commander's private cell, and a brief, furtive movement.

Reluctantly he turned his attention to the two men who had risen to their feet at his approach. One had a linen bandage around his waist. He was pale and moved with difficulty. "Greetings, Ramose," Kamose said quietly. "Are you in much pain?" The young man shook his head.

"Greetings, Kamose," he replied hoarsely. "I would be happy to see you again if the circumstances were less distressing. As for my wound, it is not serious, only uncomfortable. An arrow grazed me. Its flight was almost spent." I want to take you in my arms and beg your forgiveness for your father, for Tani, for the ruin your life has become, Kamose cried out to him silently. I am terrified that you no longer have any affection or respect for me. You know what I must do. There is no way out.

With difficulty he forced his gaze to Teti. The man was barefoot and unpainted. He was clad in nothing but a short kilt fastened loosely under the sagging mound of his belly and Kamose surmised that, having been woken suddenly by the attack, he had simply wrapped himself in the garment and then cowered here, waiting. Kamose could smell the fear coming from him, acrid and humiliating.

"Teti, I do not remember you this way," he said. "You have become an old man."

"And you are no longer the handsome, quiet boy who used to pick fruit from my garden," Teti ground out, though he had begun to tremble. "You have become a murderer, Kamose Tao.

Your delusions will not carry you much farther. Apepa will crush you in the end."

"Perhaps," Kamose replied, full of a momentary pity for the man who had presided with such pomp and self-assurance over the prosperity that had been Khemmenu. "I think you are wrong, but even if this war turns against me and I and all who support me are destroyed, at least I will have done the right thing, the honourable thing."

"The honourable thing?" Teti shouted querulously. "Honour resides in loyalty to those in authority and to the King most of all! I have been honourable all my life!"

"You really believe that, don't you?" Kamose said. "But was it honourable to corrupt my brother Si-Amun, so that he had no choice but to take his own life? Was it honourable to engineer the attack on my father through a member of his own household? To agree to take everything my family owns in payment for this so-called loyalty? Those things go beyond mere faithfulness, Teti. They belong to greed and a cold callousness. They are the acts that have signed your death warrant, not Apepa."

"It is nothing but revenge!" Teti broke in hotly. His face had flushed a hectic red and Kamose saw sweat begin to trickle under his armpits. "You would have done the same if you had been trapped in my situation!"

"I do not think so. Oh, my uncle, I know what led you into such a snare. I know that your grandfather led an insurrection against Sekerher, Apepa's own grandfather, and had his tongue cut out for his temerity. I know that your father, Pepi, served long and hard in Apepa's army and thus lifted your family out of shame. These things are clean. They belong to the realm of Ma'at, action and consequence, the promptings of conscience that cause a man to do what he believes to be right. If your deeds had been born of such roots, I could applaud them, even though I could not agree." He paused and swallowed, aware that his voice had been rising with his fury. "But you twisted that loyalty into something filthy," he went on more calmly, "the pain and death of your own kin in exchange for personal gain. You could have come to us, explained the net being cast around you, begged for help or advice from Seqenenra. You did not, and that is why I am going to execute you." Teti's knees at last gave way and he sank onto the stool.

"You do not understand the pressure, Kamose," he choked. "Everything for you is black or white, right or wrong. You do not see the subtleties of either. If you did, you would not be slaughtering innocent citizens in your mad meanderings down the Nile. Do you think I lost no sleep over the decisions I made? Felt no remorse?" Kamose folded his arms against the almost physical stab of rage Teti's words caused him. What do you know of remorse? his mind clamoured. Of the foul necessities that are haunting my couch and poisoning my food? Of the pity and horror that threaten to unseat my very ka?

"That is exactly what I do think, Teti," he managed huskily.

"Then all I can do is beseech you for mercy," Teti pleaded. "I am a broken man, Kamose. I have nothing left. I am no threat to you any more. Set me free, I beg you. For the sake of my son and of your mother, my wife's cousin," and here he put a hand up against Ramose's back, "do not bring bereavement to my loved ones." Ramose stiffened.

"Father, for Thoth's sake do not beg!" he said urgently. "Do not demean yourself!"

"Why not?" Teti blurted. "What is it to you if I grovel for my life? He will spare yours, Ramose, but he is determined to revenge himself on me, no matter what I say. There is no kindness in him." Ramose looked across at Kamose.

"Please, Highness, if you can," he said softly. Kamose shook his head once, a denial.

"No. I cannot. I am sorry, Ramose. Hor-Aha, go into the

other room and bring out my aunt." Hor-Aha made as if to obey, but at Kamose's words the woman herself appeared in the doorway. She bowed then drew herself up proudly, and with a spurt of tenderness Kamose saw that she was painted and arrayed decently in clean linen even though there was no sign of her body servant.

"I greet you, Kamose," she said bleakly. "I have heard everything that has passed here. I have lived a good life and served Thoth in his temple with honesty and devotion. I am ready to die with my husband." Kamose was taken aback. It is just as well that your husband does not possess your strength of character, he thought, looking into that aging, dignified face. If he did, I might be tempted to let him go.

"That will not be necessary, Aunt," he said. "Neither I nor Egypt has anything against you. You are free to go to the river." He had used the euphemism that described women whose husbands had been killed in battle and who had been driven from their homes, and she smiled icily.

"As opposed to those women who are forced there?" she retorted. "No thank you, Kamose. I have nowhere to go."

"My mother would welcome you at Weset." For a second she faltered, but then her chin came up.

"I have no wish to accept the hospitality of those who have conspired to ruin Egypt and murder my husband, relatives though they be," she said. "I do not deny that Teti is weak, but so are many men. Nor do I deny that he had a hand in those despicable events of which you have spoken, although I knew nothing of them until long afterwards. But I am his wife. My loyalty belongs to him. There is no life without him."

"Kamose, if you will release her to me, I will care for her," Ramose interrupted. "I will take her away. I will make no trouble for you, I swear."

"No!" Kamose said harshly. "No, Ramose. I want you with

me. I need you. Tani needs you. I want to give Tani back to you!" Misery, quickly controlled, flared behind Ramose's eyes.

"And how will you do that?" he flashed. "Supposing you win through to Het-Uart, supposing you can siege and overcome that mighty city, supposing you find Tani still alive, have you the power to restore her to the innocence of her girlhood? Wipe from her consciousness all that has passed since Apepa carried her away? Have you received one word from her? For I have not." His fingers found his side where the arrow had struck and he lowered himself onto the stool. "It was a dream, Kamose, and it belongs to the past," he finished wearily. "What you and I want does not matter any more." Kamose stared at him.

"Do you still love her, Ramose?"

"Yes."

"Then you have no right to give up that love or our hope until the future has unfolded. You will come with me." He turned to the General. "Hor-Aha, I will give my aunt some time to say farewell to her husband. Then place her in the care of one of my heralds and send them south to Weset. I will dictate a letter to my mother." There was nothing left to say. Feeling old and empty, Kamose left them. The sunlight smote him like a hot blow after the dimness of the room behind him and he paused for a moment with eyes closed against its onslaught. "Hor-Aha," he said heavily, "I am sick unto death of the word 'honour.'"

An hour later he watched from the shade of a canopy as his aunt, still stiff and unyielding, walked across the churned and stained parade ground beside the herald and out through the eastern gate. He had dictated a hurried message to Aahotep and Tetisheri, telling them of the events that had transpired since his last letter and asking them to care for the woman. He knew that his mother's conscience would not allow her kinswoman to suffer any more than she had done already, and he hoped that in Weset she might find some peace. The bodies of the dead were being hauled through the gates to east and west to be burned, and it came to Kamose that if he won this dirty war, if by some miracle he was permitted to return to Weset as King and live out the remainder of his days in peace, the memory of the stench of burning human flesh would eclipse all other remembrances of this time.

The Princes had begun to gather, their servants busy around them erecting sunshades and opening their camp stools. Iasen of Badari leaned close to Mesehti of Djawati, both men deep in conversation. Ankhmahor stood with a good-looking youth Kamose recognized after a second as the Prince's son Harkhuf. Makhu of Akhmin was speaking rapidly and with many gestures to two officers who were listening respectfully, but Prince Intef of Qebt sat alone, his brooding dark eyes fixed on the sun-fired scene before him. None of them approached Kamose. It was as though they knew that the space around him was temporarily inviolable, and he was grateful. He found himself gazing without thought at the spasmodic ripple of shadow cast on the ground when the breeze stirred the tassels of his canopy, and he came to himself with an effort, his thoughts sluggish, his heart numb. It has to be done, he told himself firmly, trying to gather up the tatters of his resolve. And I have to do it.

Ahmose came striding across the slowly emptying parade ground, Hor-Aha beside him. Both men had obviously cleaned themselves and Ahmose had donned a starched yellow linen helmet beneath whose rim his freshly kohled eyes roamed the activity going on around him. Coming up to Kamose, he nodded gravely but said nothing, settling himself on the stool his attending servant placed for him. Hor-Aha bowed, then sank cross-legged to the earth and quickly became immobile. A mood of solemnity fell on the three men and for a long time they simply watched as the interior of the fort was restored to a semblance of normality.

Then Kamose sighed and straightened. "Hor-Aha, have the work cease," he said. "Bring out Teti and Ramose. Ipi!" he signalled to his scribe, who had been waiting with the other servants a short distance away. "Prepare to take down the indictment and the execution order. Ahmose, I will have the Princes behind me." Ipi came close, while Ahmose, with a grim nod, walked across to the nobles. One by one they followed him back to cluster behind Kamose, who had come out from under the canopy.

An expectant hush fell. Presently the guards on the door of the commander's quarters fell back and Teti emerged, his arm through his son's. He had made no attempt to wash himself or change his linen and he was still barefoot. Pale and blinking, he stood irresolute until, at an abrupt word from the General, he shuffled forward. Kamose crooked a finger at Ramose. "You need not be a witness," he said gently. "Go outside the walls if you wish." At his words Teti clutched Ramose's arm with both hands and whispered something urgent in his ear. Ramose shook his head.

"I will stand by my father," he called. "But I ask you once more, Kamose, will you show mercy?" For answer Kamose turned to Ipi who was now at his feet, brush in hand over his papyrus.

"Write," he said. "Teti son of Pepi, erstwhile Governor of Khemmenu and Administrator of the Mahtech nome, Inspector of Dykes and Canals, you are accused of collusion in the attempted murder of Prince Seqenenra of Weset and of betraying and thus bringing to ruin the House of Tao, which House is allied to you by blood and the ties of familial loyalty. You are accused of treason against the rightful King of Egypt under Ma'at, Kamose the First, in that you have spied against him on behalf of the usurper Apepa. For the crime of attempted murder you are sentenced to death." The echo of his voice rebounded from the baking walls of the fort. He felt the mounting tension of the motionless Princes at his back and the heat of the sun pounding against his skull. Silence had rushed in to fill the void left by his proclamation and he fought its pressure, aware of the dozens of soldiers, their labour suspended, their eyes fixed on him avidly, waiting.

I dare betray no weakness, he thought. I must not swallow or clear my throat or glance to the ground. This is the moment when my authority is confirmed. "Teti, have you prayed?" he asked. With an outward impassivity he watched as Teti struggled to reply. The man was crying quietly, the tears tracking his plump cheeks and falling glistening upon his heaving chest. It was Ramose who answered for him.

"My father has prayed," he said. "He is ready." Kamose held out a hand and Hor-Aha laid his bow and one arrow across his palm. Kamose's fingers closed around the weapon. His own skin was slick but he knew he must not wipe the sweat away. Carefully he fitted the nock of the arrow to the bowstring and his other hand came up to cushion its tip. Placing his feet apart and turning his shoulder to the target, he began to take the strain of the draw. "Ramose, stand away," he called. Sighting along the shaft of the arrow, he saw the young man kiss his father, steady him as though he were a baby unsure of its balance, then move out of his vision. Teti alone filled it now, swaying and weeping, his lips forming prayers or admonitions or simply the babblings of terror, Kamose could not tell. He took a breath, held it, opened the fingers of his left hand, and Teti staggered and fell onto his side. A small amount of blood dribbled around the shaft of the arrow that had smashed through his ribs. Ramose ran to the twitching body and fell to his knees and from Kamose's rear came a collective sigh. He passed the bow back to the General. "Write again, Ipi," he said to his scribe's bent head. "On this day, the fifteenth of Pakhons, the sentence of death was carried out upon Teti son of Pepi of the city of Khemmenu for the crime of attempted murder. Make a copy before you file the scroll, and send it south to my mother. Akhtoy, are you there? Give me wine!"

An excited chatter had broken out as the soldiers slowly returned to their tasks, but the Princes still stood mute behind Kamose. He ignored them, gulping the wine, aware that his limbs were shaking. Wiping his mouth, he was about to hold out his cup for more when he saw Ramose approach. The man bowed and lifted an expressionless face to Kamose. The hands he had placed on his knees to make the obeisance were glossy with blood.

"Kamose, give me leave to have my father taken to the House of the Dead in Khemmenu," he said huskily. "He must be beautified, mourned, my mother must come back from Weset for his funeral. You cannot let him be burned!"

"No, I cannot," Kamose agreed, forcing himself to meet his old friend's eyes. "But it is impossible to keep the army here through the seventy days of Teti's beautification and mourning. We must move on, Ramose. Let him go to the House of the Dead and I will have your mother escorted north for his funeral. By then I expect to be sieging Het-Uart."

Ramose nodded, tight-lipped. "I understand that you can do little more, but you will forgive me if I am not grateful." He bowed again and retreated, and without Kamose's permission Hor-Aha followed him, barking orders that sent four men scurrying to bring a stretcher and lift Teti onto it. With Ramose at its side, the little cavalcade wound its way to the gate and Hor-Aha came back.

"The officers and soldiers who are to stay and destroy the fort are already moving their possessions into the barracks, Majesty," he told Kamose. "Nefrusi is over, it is done. I need your command to rank the army and get it on the march." Kamose rose and turned, scanning the faces of the Princes still arrayed behind him. All met his scrutiny calmly.

"It is about forty miles from here to Het nefer Apu in the Anpu nome," he said. "There are perhaps eight or ten villages between Nefrusi and Het nefer Apu and we do not yet know how many of them contain garrisons. We have acquired many weapons here, and chariots and horses, a great blessing, but now we need some time to assess how these things have changed the nature of our forces. I propose to go north some ten miles, then rest briefly while you see to it that your peasants learn to use and care for the axes and swords being issued to them. In that time the scouts will be able to give me a clearer picture of what lies ahead. Have you anything to say? Do you have any requests regarding your welfare or that of your divisions?" No one spoke and Kamose dismissed them, walking thankfully past the spot where Teti's life had flowed away and out onto the river path.

The barges were already loaded with the vital booty taken from Nefrusi's armoury and granaries and soldiers swarmed in a noisy mob around them. "Ahmose, send to the sem-priests in Khemmenu," he said to his brother as they swung side by side away from the dust and clamour. "Make sure they are well paid for Teti's beautification. Ramose cannot do it. I have disinherited him. And take my greetings to Meketra. Tell him I will keep him apprised of the campaign."

"Pacify him further, you mean," Ahmose retorted. "I do not trust that man, Kamose."

"Neither do I," Kamose admitted, "but he has done nothing to earn our suspicion. We must treat him as the ally he has proved himself to be."

"So far," Ahmose said darkly. They regained their boat without further conversation.

Ahmose discharged his errands and returned at sunset, together with Ramose, whom he had met in the house that now belonged to Meketra. Ramose had been collecting a few personal belongings and mementos of his family, amid what Ahmose described as a chaos of chests and furniture and harried servants as Meketra and his brood took over Teti's estate. "Meketra's wife seemed to know exactly where she wanted everything placed," Ahmose told Kamose, as they ate their evening meal in the last soft glow of Ra. "But of course she ran the house years ago, before Apepa gave it to Teti." He blew out his lips and looked across at Ramose who sat nursing a cup of wine, his food untouched on the dishes before him. "I'm sorry, Ramose, but it is nothing but the truth."

"I know," Ramose said curtly. "I only pray that Meketra can find enough peasants to tend the vines properly. Father was proud of his vintage, and without pruning this winter the grapes will be small and bitter. It will be hard, though. You have killed them all."

For a moment Kamose puzzled over how he and Ahmose might be responsible for the death of Teti's fruit, but then he understood. He made no response. Will you ever forgive me? he asked Ramose in the tumult of his mind. Can we ever be friends again or will the exigencies of this appalling age drive us even farther apart? To his relief Ahmose gave his attention to his food, and in a daze of silent exhaustion Kamose watched his brother eat.

Later that night he woke from a sodden sleep to the faint sound of crying. The boat was rocking gently as it rode the current north. Dull light came and went in fitful bands across his cot as the lamps set at prow and stern swayed with the motion, and the only other sound was the constant, sweet murmur of water under the keel. They were floating, Kamose knew, drifting slowly with only the current for propulsion until the dawn, as the captain had advised. Turning onto his back, he lay listening to that muffled outpouring of desolation. It could have been one of the sailors or an expression of homesickness on the part of a servant, but Kamose knew it was not.

The grief belonged to Ramose, sobbing out his loss and loneliness under the cover of darkness. I should get up and go to him, Kamose thought. I should tell him that I feel it too, that for me also there is no longer any safe harbour, any welcoming arms. But no. If I were Ramose, I would not want any man to see my distress.

He closed his eyes and it seemed to him that the sound began to grow, to fill the cabin and reverberate across the invisible deck, to multiply until the boat and the water and the shrouded banks of the Nile were thrashing with the misery it carried. All of them, Kamose thought incoherently, wanting to press his hands over his ears. It is all their pain, the men who have died, the women I have widowed, I am not really hearing it, it is just my imagination, it is just Ramose, oh, Ramose, how much we need to help each other! Yet he knew that he had merely conjured an ephemeral imitation of the torment Ramose was so poignantly expressing. Kamose himself felt nothing at all.

# Chapter FOUR

Tᴇᴛɪsʜᴇʀɪ ʜᴇʟᴅ ᴏᴜᴛ her hand and Uni, her steward, passed her the scroll. Taking one polite step backwards, he waited while she weighed it, frowning. "Hmmm," she said. "It is very light. Very thin. Good news or bad, do you think, Uni? Shall I break the seal or fortify myself first with a little wine?" Uni grunted non-committally and Tetisheri lowered the papyrus onto her scarlet lap. It has become a game, she thought, her eyes fixed unseeing on the view of the garden around her. Since the middle of Pakhons the scrolls have been coming, big ones, small ones, neatly penned or scrawled by Ipi from some cramped, uncomfortable place, and each time I have hesitated, lost my nerve, spent a moment or an hour trying to assess their contents before cracking my grandson's seal.

". . . It is a fat one this week, Uni. Poison or medicine?"

"Hard to say, Majesty."

"But fat means much time in which to dictate. Nothing hurried, like the one that came from Nefrusi with Aahotep's cousin."

"I am sure you are correct, Majesty. . . ."

And always the fear, the shrinking. Has someone been slain?

Wounded? Are we defeated at last? Has the dream turned to ashes?

But so far there had been no defeats. Mesore had begun, a month of harvest and stultifying heat, when time in Egypt seemed to stand still and man and beast struggled against the heavy desire to lie down, to sleep, while the river sank ever lower and the only greenery was to be found in the precincts of the nobles and the crests of the drooping palms. In the tiny fields the sickles rose and fell and in front of the granaries the air grew choking with dust from the winnowed wheat. Vines bowed down by clusters of fleshy black grapes were relieved of their burdens and the juice flowed purple and pregnant with promise into the vats.

Four months, Tetisheri sighed. Four months of this regular tension, this quick constriction of the heart, this flicker of cowardice before the wax crumbles under my fingers and Ipi's hieratic figures jump out at me. It's a wonder the constant anxiety hasn't killed me. She thrust the scroll at her steward. "You read it to me, Uni," she ordered. "My eyes are tired today." Obediently the man took it from her, and breaking the seal, he unrolled the scroll. There was a short hiatus in which Tetisheri fixed her gaze on the surface of the pond that glittered just outside the shade cast by her canopy. Uni cleared his throat.

"It is good news, Majesty," he said. "Only two lines. 'Sacrifice to Amun. I am coming home.'"

"Give me that." She snatched it back and held it open on her knee, her forefinger tracing the flow of words. "'I am coming home.' What does he mean?" she snapped irritably. "Is he fleeing from a lost battle or bringing victory with him? How can I go to Amunmose in the temple unless I know?"

"I rather think," Uni said carefully, "that if His Majesty was fleeing he would have been more specific in his message. He would have included a warning for the family, and instructions.

Besides, Majesty, there has been no hint of disaster in his letters, only frustration."

"You are right of course." She let the papyrus roll up and began to tap it thoughtfully against her chin. "Go and tell Aahotep and Aahmes-nefertari. The silly boy has put no date on the communication so we cannot know when he may appear. We must prepare to see him at any time." She graced Uni with a rare smile. "Perhaps he has taken Het-Uart and executed Apepa already."

"Perhaps, Majesty, but I do not think so."

"No, neither do I. It was a foolish hope. Go then."

She watched him stride away and disappear under the shadow of the entrance hall, aware suddenly that her heart was palpitating painfully. Any surprise, pleasant or not, agitates my body, she thought. I am beginning to feel my age. So, Kamose, beloved, soon I shall look into your face and embrace you and it will not be the hazy fantasy in which I have indulged as sleep descended. You will have changed. I must be ready for that. Your words have given me no indication of the state of your ka. They have all been of skirmishes and little sieges, of burnings and slaughters, yet under them I have sensed a more sinister battle, invisible yet grave. Beware of the damage to your ka, I told you. Did you heed me, my implacable one? Or in laying waste to this precious land have you ravaged your soul as well?

Presently there was movement by the pillars and Aahmes-nefertari came bursting out of the dimness, her linen flying as she veered around the pond. She was barefoot, clutching a thin white cloak around her naked body, and Raa came hurrying after her, a pair of sandals and a cushion under her arm. Aahmes-nefertari ducked beneath the canopy and stood flushed and panting before Tetisheri. "Uni said there is great news!" she exclaimed as her body servant placed the cushion on the ground and withdrew. "Forgive my appearance, Majesty, but I was about to take my afternoon rest. May I see the scroll?"

"No, Aahmes-nefertari, you must wait until Aahotep has seen it," Tetisheri said waspishly. "Sit down, girl!" She softened the tone of her words with a hand on Aahmes-nefertari's elbow. "Be patient. Have we not all had to learn endurance? Let an old woman keep her secret for a while longer." With the humility of instant obedience that gave her such charm, Aahmes-nefertari sank onto the cushion and dug her toes into the grass.

"They've won, haven't they?" she said eagerly. "At last Het-Uart has fallen! Week after week the news has been the same, but Uni called it great today! Oh, I have prayed and prayed for this moment!"

"Always you jump to conclusions, Aahmes-nefertari," Tetisheri said dryly. "No, as far as I know, Het-Uart is still on its feet. Here is Aahotep." The woman came on slowly, Senehat behind her, and as always Tetisheri relished the sight of her daughter-in-law. The graceful carriage, the sensuous yet discreet fullness of her hips under the yellow sheath, the evenness of her features, spoke of both the beauty and the good breeding that had captivated Seqenenra and satisfied Tetisheri's own stringent standards. Bowing as she entered the shade under which Tetisheri sat, she straightened and met her mother-in-law's eyes.

"Is it what we have hoped for?" she asked quietly. For answer Tetisheri relinquished the scroll. Aahotep unrolled it without hesitation, read, smiled, and passing it down to Aahmes-nefertari she turned to her servant. "Senehat, set down my stool and then bring wine. We will celebrate." As she settled herself, Aahmes-nefertari gave a cry.

"They are coming home! How wonderful!" She pressed the scroll to her mouth. "But have they left the Delta already or not? Ipi does not say."

"Neither does he say that they are coming home," Tetisheri

reminded her. "He says only 'I am coming home.' Where is your cousin, Aahotep?"

"Asleep in her quarters," Aahotep replied. "It would be best if this news could be kept from her for now. We do not know whether Kamose is coming because the Inundation is at hand or for other reasons. Nefer-Sakharu is unpredictable. She is still grieving. If I had not sent a bodyguard with her to Teti's funeral, she would have run to the Delta afterwards. Doubtless Kamose will send word just before he reaches Weset, and then we can warn her." Aahmes-nefertari had been listening with only half an ear. Now she sat up.

"She has grown to love Ahmose-onkh," she commented. "When she plays with him, she forgets about Teti for a while. And she is not weeping as often as she did."

"Grief cannot last," Aahotep said. "Time blunts its edges. But the deep things, the memories and the love, they refuse to die. Poor woman. Yet have we not all suffered terribly since Apepa's insulting letter came to Osiris Seqenenra? Here is the wine. We will forget the past and drink to a blessed reunion."

Afterwards, when the gentle effect of the wine had prompted the reminiscences that had long remained untold through fear of what the future might bring, the women returned to the house. Aahotep and Aahmes-nefertari drifted away to their couches, but Tetisheri sat before the table in her bedchamber and requested of her steward the chest in which she had kept all of Kamose's letters. Now I can read them again, she thought, dismissing Uni to his own couch and lifting the lid of the gold-chased box. They cannot hurt me with doubts or set me worrying about the army's next move or fill me with impotent exasperation because I am unable to question the wisdom of Kamose's decisions.

Removing them all, she set the chest aside and arranged them carefully according to the dates her scribe had written on them. The first few made her hesitate, then briskly she replaced them, not wishing to relive the intense emotions that had accompanied their arrival. We were all terrified in those days, she thought. Kamose with his miserable one division from Weset, not knowing if the Princes would go back on their word or not, and his five thousand Medjay who could have proved lethal but ungovernable. Thank all the gods for Hor-Aha! And here at home every morning had brought a shrinking, a secret, unvoiced certainty that Apepa's hordes would appear around the bend in the river with Kamose's corpse hanging from a mast. Each scroll could have held damnation, but did not, and gradually our dread began to fade. Then came the triumph of Nefrusi, and from that moment the opening of the letters became a matter of ceremony. Still worrisome, still with that drawing in of courage, but with a swift return to confidence.

I never liked Prince Meketra, her thoughts ran on as she tossed Kamose's message following the taking of the fort back into the casket. I remember him well from the very early days. There was always something faintly unwholesome about him, as though he often neglected to wash. But he has proved himself now and I suppose I ought to revise my opinion of him. After all, it has been a very long time since we met.

Choosing a scroll dated "Payni, day two," she smoothed it open. "To Their Majesties the Queens Tetisheri and Aahotep, honoured Grandmother and Mother, greetings," it began. "Tonight our boat is moored at Het nefer Apu. It has taken us a full seven days to travel here from Nefrusi due to the increasing number of villages we are encountering as we draw closer to the Delta. Our ignorance of everything north of Khemmenu has also slowed us down. We must rely on and wait for the reports from our scouts as we go. We engaged and overran one garrison, putting all soldiers to the sword, but the small fort here at Het nefer Apu surrendered as soon as its commander saw our approach. It seems that peasants from Khemmenu and Nefrusi have been struggling north to seek protection, carrying with them tales of our might and exaggerated stories of our ruthlessness."

Here Tetisheri looked up for a moment, her gaze fixed absently on the wall across from her. Exaggerated? she repeated silently. What were you trying to say, Kamose? Every letter from you has paired words of wholesale butchery together with the plea of necessity. We agreed that it was the only way you could secure your rear without thinning the ranks of the army. Then why that subtle lie? Had the killing become routine, until in the dictating of this epistle you felt a fleeting guilt? Is it even possible for the peasants to exaggerate the essential brutality of this campaign? With a grimace she resumed reading.

"Half the garrison's force was executed and the rest put to work reducing the walls to rubble. I did not want to take the commander's life but he gave me no choice, being not only of Setiu blood but openly hostile to me. I do not think that even now, even after subduing the land from Weset to Het nefer Apu, the Setiu regard us as more than a temporary revolt. I heard as much from the commander's mouth before he died, and of course Teti recited the same tired lines. We move on towards Henen-Nesut tomorrow. I wish there was time to take the track west from here to Uah-ta-Meh. I would like to explore the oasis. Pray for us. We are so tired."

Tetisheri lifted her hands and the papyrus rolled up with a whisper. Kamose's last few words had wrenched at her heart when she had first heard them read by Uni while she and Aahotep sat at meat in the dining hall. They still did. "We are so tired," she repeated the words of the scroll now in her mind. Not tired in your bodies, my dearest ones, but tired in your souls. Yes. And we do indeed pray for you, every day. Pushing the scroll aside, she unrolled the next, allowing herself a tiny spark of the same pleasure she had felt when news of Teti's death reached the estate. She had hidden it from her daughter-in-law, for although Aahotep had known her relative's execution was inevitable she was clearly distressed. "You will recite no more lines," she said aloud. "Or issue deceitful and treacherous orders. You may lie beautified in your tomb but I wager that the scales in the Judgement Hall did not balance when your heart was laid on the dish. I hope Sebek found you a juicy morsel."

This letter was headed "Payni, day thirty." "We have battled our way to Iunu," it said after the usual salutations, "and tomorrow we enter the Delta and come to Nag-ta-Hert, a mighty fort built on a mound, according to the scouts. At least ten thousand troops are quartered there. It is Apepa's bastion against incursions into his heartland from the south. I do not yet know how we will deal with it. I cannot hope for another Meketra to visit me in the night. I have spared most of the inhabitants of Mennofer, killing only the active soldiers, for the city and its nome are governed by Prince Sebek-nakht. I remembered him as soon as he emerged from the White Wall with his entourage. He came to Weset with Apepa at the time of our sentencing and he was the only Prince brave enough to speak to us publicly. He went hunting with Ahmose. Perhaps you can recall him. He is a priest of Sekhmet, an erpa-ha and hereditary lord, and one of Apepa's architects. His father was Vizier of the North before he died. His hospitality was generous and not, I think, tainted by a desire to ingratiate himself. With him we visited the ancient tombs on the plateau of Saqqara, inspected the harbour which was full of all kinds of trading vessels as well as our own boats, and worshipped in the temple of Ptah. After a long conversation that took us through the night, the Prince has sworn that if we leave Mennofer intact he will make no move to warn Apepa of our strengths and weaknesses and he will support us with any goods or weapons we may require. Ahmose trusts him implicitly, but then Ahmose bestows his admiration on any man who can bring down a duck with a throwing stick on the first try. I like the Prince well enough to believe that he will stand by his word. Ankhmahor knows him well."

Yes, I recall him, Tetisheri thought. I knew his mother, a woman who took an active and stern hand in the education of her sons. His blood is pure. But, Kamose, I like your jibe at your brother even less now than when you first dictated it. Surely you realize that a falling-out between you will spell disaster. That is one more thing that must be discussed while you are here.

The next scroll was as light as a handful of feathers and after tapping it with one long fingernail she laid it in the chest. I do not need to look at this message, she thought. I know it by heart. "Epophi, day thirty. Nag-ta-Hert. It has taken us a whole month to siege and burn this accursed place. Sloping walls, sturdy gates, all uphill. Ten thousand bodies to fire. Three hundred of ours to bury. Murmurs of mutiny in Intef's division. Why has Apepa not reacted?"

We will chew that particular bone together also, Tetisheri promised him in her mind. It is not logical that Apepa still has no knowledge of the advance. Where are his troops? He sent Pezedkhu hundreds of miles south to Qes to defeat Seqenenra. What is he waiting for this time? The stirrings of mutiny to spread? Would he presume there would be such dissatisfaction eventually in an army whose men are being asked to kill their own countrymen every day?

Well, so much the better, she said to herself as she undid the second to last letter. Kamose and Hor-Aha can deal with mutiny. They have breached the Delta's southern defences. Nothing lies between them and Het-Uart. Unrolling this missive gave her a glow of sheer triumph and she read it aloud as if to a reverential audience. "Mesore, day thirteen. I am dictating these words within sight of Apepa's great city, sitting in my boat while all around me it is as though the paradise of Osiris has come down to earth. Luxuriant greenness is everywhere, cut through by many wide canals whose water is as blue as the sky that can hardly be glimpsed for the profusion of trees. Birds make a constant musical clamour and the air is full of the odours of ripe fruit from the orchards. I understand now why the northerners call our nome Egypt's southern brazier, for Weset is arid indeed compared to this flagrant fecundity.

"The city of Het-Uart is built on two huge, low mounds, one larger than the other. Each one is defended by massive high walls with sloping outer surfaces. Both are completely encircled by canals that are dry at this time of the year but when filled must make the mounds well-nigh unapproachable. I have sent heralds to the gates of the main mound of Het-Uart, of which there are five, to shout my name and titles and demand Apepa's surrender, but there has been no reply. The gates remain firmly closed and the city, being walled in all its four-mile circumference, is impregnable.

"Our ranks have swelled to nearly thirty thousand infantry, but there is no time to lay down a siege. The Inundation will be upon us in two weeks if Isis wills to cry and I do not want the army to winter here. Therefore I have commanded a scouring of the Delta. Towns, villages, fields, vineyards, and orchards are to be put to the torch to prevent the citizens of Het-Uart from obtaining enough food to sustain them through the siege I intend to mount next campaigning season. The Inundation will do the rest. We still do not know how many soldiers inhabit the two mounds, but Hor-Aha estimates their number to be at least one hundred thousand, perhaps more. Apepa has not released them. He is a fool."

But is he? Tetisheri asked herself as she stood, put that scroll and the latest one into the box, and lowered the lid. If Het-Uart is so impossible to storm, why should he risk his army in an aggressive action? I wouldn't. Let the besieging army grow tired of patrolling those unyielding, unfriendly walls. Let them eat up their stores and then tighten their belts. Let their hearts grow cold and faint as the days go by. You will have to be very clever indeed to overcome both enemies, within and without, my Kamose, Tetisheri mused as she at last perched on the edge of her couch and called for Isis to remove her sandals. Burning half the Delta will not do it. What will? Soon you and I can grapple with this dilemma face to face.

In the two weeks that followed, no further scrolls arrived from the brothers, and Tetisheri found herself fighting once more the ogres of an over-active imagination. Apepa had opened the gates and flooded the Delta with those one hundred thousand warriors. On their way home Kamose had been ambushed by distraught peasants and murdered. Ahmose had fallen ill under the Delta's humidity and was gasping out his life while the fleet was stalled in some northern backwater.

Weset was preparing to celebrate the beginning of the New Year with great feasts for Amun and Thoth, who had given his name to the first month, and the priests whose task it was to record the level of the Nile from day to day waited anxiously for the minute change that would herald the Inundation. Aahmes-nefertari spent the anxious days in solitude, keeping her worry to herself, but Tetisheri and Aahotep made their way to Amun's temple, standing mute while Amunmose's voice was raised in supplication and the incense wreathed about the swaying bodies of the holy dancers.

It was there that the herald found them, coming over the stone flags of the outer court and bowing as they emerged from their devotions. Tetisheri felt Aahotep's hand slide into hers as the man straightened up. "Speak," she offered. He smiled.

"His Majesty will arrive before noon," he said. "His craft is even now upon my heels." Aahotep's fingers were withdrawn.

"That is very good," she said steadily. "Thank you. Are they well?"

"They are well, Majesty." She nodded gravely, but her eyes were shining.

"We will wait by the watersteps. Herald, tell the High Priest that there must be milk and bull's blood at once."

Two hours later the pavement above the steps was crowded with silent watchers. Above them the canopies billowed, white linen rising and collapsing slowly in the hot wind, and under them the whole household stood in tense expectation. Chairs had been set for the three royal women, but they too were on their feet, eyes narrowed against the relentless glare of sunlight on water as they strained to see down river. Behind them the servants and musicians clustered and beside them Amunmose, draped in the leopard skin of his sacerdotal office, rested one hand on the shoulder of the acolyte who clasped the large silver urn containing milk and blood. The censers had been fired, their smoke rising almost invisibly into the fiery air. No one spoke. Even Ahmose-onkh was quiet in his nurse's arms.

The silence was not broken even when the prow of the lead vessel nosed around the bend. It came on like the denizen of a dream, oars dipping to plough the water and rising in a glittering fall of droplets, and not until the assembly could hear the warning cries of the captain did the spell break. Like the legs of some enormous insect the oars were shipped at his command and the craft came gently to rest against the mooring pole. In a sudden whirl of activity, servants rushed to secure it, the ramp appeared, the musicians began to play with a thunder of drums and tremor of lutes, and Amunmose took the urn from the boy. Priestesses shook the systra. But Tetisheri was oblivious to the instantaneous din. Her eyes searched the men grouped on the deck. There was Ahmose, brown and sturdy in his yellow-and-white striped helmet, ringed hands on his hips, the sunlight sparking from the gold lying on his broad chest. He was grinning delightedly at Aahmes-nefertari. But where was Kamose?

Soldiers ran down the ramp to form a guard and Prince Ankhmahor followed. Tetisheri recognized him at once, but her gaze did not linger on him. Chanting the prayers of welcome and blessing, Amunmose began to pour the milk and blood in a pink stream onto the sizzling stone of the paving and a man began to descend the ramp. He was thin, the muscles of his gold-gripped arms and long legs standing out as flexing knots, and his face beneath his blue-and-white headdress seemed all gaunt hollows. Around his neck hung a pectoral Tetisheri knew, Heh kneeling on the heb sign, the Feather of Ma'at, the royal cartouche encircled by the wings of the Lady of Dread, the lapis gleaming a sultry blue in its prison of gold. Bewildered, with a terrible pang, Tetisheri lifted her eyes once more to the man's face. He had reached the foot of the ramp now and was pacing through the sticky, steaming puddles of milk and blood, looking for her, looking at her; it was Kamose himself. "Gods!" Tetisheri breathed, horrified, then she knelt in prostration, Aahotep beside her. "Rise," a voice invited, tired, thin, as thin as the body from which it came, and the women rose. Kamose held out his arms. "Am I really home?" he said, and the women fell into his embrace.

For a long time Tetisheri held him, inhaling his familiar odour, feeling his warm skin against her cheek, only vaguely aware that Aahmes-nefertari was shrieking with joy and Ahmose had passed her in a flash of yellow. Amunmose had ceased his singing, the end of his prayer drowned out by the prattle of greetings and conversation. Kamose released his kin and turned to the High Priest, gripping his hand. "My friend," he said huskily. "I have depended much on your faithfulness and the efficacy of your petitions to Amun on my behalf. Tonight we will all feast together and at dawn I will come to the temple to make my sacrifice to the Great Cackler." Amunmose bowed.

"Majesty, Weset rejoices and Amun smiles," he replied. "I will leave you to the welcome of your family." He backed away and Kamose gestured.

"Mother, Grandmother, you must remember Prince Ankhmahor. He is the Commander of the Followers and also of the Braves of the King. I have left the other Princes with their respective divisions." Ankhmahor performed his reverence and excused himself, issuing orders to the soldiers as he went. Ahmose and his wife were still clasped closely against each other, eyes shut, rocking in mutual elation. Tetisheri, struggling to conceal her shock at Kamose's appearance, was recovering her wits. Glancing behind him at the craft now choking the river from bank to bank, she asked sharply, "Kamose, where is the army? Where is Hor-Aha? Is this all you have brought home with you?" He graced her with a tight smile.

"I have brought all the Medjay," he replied brusquely. "I will discuss my disposition of the remainder of our forces with you later, Tetisheri. Now all I want to do is stand on the bathing slab under a deluge of scented water and then fall onto my own couch." The smile trembled and slipped. "I love you, both of you, all of you," he finished. "I would kiss every servant assembled here if my dignity would allow!" The words were humorous but his voice had broken. For a moment he waited, lips compressed, his gaze wandering across the façade of the house, the limp trees, the small glint of sun on the surface of the pool half-glimpsed beyond the vine trellis, then he started towards the entrance pillars. At once the Followers fell in before and behind him. Ankhmahor strode at his side. But they had not gone far when a grey shape detached itself from the shade of the vine trellis, came streaking towards them, and flung itself at Kamose. He opened his arms and bent down. Whining with joy, Behek pawed him, licking his face and nudging at his neck. Kamose remained still, only his fingers betraying any emotion as he buried them convulsively in the dog's warm fur.

"He looks driven," Aahotep said to Tetisheri in low tones. "Ill."

"He must do nothing but eat and sleep for a while," Tetisheri agreed. "What is it?" Her last words were addressed to the we'eb priest who had come up and was waiting patiently at her elbow.

"Your pardon, Majesty," he said, "but I have been commanded to tell you that the Nile has begun to rise. Isis is crying."

That night the reception hall was full, its shadows no longer melancholy reminders of days gone by. The little dining tables laden with fruit and delicacies were jammed against each other and the guests sat on their cushions almost back to back, garlanded in flowers, their skin gleaming as the fragrant oil in the cones on their wigs melted and ran down their necks. Servants threaded through the noisy crowds, wine jugs or trays of steaming food held high. Music blended with song that burst forth sweetly and intermittently as the excited conversations rose and fell. On the dais the family, resplendent in freshly starched linen, gold dust on their kohled eyelids and henna on their mouths, received the adoration of those who came to their feet to offer thanks and make their reverences. Ankhmahor sat with them, his son seated behind him. The mayor of Weset and other local dignitaries, Amunmose among them, also graced the high table. Ahmose and Aahmes-nefertari ate and drank with arms linked, chattering nonsense, intoxicated more with the sound of the other's voice than with any words.

But Kamose remained silent. With his mother on his left hand and Tetisheri on his right, he ate and drank as one famished, gazing seemingly imperturbably at the happy chaos below. Behek leaned against him and he kept one hand on the dog's grey head, passing him morsels of roast goose or barley bread dipped in garlic oil. Ankhmahor too had nothing to say. For once Tetisheri held her tongue and, after a few attempts to engage her grandson, turned her attention to her own pleasure at the occasion.

Egypt, with the minor exception of the city of Het-Uart, was back in the hands of its rightful rulers at last. Ma'at was about to be restored. Here, spread out before her in noise and laughter was the proof of Tao superiority and her grandson's victorious right to ascend the Horus Throne. It will have to be purified before Kamose lowers himself onto it, she thought, closing her eyes and inhaling the mixed scents of perfumed bodies and flower wreaths that came gusting to her nostrils on a puff of night breeze. All trace of Setiu stench must be removed, but we will have a Setiu likeness etched into the gold of the King's footstool. Yes, indeed we will. Kamose will have to marry whether he wants to or not, but perhaps we will wait until next year when Het-Uart has fallen. I wonder if Kamose has thought to send a message to the mayor of Pi-Hathor, telling him of our success. I would like to tell him myself how annoying it was to have to watch the river constantly for fear a message to Apepa might slip through. But I will tell Kamose nothing yet, she decided, painfully aware of his elbow touching hers, the near immobility of his body. He is in no state to hear me. He must recover first, gain strength. He and Ahmose have not exchanged one word since they arrived home. Now I have new things to worry about, but not tonight. With a sigh she held out her cup for Uni to fill and sipped her wine reflectively. Not tonight.

Long after the guests had staggered to their skiffs or been carried, happily drunk, to their litters, and the lamps in the refuse-strewn hall had been extinguished, Tetisheri still could not sleep. Too much wine and exhilaration had taken their toll and she lay restless and alert on her couch, listening to the pacing of the guard outside her door. The room was close and stuffy, as though the heat of the day had somehow shrunk to the confines of her four walls. Her sleeping gown irritated her skin where it clung and her pillow seemed full of hostile lumps. Sitting up, she folded her hands and gazed into the dimness, thinking how the whole atmosphere of the house had changed with the return of its masters, and hard upon the heels of that reflection came the knowledge that she herself could relax her authority. Major household decisions would be made by Kamose, at least until the flood had abated. That is both a relief and an annoyance, she mused. If I am honest with myself, I must admit that I like the power inherent in my position as matriarch of the Taos. I will try to be careful not to foist my judgements on any military discussions my grandson and I might have. And there is Aahotep. We have become confidantes in the past months and I have discovered that under her serenity lies a lake of stubbornness and implacability that mirrors my own. She must not be excluded from any policies Kamose and I devise. But the truth is that I do want to exclude her. I want to exclude everyone. Tetisheri, you are a domineering old woman.

Leaning her head against the rim of the couch, she closed her eyes, uselessly seeking the first drowsy approach of sleep, then with an exclamation of impatience she tossed back her sheet and reached for a cloak. Outside her door, she greeted the guard, assured him that he need not accompany her, and made her way out into the dusky garden.

The night air was delightfully cool, the heavens thick with a dusting of stars, the grass still damp from its evening watering. I should have put on my sandals, she thought guiltily. Isis will grumble when she anoints my feet tomorrow. But at my age one lapse does not matter. How peaceful this is! As though with Kamose's return the ineffable harmony of Ma'at has suffused Weset with tranquillity.

Drawing the cloak around her, she began to wander slowly towards the river, skirting the shrouded entrance pillars of the house where the guards rose from their stools to reverence her, and taking the short path to the watersteps. The paving, now slightly chilly to her footfalls, was still sticky with the purifying libation Amunmose had poured, and Tetisheri smiled briefly into the darkness as she went. It had been a glorious moment.

The Medjay had left the boats for their quarters and the jumble of empty craft bulked black and misshapen, obscuring the surface of the water. Several guards were gathered around a small fire in a patch of sand beside the watersteps, talking and laughing softly. At her approach they scrambled up in confusion and bowed and for a while she stood with them, comfortable in their presence as she always was with soldiers. They answered her questions respectfully regarding their welfare— were they fed enough? did their captains treat them fairly? were their physical complaints attended to promptly by the army physicians?—and Tetisheri resisted the urge to examine them regarding the details of Kamose's campaigns. Bidding them a safe watch, she turned back, leaving the path and making her way slowly past the fish pond towards the rear of the house.

Coming to the corner and starting around it, she paused. At the far reach of her vision the staff quarters showed as a low rectangle huddled against the outer wall of the estate. A little closer in was the kitchen, set at right angles to the scuffed courtyard that also met the house granary, and closer still were the shrubs and clusters of trees that marked the division between masters' and servants' domain. They had been planted thickly to protect the privacy of the family, and under the sanctuary of their leaves something moved.

Tetisheri froze, one hand against the comforting roughness of the house wall, not quite knowing what had alarmed her. A lone guard would have been upright and pacing. Perhaps the crouching shape was a servant who, like her, could not sleep. It was rocking to and fro, to and fro as though it were a woman with a baby clutched to her breast, but no woman possessed such broad shoulders. Puzzled, her senses sharpened, Tetisheri probed the dimness. The set of those shoulders was familiar, the rhythmic motion conveying an interior agitation that intensified the longer Tetisheri watched, until the space between her and the man was filled with a silent agony.

All at once Tetisheri felt a touch on her arm. Startled, she turned to find Aahotep's shadowed face inches from her own. "I could not sleep either," Aahotep whispered. "The day has been too eventful. What do you see, Tetisheri?" For answer, Tetisheri pointed.

"It is Kamose," she whispered back. "Look at him, swaying like a drunkard."

"Not like a drunkard," Aahotep responded, her eyes on her son. "Like a man trembling on the verge of insanity. He came home just in time, Tetisheri. I feel helpless in the face of such inner pain. He said nothing at the feast. Nothing at all."

"At least he ate his fill," Tetisheri reminded her in a low voice. "That is a good sign. But you are right, Aahotep. I shudder to think in what state he might have arrived if he had not been forced back to Weset by the Inundation." Taking Aahotep's elbow, she drew the other woman away. "He must not know that he has been seen," she said. "Come to my quarters and we will talk." They retraced their steps together in silence for a while, each deep in worried thought, then Aahotep said, "First he needs much sleep. Our physician can prescribe a soporific for him until such time as he is calm enough to sleep without aid. We must make sure he is not burdened with many duties."

"Senehat is a beautiful girl," Tetisheri put in. "In a few days I will send her to his bedchamber. If he can forget himself in making love, that will be a healing thing. It is all the killing," she went on more forcefully. "Necessary, we agreed on that, but Kamose has had to carry the weight of it on his conscience for months. It has almost broken him."

"Then pray that the winter may heal him," Aahotep said grimly, "or we will find ourselves in the direst predicament. I miss my husband tonight, Tetisheri. Seqenenra always seemed to know what to do. I felt secure when his presence filled this house."

"It was an illusion," Tetisheri said brutally as they went in under the shadow of the pillars and entered the shrouded entrance hall. "My son was a brave and intelligent man, but it was not within his power to guarantee us our safety, although he tried. No one can, Aahotep. Kamose also is trying and he has almost succeeded, but that is not the kind of security you mean, is it?"

"No," Aahotep said shortly. "I want the security of never having to make any decision of importance. I do not wish to be anything other than the widow of a great man." They had reached Tetisheri's door and her guard had opened it obligingly for them.

"Go and wake Isis," Tetisheri said. "Tell her to bring us beer and cakes and oil for my lamp. Come in, Aahotep. We are not going to sleep, so we might as well pass the hours until dawn in some fruitful conversation."

They were not able to sit down with Kamose for the next few days. The month of Thoth began with the traditional cele-bration of both the rising of the river and the appearance of the Sopdet Star, and all Weset participated in the festivities. No one worked. Homes were thrown open to relatives and friends and Amun's temple resounded with the shouts and songs of priests and worshippers. A stream of dignitaries kept Aahotep busy with the organization of servants and it was not until the second week of Thoth that the household emerged, relieved and dishevelled, to find that peace had once more descended.

But the flow of another kind did not abate. Scouts and heralds arriving from the north continued to dock at the watersteps and disappear with Kamose and Ahmose into Seqenenra's old office and twice between the rituals and feasts the two men had gone to confer with the officers of the Medjay, enjoying their own brand of holiday. The women and the servants had their own many duties and it was with a collective groan of satisfaction that the pace finally slowed and the family could meet together on the lawn under a canopy on a hot, cloudless morning. "I love the New Year celebrations," Aahmes-nefertari said. She was seated on a cushion at her husband's feet, leaning against his bare calf. "There is always the tiny dread that the Nile will not rise and there will be no sowing, and when it does I'm surprised that I worried at all. Besides, I like the cycle of everything beginning again, the feasts of the gods and the familiar routines in the house and in the fields." Ahmose looked down on her with fondness.

"And for me there is time to hunt and fish while the land floods," he added jovially. "You forgot to add how much you like to lie in the bottom of the skiff and daydream, Aahmes-nefertari, while the ducks fly overhead squawking scornfully at my efforts with the throwing stick!"

Tetisheri scrutinized him with a mixture of annoyance and disbelief. The weeks of tension, the dulling, brutish round of killing and burning right to the gates of Het-Uart itself did not seem to have left any mark on him at all. It was as though he had been on a prolonged visit to somewhere tedious and now was overjoyed to be home. He was sleeping well in his wife's arms, eating and drinking with pleasure, and beaming upon everyone. He always was an unimaginative boy, she thought waspishly. No wonder he cannot suffer. It is unfortunate that Kamose has inherited the sensitivity that should have gone to Ahmose as well as his own.

But no, she corrected herself immediately. I am not being fair. Ahmose may lack the visionary quality that is a part of Kamose's torture but in intelligence he is any man's equal. And I know very well that he is adept at hiding his personality behind this façade of good humour. Why does he do so?

"This year the Inundation has an added value," she said quickly. "It enables the two of you to rest and plan your next campaigns and the army to regroup." She turned deliberately to Kamose. "Where is the army, Kamose?" He smiled across at her and she noted that his eyes had become clearer in the short time he had been home. His face, though still gaunt, now showed a faint suggestion of more fullness, but the stamp of his experiences remained too evident.

"The infantry is quartered at the Uah-ta-Meh oasis," he answered. "It is a hundred miles from the Nile road and there are only two ways to approach it, both across the desert. One runs from Ta-she, the other from the river. There is plenty of water for the troops and no lack of food. Het nefer Apu sits precisely where the track to the oasis meets the Nile road, and is in full control of the navy. So no messages from the Delta can slip past and no one can trek to Uah-ta-Meh without Paheri's permission."

"Paheri? The mayor of Nekheb? What is he doing at Het nefer Apu?" Tetisheri demanded irritably. "And what is this talk of a navy?" Kamose brushed a fly from his arm. It rose reluctantly and settled on Behek's nose. The dog twitched once in his sleep by his master's foot, but did not wake. "Nekheb is famed for its sailors and shipbuilders, as you know," Kamose began to explain. "Ahmose and I decided to take five thousand soldiers and put them in cedar boats. The Medjay still occupy the hundred reed ships I commissioned. They remain in good condition."

"What cedar boats?" Tetisheri interrupted him. "We have no cedar vessels."

"Be patient and I will tell you in a moment," Kamose said. "To continue, Paheri is expert in all matters relating to the care of ships and navigation. We have given Baba Abana the task of turning five thousand infantry into fighting sailors."

Ahmose forestalled his grandmother's next question. "Baba Abana is also from Nekheb," he said. "You might remember him, Grandmother. He served under our father and now he captains one of our ships. He and Paheri are friends. His son Kay distinguished himself in the battles on the canals of the Delta. In fact he came roaring up to Kamose and me in the thick of one engagement, blood all over him, and shouted, "Majesty, how many Setiu must I kill before I am allowed to go home? I have dispatched twenty-nine so far in this little war of yours!" He made us laugh. It was the only time since leaving Weset that Kamose laughed."

Tetisheri pursed her lips. "And how many infantry are at the oasis?"

"Fifty-five thousand," Kamose told her. "Eleven divisions. I believe that we are now at our fullest strength. There will be no more recruits or conscripts. I brought the five thousand Medjay back with me."

"So." Tetisheri pondered for a moment, her eyes on the play of bright sunlight beyond the thin shade of the canopy. "But was it wise to leave the bulk of the army at Uah-ta-Meh, Kamose? The flood will of course prevent access to the oasis from the Nile, but the overland route from the Delta to

Ta-she and then to the oasis is open all year round. If Apepa learns of the troops' presence there he can march down and surround them."

"Providing he can confirm that they are there," Kamose responded quickly. "As far as he is concerned, we are nothing more than a rabble bent on burning and looting. The five thousand men I left at Het nefer Apu will be training all winter on the swollen river. They cannot hide. Apepa will presume that they are all the strength we have."

"Why should he?" Tetisheri objected. "He had the chance to assess the number of our divisions during the siege last summer."

"Not so," he answered her patiently. "The siege encompassed miles of city wall. It was not a matter of soldiers drawn up stiffly in formation day after day. The army was fluid. There was much coming and going and besides, many of my men were occupied in sacking the Delta villages. The oasis is safe, Grandmother. It is a hundred miles from Ta-she, a hundred miles from the Nile, and the people there go nowhere. Any stranger entering it will be immediately arrested. Where else could we put fifty-five thousand men without discovery?" Tetisheri was only faintly mollified. She was about to speak again when Aahotep picked the persistent fly out of her hair and swung to Kamose.

"Tell us about the cedar ships now," she said. "Where did they come from, Kamose?" The brothers looked at each other, grinning, and for a brief second the women saw in Kamose the return of the man who had left them whole and untainted.

"We have been saving this as a surprise," he announced. "While we were sieging Het-Uart, Paheri and Abana captured thirty baw-ships of cedar loaded with treasure intended as New Year's gifts for Apepa from his fellow chieftains in the east. They were taken easily. The sailors were confused, not knowing what had been happening in the Delta, for they had set sail

from Rethennu. Kamose, send for Neshi to read the list."
Kamose nodded and beckoned Akhtoy.

"He should be in the temple storerooms," he told the steward. "Have him come here, Akhtoy." When the man had bowed and walked away, he held up a hand. "Neshi has proved himself an honest and meticulous Army Scribe, so I have appointed him Royal Treasurer," he explained. "He takes his work very seriously. He calculated the long-term loss of the goods to Apepa in terms of court, army and commercial restraints down to the last uten's weight. Of course there will be nothing for Apepa from Teti-en this year. All traffic from the south has to get past Weset. I foresee a rather lean future for the usurper."

They waited in an expectant silence. Uni unobtrusively replenished the beer in their cups. Ahmose fell to stroking his wife's warm head. Aahotep took a sweetmeat from the platter on the table and nibbled at it absently while Tetisheri's ringed fingers drummed a rhythm on the arm of her chair, a frown creasing her kohled brows. "I suppose you have already decided on the distribution of this treasure," she said at last. "We are not short of food for the winter, Kamose, but we do need lamp oil and sundry household effects. We gave everything we could spare to the army."

"And you did so without grumbling, Grandmother," he rejoined, "but the needs of this estate are still low on my scale of priorities. Ah! Here is Neshi." The Royal Treasurer's litter had been lowered some distance away and he and his scribe came briskly over the dry grass, the latter struggling with a large box on top of which he had balanced his palette. Neshi came to a halt and bowed and the scribe followed suit after laying his burdens on the ground.

Tetisheri looked them over carefully. The Royal Treasurer was a young man with a downturned mouth and two deep grooves between his eyebrows that gave him a perpetually worried expression. He also had large ears, and rather than try to hide them he had accentuated their size by hanging them with fat golden pendants. Tetisheri approved. Such a man would not be easily cowed. "Greetings, Neshi," Kamose said. "Please give an accounting of the goods taken from Apepa's baw-ships." Neshi smiled and gestured to his scribe. They are all very pleased with themselves over this feat, Tetisheri thought, amused. It has been an accomplishment lifted out of its proper proportion and placed against the grinding miseries of the campaign. Truly a gift from Amun, who saw the desperation in their hearts. But as Neshi began to read from the scroll handed to him, she drew in her breath at the magnificence of the prize.

"Of gold dust, forty sacks. Of gold bars, three hundred. Five pieces of lapis of the finest quality measuring three widths of Your Majesty's hands. Of pure silver, five hundred bars. Of green turquoise of the finest quality, sixty pieces. Of copper axes, two thousand and fifty. Of olive oil, one hundred barrels. Of incense, ninety-four sacks. Of fat, six hundred and thirty jars, and of honey five hundred. Of precious woods, nine lengths of ebony and one thousand seven hundred and twenty lengths of cedar."

"And all ours!" Ahmose exulted as Neshi passed the scroll back to his scribe. "What do you think of that, Grandmother?"

"I am rendered almost speechless," Tetisheri answered, and Aahotep cut in, "Almost but not quite!" They all laughed.

"Is Amun pleased with his share?" Kamose asked the Royal Treasurer. Neshi bowed again.

"The tallying is complete, Majesty," he said. "The High Priest will doubtless come to you in person to express his gratitude."

"Thank you. You can go." He turned to Tetisheri. "The axes have already been distributed among the troops," he explained. "That was done before we sailed for home. I sent most of the oil to the oasis together with the fat and honey. The troops must not exhaust themselves foraging in the unlikely event that their supplies of those things run out, and in any case it will be well to begin the next battle season with plenty of these commodities on hand. However, the gold, silver and precious stones have been stored in Amun's treasury against the day when I ascend the Horus Throne. I have given to Amun for his own use and for the citizens of Weset ten sacks of gold dust and one hundred bars of gold."

"How did gold in such quantity get to the Delta?" Aahmes-nefertari wondered. "It cannot all have been tribute from Rethennu, for that country does not have gold mines. Only Kush and Wawat can supply that kind of wealth. And what of the lapis? That also comes from Kush. No ship has passed our watch here, Kamose." He shrugged.

"I don't know," he admitted. "The same is true of the incense. Perhaps Apepa has established caravan routes from Kush to the Delta so as to avoid Weset entirely. We can only speculate. In any case it was a marvellous stroke of luck and we must thank Amun for it."

"For the cedar in particular," Ahmose added. "We can send it to Nekheb and build more ships to replace the reed ones, use them to establish a southern branch of the navy." Tetisheri reached across and took Kamose's hand, feeling the bones under her fingers where the flesh had melted away, and skin as cold as her own.

"It was a miraculous surprise," she said gently. "A sign of approval from the gods." She hesitated, wanting to ask of Hor-Aha, how he had fared in his relations with the Princes, whether he could maintain control of them at the oasis during the months of winter, anything rather than the question that burned, she knew, on Aahotep's tongue. "But we long to hear of a greater treasure, Kamose. Is there any news of Tani?" Kamose's hand slid out of her grip and another silence fell, this one fraught with uneasiness. Ahmose shifted on his chair and folded his arms. Aahotep bent her head and began to study her fly whisk. Aahmes-nefertari was chewing her lip with henna-stained teeth.

"Tani," Kamose said heavily. "The closer we came to the Delta the more she was on my mind. Ramose and I spoke of her constantly in the long nights. We would storm Het-Uart, rush the palace, run to the harem, and Ramose would sweep her into his embrace and carry her away. Of course we knew we were dreaming, but we needed the dream. Needed it badly." His face twisted in distress. "The reality was a city girt by a long high wall and impregnable gates that we could not storm. We could see the palace, though. Its roof loomed above the wall. I gave orders that no arrows were to be wasted on the soldiers who patrolled the top of the encircling fortification. What would have been the point? And once the women of the palace realized that they were in no danger from flying missiles, they began to gather on that roof every evening to stare down at us. A flock of beautiful birds they were, in their brocades and gauzy veils." He stopped speaking and swallowed, running a hand through his black mane, and Tetisheri thought idiotically that she must order Akhtoy to see that it was cut. Kamose glanced almost appealingly at his brother but Ahmose was looking grimly away. "Our soldiers enjoyed the sight," Kamose went on eventually. "They would stand in the shadow of the wall, looking up and taunting the women. 'Come down and let us show you what a real man can do,' they would call. 'Your Setiu lord is impotent. Come down!' The women never answered the teasing, and after a time I put a stop to it for fear they would not come to the roof, for fear a chance to see Tani might be lost. But she did not come. Sunset after sunset I stood with Ramose and

Ahmose, craning up until our necks ached and our eyes watered, but she did not appear."

"Either she is dead or Apepa deliberately forbade her to show herself to us," Ahmose put in roughly. "Ramose wanted to seek admittance to the city under the excuse of a parley but Kamose would not let him." Kamose rounded on his brother.

"We will never parley with him," he said fiercely. "Never! Not for Tani, not for anyone!" Tetisheri felt Aahotep stiffen. This wound was obviously still fresh between the young men.

"You were right in your decision to have no verbal dealings with Apepa," Tetisheri said swiftly. "To do so at this stage would be seen by him as a suspicion of weakness. We are all preoccupied with Tani's fate. It is the dark river running under all our actions and conversations. But Ahmose, for the sake of our sanity we must presume that she still lives. We must hope without evidence that Amun has decreed her preservation."

"Where is Ramose?" Aahotep wanted to know. "His mother will want to see him."

"He elected to stay at Het nefer Apu with the navy," Ahmose told her. "He somehow feels that if he stays closer to the Delta than Weset, Tani might feel his presence. It is a sweet but illogical fantasy."

"Perhaps," Kamose said hoarsely. "But I understand him. I am well acquainted with the power of the ephemeral." Are you indeed? Tetisheri thought, regarding him carefully. I wonder what you mean. She eased herself from her chair, shook out her linens, and snapped her fingers at Uni.

"It is time to eat," she announced. "Aahotep, find your cousin and tell her what is happening with her son. She is probably in the nursery with Ahmose-onkh. Your news is good, Kamose. Rest now." They scrambled up obediently and Tetisheri left them, walking towards the house under the protection of the small sunshade Isis had hurriedly lifted over her head.

The sultry weight of a hot afternoon descended on the house. Servants and family alike shut themselves up in darkened rooms to lie drowsy and languorous under Ra's molten breath. Ahmose and his wife made love and then fell asleep, their sweat-slick bodies entangled together. Aahotep, after trying to staunch the flow of her cousin's ready tears, also slipped into an uneasy slumber. But Kamose lay awake, his mind far away with Hor-Aha and his army, and Tetisheri, though she yawned under the expert fingers of her masseur, had no desire to waste the hours in unconsciousness. She had too much to think about.

When the household began to stir and the first fragrant odours of the evening meal began to drift into the garden, Tetisheri made her way determinedly to her grandson's quarters, only to be told by Akhtoy that Kamose had gone out. Enquiries revealed that he had not taken a skiff, nor was he in the temple. With a glance up at a sky beginning to acquire the slightly pearly hue of the impending sunset, Tetisheri strode across the lawn and picked her way through the rubble of the wall that separated the estate from the environs of the old palace.

She seldom went there, afraid of the danger of falling bricks from which, at her age, she would not be able to flee. Besides, the gloomy rooms and empty pedestals made her both angry and melancholy, reminding her both of the depths to which her illustrious family had fallen and of her son who had loved to meditate on the crumbling roof where Apepa's long arm had at last reached out to destroy him. Seeing her intent, the guard who was with her began to remonstrate, but she thanked him warmly for his concern, told him to wait for her by the cavernous main entrance, and went forward into the reception hall.

It was always gloomy in that vast space. Footfalls echoed, whispers were magnified into a hundred ghostly voices, and everywhere the floor was littered with traps of broken stone and half-hidden holes, as though the palace mourned its ancient inhabitants and wished to capture more. Holding up her sheath, eyes on her sandalled feet, Tetisheri stepped gingerly past the wide dais on which the Horus Throne once stood and groped her way along the rear passages until she came to the open mouth where thick double doors of electrum had once heralded the women's quarters. Here there were shafts of sunlight bursting through the intact clerestory windows high above and she had no difficulty finding the rough stairs leading onto the roof. Muttering an imprecation against her grandson's predilection for odd corners in which to find privacy, she began to climb.

She found him where she knew she would, sitting with his back against the ruined windcatcher, knees drawn up, arms folded across them. There was no sign of his guard or his dog. He stirred a little when she appeared but did not look at her, and she brushed away the sharp pebbles and stone dust before settling herself beside him as best she could. For a while they rested in a companionable silence, both watching the shadows of early evening lengthen across the roof, until Tetisheri said, "Why do you think Apepa has not answered your challenge, Kamose? Why has he done nothing?" He blew out his breath and shook his head.

"I do not know," he answered. "Certainly there are enough troops within Het-Uart to have engaged us and perhaps even defeated our forces. To my mind there are two reasons for his delay. The first lies in the man himself. He is both cautious and over-confident. Cautious in that he will not take any gamble. Confident because his ancestors have been in power for many hentis and they bequeathed those years of peace to him. Neither he nor his father have had cause to lift the sword, indeed, Apepa has not even bothered to establish an efficient network of spies. He has relied entirely on sporadic information from nobles like Teti. The second reason is a logical one. He believes that we will simply exhaust ourselves with waiting and in the end give up and go home. Then he can unleash his soldiers without fear of any loss."

"I agree," Tetisheri said, pleased that he had arrived at the same conclusions as she. "But of course you will not give up. Have you any plans for the summer?" Glancing at him, she saw him smile coldly.

"All I can do is continue the siege and taunt him daily in the hope that he will become exasperated enough to open the gates and release his army," he said.

"And does Ahmose agree with you?" She had put the question tentatively and his smile became a harsh bark of humourless laughter.

"Ahmose is all for retreating from Het-Uart and fortifying Het nefer Apu," he said bitterly. "He wants to make that our northern boundary, establishing permanent troops there to prevent Apepa from flowing south. He wants to use the remaining forces to revive the towns I have decimated. He imagines that I ought to be content with ruling over an Egypt still divided, still stained with the sheep herder's feet. He would undo everything that I have done!"

Tetisheri hesitated before speaking, aware that she was trying to enter a dark place where one wrong word could slam the door in her face. "I am sorry that Ahmose wishes to pursue a different policy," she began cautiously. "I feel as you do, that Egypt will not be cleansed until the Setiu are driven beyond our borders. But I also believe that Ahmose is unchanged in his desire to see full Ma'at restored. It is just that he is more patient than we. He is afraid to proceed rashly and risk ultimate failure. It might be beneficial to build a fort at Het nefer Apu, Kamose, regardless of how you approach the problem of Het-Uart. That way the south is indeed safeguarded."

"Afraid, yes," Kamose cut in vehemently, and Tetisheri saw that he had begun to tremble. "He is afraid. He fears the purging, he fears the decisive action, always he is preaching discretion, prudence. He argues against every move Hor-Aha and I make."

"Not in public I hope!" Tetisheri said sharply. "The two of you must be seen to agree, Kamose! Dissension between you will weaken the soldiers' morale and erode the trust of the Princes!" He rounded on her savagely.

"Do you think I don't know that?" he said loudly. "Tell that to my brother, not to me! Tell him how his lack of support wounds me! Tell him how I have had to command one filthy massacre after another without his understanding, his comfort! Tell him that I am forced to contend with his tacit disapproval when I most need his strength! Must the weight of Egypt's oppression fall on my shoulders alone?" She touched his shaking arm and found it clammy and cold. Alarmed, she began to stroke it soothingly.

"You are the King," she reminded him quietly. "In your divinity you are alone. Even if Ahmose stood behind you as nothing but an instrument of your will, you would still inhabit the desert of uniqueness. No matter how Ahmose feels, and I do not believe that he is as opposed to you as you think, he cannot remove that truth. Your friends must be the gods, Majesty." She saw his chest constrict and his hand closed over her own, stilling its movement.

"I am sorry, Grandmother," he murmured. "Sometimes my reason begins to fracture and I see phantoms of betrayal where there are none. I love Ahmose and I know he loves me whether he always agrees with me or not. As for the gods..." He looked away, and all she could see was the curve of his cheek. The rest of his features were hidden by the fall of glossy hair. "I forgot to sacrifice to Thoth before I burned Khemmenu. I promised Aahotep and then I forgot. I forgot to celebrate the anniversary of Ahmose's birth, too, in Payni. Something terrible is happening to me." She withdrew her hand from his painful grip and kneeling up she took his face between her palms and compelled him to look at her.

"Kamose," she said deliberately, "it is not as important as you think. We sacrificed for Ahmose here in the temple to mark the beginning of his twentieth year. As for Thoth, he is the god of wisdom. He sees into your heart. You did not purposely neglect him. Your mind was occupied with a task of which he himself approves. If you do not try to wrench your thoughts away from these deadly fantasies, you will indeed go mad, and then where will Egypt be?" She removed her hands for fear he should sense the pounding of her heart through her fingers. "Now tell me of the disposition of the army," she ordered. "I want to hear about the navy you are forming. Describe the mood of the Princes. Are they bowing under Hor-Aha's yoke? Tell me the story of Kay Abana again. Tell me of the capture of the baw-ships. Kamose. Kamose!"

Slowly he obeyed her, and with relief she saw a frown of concentration grow between his thick eyebrows. He picked up a brick shard and began to roll it absently up and down his thigh as he spoke. His words became increasingly clipped and dispassionate, the progression of his thoughts methodical, but sometimes his voice would begin to rise, the phrases flow faster, until with a conscious effort he controlled himself. "I have a mind to build a prison here at Weset," he finished. "I will put Simontu in charge of it. He is the scribe of the prison already existing, and a Scribe of Ma'at. He administers the city's granaries. I want to put ordinary peasants under him."

"A new prison?" Tetisheri, momentarily lulled by the lucidity of his previous discourse, was taken aback. "But why, Kamose? We have few criminals in this nome." His lip curled.

"It will be for foreigners," he said. "They will work off their sentences under the authority of peasants, for surely our meanest commoners are as nobles compared to men of alien blood."

"Your father would not approve," Tetisheri managed.

"If Seqenenra had imprisoned all our servants of doubtful ancestry, he would not have been so badly maimed," he retorted. "Mersu would have been safely shut away. I will take no chances here at home, Tetisheri. I have not put Weset to the sword. I do not want to. But the Setiu threat is everywhere, even in our own city. I intend to winnow out the foreign chaff, but I will be merciful. I will segregate, not exterminate." He pulled himself to his feet and reached down. "Let me help you, Grandmother. The sun is setting and the palace below will be dark. Hold my hand." Speechlessly she accepted the offer. Now his skin burned against hers, but she could not pull away from him. She needed his guidance through the empty murk beneath them.

All that evening and far into the night she pondered his words, probing behind them in the hope that she might discover to what extent his soul had sickened. He was exhausted both physically and emotionally, that was obvious, but was his instability merely the result of a fatigue that would fade or was it rooted more deeply? If he broke, they were doomed, unless Ahmose could assume the leadership of the army. Sitting before her cosmetic table while Isis expertly laid the kohl over her wrinkled eyelids and hennaed her withered hands, she allowed the hurt to wash through her.

She loved all the members of her family, loved them with a fierce, possessive pride, but Kamose had been her favourite since the day she had gazed into his solemn little face and recognized a personality much like her own. The years of his growing had reinforced that familiarity. A bond of ka and intellect had formed between them, a consensus of often unspoken agreement. He was far more her son than Aahotep's, or so she had secretly avowed, but now she wondered if perhaps Aahotep's calmness had been transferred to her middle child as a brittleness that had only surfaced under extreme stress. To have to think of Kamose as having faults was wounding. It reflected on her powers of judgement. A remedy must be sought.

At dinner that night, while Kamose sat as before with Behek leaning against his leg, the dog's liquid eyes fixed on his master's closed face, Tetisheri watched Ahmose as the young man ate and drank, rained kisses on his wife and bantered good-naturedly with the servants. He is completely at ease, she thought. I have never really noticed before how they approach him deferentially but with the confidence that they will not be rebuffed. Kamose commands respect tinged with awe and that is right, it is correct, yet would such a cold thing as respect without affection survive the failure of a king to maintain the aloof sanity of godhead? I did not realize before that Kamose cannot inspire affection.

Sighing, Tetisheri lifted her wine cup to her mouth and drank to hide the flash of disloyalty that insight had brought. Should I approach Ahmose with this burden? she wondered. What really lies behind those limpidly placid eyes of his? Would he repel me with a superficial platitude or grant me the surprise of wisdom? I am ashamed that I do not know. I have taken him too lightly for too long, preferring to contemplate my delight in his brother. Oh, my darling Kamose, I want you to be strong, vital, embody all the virtues bequeathed to you by your lordly ancestors. I want the proud legacy of the Taos to go to you, not to Ahmose.

She requested a draught of poppy that night so that she could sleep, but the effects of the drug wore off long before the dawn and left her suddenly alert, her mind filling with thoughts that buzzed inside her head like a swarm of direction-less bees. Resignedly she left her couch, opened her Amun shrine, and began to pray. It was some time before she realized that she was addressing her dead husband and not the God of Double Plumes.

# Chapter FIVE

IN THE MORNING Tetisheri got into her litter and had herself carried north to Amun's temple. The day was fine, glittering with a brief freshness that would fade as Ra strengthened, and she travelled with the curtains open so that she could enjoy the view. The river was rising slowly, its turbid current beginning to flow faster in the cool depths where the fish lurked, but its surface rippled brightly as the wind whipped the water. The stiff palm trees and spreading sycamores seemed to lean thirstily towards it in anticipation of their yearly immersion, their branches alive with nesting birds, and in the green reed beds that choked its shallows the herons stood bemused on their delicate legs, their pristine white plumage ruffled by the warm air.

A group of naked children were running in and out of the water with shrieks of delight. They fell silent and bowed to her as she passed and she raised a benign hand to them, smiling at their unselfconscious happiness. War means nothing to them, she thought, answering yet another obeisance from a cluster of women and young girls laden with baskets of laundry. They are protected here in Weset. My son died to make it so. The bawling of oxen alerted her to more traffic on the road and reluctantly she twitched the curtains closed, hearing her guard call a warning and the litter sway as her bearers negotiated the obstruction. The odour of the animals filtered through to her, sun-warmed hide and a hint of dung, and a wave of contentment filled her. The cosmic reality of Ma'at seemed in perfect balance.

She felt the litter turn north and she was gently lowered. Waiting until Isis stepped up with the sunshade, she emerged, squinting at the sudden assault of harsh light, and walked towards the temple. To her left, the chapel of the Osiris King Senwosret lay baking in the sun, and farther along to her right his pillars soared stark and lofty against the horizon. Behind them lay the sacred lake, a pleasing stone rectangle placidly reflecting the vivid blue of the sky. Amun's precinct was straight ahead at the end of the paved path, and as she approached it, Tetisheri could hear the click of finger cymbals and the voices of priests raised in song. The morning rituals were being concluded. Amun had been washed, censed, and fed. Flowers, wine and perfumed oil had been offered to him and His Majesty had been adored.

Entering the courtyard, Tetisheri paused. Amunmose had just shut and bolted the doors to the sanctuary and was applying the seal that would remain in place until the evening rites took place. Turning, he saw her and bowed, then came to her swiftly, removing from his shoulder the leopard skin and passing it to an acolyte who bore it reverently away. "Greetings, Amunmose," Tetisheri said. "I have come to see the treasure my grandson brought home." He returned her smile and gestured to the storerooms and priests' cells lining the outer wall of the temple.

"It is good to see you, Majesty," he responded cheerfully. "The goods have all been tallied and sorted. His Majesty has been most generous to Amun and I am grateful."

"His Majesty knows how much he owes to the power of

Amun and the loyalty of his priest," Tetisheri answered as they began to walk together across the court. "You have given Kamose far more than your trust, Amunmose, and he regards you as a friend."

"When His Majesty rids Egypt of the foreigners, he has promised to make Weset the centre of the world and elevate Amun to the status of King of the Gods," Amunmose commented. "We are living in stirring times. Each one of us has been called to examine where our fealty lies." He hesitated, drew breath to continue, hesitated again, and as they arrived at the storeroom door and were bowed into the welcome coolness by a temple guard, he swung to face her. Seeing his reluctance to speak, she snapped, "Well, Amunmose? What is it?"

"It is the omens, Majesty," he blurted. "They have not been good since His Majesty returned home. The blood that poured from the bull I sacrificed as a thanksgiving was black and it stank. All the doves were rotten inside. I do not exaggerate."

"Of course you don't!" Tetisheri stared at him unseeingly for a moment. "Were the sacrifices made specifically on Kamose's behalf or in gratitude for the progress of his war?"

"They were made for His Majesty alone, a gift to Amun for keeping him safe. I fear for his life, Tetisheri, yet he is in good health, the army prospers, and most of Egypt is back in the hands of your divine family. I do not understand, but I am more than worried. What have the gods decreed? How has he displeased them? The fate of Egypt is being decided in the person of your grandson. Do the gods not care?"

"You are the High Priest! You should know!" Tetisheri barked back at him, in her panic ignoring his use of her name. "Why was I not told of this before? Kamose has been home for nearly a week!"

"Forgive me," Amunmose said diffidently. "I did not want to distress you prematurely. There was the bull first, and I sacrificed the doves the following day to be sure that the first omen was correct. When it was confirmed, I consulted the oracle." Tetisheri wanted to shake him. His expression, usually so open and artless, was a mixture of insecurity and alarm and he was fidgeting nervously with the full sleeves of his shift.

"And what," she said with obvious deliberation through clenched teeth, "did the oracle say?" His shoulders slumped and he managed a rueful smile.

"I am sorry," he said at once. "I have been fumbling and imprecise out of my own great concern. The oracle spoke these words. 'Three Kings there were, then two, then one, before the work of the god was done.' That was all."

"That was all? Then what does it mean? Did the oracle elaborate? What are we supposed to make of it and what use is it if it makes no sense to us?" Faced with her own incomprehension, her quick temper was rising and she fought to control it. "Are we supposed to sit around discussing interpretations until some ray of new inspiration strikes us? Three Kings, then two, then one. What in the name of Amun is that about?" Amunmose was used to her outbursts. Going farther into the room, he brought back a stool and set it behind her. She sank onto it absently.

"I am indeed the High Priest," he said. "I am also the First Prophet of Amun. The god speaks to the oracle but the authority to interpret is mine."

"Well, stop shredding your linen and perform your task!" He nodded.

"There were three Kings, three true Kings in Egypt," he said. "Seqenenra the Mighty Bull of Ma'at, Beloved of Amun; his son Kamose, the Hawk-in-the-Nest; and his youngest son, Prince Ahmose. We cannot consider poor Si-Amun, who sold his birthright and paid the price. Your son, Seqenenra, was killed. In that moment Kamose, the Hawk-in-the-Nest, became the Mighty Bull in his father's place."

"I know where you are going," Tetisheri interposed huskily. "The god's work has begun but is not yet completed, and before it is, there will be only one King left. Ahmose." She rose to her feet determinedly. "But the prophetic utterance has not been set into the fabric of time, Amunmose, and my whole being revolts against the presumption that His Majesty will die before old age carries him into the Judgement Hall. Supposing the work of the god will not be done until the very last foreigner is expelled from our soil? That could be long after Het-Uart has fallen and Apepa executed. Besides, what if the last King is Ahmose-onkh?"

"That would make four Kings," Amunmose reminded her. "We are clutching at straws here, Majesty. Perhaps my interpretation is faulty?" She sighed.

"No, I do not think so. But I refuse to believe that Kamose will not sit on the Horus Throne here in Weset once it has been snatched back from that upstart Apepa. The god will not be angry if we try to draw out the sentence of fate; therefore, I will command a doubling of guards upon Kamose and set a watch upon his food and drink."

"He may succumb to the prophecy in battle."

"He may." She waved an impatient hand at the sacks and chests piled all around her. "I am no longer interested in examining the treasure," she said. "Tell me, Amunmose, have you noticed any changes in my grandson since he returned?" His eyes narrowed and met hers shrewdly.

"Majesty, you and I have been partners in the service of the god and the furtherance of the Tao destiny since I came to the temple as a we'eb priest," he reminded her. "You would not ask me that question unless there were grounds for a positive answer. I am His Majesty's faithful servant and my first loyalty goes to him, but if I thought he had become other than what he is, I would let you know." He shrugged. "His Majesty seemed a trifle brusque and very preoccupied. That is all."

"Thank you. Please keep the oracle's saying to yourself, Amunmose. Kamose must not have his confidence undermined by the added weight of an impending doom to which he might not succumb for hentis. I will see you on the twenty-second of this month for the celebration of the Feast of the Great Manifestation of Osiris." Acknowledging his obeisance, she left him, walking quickly back to her litter with Isis holding the sunshade above her.

This is cruel, she thought furiously, as her litter jolted on its way back to the house. This is not acceptable, Amun, this is no way to repay my grandson's devotion to Egypt. He has emptied himself, he has suffered, and you reward him with the promise that he will be dead before you reign over a purified country. I do not like you today. Not at all. So she fumed, fists clenched in her lap so that she should not feel the deeper emotions, pain and fear, until she was ready to let them consume her.

She did not re-enter the house. Sending Isis with a message to Uni to keep back her midday meal, she ordered her bearers to continue on behind the gardens, beyond the servants' quarters and the granaries, to where the Followers of His Majesty were billeted. Here the élite guards of the King had comfortable barracks fronting their own small pond and lawn and their commander, Prince Ankhmahor, occupied a detached cell of three large rooms. Tetisheri walked straight in, startling the scribe seated on a mat on the floor, scrolls piled around him. Laying aside his palette, he scrambled up and bowed to her hastily. "Majesty," he stammered. "It is an honour. The Prince is not here."

"So I see," Tetisheri said tartly. "Go and find him. I will wait." He bowed again and Tetisheri was pleased to see that he gathered up the scrolls and placed them in their box before backing out of the room. Doubtless he had been copying information regarding the Followers for storage in the archives. Such information was not forbidden to her, but protocol required her to demand it from the commander, who would have been angry with his servant if he knew that the man had left it lying under unauthorized eyes, even those of Tetisheri herself.

She found a chair and sat facing the open door, listening to the strident blend of birdsong in the trees outside, until the light beyond was cut off and Ankhmahor strode in. He shook the dust from his sandals, then reverenced her politely, and she looked into his face with a lightening of her heart. "It is good to see you, Ankhmahor," she said. "I was glad when I heard that my grandson had appointed you Commander of the Followers. I knew your mother. She was an estimable woman." He smiled, standing easily before her, the wings of his blue-and-white striped helmet framing features that exuded the calm sobriety Kamose trusted.

"Your Majesty is gracious," he replied. "How may I serve you?" He did not apologize for being absent when she arrived, and she was secretly pleased. Any hint of obsequiousness made her irritable. She straightened her spine and with it came an interior tautening.

"I want you to tell me how Kamose seems to you," she began. "I will be honest with you, Prince. I am worried about him. Since he came home, he has been withdrawn and when he does speak his words are bitter and sometimes even unbalanced." She paused and then plunged on, quelling the spurt of disloyalty she felt. "I love my grandson and the state of his health is vital to me, but there is more at stake here than Kamose's mental condition. Is he fit to remain in charge of the army?" The question was out now, hanging in the air like a condemnation. Tetisheri felt herself diminished by it, as though some of her omnipotence had been sucked from her with the utterance, and she was suddenly very thirsty. Ankhmahor's eyebrows had shot up, and without being invited to do so he settled himself on the edge of the desk.

"I think that under any other circumstances in the fortunes of our country I would have to say no," he said frankly. "His Majesty has swept north with a ruthlessness and brutality that has horrified many. Egypt is almost a wasteland, but it is the action of a purge, planned and executed out of necessity, not cruelty. Such an action on the part of a King ruling a free and stable Egypt merely being threatened by, say, an incursion from the desert tribes, would be seen as madness. It is to your grandson's high credit that the uncompromising nature of his deeds has resulted in personal suffering. He has felt every sword thrust into Egyptian flesh and that pain has increased his hatred of the Setiu for compelling him both to do these things and to feel them so deeply." He glanced at her thoughtfully. "There is also his need to revenge his father's death and his brother's suicide. He is being tempered in the very fire he has lit, Majesty. It may consume him in the end, but not before he has completed the task. He has my total allegiance."

"How do the other Princes regard him?" Ankhmahor smiled slowly.

"At first they were terrified that he might succeed," he told her. "Even though they had pledged to him, they wanted to be spared a lot of bloodshed and inconvenience. Later they went in awe of him for what he accomplished and for his harshness." Awe, Tetisheri repeated to herself. Awe. Yes.

"And now?" she prodded him. "What of Hor-Aha?" His gaze became speculative.

"You are a Queen of surprising intuition," he said softly. "I had heard of the pride and intractability of the Tao women, but not of their masculine turn of mind. I mean you no disrespect, Majesty."

"I am not offended. We share an ancient lineage, Ankhmahor. Well?"

"The Princes do not like the General. They are jealous of what they see as his hold upon His Majesty. They resent being under his command."

"And Ahmose agrees with them."

Ankhmahor sighed. "His Highness is a man of great perception, moderate in his views and his speech. He shares his brother's affection for Hor-Aha and acknowledges his skill in matters of warfare, but he is not blind to the danger of the situation. His Majesty is. Loyalty has become the only creed by which he judges."

Tetisheri's thirst had intensified. She swallowed with difficulty. "Can Kamose hold them together?" she asked bluntly.

"I believe so, as long as he continues to give them victory. If the siege goes badly next season, they will blame the General. If His Majesty defends him, there will be trouble. But I do not like to enter the world of 'ifs.'"

"I do not like to either, but I must," Tetisheri said. "I want you to increase the guard you put on him, Ankhmahor."

"May I ask why?" Again she hesitated, and it came to her that she trusted this man as she had trusted her husband, without reservation. The knowledge spread through her like a balm.

"Because this morning Amunmose told me that the omens for Kamose were bad," she said flatly. "There has been an unfavourable oracle. I am not really afraid of an attack on his person while he is here, but it is well to take every precaution." She rose clumsily, her joints stiff. "Thank you for your candour, Prince. I do not require reports from you, indeed that might be construed as an invasion of your responsibilities." She smiled. "Look after him." She moved to the door and turned to receive his obeisance.

"He is a great man, worthy to wear the Double Crown, Majesty," he said. "I pray that he will be remembered with love."

I doubt it, Tetisheri thought, as she hurried towards the house. His mighty aim to free Egypt, the baiting of this family by Apepa, Seqenenra's bravery and our desperation, it will all disappear. Only my grandson's remorselessness will remain. Few men in ages to come will know enough to testify on his behalf.

Once back in her own quarters, Tetisheri sent Isis to fetch her meal. "But first," she ordered, "bring me beer or I shall faint." When it came, she drank deeply and gratefully before demolishing the food her servant had set before her. The conversation with Ankhmahor, distressing though it had been, had somehow comforted her, and in the increasing torpor of a blazing afternoon she took to her couch and slept without moving.

After her exchange with Ankhmahor, Tetisheri felt more settled in her mind. She agreed with the Prince that Kamose's reason, though threatened, would not collapse, and with that assurance she turned her attention to making sure that the healing of his interior wounds was not hindered by any physical want. Mindful of the oracle's words, she quietly reminded Akhtoy that His Majesty's food and drink must always be tasted, and she made sure that the finest and most varied selection of meats, dried fruits and vegetables was set before him.

With a deliberate calculation she decided that a female in his bed would bring him a healthful forgetfulness and accordingly she summoned Senehat, made her disrobe, examined her carefully, ordered Isis to wash, shave and perfume her, and sent her to Kamose's quarters, after reminding her that no law in Egypt could compel her to comply with her mistress's wishes in this matter and if she chose to decline the honour of sharing

the King's couch someone else would be eager to accept. Senehat complied, but soon returned to Tetisheri in tears. "I did
nothing wrong!" she wailed. "But His Majesty would not have
me! He sent me away! I am ashamed!"

"What for, you stupid girl?" Tetisheri said, not unkindly. "Be
off to your cell and do not let your tongue waggle about this or I
will cut it out." Senehat retreated sniffling, and in the morning
Kamose requested admittance to his grandmother's domain. He
kissed her but then stood back.

"I presume that it was you who sent Senehat to me, Tetisheri," he said. "I am not ungrateful. I know how you fret over
my welfare. But I am not interested in a sexual encounter, and
even if I was I would choose someone more to my liking than a
little servant, no matter how attractive she may be."

"Then who is more to your liking?" Tetisheri asked him
unrepentantly. He laughed, one of the few times she had seen
his face relax into lines of mirth since his return, but then a
curious expression, part sadness, part longing, filled his eyes.

"No one I have ever met," he answered simply. "Not all men
who sleep alone are fanatics or aberrants, Grandmother. I am
perhaps close to the one but definitely not the other. Please
stop trying to manipulate me." He kissed her again and abruptly
departed, leaving her disgruntled and puzzled.

In the weeks that followed both she and a worried Aahotep
continued to watch him closely. His nature had always been a
solitary one and he continued to prefer his own company,
although he appeared regularly at the family's feasts and performed the social duties relevant to his position as head of the
household and Prince of Weset with faultless grace. There was
a coldness about him, however, that did not abate, and when
he was not engaged in necessary conversation, his face became
like a closed door behind which he hid his true character.

He had rounded up those peasants who had not been

conscripted into the army and put them to work on the construction of his prison out on the desert behind the city, and he could often be seen standing just out of reach of the dust stirred up by the swarms of toiling men, Behek lying in the shadow cast by his body and his guard beside him.

Only in the temple did he seem to melt, become fluid, his supple young spine bending easily in prostration to his god, his knees flexing as he went to the floor before the wide double doors of the sanctuary. The priest who measured the rising of the Nile calculated its full height that year as fourteen cubits, a magnificent outpouring of Isis's tears, and the seven days of the Amun-feast of Hapi, god of the waters, that marked the middle of the month of Paophi, was a time of riotous celebration. Kamose remained in the temple for the full week, sleeping in a priest's cell and joining Amunmose and the other priests in every ritual. It was as though proximity to the god offered him a peace he could not find outside the holy precinct, Tetisheri mused to Aahotep, as each day they met under a canopy in the garden or in the seclusion of Tetisheri's shrouded bedchamber to share their anxiety. Somehow his demons are quietened in the presence of the god. He does not seem to be as driven as he was. There is flesh on his bones and his eyes are now clear. He speaks to me as affectionately as he used to do, yet there is now a place inside him that is completely inaccessible to everyone, including me. And I do not like the way he will sometimes sit and shiver and complain that he is chilled. He develops no outward illness. It is all inside him, in his soul, this icy darkness.

It seemed to her that her whole world had shrunk to the dimensions of Kamose's mysterious ka. Nothing but Kamose filled her mind, no matter who she was with, but she knew that on such occasions her tongue spoke safely of other things. Aahotep's cousin Nefer-Sakharu was spending less time with Ahmose-onkh as her grief began to subside, and under the pretext of allowing the woman to find peace in the retelling of her husband's execution, Tetisheri was able to gain a clear picture of the events surrounding the sack of Khemmenu and the taking of Nefrusi. Doubtless Ankhmahor would have described other clashes if she had asked him to, but she felt that she had already stretched the limits of his loyalty to his King, and besides, she recognized the urge as an invitation to spawn a preoccupation as dangerous as her grandson's.

News continued to arrive from the troops wintering in the north. Sometimes the information was from Ramose, but more often than not it was Hor-Aha who filled the papyrus with his dictation on the current state of the army. He always included respectful greetings to Tetisheri, who began to wonder if his words did not smack of a sycophantish insincerity. He was, after all, just a tribesman with a genius for military planning and the days of Seqenenra's desperate campaign were long gone. Was Hor-Aha's position going to his head? Kamose should not have made him an hereditary lord, Tetisheri decided. It would have been better to leave him a General and set one of the other Princes over him in a purely honorary capacity.

The month of Athyr began, always a time of boredom for Tetisheri, although the heat began to abate. Egypt had become a vast lake dotted with the upper halves of drowned palm trees. The fields lay under sheets of silvery water. The only building project was Kamose's prison, an ugly thing, on which the peasants laboured when they were not sitting outside their huts gazing over their inaccessible arouras and calculating the amount of seed they would broadcast when the flood receded. Aahotep was presiding over the annual taking of inventory in the house. Even the temple was quiet. There were few festivals to relieve the interminable hours.

Ahmose was happy, however. Each morning he took his guards and his skiff, his throwing stick and his fishing gear, and disappeared into the marshes, to return in the late afternoon muddy and flushed, and fling his dead booty at the servants waiting to transform the limp ducks and gaping fish into that night's fare. Aahmes-nefertari went with him sometimes, but as Athyr drew to a tedious close she good-naturedly avowed that she could no longer keep up with him, preferring to spend her mornings in her mother's company or playing board games with Raa.

On the evening of the last day of Athyr, when the family had eaten together and Tetisheri had retired to her quarters, she was surprised to learn that Ahmose was outside her door requesting admittance. Isis had just finished washing the cosmetics from her face and the henna from her hands and feet and was combing her hair. Tetisheri's first impulse was to send him away until the morning when she might greet him fully painted, but she quashed the vanity of the thought and told Uni to let him come.

"Forgive me, Grandmother, I know it's late," he said as he crossed the tiled floor and came to a halt, bowing politely. "I wanted a few uninterrupted minutes with you. I have been selfish with my days, trying to crowd a year's worth of hunting into these few months, and I have already been taken to task over it by my mother." He smiled ruefully. "Even Aahmes-nefertari reminded me that I have not been giving my family the attention it deserves."

"I am not in the least offended by your absences, Ahmose," Tetisheri replied. "We see one another every evening at dinner. Your leisure time is yours to use as you see fit and as long as you have been doing your duty by your wife I will not complain. You do, however, choose an odd time to be remembering your obligation to me." She waved Isis away and indicated the chair beside her couch. "You may sit."

"Thank you." He dragged the chair closer to where she was perched on the stool before her cosmetic table and collapsed into it with a gusty sigh. "To tell you the truth, I am becoming surfeited with killing wild things. Aahmes-nefertari says that I am growing up. She teases me."

Tetisheri looked at him speculatively in the steady yellow glow of her lamps. Broad-shouldered and stocky, his skin gleaming with health, he filled the room with masculine vigour. His curly brown hair had been loosely tied back with a red ribbon, from which tendrils escaped to coil against his sturdy neck and frame an open, eager face. But his eyes were not smiling. They met hers gravely. She turned to Isis. "Leave the comb. You can go," she said. "I will see myself to bed." After the woman had closed the door quietly behind her, Tetisheri folded her arms. "You do not fool me, Prince," she declared. "What do you want?"

"It is not a matter of wanting," he said mildly. "I really do not want to consult you at all. I know that your heart belongs to Kamose and that you look out upon an Egypt coloured by his every breath. Do not deny it, Tetisheri. It does not hurt me, but it does make me wary of closing the distance between us."

"I do not deny it," she interjected. "But if you think for one moment that I would place my love for your brother above the good of Egypt, you are mistaken. To do so would dishonour your father's memory and diminish me."

"Perhaps. I have been hoping that you would summon me to discuss last season's campaign or at least tell me what has been going on here, but no, you prefer to take your concerns to Ankhmahor and interrogate poor Nefer-Sakharu, seeing that Kamose will not talk to you. I am not blind. Are you afraid of me, Grandmother, or am I merely a witless trifle to be dismissed?" His tone did not change. It remained moderate. His hands lay loosely on the supports of the chair and there was no tension in his body, yet his very composure only served to accent the accusatory force of his words. Tetisheri struggled against the immediate flare of anger they lit in her. He is right, she thought bitterly. I should not have ignored him. I should have listened to the voice of my own intellect.

"I would have sought you out, Ahmose," she said slowly, "but I did not want Kamose to imagine that he had forfeited my loyalty. That may seem to be a petty excuse, but Kamose is the King. He makes the decisions that will affect the progress of the war. I could not afford to close off the avenue between us."

"So you took your concerns to Ankhmahor." He uncrossed his legs and leaned back, linking his fingers together. "Why was that? Because he is older than I, more mature, hates hunting, what? And no, before you begin to protest, he has not approached me. I noticed that Kamose's guard had been doubled, and when I asked Ankhmahor why, he told me that you had made the request. You must decide now, Grandmother, whether you will trust me or not. If not, then I will take my need for advice elsewhere."

For a long time they sat motionless, staring at each other, Ahmose's steady brown eyes meeting Tetisheri's reflective gaze. The young whelp is challenging me, she thought, amazed. This is not jealousy, this is a demand to be accorded what he sees as his legitimate position at last. And he is right. If I attempt to justify my doubts about him now, he will judge me as weak and relegate me to the margins of his life. I must not even apologize. So be it. "I took one concern to Anhkmahor," she began. "It was this." She told him quickly of the omens and the oracle. "It may have nothing to do with the immediate future, but I deemed it wise to take every precaution," she pointed out. "I also wanted Ankhmahor's opinion of Kamose's mental condition. If he breaks, the rebellion is doomed." Ahmose's eyebrows shot up.

"It is disconcerting to hear you move so rapidly from frigidity to complete surrender," he commented. "You are a complex woman, Grandmother. I presume that the Prince assured you Kamose's mind would remain whole, at least for the foreseeable future."

"You speak of it so calmly," Tetisheri almost shouted. "Have you lost your love for him already?"

"No!" He pounded the arm of the chair with one clenched fist. "But I have learned the hard habit of disconnecting myself from his agony! How else do you think I was able to stand beside him and watch what the orders that issued from his mouth did to his ka? He has no route of escape from his demons, Tetisheri. I am blessed. I can achieve forgetfulness in my wife's embrace, in the flailing of a fish on my hook, in the second when my throwing stick flies upward and all my consciousness flies with it. These things snare my nightmares and smother them. Kamose is not so lucky. We killed all day, every day, for weeks on end. Kamose goes on killing even as he sits on the roof of the old palace and stares at the sky. It will be better for him to take up a real sword again."

"So." She was shaken and this time she could not hide it. "Tell me everything, Ahmose. I want to know it all."

She sat very still while his voice filled the dim, warm air around them. He hid nothing from her, describing so calmly and vividly the stink of carnage, the conflagrations, the bewildered wails of the women, the restless nights often broken by the reports of scouts who moved up and down the river under the cover of darkness, that she did not even need to close her eyes to see it all unfold within her mind.

When he had finished recounting the details of Kamose's sweep north, he turned to an assessment of each Prince's position of responsibility, together with a conjecture regarding each one's loyalty and attitude toward Kamose, himself and Hor-Aha. "Het-Uart will not fall this year unless Apepa can be lured out of his citadel," he finished. "Kamose is determined to besiege the city again, but it will be time wasted. The Princes will remain with him for one more season, I think, but if there are no results by the next Inundation, they will begin to petition him to let them go home and see to their nomes and estates."

"Then what should he do?" she asked, her voice husky from disuse, her head still full of bright and terrible images. He blew out his lips.

"I want to hear your opinion first," he said. "And may we have beer, Grandmother? All this talking has dried up my throat."

*What are you?* she thought, as she called Uni from his stool outside her door and sent him for refreshments, and even as the question came clear and cold it was followed by a rush of sorrow. *You are not Kamose. You are not the King. I wish that it was your brother sitting across from me, discussing these matters with such lucidity and skill.* "He should garrison Het nefer Apu, although the town is really too far from the Delta," she said. "He should build a large fort at the Delta's root, at Iunu, and fill it with permanent troops to prevent Apepa from coming south. He should fill Het-Uart with spies, people who can take up work in the city, and thus gradually acquire a picture of everything from the structure of the gates to the number and direction of the streets to the location and staffing of the military barracks. He also needs to know the tenor of the inhabitants. All that would take time." She hesitated.

"The passage of time is driving him mad," Ahmose pointed out. "Both of you wanted a swift, sustained push north and a speedy end to the weight of Apepa's foot on our necks. But, Tetisheri, it is not to be, and it seems to me that you have accepted the fact. Kamose has not. He will not. I am tired of arguing with him."

"But you will not desert him!" she blurted. "You will not quarrel publicly, Ahmose!"

"Of course not," he retorted. "You still see me as a fool, don't you, Grandmother? I will say this to you once." He leaned forward, lifting one admonitory finger. "I hate the Setiu. I hate Apepa. I swear by my father's wounds, by my mother's grief, I will know no peace until an Egyptian King reigns again over a unified country. I do not agree with Kamose's strategies, but as his true subject I will support him because he and I, all of us, want the same thing." He sat back and folded his arms. "Kamose has become like a chariot horse with blinkers. He can no longer see to right or left, but like such a horse he is running in the right direction." With a knock on the door Uni entered, quietly setting out beer and pastries and trimming the lamps before discreetly retiring. Ahmose drained his cup in one gulp and refilled it. Tetisheri watched him carefully. After a moment she wet her lips.

"Who holds the reins, Ahmose?" she murmured. "Does Hor-Aha?" He considered the question, staring into his beer, then he looked up.

"The General is ambitious and imperious," he said. "There is no doubt that he is a brilliant tactician. He has complete control over his Medjay but not over Kamose, I think, although Kamose trusts his advice before he trusts mine. Frankly, Grandmother, I have come to dislike him. But I keep that to myself. I do not want to alienate him while he is still useful."

"His Medjay?"

Ahmose grunted. "A slip of the tongue. Hor-Aha's mother, Nithotep, was Egyptian, you know. I fancy she lived near the fort at Buhen in Wawat and made a living by washing the soldiers' linen."

"No, I did not know," Tetisheri responded. "What of his father?" Ahmose shrugged.

"Obviously a tribesman, given the General's colouring and features. But Hor-Aha regards himself as a citizen of this country. He takes pride in it. He will not betray his King." He selected the largest pastry and bit into it with relish, licking the honey from his fingers and gracing Tetisheri with a sudden wide grin. "Now that Kamose has made him a Prince, he wants a nome to govern. Kamose has promised him something in the Delta."

"How ridiculous!" Tetisheri snapped. "We cannot have a tribesman governing a nome." Ahmose's teeth gleamed at her. "Don't worry, Majesty," he said softly. "It will be a very long time before the Delta is stable enough for proper government. We need not concern ourselves with that problem just yet."

"Ahmose," she said wonderingly, "have we just become accomplices?"

"Allies, Majesty," he replied firmly. "Allies. Together with Kamose, we always were." He rose and stretched. "Thank you for your august ear. Do we understand one another a little better now? May I go?" She nodded, holding out her hand. He took it in both of his, and bending he kissed her cheek. "Sleep well, Tetisheri," he said and the door closed firmly behind him.

Her couch beckoned, its white sheet turned back. She was aware of an enormous tiredness but she did not move, sitting staring into the silence, her mind racing. Not until the last lamp began to gutter did she pull herself up, but it was only to snuff the feeble flame. Placing a cushion on the chair Ahmose had vacated, she lowered herself onto it, set her elbows on the table, and gazed unseeingly into the darkness.

The beginning of the month of Khoiak and the Feast of Hathor, goddess of love and beauty, marked the following day. Tetisheri, after a short and restless night, stood irritably with her female relatives at Hathor's shrine near the centre of Weset to pay tribute to the mild, cow-headed deity. She had never felt much veneration for Hathor, believing less in the power of beauty to sway the deliberations of men than in a woman's wit and intelligence, and she plied her whisk with impatient vigour at the flies attracted to her sweat.

The river had reached its highest level and would now begin to sink. The sun was almost imperceptibly less intense but hot nevertheless, and Tetisheri wanted to tear the incense holder from the priest's hand and finish his sonorous chant for him so that she could climb back into the litter waiting for her on the edge of the respectful crowd. Mindful, however, that Hathor had once been a vengeful goddess who had bathed Egypt in blood, she had brought a trinket to offer and a scroll detailing the amount of grain and other goods the priests might expect through the coming year. It was naturally far less than the assessment due to Amun, but Hathor's main temple at Iunet would be flooded with gifts and worshippers on this occasion and the family need only concern itself with maintaining her small shrine and its modest complement of servants in Weset.

In spite of her own lack of proper zeal, Tetisheri was touched to see Aahmes-nefertari's devotion. The girl prostrated herself on the dusty stone with genuine reverence, whispering the prayers sung aloud and kissing the feet of the statue with eyes closed as though she were approaching a lover. The reason for her devotion became apparent once the women had retired to the seclusion of the grape arbour, where Kamose and Ahmose were waiting for them, wine, dried figs and date cakes laid out on linen in the leaf-dappled shade. "I need more than that," Tetisheri grumbled as the men rose to greet them. "I ate very little and we left early for the shrine. Where is Uni? I want fresh vegetables and gazelle meat." Ahmose had poured wine for her and was holding out her cup.

"In a moment, Grandmother," he said. "Come and sit down. Aahmes-nefertari has an announcement to make." He smiled at his wife, who had not settled herself on the cushions strewn about. She smiled back and took a deep breath.

"I have been saving my news for this day, Hathor's day," she said. "I am pregnant. The physician tells me that the baby will be born sometime in Payni, just before the harvest begins."

"So let us toast the conception of another Tao!" Ahmose broke in. He put an arm around the girl's shoulders and drew her close. "No matter what the future might bring, the gods have decreed that our blood flows on." Aahotep raised her cup and laughed delightedly.

"Well done," she said. "It is a magnificent omen. I am to be a grandmother yet again!"

"And I a great-grandmother," Tetisheri observed. "My congratulations, both of you. I wonder what the sex of the child will be. We will consult the oracle, and an astrologer of course." Her words were directed at Aahmes-nefertari's flushed face, but her eyes were surreptitiously on Kamose. He was smiling with everyone else and Tetisheri could detect no shadow of sadness or resentment in his expression. He is wholeheartedly glad, she told herself. He does not begrudge Ahmose this happiness at all. He really does not want it for himself.

But Kamose, sensing her glance, turned his face towards her and that assumption quickly dissolved under a more sober realization. He knows he will not survive, she thought. Somehow he believes that his own marriage, the getting of royal children by him, is utterly unimportant because Ahmose will be the one to sit on the Horus Throne and perpetuate Tao gods in Egypt. Perhaps he has always suspected it. Oh, my darling Kamose! His smile, as he met her gaze, became wry, and he raised his wine in a salute to her before holding the cup to his mouth. "Tetisheri, what is the matter?" Aahotep asked anxiously. "You look suddenly grey. Are you ill?"

"The visit to the shrine and then my announcement has been too much for you, Majesty," Aahmes-nefertari said kindly, and Tetisheri bit back a scornful reply. I could stand forever in one place if I had to, and take the shock of any news, good or bad, better than you, she wanted to say. The child in your womb should have been Kamose's seed, not his brother's. Ahmose was watching her with a level, sympathetic scrutiny, and once again she was forced to quell the tide of bitterness she felt. This resentment will pass, she tried to say to him with her eyes. It is the death throes of an old woman's fantasies, nothing more.

"This wine is sour on an empty stomach," she managed gruffly. "Isis! Find Uni and make him bring me food! Now sit here beside me, Aahmes-nefertari, and tell me how you are faring." She patted the cushion at her side and the girl obeyed.

"The physician says that if I carry the baby high it will be female," she said eagerly. "And if low, then male. But it is too soon for him to predict either. I do not feel at all ill, Majesty." Her hands flew to her cheeks. "I'm sorry for talking so fast. I am both excited and afraid." Aahotep leaned across and patted her knee.

"You will give Egypt many children, Aahmes-nefertari," she said. "We are all so happy for you." Aahmes-nefertari gave her mother a grateful glance.

"Ahmose does not care whether we have a boy or a girl," she said. "But I think a girl would be best. That way Ahmose-onkh . . ." Her voice trailed away and her gaze dropped to her lap.

"Do not be ashamed of what you were about to say." It was Kamose who spoke. He was lying on his side, head propped on one palm, his eyes on the moving tracery of vine leaves above him. "We must never lose sight of the painful realities of these days. If you produce a girl, the divine blood will be passed to her through you, and Ahmose-onkh in marrying her will obtain his godhead. Providing, of course, that Ahmose is dead." He sat up, crossing his legs and squinting at her through the patterned shadow. "Our line is royal anyway," he went on, "and some-times there has been no sister to refine and reanimate it. But when there is, it is better, stronger. Ma'at is renewed."

"These are hard things to consider, dear brother," she said softly, still staring into her lap. "And it does not escape my attention that even though you are Majesty, you speak as though you do not intend to perpetuate our line yourself. I fear for you, Kamose."

No one broke the silence that followed. It spread and deep-ened, a weight of despondency that froze all movement. The wine remained unfinished in the cups and Uni, coming around the corner of the house with food-laden servants behind him, saw the family briefly as a collection of rigid statues.

The month of Khoiak passed uneventfully. Gods' days came and went: the Feast of Sacrifice, the Opening of the Tomb of Osiris, the Feast of the Hoeing of the Earth, the Feast of the Father of Palms; there were eleven temple festivals in all to occupy those made idle by the flood. It was a time the peasants loved, for they were exempt from building projects on holy days and could not labour in the fields because of the water.

Slowly the Nile began to return to its banks and the heat lessened. Life in the house had settled into a pleasant routine and, but for the regular reports from the Uah-ta-Meh oasis and Het nefer Apu, the family might have imagined a return to the peace and stability of earlier years. Ahmose hunted and fished occasionally but now preferred to keep his wife company as she followed her small round of domestic duties. Aahotep was busy with the gardeners and with Simontu, the Scribe of the Granaries, who had been selecting staff for Kamose's now-completed prison until he was summoned to calculate and apportion the amount of seed to be sown that year.

Tetisheri, revitalized by the cooler temperatures and deter-mined to wrench her mind from her former preoccupation with

the campaign, decided to begin a history of her family and sat
beside the pool dictating to her scribe. As for Kamose, he continued to spend many hours with the patient Behek beside him
on the roof of the old palace. Sometimes preoccupied servants
who happened to glance up and over the dividing wall on their
way through the gardens saw Seqenenra in the hunched silhouette and muttered a quick prayer before recognizing his son. But
in spite of his need for privacy, Kamose seemed to have recap-
tured much of his mental equilibrium. His face had lost the
drawn, haunted look that had so shocked his grandmother, and
new flesh overlaid his wiry muscles.

In the late afternoons the members of the family, as if by
unspoken consent, would drift out into the garden and gather
by the pool to drink wine and talk desultorily before they were
summoned to the evening meal. They sat or lay on the warm,
fragrant grass, lazily watching mosquitoes hover over the red-
dening surface of the water and calculating how soon it would
be before a fish rose with a swirl and a snap to feed on the delicate insects, or rising to pluck the newly opened lotus blooms
on whose pads the frogs squatted, croaking noisily.

An unlooked-for tranquility had descended on them all, as
though the receding waters were taking with them the agonies
and nightmares of the past weeks. Around the estate, the fields
began to emerge, deep brown and glistening with moisture, and
their husbandmen could be seen standing ankle deep in the
sodden soil as if tranced.

"It will be a bountiful year," Aahotep said. She was sitting on
the stone verge of the pond, trailing her fingers in the water.
"We will be able to sow more seed than last season and none of
the crop will go to Apepa."

"None of the wine either," Ahmose put in. He had his head
in his wife's lap and she was tickling his nose with a spear of

grass. "Our vintner tells me that there is no sign of spring blight on the vines. Where is Nefer-Sakharu? Why does she never join us?" He batted at Aahmes-nefertari's hand and sneezed.

"Her grief has turned to hate," Tetisheri said. She was tossing scrolls one by one into the chest at her feet while her scribe flexed his aching fingers and put his palette in order. "She is not grateful for the sanctuary she has found here. Senehat tells me that she heard Nefer-Sakharu speaking ill of you, Kamose, to Ahmose-onkh, so I forbade her to see the boy any more. I do not know what to do with her." She threw the last scroll down, brushed off the skirt of her white sheath, and took the wine Uni was proffering.

"There is nowhere to send her," Aahotep joined in, her eyes on the red ripples spreading out under her hand. "We could put her in a cell in the temple, I suppose, ask Amunmose to care for her, but it seems a cruel thing to do and really she is not the High Priest's responsibility."

"No, she is ours," Kamose said resignedly. He had been inspecting the irrigation waterways with his Overseer of Dykes and Canals for any signs of abnormal subsidence and had then plunged in the Nile to wash off the mud of the afternoon. Clad only in a loincloth, barefoot and unpainted, his skin glossy and his hair still damp, he looked younger than his twenty-four years. "I am sorry to give the burden of her supervision back to you, my dear women, but I have no choice. The river is ready for navigation and Ahmose and I must leave very soon. Have Nefer-Sakharu watched constantly. She is desperate to see her son, and besides, she has been here long enough to have learned a great deal about us, our state of mind, the tenor of Weset's inhabitants, the promise of our crops, things that might seem inconsequential until they are combined in the mind of a military strategist."

"Strategist!" Tetisheri snorted. "The only strategist in Het-Uart is Pezedkhu and he is choking on that coward Apepa's leash. He is the only man to fear, Kamose."

"I know. We have had no information regarding him. I think Apepa will hold him in until a pitched battle becomes inevitable."

Aahmes-nefertari sighed. "It has been such a lovely month," she said wistfully. "So quiet. Now we talk of war again. When will you take Ahmose away from me, Kamose? And will you send him home for the birth of our child?"

"I make no promises," Kamose stated flatly. "How can I? You have Mother and Grandmother, Aahmes-nefertari. You will just have to be brave." Ahmose reached up and grasped a lock of her black hair, winding it around his wrist.

"You will be brave," he repeated. "All will be well and you will send me word. I do not want to have to worry about you, Aahmes-nefertari, and worry I will unless you can promise me that you will be calm and not fret and not miss me too much."

"I am learning a fatalistic patience," the girl said, half-humorously. "Now answer my question, Kamose. When must you go?"

"Tybi begins in three days," Kamose said. "We will wait to make offerings at my father's tomb in remembrance of his birthday and, of course, the first day of the month is doubly sacred to me, being the Feast of the Coronation of Horus, but then we will be gone. I have already commanded the Medjay to refurbish their weapons and prepare to take ship." He turned a level gaze on Ahmose. "I hope to accomplish a successful siege this season." Ahmose made no reply. He continued to play with his wife's hair, and it was Tetisheri who covered the moment of tension.

"Are we to continue our watch on Pi-Hathor?" she wanted to know. Kamose shook his head.

"No. It is no longer necessary I think. We hold the country

from Weset to the Delta anyway and a messenger from Het-Uy would find it almost impossible to get through our ranks."

"Perhaps it is time to offer the mayor the hand of friendship," Aahotep suggested. She scrambled up and came in under the now superfluous shade of the canopy. "He has kept to his agreement with you, Kamose. Do not forget that he builds craft of all kinds there and moreover he has a limestone quarry. He must know by now that the time for any revolt on his part is over. We could make use of him."

"No." Ahmose let go of the thick tress he had tangled and sat up. "Not yet. We must give no one the slightest cause to imagine that we have any need. Leave Pi-Hathor and Het-Uy alone for now."

For a while silence reigned as each one of them succumbed to the beauty of the hour. Pale shadows had begun to snake across the lawn and before them the red light retreated, leaving a soft dusk still redolent with the perfume of the budding flowers. The sky was an arch of dark blue benignly fading into a pearly azure before becoming pink. Then Aahmes-nefertari stirred. "Khoiak has been like the peace that falls before a desert storm," she said. "Precious and not to be forgotten. I think we will all feed on its memory." Tetisheri swallowed the lump in her throat.

"Dinner is late," she said tartly.

# Chapter SIX

TWELVE DAYS LATER, on the ninth day of Tybi, the family met above the watersteps to say their farewells. It was a cool spring morning, with the river running fast and a strong breeze tossing the trees and whipping up the surface of the Nile. Boats loaded with the excited and voluble Medjay rocked and jostled between the banks. The brothers' craft, with its blue-and-white royal flag rippling frenetically and its prow grating against the pole to which it was tethered, seemed to mirror Kamose's own inward impatience to be gone. He stood with Ahmose beside him and Ankhmahor and the Followers behind, scanning the faces of his loved ones and the priests and servants gathered to wish him good fortune, while at his back the Medjay laughed and shouted in their own quaint tongue and the thuds and curses of the men loading last-minute supplies were snatched away by the blustery air.

Already the winter months held a quality of unreality. There had been the dream of returning home, an ache that had grown with every mile that had taken him farther away from Weset, and the burst of joy he had felt when finally the familiar and beloved contours of his home came into sight again. But after the embraces and tearful greetings, after the taste of local wine and homegrown food, after the blessed relief of his own couch, he had entered another dream, less pure. The demons held at bay by bloody actions and one consuming decision after another had slipped past a guard that was no longer necessary and danced unhindered through the caverns of his empty mind. He knew this. In a cold and detached way he had been entirely aware of what was happening to him, but the extreme fatigue he had also been thrusting back had overwhelmed him too and he could not fight. He slept and rose, ate and talked, but within himself he was supine, powerless.

Gradually the demons grew bored and wandered back into the darkness of his nightmares, but by then Khoiak had begun and it was too late to rediscover the elation of that day. Consequently he found that he had substituted dream for illusion. The four months spent in the sanity and stability of his home seemed to him now to have been a waking fantasy, a combination of wishful daydreams and disjointed turmoil that left him anxious to escape to a more tangible existence.

There stood his women, his grandmother, mother and sister, linens pressed against their legs by the force of the wind, eyes fixed on him variously with trepidation, stubborn resolve, sad affection, but they belonged to a world he could no longer inhabit, a world, moreover, that he had left a long time ago. He had tried to return to it, only to find himself a stranger.

Ahmose felt none of these things, he knew, but then Ahmose's strength lay in his ability to enter completely into his present circumstances and lay aside any contemplation of his past as a fruitless trap. If he was impelled to reflect upon it, it was for practical reasons. He would sail north with happy memories of his hours with Aahmes-nefertari, with the anticipation of his fatherhood, with hope for the coming battle season, but those emotions would not overwhelm him. He would sleep deeply wherever he found himself, eat and drink gratefully whatever was presented to him, and perform with equanimity the tasks at hand. I envy him, Kamose thought, as he moved to kiss his mother. I would not want to be what he is, but I envy him.

Aahotep smelled of lotus oil and her full lips were soft under his. With one hand she held back her gale-tousled hair and the other caressed his cheek. "May the soles of your feet be firm, Majesty," she said as he drew away. "If by some miracle of the gods you are able to get a message to Tani, tell her that I love her and pray for her safety every day." He nodded, and turned to Tetisheri.

"Well, Grandmother," he smiled. "Our parting this time is not fraught with the uncertainty of last year. The Delta is all that remains to be cleansed." She did not return his smile, only regarding him expressionlessly out of the wrinkled parchment of her face.

"I know your haste," she said. "It is mine also. But do nothing rash, Kamose. The patience of Ma'at is eternal. Send me regular scrolls. Guard your person. Watch Hor-Aha." She spread her braceleted arms. "Do the will of Amun." He was suddenly reluctant to press her ancient flesh against him, why he did not know. I am already too infected with the taint of death, he thought grimly. Tetisheri's vigour in spite of her age should be like a medicine to me, not a poison. She triumphs over every symptom of impending dissolution. Pulling her to him, he crushed her loose bones against his body, but the impulse could not quell a moment of revulsion.

"Do not withdraw your favour from me, Grandmother," he said urgently, guiltily. "We have always understood one another. I would be devastated if that should change."

"My love for you will never fade," she answered, straightening. "But Egypt comes first. I intend to survive long enough to see you mount the Horus Throne, O Mighty Bull, therefore take heed that you tread warily and with circumspection."

"You sound like Ahmose," he retorted, half-jokingly. She went on scanning him soberly, her hooded eyes narrowed.

"If you had wanted my advice, or anyone else's for that matter, you would have sought it," she said acidly. "But you have made up your mind what you will do once you reach the Delta. Be careful, Kamose. The brittle branch will snap more easily than wood that is soft with sap." You are a fine example of the brittle branch, he said to himself in his mind. There is no one more inflexible than you, dear Grandmother, with your spine as rigid as a djed pillar and your will as adamant as stone.

He was spared from replying by a flurry of activity on the periphery of his vision, and he turned to see Amunmose in full sacerdotal regalia come pacing towards him, flanked by acolytes with incense holders extended. If myrrh was being burned, there was no indication, for any fragrant smoke was being snatched away by the wind. At once the family bowed, and waited reverently while Amunmose sang the chants of blessing and parting and the blood and milk streamed onto the paving, and when he had finished, Tetisheri asked him what omen the entrails of the sacrificed bull had revealed.

"The animal was in perfect health," the High Priest assured her. "Heart, liver, lungs, all without signs of disease. The blood that streamed upon the ground formed a perfect map of the tributaries of the Delta and the first spot to dry was in fact the thickest. It had fallen where Het-Uart would be. Your Majesty may go north with confidence."

"Thank you, Amunmose. Is there an oracular pronouncement?" Amunmose shot a rapid, almost imperceptible glance at Tetisheri that Kamose did not miss. Now what is this? he thought, surprised. Collusion between my grandmother and my friend? Has Amun spoken words that I may not hear, or worse, words that would make me despair? Stepping up, he took the High Priest's arm. "I charge you on pain of sacrilege to answer me," he demanded. "If the god has prophesied to me, then as his chosen son I have a right to know! Is there a prognostication regarding the campaigns of this season?" Again a silent communication passed between his grandmother and the High Priest, this time of relief, and a puzzled Kamose realized that he had asked the wrong question. Well then, what? he thought, mystified and troubled. Amunmose squared his shoulders and at his movement the leopard's head on the end of the skin slung over the man's shoulder seemed to snarl at Kamose.

"No, Majesty," Amunmose said. "There has been no direct word from Amun on the success of this season's war. Apart from the excellent sacrificial omen, of course." He snapped his fingers at one of the acolytes and the boy came forward shyly, proffering a small bundle wrapped in linen. "I have a gift for you from Amun's artisans," he went on, taking the package and passing it to Kamose. "It was formed from the gold and lapis you captured and apportioned for the use of the god. He is grateful." Intrigued, Kamose unfolded the layers of thin cloth. Within its nest lay a box-like armlet of heavy gold. Its square perimeter encased Kamose's name in lapis within a golden cartouche that was flanked by two rampant lions whose bodies, shaped in gold, were also of lapis. The thick ornament exuded both power and a deliberately primitive beauty. Kamose stared down at it, caught up in the sparkling play of sunlight on the precious metal and the gleaming richness of the blue stone. A sturdy double cord of flax lay coiled under it. After a long moment he picked up the piece and held it out to Amunmose.

"Tie it on me," he ordered in a strangled voice and the High Priest obeyed, laying it against his upper arm and drawing the twine tight. At his touch Kamose trembled. Something in him loosened and taking Amunmose's hands in his he lifted them to his forehead. "I have had peace in Amun's house these four months gone," he said huskily. "Tell the artisans that I intend to fill Amun's storehouses so full of gold that they will need more than one lifetime to fashion it. Thank you, Amunmose." He did not look at any of them again. Turning on his heel, he ran up the ramp and onto the deck of his ship, Ankhmahor following. With a last embrace for his wife, Ahmose joined him, and Kamose called the command to cast off.

At once the craft's prow swung north, as though it had been waiting for release, and Kamose, as the boards came to life beneath his feet, felt a surge of anticipation. "It is different this time," Ahmose remarked. "We go to continue a work well begun, eh, Kamose?" Kamose looked to where, with a great flurry of yells and curses from the captains, the Medjay's boats were jockeying for position behind his. The current was running fast, bearing them all rapidly away from the watersteps, the jumbled buildings of the town, the cheering crowds lining the river's edge. Above him the huge lateen sail billowed, sank, billowed again, then filled exultantly with the warming breeze. His eyes found the forlorn little group above the watersteps, already shrunk to the size of dolls, already slipping into the past. He did not wave and neither did they.

"Ahmose," he said slowly. "Do you know anything of an oracle's prediction in the temple this winter?" Ahmose's gaze remained on the lush bank sliding by.

"You have already asked the High Priest that question," he said after a pause. "What makes you think that I know something Amunmose does not?" That is not an answer, Kamose thought, but did not pursue the matter. His ship had already entered the bend in the river that hid Weset from sight and his family was gone.

Last year it had taken the flotilla eight days to reach Qes, not including the time he and Ahmose had spent collecting conscripts on the way. This time there would be no delays. The ships would put in at sheltered bays each evening, the cooking fires would be lit on the sandy banks, the sailors would sing and drink their beer without the need for caution, and Ahmose and I, Kamose mused as he sat comfortably under the wooden sunshade towards the prow, can sleep peacefully for many nights. Heralds have gone out to Het nefer Apu and the oasis. We are expected. We hold all the land between Weset and the Delta and there will be no surprises. I do not even want to discuss the problem of Het-Uart just yet. Ahmose can fish the sunsets away and I can do absolutely nothing if I choose. I can pretend that we are on a pleasure jaunt or a pilgrimage to Aabtu or even a hunting expedition. I can close my mind to everything. "I notice that some of the peasants are on the land already," Ahmose ventured. "Few of them are men." He had been leaning over the side of the boat, alternately watching the shore and the bubbling froth of their wake, and now he drew up a stool beside his brother. "It is a little early but the flood seems to have receded more quickly this season than last. The current is certainly swift. We will make good time, I think." Kamose nodded. "The work is not particularly arduous," Ahmose went on. "Just monotonous. The women will manage the sowing quite well, and perhaps by next spring we will have been able to return their men to them. Shall we keep the Medjay, Ahmose?"

"After we have sacked Het-Uart, you mean?" Kamose responded sarcastically. "Let us negotiate the river first, Ahmose. For now I am content to remain within this hour."

"Oh very well," Ahmose said good-naturedly. "I must confess that it is good to be here on a boat in the middle of the Nile surrounded by men and embarking once again on a worthy adventure. I even feel free enough to get drunk once or twice before we rejoin the army." He laughed. "I have no fears for the coming months, Kamose."

"Neither do I," Kamose admitted. "And I agree with you. Although I love the family, I am not sorry to have left household affairs behind."

"Not that either of us have had much to do with them," Ahmose commented. "The women seem to have found a quite laudable ability to not only run the estate but keep the local soldiers in line and guard the river. Next they will be wanting to go to war."

"That is certainly true of Tetisheri," Kamose said, deliberately matching his brother's light mood and watching himself do so. "When she was young, she pestered first her father and then Senakhtenra into letting her take sword and archery lessons. Womanhood sits uneasily on her. I think she would have liked to be born male. She still often mixes with the house bodyguards. She knows them all by name."

"That is rather sad," Ahmose murmured. "Have you ever wished you were born female, Kamose?" Kamose felt his inner buoyancy collapse and grimly he relinquished the effort of sustaining it.

"Yes," he said shortly. "To have no responsibility other than that of domestic affairs, to make no decisions other than what jewellery to wear, to be nothing but a vehicle for the god's blood, to have never killed, all this I envy women."

"But our women are not like that," Ahmose objected after a moment. "You speak as though you have contempt for them, Kamose."

"Contempt? No," Kamose said wearily. His brief joy in the morning had evaporated and he knew it would not return. "I merely envy them sometimes. Women are seldom lonely."

That night they moored at Qebt. The Prince of its nome was of course at the oasis with his troops, but Kamose received

Intef's deputy and heard a report on the projected use of the town's fields and the mood of the people. The man told Kamose that Intef remained in communication with him regarding the welfare of the nome's inhabitants and Kamose, remembering the acrid exchange that had taken place between Intef and Hor-Aha, was tempted to ask to see the scrolls, but he resisted the urge. Intef would not appreciate a show of distrust on the part of his King, and besides, Kamose knew that the voice whispering potential betrayal in his mind came from his own insecurity.

He slept late the following morning, rising to find his boat already gliding north and Akhtoy clearing away the remains of Ahmose's early meal. Ahmose himself squatted in the shade at the stern, surrounded by the sailors who were standing down, and judging by the loud chatter they were having much to say to each other. A burst of their laughter pursued Kamose as he went to lean over the thickly bundled reeds making up the perimeter of the deck. "We have passed Kift!" he exclaimed in surprise to his steward, who had left his task at once as Kamose emerged from the cabin and now stood waiting behind him. "We should make Aabtu the day after tomorrow at this speed!"

"Will you wash first or eat, Majesty?" Akhtoy enquired. "There is bread, cheese and raisins. The cook begs your indulgence and expects to take on more fresh food at Aabtu." Kamose considered.

"Neither," he said. "Have the captain slow our progress. I will swim. Ahmose! Join me in the water!" he called, trying vainly to still the worm of jealousy that had begun to undulate in his heart as the lively conversation in the stern died away. The sailors scrambled to their feet, their faces becoming solemn. "You should not become too familiar with them," he said in a low voice as Ahmose came up smiling. "It is dangerous to foster the illusion that the gulf separating you from them can be crossed." Ahmose gave him a quizzical look.

"Of course it cannot be crossed," he said quietly. "But neither must it be allowed to grow so wide that they can no longer see me. Or you, Kamose. What is the matter? Are you jealous of a few rough men?" No, Kamose thought, hating himself for his pettiness. Amun, help me, I am jealous of you.

The days that drifted by were pleasant ones, the steady flow of the water under their keel, the unvarying glide of the riverbank, the simple routines of life on board their vessel, all fostered the fantasy that their journey was nothing more than a spring voyage. Even the appearance of scouts from the north and the dispatching of heralds in the same direction did little to dispel the air of relaxation that enveloped not only the brothers but the Medjay as well. Strung out in their craft, they spent the hours crowded against the edges of their decks exclaiming at the ever-changing view or dancing with arms outstretched to the monotonous beat of their small drums. At sunset the sound began to echo against the confines of the water as though the Nile was lined with invisible Medjay returning their kinsmen's rhythmic greeting in some sort of tribal ritual.

Ahmose complained that the unceasing sounds gave him a headache, but Kamose rather enjoyed the barbarity of the music. It stirred something primitive in him, insinuating itself beneath the rigid control he tried to maintain over his thoughts and scattering them to reveal a core of blind sensation into which he was plunged if the drumming went on very late and he lay drowsy on his camp cot. He often had the half-formed thought that under its sensuous compulsion the mysterious woman of his dreams might come back to him, that she might be lured into his sleep while his mental defences were weak, but though the images of his subconscious became soft with the sensuality he had long since denied himself in his waking hours, she remained elusive.

At Aabtu he and Ahmose paused to worship Osiris and Khentiamentiu and pay their respects to Ankhmahor's wife. Kamose allowed the Commander of the Followers a night and the better part of the next day in his home before casting off for Akhmin, and quickly the delightful habits of life on the river reasserted themselves. Kamose saw no need to put in at either Akhmin or Badari. The Nile had now completely regained its bed, the fields were bare, and to his practised eye the spring labours were proceeding as they should. Dykes were being repaired, irrigation canals shored up, and no day went by that he did not see the peasant women with sacks strung around their sturdy necks flinging showers of precious seed onto the waiting soil.

Qes was approached and passed without a tremor. It seemed to Kamose that the ghosts of that tragic place had been exorcised last year when his fleet had crept in breathless silence past the path leading from the village to the river and his mind had been full of his father and the heat and desperation of Seqenenra's last battle. Now it lay innocently shimmering in the morning's bright sunlight, a dusty track inviting the traveller to turn aside and follow it to the tumbled cliffs and the cluster of houses beyond. "It looks very peaceful, doesn't it?" Ahmose remarked as, side by side, they watched it dwindle. "Qes has a pretty little temple to Hathor I'm told. Aahmes-nefertari has always wanted to visit it. When we return, I must remember to take her there." He turned to glance at Kamose. "Dashlut is next," he said. "From then on we will not particularly like to keep our eyes on the bank, Kamose. The view will not be as idyllic. Perhaps you will wish to sit in the cabin with me and thrash out a policy to present to the Princes waiting for us in the oasis. We have been fallow long enough."

"I suppose we must," Kamose acknowledged. "But there is not much to thrash out. Do we move the army close in to

Het-Uart and begin another siege or do we stay in the oasis until we have devised a more efficient scheme for victory?"

"What choice do we have but to siege again?" Ahmose said. "And this time we should make sure that we have placed spies inside the city with a plan for retrieving their information." He touched Kamose's arm. "Ramose would be perfect. He is intelligent and resourceful. He has been to Het-Uart with his father. And he would do anything to put himself closer to Tani." Kamose met his eyes. Ahmose regarded him coolly.

"Ramose would be a perfect tool you mean," Kamose said thoughtfully. "But could we trust him, Ahmose? We have killed his father, sundered him from his mother, given his inheritance to Meketra. He is a man of integrity, certainly, but how far can he be pushed? Besides," he looked back to where a stand of palms shuddered in the breeze, "Ramose is my friend."

"All the more reason to use him," Ahmose pressed. "Or rather, to let himself be used. The affection between the two of you goes back a long way, Kamose. Consider Hor-Aha." His eyes left his brother's and returned to the bank. "You have made him a Prince. You have set him over the other nobles in spite of their obvious resentment because of his ability. Or so you tell them. To me you say that it is a matter of loyalty. You are ruthless enough to reward loyalty with danger but you balk at putting friendship to the same test. Is loyalty then less admirable than friendship?" Kamose turned his head sharply but Ahmose refused to look at him. His gaze remained on the placid view slipping past. "Are we not all grist to the great stone of your implacable will? Why not Ramose also?"

Because, in spite of everything, Ramose loves me, Kamose wanted to say. Because the men around me show the faces of obedience and respect but I cannot know what is in their hearts, even Hor-Aha's. Time and again he has demonstrated the loyalty of which you speak, but I know that it is tinged with ambition, not love. I do not condemn. I am grateful. Yet there are few who truly love me, Ahmose, and I value them too much to put that affection in jeopardy.

"No," he answered finally. "Loyalty can endure beyond friendship for it is a steadier and deeper emotion that will survive many abuses before it dies. But Ramose has been through enough. It is that simple."

The conversation veered into safer waters, but his brother's words came back to Kamose in quiet moments and he found himself pondering them dispassionately. Ramose was indeed resourceful and intelligent. He did indeed know the city of Het-Uart. If we were not childhood comrades, if he were one of my officers, would I be hesitating to turn him into a spy? he asked himself with as much honesty as he could muster. Am I putting my loneliness above the well-being of Egypt? In the end he pushed the questions away. There would be time to bring them out later on the long, hot trek from the Nile to the oasis.

They passed Dashlut just after sunset, when the sun had gone but its glow still lingered. A silence fell on the travellers as the village, already drowned in shadows, went by. Nothing moved. No dogs barked, no children splashed in the twilit water, no odours of cooking food wafted from the darkened doorways. A large patch of black sand filled the ground between the river and the first houses and as he looked at it Kamose felt again the arrow pressed into his palm and the smooth weight of his bow as he unslung it. The mayor's name had been Setnub, he remembered. Setnub, angry and bewildered, Setnub whose charred bones lay mingled with those of his villagers in that cold residue of fire. "Where are they?" he muttered. Ahmose stirred beside him.

"They are there," he said quietly. "The fields are unkempt but someone has been making an attempt at the spring sowing. It had to be done, Kamose. We both know that. The women

and plenty of children remain. Dashlut is not completely dead."
Kamose did not reply, and the hush that had overtaken the
Medjay was not broken until the melancholy village had disap-
peared into the dimness behind them.

They spent the night just out of sight of Khemmenu, but
Kamose sent a message to Meketra warning him of their
approach, and in the morning a delegation was waiting above
the watersteps to welcome them. Kamose, striding down the
ramp and onto the stone to receive the homage of the men
gathered there, noted with relief that the Prince had not
wasted the winter months. No evidence of the carnage of last
year met his eye. The docks were busy. Laden donkeys thronged
the space between Nile and town. Children ran and shouted,
the large communal ovens smoked, and a group of women
stood knee-deep on the edge of the river slapping their laundry
against the rocks and gossiping. "You have not been idle,
Prince," he remarked approvingly as Meketra straightened from
his obeisance and together they walked towards the town.
Meketra smiled.

"I have taken in the male survivors of Dashlut with their
families," he said eagerly. "There were not many, but I put them
to work at once. The streets are clean and the houses whitewashed. Many are empty of course. The widows have moved in
with relatives. They labour in Khemmenu's fields in exchange
for food from the granaries and storehouses. All discarded
weapons have been collected and repaired for you, Majesty, if
you need them. I cannot yet reopen the calcite and alabaster
quarries at Hatnub. There are not enough men for such heavy
labour. But Your Majesty will send us men when the war is won,
will you not?"

Kamose fought against the irritation Meketra's flood of self-
congratulatory words spawned in him. The Prince had achieved
a great deal since Kamose had ordered him out of Nefrusi and

back to the estate Teti had occupied. The streets had been raked of blood-clotted soil, the refuse cleared away, and the walls of the houses gleamed where once they had been splashed with mire. "I congratulate you," he managed, forcing warmth into his voice. "You have done very well, Meketra. I cannot promise you anything yet, of course, and even when we are victorious I will have to maintain a standing army, but I will not forget your request." They had come to the wide avenue leading to Thoth's temple and Kamose halted. "I must pay my respects to the god," he went on. "Then we will break our fast with you." He did not wait for Meketra's bow but turned from him hastily, Ahmose at his elbow.

"Be careful, Kamose," Ahmose whispered as they approached the pylon. "He must not see how you dislike him. He has indeed performed a miracle here."

"I know," Kamose said. "The fault is mine, not his. Yet something tells me that for every feat and favour he accomplishes he will expect to be rewarded tenfold, either in preferments or in kind. That is not loyalty."

"It is loyalty of a sort," Ahmose murmured dryly, "but not what one might anticipate from a noble. Still, he is useful." Loyal, Kamose thought. Useful. Are we back to that, Ahmose? He bent down, and removing his sandals, began to cross the wide outer court.

He recognized the priest who was standing just inside the inner court and watching them come. The man inclined his head, an impersonal greeting, and nothing could be read from his expression. As they reached him, Kamose held up his sandals. "There is no blood on them this time," he said. The cool eyes flicked to Kamose's hand and back to his face.

"Have you brought a gift, Kamose Tao?" he enquired.

"Yes," Kamose replied smoothly. "I have given you Prince Meketra. Let me warn you, priest. I am indulgent towards your veiled insolence because last time I entered Thoth's domain I was not purified, but here my tolerance ends. I can command Meketra to have you replaced. You are a man who is unafraid to defend his god and his concept of Ma'at and for that I admire you, but I will not hesitate to have you disciplined if you refuse to accord me the reverence my blood demands. Am I understood?"

"Perfectly, Majesty." The man stepped aside but his spine did not bend. "Enter and pay your vows to Thoth."

They crossed the smaller inner court and prostrated themselves before the doors to the sanctuary, praying silently, but Kamose doubted that his words were heard, for he could not keep his mind on them. He remembered the wounded that had lain in the outer court, the sobbing women, the few harried physicians, the atmosphere of hostility through which he and Ahmose had waded as though it were dirty water. Khemmenu will never be mine, he thought as he came to his feet. It was Teti's and therefore Apepa's for too long. And what of you, great Thoth, with your ibis beak and your tiny, knowing eyes? Do you rejoice to see Egypt re-forming or is your divine will opposed to the will of Amun? He sighed, the sound magnified in sibilant echoes, and taking his brother's arm he went out past the priest's exaggerated bow and into the brilliant sunshine.

It was unsettling to sit in the reception hall of the house to which he had come many times in his youth and see strangers leaning across the little tables to speak to him in voices that struck no chord of recognition. Most of Teti's furniture had gone, but Kamose noticed that the pieces Meketra's wife had kept were the most beautiful and costly. He thought of his own mother who in the same circumstances would most certainly have given it all away rather than profit in even the smallest way from another's downfall. I am not being just, Kamose tried to tell himself as he nodded and smiled at the conversation directed at him. This house was theirs before it was Teti's. They must regard its contents as reparation for the years of exile at Nefrusi. But he liked Meketra's wife no better than the Prince himself, and one of Meketra's young sons was wearing an earring Kamose had last seen dangling from Ramose's lobe.

Meketra sat smiling indulgently while his family prattled on artlessly, regaling the royal pair with stories of their hardships outside the fort, the coldness and rudeness of Teti's wife, and of course Meketra's monumental and selfless efforts to restore Khemmenu. In the end Kamose was forced to remind them with unmistakable authority that they were maligning his relatives by marriage and it was with considerable relief that he and Ahmose at last took their leave. "It is entirely likely that Apepa sent Meketra to Nefrusi to rid Khemmenu of that woman's gossiping tongue," Ahmose remarked as Ankhmahor and the Followers closed in around them and they made their way back to their boat. "She has got rid of Teti's servants, did you notice, Kamose? but she has kept the silver dishes Aahotep gave to Nefer-Sakharu." He followed Kamose up the ramp and flung himself down under the sunshade. Kamose waved at his captain, and at once the sailors on shore began to untie the mooring lines.

"They are mannerless," Kamose agreed. "But that is a mild annoyance beside the question of whether or not they are trustworthy. Thank Amun we do not have to worry about it just now! Akhtoy, bring me Weset wine. My mouth feels foul."

Nefrusi was only a short distance downstream and here, as at Khemmenu, great changes had taken place. As his boat tacked to shore in the late afternoon heat, Kamose looked in vain for the sturdy walls and thick gates that would have caused him so much delay if it had not been for Meketra. Piles of rubble littered the ground, cracked stone and chipped mud bricks through which the peasants clambered seeking usable pieces with which to repair their huts or grind their grain. The captain Kamose had left in charge of the demolition picked his way to the foot of the ramp and bowed as Kamose and Ahmose descended. He was dusty and smiling. Kamose greeted him affably. "There has been no trouble with the Setiu workmen, Majesty," the man said in answer to Kamose's question. "I think that in another month the site will be level. What must I do with them then? I have left the barracks standing for shelter." Kamose considered.

"Have them set up the barracks as their permanent home," he decided. "You and your assistants can move into the house Prince Meketra's family left. The Setiu can haul soil in here and after the next Inundation they can become farmers. You must know them all well by now. Kill any who are still surly or recalcitrant and continue to guard the rest so that none are able to go north. Keep them away from the local peasants at least until I have defeated Het-Uart, and send me regular reports. You have done well here. I am glad that Nefrusi can be left in your hands. Is there anything you need?" The man bowed.

"If we are to become a village, it would be good to have a physician here," he said. "Also a priest to serve the shrine to Amun I would like to build. Another scribe would lighten our load also." Kamose turned to Ipi who was writing furiously.

"You have recorded that?" he asked. Ipi nodded. "Good. You shall have what you require, captain. Ipi will draw up a requisition for you to take to Khemmenu. Use it judiciously. It will give you the authority to enter the granaries and storehouses as well, until such time as the Setiu begin producing their own wheat and vegetables. If they behave, we may supply them with wives next year." The captain looked at Kamose uncertainly and seeing the King's grin he laughed.

"Women will multiply my problems, Majesty," he said. "They are one luxury the foreigners can do without, at least for now. I thank Your Majesty, and if you will dismiss me I will return to work."

"Have wine and beer unloaded for the captain and his soldiers," Kamose instructed his scribe as he regained the deck. "And make a note that if all goes well here the captain must be promoted." He stretched. "I feel lighthearted today, Ahmose. We will not move on until the morning. Het nefer Apu is only another forty miles downstream and we are making good time. Mekhir is not yet upon us."

"I wonder what we shall see before we get there," Ahmose muttered. "Ten villages we destroyed last year, Kamose. I imagine that the fields are already full of weeds." Kamose did not answer. Turning abruptly on his heel, he went into the cabin and closed the door.

As Ahmose had predicted, the land from Nefrusi onwards had a derelict air. Acres of untilled brown earth showed between clumps of rank grass and tufts of ungainly wild growth. Here and there the irrigation canals had silted up and debris from the flood—tree branches, the bones of animals, old birds' nests and other flotsam—still lay on the untended ground. Close to the ravaged villages, small groups of bedraggled women and listless children could be seen, bent over the tiny patches they had cleared. They did not even straighten up as the flotilla went by. "Give them grain, Kamose!" Ahmose urged as they stood side by side. "We have plenty!" But Kamose, his mouth drawn into a thin line, shook his head.

"No. Let them suffer. We will give them peasant males from our own nome who will fill these miserable houses with Egyptian children, not Setiu half-breeds. Ankhmahor!" he shouted irritably to the Commander of his Followers. "Send back to the other boats and tell the Medjay to stop their noise! It does not go well with the cheerless neglect around us!" Wisely Ahmose did not try to argue with him and no other words passed between the brothers as the sad miles lengthened behind them.

One day out of Het nefer Apu they encountered their own scouts posted to permanently watch the river traffic, and it was with great relief that long before the town came in sight the sounds of the navy filled the limpid air, mingling with the dust of its camp. The Medjay began to babble excitedly. Kamose's captain ran to climb up beside the helmsman, alternately issuing orders and shouting warnings to the captains of the great cedar barques choking the river. Heralds on the bank began to join their voices to the general hubbub and Kamose heard their cries fly from mouth to mouth. "The King is here! His Majesty has arrived! Make ready for the Mighty Bull!" Sailors tumbled from the tents that lined the Nile to bow and stare, and behind the furore the town itself emerged, a press of low buildings around which streams of busy people, plodding donkeys and laden carts swirled. The clamour reached out to embrace the brothers with the arms of an optimistic normality and Kamose felt his spine loosen after the weight of the melancholy and silent vistas they had passed through.

He and Ahmose, followed by Akhtoy and Ipi, reached the foot of the ramp, and the Followers immediately took up their positions around the royal pair. After giving the Medjay officers permission for the archers to disembark, Kamose set off towards the largest tent, pitched a little way away from the others, but before he reached it Paheri emerged, Baba Abana at his side, and came swinging along the uneven path. Halting, both men knelt with their foreheads in the dust. Kamose bade them rise and together they re-entered the tent. Paheri indicated a chair and Kamose, taking it, waved the rest of them down. Ahmose sat on a stool but Paheri and Baba Abana sank cross-legged onto the worn carpet. Although the tent was spacious, its furnishings were sparse. A lamp hung from its sloping roof, swaying gently in the breeze that was lifting its sides. Two camp cots were set far apart. A table stood at the closed end and under it a large chest. Beside it a scribe was bowing profoundly. A plain travelling copper shrine had been placed behind it. Just inside the tent flap a servant waited. Akhtoy joined him. Ipi settled himself on the carpet by Kamose's feet and began to arrange his palette.

Kamose surveyed his two naval officers. Paheri was glancing about with the shadow of a frown on his face, an invisible list obviously being checked off in his mind. Everything from his upright back to his calmly folded hands and the air of worried authority he exuded spoke of his years as an administrator in Nekheb. Baba Abana, however, sat with casual ease, his kilt rumpled over his thighs, his calloused fingers tracing an absent pattern on the rug in front of his folded legs. "Give me your reports," Kamose said. Paheri cleared his throat, held out a hand to his scribe for the massive scroll, unrolled the papyrus, and shot Kamose a stern though impersonal glance.

"I think you will be very pleased with what Baba and I have done with the riff-raff soldiers you left us," he said. "All of us, officers and men, have worked extremely hard to develop an effective marine force. My shipwrights from Nekheb have made sure that each of the thirty cedar craft you left with us was kept in excellent repair. I have here an account of each boat, the names of its officers and men, and the particular skill of each one of them. Approximately one in five of the soldiers here could not swim when we began their training. Now they can all not only swim but dive as well."

"We devised a rule whereby if a man dropped one of his weapons overboard he was responsible for retrieving it," Abana cut in. "At first we had to hire some of the local boys to dive for the swords and axes and refuse beer to the guilty men, but now they have become such good marines that they do not even lose the weapons, let alone have to dive for them." Paheri had opened his mouth and was about to begin reading again from the seemingly endless scroll, and Kamose hastily stepped in.

"I presume you have a copy of your lists," he said. "Give it to Ipi and I will go over it at my leisure. That way I can absorb its contents more deeply. I congratulate you both on the swimming lessons. A man who is drowned during a battle is a stupid and unnecessary loss. I see that I have put my faith in the right men." His tone was not ingratiating and the compliment was received as just. "Now tell me of the training you devised," Kamose went on. Paheri nodded, but before he spoke he signalled to his servant waiting by the tent flap. The man bowed and disappeared.

"Baba and I mapped out a strategy together," Paheri explained, "but it was Baba who saw to its implementation. We abandoned all drilling on land. The soldiers ate, slept and exercised on the ships for the first two months and after that they were only allowed to pitch tents on the bank if they had been victorious in one of the engagements we set up every week."

"I am glad Your Majesty was not here to see those first miserable attempts at naval warfare," Abana said, a smile in his voice. "Boats ramming each other, oars tangling and snapping, soldiers losing their balance as their craft lurched, captains screaming abuse at each other across the water. And of course a veritable shower of swords, axes and daggers piercing the surface of the Nile. Those were frustrating days." But he did not look frustrated. He looked happily smug. "Your Majesty will be pleased to know that only a mere handful of weapons were irretrievable." He unfolded his legs and leaned back on his hands. "I guarantee that Apepa's marines will look like fumbling amateurs beside ours."

"I do not think that Apepa has any coherent naval force," Ahmose said. "He has left the canals to the traders and citizens and relied on the impregnability of his gates. How is the soldiers'

morale, Paheri? And how have your stores held out?" Paheri
allowed himself a polite twitch of the lips.

"Morale is excellent, Highness. It is hard to believe that the
motley crowd of grumbling peasants you rounded up has
become what you will see tomorrow. The officers have prepared
a demonstration of skill and discipline I hope you will enjoy. As
for our stores, we have been liberal. If a soldier goes hungry, he
does not fight well. We have enough grain and vegetables to
carry us through to the next harvest. All the fields around the
town have been sown already." Doubtless he would be able to
reel off the number of bushels of wheat used, the amount
remaining, even the weight of the seed scattered, Kamose
thought admiringly. He was a good mayor and he has become a
superb Scribe of Assemblage.

At that moment, a small parade of servants entered, bearing trays laden with dishes that filled the airy space with the
aroma of hot food. At another gesture from Paheri they began
to serve it, and Kamose realized that he was genuinely ravenous for the first time in many days. This man forgets nothing,
he thought as he watched roast goose stuffed with leeks and
garlic being lowered onto the camp table another servant had
placed in front of him, and bread glistening with juniper-laced
olive oil followed. Two jugs were held out below a respectfully
bowed head. Kamose chose the beer and watched with satisfaction as the dark liquid cascaded into his cup. "I think I will
remove you from the navy and set you to work organizing the
army's rations, Paheri," he joked as he licked oil from his
fingers. Paheri's face immediately took on an expression of
shocked anxiety.

"Oh, Majesty, I am yours to command, but I beg you to
consider that . . ." Kamose burst out laughing.

"I am not foolish enough to take an hereditary shipbuilder

away from his ships," he said. "I was only joking, Paheri. I am
more than content with all you have accomplished here."

While they ate, the conversation became general but did not
stray far from the interests of all military men. Abana questioned the brothers regarding the Medjay, where in Wawat they
were from, how many different tribes made up the division of
five thousand Kamose had kept with him, how they had
acquired their legendary skills as bowmen. Kamose could detect
no prejudice in his words, only a desire for knowledge, and
answered as readily as he could. "You must ask the General
Hor-Aha these things," he finally confessed. "He knows the
Medjay better than anyone, having brought them out of
Wawat. All I know is that we would not have been able to
move downstream with the speed we did last year without the
amazing accuracy of their archery. I do not even know what
strange gods they worship."

"They are intrigued by Wepwawet of Djawati and Khentiamentiu of Aabtu," Ahmose said. "Both are Egyptian jackal gods
of war. But they seem to follow some strange religion whereby
certain stones or trees contain good or evil spirits that must be
appeased and they each carry a fetish to protect them from
their enemies."

"Does Hor-Aha?" Kamose asked him, surprised at the information he had somehow gleaned. Ahmose nodded, his mouth
full of sesame cake.

"He carries a scrap of linen our father used once to staunch a
bleeding scratch. He showed it to me once. He keeps it folded
up in a tiny leather pouch sewn to his belt."

"Gods," Kamose muttered, and changed the subject.

After they had demolished the food, Paheri took them into
the town to inspect the storehouses and then into the tents of
the soldiers. Everywhere Kamose was struck by the neatness of

the men's belongings, the cleanliness of their scant clothing, and the care with which they treated their weapons. Swords gleamed sharp and spotless, bowstrings were oiled, the rope that bound axe heads to hafts was unfrayed and tight. Beneath the constant din arising from the boats and barges choking the river from the west bank to the east, he moved among the deferential men with a question for one, a word of praise for another, becoming acutely conscious as he went that he was at last the Commander-in-Chief of a fighting force that could be called a navy.

Before he retired to his ship, he arranged to be present the following day to observe the manoeuvres Paheri and Abana wanted him to see, and he received an armful of scrolls from Paheri's scribe. "These are all the reports made by our scouts in the Delta," Paheri explained. "Most were sent on to you at Weset, Majesty, but you might like to refresh your memory with the copies. There is also one scroll from General Hor-Aha. It is sealed and came with the instruction that it was to be given to you personally when you arrived. I have obeyed." Kamose passed the unruly pile to Ipi.

"Have there been any Setiu spies caught anywhere near here?" he asked Paheri. The man shook his head.

"I expected to deal with a few, but the scouts have challenged none any farther south than Ta-she. It is my opinion that Apepa simply does not care what we do because he regards Het-Uart as inviolate and he will not stir outside his city."

"That is my opinion also. Thank you." He walked up the ramp and gained the cabin in a thoughtful frame of mind, Ipi on his heels. Somehow Apepa must open his gates, he mused. He must be persuaded, but how? He sat down on the edge of his cot with a sigh. The morning had been eventful. Ahmose's shadow darkened the doorway as Akhtoy bent down to remove Kamose's sandals.

"I'm ready for an hour on my cot also," he yawned. "They have done wonders here, Kamose, the two of them. I think they deserve some kind of recognition. Will you read the dispatches now?" Kamose swung his feet up onto his mattress.

"No. Later. You can go, Ipi. Akhtoy, tell the guard on the door not to disturb us for at least an hour."

He slept like a child, deeply and dreamlessly, and his waking was childlike also, a sudden return to consciousness and a keen awareness of well-being. Summoning his steward, he had himself washed, changed his linen, ordered bread and cheese, and went out to sit under the wooden sunshade. In a few moments Ahmose joined him. They ate and drank briefly, then Kamose sent for Ipi. "Now," he said to his scribe when the man was settled beside his bare feet, "we had better begin with the scroll from Hor-Aha. Read it to us, Ipi." Ipi broke the seal and began.

"'To His Majesty King Kamose, Mighty Bull of Ma'at and Subduer of the vile Setiu, greetings.'"

"Subduer of the vile Setiu," Ahmose murmured. "I like that."

"'I have spent much time this winter pondering the matter of Het-Uart and wondering what Your Majesty's strategy might be during this season's campaign,'" Ipi went on. "'I have presumed that Your Majesty's choices are limited to a renewed siege of Het-Uart or the fortifying of Nag-ta-Hert or Het nefer Apu against an incursion from the north, coupled with a mopping-up of territory already held. I would like to humbly propose an alternative. I do so with boldness only because I am Your Majesty's General and Your Majesty has seen fit to consult me on military matters before.

"'As Your Majesty is well aware, there are only two tracks leading into and out of this oasis. One comes down from the lake of Ta-she and one runs due west from Het nefer Apu, already secured by your navy. If Apepa's troops could be informed that your army bivouacs at the oasis and if his generals could be persuaded to leave Het-Uart, they would be forced to travel to Uah-ta-Meh through the desert by way of Ta-she, because the navy holds the approach to the only other route, which leaves the Nile just north of Het nefer Apu.

" 'You would then enjoy two advantages. Firstly, the desert terrain is rocky and both trails are very narrow. Secondly, if your troops retreated from Uah-ta-Meh back to the Nile and the safety of Het nefer Apu, Apepa's officers, no matter what they chose to do, would be faced with a daunting and exhausting march either back to Ta-she or forward in pursuit of your army. It is less far to the Nile than to Ta-she. I judge that they would pursue the army. Thus by the time they were forced to engage both the army and the navy they would be fatigued and demoralized. I trust Your Majesty is not offended by my temerity in putting forth this suggestion. I await with glad anticipation either your command to return the troops to the Nile or the arrival of your royal person. I extend to His Highness Prince Ahmose my devotion.' " Ipi looked up. "It is signed 'Prince and General Hor-Aha' and dated the first day of Tybi," he finished. "Would you like me to read it again, Majesty?" Kamose nodded. He glanced at Ahmose who was staring breathlessly at the scribe.

After the second reading Kamose took the scroll and dismissed Ipi. Ahmose spoke into the moment of hiatus. "Let me understand this," he said slowly. "Hor-Aha proposes that we somehow lure the Setiu to the oasis and as they come we retreat to the Nile, so that by the time they have caught us up we are at full strength with the navy, while they are tired and dispirited after an arduous trek through the desert."

"It seems so."

"He is advocating a pitched battle here at Het nefer Apu."

"Ultimately it would come to that." Kamose tapped the papyrus meditatively against his chin. "But why would Apepa risk such a move, when he can simply close up his city as he did last year and watch us running to and fro outside like starving rats? He has every advantage. He can sit there inviolate until we are forced to create a border for ourselves at Nag-ta-Hert or here as Hor-Aha points out, thus dividing Egypt into two lands as it used to be hentis ago. Eventually we would have to disband the army and send the men back to the land or face the disintegration of Egypt's food supply, not to mention her administration." He sighed. "I had dreamed of storming the city this season, breaching the walls, smashing the gates, but my dream was not realistic. What do you think?" Ahmose chewed his lip.

"There are several problems," he said at last. "Apepa would have to be convinced that he could indeed wipe us out at the oasis. He is a cautious, not to say timid, man. He would not take such a gamble without a clear chance of complete success. Someone would have to make him believe that we thought we were safe in sitting at Uah-ta-Meh. Someone who could act the traitor convincingly. Also, why would his troops arrive at Het nefer Apu any more exhausted than ours? The oasis has plenty of water. The Setiu arrive at the oasis to find us gone. Before they follow, they replenish their supplies of both water and food and come after us in good health. There is no advantage to us in this plan."

"Except that, if it worked, we would be saved from another season of fruitless impasse," Kamose said. "It would draw them out. Apepa has made no effort to attack the five thousand soldiers we left here with Paheri and Abana. He sees us as too disorganized to bother about. He knows that the rebellion will disintegrate in time."

"Kamose, it will unless we can change our tactics," Ahmose said softly. "This suggestion of Hor-Aha's is crude, it needs honing, but it is an alternative we had not considered. We must go to the oasis instead of recalling the army from there. We know that it cannot be defended and we never intended that it should be. It was simply a fairly secret place to winter our men. But we must see for ourselves whether or not it would be suitable as a trap."

"What do you mean?" Ahmose shrugged.

"I'm not sure, but what if the Setiu were not able to get fresh water once they arrived there? What if it were possible to retire into the desert and then return to surround them? We have never seen Uah-ta-Meh, Kamose. We should at least go and study the terrain. Perhaps we can bring everything to a head, do something decisive. What use is a fine navy and a disciplined army if the enemy will not fight?"

"I had wanted to bring them east," Kamose said unwillingly. "We will waste time if we trek to the oasis only to find Hor-Aha's great plan impractical in the end. Still . . ." He laid the scroll on his cot. "Who is to say that Amun did not whisper the idea in the General's ear? Let's recall Ipi and go on with the dispatches Paheri gave us."

That evening there was a feast for the Taos and their officers in the house of Het nefer Apu's mayor. The atmosphere was rowdy and merry, the revellers optimistic. The flood had been good, a new campaign season was about to begin, and there was no shortage of beer. Ahmose gave himself over to the frenetic delights of the occasion, but Kamose, though he longed to do the same, found himself as always the quiet observer, watching the antics of his fellows with cool detachment. Already his mind was entangled in his General's proposal, turning it this way and that, searching for a way to make it work, looking for hidden difficulties. Politely he endured the festivity, knowing that it was in his honour, answering the obeisances of the men and women who came up to the dais to bow before him and press their lips to his feet, but long before the lamps began to

gutter and the drunken guests slumped unconscious and satiated over their small tables he was eager to return to the silence
of his cabin.

In the morning he and a white-faced and yawning Ahmose
sat on a raised platform beside the Nile and watched the navy
go through its paces. Abana had devised a mock battle to
demonstrate the skill of his new marines and in the glittering
sunlight they were an awesome sight. The boats moved to and
fro, the officers' commands rang out sharp and clear, and the
men obeyed with precision and alacrity. Kamose was particularly impressed with the clashes between the craft to be boarded
and the soldiers scrambling to board them. No one fell into the
water. All recovered balance and wits enough to begin to fight
at once with the wooden swords issued to them for the exercise.
Marines on the bank provided fleeting targets for the archers
lining the rocking decks and again and again the tipless arrows
fired by those men found their mark.

The Medjay, jostling in the shallows for the best vantage
points, yelled and whistled their approval. Paheri sat with the
brothers but Abana stood easily in the controlling boat, fists
on his hips, his voice carrying clearly over the turbulent water
as he called his orders. "You see Baba's son Kay standing
beside him?" Paheri almost shouted to Kamose over the
tumult. "He has proved himself a good soldier, but more
importantly he is a fine sailor like his father and knows how to
command the respect of the men. I would like to recommend
him for promotion, Majesty." Kamose nodded his understanding without replying.

When it was over and the boats had lined up side to side in
what was itself a display of the sailors' dexterity, Kamose rose
and praised them, alluding to events in their battle and giving
them the rest of the day to do as they pleased. They cheered
him enthusiastically and at their officers' word began to disperse.

Abana ran down his ramp, his son behind him, and came up to Kamose, bowing profoundly. "A little more than a year ago those men were farming peasants," Kamose said. "You have utterly transformed them. I am full of admiration."

"Your Majesty is kind," Abana replied, smiling. "It has been a pleasure for me to do more than oversee dockyards and inspect trading vessels for repairs. After serving under Your Majesty's father, Osiris Seqenenra, I must confess that my own life until recently seemed entirely mundane." He took his son's arm and pulled the young man forward. "I would like to bring my son Kay to Your Majesty's attention once again." Kamose ran his eye swiftly over the same shock of curly hair, barrel chest and rugged features as Baba's.

"You have been under your father's command, Kay?" he enquired. The young man bowed.

"I have, Your Majesty."

"And what did you think of the mock engagement today?" Kay considered, then answered boldly.

"My father's ship, *The Offering*, did well. His crew is the most thoroughly disciplined in the fleet. I was pleased to see that the *Shining in Ma'at* had improved in the area of manoeuvring quickly. Its sailors have had trouble controlling the vessel smoothly. But the *Barque of Amun* and the *Beauty of Nut* held onto their advantage by the skin of their teeth. Their marines have still not entirely mastered the art of handling their bows on the deck of a lurching ship but they work hard and they are certainly improving."

"Which craft turned in the worst performance?"

"The *North*," Kay said at once. "The oarsmen were slow, the helmsman panicked, and the marines fell over each other when the order to board was given."

"Indeed." Kamose smiled. "Then I think you must take over the captaincy of the *North* and knock its crew into better shape.

Paheri has recommended you for promotion. How old are you?"

"Majesty!" the young man exclaimed. "You are generous! I would like nothing better than to put the *North* through its paces! It will become the best ship in the fleet I promise you! Forgive my outburst," he finished more calmly. " I am twenty years old."

"Very well. I expect you to serve me honestly and to the best of your abilities as captain of your ship. You are dismissed." Kay bowed immediately and backed away, his face alight. They watched him run to the *North*'s ramp and stand gazing up at his new charge. "Do what you like with the *North*'s previous captain," Kamose said to Baba. "I presume you know his weaknesses. Put him somewhere where his strengths can be turned to our use."

"Your continued faith in my son will not be abused, Majesty," Abana said. "And thank you, Paheri, for bringing him to His Majesty's attention." Kamose inclined his head.

"You and Paheri have different talents," he said, "but I have never before seen two men who complement each other so well. I leave my fleet in good hands."

"Your Majesty is gracious," Abana responded. "Thank you. It would have been a nuisance to have to accord deference to anyone else you might have designated. As it is, I can easily shout Paheri down." The two grinned. Paheri momentarily lost his rather prim, serious demeanour.

"You are indeed generous, Majesty, and we will do our utmost to honour the trust you place in us," he said. "Have you orders for us? I presume that you will recall the army from the oasis and we will proceed downriver to the Delta."

"No, I don't think so," Kamose replied carefully, his eyes on the noisy scene around him. Beyond the sheltering bodies of Ankhmahor and the Followers the riverbank was crowded with troops handing in the mock weapons, inspecting their bruises and scratches, plunging sweaty limbs into the water, and gathering in excited groups to dissect the tactics of their engagement. "I intend to travel to Uah-ta-Meh myself," he went on. Rapidly and succinctly he laid before them the gist of Hor-Aha's suggestion and they listened attentively.

"It may work," Paheri remarked when Kamose had finished. "I have heard that the desert surrounding the oasis is very inhospitable. Moreover, any army marching from Ta-she under the very best conditions would still arrive there fatigued. We are to hold the navy here then, pending your instructions?"

"Yes."

"Have we your permission to raid downstream? These men must not be idle, Majesty. Their morale is high, but without a few skirmishes they will easily cease to believe in their abilities. Action ought to follow hard upon their training."

"I know this," Kamose agreed. "But I do not want to sting Apepa into attacking Het nefer Apu instead of concentrating his forces on the oasis. That is, of course, if we can devise a suitable plan to draw him there. If we do, then there will be fighting enough when we retreat and he follows. I will send you regular reports, Paheri. Until then you must go on drilling your men." He rose and at once the others also stood. "We leave for Uah-ta-Meh at sunset," he said. "We may as well travel at least some of the way in the coolness of night. You have lifted my spirits, both of you," he told them. "At last this campaign is acquiring a coherent shape. You are dismissed." They bowed.

"May the soles of your feet be firm, Majesty," Abana said. Kamose watched them vanish into the crowd before stepping from the platform and addressing Ankhmahor.

"We leave the ship this evening," he told his Commander. "Have two chariots ready." He turned to Ahmose. "Akhtoy can see to the baggage train and Ipi can send a message on ahead of us with a herald. Hor-Aha and the division commanders have twenty-three of the chariots we captured at Nefrusi. If we take two, we will be leaving fifty for the scouts and officers here. Did I do the right thing, Ahmose?" Ahmose looked at him curiously. There was a note of doubt in his brother's voice.

"In promoting young Abana, most certainly," he urged. "In deciding to go to the oasis, well, Kamose, we have no way yet of knowing what the right thing is. Let us sacrifice to Amun before we go. Is something wrong?" Kamose squared his shoulders.

"No," he said. "But it is one thing to lead a motley rabble of grumbling peasants. It is quite another to be King of a formidable army. Everything is coming to a head, Ahmose. I can feel it. My destiny is being fulfilled, I am waking from a poignant dream to find it mirrored in reality, and I am awed and a little afraid. Come. Let's get out of the sun and find something to drink. I must dictate to Tetisheri before we take the track into the desert." He swung away, calling for Ipi and Akhtoy as he did so, and Ahmose followed on a sudden wave of homesickness. Weset seemed a long way away.

# Chapter SEVEN

ALTHOUGH A HERALD bearing the news of their imminent arrival was dispatched with chariot and driver less than an hour later, Kamose and Ahmose did not take the track that wound away from the river until dusk. At first it ran through still-naked fields, criss-crossed by irrigation canals and lined with stately palm trees, but before long all signs of cultivation ceased. The land stretching ahead was barren and forlorn, a seemingly endless vista of sand broken haphazardly by patches of rough gravel that looked like pools of dark water in the uncertain light. The path itself was still clear, a narrow ribbon winding away into a dim nothingness, and for several hours they followed it in a silence that grew as night deepened. Kamose led, driving his own chariot with Ankh-mahor standing watchfully behind him. Ahmose followed, and beside them their bodyguard marched grimly. The donkey train brought up the rear.

Sometime towards midnight Kamose called a halt; the chariots were unhitched and the horses watered. After posting guards, the brothers wrapped themselves in their cloaks and lay down in the softer sand beside the track. Ahmose was soon asleep, but Kamose lay on his back gazing up at a sky brilliantly festooned with stars set in an all-enveloping canopy. The air was delightfully cool. No sound disturbed the profound tranquility embracing him. In spite of the many activities of the previous day and the gentle ache of muscles unused to chariot work, he was not tired. His mind, so often noisy with clamorous thoughts, was quiet. I am doing the right thing, he told himself peacefully. My doubts fell away as soon as Het nefer Apu was behind me. It is good to be here in the desert for a few precious days with no responsibilities. I feel as I did when I was a boy and Si-Amun was alive. We did little but swim and fish and make forays to hunt in the sands east of Weset. I have become old in the intervening years. Ahmose murmured in his dreams, stirring and flinging one warm arm across Kamose's neck, and the spell was broken. Smiling ruefully to himself, Kamose closed his eyes.

They rose at dawn, broke their fast quickly, and were following their long shadows west before Ra had cleared the smudged horizon behind them. The horses plodded on resignedly in the increasing heat, and soon Kamose halted so that sunshades could be attached to the chariots. In spite of the water he had drunk with his lentils and bread he was already thirsty, the sweat dampening his linen, the glare of light on the ground aggravating an already pounding head. It is just bearable for us, raised in the furnace of the south, he thought. How would it be for soldiers from the softness of the Delta, unused to anything but orchards and damp gardens? He grinned over gritty teeth. Hor-Aha's plan had begun to grow in viability as the tedious miles glided by under his chariot's wheels.

Six hours later they were forced to make camp, and they spent the remainder of the day sheltering under whatever shade they could find. "We are making good time all the same," Ahmose remarked in answer to Kamose's grumble. "We should sight the oasis in another two days, maybe less. The donkeys are drinking more water than we anticipated, but we will still have plenty left in the skins if you want to wash." He squinted into the furnace above. "For myself I will not bother until our tent is pitched beside one of the springs at Uah-ta-Meh. A winter spent out here will have toughened up the troops considerably, Kamose."

"But we ourselves have become somewhat delicate," Kamose answered. "The sun is our medicine, Ahmose. We must take it to become strong again."

At sunset on the third day they sighted a corrugation limning black against the red rim of the sinking sun on the horizon and knew it was their destination. Impatiently Kamose had ordered them to push on through the afternoon's discomfort rather than lie up to wait out the worst of the fiery heat, and it was an exhausted caravan that straggled to a halt as a scout appeared beside the track and challenged them.

The oasis of Uah-ta-Meh was one hundred miles equidistant from both Ta-she to the north-east and the Nile due east. It was a long, uneven depression running fifteen miles from north to south, with a village at either end. A beaten path snaked between them through an inhospitable panorama of jagged black rocks and sand dunes. The village to the north was a motley collection of huts leaning haphazardly between more rocks and a few springs that fed a vivid green life into an otherwise arid landscape. There were pools, clumps of straggling bushes, even a palm tree or two, and it was here that Kamose stepped down from his chariot, relinquished the reins to a waiting servant, and turned to receive the obeisance of his General.

Full dark had fallen and the air was suddenly redolent with the smell of water and the sweet aroma of the oleander flowers that bloomed everywhere. The still reflection of starlight in the pools was broken into shards as the chariot horses and the braying donkeys bent their heads to drink. Already Ipi had appeared, dusty but composed, his palette in his hands. Shouts rang out as men struggled to unload the brothers' belongings, their movements lit by the glare of orange torches, and soon their tent was being pitched beneath a stunted palm while Akhtoy stood by issuing orders. Kamose bade Hor-Aha rise and they studied one another for a moment.

"It is good to see you again," Kamose said at last. "There is much news to give and receive, but before we talk I must toss beer down my throat. When our tent is ready, I want to be bathed. I had forgotten the implacability of the desert." Hor-Aha laughed. He has not changed at all, Kamose thought as the man bowed him towards another tent and he and Ahmose followed. But then, why should he? The winter seemed to trickle by so slowly in Weset, yet it has only been five months since I watched him depart from Het nefer Apu. His hair is longer, that is all. Gratefully he walked into Hor-Aha's quarters and lowered himself onto a stool. Ahmose sank to the floor with a gusty sigh and the General's servant offered the beer Kamose craved. Outside, the furore of their arrival went on, but inside the gently billowing linen walls, lit by the glow of a single lamp, there was peace. Kamose drained his cup.

"There was not much of the oasis to see as we came up to it," he said. "It was too dark. But it seems a rather desolate place, Hor-Aha. How has the army fared?"

"Very well, Majesty," the man replied. He crossed his legs in a gleam of golden anklet, luxuriously exotic against his black skin. "There is in fact plenty of water but its source is divided. The springs are here in this village, not enough to supply all the troops unfortunately, but at the southern end there is a large well at the other village. I decided to divide the fifty-five thousand men between the two villages. That has made communication difficult for the officers but much easier for the distribution of water. They have not been idle." He leaned over and poured Kamose more beer. "Their only days of leisure have been for the celebration of gods' festivals. They have been engaged in desert manoeuvres, survival drills, mock battles, and I am proud to say that you now have an efficient fighting force." He smiled, his ebony eyes alight. "I understand that you now have a navy also."

"I have." In a moment of curiosity Kamose glanced at the man's belt. It was of shabby leather studded with pieces of milky green turquoise. Hor-Aha had worn it every day for as long as Kamose had known him and Kamose quelled a sudden urge to be shown the secret it contained. He did not want to embarrass his General, however, and he did not think that he wanted to see the piece of linen besmirched with his father's blood. Not now.

"Where are the Princes?" Ahmose wanted to know. "And Ramose. How has he fared?"

"The herald came straight to me with the message of your arrival, Highness," Hor-Aha explained. "I took it upon myself to refrain from telling them you were coming until such time as you had recovered from your trek. It is a tiring one. Ramose is in good health. He requested to be posted out in the desert as a scout along the Ta-she track and I agreed. I have sent for him." He turned an enquiring eye on Kamose. "Do you wish to see the Princes tonight?"

"No." Kamose decided. "We are both dirty, hungry and tired. Tomorrow will be soon enough for discussions of strategy. Did you lay your plan before them, General?" Hor-Aha shook his head and once more his strong white teeth flashed out at them.

"I thought I would spare myself the humiliation of their criticisms," he said shortly. "If you think the idea has some merit, then I may have your support when I present it to them, Majesty. If not, then at least I have sunk no lower in their august eyes."

"If it had no merit, Ahmose and I would not be here," Kamose said irritably. "Have the Princes been difficult?"

"No. But then they have had little to do but dictate letters to their families, hunt whatever game they could run to ground out there," he said, waving at the desert that brooded invisibly beyond the confines of the tent, "and train their divisions under my supervision. There has been no conflict between us." At that moment Akhtoy's voice broke in on the conversation and Kamose rose.

"The tent is ready," he said. "Join us in an hour for food, Hor-Aha."

He did not wait for Hor-Aha's reverence but strode out, Ahmose behind him. They crossed to their tent, and while Ankhmahor took up his station outside they surrendered to the benison of hot water and the firm hands of their body servants. "Look at this," Ahmose commented as he stood naked beside his cot. "One carpet on the sandy ground, two miserable cots, two plain chairs and a table. Not to mention the lamp. Spartan surroundings, Kamose, but they seem perfectly wonderful to me after three nights of sleeping out."

"The tent is larger than our cabin on the boat," Kamose replied automatically. He was conscious of a mild depression and it was a few seconds before he was able to trace its cause. Hor-Aha and the Princes. He swore softly. "If we can make Hor-Aha's scheme work, it will go a long way towards reconciling the Princes to his authority," he said. Ahmose's retort was muffled by the towel being applied vigorously to his wet hair.

"I do not think so," he managed. "It will simply make them more jealous. But if you are seen to issue all commands, Kamose, it will not matter. Don't call him by his princely title in their presence."

"Why not?" Kamose snapped back. Ahmose's face emerged, flushed and shiny.

"You will be seeding a disastrous crop if you do," he said calmly. "Now where is the oil? My arms are sunburned."

Later they sat with Hor-Aha by the inky pool whose surface now reflected the flare of the torches. Above their laden table the palm leaves rustled dryly. As he ate and drank, Kamose remained powerfully aware of the miles of night-hung desert that surrounded this small enclave of human activity with its utter silence. He wondered what god commanded the ocean of sand; whether Shu, god of the air, or Nut, the goddess whose body arched over the earth, or perhaps Geb himself, whose essence vivified it. Probably all three deities delighted in its awesome quality of timeless solitude. He was drawn to it himself, not in the way he had loved it as a stripling. In those days it had been a limitless playground. Now its boundlessness called to his ka, whispering of the clarity of vision it could bestow, the mysteries of the eternal it could reveal to one who surrendered to its supreme otherness. He recognized its call as an invitation to lay down the crushing obligations of the war his father had begun, to run away, and he wrenched his mind back to the conversation going on between Ahmose and the General. Hor-Aha was enquiring into the state of his Medjay and Ahmose was relating the events of the mock naval battle. Kamose listened without comment.

In the morning both brothers dressed with care. Kamose had himself arrayed in a white, gold-bordered kilt and jewelled sandals. The royal pectoral lay against his chest with its counter weight hanging between his naked shoulder blades, and the thick gold armlet Amunmose had presented to him was tied around his upper arm. A white-and-blue striped linen helmet framed his painted face and a silver ankh hung from one earlobe. His palms were hennaed. When he and Ahmose were ready, they left the tent, emerging into bright sunlight and the salute of the Followers. Hor-Aha was already waiting, together with a contingent of troops who would act as escort. Ankhmahor stood in Kamose's chariot and behind it Ahmose's charioteer was clucking softly at the little horses. Kamose took a swift glance at the surroundings that had seemed so peaceful the night before.

Beyond the largest pool beside which his shelter had been pitched were other pools, each fringed in reeds and stunted palms. Many had narrow irrigation trenches full of scummed and stagnant water leading into tiny fields around whose edges oleander bushes grew in a riot of pink and white blossoms, and everywhere the sand was littered with sharp black rocks where untethered goats picked their dainty way and flocks of geese scuttled to and fro.

The villagers had erected their shanties in a disorderly jumble at the farthest perimeter of their cultivation so that not an inch of arable ground might be wasted. No trees shaded their uneven roofs. Kamose, peering into the distance through a network of shrubs, blooms and the army's pack animals crowding the verges of the pools for their morning watering, could just discern movement in front of those desolate and impoverished huts. "We keep the villagers away from the tents," Hor-Aha said, seeing the direction of Kamose's eyes. "We cannot prevent them from fetching water from the springs in the rocks or bringing their herds of goats and cows to the pools, of course, but we do not allow them to wander about." He gestured. "The army is camped out beyond the village. Prince Intef has requested the honour of receiving you in his tent. Prince Iasen is with him. The Princes Makhu and Mesehti are on their way from the southern village. I sent for them last night." Kamose put a hand on the hot frame of his chariot and pulled himself up.

"How long?" he asked. "And what of Ramose?"

"They should arrive in four hours, Majesty. Word has not yet come from Ramose."

"Then I will inspect the troops before greeting Intef and Iasen. Lead the way, Hor-Aha."

For much of the morning Kamose directed Ankhmahor to drive him slowly between the ranks of tiny tents in which his soldiers lived, stopping often to examine their weapons and ask them if they had any needs or complaints. They no longer resembled the conscripts the Princes had dragged from their fields. Burned almost black by the desert sun under whose glare they had marched and drilled, thinned and toughened by the relentless discipline of their officers, they had a sameness about their eyes and the way they moved that gave Kamose a deep satisfaction. He received the deference of the officers and spoke to the army's physicians. There had been the usual crop of fevers, eye infections and worm infestations but no serious plague had endangered the effectiveness of the force.

Lastly Kamose consulted the Scribe of Assemblage regarding the food supplies. Only then did he have Ankhmahor turn the horses' heads towards the two large tents set a little apart from the rest. The two guards before it straightened as Ankhmahor called a warning. Kamose alighted and Ahmose walked to join him, stretching hugely. "An impressive tour," he said. "We must presume that the troops stationed at the other end of the oasis are also in excellent fighting readiness. Who would have thought it a year ago, eh, Kamose? Now I want refreshment."

"Have the horses taken into the shade and let them drink," Kamose said to Ankhmahor. "Come with us, Ankhmahor. You are my most trusted Prince and I want you to participate in this discussion. Hor-Aha, have me announced."

He walked into the shadow of the tent on a wave of trepidation. I do not want to congratulate them on their achievements here, he thought. I do not want to see smiles of self-indulgence on their faces. I still resent them bitterly for letting my father's desperate bid for freedom go unaided. Petty it may be, but I cannot rid myself of this grudge.

In the cool dimness of the interior there was a flurry of movement. The Princes had risen and as he and Ahmose strode in they bowed. All four were there. Kamose greeted them, bade them sit, and himself took a chair that had been placed at the head of the table that dominated the space, Ahmose beside him. After a moment Ankhmahor slipped in and the council was complete.

Kamose looked them over slowly and they stared back at him solemnly. They, like the soldiers under them, had been changed by their months in the desert. Beneath the kohl and gems, the soft folds of their fine linen, their skin was darker, the whites of their eyes more startlingly pure in faces etched into fine lines by the dry winds. The small movements of the two servants setting food and drink before them were loud in the sudden hush. Kamose gathered in his resolve and lifted his wine cup. "You have created an army out of a rabble," he said. "I am content. To victory!" They smiled and loosened, raising their own cups and drinking with him. There was a flurry of clinking plates and low murmurs as they began to eat.

For a while they exchanged news, spoke of the prowess of their divisions, bantered and laughed while the servants set down finger bowls and removed the scoured dishes, but at last Kamose dismissed the servers and held up a hand and an expectant silence fell. "Doubtless you wonder why I am here, and have not sent for you to join me at Het nefer Apu," he began. "The reason is this. Prince Hor-Aha has proposed a scheme that would entice Apepa from his stronghold if it can be made to work. I require your thoughts." He watched them as he went on to outline Hor-Aha's plan, his own thoughts at variance with the words flowing easily from his mouth. Their attention flitted from him to the General sitting stolidly on his left hand and he could not mistake the coolness in their glances. They had not liked to be reminded that the black foreigner bore a title that gave him an equality with them. They would argue against anything Hor-Aha submitted.

But to his surprise Mesehti's own mouth opened as soon as Kamose's had closed. "This plan has merit," he said. "None of us were looking forward to another frustrating season of siege. We have talked a great deal this winter of what could be done but could find no solution." I would wager that you talked among yourselves and did not include Hor-Aha, Kamose silently surmised.

"And neither is this a solution," Intef said sourly. "It is based on far too many suppositions. Suppose that Apepa greets the news of our presence in the oasis with delight instead of suspicion. Suppose that we can retreat in plenty of time instead of being caught in this forsaken hole. Suppose that his forces do arrive at Het nefer Apu in a state of fatigue instead of eagerness to engage. Suppose our combined army and marines can defeat what will be a superior enemy instead of being beaten back and having to regroup with heavy losses." His tone had been sarcastic. "We cannot afford to take any risk, particularly one as foolish as this." He sat back, looking smug. Makhu of Akhmin clasped his beringed fingers primly on the table.

"I also hesitate to consider such a rash plan," he said. "But our alternatives are limited. In fact, my friends, we have only one. Siege. In all the months of fruitless discussion we have had, not one of us has put forward any idea worthy of serious dissection. Het-Uart is a fortress. We cannot take it by an open method. That much is certain."

"We might as well petition Shu to lift us and fly us over its walls," Iasen said gloomily. "So let us take Intef's suppositions one by one and see if we may demolish them. How would Apepa greet the news of our presence here? With indifference, I think. He does not care where we are or what we do."

"He would care if he was told our strength and the defence-lessness of the oasis." Mesehti spoke again. He was frowning and absently sweeping bread crumbs into little hills. "He believes that the five thousand men who wintered at Het nefer Apu comprise our whole army. What would he feel if he was told of the fifty-five thousand here? First astonishment, then alarm. Following that would be temptation. He is presented with an opportunity to take advantage of the stupidity of the Tao's officers." He turned to Kamose. "Forgive me, Majesty. I am attempting to enter Apepa's mind. He will be anxious, wondering how long we intend to stay here, whether it would be better to wait and see if we move the troops to an even more defenceless position or risk a quick march across the desert to catch us here. He will consult his officers for advice."

His officers, Kamose thought. Pezedkhu. A chill ran down his spine. Pezedkhu, whom he had last seen standing in his chariot while he, Hor-Aha and Si-Amun crouched behind a rock after the disastrous engagement at Qes. Pezedkhu's words had rung out coldly, arrogantly, across the carnage. " . . . He is mighty. He is invincible. He is the Beloved of Set. Crawl home if you can and lick your wounds in shame and disgrace . . ." Kamose's fingers went to the barely visible white line across his cheek, all that remained of the slash that had cut open his face.

"But could we withdraw our men into the desert until Apepa's arrived and then sweep down on them?" he asked. "Could we keep our troops out there in that pitiless waste for days while we watched the oasis? It would be an even greater gamble than the one we want Apepa to take." He shifted in his chair and forced his hand back to the table.

"No, Majesty, we could not," Hor-Aha said definitely. "We must begin a retreat to Het nefer Apu as soon as our spies tell us that Apepa has left the Delta, arrive at the Nile in time to drink and rest, and then turn upon the other forces as they come east."

"Why would Apepa commit his army in the first place?" Ankhmahor put in at last. He had been listening intently to the discussion, his eyes going from one speaker to another, his body relaxed and still. Now he straightened and leaned forward, reaching for the jug of water before him. The heat in the tent had thickened and all present were sweating lightly. "Why would his first presumption not be that this is a trap?"

"Someone must go to him and convince him that it is not," Ahmose said slowly. "Someone he can be persuaded to trust. We must send a spy who will allow himself to be caught and who has the wit and subtlety to feign fear and confess the knowledge. A common soldier perhaps. A pretended deserter? Greedy for reward?"

"There would be no second chance," Mesehti said. "If the spy failed and we waited in vain for any word, we would be losing valuable time. The campaign season would be passing swiftly and it is no mean feat to lead fifty-five thousand men back to Het-Uart and then organize another siege."

That word seemed to settle a pall of gloom over the assembly. For a while there was a silence broken only by the intermittent swish of Intef's fly whisk and the soft conversation of the guards outside. Kamose was about to suggest that they disperse in order to think about what had been said until the morning, when a sharp challenge rang out beyond the tent and a familiar voice answered it. The flap was lifted and Ramose strode in. His short kilt clung damply to his dust-streaked thighs and his sandals left little pools of sand as he approached the gathering, went down on his knees, and kissed both of Kamose's feet. "Forgive this sweat and filth, Majesty," he said apologetically. "I received the summons and set off at once. I slept under my chariot and have not been to my tent to be washed." Impulsively Kamose bent and gripped both the hot shoulders before him.

"I am very happy to see you again, Ramose," he said. "Get up!" Ramose obeyed, scrambling to his feet and taking the cup of water Ankhmahor was holding out to him. Draining it, he saluted Ahmose, then sank onto an empty chair. He drew a battered scroll from his belt and handed it across the table.

"My soldier and I intercepted a Setiu herald heading south on the Ta-she track," he said. "He was carrying this. He is being detained in the prison hut." Amid the general murmur his announcement had prompted, Kamose took the scroll and unrolled it, reading swiftly. He looked up.

"The man was on his way to Kush," he said. "He was taking the desert paths, well away from the Nile." He grinned. "This confirms our suspicion that Apepa believes our whole force to be centred at Het nefer Apu. The herald chose the route he did so as to avoid Paheri and the navy. Thank all the gods you were vigilant, Ramose, or both Kush and the Delta would soon have known of our strength here."

"Will you give us the news?" Ahmose urged. Kamose nodded.

"The scroll says this. 'Awoserra the Son of Ra, Apepa: Greetings to my son the ruler of Kush. Why do you act there as ruler without letting me know whether you see what Egypt has done to me, how its ruler Kamose has set upon me on my own soil though I have not attacked him? He has chosen to ruin these two lands, my land and yours, and he has already devastated them. Come north therefore. Be not timid. He is here in my vicinity. There is none who can stand against you in this part of Egypt. Behold I will give him no repose until you have arrived. And then we two shall divide up the towns of Egypt.'" A gale of laughter, part derision, part relief, shook the listeners when Kamose had finished.

"What a boaster!" Mesehti chortled. 'I will give him no repose.' It is we who have given him no repose!"

" 'Be not timid'?" Ahmose quoted. "The coward sits safely in Het-Uart while we take back what is ours almost without opposition and he dares to call Teti-En the Handsome timid? Timid? He has no Setiu blood in him, so how can he be timid?"

"What do you think Teti-En would have done if the message had got through to him, Majesty?" Iasen wanted to know. "Apepa called him his son."

"He was just trying to ingratiate himself with the Prince of Kush," Kamose replied. "Teti-En is no Setiu, as my brother said. He is a mystery, the Fallen One, an Egyptian who chose to leave Egypt and draw the Kushite tribes into one union under him, but he seems to have no interest in using them for conquest." He paused, considering. "He has treaties with Apepa, but whether he would honour them, it is impossible to say. If he still thinks like an Egyptian, he would read Apepa's appeal and then wait to see what might happen. After all, in order to bring warriors from Kush to the aid of Apepa, he would have to first march them through Wawat, and the Medjay hate the Kushites. After that he would enter Upper Egypt and immediately be in land under our control."

"Fortunately he has remained quiet so far, seeing that most of the men from the Medjay villages in Wawat are here with our army," Ahmose pointed out. "No Kushite messenger has been intercepted at Weset. It might be as well to send to Tetisheri and warn her to tighten her watch on the river, although Weset does not have enough troops left to repel a concerted attack by the Kushites. We can only hope that in such an eventuality the remaining Medjay in Wawat and the soldiers still at Weset would be able to at least slow him down. The last thing we need is a battle front forming down there."

"I know," Kamose admitted. "All we can do is trust that Teti-En's inaction signifies an attitude of temporary neutrality. Remember that his capital in Kush is a very long way from

Egypt. I think that he will only come north if his own little kingdom is directly threatened."

"I agree," Ahmose said. "He will consider his own advantage first. What will you do now, Kamose?"

"I am not sure." Kamose rose and stretched. "But I am heartened by Apepa's ignorance. I hope the majority of his officers and advisers are as stupid as he." Ramose glanced around the company.

"I see that I arrived too late for a strategy meeting, Majesty. Do we march for the Nile?" Kamose shook his head and gestured at Hor-Aha, and the General briskly summarized his proposal and the talk that had followed it. When he ceased speaking, Kamose bade them stand.

"No more until tomorrow," he said to them all. "Come back with a clearer vision of how this may be accomplished. Ramose, clean yourself up and join Ahmose and me for the evening meal."

The Princes bowed and quickly scattered. When the two brothers and Ramose were alone, Ramose asked quietly, "Majesty, how is my mother?" Kamose met his eye.

"She is well but still keeps much to herself," he answered honestly. "I do not think it is grief any longer, Ramose. It is anger because I did not let her die with Teti." Ramose nodded.

"She has always been strong-willed, like her cousin, your mother. I miss her."

Riding back to their tent, Kamose found himself suddenly exhausted. After handing the scroll to Ipi for copying and filing, he lay on his cot and was soon asleep and he did not wake until the long fingers of sunset crept across the carpeted floor.

Washed, painted and freshly clad, Ramose joined Kamose and Ahmose as they ate beside the pool. Torches guttered orange in the spindled palm trees, their flames tossed in the pleasantly cool night breeze. Servants came and went, padding barefoot through the hillocks of sand, and the spasmodic laughter of unseen soldiers filled the air. High above in the velvet darkness of the sky the stars hung unblinking.

Towards the end of the meal, when the wine flagon had been emptied and the three men were picking half-heartedly at the last platter of dates, Ahmose sat back with a sigh of satisfaction. "There is optimism in the air tonight," he said. "You can hear it in the men's voices. I feel it as a wind of change, a good omen. What do you think, Ramose? You've been very silent." Ramose gave him a faint smile.

"I am sorry, Highness," he said. "I have indeed been thinking hard, but about the General's plan. It is sound. It has only two flaws."

"How can Apepa truly be persuaded to leave his city and how can we ensure that his troops will be more fatigued than ours when they reach Het nefer Apu," Kamose put in. Ramose nodded.

"Exactly." He hesitated, his gaze on the black burnish of the dates. Kamose saw his brows draw together in a frown and felt his own stomach tighten. I know what he is going to say, he thought to himself with cold certainty. It is so obvious and yet I shied away from it. Did Ahmose? He felt his brother's glance and met it. Ahmose nodded once, an imperceptible assent. Ramose's chin lifted. "I have no idea how the second objective can be achieved," he said. "But I have a solution for the first. Send me to Apepa, Kamose. I am the perfect vehicle for your betrayal."

"Go on," Kamose said tonelessly. His heartbeat had quickened. Ramose held up a finger.

"There is Tani," he began. "I am still in love with her and I ran away from you in order to see her again." He extended another finger. "There is the execution of my father, a reason to turn my affection for you into hate." A third finger rose to rest against the other two. "There is my inheritance, my estates at Khemmenu, gone to Meketra. If Apepa doesn't know that, I will tell him. I will offer him all the information he wants in exchange for a meeting with Tani and the opportunity to fight with the Setiu against you." He grimaced. "Perhaps I shall ask for Khemmenu to be returned to me for my loyalty." In the silence that followed he looked from one to the other. "My words do not surprise you, do they?" he said softly. "My offer was already in your minds." He turned urgently to Kamose. "Majesty, do not hesitate to use me, do not shrink because of our long friendship or in guilt over the destruction of my hopes. Apepa ruined them, not you, and my father was the cause of his own downfall." Kamose studied the handsome, earnest face and felt an unaccustomed sadness well up in him. It was a gentle emotion, civilized and fraught with nostalgia.

"You deserve to live the rest of your life in peace, Ramose," he managed and the young man made a savage gesture and sat back.

"So do you. It is pointless to kick against fate. To do so simply renders us less and less able to make sensible choices. It has to be me, Kamose. None of the Princes will do. With the exception of Ankhmahor and perhaps Mesehti they are too open to seduction once they leave your control. You cannot trust them completely." He heaved himself to his feet and stood with both palms flat on the surface of the table. "You cannot send an ordinary officer. He would not have the subtlety of mind necessary to spar with Apepa and allay his suspicions. It has to be me." But what is your motive? Kamose wondered. A loss of faith in your future? Revenge on Apepa? A genuine need to see Tani? Or is it a chance to flee from my presence? He shook himself mentally.

"I am loath to do this," he said. "I do not want your death or imprisonment on my conscience if something goes wrong. You have suffered enough at my hands." Ramose's eyes narrowed.

"I made my choice years ago," he retorted. "It is already the end of Mekhir, Majesty. Spring is advancing. You must decide."

"But first I must think." Kamose rose and Ahmose with him. "Go and sleep, Ramose. We will talk again tomorrow."

When Ramose had gone, Kamose drew his brother away from the torches, and when they had reached the edge of the straggling palm grove and were alone with the immensity of the desert running away from them under the pale starlight, he lowered himself onto the sand and folded his legs. Ahmose sank down beside him. For a while they did not speak, allowing the deep stillness of their surroundings to enter them. Then Kamose said, "I cannot allow him to take the risk. It is too dangerous." Ahmose did not answer at once but Kamose felt his slow appraisal.

"I do not understand you, Kamose," he said after a moment. "So far you have been ruthless in your disregard for anyone and anything that threatened to become an obstacle. The impregnability of Het-Uart has been driving you insane, yet when you are presented with an opportunity to achieve your goal, you suddenly develop a most uncharacteristic sensibility. Why?"

"I thought it was our goal, not just mine," Kamose said fiercely. "Don't you understand that Ramose is a link with the past, with a kinder time, that when I look at him I am reminded not only of the pain I have caused but also of the man I used to be?" He struggled to suppress the rage that always lurked just below the surface of his composure. "If I can keep him alive, it will be as though I have somehow preserved what is best in Egypt, as though there is something innocent and precious left after all the killing and burning." He passed a hand wearily over his eyes. "As though there is something left of myself."

"You cannot afford such self-indulgence now!" Ahmose

protested. "Kamose! Not now! Where was it when we razed Dashlut? Murdered villagers as we sailed downstream? This plan is a good one. We can use it to kill soldiers, weaken Apepa, perhaps even drive him out of Egypt! Ramose knows this. If you need the presence of a living man to remind you of who you were, then you are in grave trouble!"

A dozen cutting rejoinders rose to Kamose's tongue, cruel words of wounding and self-justification, but with a mighty effort he bit them back. He was glad that Ahmose could not see the strain on his face in the dim light. He knew his brother was right, knew it with his head, but his heart cried out in denial. Ramose was Tani, was flinging throwing sticks at ducks in the marshes on lazy spring afternoons, was family gatherings in Teti's garden at Khemmenu, he and Si-Amun and Ramose lying in the grass while the moths fluttered in and out of the glow of the lamps and the conversation of the adults was the lulling sound of security. "It is gone," Ahmose said quietly as though he had seen the bright visions filling his brother's mind. "All gone, Kamose. It can never come back. Let Ramose go too. We need him to do this. For Egypt's sake." Kamose clenched his fists in the cold sand.

"Very well," he grated. "But give me a coherent sequence of events, Ahmose. As things stand, it will not work." Ahmose exhaled gustily and Kamose, in spite of his distress, recognized with fleeting amusement that it was a breath of relief.

"It will not work if Ramose goes alone and contrives to have himself arrested," Ahmose said. "What is he there for? To spy out the city? Perhaps? But neither you nor I would swallow such a reason and neither will Apepa. Spies can come and go in Het-Uart with ease when the city is not under siege. No. Ramose must go as an escort. You must dictate a letter to Apepa and have it carried to him by the messenger Ramose caught. Ramose goes to make sure the man delivers it safely.

That way Ramose will eventually corroborate the information the man will give Apepa when he decides to turn renegade in exchange for a meeting with Tani. That way Ramose can walk right up to any Setiu guard on any gate and demand to be taken to the palace. He can begin his interview coolly, even with hostility, then begin to weaken. If we are lucky, Apepa might even offer Ramose inducements to betray us. Ramose will need to lie about nothing. He can tell the full truth."

Kamose stirred. "What will happen to him afterwards?"

"We can only guess. Apepa will not keep him in the palace. I think he will either put him in prison or demand that he prove his new allegiance by taking up arms against us under the close watch of a Setiu officer." He raised his shoulders and spread his hands in a gesture of bafflement. "Who can say? But you may be sure that Ramose understands fully what he is doing and still wants to do it. Let him, Kamose. He will willingly die afterwards providing he can have one more sight of Tani." Something in Kamose responded with an icy cynicism. How touchingly naïve, it said mockingly. How sweetly romantic. Ramose clings to his fantasy like a child. But shame brought an equally swift refutation. No. Ramose has lost everything else. Only his love for my sister remains.

"You can be pitilessly persuasive when you want to, Ahmose," he said aloud. "You are right, of course. I will dictate to Apepa, taunt him, try to make him angry and defensive so that he must release his troops or lose face. I will send it with Ramose and the Setiu herald. Ramose had better take the track back to Het nefer Apu by chariot and then sail to the Delta. Two days to the Nile and probably four from there to Het-Uart. Six days. Allow three days for audiences, discussions and so on in the palace. Nine days. Another four or five for Apepa's generals to bring his army to a state of readiness. Fourteen days. In ten days we must have scouts watching the mouth of the Delta and also the desert route at Ta-she. Amun help us if we miss the Setiu troops! As soon as we know they have left Ta-she, we march for Het nefer Apu, join Paheri and the navy, and wait to do battle. Are you satisfied?" He got up, brushing sand from his kilt.

"Yes." Ahmose joined him. "Kamose, do you think Apepa will unleash Pezedkhu on us?" There was anxiety in his voice. Kamose felt it brushing him also but he squared his shoulders.

"Pezedkhu is the best military mind he has," he replied grimly. "We have a grievous score to settle with the General. Let him come and, please Amun, let him perish under our arrows and swords. It is all a gamble, Ahmose. We can only throw the dice. Apepa and the gods must pick them up."

Back in their tent, bathed in the steady golden light of the lamp set on his table, Kamose paced while he dictated two letters. One was to Tetisheri telling her of Apepa's plea to Teti-En and warning her not to relax her watch on the river. He included greetings to the rest of the family and a hope that Aahmes-nefertari's pregnancy was proceeding normally. Next he addressed Apepa himself, beginning with difficulty but warming to the task as he recounted in vivid and derisive language every aggression he had perpetrated, every village burned, every garrison decimated. He spoke of the support he received from the Princes, those men who had taken everything Apepa had offered through the years and were now throwing it back in his face. He dwelt with genuine relish on the sacking of Apepa's fort at Nag-ta-Hert and finished with the boast that it was only a matter of time before Het-Uart itself suffered the same fate. He insulted, belittled and jeered, ending the vitriolic outpouring with the words "Your heart is undone, base Setiu, who used to say 'I am Lord, and there is none equal to me from Khmun and Pi-Hathor down to Het-Uart,'" and he signed himself "Mighty Bull, Beloved of

Amun, Beloved of Ra, Lord of the Two Lands, Kamose Living For Ever."

Ahmose had been listening from his perch on his cot. As Ipi sealed the two papyri and Kamose drank thirstily from the water by the lamp, he said, "Will you tell the Princes about the letter, Kamose?" Kamose smiled across at him. He felt as though he had taken a heavy boulder that had been slung about his neck and hurled it at Apepa. He felt light and slightly giddy.

"We are quite often in silent agreement, aren't we, Ahmose?" he said. "No, I will not. It would only worry them. After so much direct and unforgivable abuse pouring into Apepa's ears through the mouth of his scribe as he reads what I have sent, there would no longer be the slightest chance of pardon for them if Apepa proves victorious. I have implicated all of them. Ramose can take tomorrow to prepare for his journey and can be gone the following morning. They can know the rest, of course. Then you and I will explore this oasis while we wait for news from the scouts." He swept up a cloak. "I'm very restless. I think I'll walk for a while. Will you come?" Ahmose shook his head.

"Sleep for me," he said. "Take Ankhmahor. Don't be alone, Kamose." For the sake of my safety or my state of mind? Kamose wondered. He let the tent flap fall closed behind him and plunged into the night.

At the meeting the next morning, Kamose told the assembled Princes that he had decided to approve Hor-Aha's plan and that Ramose would be accompanying the Setiu soldier back to Het-Uart. He kept silent regarding the letter. He felt no guilt at withholding such information from them. He was King, under no obligation to speak to them of anything other than their orders unless he needed their advice. They gave him no argument, indeed, they seemed relieved that their long winter of idleness would soon be over.

Later he summoned Ramose, gave him the scroll, and laid out his instructions. It was to be obvious that he was escorting the herald to make sure the man did not simply run away, either to Kush in an excess of duty to deliver Apepa's message by word of mouth or back to his home, relinquishing all responsibility. "Once you are in the palace you will have to rely on your own discretion," he told Ramose. "Ask to be allowed to see Tani before you leave, having fulfilled your duty as a herald. Then show some hesitation." Kamose shrugged. "Any suggestions I may make are useless, Ramose. Lull Apepa's suspicions, tell him everything you know, but lure him out of his city."

"I will do my best," Ramose said. "If I am unable to return to you, Kamose, you must continue to trust that I have been faithful. Have you a message for Tani?"

"I could speak to you all day of what is in my heart for her," Kamose said wryly. "Tell her that all of us pray for her, that she is constantly in our thoughts, that we love her. I do not want her upset, Ramose. Nor do I want you to waste the precious time you will spend with her in talking about her family."

There was a pause before Ramose said cautiously, "Do you think she is still alive, now that you have broken the agreement with Apepa?"

"There was no agreement," Kamose said harshly. "There was only Apepa's promise that she would not be harmed as long as the rest of us did as we were told. We must presume that she lives, that Apepa would not be mad enough to kill a noblewoman. I think he is a small man, Ramose, happy to cause indignities, choosing a kind of ignoble mercy to mask his fear of any clean decision. He should have executed Ahmose and me and exiled our women. That is what I would have done. Given his careful cowardice, there is a good chance that Tani still lives." Ramose came close.

"I will escape with her if I can," he said. "Given the slightest opportunity we will run. Do I have your permission to try this, Majesty?"

"Providing you have completed the task for which you have volunteered," Kamose said evenly. "That is more vital than your personal anguish, Ramose." The two men stared at one another for a moment, tension flaring between them, then Kamose stepped forward and pulled Ramose against him. "My friend," he breathed. "We have always loved one another, but now I am King and I must put the demands of my office above the joys of brotherhood. Forgive me." Ramose pulled away.

"I love you also, Kamose," he said. "I will do my utmost to discharge the commission I have taken upon myself. But I also intend to seize Tani in payment for everything I have suffered at your hands. Affection has nothing to do with this. It is fitting."

"I understand." Kamose fought to keep his expression bland while the impulse to justify himself rose like bile in his throat. I did what I had to do, he thought savagely. Surely you can see that, surely you know! Do you think it was easy, shooting an arrow into your father's trembling breast?

But it was easy, that other voice contradicted him, the voice that increasingly drowned out the whirl of his doubts and misgivings. Easier than being torn by conflicting loyalties, O Mighty Bull, easier than enduring the gentle pain of a friend's distress. The arm of retribution must be implacable. "Then there is nothing more to say but to give you a formal farewell," he said aloud. "May the soles of your feet be firm, Ramose. Go with the blessing of the gods." Ramose bowed. Both men stood irresolute, not knowing what to say, each searching for a further word or gesture to bring what could be their last meeting to an acceptable close, but the silence between them deepened. Finally Kamose smiled, inclined his head, and went away.

## Chapter EIGHT

B Y THE TIME THE sun had lost the colour of
dawn, the oasis was a jumbled blur on the
western horizon behind Ramose. Ahead, the track to Het nefer
Apu ran straight to the east, a narrow ribbon of beaten earth
between the unforgiving flanks of the desert. Its smooth appearance was deceptive, and Ramose, sitting on the floor of the
chariot with his back pressed against its hot side, had to brace
himself as the wheels ran over half-concealed rocks and patches
of coarse gravel. Across from him the Setiu soldier also bounced
and swayed, his sandalled feet planted between Ramose's own,
his manacled hands pressed to the floor of the vehicle between
his brown thighs. He was a swarthy-complexioned man with a
shock of unkempt black hair and a tattered black beard encircling full lips. His eyes, like two shiny grapes, seldom left
Ramose's face but there was no particular expression in them.
Ramose wondered if all Apepa's servants were as dishevelled or
whether this one had been chosen to pass for a peasant or
nomad on his anonymous trek south. Above the two passengers
the charioteer stood beneath the protecting sunshade, singing
to himself and occasionally talking to the two little horses
whose gait stirred up a constant cloud of fine beige dust. Bags of
food and skins of water were piled around his legs.

Ramose fought his inclination to doze as the heat intensified. Not that the Setiu was likely to attempt an escape out here unless he was able to kill both other men and steal the chariot and the victuals, and that possibility was unlikely. His wrists were securely tied together and one ankle was loosely roped to the chariot's upper rim. He will be a continual nuisance once we reach Het nefer Apu, Ramose thought. I will be forced to tie him to a tree every night if I want to sleep. He glanced away from the man's steady appraisal, back along the wind-whipped track.

It was bad enough marching the army from the Nile to the oasis, his thoughts ran on. By the time the troops got there, the officers had to beat them away from the pools until orderly lines could be formed, and these were southerners, sturdy peasants used to privations and the unremitting heat of Shemu. How will Apepa's thousands fare after three such treks, soft Delta men, city dwellers who have known nothing but orchards and vineyards? Delta to Ta-she, Ta-she to Uah-ta-Meh, Uah-ta-Meh to Het nefer Apu? Two opportunities to replenish their supply of water, but will it be enough? Hor-Aha has conceived a very good plan.

Ramose wiped the stinging sweat from his eyes. He had kohled them heavily against the glare of the sand but still they ached. So did his backside. Scrambling up, he stood for a while beside his charioteer but he did not like the feel of the Setiu huddled down there at his feet and he soon resumed his uncomfortable position. The man was asleep, his head canted on one shoulder. He had not spoken since being removed from the prison hut. Ramose was glad that those dark eyes were now closed and he himself surrendered to an uneasy unconsciousness.

It took them three days to cross the desert, eating cold food in the evenings and lying wrapped in cloaks while the welcome cool of the hour after sunset turned to an uncomfortable chill. Before he slept, Ramose tied his prisoner to one of the chariot's spokes. The man ate and drank without comment when bidden. There was nothing sullen or hesitant in his demeanour, merely a vast indifference. They saw no one and the desert remained empty of all sound and movement save their own.

At sunset on the third day the horses' heads came up and their pace quickened. "They smell water," the charioteer commented. "We are close to the Nile." Ramose stood and looked ahead. A thin line of vegetation broke the monotony of land and sky. He watched it grow and in another hour they were jolting beneath its eaves. Beyond it lay the town of Het nefer Apu and the crowded tents and boats of Kamose's navy.

Ramose was tired, but he had himself driven to Paheri's quarters. After ordering the charioteer to water and feed the horses and see to the state of the chariot, he handed the Setiu into the care of Paheri's guards with much the same instructions and had himself announced. Paheri was alone, sitting before his evening meal. He greeted Ramose warmly. "Join me," he invited, indicating the platters grouped around him. "Or will you bathe first? What news from the oasis?" Gladly Ramose pulled up a stool, and by the time they had finished eating, he had told Paheri of Kamose's decision and his own task.

"His Majesty will keep you informed," he said. "As for me, I must sleep for a few hours and then be on my way. May I commandeer a skiff from you, Paheri? I want to travel by water, partly because it will save time but also so that my prisoner has less chance of escape. Send the chariot back to the oasis. I have a scroll here to be taken south to Weset. Give it to a reliable herald."

After the amenities had been observed, Ramose excused himself, took natron from his pack, and submerged both himself and his dirty kilt in the river. By the time he and it were

clean, the sun had entirely gone and he walked to the tent
Paheri had allotted him through groups of men clustered
around small fires whose thin smoke mingled pleasingly with
the aroma of scorching meat. He had intended to make sure
that the Setiu had been fed and allowed to wash, but changed
his mind at the sight of the blanket folded so neatly at the foot
of the cot where he was to rest. I will suffer quite enough of
that vacant stare tomorrow, he thought, untying his sandals
and lying back with a sigh. Besides, Paheri's soldiers are well
disciplined and do what they are told.

Drawing up the blanket, he closed his eyes and summoned
the fantasy that had been his comfort and hope ever since he
had stood beside his father and watched the muscles in
Kamose's strong arms tighten as he bent the bow. At first he
had conjured it to displace the memory of that day, for like a
recurring nightmare the sights and sounds, even the smells, of
the parade ground at Nefrusi would materialize against his
fierce will every time he composed himself for sleep. The feel of
his father's grip, the fingers tight with panic, clammy with terror. The acrid stench of his sweat. The utter stillness that had
fallen over the men who had been loudly busy moments before,
so that their shadows lay motionless and somehow sinister over
the baking heat of the blood-spattered earth. The Princes
ranged behind Kamose, their faces impassive, and Kamose himself, his eyes narrowing as he sighted along the arrow, the flash
of light on his rings as he gripped the bow, the steadiness of his
hands. The damning, cold-hearted steadiness of his hands . . .

Unable to banish the images that threatened to keep him in
a state of misery forever, Ramose had reached out for the only
rock to which he could cling and in doing so he had entered a
very different prison, but a prison nonetheless. He sat with Tani
on the watersteps of the Tao estate, her arm linked through his,
her warm shoulder brushing his own. A cool breeze ruffled her

curly hair and teased the glittering surface of the Nile into shards of reflected light. She was chattering away about something trivial, her small hands gesturing, her face now turned to him, now turned to the river, but he was not listening. Behind his set smile his attention was fixed on the gentle flutter of her scented linen against his calf, the feel of her skin touching his, the timbre of her voice.

There was nothing sexual about the images. Ramose knew that to allow them to become so would be to summon a greater distress than the one they were designed to supplant. So in the embrace of his fantasy he was soothed into sleep. Sometimes the fantasy merged with dream and he and Tani stayed together until the dawn, but sometimes his father returned and Tani faded away, an ephemeral ghost under the power of Teti's agony. Thus Ramose in his waking hours was convinced that only by possessing his love in the flesh, by fulfilling the promises they had made to one another in happier times, could he lay the past to rest.

He had known, with the helpless pain of a son's affection, of the disastrous defects in his father's character. He had forgiven Kamose his King for an unavoidable act of retribution, but he wrestled with the sharp division he saw between Kamose in his panoply of Kingship and Kamose his friend. He respected and feared the King but his love went to his friend. Yet there was no longer a clearly discernable contrast between the two, and Ramose was afraid that friend was slowly being swallowed up by divinity. He knew where his duty and his loyalty lay but could not easily recover the joy he had once felt in holding to those virtues. So he clung to Tani, the memories and the last reckless hope of a future resolution.

In the morning he ate a frugal meal of fresh bread, crisp new lettuce leaves and brown goat cheese before making his way to the water and sending a guard to fetch his Setiu. A small skiff lay moored to the bank, its crew of two rowers and a helmsman waiting for him, its one triangular sail still collapsed against its mast. Ramose boarded it and checked that the precious scroll for Apepa was still in his pack, then he seated himself and watched as the prisoner was led onto the deck. The man had obviously been allowed to wash and tidy himself. His hair and beard were combed and sleep had refreshed him. Curtly Ramose bade him sit with his back to the mast and ordered the guard who had escorted him to tie him to the wood. They cast off in the bright new sunlight, the helmsman seeking the current that would carry them north.

The first day took them almost to the entrance to Ta-she. They had sailed peacefully through a quietness that at first delighted Ramose. After his months in the oasis and his routine assignment as a scout in the desert, the lush greenness of spring seemed paradisaical. But soon he became aware that of the many shadufs he could see along the irrigation canals that fed the tiny fields, very few were manned by peasants lifting the water to pour on the fertile earth, and those he did see were women. Villages lay silent or partially tumbled. For every field thick with young crops, there were two where the sowing had been done but weeds had been allowed to tangle the new growth. Sometimes children appeared splashing naked in the shallows or watching while the oxen in their charge sucked up the Nile water, and at those moments Ramose could pretend that Egypt had not changed, but otherwise the country presented an air of melancholy under the optimism of the season. Kamose has done his work well, Ramose thought. He has cut a swathe of destruction so wide that there is no one left with the will to oppose him.

The second evening saw him tethered at Iunu, but he did not leave the boat to explore the city. His charge still had not spoken, apart from curt requests for water or shade. Ramose had complied, seeing to the man's needs with a view to the report he would doubtless give Apepa. He had even allowed him to swim, with the two sailors also in the water and Ramose watching him from the bank. At night he remained tied to the mast, lying in a huddle on a blanket and snoring occasionally.

Entering the Delta, Ramose took the wide eastern tributary, passing Nag-ta-Hert at noon of his third day afloat. The ruins of the Setiu fort Kamose had besieged and then razed lay empty and forlorn under the blazing sun. Evidence of Kamose's depredations lay everywhere as Ramose's boat moved north. Vineyards lay wrecked, orchards cut down, and Ramose shrank from the memory of those weeks when the troops surrounded Het-Uart and the River Raiders, so named by Kamose himself in a fit of black humour, ranged to and fro through the Delta, killing and burning where they wished. Ramose himself had been kept beside the brothers, waking each day to the looming presence of the city's mighty walls, riding with Kamose in his chariot as he circled Het-Uart, and in the hours of despair when nothing was required of him, standing gazing up at the roof of Apepa's palace and praying for a glimpse of Tani. Then Kamose had ordered the soldiers away and the women no longer clustered like flocks of multi-coloured birds to peer down at the men below.

Ramose did not doubt that the waterways of the Delta were full of Apepa's scouts, but they were also full of craft other than his and he did not concern himself with any challenge. He saw no Setiu soldiers. Apepa's influence seemed to begin and end at the gates of his city. He must know what has happened to Egypt, Ramose mused as his craft tacked to the west in preparation to enter the final stream leading to the canals surrounding Het-Uart. Doesn't he care? Or is he waiting for Kamose to exhaust himself and go home for good? The prisoner was watching him again, and this time as Ramose met his gaze, there was puzzlement and a gleam of appraisal in the eyes like black beads.

Ramose felt no desire to enlighten him. Already the sun was setting and the gates would be closing. Now the boat was nosing into a canal and there ahead, beyond the trees and shrubs feeding on the moist soil beside the water, beyond the wide expanse of water and the flat plain pounded to the rigidity of stone by the thousands of feet both human and animal passing over it, reared the southern aspect of Het-Uart's fifty-foot-high wall. All its five gates were heavily guarded, Ramose knew. Staring thoughtfully through the twisting lattice of tree branches, he debated whether or not to camp beside the canal for the night. Many other boats were tying up, their crews squatting in the grass above the waterline to undo their food packages or unrolling blankets out of the way of the loaded donkeys that would be lining up for admittance to the city at dawn. The canal's banks were alive with merchants, farmers with fresh produce, worshippers waiting to visit the great temple of Seth or the lesser shrines of the Setiu's barbaric gods: Yam the sea god, Anath the consort of Seth with her cow's horns and bovine ears in a blasphemous likeness to Hathor, Samash the sun god and, of course, Reshep, he of the gazelle's horns and tasselled skirt who brought death to the enemies of the King. Ramose remembered them all from childhood visits, but more vivid was the memory of Reshep lying in the dust of Nefrusi before Kamose's soldiers hacked him to pieces and flung him on the fire with the slain.

But there were also little knots of Setiu soldiers on the banks, men with curved swords at their belts and armoured leather jerkins, and Ramose could imagine their response if his prisoner called out to them. They might arrest him as a spy. On the other hand, they might kill him at once. Ramose approached the man. "I am returning you to your master," he said without preamble. "I have a message for him myself. Therefore I do not intend to spend the night here. You and I will go up to the gate. If you try to attract the attention of these soldiers here, I will not hesitate to cut your throat." Without waiting for an answer he turned to his crew. "Thank you," he said. "Go back to Het nefer Apu and tell Paheri that I have reached the city. Go at once. Put up somewhere quiet until the morning."

He picked up his pack, walked along the ramp, and stood on the bank, his prisoner beside him, while the sailors cast off. He knew he should be making his way towards the city while the last rays of sunlight still lingered, but he paused, watching the oars dip as the skiff backed away from the shore and then swung around with its prow pointed towards the south and freedom. A burst of homesickness shook him, a mingling of loneliness, fear of what he must do, and a longing to be sitting on the deck of the graceful little craft as it beat slowly past the other crowded moorings. The helmsman was raising the sail to catch the last of the evening wind, the north wind that would blow him to safety. With an inward shiver, Ramose took the end of the rope that bound the Setiu's wrists and together they began the approach to Het-Uart.

It had been many years since Ramose had visited the city. He had come occasionally with his parents to present gifts to Apepa on the Anniversary of his Appearing, when the governor of every nome was expected to affirm his loyalty to the King, but the journey had been tedious and Ramose, not particularly excited by the life of the court, had elected to stay at home once he reached his manhood. Still, he remembered the feeling of being dwarfed when as a child he had come under the shadow of the towering walls. That awareness had not come to him with Kamose, but it returned now that he was alone. He did his best to shake it off, but as the mighty exterior drew nearer, dim where the leaping slashes of orange light from the gate torches did not reach, it simply intensified. More than a hundred feet thick, he said to himself. The walls are more than one hundred feet thick at the top and even thicker at the level of the ground. No Egyptian army can ever conquer this place by siege, and once inside I will never get out.

Chiding himself for thoughts that could only blunt his wits, he came up to the gate and halted, glancing back swiftly at the haphazard pattern of cooking fires littering the plain through which he and the Setiu had picked their way. The citizens of the Delta and those shut out of the city were settling down for the night. There were six guards on the gate itself, brawny men in leather boots, caps and jerkins, their curved swords sheathed at their waists but vicious-looking axes propped against the wall behind them. They registered not the slightest apprehension as Ramose came up to them. "The gate is closed," one of them said contemptuously. "You must wait your turn to enter the city in the morning." In the poor light he obviously had not seen the Setiu's lashed hands.

"I bring an urgent message from Kamose Tao," Ramose replied evenly. "I require admittance immediately."

"You and a hundred others," the man scoffed. "The gate can only be opened from the inside. Where is your herald's insignia?" Ramose grabbed his Setiu's forearm and lifted it high.

"Here," he said. "I am Ramose, son of Teti of Khemmenu. Get this gate opened, you witless fool. I will not stand here and beg like any commoner." The soldier looked him over carefully and gave his prisoner a hard stare.

"I recognize you," he said directly to the man. "You left Het-Uart weeks ago by this gate. You were captured? Why is he bringing you back?"

"That is not your business," Ramose interposed roughly. "It is for Apepa. Send to him at once!"

"His name may not be spoken," the soldier said loudly, but

he had lost some of his bombast. Looking up he bellowed, "Hoi! Open the gate!" and Ramose, following his glance, saw the shadowy shapes of more armed men standing atop the wall. There was no answer, but presently one-half of the cumbrous portal began to groan inward and a small crack appeared. The soldier ushered them through and followed them hastily. "Wait here," he commanded. Ramose watched him stride up the wide, torchlit passage that ran between the looming cross-sections of the wall on either side. The gate ground closed.

Cut into the rock-hard mud on either side of the rutted road were small rooms and the man who had opened the gate waved them into one of them. Benches had been set around the bare walls and a table with a jug of beer and the remains of a meal stood in the middle. Various weapons lay beside the platters. Two other soldiers looked up with quick interest as Ramose entered. He ignored them, pulling his Setiu down beside him on one of the benches. The others soon returned to the game of dice they had been playing.

Ramose and his charge sat in silence. Several hours went by and Ramose was beginning to wish that he had waited outside the city until the morning in order to make his own way to the palace, when the first soldier reappeared. With him was an officer who bowed perfunctorily. "You are indeed Ramose of Khemmenu?" he enquired briskly. Ramose nodded. "Then the One has sent a chariot for you. Untie your prisoner." Ramose stood, hauling the man to his feet.

"Not yet," Ramose said pleasantly. "He too has words for Apepa." The officer flinched. For answer he came forward and, taking a dagger from his belt, sawed at the bonds until they fell away. The Setiu rubbed his wrists but his expression did not alter.

"Both of you, come," the officer snapped. Ramose followed him out into the fresh air.

The chariot was waiting. Without further comment they were waved brusquely up, the officer stepping up also to stand behind them. At a word from the charioteer, the vehicle began to move. They emerged from the roofless tunnel of the passage and Ramose looked about him.

They were rolling briskly along a thoroughfare crowded with empty market stalls under which was piled the refuse of the day. Behind them, the endless uneven lines of cramped and jumbled mud brick houses he remembered from his youth began. A crossroad passed under the chariot's wheels and then there were more lopsided houses, from whose naked windows soft candlelight flickered. People came and went before them or were gathered in their doorways to gossip. Sometimes the rows of homes were broken by narrow alleys, sometimes by one or two spindly and misshapen trees, under whose thin branches the dark maw of a well could be seen. Patches of beaten earth marked the presence of shrines, the small figures of the gods sheltered inside tiny porches atop stunted granite pillars with simple altars below. The hum of city life was constant, a blend of human voices, dogs barking, donkeys braying, and the rumble of ox carts, but after perhaps two miles the noise began to abate. The stench, however, did not. Compounded of donkey dung, human waste, and offal, it stung Ramose's nostrils and adhered to his skin and clothes.

The chariot had entered a wealthier area of Het-Uart. High walls broken by discreet doors lined the road and Ramose knew that behind them the gardens and homes of the rich spread out like miniature oases. The pedestrians were fewer, quieter, more elegantly dressed, and often preceded by house guards. At another crossroads, the temple of Seth reared into view, the flags on its pylons flapping desultorily in the night breeze, one pinpoint of light piercing the darkness of the outer court where some priest was conducting his reverences deep in the interior.

The officer spoke and the horses clattered left, but as they swung about, Ramose caught a glimpse of a huge gate and beyond it a vast open courtyard. The parade ground, he thought, and the barracks. How many troops does Apepa have? At least twice our number, or so the rumours say.

They were skirting another wall. It seemed to stretch ahead forever, a smooth, high bastion that Ramose placed, after several minutes, as the outer limit of the palace estate. Then the chariot slowed, swerved, and jerked to a stop before a set of tall cedar doors. A much smaller postern door stood open and here a herald was waiting, liveried in blue and white, the colours of Egyptian royalty. But his staff of office owed nothing to Egypt. It was a long white spear-like stick from which red ribbons trailed. On its tip rested the head of the god whose colour was blood. Seth grinned at Ramose beneath his conical cap and curling gazelle's horns. He did not much resemble Egypt's Set, the red-haired, wolfen god of storms and chaos, in spite of the Setiu's assurance that the two gods were in fact one and the same.

The officer who had brought them got back into the chariot without a word, but the herald smiled at Ramose and bade him enter. Yet another door closing behind me, Ramose thought as he and his companion obeyed. I must not call to mind the miles between me and the oasis. I must remember that somewhere within this maze Tani is eating or being painted or talking with a friend. I must keep thinking of her. Perhaps she senses my presence. Perhaps even now she is pausing, lifting her head as though she hears some whisper beyond the glow of her lamp, frowning in bafflement as her heartbeat quickens.

The herald was leading him along a broad path across acres of lawn dotted with many trees. Other paths branched off from it. Here and there Ramose glimpsed the glint of pale light on water. Statues lined the way at regular intervals, strange forms, many of which he could not name, although they reminded him vaguely of his own familiar gods. They were almost all bearded and horned. He had run carelessly between them as a child, that he knew, but now in the bluish moonlight they seemed cloaked in a foreign mystery. As they ended, the shrubs and ornamental flowerbeds began. The herald crossed a gravelled court where many litters had been set down, their bearers sitting or lying in the grass that bordered it, and now Ramose could hear music and the cheerful din of feasting.

The front of the palace soared to meet him, rows of pillars at whose feet soldiers and servants congregated, illuminated by many flaring torches. To the right, Ramose could make out the source of the clamour. It was spilling out from a hall that opened directly onto the pillars. He could see crowds of glittering courtiers moving to and fro, bathed in bright lamplight. Straight ahead was the reception area, but it was in semi-darkness and the herald turned left, leading Ramose and his stoical companion around the side of the palace to a small door set halfway along the wall. Opening it, he bowed Ramose inside but prevented the Setiu from following him. "There are refreshments for you on the table," the man said affably to Ramose. "Feel free to eat and drink as you wish. The wait may be long, but eventually you will be summoned. I am told that you have a message for the One. Is it spoken or written?"

"Written." Ramose drew the scroll from his pack and handed it over. The herald took it, bowed again, and closed the door softly behind him.

Ramose let out his breath and looked around. The room was small but comfortably furnished with low gilded chairs and one elegant table on which stood a platter of cold fowl, a few slices of black bread, crumbles of brown goat cheese scattered on the curling crispness of tender new lettuce leaves, various sweet pastries and a flagon of wine. Cushions of vivid colours in a tightly woven pattern of whorls lay here and there on the bare wooden floor. The ochre walls also were bare but for a frieze running near the ceiling on which the same close design of maze-like circles were depicted in black paint. A warm and steady glow came from three alabaster lamps on stands in the corners and in the fourth corner a golden shrine glinted. It was shut. Ramose did not bother to open it.

Going at once to the door through which he had come, he flung it open, only to see the head of a helmeted guard turn towards him. Closing it hastily, he crossed the room to the one other door that might have allowed a way of escape, but it too was watched, the man in the dim passage beyond it extending a warning arm when Ramose appeared. Not that I want to escape, Ramose thought grimly as he retraced his steps. I must see this thing through to its end. But I am a little afraid.

On impulse he turned his back to the opulent shrine, and going to his knees he conjured a vision of Thoth, god in Khemmenu, re-creating in his mind the portals of the temple there as he crossed the outer court and the shadow that always fell across his face as he strode barefoot into the inner court. He faced the shuttered sanctuary behind which the god with his beautiful curved ibis beak and wise black eyes stood. Deliberately Ramose brought Thoth's image into view behind his eyelids and he began to pray.

He had not addressed the totem of his city for many months, not being able to bear the memories such an act would have brought with it, but now he poured his fears and doubts into the god's feathered ears, begging for wisdom, for the right words to say to Apepa whose presence saturated this place, for strength to hold his purpose firm. When he had finished, he was suddenly aware of a healthy hunger, and drawing up one of the chairs he set upon the food, relishing the tang of garlic in the oil with which the salad had been drenched and washing it all down with wine whose dry bite delighted him. Then he sat back in the calm silence that surrounded him, aware that in praying and eating his equilibrium had returned. I'm very dirty, he thought. I need to wash myself before facing Apepa, but perhaps the omission of water here was deliberate, to put me at a disadvantage.

He had thought that he might lie on the floor with one of the cushions under his head and go to sleep for a while but found himself wide awake and peacefully alert. You are with me, Great Thoth, are you not? he said soundlessly to the god. You have not abandoned me, your son, in this place of blasphemy. He smiled, sighed, and settled himself in patience.

The night deepened. Even here in this quiet place that began to seem more and more divorced from any reality outside it, Ramose was aware of the journey of the hours towards a dawn that was still a long way off. He saw them clearly with the eyes of his ka, a succession of dark, indistinct shapes flowing away in the wake of Ra as he moved through the body of Nut in order to be reborn, taking with them the grief and loneliness of his past. There was no sense of a weight leaving him, merely a subtle buoyancy that reminded him of the effortless endurance of boyhood when he and his companions might heedlessly swim, wrestle and run all day with bodies that never tired.

He was still sitting upright in the chair when the door finally opened to admit a tall clean-shaven man in a floor-length white kilt and silver armbands. "I am Sakhetsa, herald to His Majesty," he said, the slight hesitation in his voice betraying his surprise at finding Ramose wide awake. "His Majesty will see you briefly before he retires. Come with me." Obediently Ramose got up and left the room that had somehow become a sanctuary that had held his god.

He was soon lost. Following the herald's fluttering linen, he paced one torch-lit corridor after another, passing closed doors and open ones that gave onto darkness, walking through dim courtyards in which the muted tinkle of fountains played tuneless music, gliding between rows of pillars beneath ceilings that echoed to his footsteps. Everywhere there were guards lining the monotonous ochre of the walls, large men standing motionless with their leather-gloved hands resting on the hafts of giant axes, and above them ran the labyrinthine motif that had decorated the upper walls of the room where Ramose had waited. The palace was asleep in the few hours between feasting and the renewed bustle of dawn, sunk in a fleeting hush.

After what seemed a long time, Sakhetsa paused before frowning double doors of chased cedar, exchanged a few words with the soldiers on either side of it, and Ramose stepped through it after him. Here the passage was smaller and brighter, the doors off it more elaborately decorated. At the farther end were more double doors. A man rose from his perch on a stool before them. Like the herald, he was dressed in white, but his robe was bordered in gold. One thick golden armband encircled his upper arm and ankle. He was an older man, his face seamed under the traces of paint, his earlobes sagging with the weight of the golden ankhs dragging from them. He looked tired. The kohl encircling his eyes had smudged and the eyes themselves were bloodshot. Nevertheless he smiled thinly. "I am Chief Steward Nehmen," he said curtly and nodded over Ramose's shoulder. Ramose turned in time to see Sakhetsa walking back down the long corridor. Nehmen gestured impatiently and Ramose, stiffening his spine, walked into Apepa's presence.

He had not much time to survey his surroundings, but he glanced about as Nehmen called his name. The room was large, well-lit, and beautiful in a way he could only describe lamely to himself as foreign. The walls, where they were not hung with woven mats in the same glowing colours and designs as the cushions he had seen, were painted with scenes of white-tipped mountains at whose feet an ocean lapped. Little ships sailed on that green expanse and beneath them various exotic sea creatures swam.

To the left, the panorama was broken by the outline of a door on which a massive bull was depicted with nostrils flared and horns painted gold. To the right, a servant was in the act of closing another door, on which some kind of sea god was represented, Baal-Yam, Ramose supposed, his beard entangled in weeds and his legs hidden in a swirl of white water. Tall lamps like seashells clustered in the corners. The legs of one of the chairs standing not far from him had been carved into the likeness of bare-breasted girls holding up the seat. They wore short pleated skirts and their hair was piled high in tiers of ribboned curls. The chair's backrest contained the plump curves and blunted snout of a dolphin, and more silver dolphins held up the bowls and cups resting on the table beside which Apepa sat, his legs crossed, his ringed hands folded on his knee.

For one wild moment Ramose was engulfed in terror. These are not our people, he thought. In spite of the kohl and henna, the fine linen and the titles, they are unable to completely hide their utter foreignness. These forms are Keftian, these fluid images owe nothing to the clean and simple lines of Egyptian art. Why did I not see it as a child? Why was I not even mildly curious? The Setiu make no effort to hide this pollution within their city. It is only out in the villages that they pretend to be at one with Egypt. They are enamoured with the island of Keftiu, that is obvious, but have they done more than indulge in trade with the Keftians? Is there a formal treaty of mutual assistance also? The moment of panic passed and Ramose stepped forward, wondering if he should accord Apepa a full obeisance even as he was going down, arms outstretched and face to the burnished floor.

He waited. Then the familiar light tones floated out over his head. "Rise, Ramose son of Teti," Apepa said. "You accord me the full reverence due to your King, but perhaps you mock me. I am tired and my temper is short. Why are you here?" Ramose regained his feet, and for the first time in many years looked into the face of the enemy.

The large, close-set brown eyes looked back at him meditatively. Even though Apepa was seated, Ramose could tell that he was a tall man, taller than the guards Ramose had seen so far. Middle age had not stooped him. His shoulders were broad, his legs long and shapely as a woman's under the loose linen garment draped about him. He had already been washed of his paint. A high forehead and strong black eyebrows gave him an appearance of gracious nobility that was unfortunately negated by a chin too weak and pointed, a neck a trifle too thin, and a mouth, though bordered in lines of laughter, that turned downwards in repose. His cheeks were so hollowed that the light in the room glanced off the bones above them. Any hair he had was concealed by a soft woollen cap.

A young man stood behind him, leaning on one arm along the back of Apepa's chair. His resemblance to Apepa was startling. The same brown eyes regarded Ramose with an interested hostility and the same sharp chin jutted out at him. A scribe sat at Apepa's feet stifling a yawn, brush in hand and ready palette bridging his knees. A man still fully dressed and painted, blue-and-white staff of office in his hand, stood to Apepa's left. A vizier, Ramose knew by the colours of the staff. He was grasping the roll of papyrus Ramose had carried all the way from the oasis. Carefully Ramose's gaze moved from one to the other of the four men, then he looked straight into Apepa's eyes. "I came to bring you the message your vizier holds," he replied evenly. Apepa made a dismissive gesture, a quick flick of his wrist.

"That is no message," he said contemptuously. "It is a boast-ful, insulting tirade containing not one word of conciliation or any practical suggestion to end the ridiculous situation that endures in Egypt. My Majesty is mortally offended by it. I ask you again. Why did you come to Het-Uart? Why was my mes-senger returned to me?" Ramose knew that he must not be seen to hesitate with his reply. The eyes were watching him almost without blinking.

"My Lord Kamose thought at first to send the herald back alone with his message," Ramose responded. "But he wanted to make sure that the man did indeed return to you and did not continue into Kush, to Teti-En, before retracing his steps to the Delta." He had the satisfaction of seeing Apepa's attention fal-ter for a second. "Therefore an escort was needed."

"I see." Apepa breathed in slowly, reflectively. "But why did Kamose select you, a man sorely abused at his hands, a man whose loyalty might be suspect?"

"Because we have been friends since our first youth," Ramose told him. "Because in spite of the necessity that caused him to execute my father and disenfranchise me, he knows that I am loyal to him and to his cause. He trusts me." He had put a slight emphasis on the word "trust." Apepa's eyes narrowed and the young man draped over the back of the chair straightened up and folded his arms.

"And why did you accept the charge?" Ramose stared at him in silence. It was an unexpected question, revealing a sophisti-cation of thought he had not anticipated. He answered care-fully, with the simplicity of honesty.

"My dearest treasure is here," he said. "The Princess Tani. I hoped that in fulfilling my Lord's command I might also glut my ka with a sight of her." The young man laughed once, harshly. The vizier smiled superciliously. But Apepa continued to fix his solemn, sharp gaze on Ramose's face.

"Did you indeed?" he said softly. "So you still love her, do you? After all this time, Ramose?" Sarcasm threaded his tone. At last Ramose bent his head, his eyes finding the royal foot, still stained with traces of the day's orange henna.

"Yes, I do," he confessed. "In this matter I am no more than a foolish boy and I am not ashamed to admit it."

"And what if I were to tell you that she is dead?" Apepa pressed. "That when the first word of Kamose's insane rebellion came to me I had her beheaded as a hostage in retribution for her brother's perfidy?" In a sudden rush of sheer dread Ramose fought to remain expressionless. Keep your mind on what you are really here for, he told himself firmly. Do not allow him to unbalance you.

"I would say that such an act is beneath the dignity and mercy of a King of Egypt," he replied. "Besides, the murder of a noblewoman would do little to strengthen the loyalty of your Princes, Majesty. I think you are toying with me."

"Perhaps." There was a small silence during which the rustle of the scribe's papyrus could be heard.

Then Apepa uncrossed his legs, pursed his lips, and said gently, "How is it that my herald was captured at all, Ramose son of Teti?" Ramose waited for him to continue, to say that the man had been ordered to take the desert tracks far from any possibility of discovery, that it was almost beyond the bounds of possibility that he should have been apprehended out there where there was nothing but heat and desolation. But he realized all at once that the Setiu had not yet been questioned, that Apepa was probing him not only for information but also to test his determination to guard his tongue and his wits. Ramose raised his eyebrows.

"I cannot say, Majesty."

"But of course you know." Apepa snapped his fingers and a servant glided out of the shadows, filled his cup, and retreated soundlessly. Apepa took one judicious sip of the wine. "You are a friend of the Tao brothers, as you pointed out, therefore I may presume that you are in their counsels. Did my herald blunder into an encampment of nomads loyal to them? Or are there soldiers wandering in the desert?" He took another sip, lifting a square of linen afterwards to pat his mouth. "They are either very stupid or very clever, those two young men," he went on reflectively. "An ordinary officer escorting my man to Het-Uart would not have aroused my suspicions. I would have received that ludicrous scroll and killed the officer or had him thrown out of the city before he was able to absorb any but the most superficial impressions. But they sent you, their valuable companion, with a letter so crude and frivolous that it is not even worth copying for the archives. You do not try to hide in the city and gather information as a spy. You ask to come here to the palace. Why?" He began to tap the floor with one naked foot. "There is a wealth of knowledge regarding Kamose and his little revolt in that handsome head of yours. Am I supposed to torture you to get at it, Ramose? Or will you, after a few coy hesitations, feed me erroneous facts?"

"Torture has never been the Egyptian way, Majesty," Ramose broke in earnestly, shocked at Apepa's acumen. You have underestimated him, Kamose, he thought desperately. You have judged him weak because so far he has done nothing to protect his hold on Egypt, but what if he sees farther than you? What if he cares nothing for a reputation of boldness and bravery, preferring to win by patience and cunning? Yet perhaps you do know him and that is why you are so anxious to draw him out of his shell. "I have told you," he continued, deliberately raising his voice and clenching his fists ostentatiously. "I begged my Lord to give me this assignment. I pleaded for it, and when he reluctantly gave it to me, I fell on my knees and importuned the gods that they might take pity on me and give me a sight of the woman dearer to me than my life!"

The young man who had been lounging behind Apepa now unfolded his arms, and walking to a chair he sat, adjusting his linen skirt and shaking his head. "There is something pathetic about a grown man being led about on the leash of passion," he commented. "Don't you think so, Father? And in this case led blindly into the dangerous maw of your royal teeth. I should perhaps have looked more closely at the Princess Tani when she first arrived, but as it is now . . ."

"Peace, Kypenpen," Apepa rebuked him sharply. "Led blindly? We do not yet know. You do appear a little ridiculous, Ramose," he said, a hint of humour in his voice. "But whether you are genuinely besotted with Tani or you are giving us a good performance, I am not able at the moment to decide." He came to his feet in one sudden movement, striking the gong on the table by his hand. At once the doors opened and Nehmen entered, bowing. "Find quarters for this man," he ordered. "Tell Kethuna that he is to be closely watched. He is not to leave his room until I send for him tomorrow." He extended a stiff arm, palm outward. "Ramose, I dismiss you." Ramose bowed and turned, following the Chief Steward into the passage beyond. He felt as though he had indeed been released from between a lion's teeth, but it was not until he was alone that he began to tremble.

The room to which he had been led held little more than a couch, a table and a stool. One clay lamp gave off an uncertain light that scarcely reached the dull plainness of the mustard-coloured walls and there were no coverings on the floor, but the chamber was far from being a prison cell. There were no windows, only three narrow slits close to the ceiling to let in daylight and air. Removing his belt, kilt and sandals with shaking fingers, Ramose collapsed onto the couch, drawing the coarse blanket up over him. He was past caring whether or not he was clean. I must think about tomorrow, he told himself. I must try to imagine every question Apepa might put to me, invent every plausible response. I did not much like his son Kypenpen. Something about his eyes . . . But it is Apepa who must believe me, not his offspring. Thoth be with me, protect me, give me your wisdom. Am I really such a figure of fun? Leaning over, he blew out the lamp. At once exhaustion claimed him in one great wave and he slept.

He woke to a form bending over him, and as he sat up groggily, it withdrew to become a boy with an anxious expression on his face and behind him a soldier. "You are awake now?" the boy said hastily. "I have placed food for you on the table. When you have eaten, I am to take you to the bath house." Ramose pushed the blanket aside and swung his feet onto the floor and at that the boy backed away even farther.

"What is the matter?" Ramose enquired, still half-asleep. "Is my odour that offensive?" The boy flushed and glanced at the guard.

"He listens to silly rumours passing among the kitchen servants," the man said roughly. "You are supposed to be a fierce general from Weset come to dictate terms to the One. Hurry up and eat."

"Perhaps the common people know more than their masters," Ramose murmured, drawing the tray towards him. There was bread, garlic oil to dip it in, and a cup of beer. He ate and drank quickly, uncomfortable under the silent gaze of the other two, and when he had finished, he wrapped himself in the blanket and followed the boy, the soldier bringing up the rear.

The bath house was immense, a huge room open to the sky with a sloping floor for drainage, a well, a fire pit for heating the water, and numerous bathing slabs, most of which were occupied by sleek, naked bodies. Beyond it, through an open doorway, Ramose could see more bodies, prone on benches and glistening with the oil being massaged into their scrubbed flesh. The din of voices mingled with the splashing of water was tremendous. Bath servants scurried to and fro armed with towels, boxes of natron and unguent jars. Steam rose from the cauldrons on the fire. Ramose, inhaling the damp, scented air, scanned the crowd rapidly, hoping he might see Tani's slight, graceful form, but of course she was not there. *If she lives, she will bathe in the private quarters of the royal women,* he reminded himself, shedding the blanket and mounting one of the few vacant slabs. *This bath house is for common courtiers.* A servant came hurrying at once and the soldier stepped close. "You are to speak to no one," he commanded. "Keep your mouth shut." The boy had vanished. Ramose nodded, then closed his eyes as the first ewer of hot water cascaded deliciously over him.

He returned to his room with his hair washed and trimmed and his body shaved, and with the shedding of the accumulation of filth his spirits rose. The boy had replaced his clothes with clean raiment—a spotless loincloth, a starched kilt and shirt, plain sandals of woven flax—but had left Ramose's own belt. Dressing methodically, Ramose turned to the soldier. "I wish to pray," he said. "Is there a shrine to Thoth in Het-Uart?"

"There may be," the man replied curtly. "But my orders are to keep you in this room until the One summons you."

"Well, must you hover at my elbow?" Ramose protested. The man's attitude was beginning to make him angry. The guard shrugged.

"No. I can stand outside the door."

"Go then."

When the door had slammed shut, Ramose sat on the edge of the couch with a sigh. Muted sounds came to him from the passage and drifted through the high clerestories. Footsteps, snatches of unintelligible conversation, someone singing, gave him the impression of being in an oasis of stagnant silence while life swirled on around him. He resigned himself to wait.

The thin shafts of sunlight had crept down the wall opposite and had almost reached the floor before the door opened again and an arm beckoned him. Ramose had been pacing head down, bored and impatient, and he was glad to obey the soundless summons. It was a different soldier who led him through the labyrinth of corridors and courtyards this time. The man kept looking back over his shoulder to make sure that Ramose did not melt into the flow of people coming and going.

Courtiers brushed by them in clouds of sweet perfume, jewels tinkling and linen afloat, their servants trotting behind them clutching listless cats with sapphire eyes, or cosmetic boxes, or scribes' palettes. Many were draped in tightly woven tasselled cloaks of intricate pattern and hectic colours and some wore floor-length skirts of the same thick wool. Ramose, knowing this to be a Setiu mode of dress, thought scornfully that it would look better covering a bare floor. Few took any notice of him and those that did merely gave him a disinterested glance.

At last the soldier paused before a set of double doors at the end of a wide green-tiled passage. To either side the god Seth sat, his granite eyes staring back the way Ramose had come. The horns sprouting amid his stone ringlets had been tipped in gold and many lapis necklaces hung on his narrow chest. Ramose, hating him, averted his gaze as Nehmen rose from between the statues and the soldier stepped back. The Chief Steward smiled. He seemed more rested today. The loose, haggard look had gone from his meticulously painted face. "Greetings, Ramose," he said affably. "I trust you slept well. The One expects you." He did not wait for an answer. Pulling open the doors, he waved Ramose inside.

Light smote Ramose at once, a burst of dazzling brightness that had him blinking and confused. But after a moment he realized that he was standing at one end of a vast hall whose ceiling soared up into high dimness and whose gleaming floor ran away to meet a dais at the farther end that swept from wall to wall. Behind the dais a row of pillars marched and between them the sun poured in, flooding the immense space with its glory. Ramose could see trees out there, trembling on a breeze, and hear the muted cacophony of birds. He could also see the row of soldiers lined up like statues themselves, each facing outward towards the glare of early afternoon.

But it was not these things that caused him to pause, a lump coming to his throat. A chair sat in the centre of the dais, a throne, it was the Horus Throne, alone in its power and beauty beneath its tall canopy of cloth of gold. The Staff of Eternity and the Stool of Wealth on its curved back were festooned with ankhs, the symbols of life, and the snarling lions' muzzles at the end of each arm roared a warning. The delicate turquoise and lapis wings of Isis and Neith rose like fans from the armrests and below them on each side a King strode, Crook and Flail in his hands, Hapi behind him and Ra before. Ramose could picture the great Eye of Horus that filled the rear, the Wadjet Eye set there to protect the King from any attack from behind. Oh, Kamose, Ramose cried out soundlessly. Dear friend. Glorious Majesty. Will those holy ankhs ever feed life into your skin? Will the goddesses ever enjoy the delight of holding their protecting wings around you? Do they suffer the same humiliation you endure every time Apepa settles his foreign carcase onto that cool gold and puts his feet upon the royal footstool?

Someone coughed politely at his elbow and he swung around clumsily. A man was waiting, clad all in white, holding a white, silver-tipped staff. "I am Chief Herald Yku-didi," he said. "Follow me." He paced the hall to the right of the dais, and seeing him come, the soldiers on the doors he was approaching opened them. "The noble Ramose," he intoned, the first time Ramose had heard his title called in Het-Uart, and Ramose walked in.

It seemed to him that the room was full of people. Apepa himself, resplendent in yellow linen shot with gold thread and a yellow helmet, was standing before a wide table. To his right sat a younger man Ramose did not recognize, but presumed from his resemblance to the King that he was yet another son. To his left sat someone Ramose was sure he ought to know. Swarthy, with coarse features and a nose that dominated his face, he sent a trickle of familiar apprehension down Ramose's spine. He wore no paint or jewels apart from a thick gold band on his muscular upper arm. One ring adorned his blunt fingers, a silver oval with some design on it that Ramose could not make out. A plain black-and-white striped helmet covered his head, its rim cutting across a broad forehead above sharp black eyes. Beside him another man watched Ramose cross the floor with considerable interest. He wore a red ribbon around his ringleted dark hair and his beard glistened with oil. Behind Apepa stood the same vizier Ramose had seen yesterday and at his feet his scribe had already laid his palette across his knees.

Ramose did not at first see the Setiu he had come to think of as his own. He, like the Chief Herald, was dressed all in white. His beard had gone and his hair was very short. If it had not been for the supreme indifference of his stare, Ramose might not have known him. So he was in fact also a Royal Herald. Would Kamose have released him so readily if he had known that he was more than a common soldier? Ramose mused, coming to a halt at the end of the table. He eyed its contents while he mentally calmed himself. Scrolls, Kamose's letter among them, plates of honey cakes and figs, a cluster of wine cups and two flagons, and a map of the western desert spread out under Apepa's slim, manicured, bejewelled fingers. Ramose repressed a shudder. The time of testing had come. Bowing deeply from the waist he straightened, put his hands behind his back, and lifted his eyes to Apepa's face.

"I see that you have recovered from your arduous journey, Ramose son of Teti," Apepa said, his hennaed mouth curving in a slight smile. "Washed and rested. Good. It is my wish that you should know into whose presence you have been summoned." Why must he persist in linking me with my father's name? Ramose wondered with a spurt of annoyance. He did it last night also. Does he think that in doing so he will force to remembrance my father's loyalty to him and the fate he endured as a result of it? As though I need such reminding! "To my right is my eldest son, the Hawk-in-the-Nest Apepa," the King was saying. "To my left the General Pezedkhu and beside him the General Kethuna, Commander of my personal bodyguard." Of course, Pezedkhu, Ramose reiterated to himself. The ablest tactician Apepa has. Seqenenra's doom and the spur Kamose puts to his need for revenge. No wonder my ka quivered when I saw him. "Behind me is my Vizier and the Keeper of the Royal Seal, Peremuah. You already know my herald Yamusa. And before me ..." his long fingers smoothed the map, " ... is a subject of concern to us all. Yamusa has acquainted us with some surprising facts. We wish you to corroborate them. We understand now how he was captured." The smile vanished. The royal lips set in a hard line. "How long has Kamose quartered troops at the oasis of Uah-ta-Meh?" Ramose kept his face still.

"I cannot say, Your Majesty."

"How long does he intend to keep them there?"

"I cannot say."

"How many soldiers are under his command at the oasis?" Ramose deliberately shifted from one foot to the other.

"Your Majesty," he said in a low voice. "My orders were to

deliver my Lord's message to you. That was all. I am not permitted to do more than that."

"And yet you expect me to allow you to speak to the Princess Tani? Oh yes, she lives," Apepa said impatiently, seeing Ramose's expression. "You expect this in return for—what? Dutifully delivering the crudest, most abusive missive I have ever seen?" His voice rose. "I am supposed to thank you and then fulsomely offer you your heart's desire as payment for such blasphemy? How cloddish are you, son of Teti? What secret contempt do you harbour for me, how disdainfully do you regard my intellect?" His hand came down on the map with a ringing slap. "You may thank the gods that you stand here alive today instead of being tossed headless onto one of Het-Uart's piles of offal! Answer my questions!" Ramose, listening carefully to the emotions behind the tirade of words, knew without a doubt that insecurity was there, and uncertainty, and a tinge of fear. Apepa had known nothing of the force at the oasis before yesterday. His complacency was shaken. He trusted the word of his herald Yamusa, yet he did not want the information brought to him to be true. It must be corroborated before he would believe. Ramose grinned to himself in spite of the peril of his position.

"I beg your forgiveness, Munificent One," he said softly, humbly. "But I have confidence in the honour that you, as the living embodiment of Ma'at, personify. I appeal to that honour. I have discharged my responsibility to my Lord. Therefore, let me return to him unsullied by any betrayal."

"Your mouth is filthy with a secret sarcasm." Apepa leaned across the table. "You do not believe that I am the living embodiment of Ma'at. You do not worship me as your King. Your adoration goes to the upstart son of a petty southern noble whose delusions of godhead amount to sheer presumptuous insanity. Look what he has done to you, Ramose! Killed your father, stolen your inheritance, smashed your future, and then magnanimously allowed, *allowed* you to end up here where your life itself can be taken from you. And you call this man your friend? Your Lord?" He raised his hands in a gesture of mystified exasperation. "Look around you. At the immensity of my palace, the wealth of my courtiers, the size and strength of my city. This is Egypt! This is reality! Now will you talk to me?"

He had the gift of persuasion. Ruefully Ramose acknowledged it, as the power of Apepa's argument tried to insinuate itself under his guard. The King was no amateur at the art of subtle enticement. He was inviting Ramose to see himself as a poor deluded provincial following an equally foolish provincial dreamer, and indeed Ramose had to consciously remind himself that the whole of the country from Weset to Het-Uart now belonged to the Taos, and no matter how mighty Het-Uart and this palace appeared to be, it was Apepa and his shrinking area of influence that was the mirage, not Kamose. "I am sorry, Majesty," he said diffidently. "Your words may be true, but I am honourably bound to do only what I was commanded. Your herald has surely told you everything you wish to know."

"If that were so, I would not be asking you!" Apepa snapped. "And let me remind you that according to your own account you pressed for this assignment in the secret hope that in carrying out your orders you might fulfil your own small purpose. Did Kamose know of it?" Ramose shook his head, lying easily.

"No."

"Then you are not as scrupulous as you like to pretend." He was quiet for a few seconds, his kohled eyes roaming Ramose's face speculatively, then he leaned back and beckoned Yamusa, whispering something in the man's ear. Yamusa nodded once, bowed, and strode from the room. Apepa returned his attention to Ramose. "The question is this," he went on conversationally. "Is your desire to see the Princess greater than the correct discharging of your duty? I rather think it might be." Ramose took a step forward.

"Majesty," he began, injecting a note of desperation into his voice, "I do not think that I can tell you anything more regarding the oasis than your herald. He was there, he saw everything! You do not need me! Give me a sight of Tani, I beg you, and then let me go!"

Apepa smiled. The vizier smiled. Suddenly all of them were smiling, and with a leap of his heart Ramose knew that he was about to win. At the expense of his reputation in the sight of these men, but win nevertheless. He hoped that he looked suitably agonized. "He did not see everything," Apepa objected. "And even if he did, there are many things I want to know that he could not possibly tell me. How many Princes Kamose has suborned, for instance. Whether or not he has been negotiating with the Kushites. Whether or not he has left troops at Weset." All at once he sat down and laid his arms across the map, giving Ramose a direct look. "You may have a sight of the Princess if you give me one piece of information," he said. "How long have those troops been settled at Uah-ta-Meh?" Ramose swallowed noisily, ostentatiously.

"Majesty, you swear?"

"I swear by the beard of Sutekh."

"I suppose such information can do no harm, seeing that it pertains to what is past," Ramose said haltingly. "Very well. Kamose sent them to the oasis after the last campaigning season. Then he went home to Weset."

"Thank you. Kethuna, take him through to the reception hall."

The atmosphere in the room had changed. Ramose knew it even as the General was rising and coming around the table. The eyes on him held contempt as well as relief. Bodies had loosened. There was whispering and fidgeting. Apepa's son lifted one of the flagons and poured himself wine while he passed some casual remark to his father.

Only Pezedkhu did not move. He sat twisting the silver ring on his brown finger, his head on one side, his gaze full of a cool assessment. He does not trust my little act, Ramose thought as he turned to follow Kethuna. He senses the insincerity behind it. He judges well. All I can pray is that he interprets insincerity as weakness.

Kethuna led him back the way he had come, into the huge hall and up onto the Throne dais, bringing him to a stop just behind the row of soldiers. Between two brawny shoulders Ramose could look out upon a wide and pleasant garden. Fruit trees rained their white and pink blossoms onto the green lawns. The taller sycamores cast patches of shade under which groups of courtiers, mostly women, sat or lay in a bright disorder of cloaks, cushions and board games. Directly ahead at the end of one of the many paths criss-crossing the expanse a large pool glittered in direct sunlight, its surface clotted with lily pads and the pale spears of white lotus blooms. "We will not have long to wait," Kethuna said. "She always walks in the gardens after the noon meal, before she takes to her couch to sleep the afternoon away. See! There is the vizier! He is looking for her."

Wildly Ramose cast his eyes this way and that. So many women out there, he thought incoherently, so many colours, faces, yet I will know her the moment I see her. Tani! I am here! Suddenly he spotted Peremuah with his blue-and-white staff, parading slowly among the chattering butterflies, pausing to speak to this one or that. He was bowed to as he went. Twice Ramose saw a braceleted arm raised to point a direction. Then the vizier glided out of sight. Ramose found himself clutching his kilt with both hands. He could hardly breathe.

Peremuah reappeared, and this time he was walking beside a slight figure swathed in a multi-hued cloak whose tassels spread out on the ground behind her as she moved. Her hair crowned her small head in tiers of dark curls wound with yellow ribbons and a fillet of gold spangled across her high forehead. More gold wrapped her ankles and glinted on her wrists as she gesticulated to the man beside her. Her face was turned away but it was Tani, Tani in the lively gait, Tani in the tilt of her head, Tani in the well-remembered fanning of the quick fingers.

Peremuah touched her elbow, bringing her to a halt directly in front of the open reception hall. He stepped to one side, forcing her to shift her body as he spoke to her, and at last Ramose could drink in the face whose delineaments were scored into his heart. She was fully painted, the generous, laughing mouth red with henna, the eyelids green and sparkling with gold dust, the black kohl accentuating her large, fine eyes. At nearly eighteen years old she was no longer a wiry child beginning to bud. Maturity had widened her hips and swelled her breasts, given her a portion of the dignity and regality of her mother, but in her quick movements and unselfconscious laughter she was still the girl who had sat beside him and slipped her arm through his, squinting across at him in the white sunlight, inviting lips parted over strong young teeth.

Why are you laughing, Tani? Ramose cried out dumbly. I love you, love you still, love you always, my own laughter has been tinged with this grief ever since Apepa took you away. Is your mirth a dutiful deceit, like mine? I am here. Can you not feel my presence? I could call to you from these mighty pillars. Would you recognize my voice? As if reading his loud thought, Kethuna put a warning hand on his arm, and at that moment Peremuah bowed to Tani and walked briskly away. Ramose saw her wave impatiently behind her and a flock of attendants came into view, following her as she strolled out of his sight. One of them was Heket, a servant Ramose vaguely remembered from his visits to the estate in Weset.

Something about Tani's imperious gesture and the response of the servants made Ramose apprehensive as he trod the echoing hall after Kethuna's sturdy back, but he did his best to quell it before facing Apepa's searching glance. He needed his wits about him to play out the next scene in this critical drama, but for a few blinding minutes he was lost in the overwhelming force of a dream brought intensely to life. He did not have to fabricate his distress and confusion as once more he approached the table.

This time Apepa invited him to sit, and as he did so he realized that he was bathed in sweat. "Well, son of Teti," Apepa said smoothly. "What do you think?"

"She is incomparably beautiful," Ramose replied huskily.

"Yes, she is, and still full of the fire of her southern deserts. She has become very popular with my courtiers." He was watching Ramose carefully. "Would you like to speak with her?" Oh gods, Ramose thought despairingly. I do not have to be an actor any more. I do not have to hide. Even if I had indeed come to Het-Uart with Kamose's stern warning not to reveal anything to the enemy, I would be ready to forfeit my honour right now. He licked his dry lips.

"On what terms?" he croaked.

"No terms," Apepa said emphatically. "You answer every question I or my generals put to you. When I am satisfied that you have been emptied of all information, I will arrange for you to see Tani alone and uninterrupted. Are you agreed?" Emptied. The word rang hollow in Ramose's mind. Emptied. Empty me then as Kamose wished, for I have become nothing but a shell holding love for Tani and the means of your downfall, vile Setiu. Everything else has gone. He did not need to prolong the moment before he conceded but he let it draw out so that Apepa could see a struggle on his face. Then he gave in, lowering his head and letting his shoulders slump as he did so.

"I am agreed," he said. At once Apepa tapped a gong and Nehmen entered.

"Have food brought, something hot," Apepa ordered. "Afterwards keep everyone away from this door." He crooked a finger at Ramose. "Come close and look at this map," he ordered. "Itju, are you ready to take down the words?" From the floor where he still sat the scribe assented. "Good," Apepa continued. "Now, Ramose, how many soldiers are at the oasis?" Ramose got up and went to stand beside him.

"Kamose has forty thousand troops there," he lied.

"Under whose command? Which Princes?"

"Under his Wawat General Hor-Aha, and beneath him are the Princes Intef, Iasen, Mesehti, Makhu and Ankhmahor."

"I remember the Wawat General." The deep voice belonged to Pezedkhu. "He fought for Seqenenra at Qes. He has Medjay archers under his black thumb. Where are the Medjay, Ramose?"

"Kamose took them to Weset with him during the Inundation," Ramose answered. "They returned north with him and now they have joined with the navy at Het nefer Apu."

"We know of the troops at Het nefer Apu," Pezedkhu went on thoughtfully. "So Kamose is trying to train a navy, is he? Under whom?"

"Paheri and Baba Abana of Nekheb." Ramose watched the General's finger trace the track from Het nefer Apu across the desert to Uah-ta-Meh.

"What are Kamose's plans for these forty thousand men?" Apepa asked.

"Another siege, Majesty," Ramose told him glibly. "He intends to join them with the forces at Het nefer Apu and surround Het-Uart again but this time with boats full of fighting sailors as well as infantry. He believes he will succeed this year if he can use the boats to fill the canals around the city." Apepa laughed without humour.

"The fool! Het-Uart is impregnable. It cannot be successfully sieged. Why did he send them to the oasis in the first place?"

"To keep them a secret from you," Ramose said promptly. "It would have required an enormous effort to take them to Weset and bring them back when the river receded. Besides, they are still a rabble. Hor-Aha needed a winter and plenty of space to continue their training."

"It is already Phamenoth," Pezedkhu said. "We are two months into the campaign season. Why has Kamose not moved?" Ramose met those perceptive eyes steadily.

"Because the men are not quite ready and because the Princes have been quarrelling," he said flatly. "They resent Hor-Aha. Each wants precedence over him. When Kamose arrived, he had to put down a small mutiny." Apepa exclaimed in satisfaction but Pezedkhu's expression did not change.

"You are suddenly very free with your information, Ramose," he almost whispered. Ramose drew back.

"I have betrayed my Lord for the sake of a woman," he said simply. "What use is there in fastidiousness now? I have already ensured my ka an unfavourable weighing in the Judgement Hall of Osiris."

"That depends on whose cause is just," Apepa said impatiently. "I wonder how much longer Kamose will stay where he is." He glanced at Pezedkhu, and Ramose saw the gleam of speculation in his eyes. Pezedkhu shook his head.

"No, my King."

"Why not?"

"Because I do not trust this man." He pointed at Ramose.

"Neither do I, but Yamusa's testimony agrees with what we have heard. Kamose is there. His army is there. The oasis is indefensible, wide open. In eleven days we could fall upon Kamose with twice the number of troops he has, and wipe him out."

"No!" Pezedkhu had risen. "Listen to me, Mighty Bull. Here

in the city you are safe. Your thousands of soldiers are safe. Kamose can be defeated without any risk. As long as we sit here patiently and let him exhaust himself with siege after fruitless siege we are sure to regain Egypt in the end. Do not be swayed by this temptation!" For answer Apepa's finger slashed at the map.

"From the Delta to Ta-she, six days. From there to the oasis, another four. Think of it, Pezedkhu. In two weeks victory could be mine. What is the risk? Only slightly greater than no risk at all. Fall on the oasis, slaughter the rabble, then march another four days and take the troops at Het nefer Apu by surprise."

"Water, Majesty."

"But there is water at Ta-she, water at the oasis, water in the Nile."

"And supposing Kamose is waiting for us? Fresh and rested while we have marched from Ta-she four days across that accursed waste?"

"We could overwhelm him with numbers alone." Apepa sat back. "Even if Ramose is lying regarding the count of men and Yamusa's eyes deceived him, we have enough soldiers to predict the successful outcome of any engagement. The gods have sent us a precious opportunity. In the oasis we would face Kamose in pitched battle with a distinct advantage and we would win."

"This recklessness is not like you, Majesty," Pezedkhu pro-tested. Apepa had opened his mouth to reply when Nehmen entered, coming across the room with a train of laden servants behind him. Quickly and efficiently they placed the trays of steaming dishes on the table, removed the used cups, filled bowls with scented water and laid linen beside them, before bowing themselves out. Apepa gestured.

"You may eat also, Ramose," he said. Ramose was not hungry in spite of his meagre breakfast, but he did not want to appear arrogant. He picked politely at the food.

"How well armed are Kamose's troops?" Kethuna asked. He was scooping out the flesh of a pomegranate, the gelid red seeds heaped on his spoon.

"They began with whatever weapons Kamose had to hand," Ramose told him. "Later, as they plundered the garrisons and the forts, they acquired axes, swords, bows, and the chariots and horses they found at Nefrusi and Nag-ta-Hert. My Lord's problem has always been teaching his peasants to use what they took. Only the Medjay and Kamose's Weset soldiers needed no time for that." He did not elaborate, knowing that the listeners would remember the reasons he had given them for the army's long sojourn in the oasis.

"What are the brothers like?" The question came from Apepa's son. Ramose, thinking rapidly, decided to tell the truth.

"My Lord Kamose is a harsh but fair man. He likes to be alone. He is brave. He hates you Setiu for what you have done to his father and what you have tried to do to his family and he wants revenge. He will not stop until he gets it or dies in the attempt. He is loyal to those who give him loyalty in return. His brother is more subdued. He is a thinker. He sees farther than Kamose."

"He is more dangerous then," Pezedkhu interposed and Ramose thought with a shock, why yes, I suppose he is. He stands in Kamose's shadow. Most of the time he is barely noticed, yet his presence is always felt.

Apepa dabbled his fingers in one of the bowls and wiped them studiously on a square of linen. "We have decisions to make," he said. "Ramose, you will be taken back to your room for the present. I have two more questions, however. Where is Prince Meketra? And does Kamose have a large concentration of troops anywhere other than the oasis and Het nefer Apu?"

"Khemmenu and the governorship of its nome have been given back to Meketra," Ramose said with a stab of bitterness he could not conceal. "Kamose has left no forces of any note anywhere but Uah-ta-Meh and Het nefer Apu, but his home is well defended by his household guards." He rose. "When may I speak with Tani?"

"That depends on whether or not we have finished our talk," Apepa said affably. "You will be sent word tomorrow. The soldier on your door will see that you are brought anything you need. You are dismissed." With a curt nod Ramose turned on his heel and strode towards the door but he still heard the young Apepa say in a low voice, "Father, you are not going to leave them alone together are you? Her person is now sac—"

"Peace!" Apepa hissed. The doors closed quietly behind Ramose.

# Chapter NINE

THE REST OF THE day dragged for Ramose. Escorted back to his room and firmly sequestered, he had nothing to do but pace and think. He was pleased that he had acquitted himself so well with regard to Kamose's instructions. He had convinced Apepa that the army was smaller than it really was, less battle ready, less disciplined, and he had blown up the mild dissatisfaction of the Princes into a mutiny that Apepa was eager to exploit. General Pezed-khu was not so readily persuaded. It was his responsibility to be cautious, of course, but unless he could produce compelling arguments to support his suspicions that all was not as Ramose had described, Apepa would override his objections and push for the emptying of Het-Uart. And Apepa had the last word.

The worst was over. I have done my part, Ramose thought, as he wandered about the room, his fingers absently brushing the walls, his eyes moving unseeingly over the sparse furnishings. Now if Apepa keeps his word, I may freely look forward to a meeting with Tani. Beyond that, my future is dark. Obviously Apepa cannot set me free. Will he execute me or imprison me permanently in the palace? Will it be possible to plan an escape with Tani? So much depends on what we have to say to each other, whether her love for me has survived.

And why would it not? he asked himself worriedly. Why should I presume that her affections have altered in a little less than two short years? Because of what you saw in the garden, he answered himself. The vizier bowed to her as though she were a woman of authority, and her entourage was large. Well, Apepa himself said that she had become very popular with the courtiers. The bow might have been merely a mark of friendly respect. And what can I make of the young Apepa's quiet protest to his father? 'Her person is now sac—' Her person is now what? Sacred? If so, then how? Why? Sternly Ramose put a stop to the flow of anxious speculations. I have only to wait, he said to himself, and all will become clear.

Going to the door, he opened it and addressed the guard outside. "Have beer brought to me," he said. "And if there are any scrolls of stories or histories in the palace archives I want them also. I am bored." The things he requested were promptly provided and he spent the remainder of the day reading. Gradually the light blurred on his wall and finally faded, but he did not bother to light the lamp. When he could no longer see to read, he took off his clothes and curled up on the couch.

He was woken, as before, with food and then escorted to the bath house, washed, shaved and oiled. Fresh clothes were provided for him and once more he was left alone. The solitary inactivity began to gall him, and he found his thoughts circling the prospect of imprisonment here, not only days of his own company but weeks, perhaps even years. I would rather die, he told himself fiercely. Attempting to remain calm, he said his prayers to Thoth and moved through the physical exercises for strength and flexibility he had learned as a boy, but nothing could prevent the flow of anxiety and in the end he succumbed to it, sitting cross-legged on the floor and watching the squares of sunlight pattern the wall.

More food was brought to him at noon but he was not

hungry, although he drank the beer also provided and it was with a relief bordering on panic that some time later he saw the door flung open and the soldier's beckoning arm. I must re-establish an inner discipline, he chided himself as he paced the crowded halls behind his guide. I was in the desert all winter. My ka expanded to fit that limitless space. I must prepare to have it shrink to the dimensions of a prison cell.

He was admitted to the same room where he had been questioned the day before, but this time more men were gathered around the table, military officers, Ramose judged, by the similarity of their attire. The table was a litter of used dishes and cups, scrolls and maps. Ramose made his reverence and stood waiting. Apepa addressed him at once. "I have decided to release twenty-four divisions to move against Kamose," he said crisply. "Sixty thousand men under Pezedkhu's command will travel from Het-Uart up to Het nefer Apu and engage his so-called navy there. The other sixty thousand will leave the Delta and march across the desert to Ta-she and from there to the oasis to destroy the enemy's army. Kethuna will have the ordering of those troops and you will go with him. If all goes well, we will have effected a perfect pincer." Twenty-four divisions, Ramose calculated rapidly. One hundred and twenty thousand men divided equally. Kamose has fifty-five thousand at the oasis and ten thousand at Het nefer Apu. The odds are two to one against him, but if he can join up with Paheri and the navy he may be victorious. It is a terrible risk. "I have already despatched scouts along the desert route," Apepa went on. "It will take my generals five days to ready the army and in that time I expect word as to whether Kamose is still dithering at Uah-ta-Meh or has left it for Het nefer Apu. I am confident that he is still there. What do you think, son of Teti?" I think that I despise you, son of Sutekh, Ramose thought so clearly and vindictively that he was afraid he had spoken the words aloud. You tell me these things because you will make sure that I will die in the forefront of the battle. Well, I will tell you what you are, but not until I have seen Tani.

"He may indeed still be at the oasis, Majesty," Ramose answered evenly. "But not for much longer. Otherwise the campaigning season will be too far advanced for any engagement."

"Leave him there," Pezedkhu muttered. "Let him march to and fro with his illusions. This is madness." Apepa ignored him.

"A bland and non-committal comment," he said. "But I suppose that you now know nothing more than we do." He studied Ramose for a moment and Ramose stared back at him. "I did not express my sympathy for you on the execution of your father," he went on. "Teti was my loyal subject. It is a pity that you chose to conspire in his downfall. My generals will wipe out Kamose and his deluded followers and then there will be great rewards for those who had the courage to remain faithful to me, their rightful King. You might have seen your lands restored to you. As it is, you betrayed first me and now Kamose. You are not to be trusted and I do not need you any more."

"Between a purpose and its fulfilment there is a gulf that must be bridged, Awoserra," Ramose declared through teeth clenched against the fume of rage curdling in him. "It cannot be leaped with fine and empty promises. Take care lest your splendid generals tumble into that abyss." The men around the table murmured angrily, all but Pezedkhu, who was sitting expressionlessly with his chin in his hand. Apepa did not seem insulted. His cold smile managed to reduce Ramose's words to the level of mere bluster.

"I have no wish to keep you sealed up for the next few days," he said. "You may enjoy the freedom of the palace, with your guard of course. The Princess Tani will be keeping to the women's quarters for the time being. You will be sent to her on the eve of your departure. You are dismissed." I rather doubt that he has widened the bounds of my prison through any pity, Ramose thought grimly as he walked away. I am to die and he knows it. He is maliciously providing a condemned man with a last vision of all that will be taken from him. But I will thwart him. I will not look on the pleasures of this place with the eyes of a walking corpse but with the delight of a man in love with life. You pathetic sheep herder, he scorned Apepa in his mind. What do you know of the soul of an Egyptian? I refuse to be humiliated. I will take what you offer and more, and if there is any justice among the gods, Kamose will crush you like the ugly beetle you are. I only wish that I might survive to see it happen.

He did not go back to his room. Resolving to shut out the constant, silent presence of the soldier at his elbow, he roamed the halls and courtyards of the palace, letting his feet take him wherever they would. When he was tired, he sat on the grass in a small open court beside a fountain, curtly sending a passing servant for fruit and wine, lifting his face to the slanting after-noon sun as he waited. He ate slowly, with relish, afterwards making his way to the bath house and commanding a massage. He lay on the bench while the masseur's firm hands kneaded his muscles and heated his skin, inhaling the mixture of per-fumed oils and letting himself drowse. The man finished his work and Ramose thanked him, then asked him for directions to the gardens.

By the time he stepped out into the warm air of early evening, the sun was going down and the trees were casting long shadows across the many paths that ran in all directions through Apepa's domain. But a few birds still sang and the hum of late bees in the fruit blossoms pursued Ramose as he wan-dered the pleasant arouras, pausing to shake the fragrant petals onto his head or drink in the riotous colours of the flowerbeds. Courtiers were drifting towards the palace as the sun sank lower. They glanced at Ramose and his tired escort curiously, greeting him politely as they passed. Ramose went on until he came to the frowning enclosure wall. Soldiers stood above it facing outward and beyond it the invisible city clamoured. He turned back, and by the time he re-entered the palace, full dark had fallen and the lamps and torches had been lit.

He thought of mingling with Apepa's guests, even now streaming towards a night of feasting in the great hall from which arose a babble of voices and laughter. There would be entertainments. Magicians perhaps, or jugglers. Certainly there would be dancers and good music. He would have gone in if he had really wanted to, but examining his true desire, he found himself craving the silence that always fell over the oasis once the troops retired to their tents. Nothing but the intermittent, quiet challenges of the men on watch ever broke that dreaming hush.

Smiling wryly to himself, he sought the empty passages. Sometimes his way was barred by armed men guarding closed doors and at such times he realized that he had blundered close to the royal apartments or the treasury or the administrative offices, but more often he was free to simply meander through the painted maze that was the heart of Het-Uart. He returned to his room very late, and as soon as he entered it, he heard the exhausted soldier relinquish his responsibility to another. Grinning to himself, Ramose lay down and was instantly asleep.

Making his way to the bath house the following morning, he became aware that the mood in the palace had changed. Little knots of courtiers stood about in various stages of disarray, talking excitedly. Servants moved with fresh purpose. Women whispered behind their hands. Ramose, mounting a bathing slab, found himself standing next to a young and very pretty woman whose body servant was pouring hot water over her long black hair. She smiled at him, unselfconsciously running an eye over his nakedness and then looking into his face with a

glint of brazen approval. "I've seen you here for several mornings," she said. "You're not a guest or you would be using a private
bath house. Are you a new retainer?" Ramose felt his soldier
come closer.

"Not exactly," he replied carefully. "You could perhaps call
me a messenger. I will not be enjoying the King's hospitality for
long."

"That is a shame." She stepped down from her slab and held
out her arms so that her servant could wrap a towel around her.
"Where are you from?" she went on, pulling her sopping hair
forward and wringing it vigorously. "You don't look like a Keftian. There are always a few of those in the palace." Suddenly her
busy hands were stilled. "Perhaps you're a southerner. Are you?
What news is there from beyond the Delta?" Ramose laughed.

"You speak as though everything south of the Delta is a wild
wasteland," he chided her. "Have you never seen it?"

"No. I've been no farther than the city of Iunu. My father is
an assistant scribe in the office of the King's Overseer of Cattle,
and all the King's cattle are in the Delta. Besides," she shrugged,
"what can there be to see but little villages and a temple or two
and miles and miles of nothing but fields? They do say that even
those things don't exist any more, that the Prince of Weset has
raged through it all like a rogue beast." Taking a comb from the
servant, she began to tug it through the heavy tangles of her
mane, giving Ramose a sidelong glance. "I would like to meet
such an animal," she purred. "But I don't suppose I shall ever
have the opportunity. The palace is buzzing with the news that
the King is releasing his army at last against this Kamose."
Ramose feigned astonishment.

"The whole of the army?"

"Well no," she began, "not the whole army, of course not,
just . . ." Before she could finish, the soldier pushed his way
roughly between them.

"This man is the King's prisoner," he said loudly. "Tell him no more. Get about your business." Her eyebrows rose and she did not so much as glance at the guard.

"Really?" she said, completely unperturbed. "Then why are you allowed the freedom of the public bath house? Will you be whisked back to a cell when you are clean? What have you done?"

"Nothing criminal," Ramose assured her. "I am from the south." A sudden thought occurred to him. "If you see the Princess Tani today, tell her that Ramose is here. Ramose. I have been granted a meeting with her but if it happens that..." This time the soldier grasped the girl's arm roughly and pulled her away.

"Enough!" he bellowed. "One more word and I will have you arrested also!"

"I know of no one answering to that name," she called back over her shoulder as she was propelled towards the massage room. "But I am Hat-Anath, and if you should escape, come to my quarters! Oh take your hand off me!" The guard released her and she vanished into clouds of steam.

Ramose endured his ablutions in a puzzled frame of mind. Why was it that Hat-Anath did not at least know of Tani? But then, the palace was huge, full of hundreds of courtiers and their hangers-on, and perhaps one little Princess from an obscure town far to the south would excite no interest. There was the matter of Apepa's army, too. If twenty-four divisions did not make up its total, as the girl had implied, then how many troops did the King in fact control? Twice that number? And where did they all come from? Ramose inwardly cursed the interfering soldier. One more moment and he would have heard something valuable. But of what use would such information be, seeing that I cannot get out of here to take it to Kamose? his thoughts ran on. Besides, he must deal with

Pezedkhu and Kethuna before he can turn to the remnants of Apepa's forces.

In spite of his determination to make the most of his few days in the palace, those two enigmas nagged at him as he continued his explorations. By the end of his second day of relative freedom he had traversed the precincts from one end to the other, and on the third day he was content to move from a secluded corner of the garden he had particularly liked to a part of the roof where he could sit in the shade of one of the windcatchers and look out over the whole of the palace grounds. His view encompassed part of the barracks. A constant cloud of dust spoke of the frenetic activity going on there as the army prepared to mobilize. Sometimes the sharp commands of the officers came faintly to Ramose's ears and occasionally he caught the glint of hazy sunlight on the spokes of a chariot's wheel.

The roof was a favourite place for many of the women, who had mats and cushions spread out for them under their fringed canopies. At first they pretended to ignore him. They gossiped and played board games and worked idly at their looms, weaving the many-coloured fabrics so many of them wore. But by the fourth day they welcomed him warmly, offering him wine and sweetmeats and including him in their conversations. Ramose talked to them cautiously, the soldier always breathing at his elbow. He did not dare to ask about Tani, afraid that the soldier would report his words and Apepa would deny him the interview he had been promised. Neither did he look for her among the soft, painted faces. He knew that she had been ordered to keep to her rooms.

No further summons came from the King. Nevertheless, on the evening of the fourth day Ramose had himself washed again and donned fresh linen. Asking for the services of a cosmetician, he sat docilely while the man kohled his eyes and temples and oiled his unruly hair. He had no jewellery to put on, no earring to brush his neck, no rings or bracelet to emphasize the grace of his strong fingers, but he did not imagine that Tani would care about such things. Alone again he lit the lamp and sat on the edge of the couch to wait.

Perhaps an hour went by and Ramose was beginning to wonder with despair whether Apepa had decided to go back on his promise, when the door opened. The herald Sakhetsa stood there, resplendent in his white robes. "You may come with me now," he said. "She has been warned." The words struck Ramose as ominous, but with beating heart he got up and followed Sakhetsa into the passage.

The way was familiar to him now. In his wanderings he had in fact already approached the imposing double doors to which he was led and had been turned away by the blue-and-white liveried guards before them. But now they bowed to Sakhetsa and swung the doors open. Ramose entered on his heels.

The apartment was sumptuous. Everywhere there was the glint of gentle lamplight on gold. Soft rugs embraced his sandalled feet. Delicate cedar chairs chased in silver exuded a faint perfume. A low table of ebony, topped in ivory squares for playing dogs and jackals, sat beside a tall golden lampstand, and the tiny animals used in the game had been intricately carved out of delicately striated alabaster. The walls were decorated with paintings of jagged mountains and a tossing ocean, all white, blue and green.

Through an opening on his right Ramose caught a glimpse of the bedchamber, its couch hung with gold-bordered linen, the chest at its foot resting on rearing golden fish whose open mouths supported it. A cosmetic stand inhabited the shadows, the pots and jars on its surface all shaped like shells but gleaming with the richness of desert gold. Someone was moving in there. Ramose saw the flick of a short kilt and heard a muted clatter, but it was not the person the herald was now addressing.

A woman stood in the centre of the room, white-faced but composed, hands loosely clasped before her. Rings winked on her hennaed fingers. Gold bands encircled her bare arms. The red sheath that fell to her ankles flashed and glittered with the gold thread woven into it. Across her forehead and entwined in her high-wound hair went a thin fillet of gold with one long drop resting between her black eyebrows. The orange-hennaed mouth was parted. She was breathing rapidly, the rise and fall of her breasts making her lapis earrings tremble. "Majesty, this is Ramose son of Teti," Sakhetsa was saying, his words muffled by the sudden pounding of blood in Ramose's head. "Ramose, do reverence to Queen Tautha." Ramose turned to him help-lessly. There must be some mistake, he wanted to shout. This creature looks like Tani, she resembled Tani from a distance in the garden and I was fooled, but something is wrong. Apepa has tricked me. Where is Seqenenra's daughter?

"Thank you, Sakhetsa, you can go." The woman was speak-ing with Tani's voice. She snapped her fingers and turned with Tani's familiar tilt to her head as a servant came out of the bed-chamber and bowed. "You go also, Heket," she said. "Wait out-side." Ramose stood stupidly as the room emptied and the doors closed quietly, his thoughts chaotic. I am dreaming, he whis-pered to himself. This is a nightmare and soon I will wake to find myself back in that little cell, still longing to see her.

The woman before him took one step, her gown shimmer-ing. She smiled wryly, faintly. "Ramose," she said. "Apepa only told me a short time ago. He enjoys his small surprises. It is one of his few traits I dislike."

The interval stretched. Ramose felt its strain in every nerve. The luxurious room seemed out of focus, its dimensions dis-torted, its furnishings flimsy and ephemeral. Desperately he fought for an interior balance, a centre where he was sanely himself. At last he found it, and with the finding, reality fell upon him. He almost heard its crash as his surroundings regained their proper dimensions and the woman resolved herself into, into . . . His throat was as dry as a desert storm. "Tani?" he rasped. She bit her lip.

"He didn't warn you either, did he?" she said. "I'm sorry, Ramose. That was cruel of him." Ramose swallowed.

"Warn me of what?" he whispered. "Why did the herald call you Queen?"

"Because I am one," she said flatly. "Come and sit down, Ramose, you are swaying like a drunken man. Let me pour you wine." Woodenly he obeyed her. His legs felt disconnected from the rest of his body and he almost fell into the chair. He watched her lift a jug, watched the dark red liquid cascade into the cup, watched her push it across the table towards him. Carefully he raised it to his mouth. The wine tasted sour and burned his parched throat.

"Make me understand," he croaked. "I do not understand." She drew up another chair and sat looking at him solemnly. As the wine began to calm him and his interior stability grew, he thought he saw pity in those large, kohl-rimmed eyes. Pity? he repeated in his mind. Oh gods, not pity! Anything but that!

"I signed a marriage contract with Apepa," she told him steadily. "I am now a Queen. Queen Tautha." He was certain now that it was indeed pity in her glance. Disbelief flooded him, and a cold desolation, but the knowledge also spawned anger.

"Why?" he demanded. "Did he threaten you, Tani? Was a contract forced on you because of Kamose's uprising? Marriage or death, was that the choice he gave you? Was it a revenge against your brother? If so, it means nothing. It can be undone, ignored. Gods! If you only knew how the thought of you has kept me sane through all the terror of the last two years, how the memories I have cherished have been my pillow at night and my sword during the days! And you married him!" She held up a hand.

"I was not threatened or coerced," she said in a low voice. "I wish I could make it plain to you, Ramose, to make you see..." She paused, groping for the right words and he, his attention fixed urgently on her face, grappled with an exploding rage. "I came here friendless, afraid, knowing what Kamose was planning and sure that when news of his rebellion reached Het-Uart I would be killed. I tried to live for each day, each hour. I had made up my mind that if I was to die I would succumb bravely." She turned her hennaed palms up in a gesture of supplication or surprise. "But he was kind to me. More than kind. None of it was my fault, he said. I was not to blame for the ingratitude of my family. When Khemmenu fell, he came to me in great distress, knowing how I loved you, and he prayed that you were still safe. He gave me presents, invited me to accompany him to Sutekh's temple, allowed me to sit on his left at the feasts. He treated me with honour, not as a hostage. I was overwhelmed. He confessed his affection for me..." Now it was Ramose's turn to raise a hand in horrified rebuke.

"He seduced you," he said savagely. "And you didn't see it. He accomplished the most exquisite revenge against Kamose that he could possibly have devised, and in spite of your intelligence, the honour you swore to uphold, you fell for his ploy! You let him give you a Setiu name. You let him take you into Sutekh's domain." He slapped the table violently and the wine jumped in his cup. "Damn it, Tani, you let him into your bed! How could you? How could you? You gave him what you had promised to me, gave it to a filthy foreigner! Where is the honest, fearless girl I adored? She has become Setiu and I have lost her!"

"It was not like that," she faltered, but he cut her off.

"No?" he said sarcastically. "Then how was it? Did you fall in love with him like some vapid peasant girl or did common greed dictate your actions? It had to be one or the other!" He flung himself away from the table and began to pace, unable to remain still any longer. "I see that I have misjudged you from the start," he went on bitterly. "You are shallow, Tani. I mistook your superficiality for lightheartedness and cheerful optimism. So did your family. Have you any idea what this news will do to Kamose, to your mother, when it reaches them? And believe me, it will. Apepa will wait to use it until a moment when it can do the most damage to the cause of freedom for Egypt." He rounded on her, coming close and bending over her where she sat, wanting to hurt her, wanting to see her bleed as he was bleeding, the torrent of dying hopes and disillusionment swirling invisibly around him. "Do not be deluded into believing that the serpent loves you," he grated. "You are nothing to him, a weapon to be used against his enemy." She pushed him away and struggled to her feet, clinging to the arm of her chair with both hands.

"Stop it, Ramose!" she shouted. "Enough! Enough! You are wrong! Hurt me all you want, since you feel that I deserve your condemnation, but you are wrong." Her lips quivered. "I loved you then. I love you still. We had a dream, you and I, but that was all it was. A dream! In another age we might have married and been happy. In another age donkeys might sprout wings and take to the air. The gods propose these things, and for us they decreed a time in which our love could not mature. Larger issues are at stake."

"Larger issues are at stake," he mimicked her brutally. "And how would you know that, wombed here in your brocades and gold? Do you nurse the arrogant delusion that you have made some kind of sacrifice in a grand cause by becoming a Setiu Queen? What makes you think that you are so important?"

"I know that you can never forgive me for the anguish I have caused you," she said in a low voice. "But, Ramose, look around you. You have been in Het-Uart for only a few days. I have been here almost two years. Apepa is releasing one hundred and twenty thousand troops against Kamose. There are more than two hundred thousand quartered here, more than half of them new men from Rethennu. Apepa sent to his brothers in the east for reinforcements and the Delta is full of them. Kamose cannot win. He was doomed from the start. I began to realize that within a few months of my enforced stay. I held out against Apepa's blandishments for a long time, during which I did much thinking." Her eyes filled suddenly with tears. "I wanted you. I wanted to go home. I wished that Apepa would order my execution. But I decided both to survive and to sign the marriage contract when I knew that in the end Kamose would be brought down in defeat. As a legal Queen I have many rights that a mere hostage or even a concubine does not have. I took advantage of Apepa's affections, yes, but not for the reasons you suppose. Kamose will fall. He will be brought here a prisoner. Then as a Queen I can intercede for him and for my family from a position of power." She shrugged. "That is all. Believe or not, as you wish."

"But, Tani," he said urgently, "what makes you think that Kamose has no hope of winning Egypt back? You have been infected with the blindness that seems to be affecting everyone in the palace and probably also in the city. You see only the richness of this place, the number of soldiers in the barracks, the impregnability of the city. Do you even know that Kamose now holds the whole country except for Het-Uart? That he has campaigned ruthlessly and there is only Apepa himself left to oppose him? Apepa knows this, but his courtiers obviously do not. Including you." He opened his mouth to go on, to tell her of her brother's plan to tease Apepa's troops out of the city and into destruction, but all at once he saw the danger in doing so. He could not trust her, and that knowledge broke his heart. His anger fled.

"No, I did not know," she said quietly. "I knew of Khemmenu and the fall of the fort at Nefrusi, but I was led to believe that these were isolated victories, that Kamose could not control the peasants and the towns and villages would give him no aid."

"He burned them all," Ramose told her curtly. "He is taking no chances." She raised her eyes, huge with unshed tears, to his.

"I am glad," she whispered. "Oh so glad, Ramose. Perhaps I have been duped, as you say. What will Kamose do now? And what about you?" Ramose deliberately ignored her first question.

"I am to march with General Kethuna to the oasis of Uahta-Meh," he said matter-of-factly. "Apepa means me to die there." She pursed her lips and searched his face thoughtfully.

"Kethuna is a reasonably good general but a petty man," she said. "Pezedkhu would make sure that you had a fighting chance for life but Kethuna will not. I can try to bribe him."

"No." Ramose slumped back into his chair and drained his cup, setting it carefully and studiously on the table before him. "Perhaps Apepa expects you to do just that and it would be a kind of test of your loyalty." He smiled up at her faintly. "Believe me, Tani, I am not stupid. I will do everything I can to stay alive."

"If you do, if you can," she began haltingly, "please do not tell Kamose what I have become. To see you is punishment enough for me." He ran both hands over his face, a gesture of fatigue and resignation.

"What a tangled toil all this has become," he said wearily. "I had foolishly imagined that when we met you would fall into my arms with cries of joy and together we would plan an escape from Het-Uart, running free to Kamose, then back to Weset. My mother is there now, you know." She was silent, staring at him without expression. He waited for a response, and receiving none, he rose. "Apepa has kept his word," he remarked. "I have spoken with you. How he must be laughing! You have become even more beautiful than I remembered, my Tani. I think it is time for me to return to my miserable little room."

"I do not want you to love me any more, Ramose," she said soberly. "There's no future in it." He grunted.

"There is a future," he corrected her. "But neither of us may be in it. May the totem of your nome take care of you, Tani."

"And may Thoth of Khemmenu go with you, Ramose," she replied, her voice shaking. "May the soles of your feet be firm." If she had taken one step towards him, however hesitant, he would have pulled her into his arms. But the moment passed. He walked to the door and glanced back. She was standing stiffly, her hands at her sides, crying quietly. He was not able to close the door behind him.

Once back in his cell he called for wine, and when it had been delivered, he sat on the couch and proceeded to get drunk, filling the cup and draining it with cold deliberation. He could not think, and he did not want to feel.

He woke at dawn with a pounding headache and a raging thirst, both of which he welcomed. It was better, he reasoned as he ate, was bathed, and dressed for the last time in the palace, to suffer physical distress than to inhabit a sound body that would allow the howling pain in his soul to come forward. As soon as he had finished tying his sandals, the soldier watching him handed him his pack and ordered him out. Ramose followed him through the still sleepy halls and into a garden glittering with early sunlight on dew. There they halted, for Apepa himself was waiting, surrounded by his yawning entourage. Ramose, his head splitting and his eyes throbbing, did not bow.

"You do not need to worry, son of Teti," Apepa said by way of a greeting. "I will take care of her. My Chief Wife Uazet is very fond of her." Ramose stared at him defiantly. He knew that he was being baited and he should not respond. He did not want to give Apepa the satisfaction of knowing that his goad had found its target but mulishly he no longer cared.

"I hate you," he said clearly, his voice ringing out in the limpid morning air. "The whole of Egypt hates you. You do not belong here and one day you will be driven from this sacred soil." He stepped closer and with an almost insane delight he saw Apepa move back. "Your god is powerless against the combined forces of the holy divinities who have decided to engineer your downfall," he finished. "I bid you farewell." He expected an immediate reaction, a sword to sever his aching head from his neck, perhaps, or at least a roar of rage, but Apepa did no more than raise his plucked eyebrows. The attendants' murmurs died away into a shocked silence. Turning from them with disdain, Ramose strode towards the palace gates, his soldier escort hurrying at his heels.

He was led to a waiting chariot where his guard handed him over to an officer and retreated without a word. Then his hands were tied together and he was taken back the way he had first come, down through the city streets and straight out onto the narrow plain between Het-Uart and its protecting canal.

He entered chaos. Clouds of dust obscured his view and in it men and horses resolved and dissolved suddenly like phantoms. Everywhere there was noisy confusion. Men shouted, horses whinnied, donkeys being loaded with provisions caught the prevailing mood of agitation and set up a hoarse and continuous braying. Ramose's charioteer cursed under his breath as he tried to negotiate a way through the choking mob. I could escape now, Ramose thought. I could jump from the rear of this vehicle and vanish into the pandemonium before this man could turn his head. But just as he was tensing to launch him-self to the ground the chariot stopped, the charioteer flung the reins to a boy already holding other harnesses, and the moment passed. Deftly the officer took the thong trailing from Ramose's imprisoned wrists and knotted it to the chariot's rim. "Stay here," he said unnecessarily, and disappeared. Sighing, Ramose sank to the floor, ignoring the boy's curious glances. His head still ached.

He had no way of telling how long he sat there, for the murk stirred up by the soldiers forming ranks continued to obscure the sun, but his joints had begun to protest their confinement long before. He was brought a full water skin and a bag of bread, which he put in his pack, and then he was led to stand in the centre of a troop of infantry waiting quietly for the order to march. One of his wrists was tied loosely to the soldier on his left. He saw Kethuna whirl by in his chariot, but the General did not even glance his way. Far ahead a standard was raised, a large, red-painted wooden fan on a tall pole, and at once a command was shouted. "At last we set out," the soldier mut-tered. "It's bad enough that I became betrothed last week, and now I must shepherd you and see that you don't make a run for it. What's your name?" The column began to move. Ramose shrugged his pack higher on his shoulder.

"I don't think my name matters very much any more," he replied curtly. "But I am Ramose, late of Khemmenu in the Un nome."

"I hear Khemmenu is in the nothing nome now," the soldier grunted. "The enemy sacked it. Did you lose relatives in that fight? Or were you in on the slaughtering?" He shook the length of leather joining them. "Are you a common criminal or a spy?"

"All of us here are in the nothing nome," Ramose said grimly, and at that the soldier pressed him no longer.

If he had been free to swing both his arms, Ramose might have almost enjoyed the first few days of the expedition, as Kethuna's sixty thousand men snaked through the Delta. It was the end of the month of Phamenoth, the weather cool, the orchards dropping the last of their blossoms, the vineyards making patterns of different shades of green with the dark grape leaves stirring over the lighter hue of the tiny grapes themselves. The water in the canals and tributaries calmly reflected a high, blue sky. Around Het-Uart, the depredations caused by Kamose's Raiders the year before could still be seen. Burned trees stood black and skeletal. Withered vines rustled sadly in the scented breeze. Patches of scorched earth marked the places where bodies had been fired and occasionally the bones of cattle littered the paths, but as the host neared the western edge of the Delta's lush cultivation the paradisiacal nature of Lower Egypt was restored.

On the evening of the third day, they camped under the shelter of the last grove of palms before the desert began. Ramose and his jailer joined a group of soldiers sitting around one of the many cooking fires that lit up the deepening twilight. The other men talked as they ate, but Ramose was silent, his eyes on the hillocks of sand stretching away before him. His wrist was chafed but he did not mind the small niggle of pain. His thoughts flowed from Tani to Kamose to the probability of his impending death and back again. Examining his heart, he found no bitterness towards the girl he had loved for so long, indeed, it came to him that he had exaggerated the emotion to enable himself to survive the horror of Khemmenu and the following days of despair. Nevertheless, the core of his tenderness for her was still there, warm and steady, and he knew that it would outlast his death and the weighing of his ka. It was a thing of eternity, fated within the rightness of Ma'at.

As the dimness began to thicken into darkness and the desert became indistinct, he fancied that he saw the furtive shapes of men out among the dunes. He wondered if Kamose would send scouts as far as the Delta. The phantoms dissolved as he tried to focus on them, but one took on solidity and became an advance scout who came up unhurriedly and passed through the line of cheerful blazes on his way to report to Kethuna.

Early the next morning they set off towards Ta-she. Each soldier had been warned to fill his water skin and to drink only when rest halts were called. There was no danger in the trek, for the path was well travelled during Inundations when the river road was flooded and an ample supply of water waited for them. Still, by the end of the first day there was grumbling in the ranks. Many of the soldiers were too exhausted to eat, preferring to cast themselves down in the sand and go immediately to sleep. Many had surreptitiously disobeyed their officers and had emptied their skins long before the fiery desert day relinquished its hold.

They had become more sensible by the time a camp was made on their second evening, but Ramose, noting blistered feet and the angry red swellings of sunburn on exposed shoulders and faces, felt an impatient scorn. Apepa's generals were idiots. Their troops had not experienced desert drilling. Delta-born and raised, or fresh from the temperate country of Rethennu, their training limited to mock battles within Het-Uart, they were too soft to embrace the rigours of hot sand and a sun undiluted by any sweet humidity.

He himself was tired. His muscles ached from the march, but that was all. The soldier to whom he was tied had not suffered much, but he also complained of a mild headache and chills to one of the army physicians who moved among the men with salves. When the physician had gone, the man hailed a passing officer and asked if he might be released from Ramose at least during the day, but the officer, returning from the General's tent, told him that Kethuna had refused his request. "They could at least tie you to someone else and give me a rest for a while," the soldier said resignedly. "I hope they remember to cut you loose before I need both my arms to heft my axe." Ramose found the situation suddenly very funny but he knew better than to laugh. It occurred to him that the desert might prove a more implacable enemy than Kamose and his hardened troops.

Ta-she appeared on the horizon soon after sunrise on the seventh day out from Het-Uart, but it was not until late in the afternoon that the vast oasis was reached. By then the soldiers broke ranks without waiting for permission and ran towards the glint of water between the clustered palms, ignoring the shouts of their officers. Ramose watched them go with a secret delight. Hot and thirsty himself, he walked forward calmly, his soldier stumbling beside him. Once among the cultivated fields the Tjehenu villagers came out to stare at this wave of undisciplined military might and Ramose scanned them quickly for someone familiar, sure that here at Ta-she there would certainly be Kamose's spies. But he recognized no one among the dark, withdrawn faces.

The army remained at Ta-she for the next day and night while equipment was checked and the men enjoyed a brief respite. They swam, ate and slept with renewed and noisy good spirits but their hurts were not healed in such a short time, and although the next leg of the march began optimistically, the unforgiving earth beneath already blistered feet and the brazen heat pouring on peeling skin soon reduced them to a plodding misery.

Ramose found himself enveloped in a deepening peace as

the miles slid away under his sandals. Life in the desert was still life. Aware of each hot breath he drew, each grain of sand clinging to his calves, each bead of sweat that trickled down his spine, he marvelled at the mystery that had been his existence, the memories that were his alone. This desert journey would be his last before the one whose gate opened onto the Judgement Hall. It would end as no other he had ever taken, yet he was not afraid. I will not live to see Kamose victorious and crowned in Weset, he thought, unperturbed. I will not greet my mother again until I stand beside my father to do so. I will never hold Tani naked in my arms or see my offspring grow like sturdy weeds in the garden of the estate that might have been mine. Yet I am content. I have loved. I have kept my honour. I have proved my worthiness in the sight of gods and men. Will the desert, this place of a unique and arid magic, preserve my body so that the gods may find me? All I can do is pray that it might be so.

The army spent the night of the fourth day out from Ta-she in a state of battle-readiness. The oasis of Uah-ta-Meh loomed close, an ominous wide blackness against a star-strewn sky. Word had come down from the General that his scouts had detected no activity there, but they had not ranged too close for fear of discovery. Nothing could hide the approach of sixty thousand men in any case, but a few hours' warning was better than a whole day. The infantry was now formed up in fighting blocks, each division behind its squadron of twenty-five chariots, its standard bearer before.

The men slept uneasily without breaking ranks. Ramose did not sleep at all. He knew that Kamose and all his troops had gone, that Kethuna would find no one but villagers in the oasis and would have to begin yet another long trek across the punishing sand, this time towards the Nile. His men had nerved themselves for action in the morning. When it did not come, the let-down, coupled with the prospect of more heat and pain, would be demoralizing. Kamose and Paheri, fresh and eager, would be waiting for their dispirited arrival. I wonder whether I will still be alive by then, Ramose thought. I doubt it. Kethuna will order me killed when he finds the oasis empty. Well, at least my bonds will be loosed!

# Chapter TEN

AT DAWN THE MEN were roused and told to eat and drink. They did so quietly, each turned inward upon his own thoughts as the time of battle drew nearer. Some prayed. Others fingered amulets or charms while they stowed the remainder of their rations and tightened their sandals.

An officer appeared and to Ramose's great relief severed the thong that had bound him to the soldier. The feeling of freedom did not last long, however. Curtly he was told to accompany the man to the front ranks, where Kethuna already stood in his chariot behind his charioteer, his squadron around him. New sunlight flashed on the spokes of the vehicles as the restless little horses shuffled and tossed their plumed heads. Already the boulder-strewn desert gave off a blinding glare. Ramose shaded his eyes as he looked up at the General. Kethuna surveyed him impassively for a moment. "My orders are to set you in the forefront of my troops," he said. "I am commanded to do no more than that. If you are recognized by the foe before you are killed, then so much the better for you. But if I discover that you have lied to the One or misrepresented the situation here at the oasis, I am to execute you at once. Walk beside the horses." For answer Ramose bowed and took his place in front of the chariot. Outwardly calm, his thoughts seethed. There would, of course, be no one to give battle. The oasis would be barren of soldiers. Would Kethuna blame him, or would he simply presume that they had set out too late to intercept Kamose as he moved towards a siege of Het-Uart, and it would be up to Pezedkhu to engage his combined army along the Nile? Would there be an opportunity to disappear into one of the villages in the oasis during the first moments of confusion? The word to march was being shouted down the lines and the standards were being raised. Ramose mentally shrugged. I will not allow myself to hope, he told himself. Today will unfold as the gods desire and with that I will be satisfied.

The chariot began to roll and doggedly Ramose went with it, inhaling the comforting, sane smell of horseflesh and leather. The oasis slowly took form, becoming smudges of green on the ground and haphazard clusters of palms against the blue sky. Nothing moved out there where the horizon shook in waves of heat. Ramose's responsibilities as a scout had been carried out along this track and he saw that the tents once sprouting at this northerly approach had gone. The horses stumbled as they trod the sharp gravel that lay black and glinting under their hoofs. The charioteer spoke to them soothingly. The sound of the thousands of men behind was a low susurration of footfalls.

For perhaps two hours they marched, while the oasis grew and continued to fill their vision. It lay silent and peaceful. No cries of warning echoed from its limpid palms. No forms scurried to give an alarm. A collective murmur began to rise from the infantry behind Ramose and he heard Kethuna curse and then say, "He has gone. The oasis is empty." Raising his voice, he called a halt, and gratefully Ramose sank to the ground in the shade of the two sweating beasts. The General seemed to have forgotten him for the time being. A scout was summoned and Ramose watched him vanish along the pebbled track that led between high dunes and into the village.

A babble of conversation broke out, a tide of cheerful excitement as the men realized that no engagement would take place that morning, and their optimism was confirmed by the return of the scout much later. Ramose, still crouching by the chariot, smiled slowly at his words. "Lord, I have been longer than I should," he said breathlessly to Kethuna. "There is a mystery here. The oasis is abandoned. No soldiers, and no villagers either."

"What do you mean?" Kethuna snapped. The man hesitated. Ramose could see his feet as he shifted his weight uncertainly.

"The villagers have gone," the scout repeated. "The huts are empty. So are the fields. There are no animals, just a few goats." The scout, and Ramose, waited. The silence lengthened. Ramose could almost feel the General thinking while the officers around him shuffled and whispered. Finally Kethuna dismissed the scout and called Ramose.

"Either Kamose has already withdrawn to Het nefer Apu or he is sitting beyond the oasis, waiting for us to occupy it so that he can surround us," he said crisply. "The oasis is not easily defensible. Yet the scouts ventured far afield yesterday and reported no movement of troops at all." He fixed Ramose with a hostile stare. "Which is it, son of Teti?"

"There is no point in asking me," Ramose retorted. "I told the King the truth. Kamose and his army were here when I left. If he has changed his plans in the weeks since I saw him, then how would I know?" Kethuna was breathing heavily.

"Kamose's scouts could have detected us days ago and alerted him," he said. "I must choose whether to risk the oasis or go around it and continue on towards the river." One of his officers spoke up.

"The men need water, General," he reminded him. "They

cannot hope to reach the Nile otherwise." Kethuna continued to scrutinize Ramose's face, his gaze pensive.

"It seems obvious that we are simply too late to trap Kamose here," he said slowly. "Yet I am uneasy. Something about this situation is not right, not clear. What am I missing, Ramose?"

"You are the General, not me," Ramose shot back at him recklessly, though he also felt a curious threat emanating from the tranquil scene beyond. "As I have told you, I know nothing of my Lord's plans beyond another siege."

"If he has gone, why did he take the villagers with him?" another officer queried. "What did he need them for?"

He did not need them, Ramose thought suddenly. But he could not leave them. Why? The reason is there, prowling in the back of my mind, but I cannot bring it forward. Oh, Kamose, implacable and devious, what have you done? He dropped his eyes so that Kethuna would not see them light up.

"Perhaps he took their flocks and herds, not them," Kethuna mused. "Perhaps he was short of food and the villagers were forced to follow him or starve." He shook his head in annoyance. "These speculations are vain," he said irritably. "I must decide on a course of action. The sun is close to its zenith. Have the men rest here and eat. By the time they have finished, I will have made my decision." His officers bowed and scattered and he himself got down from the chariot. "Watch this man," he ordered his charioteer, pointing at Ramose, then he too strode away.

Ramose regained his spot in the shade. The shadows cast by the patient animals were shorter now and paler. Opening his pack, he took out some bread and his water skin. It was more than half-empty. He shook it, wondering whether to drink or not, then chided himself for being foolish. Kamose was on his way to link up with Paheri and the springs and wells of the oasis lay waiting for Kethuna's thirsty troops, including himself.

Yet he paused, the skin to his mouth. Out of the corner of his eye he saw the other men drinking copiously, tipping the precious liquid over hot faces, obviously reasoning as he did that abundant water lay close by. One of the horses, smelling the water being spilled all around it, whickered softly.

Ramose lowered his skin. His heart had begun to pound. How much water is left for the horses in the donkey carts? he wondered. Horses hate the desert. They have no stamina for arid places. All around me the men are wasting water because they believe that there is plenty more to be had a mere stone's throw away. Hor-Aha would never allow such presumption, but Hor-Aha is a child of desert places and Kamose himself was raised on the edge of a pitiless barrens. Not like these sore, sunburned sons of the Delta.

Sore.

Sunburned.

And soon to be thirsty again.

Ramose sat very still. But is it even possible? he asked himself as the unformed thought that had been stalking him sprang forward and took on the shape of fear. Could it be done? And sufficiently completely that a whole army would be destroyed? No wonder you took everything with you, even the animals, my ruthless friend. Never in his moments of wildest conjecture could Kethuna arrive at such a startling conclusion. Pezedkhu might, but even if Pezedkhu was here instead of Kethuna, even if he suspected the truth, he would still find himself trapped at the point of no return.

But was it the truth or was he having a fit of insanity? Ramose's gaze travelled the sun-drenched road, the humps of the rock-strewn dunes, the half-hidden trees. His throat was parched and he longed to drink but he did not dare.

It was not long before Kethuna returned, his officers straggling behind him. A decision had obviously been made. Shouts rang out and the soldiers began struggling to their feet. The standards waved. Kethuna mounted his chariot. So they were going forward. Ramose checked the stopper of his water skin as he stood, and Apepa's army began to cover the last few miles between it and the oasis.

Just before they passed between the dunes, Kethuna's vanguard surged ahead and fanned out, the chariots rolling swiftly, their occupants with bows unslung and arrows at the ready. Glancing back, Ramose saw the loose lines of soldiers draw together and become a thick snake in order to keep to the track, its rear winding to be lost to sight in the dust. A mixture of anxiety and exultation gripped him as he himself was forced to walk closer to the horses. Putting out a hand, he touched the nearer animal, its flank warm and wet. At once he felt the sting of the charioteer's whip on his wrist and he withdrew.

The northern village was in view now, a collection of mud huts beyond the hectic green of sturdy crops, the small dwellings half-obscured by palm trunks and sparse shrubs. Nearer was the pool where Kamose's tent had been pitched, the ground around it disturbed and littered with the detritus of the departing troops. Kethuna's horses, once again smelling water, picked up their pace so that Ramose was forced to break into a run. The charioteer was trying to hold them in, without much success, and Kethuna, clinging to the swaying sides of the vehicle, was shouting at him angrily.

Panting and stumbling, afraid of the lick of the whip, Ramose strove to keep up. The pool was closer now, they were almost upon it, and in spite of his discomfort a puzzlement grew in Ramose. The shrubbery around the water had been cut down. Raw stumps showed yellowish above the sand. In many places the plants had been actually ripped up by the roots, leaving untidy depressions where they had been growing.

The horses came to the verge of the pool and halted. Their heads went down. Behind the chariot the soldiers broke rank, water skins at the ready, hands cupped and knees already bending. Breathing hard, Ramose scanned the surface of the scummed water. Twigs and white petals floated on it gently and thicker branches, crushed to reveal the fibres within the bark, stuck out like brown bones. Someone has killed the shrubs, hacked them up and tossed them methodically into the pool, Ramose thought. But why? It looks like an act of petty spite but to what purpose? The horses' muzzles were hesitating just above the murky liquid, their nostrils distended, whinnying softly. Soldiers were kneeling to lift the glittering wet life to their lips. Behind them their fellows waited eagerly for their turn to quench their thirst. The whole area was crowded with cheerful, jostling troops.

But Ramose, catching a whiff of sweet flower perfume brought to him on the hot breeze, drew back on a wave of horror, his own knees suddenly weak. It was death that the horses scented in their distress, death slipping down the throats of the men leaning over that seemingly innocuous expanse. Frozen to the spot by sheer dread, he watched the happy confusion. The oasis is full of it, he thought. From here to the southern village, around every spring it grows in profusion, beautiful and harmless unless, of course, its leaves are inadvertently chewed, or its seeds crushed, or one eats honey made from its flowers.

Or unless one drinks the water in which it has been immersed.

A bubble of hysterical laughter expanded in him and he clenched his teeth against it. How perfect, he thought again. How amazingly, logically, damnably perfect. Oleander, so white and delicate, yet even touching it can make a man's palms itch. Did the inspiration come to you, Kamose, or to Ahmose, or perhaps to Hor-Aha? No. This is not the work of the Prince or the General. This bears the stamp of a sophisticated mind that revolves coldly and inexorably around a victory at any cost. Kamose, I salute your cunning.

There was a thud behind him as Kethuna jumped to the ground, then the General was beside him, his charioteer's whip clutched in his hand, his face gone suddenly haggard. "Get away from the water!" he shouted, his voice hoarse with panic. Rushing to the edge of the pool he began to flog the men who were already drinking, the ones pressing forward. "It's poisoned, you fools! Get back! Get back!"

Ramose came to himself with a jolt and looked swiftly about. Already the soldiers who had been first to the water were lying doubled up on the ground, retching. The horses were neighing, the perplexed officers milling about, and the thousands flowing in from the desert, not knowing what was happening, were noisily demanding to fill their skins. When Kethuna regained control of his army, he would send scouts through the oasis to the south to see if the wells there were pure, but Ramose knew that the spiking would have been thorough, that Kamose would not have left one spring, pool or well unsullied in all the fifteen miles that comprised Uah-ta-Meh, and Kethuna and his men were doomed.

True there was another oasis at Ta-iht, a hundred miles farther south, but once there the General's army would be trapped. From Ta-iht to the Nile the distance was almost twice as that from Uah-ta-Meh, and even if the troops could endure the trek to Ta-iht without water and then by some miracle survive the even longer march to the Nile, they would emerge from the desert near Khemmenu and be faced with dragging themselves north to where Kamose waited at Het nefer Apu. No, Ramose thought, as he backed away from the chaos of vomiting, terror-stricken men, Kethuna will try to cut his losses. He will make straight for the Nile, taking the track to Het nefer Apu. And without water, most of these men will die.

Using trees and the tumble of boulders everywhere, Ramose gradually worked his way towards the deserted village. He was little better off than the soldiers who had not drunk the contaminated water, although his instinct had been to conserve the meagre supply remaining to him while the others had been almost literally pouring it onto the ground. He knew that he did not have enough to sustain him until he reached safety. He also knew that Kethuna would send officers to ransack the village for any pure water the villagers might have left, and he wanted to find it first. It would be hours before the General could re-establish any sense of order.

Going from hut to hut, Ramose searched every corner, peered into every pot, but only succeeded in adding perhaps half a cup of stale and brackish liquid to the precious drops in his water skin. He had not drunk since early morning. His whole body screamed for relief, but he knew the symptoms of a thirst that has become life-threatening and he was not yet in such extreme danger. The mud shacks were dim and cool, but he forced himself to leave them. When Kethuna came to his senses, he would want Ramose's blood, believing that Ramose had known from the beginning what Kamose would do. Walking out behind the village, Ramose found a semi-circular dune with a scattering of black rocks at its foot. Here he curled up in such shade as it afforded, digging himself a depression between sand and stones and pulling his tattered cloak over his head. He fell into an uneasy sleep.

He was woken by the sound of voices close by, and lifting a corner of his cloak he saw the desert flooded in red light. The sun was going down. The ground transmitted the vibration of the soldiers' heavy footfalls as they sought him and he lay very still, trying to breathe quietly, until they went away. Then he crawled out of his hole and came cautiously to his feet. Stiff and sore, he stood for a moment while the blood flowed back into his limbs before scrambling to the top of the dune and peering carefully down into the village and beyond it to the pool. The whole area seethed with activity but it was now brisk and purposeful. Kethuna had obviously reimposed his authority. Soldiers moved in and out of the villagers' huts and to and fro by the water, but Ramose, after observing them for a while, realized that the scene was strangely silent. No one was laughing or talking. No cooking fires had been lit. Poor devils, he thought. Are they aware yet that they are already dead? Sliding back down the dune, he unstoppered his water skin and allowed himself one scant mouthful, then he settled down to wait.

Twilight and then full darkness came. One by one the stars winked into life until eventually the great dome of the sky blazed with glimmering points of light. The moon was new, an indistinct sliver among the brilliant clusters around it. Ramose lay with his knees up and his arms outstretched, caressed by the blessed coolness of a desert night. He heard shouts now and the subdued, formless sounds of the thousands of men preparing to march. The horses were protesting, their neighing edged with an animal pleading. They would die also in a mute incomprehension somehow more pitiful than the vision of the men stumbling to their end. Kethuna was taking the only solution open to him. He was leaving the oasis while the sun was down. He would lead his army a little way south until he struck the track to Het nefer Apu and then he would head east. And I will follow, Ramose told himself. I have no intention of trudging ahead of them to perhaps be caught and put to the sword. I alone have a chance to survive. He had no desire to watch them go. He continued to lie quietly looking up at the sky until the last sound of their passing had died away.

It was hard for him to repress the urge to jump up and pursue them at once, but they would be travelling more slowly than he could alone and he had no wish to catch up to them. He was afraid to be the only living thing left in that accursed place, afraid of the heat of the day when he would have to struggle against the temptation to drink his meagre supply of water, afraid of whatever ghosts and spirits were now free to roam the oasis invisibly, but he said his prayers to Thoth, and leaving his hollow he went into the village.

Utter silence reigned. No dog howled, no tethered ox rustled, no child cried out in its sleep. The doorways gaped like black mouths and the beaten earth before them lay stark and bare in the starlight. Ramose had decided to spend the rest of the night in one of the houses but their daunting air of abandonment changed his mind. Entering one, he quickly dragged out a reed mat and a blanket he found and he passed the remaining hours until dawn under a tree.

When the first rays of the sun smote him with its fire already stoked, he retreated to a hut that welcomed him in daylight with the promise of shelter and coolness. He ate some of his bread and allowed himself another mouthful of his water. He knew better than to expend his strength by wandering about. Resigning himself to the boredom interspersed with bouts of near panic that the interminable hours of heat would bring, he sat in a corner of the bare little room and made his mind fill with thoughts of Kamose, of Tani, of the wonders of the palace at Het-Uart. He imagined himself standing in the warm humidity of a bath house, walking in a flower-burdened garden, leaning on the deck rail of Kamose's boat while the tumult of his army swirled happily around them.

Only once did he start up, his heart beating wildly, at the sound of someone's approach beyond the walls. Creeping to the doorway he peered out, but his visitor was only a goat that on seeing him bleated twice and trotted away. Goats were immune to the poison of the oleander, Ramose remembered, with an inner laugh at his moment of trepidation. Goats could and did ingest everything without harm. He wondered how Kethuna's troops were faring and the thought sobered him. He returned to his corner.

He slept again, out of boredom, not tiredness, while the day wore away, and at sunset he emerged, took bread and more water, then shouldering his pack and slinging his water skin about his neck, he set off along the path that ran down the centre of the oasis. Not until he turned onto the Het nefer Apu road did he breathe a sigh of relief, for the way had been bordered by springs choked with smashed oleander shrubs, and broken branches littered his progress.

He walked steadily in the smoother sand beside the turmoil left by the multitude of sandalled feet that had plodded over it such a short time ago. Occasionally he stumbled where the chariots had veered from the firmer earth of the track and left deep ruts. As Ra sank redly into the horizon and the desert took his colour, Ramose's shadow grew long and misshapen before him, a reassuring vanguard flowing over the hillocks and darkening furrows. Far in the distance, he thought he could discern a patch of haze that might be the rear infantry of Kethuna's miserable army, but he could not be sure. For a while when the sun had gone and the stars were still pale he doubted his way, for the light was uncertain and the whole land seemed in silent agitation, but soon the shimmer of the stars strengthened to a white, pulsing brilliance and he struck out with confidence. The air was pleasantly cool. He measured his breath and his stride carefully, not wanting to prompt a thirst, and refused to translate the irregular depressions all around him into pools of dusky water.

He had no way of telling the hour. Time meant nothing out

there where there was only rock and sand in the night. It had taken him a little more than two days to reach Het nefer Apu in a chariot. He knew that he could cover the same distance on foot in about four days if he kept up his pace and did not run out of water, but what of the soldiers? Tired, afraid and dehydrated, what would their speed be? How soon before they began to falter? He gave the survivors six days to stagger into the waiting arms of Kamose's men. And stagger they would. He smiled grimly to himself as he plodded on. Fighting would be the last thing on their minds. They would die with throats swollen with their need and the smell of the Nile in their nostrils. But I don't want to overtake them, he thought suddenly. I must resign myself to their speed and therefore ration my own water still more severely. His heart sank and all at once the soft sound of his sandals became ominous. I can do this, he told himself firmly. Providing I do not succumb to panic, I will easily be able to reach the river.

Shutting his ears to the rhythmic inexorability of his progress, he forced himself to think of Pezedkhu. It would take him approximately ten days to march his thousands from Het-Uart to Het nefer Apu. He left the city at the same time as Kethuna. If Kethuna's soldiers used up six days trudging across the desert having already spent eleven days journeying to the oasis by way of Ta-she, it meant that Pezedkhu had already been at Het nefer Apu for seven days. Had he attacked Kamose? Or, on discovering that Kamose had linked up with Paheri, would he gather in his forces and wait for the reinforcements he presumed Kethuna would bring him from the oasis? Gradually Ramose became wholly absorbed in his figures and suppositions, so that the first glimmering of dawn took him by surprise. Coming to a halt, he raised his arms and gave thanks to Ra for the god's majestic rebirth. Then, realizing that he was hungry, thirsty and very tired, he looked about for a place to lie and sleep the day away.

A cluster of rocks on his left offered him some shelter, but walking towards them he was all at once reminded of the scorpions that liked to lurk in the same shade he was seeking. He thought of their ugly bullish heads, their scuttling legs, their stiffly curved tails. With a shudder he thought of their stings and how he would grow sick and weak and be unable to walk any more if he became their victim. The intensity of his fear blinded him for a moment, but he quickly regained his sanity and berated himself. It was better to take a chance with the scorpions than lie exposed to the sun. Going forward he purposefully explored the tumbled stones, turning the smaller ones over, and finding nothing living he lay down, pulling his cloak over his head. I must be alert for a return of such dread, he thought as he closed his eyes. The desert can drive a man mad if he travels alone. Now let me sleep and forget that I want to eat and drink.

He slept deeply for a while and then more fitfully, forcing himself back into unconsciousness each time he woke and saw that the sun still shone in the sky, but at last he sat up to another sunset. Stretching, he rose and shook out his cloak. A pale scorpion tumbled to the sand and scurried back into the damp shade. With a shudder Ramose hurried back to the track. As he walked, he chewed a little dry bread and washed it down with a scant mouthful of tepid water. Neither was enough, but he felt a surge of optimism nevertheless. Once more his shadow preceded him as Ra slipped into the mouth of Nut, and twilight briefly confused him. Then it was full night and he set himself grimly to his task.

As far as he could judge by the degree of his fatigue, he had walked half the hours of darkness when the breeze brought him the acrid scent of charred wood. Coming sharply alert from the trance into which he had fallen, he peered ahead, but the desert ran on, still and silent before him. For a long time he

continued on his way with his senses straining. The odour grew
stronger. At last he could discern a huddle of angles that did
not match the harmonious flow of the dunes, but it was many
minutes until he came up to it. Then he stood and stared.

Kethuna had burned his chariots. They lay in a great mound
of smoking ruin, blackened axles pointing at the sky, splintered
shafts poking through the ashen shreds of wickerwork, great broken wheels whose spokes looked intact until Ramose gingerly
kicked one and it crumbled in a shower of hot charcoaled dust.
Twelve divisions with twenty-five chariots in each squadron,
Ramose thought. Three hundred chariots. There are the ruins of
three hundred chariots here. Gods. What Kamose could do with
them! But of course that's why the General fired them. His
plight is desperate, and he knows that if he simply abandoned
them, Kamose would send men out to retrieve them. What a
waste! Yet under Ramose's shock was a core of pure delight and
his step was lighter as he left the pitiful destruction behind.

Towards the second dawn he came across the first bodies. In
the cold grey hue that heralded Ra's approach he saw them
lying sprawled over one another, perhaps twenty of them,
before a donkey cart. There was no sign of the animal and the
water kegs it had hauled were lying in the sand, but before he
examined the corpses, Ramose went straight to the kegs. They
were not only empty but completely dry inside. Ramose
thought that they must have been left where they had fallen at
least a day ago.

Disappointed, he turned to the soldiers. These men had not
died of thirst. It was obvious to Ramose that they had fought
and killed each other over the water that had been intended for
the horses. Most of their wounds were erratic, but many of
them had died from the arrows still protruding from their
chests. So Kethuna is managing to maintain some discipline,
Ramose thought as he systematically ransacked the bodies. I

presume that his officers were ordered to distribute whatever water was left in the kegs but the men were too thirsty to accept the dribble they received and they began to attack one another. After all there was no water at the oasis to fill the horses' supply. Horses drink a great deal and I would wager that almost nothing remained of the hekets taken on at Ta-she. Not enough for six thousand men, let alone sixty thousand. Poor Setiu. Poor Delta lovers. And poor Ramose, he finished mockingly as he tossed the last water skin away. Not a drop for me. They could have waited to tear each other apart until at least a few of them had lined up to get what I need so badly. I have worked through them for nothing. I am sweating and exhausted and they are forcing me to keep going until they are well out of sight, for the hyenas and vultures will come to feast on them with the morning and I do not want to rest where I can hear them being consumed.

Frustrated and resigned, he walked on into the increasing glare of the rising sun. At last, glancing back for the hundredth time, he realized that there was nothing to see any more. He was too tired to seek shelter. Anger made him reckless. Taking two swallows of water from his goat skin, he lay down where he had stopped, twitched his cloak over his face, and went to sleep.

In the evening he ate a little and moistened his mouth, briefly regretting his rashness of the morning as the skin hung flaccid from his grasp. Then he dismissed the thought and set off. He was already tired and dispirited. His stomach growled a protest at the unappetizing bread and it came to him that he might be better advised to throw the remainder away, seeing that it could only make him thirstier. He had no fear of marching hungry. Only the lack of water could kill him now.

It was not long before he came upon the first of the horses. It lay in the harsh blaze of starlight, a black hump angled across the track. Ramose presumed that it had fallen from dehydration until he bent close to it and saw that its jugular had been neatly and deeply sliced open. There were a few patches of dark sand where it had bled, but not enough for the copious flow of blood that would have spurted forth. Straightening, Ramose looked about. More animals lay at random among the rocks and pounded sand. All of them had suffered the same fate. Ramose circled them thoroughly before setting off east again. He did not need a seer to tell him what had happened. The fools had slit the horses' throats and drunk their blood. Well, it will not quench their thirst for long, he thought grimly. Blood is salty. All they have done is lengthen their agony and shorten their lives. Did Kethuna allow this or is he pressing on as fast as possible, leaving the stragglers to fend for themselves? And how soon will I begin to encounter a living rearguard? I do not want to overtake the soldiers. If I do, they will certainly kill me. But if I slow my pace, I am in danger of dying anyway. I am almost out of water. He cursed aloud, mentally shrugged his shoulders, and kept walking.

He had hoped to breathe more freely once the pitiful, drained remnants of the horses were left behind, but from then on he was not alone. He began to pass through a grotesque and silent company made more sinister by the stark contrast of form and shadow lying over the desert. Dead men lay haphazardly everywhere. Stiff fingers dug into the sand, cold eyes reflecting the starlight, some even propped against each other in a ghoulish imitation of comradeship, they populated the dreaming expanse with a motionless pollution. It was as though a war had been fought between human beings and some malevolent supernatural power able to slay without a blow.

And that is a kind of truth, Ramose mused, as he glided slowly, too slowly, through that horror-filled landscape. They have provoked the desert itself. I did not do this to you! he spoke in his mind to the bewildered ghosts he felt drifting around him. Blame the ignorance and idiocy of your superiors and the callous brilliance of my Lord, not me! Walking, praying, and doing his best to quell the spurts of panic rising in him, he stumbled towards the dawn.

Though the sun rose, Ramose did not pause until compelled by sheer exhaustion to do so. It was the beginning of his fourth day out from the oasis. If he had been fully victualled and moving fast, he might have seen the horizon broken into the blessed outline of palms heralding the verges of the Nile. As it was, he had no idea how far Het nefer Apu might be. In spite of his feverish desire to escape from the mute army surrounding him, he knew he must deliberately slow his pace. It was too much to hope that all sixty thousand of Kethuna's troops would perish out here. He tried to estimate the number of sand-blown corpses spread out on either side of his way, but it was impossible. There seemed no end to them. Baking stiffly in the heat, swelling under an indifferent sun, they offered themselves as fodder for hyenas and vultures—and for Kamose. Their useless weapons, already half-buried, glinted impotently around them.

To try and sleep in their midst was inconceivable. Ramose was even loath to take his eyes from them for fear they might rise and come creeping silently towards him. This terror he could not overcome. Draping his cloak over a rock, he sat with his back against the hot stone and his knees hunched up, the tattered garment drawn down to his eyebrows, and watched the cautious approach of the desert scavengers.

Several times he dozed, only to be jerked awake with his heart pounding, to see the hyenas slinking between the bodies with full mouths and hear the vultures croaking from their perches on leather-clad scalps. He forced himself to stay where he was until just before sunset, knowing now that he would not walk out of the carnage until he left the desert behind. Still, it was with thankfulness that he at last got up and gave his own body something to do. He did not eat. Throwing the bread away, he drank the last of his water, emptied his pack of everything but his dagger and the skin from which he might manage to squeeze a few more drops, and forced himself forward. His head had begun to throb with every step and his sweat was cold. He knew the warning signs of extreme fatigue. If I die out here, the gods will not find me, he thought. Without beautification I will not reach the paradise of Osiris. I can only hope that Kamose remembers to have my name carved in some place where it cannot be defaced.

He did not imagine that he could endure anything more, but in the deepest night, when he had paused and bent down to retie a loose sandal, someone whispered. For a moment Ramose was frozen, not daring to stand straight, not even daring to move his eyes. The sound was repeated faintly, the calling of a phantom, and there was a tiny movement to Ramose's right. He turned his head. Living eyes met his. The man's parched lips twitched. "Water," he breathed. Ramose knelt beside him.

"I have none," he said clearly. "You must believe me. I am sorry. I drank the last of my own some hours ago." He did not know why he felt the urge to justify his denial to the dying man. After all, he had spoken nothing but the truth. "Who is your god?" he asked. The mouth opened and closed but no sound emerged. The eyes begged with incomprehension. Ramose got up abruptly and left him.

He was only the first. From then on Ramose heard the croaks and whispers of the dying and he knew that the survivors of Kethuna's army were not far ahead. His suspicion was confirmed when yet another dawn began to fill the sky, for limned against the rising sun ahead of him was a cloud of red dust. In its midst he could discern crowds of black figures. The earth around him continued to be littered with the dead and near-dead, discarded weapons and rifled packs. He felt nothing as he plodded after the living and it was with mild surprise that he found his legs giving way before he had made a conscious decision to rest. Very well, he told them tenderly. We will try to sleep now. He stretched out where they had decreed, and covered his face with his hands. He could smell the dead but he no longer cared.

It was full night when he came out of a drugged insensibility. His body ached. Sharp pains shot down his legs and through his hips as he rose trembling. Give us water! his throat, his stomach, his bowels cried. His tongue was as dry as papyrus against his teeth. Not yet, he told them sternly. We must walk first. We must earn our drink. Swaying, grimacing, he battled to regain control of his mind and then his body. It was hard stepping into the fierce hatred of the stars, but he did it, haltingly at first but then with greater ease. Surely I have two more days in me, he thought. I remember calculating six days for the army to stagger to the river. Today, tonight, yes, tonight is my fifth night. I can do this. He made it a chant for his feet, I can do this, I can do this, and lowering his head, he ploughed on.

He had no idea how long he had been walking before he came to himself with a shock and realized he had no memory of the hours since sunset. The scene looked no different. Have I been moving at all, he asked himself, or have I been standing dazed in the same place? Moving, of course, he said firmly, and indeed there were subtle signs that he had covered some ground. A light wind brought to his nostrils, sensitive now to the slightest hint of moisture, the faintest whiff of humidity out of the east where the track ran on monotonously. Something was missing, however, and with gladness he saw that the desert was clean again. No bodies corrupted the air or the ground. The soldiers who had been fortunate enough to be given the horses' water or wise enough to refrain from drinking before entering the doomed oasis, had won through. So there will be a

battle of sorts, Ramose thought, engaged in trying to coerce his
foot to lift and set itself down in front of the other. Unless
Kethuna surrenders at once. No use in that. Kamose will ignore.
He will slaughter. The foot rose. Ramose smiled. The other foot
followed. He walked on, not knowing that he was meandering
like a drunken man.

The sun rose but Ramose was aware of it only as an increased
discomfort. Teeth clenched, his mind clinging tenuously to the
merest thread of sanity, he struggled on, hardly knowing why
any more. He did not look up. When it seemed to him that the
glaring sand was closer to his face than it should have been, he
realized that he had fallen. His legs did not want to get up, so
he let them stay where they were. Groping for his cloak, he
could not find it, nor his pack either. He did not remember losing them. He lay with his cheek pressed into the hot sand, listening to a dull roar coming to him from somewhere far ahead.
Men's shouts and screams pierced the din, all of it muffled by
distance and the sound of his own frail breath. I hear Het nefer
Apu, he thought dimly, incoherently. I hear the Nile flowing. I
hear my Lord joining with the Setiu at last. You nearly saved
yourself, Ramose son of Teti. You nearly did. You did everything
you could but it was not quite enough.

He fell into a stupor in which Kamose was offering him a
bowl of sparkling water with both hands. He could not quite
reach it and His Majesty was becoming impatient. "What is
wrong with you, Ramose?" he was asking. "I thought you were
thirsty." No, Ramose thought. I am only sleepy. But Kamose
would not let him sleep. "This one's not dead," Kamose said.
"Finish him quickly and then let's find some shade to sit out the
rest of the day until the fighting stops. Listen to the noise!"

"Wait," another voice said. "I recognize him. He's no Setiu.
It's the Noble Ramose. I've scouted with him. What is he doing
half-dead out here? Hand me the water skin and then pitch

the tent. If we let him die, the King will have strong words to say to us."

Drowsily Ramose opened his eyes. He was lying on his back. A man's shadow was falling over him. Something bumped gently against his sore lips and he was forced to part them. Water gushed into his mouth. He swallowed frantically then turned his head to one side and vomited into the sand. "Careful!" the man warned. "Sip it, Ramose, or it will kill you." Ramose did as he was told. He had not had his fill before the skin was taken away. Capable hands lifted him by the shoulders and dragged him into the shelter of a tent. He wanted to ask for more water but he was too tired.

# Chapter ELEVEN

KAMOSE SAT ON A small hillock of tufted grass in the sparse shade of a spindly tamarisk, his knees drawn up under his chin, his anxious gaze on the shimmering expanse of desert to his left. Before him his chariot gleamed hotly, the two horses standing patiently with heads down, the charioteer squatting beside them. To his right, where the track disappeared into the kinder depths of palm trunks and irrigated vegetation before reaching Het nefer Apu and the river, his brother and Hor-Aha also waited, the General cross-legged and motionless, Ahmose idly piling small twigs into a haphazard pattern and humming tunelessly under his breath.

Eleven days after Ramose had left the oasis, word had come back that he had entered Het-Uart. That was a month and one week ago. Pharmuthi had come and gone and now it was Pakhons. The fields around Het nefer Apu, showing the first tender and tentative shoots of new crops when Kamose and his brother had driven through them on their way to Uah-ta-Meh, were now thickly lush with the tall green promise of a good harvest, but Kamose had paid them little heed on his return.

Seventeen days after Ramose had vanished into the ant heap that was Apepa's city, a weary scout had reported a host approaching Ta-she from the north. Apepa had taken the bait. Kamose, tense with worry and excitement, had questioned the scout brusquely outside his tent. "How great is the force?" he demanded.

"I judge it to be approximately the size of Your Majesty's army quartered here," the man answered, his voice gravelled with fatigue. "It was difficult to make a more accurate assessment without risking capture." Kamose nodded.

"Had they moved off before you left?"

"Yes." The scout grinned, his face breaking into grit-streaked lines of pleasure. "I shadowed them for the day it took them to fill their waterskins and the barrels for the horses. As soon as they left Ta-she and struck out along the track south, I ran. That was a day and a half ago." Kamose regarded him in silence for a moment. He had travelled a hundred miles on foot in thirty-six hours. Had he even stopped to sleep? "They will make good time, Majesty," the man went on. "They will be here in another three days." Panic shot through Kamose and was gone.

"Who is commanding them?" he asked.

"I am sorry, I was not able to discover what General is with them," the scout apologized. He was swaying on his feet. Kamose dismissed him, telling him to rest for as long as he needed, and turned to Hor-Aha, who had come up behind him.

"You heard?"

"Yes, Majesty. We must move on at once."

"See to it then." He had wanted to say more, to share the excitement rising in him, to indulge in the flood of conjecture filling his mind, but Hor-Aha was already striding away in a flurry of shouted orders. Kamose paused before sending one of the ever-present bodyguards to find Ahmose, his eyes narrowing as he scanned the hot, placid desert with its rows of tents stretching away beyond the pool and the sparse shrubs and the motley cluster of village huts.

So Ramose had fulfilled his mission. Where was he now? Hiding with Tani in some anonymous place close to Egypt's eastern border? Dead, perhaps? Or was he being forced to march with Apepa's army? Already the sounds of an imminent departure had begun to fill the air. Kamose saw a chariot thunder south along the path linking the two villages of the oasis. The tents that a moment ago were sitting like a vast collection of tiny pyramids were now disgorging streams of men before trembling and collapsing in puffs of dust. Closer in, the area around the pool began to fill with men whose officers had shepherded them into obedient lines. Kneeling, they held their water skins below the surface of the water, and Kamose knew that everywhere, at every spring, well and pond, the same ritual would be carried out in the next few hours until every one of his fifty thousand men had enough water to reach the Nile. It was a pity, he thought, as he ordered his guard to search for his brother amid the increasing turmoil, that the Setiu troops would soon be doing exactly the same thing. How much more satisfying it would be if somehow they could be deprived of what they would need most when they arrived. Calling for a stool, he sat and watched.

It was not long before Ahmose joined him, putting a hand on his shoulder as he lowered himself onto the ground beside Kamose. "I heard the news," he said. "It will take the Princes the rest of the day to muster the troops, victual them, have all the supplies replenished and packed. We can march at dawn tomorrow. Why has Apepa only sent a contingent whose number matches our own, Kamose?"

"I have been wondering the same thing," Kamose confessed. "It appears to be an arrogant and very stupid move on his part. I don't like the feel of it."

"Neither do I." Ahmose shifted uneasily in the sand. "There is only one explanation. He has divided his army and sent the other half upriver to Het nefer Apu to engage Paheri and Baba Abana, defeat the navy before we can reinforce it with the infantry, and so catch us between a hostile force behind us and one in front, waiting for us to emerge from the desert."

"He is surely not capable of such subtle thinking," Kamose said slowly.

"No," Ahmose cut in. "But Pezedkhu is. I am afraid of that man, Kamose." Kamose looked down on his brother's bent head.

"So am I," he agreed. "Well, all we can do is keep to our plan. It is too late to formulate another. I wish that there was some way in which we could weaken the army coming after us. I have confidence in Hor-Aha's training, and of course the Setiu will be tired, but will weariness be enough to tip the scales in our favour? If you are correct in your assumption, if we arrive at Het nefer Apu to find Paheri and Abana overcome, it will not. The odds will be two to one against us."

Ahmose did not reply and a gloomy silence fell between them, isolating them from the orderly chaos going on around the pool. Soldiers with skins at the ready pushed and jostled those already backing away from the water. Officers standing at the edge were shouting, donkeys tethered to the trees behind, infected with the confusion, had set up a raucous braying. Even as Kamose watched, an officer sporting the armbands of an Instructor of Retainers was accidentally elbowed by a man struggling away from the water. The officer teetered, grasped for one of the sturdy oleander bushes growing on the verge of the pool, and managed to regain his balance. Cursing, he began to examine his hand and forearm while others waded into the water and quickly retrieved the few spear-like leaves that had been pulled from the bush and now floated innocently on the surface.

Kamose felt himself go cold, then hot, and at the same moment Ahmose gave an exclamation and clutched at his thigh. He looked up and their eyes met. Ahmose raised his eyebrows. Kamose nodded. His heart had begun to pound. Turning, he shouted, "Ankhmahor!" After a minute the Captain of his Followers appeared, emerging from the shadowed entrance of his tent. Kamose rose. He found himself trembling. "Choose senior officers, men who will understand the purpose of these instructions," he said urgently. "Send them to every spring, well and pond in the oasis. Detail one to go into each village. As soon as every man has filled his water skin and the barrels for the horses are full as well, I want the oleanders cut down, ripped up, and tossed into the water. Do whatever is necessary to make sure that all sources are contaminated. All sources, Ankhmahor. Not one must be missed or we might as well not bother. Crush the bushes so that the sap oozes out. Make sure that the soldiers do not approach the water afterwards. And no one is to drink from their skins until the first halt tomorrow so that there is no waste tonight." Ankhmahor had listened with barely concealed astonishment, but by the time Kamose had finished speaking his expression had become grim.

"You are condemning them to almost certain death if they cannot quench their thirst here, Majesty," he said. "It will be a cruel end."

"War is cruel," Kamose replied curtly. "I know that you have considered the implications of the number sent against us here. We must increase our advantage by any means possible." The Prince bowed and strode away.

"What of the villagers, Kamose?" Ahmose had come to stand beside him. "Without water they will die too."

"It is their misfortune to be caught in the centre of this brutality," Kamose said roughly. "What would you have me do, Ahmose? Leave them a spring somewhere? That would be ridiculous. The Setiu would waste no time in sucking it dry and then crawling after us refreshed and ready to pound us into oblivion."

"I know. But if you abandon the peasants to such a terrible fate, you will incur the contempt of every common soldier in your army, let alone the Princes, who will begin to debate their decision to trust you. They strongly disapproved of the slaughter of last year. You will make more enemies than you already have. Please, Kamose!" Kamose found himself once again battling the rage that seemed to be always simmering just under the border of his control. I don't care, Ahmose! he wanted to shout. Don't make me care! I cannot afford such a gentle emotion! But as he had so often done, he swallowed the madness and faced his brother calmly.

"Then what would you have me do?" he repeated.

"Order a few men to see that the villagers pack up their belongings, gather up their animals, and march with us. They are hardy folk, these oasis dwellers. They will not hinder us. They are innocents, Kamose. They do not deserve such a fate." And neither did the inhabitants of Dashlut or any of the other villages you ordered razed, his eyes said. Or am I imagining his accusation? Kamose thought. Does he even suspect the pain I endured last year and learned to dull with the opiate of necessity?

"You are right," he made himself say. "You can see to it, Ahmose." Then he smiled. "Spiking the water supply with oleander was a inspiration sent directly from Amun to both of us, was it not?" Ahmose's face broke into an answering grin.

"It was indeed!" he said. "Now let us quit this arid place and give Apepa the thrashing he deserves!"

By evening the mustering was complete. All day the troops had been dribbling in from the farther reaches of the oasis where they had been billeted, an orderly stream of sun-hardened men carrying weapons as familiar to them now as the hoes and winnowing flails they had once wielded. Obedient to their officers, they ranged themselves along the eastern track in their several divisions, and sitting on their wooden shields, fell to gambling and gossiping as they waited for night.

Just after sunset Ankhmahor returned to Kamose to report that Uah-ta-Meh's water supply was now undrinkable. Kamose acknowledged the news coolly. He knew that he did not need to press the Prince. The pool before which he now paced was choked with the debris of the dying plants and the petals of the flowers rocked gently on the darkening surface, still glimmering white in the fast-fading light.

The tent the brothers had shared would not be struck until dawn, and as Ankhmahor deployed the Followers around it and Kamose and Ahmose turned to enter its welcoming shelter, there was a commotion on the far side of the pool. With a snap of his fingers Ankhmahor directed two of his men to investigate. Kamose watched as the brawny soldiers walked to the place where a half-naked peasant was shouting at the officers who were holding him. After a moment the Followers returned. "It is the headman of this village, Majesty," one of them began to explain. "He wishes to speak to you."

"Then let him come." At the guard's call, the officers released the man, who immediately sped across the cooling sand and fell in an ungainly heap at the brothers' feet. "Get up," Kamose said impatiently. "What do you want?" Before rising, the man planted a kiss on Kamose's dusty sandal. Kamose found himself looking into a leathery, seamed face and one sunken brown eye. The other peered at him sightlessly, a pale blue, filmy orb.

"Majesty, Great One, Favourite of the Gods," the man blurted. "It is not for me to question your inscrutable judgements for you are infallible, chosen by the immortal ones . . ."

"I have not eaten since this morning," Kamose broke in, "and my meal sits within, getting cold. What do you want?" The headman pursed his lips and looked at the ground.

"The people of my village have lived in harmony with your

soldiers for many months," he stammered. "We have shared meat, grain and water. We have not stolen from them. And in return they taint our pools and command us to leave our crops and our homes and follow them into the wasteland. We are bewildered and afraid. What is to become of us? What is your immaculate purpose for us, Beloved of the God of Weset?" Ahmose tensed and opened his mouth to speak but Kamose held out a hand and forestalled him.

"The God of Weset is Amun the Great Cackler," Kamose responded equably. "Today you have learned something new, headman. As for your concerns, it was necessary to taint the water. I do not need to explain myself to you but I choose to do so. A force of Setiu is on its way here to your precious oasis to destroy me and very probably you. By poisoning the water, I trap them. I had no wish to condemn innocent Egyptians to certain death also; therefore I ordered the evacuation of your village. When we reach Het nefer Apu you will be placed in the care of the mayor of that town." The headman swallowed, his adam's apple working convulsively against the scrawny skin of his neck.

"But, Majesty, we do not want to live by the Nile. How soon may we return to our homes here?" Kamose sighed.

"Find one of the army physicians and ask him when the waters will be cleansed," he said. "It is that or die of thirst. Be grateful that I have spared a thought for your fate in the midst of weightier matters." Signalling to one of the listening Followers, he turned towards the glow of lamps spilling out of the tent. "Well?" he snapped at Ahmose, as they sat before the laden table and Akhtoy moved to serve them. "Are you satisfied? Was I magnanimous enough? Will the peasants love me now?" His tone was savage. Ahmose held out his cup to be filled and did not answer.

They had crossed the desert in four days without mishap and

were welcomed eagerly by Paheri and Abana. Kamose ordered the army bivouacked on the edge of the cultivation, set up a strong perimeter of sentries, and ordered scouts back along the track to watch for the approach of any Setiu survivors. No word as to Ramose's fate had come to Paheri. Kamose knew that if his friend had managed to escape, he would have found a way to let him know; therefore it was likely that Ramose marched with the Setiu and would perish with them. Yet Ramose is no fool, Kamose told himself as he sat outside Paheri's tent in the shadow of the ships while the daily reports were read to him. If anyone can win through, he will. I must put him out of my mind for the present and concentrate on what is, not what might be.

For one day he and Ahmose moved among the troops that had been left at Het nefer Apu, met with all the Princes and the commanders of both arms of the army to discuss every contingency of engagement should a large force of Setiu win through to the Nile, dictated letters to the women at Weset, and swam and drew bow together.

Then Pezedkhu had come. Just before dawn on the second day, Kamose was woken by a hand on his shoulder. Ankhmahor's worried face loomed in the dimness and a taller shadow filled the tent's opening. At once Kamose sat up. Ahmose was groaning and reaching for the water by his cot. A flame flared, momentarily blinding them. Akhtoy replaced the now burning lamp. Ankhmahor bowed. "Majesty, the enemy is here," he said without preamble. "Your scout waits to give you the details. I have taken the liberty of alerting all your commanders. Hor-Aha is already outside."

"Bring him in." Kamose ran a furred tongue over his teeth. As he stood, Akhtoy quickly wrapped a kilt around his waist then turned to Ahmose. The scout stepped up and bowed, and behind him Hor-Aha's black face appeared suddenly in the yellow light, his hooded eyes swollen with sleep, his thick braids dishevelled. "Speak," Kamose invited the scout. The man nodded.

"Majesty, it is the General Pezedkhu," he said. "He sits just north of here with perhaps ten divisions. At present he is deploying his troops west to east from the edge of the desert to the river, with the bulk of his army concentrated by the desert. His sentries and ours are so close to each other that they could exchange conversation if they shouted. He has a full complement of chariots. You can hear the horses if you walk twenty paces along the riverbank. There is no attempt at secrecy." Kamose folded his arms, cradling his naked chest. The air in the tent was chilly.

"How do you know it is Pezedkhu?" he demanded.

"I stripped off my insignia, left my weapons with one of my soldiers, tied back my hair, and joined the townsmen who had begun to congregate to see what was going on," the man said laconically. "There does not seem to be any desire to come to battle readiness yet. I had no opportunity to talk to any of the Setiu. The officers soon drove us all away."

"Thank you," Kamose managed. "You can go. Hor-Aha, direct the Princes to gather outside Paheri's tent. Akhtoy, rouse the cooks. We need hot food. On the way, tell Ipi to wait on us with the army scribes. Send in my body servant." The steward bowed and left with Hor-Aha. Ahmose, Kamose and Ankh-mahor were left. For a long moment they simply stared at one another. Then Ahmose blew out his cheeks.

"Why has Pezedkhu not attacked?" he wondered aloud.

"Because his scouts are in every way as good as ours," Kamose replied. "He has been told that the infantry is here, not at the oasis. He knows that no engagement took place there. If he had arrived before us, he would have attacked Paheri and been victorious, then he would have sat and waited for either the other half of Apepa's force to arrive from Uah-ta-Meh having defeated us, or for us to march out of the desert with that same force behind us and an equally large army in front. As it is, he has calculated his odds and found them wanting. He has his sixty thousand men. We now have a combined force of eighty thousand."

"He will consolidate his position," Ankhmahor put in. "He will do nothing until his fellows join him."

"And if all goes as we planned, they are even now dying of thirst," Ahmose remarked with an uncharacteristic relish that betrayed both his fear of the Setiu General and his relief that the odds were now overwhelmingly in the Egyptians' favour.

"We can be sure that the plan to trap us in a pincer was not Apepa's," Kamose said. He was rubbing his upper arms vigorously. "Gods, it is cold this morning! Leave us, Ankhmahor." The body servant had entered and was waiting with a bowl of steaming water. Behind him his assistant carried towels. Akhtoy had returned and was laying out clean linen. As the Prince lifted the tent flap, Kamose saw his frame clearly outlined against the sky beyond. The sun was rising.

Less than an hour later, washed, dressed and shod, the brothers joined the crowd of commanders waiting in front of Paheri's tent. As they were reverenced, Kamose noted the bent back of Abana's son Kay. "What are you doing here?" he addressed him sharply, taking his seat and motioning the others to do the same around the large table. The young man smiled at him apologetically but with a hint of polite defiance.

"They say that the Setiu General has a fleet of powerful ships hidden on the Nile, Majesty," he replied. "If my marines are to engage the enemy, I want to be well prepared."

"The ship *North* turned in the worst performance of all during the mock battle," Kamose remarked dryly. "Besides, it is not true. Pezedkhu brought no ships. The Medjay and the marines will be fighting on land. And you, Kay Abana, are not a senior commander. Stop wasting my time here." The other men were listening to the exchange with barely concealed and superior smiles. All at once Kamose felt sorry for Kay. "Still, you are a talented ship's captain, highly regarded by your superiors," he conceded. "You may stay as long as your mouth remains closed. Now have us served, Akhtoy. We will debate our situation while we eat."

As food was placed before them, Kamose related the report, and they had barely begun the meal when they were interrupted by the first in a steady stream of scouts bringing a swiftly multiplying picture of Pezedkhu's deployments. The General was not preparing an attack. As Kamose had surmised, he was posting sentries and sending out a stream of his own scouts who would bring him word when the rest of Apepa's army appeared. "I want the Medjay off the boats and free to manoeuvre in the desert," Kamose told Hor-Aha. "They will harry the flanks of whatever force does come from the west. Paheri, the remaining marines must stay on the river to strengthen my eastern detachments should Pezedkhu try to push through that way. Intef, Mesehti, Iasen, your troops and most of the chariots are to muster along the edge of the fields, looking west. I am not so concerned with the ground in between. It is very difficult to push across fields of crops slashed with irrigation canals and lines of trees. But we will have a small force placed north of the town just in case. I do not think it will be needed. Pezedkhu will come against us in an arc, heavy at either end and thin in the centre. His western arm will contain the bulk of his troops."

While he was speaking, the area in which the men sat became gradually full of limpid morning light. A breeze sprang up, the air tinged with a warmth that would rapidly grow to heat, and the surrounding vegetation rustled and quivered at its touch. All along the bank the soldiers were rising, moving towards the water to wash, and the cooking fires of the night before were being coaxed back into life. For a while Kamose answered the Princes' questions as the details of their deployments were elucidated, then he dismissed them to their duties and they scattered. "Will you attempt to parley with Pezedkhu?" Ahmose asked him as they left the table and walked along the shade-dappled track to their tent, the Followers around them. Kamose glanced across at him sharply.

"No, of course not. What purpose would talking serve?" he asked. Ahmose shrugged.

"I'm not sure. It was just a fleeting thought. Pezedkhu, more than his master, will know that all of Egypt but for the Delta is in our hands. He might be persuaded to change sides." Kamose chuckled, startled. "It is an interesting idea," he replied. "But I suspect that the General is a loyal man. It would be as if Apepa tried to corrupt Hor-Aha. Beyond imagination. Let us see what happens in the next few days. If we enjoy a total victory, we will shake Pezedkhu's confidence and perhaps his fidelity also. Let us set up our own watch in the sand, Ahmose, but first we must pray."

That had been two days ago. Now Kamose, trying to quell his irritation at the sound of his brother's formless humming, sighed inwardly. Pezedkhu had made no further moves. The dust cloud sent up by the daily activities of his army hung in the distance like a mildly menacing threat, neither growing nor abating. His scouts could often be spotted, black specks that trembled far away on a horizon distorted by the heat and the glare of light on the desert dunes. Kamose's scouts ranged those miles also, gaining solidity as they approached him and then slowly vanishing back into the wasteland after reports that held little substance.

After so many hours spent peering towards the oasis, Kamose's eyes had begun to trouble him, but he was reluctant to relinquish his perch, and he knew that all his men, from Ankh-mahor to the lowliest infantryman, felt the same undercurrent of tension. He also knew that none of them could maintain this attitude of interior watchfulness coupled with physical inactivity for much longer. The edge of their battle-readiness would become blunted. Fear of the unknown would creep in and fantasies would begin to weaken them.

Each morning Kamose held a meeting with his commanders and the Princes, but there was little to say. All preparations for engagement were complete, and Kamose was beginning to wonder secretly what he would do if Pezedkhu simply continued to sit there passively, if the army trudging from the oasis by some miracle did not arrive at all. Would he himself take the initiative and attack the General? The prospect was enticing. His fingers ached to draw his bow. The weapons hanging from his belt, dagger and sword, protested their impotence. If he shifted his gaze from the shimmering sand, he could see his men strung out thickly along the irregular line where green met beige, thousands of them sitting or lying in the scant shade of the palms and acacia, gossiping, gambling, dozing under the eye of the patrolling officers, all of them waiting, like him.

But, at last, in the middle of the afternoon of the third day, when the citizens of Het nefer Apu lay on their cots sleeping away the worst of the heat and Kamose's head swam with the need to join them, he saw a chariot come careening along the track, its spokes flashing in the sun. It came up to his knoll and halted in a shower of dirt, the horses lathered and panting, and the scout jumped from its rear and ran towards him. Kamose came to his feet. "They are here, Lord!" the man shouted. "Two hours away but no more! They are in terrible condition! It will be like killing cattle in a pen!" Kamose felt the drowsiness seep away. His head cleared and his heart settled to a steady, strong stroke. Ahmose and Hor-Aha had come up to stand beside him.

"How many?" Kamose barked back. The man was almost dancing in his excitement.

"Not enough!" he called. "You will take the day, Majesty! My horses need water. Give me leave?" Kamose dismissed him and turned to Hor-Aha. The black eyes squinting into his were alight, the white teeth gleaming between parted lips.

"It worked, General," Kamose breathed. "It worked. Alert the commanders. Get the Medjay moving. I want them circling out there to keep the enemy bunched together as they approach the river. Send to Paheri to stand ready, and form up my divisions here on the track. Warn the officers closest to Pezedkhu's forces first. He will have received the news also and I expect him to strike quickly." Ahmose was already striding away and yelling for his chariot. They had argued regarding Ahmose's place in the forthcoming clash. Kamose had wanted him to lead the divisions that would in a very short time be pouring out onto the desert but Ahmose had wrinkled up his nose in disgust. "I do not want to be safe," he had retorted in answer to Kamose's importuning. "I intend to captain the divisions facing Pezedkhu unless you give me a direct order to the contrary, O Mighty Bull. Stop trying to protect me!" Kamose had given in with poor grace and he regretted it now, watching his brother swing himself up behind the charioteer and the vehicle wheel away in the direction of the massed and hostile forces to the north.

Well, it was too late to reverse any orders now. Already the long line of men to his right was wavering and re-forming as the soldiers scrambled for their weapons and began to converge on the track under the yells of the officers. More men had begun to pour out from the trees behind Kamose, the crowd parting as the chariots raced through it to roll ahead. Kamose walked down to join them, and seeing him come, his own charioteer picked up the reins. Kamose sprang up behind him and at a word they began to move to the forefront of the noisy throng.

The horizon to the west was no longer clear. It was marred by a wavering grey haze. Kamose imagined that he could discern shapes within it, but their nature was not yet clear. Did any horses survive? he wondered anxiously. Chariots? How many officers are still on their feet? Are they captained at all or have they become nothing but a rabble? And is Ramose among them? He had no more time for conjecture. Hor-Aha's chariot had come abreast. "All the divisions are moving into their appointed positions, Majesty," he called across. "Pezedkhu's men have also come to readiness but as yet no arrows have been fired. His Highness has control on the northern front. Scouts are hurrying into the enemy's area." Kamose acknowledged the General with a gesture. Pezedkhu is learning even now that the tables have been turned against him, he thought. Now he is the one outnumbered. Will he act rashly, throw himself at us? If he does, then Ahmose will be fighting the real battle.

The cacophony around him was abating. The officers' orders came crisp and clear in the hot air, a chorus of calm, controlled voices. To right and left his squadrons rolled, and behind him as he glanced back the divisions marched, the sun glinting off the forest of spears and sliding along the blades of the thousands of drawn swords. Pride swelled in him. You have done this, Seqenenra my father, he thought with a lump in his throat. These men, these sturdy brown Egyptians marching steadily towards victory with their black hair swinging and their white kilts swirling, are here because you dared to defy the power of the usurpers. Your vision has transformed the face of this country, turning peasants into soldiers and lifting the shamefaced gaze of Princes from the ground to the rich vista of a rediscovered dignity.

Sweat began to trickle from beneath the rim of his helmet

and he raised one gloved hand and wiped it away. Reaching behind him, he withdrew an arrow, holding it loosely, his eyes on the distance where the haze blurred the sky. The shapes within it were now clearly men but how many and in what condition he could not say.

He could see the Medjay now, strung out and loping effortlessly ahead of the chariots. Here on their own ground, their bare feet impervious to the burning sand, they looked like lean black hyenas. Even as he watched, Hor-Aha's chariot broke away and began to angle to the right. Leaning forward, he spoke to his own charioteer and their vehicle veered left, away from the track, Ankhmahor and the Followers turning with them.

Now Kamose could see the full panorama of the impending engagement, Medjay in seeming disarray but moving to outflank the enemy, chariots spread out to either side, and in the middle the infantry, rank upon rank of marchers churning the earth in their inexorable progress. Kamose spared one thought for his brother then pushed the familiar protective concern away. Ahmose would command well, and he was supported by fine officers and disciplined men.

Someone began to sing, the light tenor voice rising above the creak of harness and the low swell of the thousands of plodding sandals. "My sword is sharp but my weapon is the vengeance of Wepwawet. My shield is on my arm but my protection is the power of Amun. Truly the gods are with me and I shall once again feel the waters of the Nile embrace my body when the enemy of my Lord lies lifeless at my feet ..." Others took up the words, the song swelling through the ranks. Kamose smiled across at the captain of his bodyguard.

"That is no farmer's song, Ankhmahor," he called. "It belongs to the serving soldier." Ankhmahor grinned back.

"They are all soldiers now, Majesty," he answered, his words almost drowned in the flood of music. But before long a command for silence rang out and the stirring sounds died away.

Now Kamose's attention was no longer on the cloud of dust but on its cause, a wide body of men coming slowly towards him, engulfing the track and the sand to either side. At first Kamose felt a twinge of fear, for they appeared to be marching in formation, but as they drew closer he saw that they were stumbling over hummocks of land any healthy soldier would have ignored and their pace was painfully ragged. As he watched, he clearly heard an order issue from somewhere in their front ranks and swords were drawn, but the actions were clumsy and unco-ordinated and Kamose distinctly noted one man on the outer perimeter who was desperately and drunkenly trying to obey without the strength to pull the weapon free of his belt.

They are almost spent, Kamose thought with a rush of uncharacteristic pity. I should order them surrounded and disarmed, it would not be difficult, but then how to feed them and what to do with them afterwards? Besides, my men crave action, they need to fight, and I need to send an uncompromising message to Apepa.

The Medjay were now ranged in a half-circle to either side of the enemy, bows unslung and arrows fixed. Hor-Aha's chariot had slowed and Hor-Aha himself stood looking in Kamose's direction, his arm raised, waiting. Kamose lifted his own arm, for one moment powerfully aware of the relentless force of the sun, pouring heat and a dazzling light on the glistening sand, of the grim silence that had fallen on his troops, of the salty taste of sweat on his lips, then he gestured. With a shout Hor-Aha signalled the Medjay and his cry was answered by a roar issuing from the throats of his tribesmen. Kamose turned and his sign was acknowledged. Hoarse shouts filled the air, and with a howl his army flung itself on the Setiu.

It was no battle but a slaughter of men half-insane with thirst, weak and emaciated, who dazedly tried to obey the commands of officers as exhausted and confused as they. Staggering and reeling, swords dangling from shaking hands, they were cut down remorselessly. Kamose, watching the brutal massacre from his chariot, felt nothing as all the pent-up frustration of his troops was released in one deafening torrent of bloodlust and the Setiu fell in their hundreds, scarcely uttering a sound. They had no chariots. They had obviously survived this far on the water intended for their horses, and when Kamose realized that there would be no resistance, he waved his own chariots back. The Medjay also, after waiting in vain for running targets, simply stood with their bows in their hands beside the chariots, visibly disappointed.

Long before sunset it was over. As the noise began to abate, Kamose had himself driven around the edge of the carnage, Hor-Aha and Ankhmahor beside him. His men were picking over the dead for any booty they might acquire, treading carelessly through the dark pools and rivulets already sinking into the greedy sand, their own half-naked bodies mired in blood. Ankhmahor glanced up. "The vultures are circling," he said, and Kamose heard his voice quiver. "The scavengers waste no time, Majesty." He returned his gaze to Kamose's face. "This was more terrible than anything we have done so far."

"Hor-Aha, let them keep whatever they can find," he said. "Remind the officers to take the hands. I want to know exactly how many Setiu fell here today. Send scouts back along the track. I also want to know where the chariots are. If they are still whole, we can use them." Hor-Aha nodded and jumped down and presently Kamose saw the officers disperse among the dead. The axes began to rise and fall, chopping off the right hands of the dead for the body count. Kamose let out his breath. "Well, Ankhmahor, it is done," he remarked with a deliberate lightness he did not feel. Indeed he felt only a kind of numbness as though he had drunk too much poppy. "Bring the Followers and we will find Ahmose. There is no point in mustering these men to reinforce my brother unless he and Paheri are faring badly. I am worried that no word has come from our second front." He thought the Prince would speak. Ankhmahor's kohl-rimmed eyes were huge and troubled. A shard of anger pierced the armour of Kamose's indifference and he grasped Ankhmahor's wrist. "Perhaps now we can afford the luxury of an honourable war with rules that both sides recognize," he hissed. "But I doubt it, Prince. This has been a revolution fought without a code and it will continue thus. I am well aware that when the history of Egypt is written I will not fare well. Yet surely there will be readers who can grope behind my actions to the principles I hold dear." He thrust a finger at the carnage just beyond them. "Those Setiu were soldiers. Soldiers understand that they are paid to fight, but also to die. No one tells them in what manner they may die. I salute the bravery of those men who crossed the desert dying with every step and stood to be finished off by other soldiers, but I hold no sentiment towards them. They did their duty." He released the Prince and as he did so a wave of mental fatigue flooded him. "I love you, Ankhmahor," he said dully. "I love your devotion to Ma'at, your intelligence, your steady, quiet support. Do not remove it from me, I beg you. I need your heart as well as your outward obedience."

A small smile came and went on Ankhmahor's mouth, and nodding once, he stepped from the chariot. Bowing low, he walked to where his own charioteer waited. Kamose watched him spring up onto the floor of the vehicle, white kilt swirling about his long thighs, golden commander's armbands flashing in the brightness of the afternoon. "Let us go," Kamose said to his own charioteer. With a jerk, his chariot pulled free of the clotting sand, and with Ankhmahor and the Followers behind he set off towards Het nefer Apu.

He had just rolled in under the shade of the trees when he saw his brother's chariot coming towards him. He had scarcely come to a halt before Ahmose began to shout. "Pezedkhu has pulled his troops! He is leaving, Kamose! The scouts told me that you have made a massacre. Re-form your divisions and let us give chase! Eighty thousand men against his sixty! Look!" He was pointing excitedly north to where clouds of dust were blowing. Kamose thought quickly.

"Did you engage him at all?" he snapped.

"A few skirmishes, nothing more. Kay Abana took his men off his ship and chased Pezedkhu's eastern flank as it withdrew. There was some bloodshed but I have no details yet. Pezedkhu would not commit to a battle, Kamose. He knew the state of the men coming out of the desert. He weighed the odds and decided to flee. Hurry!" The chariots were abreast now. Ahmose was beating the rim of his vehicle with the flat of his hand in an agony of impatience, his entourage tense behind him, their faces upturned to Kamose. A dozen scenes were played out in Kamose's mind before he spoke. He shook his head.

"No, Ahmose. Let him go. It would not be eighty thousand against sixty. Four of our divisions are out there tired and filthy, with blunt swords and spent arrows. They need rest and refurbishment before they can chase any more Setiu. That leaves forty thousand men. Of those, twenty-five belong to the ships. We would have to take them from the river. Pezedkhu will be moving fast. Have him scouted, but I think we must let him return unharmed to Het-Uart."

"The coward!" Ahmose blurted. "He did not send one man to help his fellows. Not one, Kamose!"

"Of course not," Kamose replied quietly. "And neither would we. He knew that they were doomed and he would not send good men to die as well. He will have a disturbing report to make to his master, Ahmose. I pity him. But think. We have reduced the Setiu strength in Egypt by at least sixty thousand. Turn your chariot around and I will meet you in the tent."

They were cheered as they approached the Nile. Townsmen as well as the troops that had waited with Ahmose set up a cheerful clamour. Paheri and both Abanas stood before the brothers' tent. Only the younger Abana looked sour, his expression pained as he rose from his obeisance. Kamose paused and looked him up and down. "I am told that you emptied the *North* and pursued the enemy," he remarked. "Who ordered you to do that, my impulsive young firebrand?" Kay flushed.

"Majesty, I could see them flitting through the trees, angling west towards the desert," he answered hotly. "Our orders were to remain where we were for the present, but my ship was berthed in the most northerly position on the river. I saw the Setiu moving to enter the desert fray. I could not wait to be told what to do! I had to harry them!"

"They were in fact retreating towards the desert so as to leave Het nefer Apu and return to the Delta," Kamose pointed out gently. "Did you lose any of my marines?" Kay was affronted.

"Certainly not, Lord! We managed to kill twenty-eight Setiu. They refused to stand and fight. They kept running away."

"And you were compelled to restore the reputation of your ship after its poor showing at the mock battle," Kamose said. "Did you take the hands?"

"No, Majesty." Kay's face lit up. "But we stripped them of some very fine swords and axes." There was a burst of spontaneous laughter from the assembled men.

"It was bravely done but very foolish, Kay," Kamose warned.

"In the future I expect you to follow the orders of your superiors, who might perhaps know a little more than you regarding the strategies of engagement. Do not be impatient. Your day will come." He pushed past them, knowing that unlike theirs, his laughter had been forced. The anger that had burst forth at Ankhmahor was the only spurt of emotion he had felt and his heart had returned to a stony insensibility.

Ankhmahor had followed them inside while the Followers took up their station around the tent. Kamose motioned him to a stool and himself sank onto the edge of his cot. "Wine, Akhtoy," he requested. "But not too much. We must absorb the reports that will begin to pour in soon from the battlefield." There was a silence fraught with a sense of anticlimax while the steward poured. Then Ahmose stirred and raised his cup.

"A thanks to Amun," he said solemnly and they drank. The bitter liquid caught in Kamose's throat, scoring its way into his stomach and spreading its instant warmth, but it did not quench his thirst. With a strange compulsion he reached for the jug of water kept fresh beside his cot and drained it, allowing the last few drops to splatter onto his neck and trickle down his chest. "What happened out there?" Ahmose wanted to know. "Have we lost any men?"

Kamose did not reply and after some hesitation Ankhmahor spoke.

"I do not think so, Highness, but we will know better when the officers make their reports," he said. "Nor do we know what strength we defeated. The hand count will tell." Kamose grunted.

"Defeated?" he said harshly. "I will not use that word until Het-Uart is ours and Apepa strung up on his palace wall. No one was defeated. Many men were slaughtered, massacred, butchered, however you wish to say it." He emphasized his speech, trying to take its meaning into himself, but it remained without and himself invulnerable. "I want to know what fate has overtaken Ramose. None of this would have been possible unless he had seduced Apepa."

"We may never know," Ahmose said. "What now, Kamose? Do we march north and institute a belated siege on Het-Uart? Do we have any idea how many soldiers Apepa still has?" Kamose sighed. The jug was empty, yet still he craved water.

"We will assess this day, allow the men to celebrate and sleep, hold a meeting with the Princes, and then decide what to do," he told his brother. "I must dictate a letter to Tetisheri, but later. Truthfully, Ahmose, all I want is to be lying in our bath house in Weset while the masseur pounds scented oil into my skin and my skiff waits by the watersteps with my fishing rod and throwing stick." A voice requesting admittance came muffled through the tent flap and Kamose roused himself with a sigh. "The first report is here," he finished. "Let him come in."

For the rest of the afternoon and long after sunset the brothers listened to a steadily multiplying account of the victory. First in the tent and later in the coolness of the evening beside the river they received one officer after another. The hand count had finally been made. Ten thousand and nineteen Setiu lay slain, their bodies now food for the desert predators, their weapons in the possession of the exultant Egyptians who began to drink and sing as soon as the cooking fires were lit. There were no serious injuries among Kamose's divisions. Not a man had been lost.

The Princes began to gather under the torchlight where Kamose and Ahmose sat sipping their wine, answering Kamose's queries with the assurances that weapons were being cleaned and sharpened, harness repaired, and the soldiers fed. "They will whore and carouse until dawn," Intef grumbled, "but I suppose they deserve it. I only hope that in their drunkenness they do not antagonize the townspeople."

"The officers patrol the town tonight," Iasen answered him. "I do not think we need to worry. Indeed, the citizens of Het nefer Apu seem almost as relieved as we are to see the Setiu destroyed. Pezedkhu would not have been kind to them if he had won."

"What a noise!" Makhu exclaimed, looking beyond the area of peace around them where the Followers formed a circle of protection to the darkness under the trees and the fitful glare of the fires along the bank. "They will be a sorry sight tomorrow. Will you give them a day of laziness, Majesty?"

"Yes." Kamose straightened in his chair. "One day to sleep. Perhaps two. I am waiting for word regarding the Setiu chariots before we quit this place." He smiled. "I envy the soldiers their celebration," he went on. "If we get drunk, it must be politely, in the privacy of our tents and at a time when we expect no threats. Where is your son, Ankhmahor?"

"Patrolling the streets," Ankhmahor told him. "Majesty, I think I speak for all of us when I ask to know your mind regarding the remainder of the campaigning season. The month of Pakhons is now far advanced. In another three the river will begin to rise. You command a vast number of troops, and if you intend to continue north to Het-Uart, you will have little time for a siege." He hesitated and Intef stepped in.

"We are your nobles," he said bluntly. "Your mind is opened to us first." He cast a sidelong glance at Hor-Aha sitting quietly on the ground just out of reach of the light from the two lamps flickering on the table. "In return we are honoured when you seek our advice. May we give it now?" Kamose sighed inwardly, seeing the anxious set of their faces.

"Very well," he responded. Intef leaned forward eagerly.

"We have struck a formidable blow against Apepa this year," he began. "Not only has Pezedkhu been forced to retrench but there is no longer any doubt that all Egypt but for a portion of the Delta is in your hands. We wish you to relinquish any thought of another siege until next year." His gaze travelled across his companions. Iasen nodded. "We have all been receiving regular letters from our nomes and our families," Intef pressed on. "We are needed elsewhere, Majesty. The harvest approaches and the men who should be in the fields are in your army. The task is too great for the women alone. Every grain of wheat, every bulb of garlic is precious, given the depredations of the campaign last year."

"So you want me to disband the army, temporarily of course, and let you take your peasants home for the harvest." There was something in Intef's avidity that Kamose did not like. The man's eyes, feverish in the yellow glow, were roving restlessly and his beringed fingers scraped against one another. "When did you have the time to discuss this proposition, my lords?"

"While we waited for the arrival of Apepa's eastern army, Majesty," Iasen explained, his voice soothing. "We debated the matter and decided that if we were victorious we would ask this of you."

"And if not?" Ahmose's tone was cold. Iasen spread out his hands in a questioning gesture.

"We did not doubt that His Majesty's plan for the destruction of the enemy would work, therefore we spent little time on the alternative," he said. "As it happens, the plan did work."

"You have not answered His Highness," Kamose said curtly. "And do not forget that my brother and I were only responsible for the details of the plan. Its overall conception belonged to the Prince Hor-Aha." There was an uncomfortable hiatus. Intef looked down at his busy fingers. Iasen made a small moue. Mesehti, Makhu and Ankhmahor simply watched Kamose, who after a moment began to smile slowly.

"As you have probably noted, there have been promotions among my sailors and marines," he said conversationally and

with a seeming irrelevance. "For instance, on the recommenda-
tion of Paheri, I appointed Kay Abana captain of his own ship.
There have also been promotions among the ranks of your soldiers, particularly of common men from infantry to charioteers
with the concomitant title of officer, on your advice. But I have
done nothing to elevate any member of the Medjay archers in
spite of the fact that they have acquitted themselves with exem-
plary skill and obeyed their Prince without demur." He inclined
his head at Hor-Aha who had remained motionless, his dark body
blending with the night around him, only the shine of his eyes
and the white smudge of his kilt betraying his presence. Ahmose
placed a warning hand on Kamose's knee but he ignored the gesture. "The captains of the ships in which they sailed have spoken
highly of them but their Prince has said nothing," Kamose went
on crisply. "Why is that?" He leaned across the table and fixed
them with a stare. "It is because, like a good commander, the
Prince has no wish to cause dissent among his fellows." His palm
came down on the surface of the table with a resounding slap. "I
had thought that by now, having marched and fought together,
you were beyond this dangerous prejudice," he almost shouted,
"but I can see that I am mistaken. I intend to promote one hundred Medjay to the rank of Instructor of Retainers and distribute
them among your divisions. They will each have one hundred of
your best archers under them and they in turn will train others.
They will be given officer privileges and responsibilities. Now you
will hear my will." He sat back again and folded his arms. "You
may disband your divisions. Three thousand of your troops may
go home until the Inundation is over. One thousand stay here to
guard us from the north. One thousand come to Weset with me
on active duty. Thus I leave eleven thousand men at Het nefer
Apu and take eleven thousand to Weset. I will discuss with
Paheri the disposition of the navy. All of you will travel with me
to make sacrifices in the temple of Amun before you go to your

several nomes. While you fritter away your time before the next battle season, you will send me regular reports on the state of your governorships and other holdings. Are we agreed?" It was obvious that they longed to meet each other's eyes but did not dare. Solemnly they regarded Kamose, sitting smiling across at them, until Intef cleared his throat.

"We are your servants, Majesty," he croaked. And then more confidently, "It is wise to secure our northern border with the Setiu and of course with Teti the Handsome in Kush, and we thank you for allowing us and our peasants a chance to greet our loved ones again. As to the matter of the Medjay . . ." He swallowed, and it was Iasen who continued.

"I think we would all agree that the tribesmen have acquitted themselves magnificently, Majesty," he said. "Many deserve promotion. But let it be within their own ranks. Let those selected to be officers command their own kin. If you place them over Egyptians, there will be trouble." Kamose inclined his head mockingly.

"I seem to remember a similar objection many months ago," he said. "It was pointless then. It is merely stupid now. A gaggle of peasants has been forged into an army with which the Medjay have merged. Indispensably, I might remind you all. I have spoken. It will be done." He rose and at once they rose with him, reverencing him silently, but he read anger in their stiffly bending spines.

Beckoning Ankhmahor and Hor-Aha, he left them, entering his tent while Akhtoy scrambled to bring the lamps. Ahmose turned to face him.

"Kamose, I do not think . . ." he began, but Kamose put up a hand.

"I do," he said distinctly. "You know that it is just and proper, Ahmose."

"Yes, but there are more tactful ways of reminding the Princes that they are under your thumb," Ahmose muttered. "Trouble in the ranks is one thing. Trouble among the bluebloods is quite another. Let us hope that the glory of this day will temporarily appease their ire."

The four men settled themselves comfortably on cushions scattered over the carpet that hid the hard earth beneath. Kamose dismissed the servants. The noise of merrymaking along the riverbank was a constant undercurrent to their desultory conversation. Music came fitfully floating to them in the occasional lulls between the shouts of the soldiers, by now happily drunk, and the shrieks and laughter of the women who had joined them. "I hope the mayor of the town and the officers can indeed keep control of the situation," Ahmose remarked. "It would be sad to march out of Het nefer Apu on a tide of ill-will after the months of good co-operation between army and townsfolk."

"I do not think we need to worry," Kamose answered absently, his mind returning to Ramose in anxious impotence. "The men are cheerful and therefore compliant. They will grumble and bicker tomorrow when their heads ache, but not now." He was sitting on the floor with his back against the edge of his cot, one arm up along the mattress, the other cradling his wine.

"I have had word from my tribesmen in Wawat, Majesty," Hor-Aha said unexpectedly. "It came yesterday. Forgive me for keeping it from you, but we were all occupied with Pezedkhu. There is trouble brewing in the south."

"What kind of trouble?"

Hor-Aha put down his cup and drew a finger across his mouth. "The Kushites are taking advantage of the fact that many men from Wawat are here with you. They are pushing north into Wawat territory. I have not told my Medjay of this. They would want to leave at once and go home to defend their villages if I did." Ankhmahor frowned.

"I know little of the territory beyond the cataracts," he said, "but I remember my history lessons. The men of Kush have always coveted Wawat. Why?"

"Gold," Ahmose drawled. He was lying on his side, his head propped on one elbow. "Wawat has gold and Kush wants it for trade. Our ancestors built several forts in Wawat for the single purpose of protecting the gold. I too remember my lessons. The history of the land beyond Weset is of great importance to us in the south. Wawat is our neighbour."

"How pressing is the need for action?" Kamose asked his General with a sinking heart.

"It is not yet imperative," Hor-Aha told him. "But if Your Majesty will not allow the Medjay to go home, they will no longer fight well." Kamose was thinking swiftly.

"I wonder if Teti-En is behind the unrest in Wawat," he mused. "I have been pondering the advisability of another assault on Het-Uart, particularly now that Pezedkhu knows our full strength. I did not want to give him a chance to adjust and prepare a more successful campaign. But I cannot go north with the possibility of another front opening in the south. Does Teti-En have his eye on Weset?"

"I do not think so," Ahmose objected. "He has appeared to be quite indifferent to Apepa's plight. It is more likely that he is using our preoccupation with the north to march on Wawat and annex it for his own ends. Once he has control of it, then he of course also controls the ancient forts. Will his ambition grow? That is the question."

"Your pardon, Prince, but that is not the question to me or to my tribesmen," Hor-Aha put in vehemently. "The Medjay have been indispensable to you. They have come a long way to fight for you. They will expect you now to fight for them."

"What, go into Wawat?" Ahmose blinked. Kamose took his arm from the cot and ran a hand through his hair. He met

Hor-Aha's gaze and read a challenge there for the first time. The knowledge jolted him.

"Tell me, General, are the Medjay members of my army or are they merely allies?" he asked evenly. "Who ultimately has command of them, me or you? Are we speaking of mutiny in my ranks or the rights inherent in an alliance?" The room went suddenly still. Ankhmahor sat with both hands around his cup, his eyes resolutely downcast. Kamose and Hor-Aha continued to stare tensely at one another. It was Ahmose who broke the uncomfortable silence.

"It is indeed a delicate point," he said soothingly, "one we have not had to consider before. Let us think of it as irrelevant, Kamose. If Wawat is in danger from Teti-En, then Weset may also be threatened. It would make sense to take a small punitive force down there. After all," he finished reasonably, "you have told the Princes that you intend to leave eleven thousand troops here at Het nefer Apu. If Apepa remains true to form, he will not leave the Delta. Our northern flank is safe for the present. We can go south during the Inundation."

*My dear Ahmose, ever the peacemaker,* Kamose thought hotly but he did not say the words. Instead he made himself nod at his General, raise his eyebrows, and purse his lips as though in reflection.

"I owe you and the Medjay a debt," he said as calmly as he could. "All you had to do was request my help, Hor-Aha. I have always trusted you. Could you not trust me?" He had the pleasure of seeing the man's eyes falter and drop.

"Your pardon, Majesty," he said in a low voice. "I am anxious that the Medjay not be seen as flighty savages by the Princes who scorn them and me. Their homes are threatened. They cannot put the good of Egypt ahead of that. In some respects they are indeed as primitive as children. I humbly beg your help in Wawat."

Humbly? Kamose thought, upending his cup and drinking to hide the expression of disdain he could not repress. There is not a humble bone in that powerful black body of yours, my clever General. If I choose to go into Wawat, it will not be to restore a few ramshackle huts to your half-wild aliens. "Bring me the message you received," he said. "I want to see it. What you are asking requires at least some planning, Hor-Aha, and I am tired. It has been a long day. Bring it tomorrow morning." It was clear that Hor-Aha had understood completely. Setting down his cup he rose to his feet and bowed.

"Your Majesty is gracious," he said tonelessly and turning he stalked out of the tent. Ankhmahor also stood.

"I must undertake a last inspection of your guard before I sleep," he explained. But on reaching the tent flap he hesitated. "Be careful, Kamose," he said quietly. "Be very careful." His obeisance was slow and deliberate, a mark of genuine respect. Then he was gone.

The brothers looked at one another in a lull that only extended as far as the limpid circle of friendly lamplight. Outside, the cacophony of revelry went on. Then Ahmose said, "What just happened here, Kamose?" Kamose flung himself onto his cot, kicking off his sandals.

"What happened is that our beloved General made an error," he said shortly. "Hor-Aha let slip a glimpse of the true nature of his ka."

"He is concerned for his countrymen," Ahmose protested. "His worry and his fear that you would not understand them made him incautious."

Kamose laughed bitterly. "Incautious? Yes indeed! He threatened us, Ahmose! Or did you miss that small fact?"

"You are being overly suspicious," Ahmose said, coming over to him and perching beside his legs. "Look at it sanely, Kamose. Kush is encroaching on Wawat. Hor-Aha wants to release the

Medjay to deal with the problem. He is loyal to us but he understands his men. He tells us exactly what he fears if we neither let them go nor agree to help them. What is wrong with that? Do you not value such honesty?"

"Of course I do!" Kamose snapped. "It was not the words he spoke but the thing I heard in his voice and saw in his eyes, a flash of something arrogant yet sly. We are sensible men. Both of us appreciate the need to do something about the situation. Both of us see how we may further earn Medjay loyalty by sending or even leading Egyptian troops into Wawat, at the same time curbing any ambitions Teti-En may have and securing those old forts. Hor-Aha is an intelligent man. He sees all this. He could have put it to us differently." He folded his hands on his naked chest and turned his head to look at Ahmose. "But somehow he made a mistake. He let us see a flash of his well-hidden ambition. I think that he wants to set himself up as an independent Prince of Wawat. Not now, perhaps, but in time. With our inadvertent aid."

"But, Kamose, he carries our father's blood on his belt," Ahmose reminded him. "He loved Seqenenra. He has served us with unswerving fealty."

"All that is true," Kamose admitted. "But years have passed since our father died. Men change. Circumstances change. Opportunities arise that can sometimes waken dark regions in a man's soul that tendril through everything that he is."

"That is insane!" Ahmose exclaimed. "You are speaking of someone you have befriended, indeed championed against our own countrymen, Kamose! Hor-Aha is like our own kin!" Kamose gave an odd smile.

"Is he?" he whispered. "I do not know any more. In any case, Ahmose, we have a much better reason for marching into Wawat than the rescue of the Medjay, although we do want to stay in their good graces. We need gold." He struggled to a sitting position. "Gold for trade with Keftiu. Gold to pay the Princes. Gold to restore the old palace. So far Wawat's gold has gone into Apepa's coffers, but no more. We will not tell Hor-Aha this, of course. We will be all concern for our Medjay allies. Do you think we might offer the Medjay a home in Egypt, Ahmose? Build them a town where their families can live, and make them a part of the permanent army I intend to establish? Hor-Aha knows perfectly well how important they are to us. Damn him! Is there no one I can fully trust?"

"Perhaps not," Ahmose responded thoughtfully. "But what King could ever ultimately depend on anyone but the gods? You are wrong about Hor-Aha, Kamose. You need to sleep on these misgivings of yours to see how insubstantial they are. You need to go home for a while." He sighed. "So do I. I would like to be there for Aahmes-nefertari when she gives birth next month." Kamose's expression softened.

"I had forgotten," he said apologetically. "Pezedkhu drove the remembrance from my mind. We will go back to Weset and then south to Wawat. Oh, Ahmose." He closed his eyes. "Will there ever come a day without alarms of any kind?"

He slept fitfully and then more deeply, as somewhere in his dreams he became aware that the cacophony outside had finally died away. When he woke, it was to full sunlight and an unnaturally quiet atmosphere. Ahmose was still on his cot and snoring gently, curled up on his side, one cheek pillowed in his palm. Slipping his feet into a pair of worn reed sandals and wrapping his limp kilt of the day before around his waist, Kamose stepped out into the blinding glare of the morning.

The Followers to either side of the tent's entrance came to attention and saluted him, and a man who had been crouching a little way away rose and stood smiling, a cup in one hand and a hunk of bread in the other. He was thin, with dark smudges under his eyes and an unfamiliar gauntness to his features, but with a rush of pure joy Kamose recognized him. "Ramose, Ramose!" he cried, and striding forward he enveloped the younger man in a crushing embrace. "How is it that you are here? Have you been squatting outside the tent all night? But surely not! I thought . . . Well, I do not know what I thought! Akhtoy, where are you? Hot food at once!" He released Ramose, who set his cup on the ground and shook the spilled droplets of water from his hand.

"Two of your scouts found me out on the desert," he explained. "They brought me in yesterday, but they had to wait until the battle was over. I was exhausted, Majesty. I had to sleep." Kamose wanted to hug him again. If the guards had not been watching, he would have danced his way back into the tent. Instead he put an arm around Ramose's shoulders and drew him inside to where Ahmose was sitting up, bleary-eyed.

"I wondered what all the shouting was about," he mumbled. "Ramose! I knew you would turn up eventually. You look terrible." He gave a yawn that turned into a wide grin. "Welcome back. Give me a moment to appreciate the morning and then share your news."

"Believe me, Highness, I am here against great odds," Ramose said. "I am in no hurry to recount my adventures. I am still savouring the delights of safety and freedom." He was smiling, but Kamose noticed that his knees trembled as he lowered himself onto a stool. Akhtoy, prompt and self-effacing as always, had entered with his servants behind him bearing the first meal of the day. He began to set it out. The bread was still warm from the town ovens and the fresh dates gleamed on their bed of lettuce leaves, the first of that season. Inet-fish and Nile perch sent out a fragrant garlic-scented steam. Dark beer frothed in the cups. At Kamose's gesture the three men began to eat, and not until the dishes were scoured did Kamose fling his linen napkin onto a tray and invite his friend to speak.

"But tell us of Tani first," Ahmose said. "Did you see her? Is she well?" A shadow passed across Ramose's sun-ravaged face. He took a mouthful of his beer and swallowed it slowly before replying. Then he sighed.

"You will not like what I have to say," he told them. "Tani is now a wife to Apepa." He continued to speak, recounting his meeting with their sister, giving them her words and his with clarity and bitterness. It was obvious to Kamose, himself listening with a mounting incredulity, that the intensity and immediacy of the interview had branded Ramose forever and its scars would never fade. "I did not try to persuade her to escape with me," Ramose said. "There would have been no point. She has been utterly duped by that foreign scum." He clenched his teeth and fought for control before going on. "She sends you her love and begs for your understanding."

"Understanding! She is insane if she imagines that I will either forgive or forget her betrayal!" Kamose exploded. "This news will destroy her mother! What can I say to you, my friend? Nothing can touch your grief."

Ahmose had gone white to his lips. "We will think of her as a casualty of war," he said huskily. "We must, Kamose, or we shall be reduced to impotence every time we remember her. She is a sacrifice, one of the costs the family has paid to the gods in return for victory." He swallowed noisily. "At least she still lives. That is something for which we must be grateful."

"I do not wish to discuss her any more," Kamose retorted. His incredulity had turned to a rage that sent the blood pounding in his ears, his eyes, so that he could hardly hear or see for the force of its drumming. "I will remember her as she was in the days of her innocence. Everything else I deny!" Ramose looked at him bleakly.

"I have had time to absorb the shock, Majesty," he said. "Since I stood before her in that luxurious room and saw her so beautiful, so unapproachable ... Since then I have walked with death holding my hand. Her words will remain as sharp as a serpent's fangs in my memory, but I will no longer dwell on the time when I loved her and we planned our future together. To do so would be to reject the gift of life the gods allowed me in the desert. I am resolved to keep my attention fixed on the present as far as my wounded ka will bear."

"But I do not understand it!" Kamose roared. "I will never understand! She is a Tao! How was she able to jettison her family pride in favour of that ... that ...." He was being strangled. He could not breathe.

"Our revenge will be in driving every Setiu from our borders, Kamose," Ahmose said urgently. "We will not dissipate our energies in recrimination. We will not lose sight of our goal. Now, Ramose. We need to hear of Het-Uart, the palace, the troops still quartered there, your experience with the eastern army." His words were calming but his voice shook. "Who commanded the army that perished out there?" Ramose nodded and glanced at Kamose.

"The General assigned to the eastern army was one Kethuna," he said. "He is dead. I saw his body on the battlefield as the scouts were bringing me in yesterday. Pezedkhu did not like the plan, you know, but Apepa insisted on it. He is truly a fool. The one hundred and twenty-four thousand troops that left Het-Uart represent perhaps one-half of Apepa's combined forces. He has been sent reinforcements by his so-called brothers in Rethennu. They continue to enter the Delta along the Horus Road ...." He talked on.

Kamose did his best to concentrate on what Ramose was saying, but the fires of his rage and hurt continued to scorch him and it was not until Ramose began to recount the panic and dismay of the army when it found the waters of the oasis undrinkable that he came completely to himself. Then he listened attentively.

"I wish I had been with you as you walked towards the Nile," he said with malicious fervour. "The chariots fired, the soldiers staggering and falling and gasping for water. I wish I had been there. I gloat, Ahmose. I rejoice. Forgive me but I cannot help it." Ramose had paused to drink again, his voice hoarse from so much talk. "We will go home now," Kamose went on. "The scouts will return today with the news that the chariots are irretrievable. The hand count is complete. The enemy's weapons are in our possession." He rose carefully, nursing the sudden pain that had blossomed in his gut. "Thank you, Ramose," he managed. "You are a brave man, an Egyptian worthy of this mighty country. You have earned a royal wife, a princely title, a fertile estate. It is my shame that I cannot yet bestow these things upon you."

Ramose stood also and faced him. "Majesty, I am tired in body and soul," he half-whispered. "It is said that the gods take those they love and hone and temper them until they become as bright and pure and indomitable as new swords in the hands of mighty warriors. Perhaps they love me inordinately, for I have taken all that any man may be expected to bear, yet I survive. I want them to leave me alone now. Let me swim and hunt duck in the Weset marshes and make love to faceless women. Let me hold my mother in my arms." He gave a twisted half-smile. "Take me home with you, Great One, take me home. I need to heal." He bowed, placed both palms tenderly on Kamose's chest, and left the tent.

# Chapter TWELVE

TWO DAYS LATER, THE army set out for the south. Thirty-three thousand jubilant men received the news that they were to be returned to their homes until the harvest and the next Inundation were over, and they stowed their packs and struck their tents with alacrity. The eleven thousand remaining at Het nefer Apu were less pleased, but Kamose had wisely decreed that any leave they had accrued might be taken in staggered periods of time, during which they might go back to their villages temporarily. He intended to keep all the Medjay close to him, quartering them on the west bank opposite Weset. He had told Hor-Aha that he would indeed mount a punitive expedition into Wawat, but that it would be after the celebrations at Weset. Hor-Aha had received the news with his customary cool attention. Kamose had seen no trace of the spark of arrogance the General had betrayed before, but unlike Ahmose, he did not dismiss what he knew Hor-Aha had inadvertently revealed. He filed it away in the back of his mind for future contemplation.

After much deliberation he had decided to leave the navy, too, at Het nefer Apu, suggesting to Paheri and Baba Abana that they rotate the marines to allow them also to spend some time in their villages. But he insisted that the captains of the ships, including the two friends, accompany him to Weset together with all the Princes and their senior officers. The bounty from the treasure ships he had captured lay waiting in Amun's treasury and there were rewards to be handed out and promotions to be honoured.

He forced himself to fill the hours with the details of departure—dictating scrolls to his family and Amunmose to warn them of his coming, reading the final inventories of weapons and supplies, inspecting the horses, meeting with the mayor of Het nefer Apu to hear any complaints the townsmen had regarding the continued presence of a portion of the army and to grant him the right to requisition idle soldiers to aid in the coming harvest. He did not give himself time to grieve for Tani. He recognized the danger in turning his inner gaze upon the glowing embers of pain and rage that still smouldered deep within him. There would be time to let it engulf him when he closed the door of his own room in the house at Weset and was at last alone.

So the great mass of men, chariots and animals began to wind south, some in the boats, some marching on the shore, with much singing and laughter. As the days passed, the ranks gradually thinned, men saying farewell to their companions and melting away to come at last to their own houses, and it was a comparatively small flotilla that approached Weset in the bright heat of a summer afternoon. This is almost how we began, Kamose thought as he stood in the bow of his craft with Ahmose and Ramose silent behind him and the Princes clustered on cushions in the shade of the cabin. We had nothing but five thousand foreign archers and a wild hope to sustain us. Now Egypt is almost ours, with only Het-Uart remaining like one spot of decay on a plump grape. Above him the lateen sails bellied out on the hot north wind and the wake of his craft folded away in foaming crystal below. White ibis stalked in the rushes by the bank with a slow, lordly dignity, and beyond the tangle of shrubs the crops of his nome stood thick and golden. For one ecstatic moment his heart swelled with joy and pride but such emotions had become alien to him and he was unable to make them stay.

Long before the town became visible the men craning forward began to hear it, a low mutter of confused sound that grew as the rowers beat their way upriver. The Princes scrambled to their feet and came to stand elbow to elbow along the railing. The noise grew louder, became a constant roar, and suddenly Kamose could see the people lining the east bank of the river waving and shouting a welcome, throwing blossoms that rained down on the undulating water. The Medjay answered their tumultuous greeting, yelling back at them and dancing delightedly on the deck. Kamose raised an arm in acknowledgement of their frenzied homage and the noise rose to a mighty crescendo.

As the royal craft drew level with the canal leading to Amun's temple, Kamose saw that the priests had gathered, their loose white robes blowing and gleaming in the strong sunlight. They were silent, but as Kamose's boat drew level with them they knelt with one accord, arms outstretched, and pressed their foreheads into the earth. Ahmose drew in a sharp breath. "I had thought that our victory was real to me," he half-whispered under the continuous din, "but it was as though I dreamed it until this moment. We did it. We did it, Kamose!"

Kamose did not reply. We have not done it, Ahmose, he thought clearly, coldly. Like skilled physicians we have contained the rot but it can still spread. Oh why can I feel nothing? I eat and sleep and breathe and yet I am dead inside. The fever of my townspeople, the excitement of the Princes, does not touch me at all unless it is with the chill finger of fear. What of next year? How may we breach Het-Uart's defences? What counter measure is Apepa plotting? Do these fools imagine that the worst is over?

The crowd had thinned and the dense growth between the limits of the town and his own estate was drifting past. Kamose tensed. He heard Hor-Aha give the command for the Medjay's boats to begin to angle towards the west bank where their barracks still stood. All at once he wanted to crouch down, to hide his eyes so that he need not receive the burden of his family's faces. Panic assailed him. Now there were the massive ruins of the old palace baking in ravaged splendour behind its crumbling walls. His watersteps were coming into view, glittering as the water lapped over them, and above them the pavement, the short path disappearing into trees, the bulk of the rambling house beyond.

They were there, his kin, with the servants clustered behind them, even his grandmother and Ramose's mother, Nefer-Sakharu, anxiously smiling, wigs and linens stirring in the breeze. As the captain began to issue orders and the craft nosed in to the steps, Aahmes-nefertari struggled out of the chair in which she had been sitting, her sheath stretched tightly over the swollen belly of her pregnancy. At another word from the captain a rope was flung to shore and the ramp was run out. They were home.

But Kamose could not move. Heavy and stone-like he stood rooted to the deck while Ankhmahor and the Followers walked down the ramp, up the watersteps, and formed a protecting avenue along which he knew he must go. Ahmose touched his arm. "We can disembark now, Kamose," he whispered. "Why do you wait? Is something wrong?" Kamose could not answer. Panic began to seep into his mind. I do not want to be here, he thought. This is the womb from which I have already crawled. This is the dreamland from which I may never wake again. "Kamose!" Ahmose said sharply, and at that moment Behek came bounding down the steps in a shower of spray. With a leap he gained the ramp, skidded, righted himself, and to a ripple of laughter from the gathered men he flung himself on his master. Kamose felt the cold nose thrust into his hand and found himself looking into the shining brown eyes of his dog. The spell left him. Bending, he rubbed the soft head, and when he straightened he was able to make his legs carry him across the planking, along the ramp, and onto the hot paving, Behek padding delightedly at his heels.

Soft arms enveloped him. Perfumed hair brushed his cheek, his neck. Murmurs and cries of welcome filled the air. Out of the corner of his eye he saw Ahmose and Aahmes-nefertari locked together, rocking to and fro, and Ramose embracing his mother, and he wanted to weep for the hollow place inside him where there was nothing but emptiness. Tetisheri, after pulling him briefly against her desiccated body, surveyed him calmly. "You are burned as black as a desert peasant," she said at last. "But you seem well, Majesty. It is very good to see you again."

"I am very well, Grandmother," he replied dutifully. "As for you, I think you will live forever. You do not change at all." She gave one of her sudden, rare laughs.

"The gods only claim the virtuous," she chuckled. "I see that you have brought the Princes with you. Where shall we put them all? But come. Uni has set up canopies by the pond. We will eat and drink and I will assess the worth of these men crowding us. Have you turned them into effective commanders, Kamose, so that you will be able to stay at home while they campaign next season? Have you any plans yet for the taking of Het-Uart? And Tani. Your reports said nothing of her, although Ramose spent some time in the palace. It is bad news, isn't it?" They had begun to walk along the path towards the lawns. Aahotep had come up and slipped her arm through his, and behind them the rest of the entourage drifted in excited conversation. Kamose wanted to tear himself from the grip of the two women and run into the trees under whose shade they were passing.

"Not now, Tetisheri," he said tersely. "This is not the time. I, we, all of us need to rest. Amun must be officially thanked, rewards must be bestowed, we must all be nourished with diversions before we return to a contemplation of the future!" His voice had risen.

"Forgive me," Tetisheri said, and he stopped and turned to her in desperation.

"No. It is I who must apologize," he managed. "You are right. The news regarding Tani is very bad and neither of you should have to wait to hear it. Yet the Princes must be fêted this afternoon. I will tell you everything tonight."

They had come to the pond and the pleasing, leaf-dappled grass surrounding it. Large canopies billowed in the heat. Cushions had been piled on the shaded ground beneath them. The family settled themselves while Uni, with many bows, directed the others under the adjacent shelters. Servants appeared from the house bearing trays laden with dishes, napkins and jugs. The musicians took up their stations by the lily-choked water. Tetisheri rose and held up an imperious hand. At once the chatter ceased. "Princes of Egypt, commanders and friends," she began. "I welcome you here to the heart of Egypt. Victory has come out of great suffering and despair. Now is the time for celebration. Let us eat and drink together and remember that if it were not for the courage of my son Osiris Seqenenra this day would be like any other. My steward Uni is at your disposal while you are here. Long life and happiness to you all." She sat down again amidst a storm of clapping. The servants began to fan out. The musicians sent a lilting melody piping through the air.

Aahmes-nefertari was sitting in a chair. Ahmose, who had

made himself a nest of cushions at her feet, knelt up and laid his face against her belly. "I have missed you so much," he murmured, reaching for her hand. "I am so glad that this baby waited to be born until I returned. Has your health been good, my sister?" She stroked his head then pushed him gently away.

"Ahmose, did I not dictate many scrolls to you, full of how boringly predictable this pregnancy was?" she teased him. "Now that you see me so fat and ungainly do you still love me?" Her gaze met Kamose's. What is she saying to me? Kamose wondered. Her mouth smiles but not her eyes. Has her health not been good? A servant bent before him offering food and the connection between Aahmes-nefertari and himself was broken.

He ate the fruit of his nome and drank its wine, feeling a fragile equilibrium return to him as his nostrils filled with the summer odours of his childhood and his ears received the voices that had meant security and peace to him in his growing years. Before him the house squatted, its whitewashed walls protecting its memories, its doorways inviting inhabitants who would create even more, yet he knew that when he stood and crossed the grass and entered his home, it would no longer recognize him. It had not changed. It was he who had sailed away with a dark spawn growing inside, and now it exuded from his very pores, an invisible cloud that diminished the glory of the golden afternoon and made the cheerful crowd around him seem like dull paintings on brittle papyrus.

He watched Ramose and Nefer-Sakharu sitting knee to knee under the canopy where the Princes drank and laughed. Man and mother were leaning towards each other, their expressions solemn, their unheard conversation obviously serious. His glance strayed to Ankhmahor beating time on his folded ankle with one finger as the drums pulsed their rhythm over the garden. Beside him his son Harkhuf was talking to him animatedly, and occasionally the Prince would nod or smile briefly, but his thoughts were not on his offspring's words. Kamose sighed, and in an effort to shake off the mantle of depression and dislocation still enfolding him, he sat straighter and called for more wine.

As appetites were assuaged, the Princes began to leave their canopy and come one by one to pay their respects to Tetisheri, bowing before her and kissing her hand. She spoke to them all, enquiring about their families, asking them what division they commanded, what they had done, and Kamose thought what a great lady she was, intelligent and gracious, indomitable and proud. In his detached frame of mind, however, he did not fail to notice that Prince Intef and Prince Iasen, after exchanging these polite pleasantries with his grandmother, made their way to Ramose's mother and spent the remainder of their time speaking with her. Rousing himself, he beckoned to Baba Abana, Kay and Paheri, and when they had come, he presented them to his family. The stern lines of Tetisheri's face relaxed at their names. Bidding them sit, she began an animated discussion involving Nekheb, shipbuilding and the strategy of warfare on water. Kamose's mood lifted a little. Excusing himself and calling to his dog, he left them all.

In the evening the members of the family gathered in Tetisheri's quarters. Akhtoy and a harried Uni had found accommodations for the guests and appointed house servants to them. Hor-Aha had crossed the river to report that the Medjay were settled in their barracks and glad to be back on dry land. Anhkmahor had taken charge of the household guards, putting them under the command of the Followers and ordering the watches before choosing to sleep with his men in their compound.

Ramose had asked to be allowed to share his mother's rooms and after some hesitation Kamose had agreed. He knew that the pause between Ramose's request and his granting of it had hurt and puzzled his friend but something about the way the two Princes had approached Nefer-Sakharu and the way in which she had greeted them troubled Kamose. He could not say why. After all, he had told himself irritably, Teti made himself a friend to almost all the Princes up and down the Nile. Intef and Iasen have known his widow for years. It must have been a joy to her to see them again, to be free to talk about Teti with them and with Ramose, to relive happier times. By all accounts she has not been able to find much peace here with the family of her husband's executioner. Yet his reasons sounded forced to his own ear and the tiny kernel of anxiety did not go away.

However, he had dismissed it temporarily by the time he sent Behek back to the kennels with a servant and made his way through the quiet torch-lit passages of the house. Uni admitted him to his grandmother's quarters. The rest of the family was already there. Tetisheri sat by her table, her feet on a footstool, her ringed fingers curving loosely around the winecup beside her. Opposite her, Aahmes-nefertari also occupied a chair. The girl had had her paint removed and her own black hair cascaded to her shoulders. She was wrapped in a thin white cloak which she held close to her across her stomach. Kamose thought that she looked like a tired child. Seeing him come, she gave him a slight smile. "Raa caught Ahmose-onkh dragging the house snake through the reception hall," she told him. "He had it in his fist, just behind its head fortunately. He screamed when she took it away from him and tossed it into the garden. He could have been bitten, the silly little boy." She made a face. "I pray that the snake will not take offence and refuse to come back. That would be very bad luck indeed." Again Kamose caught a look from her, half-speculative half-fearful, before she looked away.

"The snake did not bite him because it knew he was just a baby," he commented. "And it will return for its milk for the same reason." He slid to the floor with his back to the wall beside Ahmose.

"It is not an omen, Aahmes-nefertari," her mother said. She was sitting on the stool in front of Tetisheri's cosmetic table, the thick rope of her luxurious braid pulled forward over one shoulder and hanging against one red-clad breast. "Ahmose-onkh is becoming spoiled. Now that you are home, Ahmose, perhaps you can impose some discipline on him."

"Me?" Ahmose laughed in astonishment. "What can I do with a two-year-old child? He terrifies me!"

"Think of it as training a dog," Tetisheri offered. "Reward him when he is obedient. Punish him when he is naughty. A lazy and indulgent master makes an unruly dog and I cannot see that children are so very different from dogs." She turned her severe gaze on the luckless Aahmes-nefertari. "You are not lazy, my dear, but you have certainly been over-indulgent with the boy. So has his nurse. From now on you must imagine him with grey fur and a tail when you look at him." They all burst out laughing but sobered quickly, the moment of family cohesiveness and understanding giving way to a wary silence fraught with their unspoken questions. Kamose thought of Ramose's mother, who had spent so much time with Ahmose-onkh when she first came to the house.

"Tell me of Nefer-Sakharu," he said. "Does she still grieve?" Aahotep tut-tutted.

"Grieve?" she repeated almost contemptuously. "If sullenness and a very pointed desire for seclusion can be interpreted as grief then yes, she still grieves. We had to take Ahmose-onkh away from her if you remember, Kamose. The servants heard her belittling us all to him and one never knows how much of what is said to a young child remains in his mind. She is an ungrateful woman." And perhaps dangerous also, Kamose added to himself. He made no rejoinder. Tetisheri's rings rapped the table.

"No more chatter," she said briskly. "We want to hear of Tani.

You dictated many words regarding Ramose's foray into Apepa's palace, Kamose, but what you did not say has caused us many worried hours. Tell us now. Tell us everything." Kamose looked up at her from his position on the floor. She was staring down at him, her expression carefully composed, but he knew her well enough to sense apprehension beneath the motionless lines of her age-scored face. The knowledge increased his reluctance to speak, but he swallowed, drew up his knees, and began to recount the events Ramose had repeated to him with such bitterness.

His words were arrows, each finding a mark in the listeners and burying deep and painfully. Aahmes-nefertari's hands unfolded, found their way to the arms of her chair, and began to grip the gilded wood ever tighter. The colour gradually drained from her face. Aahotep slowly bent lower and lower on the stool until her forehead rested on her knees. Even Ahmose, who already knew of the fate his sister had chosen, felt the sting of Kamose's voice as he told of Tani's marriage to their enemy, her new title of Queen, the name the Setiu called her. He was pleating and then smoothing out the hem of his kilt repeatedly and scrutinizing the ceiling. Only Tetisheri sat immobile, scarcely blinking, her hooded eyes never leaving Kamose's mouth. But it seemed to him that as the moments slipped away they carried her vitality with them, leaving her an ancient husk in which the life force had sunk to a flicker.

He was not sure how long he spoke. The words could change nothing. At last he closed his mouth and a heavy silence rushed in.

He expected an outburst of furious indignation from his grandmother, but when she spoke it was gently. "Poor child," she croaked. "Poor Tani. She went to Het-Uart with such courage, not knowing what would become of her, determined to keep faith with the family through any torment Apepa could devise. But she was not prepared for a subtler kind of torture, one that was not recognized as an attack on her innocence. And poor Ramose. His alliance with this family has left him accursed." Aahmes-nefertari had begun to cry.

"How could she do such a thing?" she burst out hysterically. "How could she give her body to that . . . that aging reptile, the murderer of her father, the blasphemer!"

"Calm yourself, Aahmes-nefertari, or you will disfigure your baby with your violence," her mother said thickly. She had struggled upright and was clinging to her braid with both hands as though it might be a lifeline. Aahmes-nefertari continued to sob.

"The thought of our blood mingling with Apepa's in some bastard child Tani may produce makes me sick!" Aahotep said loudly, with such venom that Kamose was shocked. "Tell me she is not pregnant, Kamose! Tell me she has not been so stupid! What would Seqenenra say?"

"He would say that she is a casualty of war," Kamose responded harshly. "And no, as far as Ramose could ascertain she carries no child, nor has she given birth. If it were so, I think Apepa would have taunted him with the fact. Tani has no Setiu blood in her. The title of Queen is an honorary one. Apepa already has a Chief Wife who is fully Setiu and whom he regards as therefore fully royal, not to mention numerous secondary Setiu wives. Apepa's sons have no tincture of Egypt running through their veins. To him they are pure. You know in what disdain the Setiu hold us. Tani must know it also. Surely she would not risk giving birth to a baby of mixed parentage, even if Apepa was intelligent enough to see such an event as an opportunity to lay claim to a heritage that has always been ours. Besides, it is much too late for him to rally any support by considering that particular alternative." Noting the hectic flush on Aahotep's cheeks and the unnatural brightness of her eyes, he pulled himself to his feet and taking the winecup from his grandmother he carried it to his mother, winding her trembling fingers around its stem and helping her to lift it to her lips. She gulped at it, then pushed him away.

"It is easy for you to talk that way," she said shrilly. "Casualty of war! We are all casualties of war yet we have clung to our integrity." The wine glistened on her mouth. A few drops hung quivering, netted in the dark strands of her braid. "You men," she went on more coherently. "You are able to purge yourselves of your suffering by action. March, sweat, swing your swords, engulf your pain in the mindless exultation of bloodlust. But what of us? Tetisheri, your sister, myself? How may we rid ourselves of this hurting? May we hunt? Net fowls in the marshes? Swim? Eat too much? Sleep too often?" With one motion she threw back her head and drained the cup, then set it upside down on the table with a crash. "Those polite pursuits are too weak to burn away a pain that grows and grows in the heart. You are fortunate, my sons. You can kill by killing." She rose clumsily, the stool tumbling to the floor behind her, and walked to the door. The others watched her in a dumbfounded silence. When she had gone, Tetisheri cleared her throat.

"Tani is her daughter," she said. "She feels this more than any of us, even me. She will view it more sanely in the morning. Ahmose, take your wife to her quarters and have Raa put her to bed. Eat a spoonful of honey, Aahmes-nefertari, it will soothe you and help you to sleep. Go now." The girl nodded and allowed her husband to assist her out of the chair. She had stopped weeping. Together they reached the door.

"May I return, Tetisheri?" Ahmose asked. She looked at him for a long time, and presently her face was lit by a slow smile.

"You may indeed," she said, "and not a word will pass between your brother and myself until that moment." Her tone held no sarcasm. Ahmose nodded and he and Aahmes-nefertari left. Uni appeared around the open door.

"Has Your Majesty need of anything?" he enquired.

"Yes. Bring more wine and two clean cups and whatever sweetmeats remain from the meal in the garden," she ordered. "And make sure Kares and Hetepet are with Aahotep. Ask Kares to bring me word on his mistress's condition in an hour or two. Tell Isis I will undress myself tonight. She can go to bed." The steward bowed himself out. Tetisheri rose stiffly and began to pace. "My joints ache," she murmured. "Why do they ache in summer? It is usually the cold winter nights that seep into them." She sighed. "Ah, Kamose. The news of Tani has taken the bloom from your victory. We must bring her home when you finally kill the impostor. Pick up that cushion from the floor and put it on my chair for me. The bones of my old buttocks jut out like a donkey's pelvis. Thank you. The three of us have much to discuss when your brother returns." She continued to walk up and down until with a discreet knock Uni and a servant entered and set pastries and wine on the table. Ahmose came back as they were withdrawing. The door was closed. Tetisheri lowered herself into her chair. "Is she asleep?" she wanted to know.

"Not yet, but she is more peaceful," Ahmose replied. He took up a platter and a cup, filled them both, then regained his position on the floor. Kamose joined him.

"We will put Tani out of our minds," Tetisheri said determinedly. "Not out of our hearts or our prayers, of course, but it will do no good to endlessly hurl imprecations at Apepa and accusations at Tani. I want to hear of the campaign and the battle. The oasis, the desert march, the spiking of the wells and springs of the oasis, everything. The Abanas and Paheri gave me a clear vision of your navy's composition, morale and purpose this afternoon, so do not bore me with things I have heard already. You have good men there, Kamose." The brothers looked at each other, then raised their cups in unspoken agreement.

"We salute you, Grandmother," Ahmose said with a grin. "You are truly an unstoppable force."

"Do not be impertinent," she retorted as they drank, but she was obviously pleased.

Their gesture had lightened the sombre atmosphere that had lingered in the room. All at once it became a cozy haven. The lamps sent out a steady glow, softening the grooves in Tetisheri's face, creating warm shadows, serving to draw the three of them together. The food on the table smelled sweet, its odour mingling with the faint tang of the wine, and Kamose thought briefly how it was the memory of simple sensual pleasures accumulating over a lifetime that yielded an ultimate sanity and wholeness. He was not hungry. As Ahmose cleared his plate and refilled it, Kamose drank his wine and began an account of all that had happened since he last left Weset. There was much to say that had been impossible to express in the regular reports he had dictated. Tetisheri listened attentively, interrupting him sometimes with abrupt questions.

When Ahmose had finished eating, he joined in and gradually Kamose realized that Ahmose was taking over the conversation. Neither his grandmother nor his brother seemed to notice that he himself had fallen silent. There was a harmony between them that Kamose had never seen before. Ahmose talked easily and vividly, answering Tetisheri with smiles and gestures, and she in turn became animated, leaning forward, her own withered fingers moving like fans through the still air. Kamose watched them bemused, but slowly his surprise dwindled and the sense of dislocation that had almost unmanned him on the boat returned.

They have an understanding, he thought. After years of polite distance between them they have suddenly learned to respect each other. When did this happen? And how? Grandmother always regarded Ahmose as sweet but rather stupid, and

Ahmose himself chafed under what he saw as her domineering ways. I have lost my place in her esteem. I have been demoted. Jealousy surged up in him and just as quickly vanished. I am not a part of the fabric of this family or this place any more, he told himself sadly. I am a Tao, I rule this nome, but the boy, the young man I was, no longer exists. It is as if he died and I, this imitation Kamose, have come from somewhere far away to replace him. It is not simply that war has changed me. It has changed me, but I think I have been moving towards this moment since the day Si-Amun killed himself. I love them all, my royal kin, but I can never stand among them again.

He came to himself to realize that conversation had ceased and they were both staring at him inquiringly. "I'm sorry," he said with an effort. "What did you say?"

"Grandmother asked you what plans you have for next season," Ahmose explained. "After the thanksgiving and celebrations we must endure the Inundation but what then, Kamose?" Kamose had been so far sunk in his own reflections that he did not know whether they had discussed Hor-Aha's request on behalf of the Medjay. He broached it hesitantly. In spite of the wine he had drunk he was coldly sober and his throat was still dry.

"Wawat is being threatened by the Kushites," he said, pulling his thoughts together. "Hor-Aha wants us to take a punitive force south on their behalf. It might be a good idea." Immediately Tetisheri bristled.

"Why?" she demanded. "Let the savages sort out their own problems. We cannot afford to draw the Kushites' attention to us. We cannot open a new battle front to the south and thus dissipate our divisions."

"You do not feel that we owe a debt to Hor-Aha?" he suggested wryly. "That if we do not aid the Medjay, they will desert us or worse?"

"Hor-Aha has been well rewarded for his loyalty to this house by his promotion to General and then by a princely title and the promise of a nome to govern in the Delta," she retorted. "That was a very foolish move, Kamose. It will ultimately antagonize every Egyptian noble."

"Hor-Aha's mother was an Egyptian," Kamose reminded her, "and he regards himself as Egyptian, notwithstanding his colour. As for a Medjay revolt, I do not fear it. They are more likely to simply disappear if they are disaffected." He straightened his legs and getting up from the floor he poured himself more wine, then took the chair Aahmes-nefertari had vacated. "No," he went on. "There are better reasons for leading a punitive expedition into Wawat and rescuing the Medjay's families from their nasty neighbours."

"Teti-En," she said at once. It was a statement, not a question. Kamose nodded.

"He is one. You know of the messenger who was intercepted near the oasis. He was carrying a plea for assistance from Apepa to Teti the Handsome. Obviously that request did not get through, but if Teti-En does indeed regard himself as Apepa's ally, we cannot discount an attack from the south at some time. He must be aware of what has been happening in Egypt."

"But surely that very awareness will keep him quiet," Ahmose objected. "We have talked about this before, Kamose. Teti-En might have been able to make a small incursion into Egypt, perhaps even capture Weset. He would have had to subdue Wawat first but he might have managed it. It is too late for him now that we hold the whole country but for one city and its environs. Defeat would be certain for him."

"All the same I do not like a threat, no matter how small, at my back," Kamose said. "But there is an even better reason why I have decided to aid the Medjay." His cup was empty again, although he did not remember drinking. "I am going to claim the gold routes. We need gold and plenty of it, for the gods, for ourselves if I am to be crowned King, to pay the Princes and rebuild Egypt. We know nothing of the forts our ancestors built to safeguard the gold sources, whether they still stand, whether the tribesmen have taken them. The Setiu have cared nothing for them because they and the gold have straddled both Teti-En's territory and Wawat and Teti-En has a treaty with the Setiu. I will take them back."

"So it seems that you have made up your mind," Tetisheri said. "The Princes will not like it. They will want to siege Het-Uart yet again next winter." Ahmose shot her a warning glance that Kamose did not miss.

"The Princes cannot see farther than their own aristocratic noses!" he exploded. "They will do as they are told or suffer my extreme displeasure! I hold almost all of Egypt and yet they are still looking over their shoulders, afraid that they will wake up one morning to find that Apepa has somehow magically taken it all back! They are cowardly mice terrified of the snake!"

"Alienate them and we could still lose everything," Ahmose warned at once. "There is a fine balance between keeping them reassured and making them do what you want, Kamose." Kamose, his anger evaporating, only grunted. Tetisheri pushed herself out of the chair.

"Go to bed, both of you," she said. "I am tired now. You will go to the temple tomorrow, Kamose, and arrange the thanks-giving?"

"Yes." He and Ahmose had also risen and were at the door. "Sleep well, Grandmother." She waved them away and the door closed softly behind them.

The guard in the passage saluted them as they walked side by side towards their own quarters. "You have come to an agree-ment with Tetisheri," Kamose remarked as they paused outside Ahmose's rooms before parting. Ahmose smiled.

"I suppose you could call it that," he said. "It is certainly more than a truce. Last time we were home I was brave enough to march into her den and demand recognition. She took it well. I think she even learned some respect for me because I stood up for myself. It has taken me a long time to grow up." He shrugged and gave Kamose a shrewd look. "However, you need not fear that you have lost her greater affection," he finished. "I will always be on trial to her, proving myself without hope of a final verdict." His words made Kamose feel petty. He returned his brother's smile and left him.

He entered his own quarters and stood for a while absorbing the familiarity. It had been many months since he had lain on that couch, sat in that chair, watched his body servant raise the hanging on that small window. He had longed to be here, indeed, in his imagination he had often closed his door and turned to face the things that spoke to him of his true identity and in whose mute embrace he would be able to think of Tani, even cry for her. Now that his comforting fantasy had become reality, the invitation was there but his willingness to answer it was not. I am not ready, he told himself resignedly. I will sleep in my cabin on the boat. Taking up his headrest and a blanket, he blew out the lamp Akhtoy had left burning for him and left the house, intending to make his way to the watersteps, but somehow his feet found the narrow, uneven little track leading to the break in the crumbling wall surrounding the old palace and so to the ancient pillars marking the entrance to the reception hall. Behek materialized from somewhere close by and padded after him.

The thick darkness within reached out to enfold him but he was not afraid of it, nor of the rubble and treacherous cavities that waited to wrench ankles or even break bones. The delineaments of the vast rooms held no secrets for him. He whispered a reverent greeting to the ghosts thronging the majestic spaces as he passed through and then climbed up the dusty stairs to come out at last on the roof. Scuffing aside the small loose stones, he folded the blanket, laid it down, and eased himself onto it. His neck relaxed onto the headrest as Behek stretched out beside him. For a long time he lay gazing up at the stars pricking silver in the immensity of blackness above him. Slowly his mind emptied. The peace he knew he could find nowhere else but here in this melancholy ruin began to steal over him and at last he sighed, closed his eyes, and slept.

As soon as the dream began, he knew what it was, and although he was asleep his conscious self quickened in joyful anticipation. He found that he was standing in the spot where he had believed that he was lying, and it was a bright, hot sum- mer morning. Beyond the lip of the palace roof the tips of palm trees swayed in the gusty wind and he was able to catch glimpses of the river, its surface glittering in the sun. But it was not the view that delighted him. A strong impulse was causing him to turn towards where Amun's temple lay. He knew, some- where in his dreaming mind, that he should not be able to see the canal leading to the paving before the outer court but his eyes found it quite easily. He waited, scarcely breathing.

She came out from the thin shadow of the pylon and began to walk along the edge of the god's waterway. Her head was down. In one hand she held a bow and an arrow, both flashing with the sheen of gold, and in the other a tall spear of silver tipped in gold. Her garb was military: a short, coarse linen kilt, wide leather belt, leather sandals and a leather cap hiding her hair. Last time I saw her she was also carrying weapons, Kamose thought breathlessly, but they were mine and she was walking away from me. This time she comes towards me. If she looks up, I will be able to see her face! He ran to the edge of the roof and peered down, heart pounding, everything in him tensed on the vision that had now reached the river path and had turned in his direction. Clenching his fists, he willed her to lift her head, but she continued to give him nothing more than the top of her helmet and her long, exquisitely fashioned body as she strode through dappled sunlight.

She was almost abreast of him now and he became aware of a box lying in the dust beside the track, its lid thrown back to reveal the contents. For one awestruck moment he forgot the woman, for within it, on its bed of padded damask, lay the Royal Regalia. Light moved slowly over the curves of the white and red Double Crown and sparked off the gold, lapis and jasper of the Crook and the Flail resting to either side. As he stared at it almost tranced, two sandalled feet entered his vision. The woman had come to a halt. She is going to pick up the box, Kamose thought excitedly. She is going to bring it to me. The woman bent down and placed the weapons carefully and reverently to either side of the box, then she raised her naked arms and bowed low to the holy symbols of Egypt's Kings. But she did not touch them. Straightening, she turned in through the wide gap in the palace wall where the main gate used to hang and disappeared from Kamose's sight.

With an exclamation he spun round and hurried to the stairs that led back down into the women's quarters, intending to rush to meet her, but at the first step a paralysis fell on him and he could not move. Clenching his teeth in a paroxysm of anxiety and haste, he willed his feet to obey him. He fancied he could hear her coming through the dimness below. Her feet were on the stairs. She was climbing, her tread soft and sure. She is coming to me! he was shouting silently. At last my heart's desire will be fulfilled, my soul's wound healed. I have been faithful to you, mysterious messenger of the god. I have craved no other embrace but yours. Heal me. Heal me!

She had reached the top. One delicate hand curled about the rough corner of the windcatcher. One brown knee was flexed. He caught the blur of her face, one swift glimpse of dark almond eyes, the curve of a cheek. She was singing to him, her voice high and piping like a bird, then he found himself awake and panting, clinging to the windcatcher with both shaking hands in an early, windless dawn. His feet were tangled in the blanket on which he had slept. His headrest had tumbled across the roof. Birds swooped around him, filling his ears with their early morning melodies as they fed.

Confused and aching with loss, sweat pouring from him, he staggered to where he could look down on the gaping hiatus in the old wall. Briefly he thought he saw the box still there beside the dawn-deserted path but he blinked and there was nothing but beaten earth and straggling grass and the cool flow of the river. He fell to his knees. "Amun, no, Amun, no," he groaned, over and over again, until the pain in his ka overwhelmed his tongue and he could do nothing but rock with his arms around himself as the sun pulled itself ponderously free of the desert horizon behind him and began to fill the air, already stale, with its fire.

He had intended to bathe, eat, and then walk to the temple to greet Amunmose and consult with him regarding the great thanksgiving to take place, but instead he paced in the garden until he had ceased to tremble and his mind had cleared. The house was stirring as he made his way to his sister's apartments. Servants burdened with fresh linen, jugs of water and trays that exuded the wholesome odour of newly baked bread bowed to him as he went. The guard was changing, the night watch wearily giving up their posts to the soldiers of the morning. Twig brooms stirred up dust. Doors stood open. Kamose heard Behek's deep, commanding bark coming from somewhere outside.

Reaching Aahmes-nefertari's door, Kamose knocked. After a moment it was opened and Raa looked at him inquiringly.

"Is my brother within?" Kamose asked. The servant shook her head.

"No, Majesty. His Highness has just gone down to the river to swim."

"If Aahmes-nefertari is awake, I want to speak to her. Please announce me." Raa bowed and closed the door. Kamose waited. Presently she admitted him, slipping past him into the passage as she did so, and Kamose walked up to his sister's couch.

The room was east-facing, as were all the family's bedchambers, so that the gentler morning sun might be enjoyed but the heat of the afternoon sun could not penetrate. Raa had already tidied any litter from the night before and raised the hanging on the small window so that a shaft of white light lay across the blue-tiled floor and filled the pleasing space with a cheerful glow. A chair draped with the sheath Aahmes-nefertari would wear that day sat a little way away from the window and next to it her cosmetic table was open, displaying the pots and jars that held her perfume and face paint. Under it her sandals stood neatly in pairs. In one corner her shrine to Sekhmet, the lion goddess, was closed, the incense stand before it full of grey ash, but beside the couch a small likeness of Bes, fat and smiling protector of families, presided. Kamose remembered it. Bes occupied a place of honour in Tetisheri's quarters until called upon to protect the pregnant members of the family, and Kamose, who had been three years old when Ahmose was born, could see Bes squatting in a similar spot close to his mother's couch. The memory included his father's laugh and Si-Amun's unbroken treble and he pushed it away before any emotion came with it.

His sister was still in bed, propped up on cushions under a disorder of sheets, her face somnolent with sleep, her long hair tousled about her white-clad shoulders. She held out a hand to him as he crossed to her, but her welcoming smile faded as she looked at him. "Kamose!" she blurted. "What have you been doing? Were you drunk last night?" Her eyes scanned him again and the smile returned. "You slept in the old palace, didn't you? You have stone dust all over you." He took the proffered hand, finding it hot, and kissed it tenderly.

"You are right," he admitted. "I love the old palace. I go there for privacy and to think, Aahmes-nefertari. Are you well this morning?" She made a face.

"I am perfectly well but very uncomfortable. I wish that this baby would hurry up and decide to be born. I feel so ugly. And I'm often too lazy to get up." Kamose raised his eyebrows.

"Ahmose adores you," he said. "You can never be ugly to him. As for being lazy, why should you get up until you are ready to come to my great thanksgiving ceremony?" She sighed and lay back.

"Yes," she nodded. "Thanksgiving. It has been quite a wonderful year, hasn't it? Babies conceived, battles won, you and Ahmose home once more." She bit her lip. "But Tani . . . I forgot at first when I woke and then your news came back to me and, Kamose, the anger was still there. I did not sleep it away. I try to feel the love I once had for her but it is gone. Not even pity remains. She betrayed us all. I suppose I imagined that you and Ahmose would defeat Apepa and rescue Tani and you would all come home in triumph and she would marry Ramose and everything would be as it was before. But it never will." She ran a hand across her face and up into her uncombed hair. "I was wandering in some childish dream but it has fled. In one evening I grew up." Her words mirrored those of her husband. Kamose scrutinized her carefully. There was indeed something different about her, in the eyes perhaps. They were as clear as ever but their brilliance seemed to have taken on a hard shine.

"Try not to let it make you bitter," he said quickly and she laughed. The sound was harsh.

"Bitter? This from the King whose pursuit of vengeance has disembowelled Egypt like a sacrificial bull? Oh, do not be alarmed, Kamose," she added as his expression changed. "It was a means to an end we all recognize as entirely necessary. Egypt is now being reborn. For this you deserve all honour. But you cannot deny that there is much bitterness in your own heart." He shook his head.

"I do not deny it, Aahmes-nefertari. Forgive my patronizing words."

They sat for a while in a silence filled by the last of the dawn chorus and the far-off murmur of the gardeners' voices as they began their morning chores. Then Aahmes-nefertari said, "You have not often come to my room, Kamose. Was there something in particular you wanted to discuss?"

"Yes." He looked full into her face. "I want you to tell me the thing you are keeping from me."

"What thing?" She seemed utterly bewildered, but Kamose thought he caught a gleam of something, a shrinking, perhaps even a spasm of fear in her face and the minute twitching of her fingers against the rumpled sheet.

"You know what thing," he said roughly. "The thing I have seen twice in your eyes since I returned. Twice in one day, Aahmes-nefertari! Please do not lie to me." She pursed her lips.

"I try never to lie, Kamose," she faltered. "Really, I am not sure I know what thing you mean."

"Then let me help you. I will confide in you, my sister, and in return you will tell me everything. Are we agreed?" She nodded hesitantly. Kamose left the couch and went to stand by the window. Now that the time had come to unburden himself, he found it difficult to begin. He kept his face turned away from her. "I have always been happiest when alone," he ventured quietly. "Even as a child, though I loved you all and played and swam and hunted, there was something in me that could only be satisfied in some solitary place."

"The old palace," she suggested. "Even when we were small and Father warned us to keep away from it, you defied him." Kamose turned long enough to smile at her.

"Yes. But it is not my aloneness I want you to understand. It is my continual reluctance to marry, to take a wife. That reluctance is certainly allied to my desire to live a celibate life but it is not the chief reason. I am not a virgin, Aahmes-nefertari. Neither did I refuse to marry you, although that was my right, because I found you distasteful. Far from it! I could not consider such a thing, dearest, because of another woman."

"But, Kamose . . ." He held up a hand.

"Wait. She is not flesh and blood, this woman. She visits me in dreams, very rarely. It was she who showed me how to mount our rebellion after Apepa had come here to pronounce sentence upon us and all hope seemed lost. Before that I used to think that she was nothing more than the embodiment of all I wanted, the perfect female constructed from the yearnings of my ka, but not any more."

He paused, looking out over the sun-drenched garden. It is one thing to come to the conclusion that she has been sent to me by Amun himself, he reflected, and quite another to voice such a deduction aloud. It is frightening to have evidence that I am under the direct scrutiny of a god, even though I address prayers to him every day. "I did not see her again until last night," he went on. "All through the months of campaigning I missed her and longed for her as though she were a lover. I have never seen her face, Aahmes-nefertari. Only her beautiful, lithe body and her magnificent hair. But I have come to believe . . ." He swung back into the room. Aahmes-nefertari was staring at him with rapt attention. " . . . to believe that she comes to me with messages from Amun himself," he managed. "I will tell you what she did last night and then you will interpret her actions. I have the distinct feeling that you can."

"But, Kamose, I am not priestly, I am not one of the Purified," Aahmes-nefertari protested. "You should go to the temple for an interpretation." Her words seemed nothing more than a desperate defence to Kamose. He smiled thinly and ignored them. Carefully he recounted the dream, leaving out no detail and as he relived it the sadness and frustration welled up in him so that several times he was forced to stop speaking. Aahmes-nefertari became more agitated as he went on, until by the time he had finished she was sitting bolt upright, the sheet clutched in both hands. "Now," he said, coming forward and pulling the chair close to the couch. "I have confided in you, my dear one. It is your turn to be honest with me."

He expected a continued resistance, denials, even the tears to which she had always been prone, but slowly her grip on the bedclothes relaxed and her stance loosened. She folded her arms across the bulge of her belly. "People think that you are not perceptive because you are so silent most of the time," she said after a long hiatus. "They think that you are continually turned in upon yourself and simply do not notice the words that fly around you, let alone the half-hidden meanings behind a look or a gesture." She sighed. "You are an intelligent man, Kamose. A great warrior, with your own kind of integrity and an unyielding disposition that makes you easy to respect but hard to love. I do not speak of the family of course. All of us seem to have underestimated your power of discernment. Forgive us for wanting to spare you misery." She was hunting for a way to express something terrible, Kamose realized.

"Go on," he said tersely.

"When you were home last winter, before you set out again

for the north, Amunmose made two sacrifices for you, a bull and some doves. The bull's blood was diseased and the doves were rotten inside. Amunmose was distressed. He approached the Amun oracle for an explanation." Kamose's gut began to churn.

"These sacrifices," he interrupted. "Were they for my success in battle or for me alone?" She swallowed audibly.

"For you alone. The oracle pronounced and Amunmose as one of the Purified interpreted. Oh, Kamose!" she burst out passionately. "You know what the oracles are like! They couch their messages in obscure language that can easily be misread! Please agree to take lightly what I must say!"

"That depends on what it is and whether or not it accords with my reading of the dream," he answered. "How do you know all this?"

"I overheard Mother and Grandmother talking about it one afternoon by the pond. They thought I was asleep. They presume that I am light of mind, you see, and do not care to retain what I hear, much less ponder it."

"I am sorry," Kamose said softly, and she shrugged.

"It does not matter. Ahmose knows better, and that is all I care about."

"Have you told him about the oracle?"

"Yes. I needed to share its weight with someone, and I did not want to go to Mother or Grandmother to admit that I had been eavesdropping, however inadvertently."

"And what was the oracular pronouncement?" He did not want to hear it, not really. Now that the moment had come, he shrank from it as though it were the breath of some vile pollution and in his shrinking he recognized the knowledge that the words would be true and his fate inescapable. Aahmes-nefertari looked down at her folded arms.

" 'Three Kings there were, then two, then one, before the

work of the god was done,'" she half-whispered. "It is not so hard to untangle, Kamose."

"No," he agreed after a while, suddenly aware that the room was becoming hot as the summer sun rose higher, but his feet and hands were very cold. "I watched her stop by the box," he murmured. "My heart leapt. I thought she would pick up the Royal Regalia and bring it to me after laying down the weapons. The fighting is almost over, I told myself in my dream. Soon I will be crowned Beloved of Ma'at, Ruler of the Two Lands. But she left it there. She came to me empty handed . . ." With an effort he controlled his voice. "I will never sit on the Horus Throne, will I, Aahmes-nefertari? Never wear the Double Crown. That glory will belong to Ahmose. Then am I to die soon?" She threw back the sheet, and pushing herself to the edge of the couch, she bent forward and embraced his neck.

"Perhaps 'the one' referred to is not Ahmose at all," she said. "Perhaps it is Ahmose who will die." He held her tightly in acknowledgement of the generosity of her statement but he shook his head against her warm cheek.

"That does not agree with my dream," he said. "No. Ahmose and I together have almost completed the work of freeing Egypt but it will be his privilege to claim the ultimate reward, not mine." Gently he set her away and got up. "Thank you for telling me," he said. "Thank you for not treating me as Tetisheri and Aahotep treat you." He was able to conjure a smile as he kissed her and made his way to the door. "I love you, my sister."

"And I you, Kamose." Her gaze was level, an interchange between equals. It comforted him a little as he closed the door quietly behind him and made his way to his own quarters.

# Chapter THIRTEEN

THE FORMAL THANKSGIVING to Amun for the inspiration and aid to the house of Tao that had culminated in the great victory on the desert outside Het nefer Apu was the most sumptuous celebration within living memory. Gold from the stolen treasure ships that had been stored in the temple was used by Kamose to ensure that the ceremony, those invited to it, and the feasting that followed, was spared no expense. The homage he himself would perform before the thousands expected to crowd the outer court and the select few invited to stand in the inner court was to take place in the late afternoon, but on the chosen morning Kamose, simply clad in kilt, linen headcloth and sandals, walked by himself through the pre-dawn hush in order to greet Amun early as a mark of especial respect.

The river path was empty and shrouded in the peculiarly expectant silence that precedes the rising of the sun as Kamose swung along it, came to the canal, and turned along its placid verge. Ahead, the twin pylons loomed, darker shapes against a sky still thick with night, although the stars were fading, and the walls enclosing the sacred precincts ran away to either side to be lost in the gloom. But a pinprick of light danced just within the outer court. Coming up to it, Kamose halted and

Amunmose bowed to him briefly. "Purify yourself," he said, passing the lamp to an acolyte, and obediently Kamose followed the boy back under the pylons and round to where the sacred lake lay, its inky surface calm. Here he removed his clothes, and walking down one of the four stone ramps leading into the water he submerged his body fully, letting the liquid flow into his mouth and eyes. Regaining the paving, he took fresh linen from the boy, quickly patted himself dry, put on his sandals, and returned to where the High Priest waited.

"I am purified," he said. Amunmose gestured and Kamose followed him across the deserted outer court and into the inner court.

Here the roof kept out any light but the brief slanting rays of a setting sun and at this hour the pillared darkness was illuminated by torches. The lesser priests had just completed the regular procession to the centre altar with their offerings of food, beer, wine, oil and flowers, which were being purified with sprinklings of water from the sacred lake and consecrated with incense. Kamose inhaled deeply. The temple, like the old palace, had always spoken to that part of him needing the sanity of divine order and the reassurance of continuity. Now as the scent of the fresh blooms and the sweet-acrid odour of incense infused him, he felt everything in him loosen. Behind him he heard the temple singers gather, a rustle of whispers and quiet coughs, but he did not turn around.

In the flare of the torches Amunmose approached the sanctuary, his long white tunic glowing, the snarling head of the leopard skin flung across one shoulder bumping gently against his hip. At the doors he paused, waiting for the signal from an acolyte high above on the roof of the temple to signal that the sun had just appeared on the horizon. In a few moments the cry came, and breaking the clay seal to the sanctuary, he flung the doors wide. At once the voice of the priestly chanter broke out. "Rise, thou great god, in peace! Rise! Thou art in peace." The singers clustered to Kamose's rear burst out in response, their music rising in a crescendo that filled the inner court. "Thou art risen! Thou art in peace! Rise thou beautifully in peace! Wake thou, god of this city, to life!" Again the lone chanter sang and again the chorus replied, "Thy brows wake in beauty, O radiant visage which knows not anger!" Amunmose beckoned and Kamose stepped with him into the presence of Amun.

In the Holiest of Holies, the small, secret heart of the temple, Amun sat smiling kindly, the orange flames of the torches sliding like precious oils over his golden skin. The two ostrich plumes denoting his ancient personification as the Great Cackler rose delicately from the crown rimming his forehead. Hands on his knees, he gazed at Kamose with mild recognition. To his left the sacred barque in which he made his infrequent journeys rested on its pedestal. To his right lay the exquisitely carved cedar chest that held the various utensils Amunmose needed to perform the god's ablutions and another altar, on which lay the previous evening's offerings.

Swiftly Kamose bent to kiss his totem's fingers and feet and then stood back. Amunmose, in a ritual gesture that was nevertheless fraught with a touching affection, embraced the god, thus bringing his soul back from the sky to his place in the temple. Four times he softly sang, "I worship thy majesty with the chosen words, with the prayers which increase thy prestige, in thy great names and in the holy manifestations under which thou revealed thyself the first day of the world," and weaving over and under the devout salutation was the flawless harmony of the singers.

Amunmose began the required tasks of his office: removing the night's offerings and replacing them with the gifts from the altar in the inner court, washing, painting and clothing the god and presenting to him the strips of white, blue, green and red linen representing the totality of Egypt. Under cover of the High Priest's movements and the surging music outside the sanctuary, Kamose spoke quietly. "My Lord, my totem, protector of Weset and upholder of my family," he said, a lump rising in his throat. "I acknowledge your omnipotence. I worship your benign power. Later I will come to you in all the pomp and glorious array of my kingship, but now I stand before you humbly as your son. I thank you for the victory you have been pleased to bestow on my armies. I thank you for the holy dreams you have sent me in which your desire has been made known. I thank you for the privilege of removing from this country the stain of foreign feet, so that you may walk upon Egypt's soil without pain, and I vow to you that if you give me Het-Uart I will raise you above every god and you will see every knee in Egypt bend before your glory."

But I will not thank you for your oracle, he said silently. Ahmose may one day have cause to stand where I am standing and give you homage for the words but your will for me seems hard, Mighty One, though of course it is just. Forgive me this tiny corner of fear lurking in my soul.

He watched as, through the pleasant grey murk of incense smoke, Amunmose took up the alabaster bowl of medjet oil, dipped the little finger of his right hand in it, and reverently touched the god's forehead so that he might be protected from all evil and impure influences and do his divine work unimpeded. The salts were being proffered: five grains of natron from Nekheb, five grains of resin, five grains of lesser salts. Oh let it be that I come here with the Double Crown on my head to have my own divinity sanctified in spite of that dreadful pronouncement! Kamose thought passionately. Pity my agony, Amun! Grant that I may indeed reap the ultimate reward for my sleepless nights and death-filled days! But in the god's mild, enigmatic smile he read no alteration, no sense that the power filling the sanctuary would relent.

Amunmose had almost completed the morning rites. Several times he sprinkled the floor and walls of the sanctuary with holy water, then he veiled the face of the god. The unused incense was emptied onto the ground. Taking a broom, the High Priest began to back out of the room, sweeping away his footprints as he went. Kamose, with a last look at the sublime being who had somehow become his soul's companion as well as his god, preceded Amunmose who then closed and bolted the doors and sealed them with clay once again. The singers closed their mouths, prostrated themselves before the doors, and began to disperse. Amunmose turned to Kamose and smiled. "Come into the sacristy, Majesty," he said. "I have something to show you."

The outer court was now bathed in limpid early sunlight and the sky above was a delicate shade of blue. Kamose's stomach growled. He was suddenly ravenous, but he accompanied the High Priest to one of the small lateral rooms running around the inside of the court. An acolyte was waiting to relieve Amunmose of the leopard skin. Amunmose shrugged it off, and walking to one of the huge storage chests against the walls, he lifted the lid and drew out a necklace. Even without direct light it glowed. "Amun's jewellers have taken the liberty of preparing ten of these," he told Kamose. "Amun decreed victory for you. Therefore the men worked in the certainty that you would want to distribute the Gold of Favours to those under your command who had distinguished themselves."

The Gold of Favours. Kamose was unable to speak for a moment. Taking the heavy thing from his friend, he stared down at it overcome with emotion. Each one of its golden rings, though thick, was intricately filigreed. Kamose knew the hours of dedicated work such a treasure represented. "I do not know how to thank you, Amunmose," he said huskily, placing the necklet back on the High Priest's upturned palms. "Neither the Gold of Favours nor the Gold of Flies has been awarded within living memory. I can only promise you that more gold will pour into Amun's coffers than even he could imagine." Putting his arms around the other man, he held him tightly. "Have them sent to Akhtoy," he decided. "I will indeed distribute them at the feast tonight. Bring the jewellers. It is not an accepted custom for mere artisans to be invited to such a formal occasion but I wish to publicly recognize their faith in me."

In the instant of intimacy he was tempted to unburden himself to the High Priest, question him about the oracular saying, give voice to his insecurities, but he held his tongue. Whether he liked it or not, there was a small but unbridgeable gulf of blood and station between himself and the smiling man he had just released. Taking his leave, he crossed the main body of the court and emerged from the shadow of the pylons into the full bright heat of the summer morning.

In the afternoon, arrayed in gold-shot linen, a gold and lapis circlet on his wig and the royal pectoral resting against his brown chest, he was carried to the temple through the near-hysterical accolade of the crowds thronging the river road. Behind him his women swayed in their litters, the curtains raised on his orders, although Tetisheri had protested against being exposed to the public gaze. The Followers of His Majesty went before and behind. Ankhmahor strode beside Kamose's conveyance. Heralds went ahead calling Kamose's titles. The Princes came behind, walking easily in their spotless kilts, their jewelled sandals scuffing up the dirt of the path. With them were their officers.

All along the route the vendors had set up their rickety stalls, selling everything from crude clay likenesses of Amun to lucky amulets that would impart to the wearer something of the magic of the blessed day. Others hawked slices of hot hyena meat, fish fried in safflower oil, the tender fresh vegetables just coming into season and dressed with dill, parsley or mint, strong dark beer, everything to fortify the people who had begun to assemble not long after Kamose had made his thoughtful way back to his house and who had waited patiently but noisily for a glimpse of the glittering procession. Small craft of every description jostled on the river. Flower petals tossed by the children rained down on water and onlookers alike.

The outer court of the temple was jammed with the lucky who had managed to elbow their way to good vantage positions. Young men sat high above the pillars shouting impudent encouragements to those struggling below. It took the heralds some time to clear a path for the royal entourage but in the end the litters were set down just within the inner court. Here the mayor of Weset and other local notables stood in their own finery. Prostrating themselves to Kamose, Ahmose and the other members of the family, they rose to watch His Majesty approach the closed doors of the sanctuary and light the incense burners held out reverently to him. Once they were lit, Kamose took them from the acolytes and, holding them high, began the rite of formal thanksgiving, his deep voice rising above the clamour in the outer court and gradually subduing it. The temple singers took up his theme as he fell silent, pouring out their praise. "Hail to thee, Amun, Lord of the Red Land, vivifier of the Black Land! Hail to thee, Amun, who has caused the invader to be crushed beneath the feet of thine appointed son Kamose! Hail to thee for whom Egypt lives, by whose heart Egypt is sustained!" The holy dancers, their long black hair loose and their fingers tinkling with castanets, twirled and bent in adoration, and Kamose, kneeling and then stretching himself full length on the warm stone paving, paid public homage to the god of Weset.

He had brought no tribute. This time he had nothing

material to offer. But in his mind, as he lay with eyes shut and cheek pressed to the dust, he lifted up to Amun the desiccated bodies of the Setiu shrivelling in the desert east of the oasis and the foreign blood that had flowed outside Het nefer Apu. Take it, Amun, he begged. It is seemly food for a weakened Ma'at. Accept it as a token of the time when the whole of Egypt will be cleansed.

After the ceremony they were carried back to the house through a thunderous acclamation. Ankhmahor posted guards at the watersteps and around the wall enclosing the estate to discourage any over-zealous citizens who might wish to give their thanks in person, but the throngs began to disperse not long after Kamose and the family had disappeared from view. The late afternoon had taken on the breathless timelessness of summer in the south and the sun's heat was fierce. No one wanted to linger away from their cool mud dwellings. Within the Tao domain a heavy quiet descended. The inhabitants sought their couches and even Kamose slept away the stress and excitement of the occasion, waking to the first faint bronzing of the sky that heralded a welcome sunset.

The feast that followed in Kamose's reception hall would be remembered by the invited guests for many years to come. Hope and triumph hung in the warm, torch-lit air, mingled with the scent of the many flowers strewn on the little tables and quivering about the necks of the noisy diners, rose in heady exuberance with the steam from the huge variety of foods and wines presented by deferential servants dressed in the blue-and-white livery of a royal House.

The harvest was about to begin, and so the dishes were laden with long spears of lettuce, gleaming green peas, nests of onion shoots, red-rimmed white slices of radish, knobbed chick-peas, all glistening with olive, sesame and ben oils and tangy with the dill, fenugreek, coriander, fennel and cumin grown by

Tetisheri's gardeners. Ducks, geese, inet-fish and gazelle meat—roasted, steamed, broiled—were piled high for greedy fingers. Purple pomegranate juice stained fine linens. The dusty grapes that had hung from the trellis arching over the path from the watersteps to the house burst in eager mouths with an unsurpassed sweetness. There were figs dipped in honey and shat cakes and nut-encrusted pastries. Jar after jar of yellow or dark red wine was unsealed and poured into cups that were waved high above men and women who sat cross-legged or sprawled on the cushions.

The musicians' efforts were drowned in the hubbub and loud laughter that echoed to the painted ceiling but sometimes in the infrequent lulls the tapping of drums and wail of pipes could be heard before the cacophony drowned them once more. As the evening progressed, the heat began to melt the scented wax cones tied to the wigs of the revellers, adding yet another strong odour to the aromas flowing on the eddies of night air from between the open pillars.

The members of the family, together with the Princes and the High Priest, sat on a dais at one end of the room. Aahmes-nefertari, flushed but obviously happy, ate little and then sat back and watched the chattering, high-spirited mass of jewelled and painted celebrants below. She kept one hand on her husband's thigh. Ahmose consumed everything placed before him with a cheerful dedication, occasionally offering her some titbit or a sip of his wine. Aahotep finished her meal with her usual methodical dignity, conversing desultorily with Prince Iasen as she did so. Tetisheri picked at the delicacies Uni presented to her, ordered beer instead of wine, and pointedly ignored Nefer-Sakharu, who had become drunk quite early in the evening and was complaining that her meat was not sufficiently cooked. Ramose watched her with an indulgent smile. Since their reunion he had spent most of his time with her, walking in the garden, taking her out on the river in one of Kamose's skiffs, playing board games with her in her quarters. He did not seem to mind her hectoring tone as she addressed a harried under-steward. Ahmose-onkh, dressed in little more than a bulky loincloth, was crawling and tottering delightedly among the guests, snatching food from their plates in his chubby fists and babbling nonsense as he stuffed it into his mouth. His nurse trailed after him anxiously.

Kamose himself ate his fill, then put his elbows on his table, and with a cup of wine between his palms he surveyed the hall that had been empty for so long. It had gradually acquired a melancholy atmosphere so that the household avoided it, pre-ferring to come and go through other doorways, but now it was fulfilling its proper function and the whispers of a dismal past were silent, overwhelmed by the happy chaos of the present.

Nefer-Sakharu's sharp voice cut into his reverie and he looked across at her thoughtfully. She was so brave, so quietly regal on that dreadful day when I was forced to execute Teti, he mused. Since coming here she has changed, become fretful. I cannot blame her, but tonight I do not want to consider whether she represents a threat, whether she is able to subvert Ramose's loyalty to me, whether her woman's tongue can sway a Prince. Or two. He sighed. It is one more thing to try to hold in my mind. An ant's bite may not be as painful as a scorpion's sting but one feels it nonetheless.

"What is the matter with you, Kamose?" Tetisheri asked him abruptly. "Such a sigh belongs to a child being dragged away from his toy in order to take a bath. Which is what Ahmose-onkh needs at this moment. Look at him! A princeling smeared in honey."

"I was thinking of Teti," Kamose answered. Tetisheri glanced at Ramose's mother, now apparently but sullenly mollified, a dish of herbed fish before her.

"No you weren't," Tetisheri retorted. "I agree with you, Kamose. She will have to be observed while the Princes are here. She is an ungrateful peasant and a nuisance. It is a pity. I remember her so well in the days when she was a gracious hostess and a kindly governor's wife."

"The war has changed us all," Kamose said. "We have travelled a long, dark road to reach this hour, this gathering. We rejoice, but all the same we are wounded."

"Not as severely as Apepa," she said tartly. "He has lost this country. And speaking of that serpent, did you know that the house snake has not returned? Aahmes-nefertari is concerned. She sees the rejection as a curse upon her pregnancy." Kamose laughed.

"Dear sister!" he chuckled. "No matter what, she will always be overly superstitious. I pity any new snake lured by the scent of milk. It will have Ahmose-onkh to contend with." He rose and nodded at the herald perched on the edge of the dais and at Akhtoy hovering behind him. As he stood up, the level of noise in the room began to drop and at the herald's strong voice it ceased altogether.

"Silence for the Mighty Bull of Ma'at, Vivifier of the Two Lands, Subduer of the Setiu, Beloved of Amun, His Majesty King Kamose Tao!" In the immediate hush Kamose surveyed the sea of upturned faces, indistinct in spite of the torches flaring around the walls. The orange light picked out an earring here, a hair ornament there, the gleam of a silver cup, and sent long shadows reaching across the dishevelled company. The prevailing mood was still one of vibrant joy.

"Citizens of Weset, servants of Amun, lovers of Egypt," he called. "Tonight we celebrate the culmination of two years of struggle, heartbreak and victory. Tonight we see, as though we peer through the blinding force of a desert storm towards an oasis, the end of Setiu domination and a return to the sanity and glory of a Ma'at fully restored. All of you have followed me in faith. You have given me your trust. Your weapons have been raised on my behalf. Therefore I pledge to you in return a fair and just administration when the Horus Throne rests once more in its place of honour here at Weset and a true and holy Incarnation sits upon it." He paused, aware suddenly of his brother's eyes upon him. Turning, he signalled to Akhtoy who placed a small, fragrant cedar chest in his arms. "In the days of my ancestors, before the Setiu came with their corrupt gods and forced us to fight like wild beasts instead of men, it was the custom for the King to reward the warrior with the Gold of Favours and the brave with the Gold of Flies. I am proud to revive this ancient and honourable practice." Lifting the lid of the box, he drew out the first necklace, weighing it deliberately in his fingers. "The jewellers of Amun, in anticipation of our victory, have created the Gold of Favours once again. They are here tonight. To them I offer my thanks for the beauty of their work and for their belief in me and in the power of Amun that never wavered." A murmur of surprise and admiration went up as he held the necklace high. Its wide, tight rings were worth ten years' grain harvest on any one of their holdings and they knew it. "Ramose!" Kamose shouted. "Come forth and be the first to receive the gratitude of your lord. I bestow the Gold of Favours upon you for voluntarily putting your head between the serpent's jaws so that the routing of the enemy in the desert was made possible. Be assured that when our conflict is finally won you will find yourself among the most powerful in all Egypt." Ramose had left his mother and approached the dais. He stood awkwardly looking up at Kamose, a smile on his lips.

"This is most unexpected, Majesty," he said. "I only did my duty."

"And in doing it, you lost everything," Kamose replied quietly. "Come closer, my friend. This gold will suit you perfectly."

Leaning down, he slipped it over Ramose's head. "Receive the Gold of Favours and the favour of your King," he said loudly. Those words had not been heard in Egypt for hentis and everyone knew it. A reverential hush filled the hall. For some moments no one moved, then all of a sudden a gale of clapping broke out, accompanied by cries of "Ramose, Ramose!" and "Long life to your Majesty!" A hail of wilting blossoms torn from the battered remains of the festive garlands rained on Ramose as he bowed and sought his place beside Nefer-Sakharu. She was staring at him bewilderedly. Her arms went around him as he sank down beside her.

"Now it is your turn, Prince Ankhmahor," Kamose said. "All evening you have been pacing the room, watching that the Followers are alert. Have you even eaten? Come here." Ankhmahor had indeed been at the far end of the hall, peering out into the palm-tossed darkness beyond. Startled, he swung round at the sound of Kamose's voice and skirting the crowded disorder in the centre of the hall he moved forward. "Ankhmahor, Commander of the Followers of His Majesty," Kamose said. "You followed me without demur although you had a great deal to lose by doing so. Your presence has been a comfort and a bastion of strength to me. Your courage in battle is unsurpassed. Receive the Gold of Favours and the favour of your King." Ankhmahor gravely lowered his head and the heavy necklet settled on his breast.

"Your Majesty is generous," the Prince said quietly. "I do not deserve this honour, but I vow to serve you as long as I have breath. I and my family are your servants always."

"I know," Kamose told him. "It is pointless for me to offer you more land or greater riches for you are already a wealthy man, but to you I promise a vizier's position if the god wills that I become the One. You are wise and trustworthy." He scanned the hall as Ankhmahor melted back into the shadows on the periphery of the multitude. "Kay Abana, are you here?" he called out. "Where are you?"

"I think I am still here, Majesty," Abana's voice boomed out from somewhere to the rear. "But I confess that the quality of your wine has made me doubt my very existence this night." Amid a gale of laughter he struggled to his feet. Kamose regarded him with mock solemnity.

"Who is the woman clinging to your leg and attempting to whisper warnings in your arrogant ear?"

"This is my future wife, Idut," Kay responded promptly. "The females of Weset are indeed very comely. I have been admiring them since we arrived here. Idut is the loveliest of them all and I shall be taking her home to Nekheb with me. A ship's captain should have respectability."

"Be sure that her father approves," Kamose said, amused. "Now come here." Kay moved unsteadily to the dais. "You deserve a show of my royal displeasure," Kamose went on. "You were the only officer who disobeyed an order."

"I displayed initiative," Kay protested, affecting an injured look. "I behaved as an officer should."

"Then you have my royal thanks and that should be enough for any man," Kamose shot back at him.

"But, Majesty, did I not captain one of your ships in a most excellent display of competence?" Kay objected jokingly. "Was I not the only officer to lead my men against the fleeing Setiu? Do I not also deserve a show of your royal gratitude?" Kamose began to laugh. There was something so clean, so sane and reassuring about Kay. He forced a severe expression.

"Paheri tells me that you are a man of modest means, content with your little house and your work building boats and your two arouras of land on the outskirts of Nekheb," he said. "You do not need rewards. You prefer a simple life." Abana bowed somewhat unsteadily.

"Paheri perhaps overstates the degree of my contentment," he drawled. "Nekheb is as close to the paradise of Osiris as I could wish to come in this life, but perhaps there is somewhere closer. As for building boats, what would your Majesty have done without my expert knowledge and that of my father?"

"What indeed?" Kamose agreed, returning Abana's wide grin. Amid cries of, "Nekheb is an arid pit!" and "Boatbuilders stink of rotting reeds!" Kamose settled the gold around the man's neck.

"Receive the Gold of Favours and the favour of your King," he intoned. "And as an added punishment, Kay Abana, I deed to you seventy acres of land in your home district and nineteen peasants to work them. Once Het-Uart falls of course." Kay bowed again.

"Of course, Majesty. Therefore as night follows day it is certain that I will be able to claim your Majesty's generous gift. I wish you life, health and prosperity." He wove his way back to his place considerably more sober and allowed Idut to pull him to the floor. Kamose squared his shoulders and continued with the awards.

One by one the remaining Princes came up to have the gold slung around their necks. Kamose told them that like Ankhmahor they had no need of more land, but he promised a redistribution of governorships in time and with that they had to be content. They received their accolades with mute composure.

Hor-Aha was the last Prince to be honoured, and Kamose, seeing him striding confidently to the foot of the dais, found that he had no words for his greatest strategist. Placing the gold over the General's black braids, he touched the dark cheek before stepping away and their eyes met. Hor-Aha raised his eyebrows and smiled. In spite of his festive kilt, the carnelian Eye of Horus on his chest and the bulky rings on his fingers, he still wore the plain leather belt with its worn pouch containing his secret totem, the blood of Seqenenra, and with a thrill of distaste Kamose willed himself not to let his gaze stray to it. Then he was gone and those commanders worthy of the Gold of Favours took his place, Paheri among them.

Finally it was the Medjay's turn. Two of them had been singled out for bravery. They glided to the dais on their light, soundless feet, looking up at Kamose with bright eyes like shiny beads, their cheap clay necklaces and the gaudy ribbons they had tied in their hair in honour of the feast making them seem even more incongruous among the nobles and Weset notables than they were. Kamose smiled at them, speaking of the Medjay's skill and fearlessness and thanking them for what they had done, but he could not ignore the embarrassed silence that had fallen or the resentful mutters that filled it.

"To Set with them!" he grumbled at Ahmose when the ceremony was over and he sat down and gestured for Akhtoy to fill his cup. "Their fine lineage chokes them! Why can't they see that without the Medjay they would still be out there hacking their way towards Het-Uart and perhaps in danger of actually having to spill some of that precious blue blood of theirs? Sometimes I actually hate them, Ahmose." His brother let go of Aahmes-nefertari's hand and turned to fully face him.

"We have been over this a thousand times before, Kamose," he said in a low voice. "Their suspicion and prejudice cannot be changed. All we can do is limit it as best we can by taking care not to rub their noses in your preference for Wawat warriors and a black General. Keep them feeling safely superior and it will not matter." He pursed his lips and tapped Kamose on the knee. "There was no Gold of Favours for Prince Meketra," he went on. "He is not even here. Why?" Kamose shifted restlessly.

"He fought no battles for me," he answered roughly. "All he did was betray Teti. The Gold of Favours is not for such as he."

"He should at least have been invited to the thanksgiving

and the feast," Ahmose urged. "All his fellow Princes are here. Word will reach Khemmenu soon that there were great celebrations in Weset from which he was excluded. How do you think he will feel? Glad that he was left in peace at Khemmenu? No. He will be bitter and offended. He will not consider that he does not deserve the Gold of Favours. He will believe that you have deliberately slighted him, that you hold him of little account."

"Then he will believe the truth," Kamose returned. "I have not deliberately slighted him, Ahmose, but I neither like nor trust him. I cannot help it."

"I agree with your assessment of his character," Ahmose sighed, turning back to his wife. "I only hope that we are not creating trouble for ourselves later. You do not trust Intef or Iasen either, but they are here." To that there was no answer. Kamose hurriedly finished his wine, and bidding the guests continue to enjoy themselves, he quietly left the hall. He had had enough.

There was nowhere in the house to which he could retreat from the crescendoing din of the feast. Even in his own quarters with the door closed he could still hear the drunken squeals and laughter of his guests, and the garden, when he escaped outside with a cloak over his arm, was no more peaceful. Light and noise streamed out from between the pillars of the reception hall to be slowly dissipated in the shrubbery between the house and the protecting outer wall. Wandering towards the river, answering the challenge of the guards as he went, Kamose came at last to his watersteps where the family's barge and a couple of skiffs rocked peacefully against the mooring poles. A distance away to right and left the larger ships lay, dark hulks whose masts reared into the starry sky. For several moments Kamose considered crawling onto the tiny cot within the cabin he and Ahmose had shared for so many weeks but he was wary of the desire to retreat into so comfortable and familiar a place, both physically and mentally. With a word to the patient soldier watching the river he wrapped his cloak tightly around him and lay down in one of the skiffs. He was asleep almost immediately.

He did not hear the hall empty as towards dawn the drunk and satiated crowd dispersed towards the town or the accommodation Tetisheri had provided for them. Nor did he stir when with the first rays of the new sun the servants began to prepare for another day. He came to consciousness only sluggishly to find Akhtoy bending over him, sheath held high around his thighs to keep his linen out of the water, calling his name. Kamose sat up blinking in the bright morning light. "I have been searching for you for hours, Majesty," the steward said with a note of irritation. "Her Highness's labour began shortly after she retired for the night. The physician and her mother are with her. His Highness is breaking his fast by the pond if you wish to join him."

"Thank you, Akhtoy." Kamose stepped out of the skiff. The water lapping over his feet felt cool and his head began to clear. "I will eat with Ahmose. Please send my herald to me. And do not look at me like that. I will bathe later." With a bow Akhtoy regained the paving above, slipped on his sandals, and disappeared along the path. Kamose followed more slowly.

He found Ahmose sitting on the grass under a canopy, bread and cheese and a bowl of fruit beside him. He waved Kamose into the shade. "She woke me just as I was falling asleep," he said without preamble. "She is not worried, only glad that she does not have to endure another day of pregnancy in this heat. Mother will make sure all goes well and a priest is there to burn incense for Bes." He deftly sliced open a pomegranate and began to spoon out the seeds. Kamose looked at him curiously.

"And you," he said. "Are you worried?" Ahmose set down the spoon and frowned.

"Not for Aahmes-nefertari," he decided. "This is her third child. She is young, healthy and strong. But I worry for Egypt." He turned anxious eyes on Kamose. "We still face the possibility of death in battle," he went on soberly. "You or me. If we are both killed, the only heir to the Horus Throne whether we have recovered it or not, is Ahmose-onkh. Children are vulnerable, Kamose. They die easily. They die suddenly." He pushed the plate of fruit away. "Ahmose-onkh is fine today. He toddles about happily molesting snakes and driving the servants to distraction. But tomorrow he may have a fever and the next day be carried to the House of the Dead. Then who is heir to Egypt? You refuse to marry and get sons. We Taos must have sons." He scowled. "If Aahmes-nefertari gives birth to a girl, we are in a precarious position."

"I know," Kamose admitted, his mind filling with the memory of his father and Si-Amun. Seqenenra had produced three sons. Two were left. And one of us will not survive, he thought grimly. According to the oracle it will be me, but have I not always known somewhere deep in my ka that to Ahmose alone will go the glory of a long life at the pinnacle of Egypt's nobility? "You can take a second wife, Ahmose," he said carefully.

There was a long silence. Both men fixed their gaze on the cloud of flies that had begun to hover and then crawl over the disembowelled pomegranate and its oozing purple juice. Then Ahmose cleared his throat.

"You do not believe that you will live much longer, do you, Kamose?" he said softly. "You know about the oracle. So do I. Aahmes-nefertari told us both. Yet I pray fervently that it may be a mistake, that we are fretting over a phantom future." With savage, quick gestures quite unlike him he began to slash at the flies with his whisk. "I have thought about taking another woman," he grunted as he flayed the air. "But I will not tempt Ma'at. Not yet. You may reconsider your duty, Kamose, and marry yourself, and give us royal sons." He tossed the whisk onto the grass and at last looked directly at his brother. "Besides, no matter what my legitimate right may be, Aahmes-nefertari is not ready to accept the planting of my seed elsewhere. She has suffered a great deal, losing Si-Amun, losing her first child, being handed to me instead of to you, trying to come to terms with Tani's betrayal. She and Tani were close in a way that brothers cannot understand. Her life has been one deprivation after another. If she seems weak and prone to emotional outbursts, we should not be surprised."

"She has changed," Kamose broke in unthinkingly. "When I talked with her after I gave the news about Tani, there was something in her I had not seen before. A steadiness. Almost a detached coolness. Whether for good or not I can't say. She said that she has grown up." The flies were back mindlessly circling the fruit and this time Ahmose ignored them.

"The waiting is hard," he remarked, and Kamose realized that the subject under discussion was now closed. "Shall we swim, Kamose? Already the garden is like a furnace. Or will you eat?" Kamose shook his head, looking with distaste at the stiffening bread and sweating chunk of brown goat cheese. Glancing up, he saw his herald approaching. He and Ahmose came to their feet as the man bowed.

"You sent for me, Majesty?" Kamose nodded.

"Take a message to all the Princes and commanders," he said. "They are free to go home and see to their harvests and their family affairs. I shall expect regular reports from them on the state of their holdings, to be addressed to my grandmother. They must be prepared to be summoned after the Inundation. My permission extends to Prince Ankhmahor in particular. Tell him to delegate his authority over the Followers to his second.

Prince Hor-Aha will not be leaving yet, however. I will speak with him myself later. That is all."

"You will miss Ankhmahor," Ahmose said when the herald had gone. "But at least you are keeping Hor-Aha. I wish you would change your mind about Wawat. I hate the south. Unbearable heat and uncivilized tribesmen. I do not want to go there." Kamose was removing his kilt and sandals. Naked, he moved off along the path to the river.

"Neither do I," he called back over his shoulder. "But think of the gold, Ahmose!" Yet it was difficult for him to keep his own mind centred on the gold. As he plunged into the tepid water of the Nile, he was imagining the miles that would separate him from Weset, the amount of time it would take for reports from Tetisheri regarding the Princes to reach him far away in the desert wastes of Wawat, the dangerous void he would leave that anything might fill. Anything. Or any one.

There was still no news from the house when the brothers had scrambled, dripping, onto the watersteps and had made their way back through the garden. Once painted and dressed, Kamose asked Ahmose to accompany him to the west bank to see how the Medjay were faring. Together they were rowed across the river and carried in litters to the stark site of the barracks. No grass grew here on the sweep of hard-packed sand beneath the western cliffs. No trees afforded shade. Yet the Medjay did not seem to care.

Hor-Aha came out to greet Kamose and Ahmose from the doorway of the small house Kamose had ordered built for him, and the three of them walked between the rows of dun-coloured mud dwellings, greeting the archers and listening to any complaints they might have. There were few. The Medjay were an unquestioning, pragmatic group of men, easily controlled by a firm hand, but Hor-Aha warned Kamose as they paced side by side in the blistering heat under the entirely inadequate shelter of the sunshades held over them by their servants that his countrymen were restless. They wanted to go home to Wawat and see for themselves how their villages were faring under the onslaught of the Kushites. They would submit to his command but eventually they would begin to slip away. "They have heard rumours that the Princes are going," Hor-Aha said frankly. "They say that they have fought more bravely than the Princes. Their officers wear the Gold of Favours. Why can they not go home?"

"They wear the Gold?" Ahmose queried, amused. "It is not supposed to be actually worn! What odd savages they are!"

"I know that they deserve to leave," Kamose said. "But, Hor-Aha, I am afraid that they will not come back."

"They will return to fight again if you go with them into Wawat and set their land to rights," Hor-Aha insisted. Kamose wiped a trickle of sweat from his temple and squinted across at his General.

"We will go at the end of this month then," he capitulated abruptly. "That will give us time to look at any maps of Wawat that still exist in the temple archives. Apepa knows the gold routes but they have been lost to us for a very long time. I must leave some defence at Weset, Hor-Aha! Surely you see that!"

"Then let local soldiers do their duty, Majesty," Hor-Aha finished emphatically. "My Medjay must go home." Kamose felt Ahmose's quizzical gaze on him. He wanted to reprimand the General for his disrespectful language but he resisted the urge. He recognized the fuel of his ire. It was fear, not offence.

He and Ahmose ate the noon meal together in the coolness of Kamose's quarters. The women had not appeared. The house was quiet. Kamose expected Ahmose to go to his own rooms for the afternoon sleep but to his surprise Ahmose simply stretched out on the floor, a headrest under his neck. "If I am alone, I will worry," was all he said before closing his eyes. For some time

Kamose, lying on his couch with his head propped on one palm, looked down at his brother, watching the slow rise and fall of his chest under the loosely crossed hands, the flutter of his eyelids as he dreamed. I love him, he thought fondly. In spite of all the tragedies the years have brought us I take him for granted because his nature is so constant. He is always present, always in the moment, his steadiness seems rock-like and I rely on it without reflection. Yet he deserves more. He deserves to be treasured and told that he is precious to me. His brother's regular slow breaths were soothing. Kamose rolled over onto his back and fell asleep.

When they woke, the long, hot slide towards sunset had begun. Slaking their thirst, they wandered out into the garden and sat drowsily watching the fish in the pond now shadowed by the surrounding trees break the surface of the water with mouths agape to snap up the first mosquitoes. "There is something about the summer that returns me to my mother's womb," Ahmose murmured, yawning. "I feel ageless, timeless, unconcerned about anything. I feel utterly lethargic." And I feel like a ghost haunting an illusion, Kamose thought. He did not reply.

At sunset the house stirred. Appetizing aromas began to waft from the kitchen to the rear. The clatter of the servants as they prepared for the evening meal brought a return to normality. Kamose, realizing that he had not eaten all day and that he was at last hungry, was making his way back inside when Ankhmahor came up to him. "I have done as your Majesty requested," he said in answer to Kamose's question. "My son will stay and command your personal guard. He is eager to do so. I will return as soon as the harvest at Aabtu is over. I can come by the desert route if the Inundation has already begun." Kamose's heart sank. Even though he knew Ankhmahor deserved to be released, he wanted to beg him to stay. Five months without him to order the Followers was a very long time.

"There is no need for you to hurry back," he said. "I am going into Wawat soon to set the Medjay's villages to rights. I will not be back until the force of the Inundation has lessened." Akhmahor looked at him thoughtfully.

"Your pardon, Majesty, but is that wise?" he offered. "What might Apepa do if he learns that you are far away and cut off from Egypt by the flood?" Kamose shrugged.

"The flood will hamper him also," he reminded him. "The country becomes a vast lake and all troops must move on its perimeter. I think I will go down by boat so that I may use the shrinking waters to return home more quickly." He blew out a gust of breath. "I do not want to do this," he confessed. "Everything in me screams a warning. But I must. It is a matter of obligation." Ankhmahor opened his mouth to voice what would obviously be a protest but closed it again. There was a moment of silence before he spoke.

"That I do understand," he said. "It is a part of the harmony of Ma'at that must be maintained. I have been talking to the other Princes. They are concluding their preparations to leave. They would make their farewells if it were not for the imminent birth in the house." He smiled. "It is a great day for your family." Kamose embraced him.

"May the soles of your feet be firm, Ankhmahor," he said. "Take my greetings to your wife."

"Make my farewell to your grandmother," Ankhmahor requested. "I will not disturb her now. I wish you a bountiful harvest, Majesty, and a safe journey into the southern lands." Kamose watched him stride away with a deep sense of regret.

Aahmes-nefertari gave birth to a girl an hour later, and Kamose and Ahmose left their evening meal to answer Uni's summons. Their sister had left the birthing stool and was propped up on her couch with the baby already at her breast when they entered the room. Sweat-dampened hair straggled her cheeks and hung in strings over her bare shoulders. A thin haze of incense from the burner before the image of Bes lingered in the hot closeness of the air and Raa was in the act of raising the window hanging as Kamose approached the girl and kissed her hot forehead. "Well done," he said and stepped aside. Ahmose sank onto the disordered sheets, and taking one of her hands in one of his, he began to stroke his daughter gently with the other.

"Look at the black mop she already has on top of her head!" he said admiringly. "And what a delicate little snub nose! She is already very pretty, Aahmes-nefertari." His wife laughed.

"She is red and wrinkled and very greedy," she replied. Then her features became solemn. "Ahmose, I know you wanted a son," she half-whispered. "Please forgive me. Do you think that I was carrying a boy and that perhaps my rage at Tani caused him to become so distressed that he retreated behind a female form?" Ahmose leaned forward and enveloped them both in a tight embrace.

"No, my dearest," he said emphatically. "And do not fret. I love you. I love this child. We can make many more babies, male and female. How can this tiny one not be precious whatever its sex? How can you blame yourself for something the gods have decreed? We will rejoice together in your safety and her health. She is perfect, is she not?" They went on murmuring to each other while the baby let Aahmes-nefertari's nipple slip out of her mouth and fell asleep. Kamose, after watching them fondly for a while, quietly retreated into the passage and from there into the coolness of the reception hall. Here he found his mother and grandmother already eating.

"Aames-nefertari looks well, doesn't she?" he remarked.

"Yes, she does," Aahotep replied as he folded himself onto a cushion beside her and pulled his own neglected platter forward. "However, the labour was long for a third pregnancy and the heat did not help."

"It is a pity that the child is female," Tetisheri cut in. She looked tired. The network of fine lines criss-crossing her face seemed more pronounced. Her blue-painted eyelids had swelled and beneath the kohl her eyes were darkly patched. But the glance she darted at Kamose was as keen as ever. "One male offspring is not enough. Ahmose-onkh is thriving but one never knows. We need another two or three for the line to be secure."

"Not now, Tetisheri," Aahotep begged with weary humour. "I need to finish this meal and then sleep for a very long time. We will consult the astrologers. They will give the baby a name and a prognostication for the future, but neither will matter very much. You know as well as I do that Aahmes-nefertari will be pregnant again by the time the Inundation sinks. There will be male Taos in plenty."

"I hope you are right," Tetisheri said dourly. She chewed reflectively for a moment and then turned to Kamose who was scouring his dish with a piece of black bread. "The Princes and their retainers have gone," she stated. "I heard the commotion of their leaving from Aahmes-nefertari's quarters. It is already the beginning of Epophi, Kamose. Have you really decided to go into Wawat? Ankhmahor seems to think that you should not go." Kamose nodded. Reaching past her, he poured himself a cup of beer.

"I know," he commented. "He intimated as much to me. Do you and the Commander of my Followers have secrets, Grandmother?"

"Not really," she said with evident relish. "But we like each other and we have a concern for your welfare in common. Did you ask him for his opinion?"

"Really, Tetisheri, your urge to control us all is sometimes intensely annoying," Kamose responded, not sure whether to be irritated or amused. "The decision is not Ankhmahor's to make."

"No, but his advice is sensible. He is a wise man." Kamose drained his beer.

"I do not need his advice," he retorted. "And I am not going to ask you for yours either. Wawat cannot be ignored if we want to keep the Medjay happy." His mother had been listening quietly to their interchange. She broke in quickly.

"The concern is defence," she said slowly and firmly. "For two campaigning seasons Tetisheri and I have ordered the soldiers here and watched the river. We have organized spies in Pi-Hathor. We can do it again, but it is a great responsibility, Kamose." Kamose fumbled his cup and almost dropped it.

"You have spies in Pi-Hathor? But why didn't you tell me?"

Aahotep shrugged. "There was no need. You had too much weighing on your mind already. Besides, Het-uy, the mayor, has been honouring his agreement with you and will continue to do so given your overwhelming success this winter. You asked us to watch and it seemed sensible to us to do a little more. That is all. And speaking of spies, have you considered recruiting men in Het-Uart? There must be some way to breach those walls. No defence is completely impregnable. Besides, spies could bring you the mood of the citizens there, the number and disposition of Apepa's remaining troops, what trade is still going on, all sorts of important information." She smiled thinly. "You might even find men willing to whisper words of sedition and uncertainty in the city. All Egypt knows that Het-Uart is the only thing standing between you and a united country. Demoralize them, Kamose. Give them bad dreams."

She glanced at Tetisheri and a spark of mutual complicity passed between them. Kamose saw it with wonderment and a tiny chill. For a fleeting second he ceased to recognize them, these women who had governed his childhood and ruled the household. Briefly their sex and even their age had vanished to leave an impression, there and instantly gone, of two fleshless predators facing each other in an emotionless agreement that shocked him.

"I think I will leave that matter in your hands," he said somewhat dazedly. "You are obviously more than capable of administering such a scheme. It is true that women far outstrip men in the practice of subterfuge, manipulation and deceit." His mother laughed.

"You look like a bewildered sheep, my dearest," she chided him. "I do not know whether to be flattered or insulted at your astonishment. We may be women, but we are also Taos. We do not lack for courage or intelligence. Shall I pour you more beer?" He nodded dumbly, his gaze fixed on her long, graceful fingers as she tipped the dark liquid into his cup. "That is why I will never forgive Tani," she went on conversationally. "Never. Now, Tetisheri, we should take to our couches and later we will visit Aahmes-nefertari. Should we engage another nurse, do you think, or will Raa be able to cope with the new baby as well as Ahmose-onkh?" She was rising to her feet as she spoke, and Tetisheri, with many groans and complaints regarding her stiff joints, followed suit. Bowing to him absently, they passed out of the hall, still talking lightly, and Kamose was left to stare pensively into a dimness that seemed decidedly smug.

# Chapter ✺
# FOURTEEN

KAMOSE SENT IPI to the temple archives for any maps of Kush and Wawat that might have survived the turbulence of the years since his ancestors had built forts in the south and established regular trade routes. Originally the lowliest Setiu had obtained permission to pasture their flocks in the Delta during Rethennu's dry seasons, after which they would return to their own land. Gradually they stayed longer in the Delta's unfailing vegetation and established permanent villages. They were followed by their more affluent brothers, men of ambition and intelligence who took an active and predatory interest in Egypt's weak administration. They had been known throughout the world as traders, disseminating goods between the islands of the Great Green and venturing as far away as Naharin in the quest for wealth that had earned them the Egyptians' contempt. They were middlemen, purveyors of commodities, hagglers and shopkeepers whose ships and caravans supplied anything to anyone for the right price.

Pragmatic to the core, they adapted their gods, their way of life and their ideologies to suit whatever nation welcomed what they offered. Like chameleons their colours changed depending on the circumstances in which they found themselves, but underneath their polite camouflage they were a race alien to everyone but themselves. When their eyes had alighted on the Delta, rich and secure and central to their business affairs, they had lulled the lazy and complacent Egyptians into a sense of security and then gradually, almost imperceptibly, had lifted the reins of government, and control of the trade routes, from the King's fingers.

The forts in Wawat and Kush meant nothing to them and were allowed to sit empty, slowly crumbling in the fierce southern climate. But the wealth of those countries, the gold, leopard skins, elephant tusks, spices, ostrich eggs and feathers, drew them like flies to honey. So did the supply of slaves. Egypt had no word for the full ownership of another human being until the Setiu taught it to them. Helplessly the Egyptians watched the abundance of the south pass quickly and efficiently into the grasp of their masters.

But now they would take it back. Ipi had returned from the temple with three maps, the most recent still many hentis old, having been drawn up by the great King Osiris Senwasret, the third of that name, who had hacked a canal called the Way of Khekura through the first cataract leading south so that his soldiers and treasure boats could come and go more easily. He and his predecessors had built the chain of forts on the border between Wawat and Kush to protect the gold sources from local marauders, but they could not have foreseen my own necessity, Kamose thought grimly as he bent over the brittle papyrus. "This information is scanty," he remarked, letting the map roll up. "Hor-Aha, in what condition is the largest fort at Buhen?" The General hesitated.

"Buhen is the northernmost member of the chain," he replied, "but it marks the southernmost limits of Wawat territory. I have not seen it for some time. It has been taken over by native villagers who will not have a significant means of defence.

They can easily be routed if Your Majesty desires to repair and man it again."

"I may do so," Kamose said. "However, putting Wawat to rights must come first. Is my ancestor's canal still navigable?"

"That I cannot say." Hor-Aha shook his head. "I and the Medjay travelled overland to and from Wawat. Perhaps the sailors at Nekheb will be able to tell you."

"Gold has still been coming up from Kush by water," Ahmose pointed out. "The Setiu have been mining it. Did they bring it past the first cataract by caravan or use the Nile the whole way?"

"It is time that is worrying me," Kamose said. "The river will begin to rise in a little over a month but I have things to do here before we leave. If there are no unforseen obstacles below Swenet, we can be in Wawat well before the flood. If not, and we take boats, we might be trapped."

"Take the boats anyway," Ahmose urged. "We can ride the river home once the Inundation begins to subside. I like this venture no more than you, Kamose. We will be far from home if there is trouble." Silently Kamose agreed. Handing the maps back to Ipi, he signalled that the meeting was over.

In the two weeks remaining before the month of Mesore began Kamose did his best to give local matters his attention. He inspected the prison he had ordered rebuilt the previous year, the motive for which he could scarcely recall and which filled him now with a mixture of foreboding and anxiety. He listened to the crop assessments for the harvest that had just begun. It would be a bountiful year and he reminded Ipi, writing furiously at his feet while the various stewards made their reports, to carefully note the tithe that was to go to Amun.

He crossed the river to the west bank, ostensibly to see how work on his tomb was progressing. Like every other noble he had begun it as soon as he reached his majority. The masons and artists involved in its construction and decoration welcomed him effusively but the visit depressed him. He was still young, only twenty-five years old. There was no urgency to the tasks the brawny stoneworkers were performing, no need to hurry the smoothing and plastering of the still-jagged walls between which he descended to the dank coolness of the room where he would eventually lie.

How will the artists fill these voids? he wondered with despair. I have no wife or children. There will be no pretty scenes of family felicity, no peaceful accomplishments completed over a lifetime of service to my nome. Instead I have killed and burned and battled. The paint laid so brightly here will glow with the red of blood, the blue of tears, and that will be the story of my life. Do I dare to command the recording of such an account seeing that I have not freed Egypt and my deeds will probably not be redeemed by a King's burial? With an effort he gave the artists his attention, looking at their sketches and answering their questions, assuring them that they need not hurry their work, when all he wanted was to tell them to put down their tools and go home.

Emerging half-blinded from the dimness of the passage, he stood gazing out over the sandy plain that lay between the cliff of Gurn behind him and the thin ribbon of green beyond which marked the Nile. To his right the pyramid of Osiris Mentuhotep-neb-hapet-Ra hugged the tumbled rocks and before him, scattered here and there in the baking aridity, other small pyramids jutted, each with its courtyard and low surrounding wall. Here his ancestors lay, beautified and justified, the royal Kings of his beloved country, in whose shadow he lurked like a dwarf. These were not the mighty gods of the beginning whose monuments reared in all their awesome immensity near the entrance to the Delta. They were closer to him in time and familiarity, men of strength and wisdom whose divine blood, though diluted, provided a tincture to his own. I need not be ashamed in your presence, he spoke in his mind to the stubby structures shimmering in the noon heat. I have done what I can and I will do more if Amun wills it. I envy you the ages in which you lived, no matter how turbulent they might have been, and the peace you now enjoy.

The astrologer priests, after consulting their charts and each other, decided that Aahmes-nefertari's little baby should be called Hent-ta-Hent. It was a safe, non-committal name with no negative connotations. They were equally conservative in their predictions for the child's future, saying merely that she would enjoy good health in such years as the gods would give her. "It is not enough," Aahmes-nefertari complained to Kamose on one of his frequent visits to the nursery where Raa was tending to both Tao children. "First they give her a name that is completely anonymous and then they fall over themselves in stepping delicately around any definite prognostication." Leaning over the sleeping baby, she gently pressed the tip of one finger to a bead of sweat that had gathered on its temple. "If she is to die, then they should say so. I have lost one child. I do not want to pour my heart into this one if she is to be taken from me." There were no tears in her voice. She spoke calmly, and her expression when she straightened up and regarded her brother was composed. "Besides," she went on. "Ahmose wanted a son. The family needs another boy." Kamose put his arm around her hot shoulders, his eyes on the tiny bundle so blissfully unconscious.

"The astrologers can be wrong," he said. "You must not shut up your heart on the words of a few old men, Aahmes-nefertari. Hent-ta-Hent is innocent. She needs your love."

"And I need Ahmose." She shrugged out of his embrace and looked at him coolly. "Our marriage has been nothing but a series of farewells followed by periods of intense fear and interspersed with brief moments of joy. If you were taking him back to the Delta to attack Het-Uart, I would not feel as I do, but why must you drag him with you into Wawat?" She spread her hands. "Is this all I may look forward to? Boredom, child-rearing and a kind of widowhood? Let him stay home with me this time!"

"But I need him," Kamose answered her. "I am taking all the Medjay and one thousand local troops into Wawat with me. The Princes and commanders have gone. I cannot control events in the south by myself."

"You have Hor-Aha." He did not respond at once and she pounced on the delay. "You no longer trust your General com-pletely, do you, Kamose?" she said. "Why not? Did something happen during the last campaign season?" He shook his head, briefly unbalanced by her perception.

"No," he said. "Nothing happened. I would certainly put my life in Hor-Aha's hands and I know that he would defend me with his last breath. It's . . ." He could not put what he felt into words. "It's nothing more than a very faint uneasiness. Perhaps a reflection of the Princes' antipathy towards him."

"Perhaps. Does Ahmose share it?" The baby was stirring at the sound of their voices and they moved together to the door.

"I am not sure," Kamose replied once they had gained the hallway. "It is often difficult to know what he is thinking." She faced him squarely.

"No, it isn't," she said. "Not for me." There was an angry glint in her eye. She swung away, and Kamose watched her stride towards the square of white light at the end of the pas-sage. Even her walk is different, he thought. The seeds of Tetisheri's character are beginning to sprout in her. Something of her vulnerability is gone and with it much of her modesty. She will be a formidable woman one day, yet I grieve a little for the tender girl who was so prone to nervous tears.

One task he performed with pleasure was the dictating of two texts to be carved on two stelae and set up within the sacred precincts of Amun's temple. Pacing the floor of his father's office with Ipi cross-legged on the floor by the desk, he did not mince his words, finding in them the cloak of pride that was becoming more and more difficult to draw around himself. On the first stela he described the first council he had held with the Princes in the dark and uncertain days before the Medjay had come and he had begun his desperate trek north. He spoke as a King, repeating the titles he longed to hear called out in his honour as he mounted the Horus Throne. "Horus Manifest on His Throne, Beloved of the Two Goddesses of the Repeating Monuments, the Horus of Gold, Making Content the Two Lands, King of Upper and Lower Egypt, Uaskheperra, Son of Ra, Kamose given life forever and ever, Beloved of Amun-Ra, Lord of Karnak." In the formal language of official documents and pronouncements he went on to describe the words, decisions and events he remembered so well. "Men shall hail me as the mighty ruler in Weset," he finished in a burst of desire that he knew was nothing but self-deception. "Kamose, the Protector of Egypt."

The second stela began with his assault on Khemmenu and went on to chronicle the interception of the letter from Teti to Apepa, the march north, the bloodless destruction of the oasis, and the subsequent victory over Kethuna and his exhausted men. "Take the texts to Amunmose and have him appoint a temple stonemason to carve them," he told his scribe. "They are to be erected within the bounds of the outer court so that all may know how I have tried to give Egypt back to the Egyptians." Flinging himself into his father's chair, he watched as Ipi wiped his pens, closed his ink, and scrambled to his feet, flexing his tired fingers. "It is really for the generations to come," he said quietly. "I want to be remembered kindly, Ipi. I want the people to understand."

"I know, Majesty," Ipi replied. "I also know that you believe you will soon stand in the Judgement Hall. Your words cannot hide the things I see beneath them. Yet if Amun wills, it may not be so. I very much desire to sit at your feet beside the Horus Throne!" Kamose summoned a smile.

"Thank you, my friend," he said. "Go about your business." When Ipi had bowed himself out, palette under his arm, Kamose sat on, staring at the blurred reflection of his clasped hands on the gleaming surface of the table. I do not want to stand in the Judgement Hall, he thought wearily. I want to ride in the Heavenly Barque with the other Incarnations of the God, having laid aside the Double Crown and the Royal Regalia for my successor to a united country. Do not do this to me, Amun my Father. Let the oracle be deceived and in the years to come I will look back on my agonies and laugh.

With a deliberate act of the will he tried to allow the peace of high summer to enter him. It slowed the pace and speech of the inhabitants of house, temple and town, hung drowsily in the limp leaves of the trees, weighed heavy on the drooping, dusty vines from which the gardeners plucked the great purple grapes, but try as he might, it skirted him as though it had a consciousness and knew that he was no longer a child of stillness. He swam, stood in the temple to pray, ate the increasingly bountiful food placed before him as the harvest proceeded, he even played with a delighted Ahmose-onkh, but he was an impostor, an actor longing to live his part yet forced to count the minutes until his performance might be over.

It was with a guilty relief that he received word from his Overseer of Ships. The vessels going into Wawat had been inspected and repaired and were ready to sail. At once he ordered the Scribe of Recruits to the Medjay camp and his under-scribes into the town and the surrounding countryside to gather the thousand conscripts he needed to augment the tribesmen. Summoning the Scribe of Assemblage, he listed the provisions of food and beer to be loaded and the weapons to be cleaned, sharpened and distributed. There was no sense of excitement or even fear in these preparations, only a dull feeling of familiarity. Wawat would present no challenge. It was a punitive expedition and nothing more. Kamose sent word to his brother that they would sail at dawn the following morning, but he did not give him the news in person. He did not want to see his sister's face.

He requested a meeting between himself, his mother and his grandmother in Tetisheri's apartments following the afternoon sleep. Uni admitted him to a room full of eddies of hot air from the fans in the hands of two girls standing by the window. Tetisheri had obviously just left her couch. The sheets were rumpled and her headrest lay on the floor. She herself was sitting in a loose diaphanous tunic, her wiry grey hair dishevelled, her face paint smudged. She was drinking water from a large cup. Aahotep was leaning on the window sill, the ostrich plumes of the fans almost brushing her back as she surveyed the tired garden beyond. She turned as he entered and gave him a smile. "I heard all the activity on the river," she said by way of a greeting. "I presume that it presages your departure, Kamose. I was not able to sleep this afternoon." He came to her swiftly and kissed her smooth cheek. She smelled of lotus oil and acacia blossom essence.

"I am sorry the noise disturbed your rest," he responded dutifully and she laughed.

"No you are not, for it is unavoidable. Besides, I was too restless to close my eyes."

"Well I was not," Tetisheri grumbled. "I slept as one dead.

Look at me! You could have waited an hour to allow me time to bathe and dress, Kamose."

"I am sorry," Kamose repeated. "But you allowed Uni to admit me. Please dismiss your fanbearers, Grandmother."

"Oh, it is to be like that is it?" She brightened and waved a hand at the young women, who immediately laid down the fans and bowed themselves out. "A council of war." The atmosphere had become breathlessly still once the servants had left. Kamose felt sweat break out along his spine as he drew up a stool for his mother beside Tetisheri and positioned himself on the edge of the couch.

"Of a kind, I suppose," he agreed. "I leave for Wawat early tomorrow and expect to beat the Inundation. But once I am in the south, I will be trapped by the water until it begins to sink. I intend to ride home on the remnants of the flood but that may not be until the end of Tybi."

"Six months from now," Tetisheri put in thoughtfully. "Quite enough time to subdue the savages who are preying on Wawat villages, inspect Buhen, find out what Teti-En is doing, and bring home a cargo of gold."

"Why would I inspect Buhen?" Kamose enquired, testing her.

"Because Buhen repaired and refortified will secure your southern border against that renegade Egyptian," she said slowly and distinctly as though speaking to a child. "Then you can come home and concentrate your energies on Het-Uart without worrying about a second front opening against you." He nodded.

"I will send you both detailed reports on what is happening," he said. "While I am gone, I leave you both in full control of my nome as I did before. When the harvest is over, I want you to instruct Ankhmahor's son Harkhuf to command war games out on the desert. Use the remainder of the Weset troops. There are two thousand still here. They must not waste the

Inundation in idleness. They must stay fit. Consult with him regularly." He paused for their response and when there was none he went on. "I have been thinking about your suggestion to recruit spies for Het-Uart. It is a good one. Seeing that you are already acquainted with this particular stratagem of underground warfare, I will leave it also in your hands. Ramose can help you."

"You are not taking him with you?" Aahotep interposed. "I wish you would, Kamose. For one thing he will be disappointed to be left and for another I do not like the amount of time he spends with his mother." Kamose raised his eyebrows.

"What do you mean?"

"She means that Ramose has been in his mother's company every day since you returned," Tetisheri broke in. "He has eaten with her when she refuses to eat with us, taken her on litters into Weset, boated with her, and read her to sleep at night." Her tone was contemptuous. "She has demanded his attention at every moment. Nefer-Sakharu hates all of us. She is trickling poison into his ears at every turn." Kamose cursed himself for not noticing these things himself. In spite of his growing respect for the women of his family he did not like to be put at a disadvantage.

"How do you know this?" he demanded. Aahotep put a conciliatory hand on his knee.

"Do not blame yourself," she said. "You have been preoccupied with larger matters. Ramose is sleeping with Senehat. She tells us everything." Kamose looked from one sober face to the other. Two pairs of shrewd brown eyes stared back at him.

"Am I to understand," he said carefully, "that Nefer-Sakharu aroused your suspicions and that you deliberately set Senehat to seduce Ramose and spy for you?"

"No, they didn't," came a voice from the doorway. Startled, Kamose swung round to see Aahmes-nefertari coming across the floor, her lips set in a thin line. "I did. I object to being omitted from this deliberation, Kamose. I object to being indulged and protected like a little girl. Perhaps you see Tani when you look at me, but I assure you that I am nothing like my sister. I am tired of not being seen by you." Going to the window she turned back into the room, leaned on the lintel, and folded her arms. "Throw me out if you like, but Grandmother will only tell me everything passing here later on. I take responsibility for Senehat. I consulted with Mother first, of course." She smiled grimly. "Senehat is clever and Nefer-Sakharu is very stupid. She suspects nothing. Neither does Ramose. Senehat is pretty and vivacious. Perhaps she reminds Ramose of Tani." Kamose held up a hand. He felt slightly sick.

"Are you trying to tell me that Ramose is on the brink of betraying me in some way?" he managed. Aahmes-nefertari shook her head vigorously.

"No no! But how long can he go on listening to his mother's vituperative words without some sort of action? His loyalties will be once again divided. He already suffers. It does no good for him to tell her to be silent. She takes no notice. But, Kamose, neither does he come to you and warn you that his mother genuinely wishes us harm. He should have done that."

"I cannot imagine Ramose in the same light as Meketra or even his father," Kamose said shakily. "Gods! He went to Het-Uart for me. He has fought beside me."

"We love him," Aahotep emphasized. "We hate to see him continually stung by that ungrateful wasp of a woman. Do not make this a mountain. But do not leave Ramose here with her."

"Then what do you suggest?" he asked. "Seeing that the three of you are better informed regarding the secrets of this household than I am!" His tone was caustic to hide the momentary panic, the sense of sudden forsakenness he felt.

"Take him with you," Tetisheri urged. "He would, of course,

be very useful to us in setting up spies for Het-Uart, but it would be cruel to send him back there. He is a good man. I will sleep deeper if I know that he is with you." To protect me or to remove him from temptation? Kamose wanted to ask. Instead he inclined his head.

"Very well. Now let us move on. I want you to send for the Princes at the end of Khoiak. They are to be here and waiting for me when I return from Wawat. Het-Uart must fall next winter. They will be sending their reports to you, Grandmother. Read them carefully and reply to them in my name. Give me your own thoughts on their words when you dictate the news to me. I also want you to request news of my navy at Het nefer Apu. I will visit Paheri and the Abanas at Nekheb on my way south, and when I have picked their brains regarding the river below Swenet, I will send them north to rejoin their sailors and tell them to report to you." He surveyed their intent expressions. "I am putting a great load on your shoulders," he confessed, "but I am not sorry. You have shown yourselves well able to carry it." His glance included his sister and he smiled at her in apology. "Beware the Princes," he repeated. "Particularly Intef and Iasen. Intef is not far away. Qebt is only twenty miles or so downriver from Weset. Any hint of subversion on his part can be quashed by a formal visit from one or all of you. But Iasen at Badari is out of your direct control. So is Meketra, Mesehti and the others."

"Subversion?" Aahmes-nefertari said. "That is a strong word, Kamose."

"I know. Probably too strong to describe the intermittent grumbling and resentment most of them have indulged in ever since I first called them to council. They wanted to go on enjoying the peace and prosperity of their little domains. The Setiu have left us alone, they said. Why should we stir up trouble? Why should you? Even though they knew of the fate

Apepa had planned for us. I do not forget their words. Neither must you. Once allowed to go home, they might try to defy me and stay there."

"Not Ankhmahor surely!" Aahotep expostulated.

"No, not him," Kamose admitted. "He sees the true nature of Egypt."

"Part of the problem has been the power you have given to Hor-Aha," Tetisheri said. "I have warned you about that before, Kamose. Keep him on a very tight rein. Perhaps you could even leave him behind in Wawat. Make that his princedom."

"Is Ahmose aware of the tasks you have set us?" Aahmes-nefertari wanted to know.

"I will tell him later," Kamose said. "Otherwise there would be discussions and arguments and further instructions. I wanted to keep this meeting simple." He left the couch. "Mesore begins tomorrow," he finished as he moved towards the door. "I will not be here for the Beautiful Feast of the Valley. When you go to Father's tomb to eat the meal and make the offering, do so for Ahmose and me as well. Thank you, all of you. For everything. I will send the fanbearers back in." Bowing to them shortly, he left them.

The members of the family ate the evening meal together quietly then scattered to their several quarters. Kamose, as had become his habit, took bedding and climbed to the roof of the old palace. The Medjay were sleeping aboard the ships together with the thousand extra soldiers culled from Weset and the surrounding districts. They were cramped but resigned and their subdued sounds floated quietly and comfortingly to Kamose's ears on the still night air.

It is good to think of tomorrow, of being on the move again, he told himself as he lay listening to his archers and infantry jostle for places on the decks and roll themselves in their blankets. I would rather be sailing north, but Wawat is preferable to fidgeting through the Inundation here at Weset. I am not needed here. Perhaps I am not really needed anywhere. But that thought carried no emotion with it and he soon drifted into unconsciousness.

Even the leave-taking was becoming familiar. The women stood on the top of the watersteps as they had done before and Kamose kissed them dutifully, including the baby in his sister's arms. Amunmose was there with acolytes and incense. Ankhmahor's son waited by the ship's ramp with the Followers. Akhtoy looked glum as he stood on the deck in the early light. The ritual of parting proceeded with no great storms of regret, no tears. Wawat would not be dangerous. Only time lay between the embarking and the coming home. "This little scrap will be sitting up all by herself in five months," Ahmose remarked to his wife. "Do not let Raa give her honey, Aahmes-nefertari. It will ruin her taste for other food later on. Look how Ahmose-onkh howls for sweet pastries." He kissed her. "Do not worry if my messages take weeks to reach you," he said. She patted his cheek.

"I have no fears for you or myself," she replied calmly. "I will pray for you, of course, but I will be fully occupied, Ahmose. Bring me back some gold dust for my eyelids. I hear that you can scoop it up out of the river in great handfuls in Wawat."

Amunmose had stopped chanting. The captains were waiting and the helmsmen had clambered to their perches. Sailors prepared to hoist the sails that would fill with the summer wind that blew with reassuring constancy out of the north. Only Nefer-Sakharu, standing apart from the others, cried and held onto her son with an embarrassing determination until Ramose had to tear himself out of her arms. The three men passed through the protecting lines of the Followers and ran up the ramp, and the order to cast off was given. With a sense of guilty relief Kamose saw the expanse of water between him and his kin begin to widen. He waved once and turned his face to the south.

◎﹚

MESORE, DAY 3. To the Great Queen Tetisheri, my grand-mother, greetings. The bearer of this letter should be Kay Abana, who with his father, Baba, is on his way north to Het nefer Apu. Having taken on a quantity of natron and pilots who will guide us safely to Swenet, we expect to depart Nekheb tomorrow morning. I have made sacrifices in the temple of Nekhbet, asking her in her capacity as protectress of Kings to spread her wings over me. As we passed Pi-Hathor I debated whether or not to stop and remind Het-uy of his oath but it seemed an unnecessary waste of time. I do not doubt that he is well acquainted with the fact that I now hold three-quarters of Egypt in my control. I ignored Esna also. Both these havens of Setiu sympathy are isolated by Wawat and by us and are thus impotent. Treat the Abanas with every courtesy and do not for-get to arrange correspondence with them when they reach the navy. Be sure to share my news as you receive it with my mother and sister. Dictated to the Chief Scribe Ipi and signed by my own hand. Kamose.

MESORE, DAY 10. To the Great Queen Tetisheri, my grand-mother, greetings. This town of Swenet is dusty and barren, surrounded by nothing but the arid heat of pure desert, yet its cemetery contains the tombs of many of Egypt's mighty Kings and there are vast granite quarries here stretching east a con-siderable distance from the centre of the miserable collection of houses.

Just before coming upon the island we saw the Nile widen, and the island itself rears majestically out of a river full of eddies and whirlpools. I am very aware that this place marks the formal boundary between Egypt and the south, for just beyond Swenet is the first cataract where the Nile becomes very troubled, splintering and dashing itself over and between black, smooth rocks so hard that the current can only polish them. They are beautiful, however. They contain some kind of crystalline substance making them flash red and pink when Ra strikes them. Ahmose remarked that their colour reminds him of the pink grapes of Ta-she, so far away from us here in distance as well as in memory.

The pilots we engaged at Nekheb have gone home and I have local men who will take the ships through this maelstrom. They tell us that the Osiris King Senwasret many hentis ago caused a great canal to be cleared through the cataract. We have heard of this and, of course, I have seen it marked on the maps but a few pen strokes on papyrus do not convey the power and danger of the rocks to our ships. I am in grave doubt as to whether we can trust either the Divine One's engineering abilities or the knowledge of the new pilots, though I have little choice.

The name of Teti of Khemmenu is well known here. I had already forgotten that Teti was Apepa's Inspector of Dykes and Canals even though he lived in Khemmenu. Of course few Setiu have ever ventured farther south than the root of the Delta. Their concern was a practical one. Keep the canal open so that the gold might flow. So perhaps we will brave the turbulence unscathed.

I trust that you have been given the first reports from the Princes regarding their harvests and the ordering of their nomes. Do not wait too long to remind those who are still silent of their duty. Renew your watch on the river. It may be that Het-uy will try to send a message to Apepa on seeing my fleet go past. I do not think the serpent has the foresight or the courage to assemble a force to retake Egypt while I am gone, but the gods favour those who are humble enough to take every consequence into consideration. Dictated to the Chief Scribe Ipi and signed by my own hand. Kamose.

MESORE, DAY 19. To the Great Queen Tetisheri, greetings. By now the Beautiful Feast of the Valley will be over. I said prayers for my father's ka and imagined the crowds of people invading the west bank laden with flowers and food for their dead, the priests in their flowing white linens, the singing and the faint breath of incense tinging the air. I also prayed for Si-Amun. I trust you did also.

However there has been little time for prayer. Our progress has been slowed by the need to probe for hidden sandbanks where the river widens and becomes shallow. According to the pilots these sandbanks shift from time to time and therefore cannot be mapped. This is particularly true in summer when the level of the water is low. Twice we have used up a day in having to disembark while the boats were dragged onto the shore and then along slipways to avoid rapids and sandbanks.

Wawat is a place of harsh beauty. Great rocks that resemble rough pyramids rise out of land that is light brown, and some-times we drift past jagged rifts that split the heights open to reveal desert running away to a naked horizon. When the cliffs retreat, we come across huge plains tormented by winds that have formed mighty golden dunes or that whine around curious rock formations jutting from the sand.

We are at present moored at Mi'am. Here there is a large cemetery and a fort in disrepair but I have explored neither. The heat is indescribable, a furnace that saps moisture from the body and takes away the desire for movement. The Medjay are less affected by it and I have sent out Medjay scouts to ascertain the state of the villages under attack. Mi'am is in the centre of

Wawat, a good position from which to operate. Our Egyptian troops are dispirited. The heat and the immensity of this bleakness make them so. I also feel my ka loose within my body, but I cannot allow this dullness of mind to conquer me. I await the reports of my scouts and some news from you. Dictated to the Chief Scribe Ipi and signed by my own hand. Kamose.

MESORE, DAY 21. To the Great Queen Tetisheri, greetings. I received your letter yesterday together with one for Ahmose from our sister and one for Ramose from his mother. I congratulate you for the vigilance that resulted in the interception of the message from Nefer-Sakharu to Prince Meketra at Khemmenu begging him to send an escort for her so that she may return to her city. She also asks him for a house there and his protection. From us, I presume. You say that the tone of the letter was curiously formal, as though she had already concluded some kind of contract or agreement with him and that a similar one was to be delivered to Prince Iasen at Badari. I am surprised that she did not include Intef in her correspondence, but perhaps Intef's estate at Qebt is too close to Weset for her comfort. I wonder what is in her mind? I trust that you had the letters resealed and allowed the heralds to take them north. If the two Princes mention her contact with them in their communications with you, then we may know that they are to be trusted. If they do not, then we must presume that the time she spent in their company has borne a dangerous fruit. Perhaps it is no more than a fervent, even desperate desire to escape into the company of old friends, but I suspect something darker. If Apepa regains control of Egypt, Nefer-Sakharu stands to gain more back than she has lost. Am I full of vain imaginings, Tetisheri? Continue to watch her but do nothing. She is a disagreeable woman, but if I am wrong I risk the disapproval of the gods.

We have spent the last eleven days in skirmishes with the desert predators who have been harassing the Medjay villages. It seems that they came up from Kush some time ago and they have been gradually pushing north into Medjay territory east of the river, from Buhen almost to the first cataract, in the large tract of land called Khent-hen-nefer. They terrorized the Medjay women and children but there is no evidence that they have done so under orders from Teti-En. Hunting them down has been a hot, dirty and brutish affair. They are good marksmen but not as adept as the Medjay, who are taking to this little foray with the ferocious glee of cats let loose on the rats in a granary.

The Kushites are poorly armed. Most of them carry clubs alone. Some have knives. A few wield swords that look suspiciously Egyptian in design. Looted from the forts in hentis past, I think. They wear nothing but loincloths made from the hide of gazelles and go barefoot on sand that would burn the skin from the soles of all but our hardiest peasants. They yell a great deal and shake their clubs. The Medjay scream back at them and then there is the usual confusion of running, shooting and slashing, blood and sweat and wounds. In the night the hyenas come for the corpses. Our losses have been so slight as to be negligible. Tomorrow I am sending a thousand Medjay under Hor-Aha into the north-eastern portion of Khent-hen-nefer to destroy any straggling Kushites. We cannot have them creeping close to our own border. Wawat is an excellent buffer zone and we must continue to keep it peaceful.

Send to the masons' workshops and make sure that the carving of my two stelae is proceeding well. I want them set up in the temple by the time I come home. Dictated to the Chief Scribe Ipi and signed by my own hand. Kamose.

THOTH, DAY 3. To the Great Queen Tetisheri, my beloved mother and dearest sister, greetings on this, the third day of the New Year. I wanted to be with you all on the first day of this month when all Egypt celebrates the Rising of the Sopdet Star and we in Weset make solemn sacrifices to Amun. I long to know what auguries Amunmose discovered regarding our fortunes during the coming year and how little Hent-ta-Hent is faring and what the final tallies of the harvest were. There is no sign here yet that Isis is crying, but I trust that she will honour our endeavours on behalf of Ma'at and provide us with an ample flood.

I am dictating this at sunset from the deck of my ship. The whole desert, the old fort, the mud huts of Mi'am, the motionless palms, everything is on fire with the lingering red glow of Ra as he is swallowed by Nut whose mouth here in Wawat seems as wide as the whole world. This is the hour when our spirits begin to rise. A desert coolness begins to creep in on an ephemeral breeze. Fires are lit and before long the odour of cooking food wafts over us. Akhtoy brings cool beer that has been sunk in the river all day. The villagers sidle close to receive whatever the cooks will give them, and when they have eaten, they bring out their little drums and sing and beat rhythms so that the Medjay will dance. So much seems familiar after two seasons campaigning along the Nile, yet the flavour of this country is foreign, wild and inhospitable outside the boundary of civilization we take with us and set up wherever we go.

Hor-Aha and the troops returned this morning with six prisoners, the headmen of the villages they sacked and burned. I think I will bring them to Weset and show them the power and riches of Egypt as a warning not to attempt future incursions. Hor-Aha is able to speak to them in their own language, a mixture of the Medjay's tongue and something more guttural. Once captured they become very meek, but Hor-Aha has put them under constant guard all the same.

Tomorrow I intend to leave some five hundred men here and take the rest farther south to Buhen. There is little more to be done in this area. We must go on foot, for the Nile shows a slight rise and the boats must be hauled high onto the bank to avoid the coming flood. We expect a long, slow progress because there are many villages on the way and they are all infested with Kushites. I am anxious to see the great fort at Buhen, whether it will be worth repairing and garrisoning, and I hope to investigate the possibility of taking back the retrieving and shipping of gold at once. I trust that you have been receiving the letters Ahmose has been dictating. I am sure he has told you, Aahmes-nefertari, that where we are going gold can be picked up from the bank of the river even as we walk along it, and can be seen glittering under the water. I love you all. Dictated to the Chief Scribe Ipi and signed by my own hand. Kamose.

PAOPHI, DAY 7. To the Great Queen Tetisheri, greetings. I wish that you could see the sheer grandeur of this place. The fort of Buhen is situated in the centre of a kind of bay of low sand hills, the bay itself being a very fertile plain that extends on both sides of the Nile and supports many fields and groves of palms. The river runs long and straight here. There are no narrows, no rocks or dangerous currents, so that the ancients were forced to build stone quays for the berthing of large ships. The quays themselves are not in a good state of repair and are at present largely just under the surface of the flood.

However, it is the fort itself that draws the eye. I will not describe it in any detail save to say that perhaps a third of the population of Weset could be poured into its brick walls. It is like a small fortified town. Within its perimeter there is a walled citadel containing residences, workshops, granaries, all surrounded and protected by walls thicker than two men lying head-to-feet. Ramose told me that it reminded him of the citadel in Het-Uart. Apepa's predecessors chose to build their palace behind a shield our own ancestor provided all unwittingly for them, that same ancestor who had this invincible place erected.

Two great gate-towers give access to the two stone quays but the mightiest gateway opens out to the desert on the western side. I will say no more regarding its dimensions. Ahmose is having it mapped for further study when we return home. He urges me to revive it, leave troops here, but I cannot see the necessity at present. Teti-En's capital, Defufa, is over two hundred miles farther south. I no longer believe that he is a threat. The barbaric inhabitants of Kush belong to several different tribes and none of those tormenting the Medjay belong to Teti-En. Besides, my soldiers must be concentrated on routing the remainder of the Setiu before I seriously turn my attention to Kush. Soldiers stationed here would be able to provide themselves with fresh vegetables and meat but grain and all other provisions would have to come regularly from Egypt and Egypt is in no condition yet to bother with Buhen.

It has taken us more than a month to battle our way here. The river from Mi'am south is thick with Medjay villages, all of them more or less controlled by Kushites to be flushed out, all of them containing the families of our archers, so not only have we fought but we have also been compelled to remain a day or two in each village while Medjay reunions took place. We are storing up much goodwill for the future, but I chafe under the yoke of this necessity.

Buhen itself had been overrun by Kushites who put up a fierce defence against us and held the fort for a full three days, their success due more to the excellent design of the complex than their proficiency in warfare. There was a prodigious slaughter once we gained entry, and our men are still engaged in dragging bodies outside to be burned and cleaning out the mess of reed huts, firepits, rickety animal stalls and other foul debris in which the savages lived. I have sent their women and children back to wherever in this pitiless waste they came from.

Ahmose and I have talked much about the gold. It was collected by Teti-En at Defufa and shipped north for Apepa on barges drawing a very shallow draught. There is no sign of such barges anywhere, so we presume that they are all at Defufa, probably rotting away during the two years of our campaigns. We can use the next month or so to build more, and organize the local Medjay to fill them. It is quite true that gold can be literally picked up from the ground and sifted from the Nile. But where are the Egyptians who will organize the undertaking? We can begin the venture but officials will have to be despatched from Weset to keep the people working. Buhen marks the boundary of Wawat with Kush. Unless we conquer Kush, we cannot obtain the gold that is available right down as far as Defufa and I cannot waste the time or men at present. Not until Apepa and his brood are gone. I do not want to stir up Teti-En. He is too much of a mystery. We do not know what forces are at his command. So far he has shown himself indifferent to events in Egypt. Let us leave him alone. I could perhaps attempt to treaty with him, but if he is an honourable man he will hold to his agreements with Apepa.

I am pleased that the harvest tallies are so high and the granaries full. Also that you have received letters from all the Princes, including the commanders of the navy. However, the fact that neither Meketra nor Iasen have acquainted you with their communication from Nefer-Sakharu fills me with suspicion. They have remained silent on the matter either because they are loyal to me but do not want to stir up trouble for the wife of their dead friend, or they are indeed plotting against us. Of course I cannot form any judgement on the matter just yet. It seems that I will be able to begin a march on Het-Uart as soon as I return. This year may see the end of the Setiu presence in Egypt if Amun wills it. Dictated to the Chief Scribe Ipi and signed by my own hand. Kamose.

ATHYR, DAY I. To the Great Queen Tetisheri, greetings. It is difficult to believe that we have been away from Weset for only three months. It seems like three years. Since my last letter to you I have ventured a little way south to view the second cataract, which begins not far above the smaller fort at Kor. Although the floodwaters continue to rise, it is possible to see why the ancients considered it necessary to build a slipway. The cataract itself, called the Belly of Stones, stretches upriver for many miles through granite boulders tossed and tumbled like teeth waiting to rip apart any ship foolhardy enough to try a passage. At its northern end it is barely passable with the use of towing ropes at high water, but vessels cannot be hauled through all of it.

The slipway at Iken runs for perhaps slightly more than a mile where there is a group of rocks almost large enough to be called islands, blocking all progress. Ahmose and I walked its length. It is in good repair even though it has not been used in two years. It would seem to me more sensible to unload the gold at the southern end of the cataract, have it carried to the northern end, and then put on other ships waiting to receive it. But perhaps the sheer volume of the cargo would make this impractical.

My business here is largely concluded. Akhtoy has made my quarters at Buhen in the commander's house very comfortable. I share it with Ahmose but see him only in the evenings. He spends much time exploring the area and talking to the villagers or putting the troops through manoeuvres to prevent boredom, theirs as well as his.

Ramose and I walk the ramparts of this lordly site and watch the river flowing north to you, or sit in the shade of its soaring walls and talk. He speaks of many things but not of his mother, therefore, Tetisheri, do not relax your vigil. I do not say that Ramose has something on his conscience that engenders a personal guilt, but Nefer-Sakharu may have spoken malicious words to him that would anger me and he dares not tell me out of fear for her well-being. You do not report any further letters between Nefer-Sakharu and the Princes. Either she has not written or the contents are not important enough to acquaint me of them. Yet I feel uneasy. Make sure that the Princes are gathered at Weset by the end of Khoiak as I asked. I do not want them spending more time on their estates than is absolutely necessary.

Hor-Aha has gone to visit his mother, Nithotep. He looks forward to the day when he can invite her to live in the house I shall give him, on the arouras he will govern. Did you know that he carries on his belt a token of his service to my father? He is very pleased at the cleansing of Wawat. We have ensured the Medjay's loyalty at very little cost to ourselves.

The Festival of Hapi approaches. We will make our sacrifices here, but please pray fervently to the God of the Nile that he may bear us safely on his breast and speed us home when the flood abates. Dictated to the Chief Scribe Ipi and signed by my own hand. Kamose.

KHOIAK, DAY 11. To the Great Queen Tetisheri, greetings. Today finds us back at Mi'am, having trudged through the desert along the fringes of the flood to get here. The water is still too high to launch the boats but it has begun to sink. In another week we will risk the return to Swenet and the difficulties of the first cataract. I pray that it will be passable.

Since receiving your last letter I have been in a state of anxiety. Why has Intef not written to you for so long? Qebt is a mere twenty miles from Weset. I am glad that my mother decided to take an escort and visit him in person and her excuse for doing so, a concern for his welfare, was a plausible one. His own excuses for his silence seem too glib. What Prince does not find his hours taken up with settling the petty squabbles of his subjects and arguing with his stewards regarding the disposition of the crops after the harvest? At least he assured her that he would arrive in Weset at the end of this month. The other Princes should be preparing to travel as well.

I am not happy, Tetisheri. I sense something wrong. I have vague premonitions and wish I could consult Amun's oracle. Do it for me, although nothing can be as disheartening as his last pronouncement. I try not to dwell on it, but in this vast, heat-seared aridity death does not seem so very far away in spite of the small routines and duties of a life on the march. They ought to comfort me but their protection is illusory. One disaster, one mistake, one outbreak of fever, and we are at the mercy of implacably hostile surroundings. I am losing control over my own thoughts and I certainly have no control over whatever is happening in Egypt. I am desperate to leave Wawat behind me.

Ahmose is bored but he does not brood. As we passed Toska, a Medjay village on the east bank, he commandeered a reed skiff and poled himself across the current in order to hack our names into the rock there. I was angry with him for taking such a risk but he just laughed. "I am ensuring that the gods may find us if things go badly and our tombs are destroyed," he said, but I think he did it out of sheer high spirits. The soldiers cheered him all the way.

I am surprised and pleased that Aahmes-nefertari has taken to watching the troops drill out on the desert and that she has been offering little rewards to those men who excel at the mock battles. She has taken my instructions to heart. Tell her of my approval.

I will not write again, Grandmother. If all goes well, I will embrace you sometime in Tybi. Dictated to the Chief Scribe Ipi and signed by my own hand. Kamose.

# Chapter FIFTEEN

THERE WAS SOMETHING different about this homecoming. It was not in the wide, turbid flow of a Nile still lapping just above its banks, nor in the burst of new green life flushing along the east bank. It was not in the dazzle of his watersteps where the mooring poles, blue and white, broke the water into crystal rivulets as his boat approached them. The vine trellis still arched above the path that meandered to the house through spreading sycamores. The house itself, glimpsed fitfully through the entangled branches, still extended comfortably amid its flowerbeds and sparse lawns, its walls gleaming with the fresh whitewash the servants applied every spring. The wall dividing the garden from the old palace was still crumbling and the palace itself continued to rear above it with a worn, aristocratic dignity. Kamose, his hands gripping the deck rail, Ahmose and Ramose to either side, felt his heart expand as his gaze travelled the familiar scene. A little farther north he could see the top of the temple pylon, pale stone caught between deep blue sky and the quivering spears of the palms. To his left on the west bank, sand flowed towards the brown cliffs and he could just make out the mortuary temple of his ancestor Osiris Mentuhotep-neb-hapet-Ra tucked shimmering against the base of the rocks.

Heart pounding with a strange joy, he scanned the sun-drenched panorama for change, something different, something to explain the loosening of every tension within his body and the lightening of his mind, and found nothing. All was as it should be, as it had always been, house, old palace, temple, town, blending together in a sanity of perspective he had known from his childhood. True, the river was choked with craft of every description and the banks were alive with soldiers so that he knew the Princes had come, but boats and men could not account for the relief and exultation he felt.

No, he thought suddenly. No. Blessed Weset has remained the same. It is I who have changed. Something happened to me in Wawat, a shift in my ka so subtle that I did not detect it. When? Why? Was it a swift unnoticed progress or an infinitesimal turn because I glanced a certain way in a certain patch of sunlight towards a certain hill? O Great and Mighty Amun, does this mean that everything will be all right? That the thing weighing so heavily upon me has been lifted and I may dare to look forward, to conquer Het-Uart, to bring the Horus Throne back to the old palace and feel the Double Crown settle on my brow? He clutched his brother's wrist. "Ahmose," he said thickly. "Ahmose . . ." and could get no further for the lump in his throat.

The boat nudged the steps and at a cry from his captain the ramp was run out. The Followers formed a guard. Without hesitation Kamose ran across the deck and down the warm wood onto the stone flagging where Behek was, as usual, the first to welcome him. At the end of the path he saw his women hurrying towards him. Briefly he examined his ka and found there no stain of dislocation, no shrinking. Smiling, he held out his arms. "Wawat is a wondrous place!" he called. "But Weset is better!" He enfolded them fiercely, glad for the feel of their soft flesh, the smell of their perfume, their high, excited voices.

Only Tetisheri looked at him askance. Disengaging herself, she stepped back, scrutinizing him carefully.

"You seem to be pleased with us, Majesty," she said dryly. "Well, you will not be pleased for long. The Princes are here and they have brought many soldiers with them. Too many. The barracks are crowded to overflowing and the distribution of food has become a headache. Of course I did not know that they would arrive surrounded by their own private armies or I would have forbidden it." She squeezed his forearm. "I do not like it, Kamose." At any other time he would have rebuked her for thrusting concerns on him before he had even had time to bathe, but now he merely frowned and patted her gaunt fingers.

"I do not like it either," he replied after a moment. "But much depends on why they have seen fit to provide themselves with armed protection. Has there been trouble, Tetisheri? Is Apepa stirring? What of Pi-Hathor and Esna?" She shook her head vigorously.

"Nothing like that. Word from Abana in the north is good. The Delta has lain quiet. Pi-Hathor likewise. The Princes had no good reason for all these hundreds of extra mouths we have been trying to fill."

He pulled her to a halt. Behind them Aahmes-nefertari was exclaiming with relish over the small bag of gold dust her husband had gathered from the edge of the river for her with his own hands and Ramose, his arm around his mother's shoulders, was talking to her in a low voice. Ahmose-onkh was toddling in the rear, Behek now pacing beside him, the dog's ear grasped firmly in the child's little fist. "What is it, Grandmother?" Kamose said in a low voice. "What do you sense? Have the Princes not been fully respectful and obedient?" Tetisheri shrugged.

"I have noticed no change in their attitude towards me," she declared, "but they have refused to entertain Ankhmahor's suggestions regarding the bivouacking of their troops on the west bank instead of the desert behind our enclosure wall. He returned a little earlier than the rest of them. He has been trying to establish some order, but naturally they regard him as one of themselves and he does not have the power to command them without your permission. It has been all he could do to keep them and their retinue out of the house." Kamose felt a stab of genuine alarm.

"Could you not issue commands yourself, through him?" he demanded.

"I have certainly tried," she answered forthrightly, "and to some degree I have been successful. Aahmes-nefertari has segregated our men and used them to patrol the town and of course the estate itself. There have been no outward incidents, Kamose," she finished in exasperation. "It is all intuitions, annoying hints, vague suspicions that all is not well. I am relieved that you are home."

They had reached the portico of the house. Turning, Kamose signalled to Hor-Aha, far back in the chattering throng. "Take the Medjay across the river and settle them down," he said when the man had come up and bowed. "Then leave your second to deal with them. I need you here. Put the Kushites in the prison. Tell Simontu to treat them kindly." He swung to his herald. "Khabekhnet, go to the temple and tell the High Priest that I am anxious to view my stelae and perform a thanksgiving to Amun for a successful foray into Wawat. I will come tomorrow morning." He turned back to Tetisheri. "Tonight we will feast and I will address the Princes," he told her. "But now I wish to bathe, break my fast, and tour the barracks." He grinned wryly. "It seems that I must take my sister with me so that I may become acquainted with the progress our men have made," he remarked. Tetisheri regarded him shrewdly.

"She has changed," she said. Kamose nodded.

"So it seems." He reached out for his mother standing patiently behind him. "Sit with me when I return from the bath house, Aahotep," he requested. "I want to talk to you."

Bathed and freshly painted, he ate under his canopy beside the pool and presently Aahotep joined him, folding easily and gracefully onto the cushions beside him, fly whisk in hand. Kamose thought how well she looked. Her burnished skin gleamed. The full mouth, orange with henna, revealed the glint of white teeth as she smiled a greeting and the tiny lines around her eyes, partially camouflaged by the black kohl, served only to emphasize their dark, mature beauty. "You should marry again," he said impulsively. Her smile widened in surprise.

"For what purpose?" she asked. "And to whom?" He laughed.

"Forgive me, Mother. A fleeting reflection reached my tongue before it vanished. Would you like wine? A pastry?" She shook her head. "Then give me your opinion of the reports Tetisheri has been receiving from the Princes over the last five months. I presume that you read them. And tell me of Aahmes-nefertari." The fly whisk began to move to and fro, too slowly for the horsehair to ruffle the warm air.

"The reports have been formal, dutiful and entirely blameless in their wording," she said meditatively, "yet both Tetisheri and I found them disturbing, why we could not say. We could not fathom exactly what it was about them that rang false." She raised her eyes to his. "You must read them yourself, Kamose. Perhaps we have lived with treachery and betrayal too long and are starting at shadows that do not exist. I do not know. We feel the same polite distance from them in person since they have been here. They are not lacking in respect, but there is something not quite right behind their fine manners, something cold. Even calculating?" The whisk fell into her lap and she stroked it absently. "They remind me of Mersu."

A silence grew between them and in it Kamose saw the

closed, enigmatic face of his grandmother's steward whose bland obedience had hidden a murderous hatred. He sipped his wine pensively. "They are arrogant and often argumentative," he said, "but they know what I have done for them, for Egypt. I have abolished the fear that at any time their birthright might be removed from them. I have rewarded their faithfulness with gold. I will do more for them once Het-Uart is cleansed. They know all this. Yet I do not discount your impressions. Now what of my sister?"

Aahotep's fingers fluttered in bewilderment. "She speaks often of Tani. Not with anger any more but with a kind of terse dismissal and it is as though the knowledge of Tani's betrayal feeds a new energy within her. She goes about her household duties with the same attention and concern but she despatches them quickly, very efficiently, and then spends her time with the soldiers. No," she said emphatically with a sharp gesture, "it is nothing lewd, nothing morally reprehensible. There is not the slightest suggestion of that. She sheds her jewels, puts on sturdy sandals, and goes to stand on the reviewing dais while the men parade and fight their mock battles. She talks to the officers."

"But why?" Kamose did not know whether to laugh or be annoyed at the vision of Aahmes-nefertari, delicate and fastidious, engulfed in clouds of dust while the troops wheeled and the captains shouted. "She must not make herself look ridiculous, Mother. It will be very bad if the common men think they can regard royal women with familiarity."

"They like her," Aahotep replied. "They drill more smartly when she is there. I went with her several times, seeing that I could not divert her by argument." She smiled ruefully. "She has developed a most unfortunate stubborn streak. The men salute her, Kamose. She calls to them, jokes with them. I think she began it because she wanted to prove to you that your trust was not misplaced but she discovered an enjoyment in it. If she were male, she might make a good commander." Now Kamose did laugh.

"Ahmose has returned to a wife he does not know," he chuckled. "That should add some spice to their reunion." Becoming aware that they were no longer alone, he turned to see Ankhmahor, Hor-Aha and Ramose waiting for him a polite distance away. He sighed and made as if to rise, but Aahotep put a restraining hand on his wrist.

"I know you have much to attend to," she said. "But there is one other thing. It may be nothing, but . . ." She bit her lip. "Nefer-Sakharu has been going among the Princes constantly since they arrived, entertaining them in her quarters, sitting among them at meals, taking her litter into Weset with those who wanted to divert themselves in the town. I know she is lonely. It has all been very frivolous and probably harmless. I had no excuse to try to prevent it and I could not very well confine her to her rooms out of spite." She met his eye. "I was ready to, several times, but after all she has done nothing wrong unless one can call ingratitude and dislike an offence." Kamose lifted her soft hand and kissed her fingers as he rose.

"I should have sent Ahmose down south and stayed here myself," he said heavily. "Although it is doubtful how I might have done more than the three of you. I must go. I will see you this evening." He walked towards his men in a sober frame of mind.

The Princes and their personal retinues were all present in the reception hall that night. Kamose, his sharp gaze travelling the wigged and gold-spangled heads, suddenly saw a tall, rather stooped form lean back and hold up a winecup to be filled. "What is Meketra doing here?" he said quietly to his mother. "I gave him no command to join my army!" Aahotep, tearing apart a piece of chickpea bread beside him, paused and glanced out over the company.

"He arrived with Intef," she said. "He has been boring me with all the wonderful restorations he has personally sanctioned in Khemmenu. One would think he had trodden the mud and straw himself. I am sorry, Kamose. I did not know that he had no permission to leave his city. He spoke as though he had received a direct invitation from you."

Kamose watched him thoughtfully. He and the other nobles appeared to be in high spirits, trading sallies and witticisms with each other, drinking plenty of wine and tossing the abundant spring blooms that lay on their small tables at the servants, but their behaviour seemed to him to have an unpleasant undercurrent of impudence about it as though they were using their very exuberance to shut him and his family out.

After reverencing him as he entered the hall, they had ventured him no further attention, answering him when he spoke to them but otherwise conversing among themselves. "They have been like this almost every night," Tetisheri had muttered in his ear. "Getting drunk and bothering the staff like a crowd of undisciplined children. The hotheads! I will be more than glad to see you take them all north, Kamose. A few forced marches will dampen their enthusiasm for nonsense." But Kamose decided, surveying them carefully, that there was nothing hotheaded about their noisy behaviour. Rather, their loud cacophony had an undercurrent of coldness to it, almost of calculation. The women are right to be uneasy, he told himself. Something is wrong here.

Later he rose and addressed them, recounting all that he had done in Wawat and warning them that on the following day they were expected to attend the thanksgiving in the temple and the dedication of his stelae and the day after that they would be leaving to resume their war against Apepa. They listened politely, their painted faces turned up to him, but their hands and bodies were restless. "Tomorrow afternoon we will counsel together in my father's office," he ordered them crisply. "Tybi is advancing. I want to be outside Het-Uart by the beginning of Mekhir."

He wanted to shout at them, break through the invisible but keenly felt circle they had drawn around themselves, berate them for flooding his domain with unnecessary soldiers, but he sensed that such a display of anger would put him at a disadvantage. Why do I feel as though they are lions waiting for me to break and run? he wondered anxiously as he regained his cushions and waved at the musicians to continue playing. I must ask Ahmose if he shares these imaginings.

But he was unable to speak with his brother that night. Ahmose had retired early and was closeted with his wife, and Kamose did not have the heart to disturb them. Taking Ramose and Ankhmahor, he made a slow circuit of the house, all three men silently absorbed in the cool beauty of the moon-washed gardens. They parted, Ankhmahor to check on the Followers taking the watch and Ramose to his couch where, Kamose mused, the enticing Senehat was doubtless waiting. Yet he did not feel deserted. With his arouras to himself he wandered under the trees, circled the moonlit silver of the pool, and finally took the passage to his own quarters. His sleep was deep and untroubled.

In the morning the house and grounds emptied and the temple filled as Kamose once more prostrated himself before his god in thanksgiving for his success in Wawat. His stelae had been erected, two sturdy blocks of granite almost as tall as he, their surfaces incised with the chronicles of his campaigns. Standing before them, he read their message aloud himself in proud tones that rang throughout the sacred precincts. Under the words he called out, those listening heard other truths. This is what I, Kamose Tao, have done. I have lifted shame from the shoulders of my family. I have avenged my father's honour. I have proved myself worthy of the blood of my royal ancestors.

When he had finished, he turned to the six Kushites who had been brought into the temple and who now stood awed and awkward between their guards, their black eyes shifting rapidly among the press of sumptuously arrayed worshippers. "I have seized your land," he said to them slowly and deliberately. "That knowledge will be carved into my stela so that all who come here may read it. Look around you. You have had an opportunity to assess the might and majesty of Egypt. You see how any further attempt to invade Wawat will be met with all the hostile power of this country. Go home and tell your tribesmen that to those who merit it Egypt is merciful and just but retribution will be swift to those who try to threaten her. You are free. My soldiers will give you food and send you on your way."

As the crowd was flowing out of the temple on a cloud of incense and the last strains of the holy singers, Kamose found his sister beside him. She had come up behind the Followers and at a word they had let her through. "Ahmose has gone ahead with Mother," she said. "I wanted to speak to you before your meeting with the Princes this afternoon, Kamose."

"I had intended to talk to you before I left Weset in any event," he answered her. "There is not much time for anything. Have you been able to establish spies in Het-Uart?"

"We have begun to organize something but it is a slow process," she said. "We have been working through Paheri and Kay Abana in the north while the navy has been idle. They must find inhabitants of the city who can be trusted. You are not loved in the Delta, Kamose. You destroyed too much." They had been approaching their litters. The bearers sprang up but Kamose waved them away.

"We will walk," he shouted. "So you do not yet have any useful information for me," he said as he dropped his tone. "It was too much to hope that some obliging citizen of Het-Uart was already eager to open the city gates. Keep working at it, Aahmes-nefertari. Eventually the greed of the Setiu will win out. After all, making a profit is what they do best." His tone was light and the girl laughed. "I hear that you have joined the army," he went on. "Do you want me to make you an officer?" This time she did not respond to his humour.

"You could do worse," she said soberly. "It is the army I need to talk to you about, or rather, our local troops. Mother has obviously told you that I have taken a very great interest in their activities while you were away." She glanced up at him and then down to where her sandalled feet were leaving soft impressions in the dirt of the path. "It began because I thought that Ahmose-onkh might be amused for a while if I took him out to the parade ground by the barracks. Raa has been very occupied with Hent-ta-Hent. So I asked the commander's permission to sit on the dais with Ahmose-onkh and watch what went on. Of course the little brat became bored before too long and wriggled and whined but I was fascinated." She put up a hand to push one wind-whipped braid of her wig away from her mouth. "I talked to the Scribe of Assemblage, the Scribe of Recruits, the local officers. I know what the men eat and how much. I know how many pairs of sandals need mending every month. I know how many arrows get broken during archery practice. And I can sharpen a sword." She looked across at him hesitantly as though he might laugh at her, but what she saw seemed to reassure her. "I have been inventing mock battles for them to fight," she told him almost in a whisper, "but I am not very good at strategy, having had no experience in the field. I divide up the men and put some of them behind rocks or on top of hills, that sort of thing. I like it all very much, Kamose."

He did not know how to respond, so great was his astonishment. "I requested permission from the captain of the household guards to draw up a plan whereby the men who have been responsible for our safety might spend some time out on the desert with the other troops and so refresh their skills, and be replaced in rotation with some of the soldiers who are very competent but have not had the privilege of guarding us. He allowed me to do this. It is working well." Kamose allowed himself a private grimace.

"Aahmes-nefertari," he said gently, "you were right to reprimand me for disregarding your abilities, but do you not think that you are taking this a little too far? You need not prove yourself to me. I trust you fully." She showed him a flushed face.

"You have not listened," she protested hotly. "Your captain approves of my involvement. The men expect to see me every day. I enjoy them. Do not imagine that I have immersed myself in their training and welfare because I miss my husband or do not have enough household chores to perform." She took two hurried steps ahead and then rounded on him, bringing him to an abrupt halt. "I do not ever want to find myself as weak as Tani," she said in a low voice. "I do not ever want to wake up one morning and find myself incapable of courage, drained of assertion or unable to make an act of the will because I have allowed childbearing and the gentle arts of womanhood to soothe me into an inappropriate submission. I have been close to that danger, Kamose. Yes I have. But no more. Oh please do not forbid me this service!" Kamose refrained from pointing out that it was neither childbearing nor the gentle arts of womanhood that had undone her sister, but a wily and unscrupulous adversary. Her reasons were irrational but perhaps her fear was not. After all, Kamose thought quickly, she has had a powerful example of uncompromising authority in her grandmother.

"Is this why you accosted me today?" he asked her again. "If so, you need not fear. I will speak with my commander and my captains. If they sing your praises honestly, you may continue to work with them on the understanding that the word of my commander is your law. Of the two thousand troops I left here in Weset, only one thousand will remain. I intend to take the rest north with me, together with the Medjay, of course. Will that satisfy your thirst for death and destruction?" For a brief moment the Aahmes-nefertari of his earlier days shone through. Tears had come to her eyes and her lips trembled. Standing on tiptoe, she kissed his cheek.

"Thank you, Majesty," she said. "No, that is not why I accosted you today, but I am glad the matter is settled." She resumed her pace and he began to walk also.

For a while there was a companionable silence between them, broken by the measured thud of the Followers' sandals. Far out on the river a small craft moved slowly by, its triangular sail flapping, its progress marked by the rhythmic tapping of a drum held under the arm of a young boy sitting in the stern. Its wash lapped the sandy bank in glittering waves. Kamose was in no hurry to hear what his sister had to say. In spite of the coming gathering with the Princes he was aware of a spreading contentment. The bounty of his harvest would be arrayed under the waiting canopies in his garden. The wine would be unsealed. Dark beer would be poured to quench his thirst. And tomorrow he would leave Weset once more for the north. He was not sorry to be going, but he knew that he would take with him the healing that had been so mysteriously accomplished in his soul and while he was away the thoughts of his home would be warm and guiltless.

Then Aahmes-nefertari spoke without turning her head. "You should know that there has been trouble between myself and the Princes Intef and Meketra," she said. "Grandmother, Mother and I had decided that since we were able to contain it we would not bring it to your attention but I have been pondering the matter, Kamose. You will be relying on all the Princes during the coming siege. Some more heavily than others." She drew a deep breath. "If you leaned on a branch that broke, I would feel responsible. It was not a large storm," she said hastily. "A puff of desert wind, that is all."

"You are painting a confusing picture," Kamose interrupted impatiently. "We are nearly at the watersteps and I am hungry." He spoke more harshly than he had intended out of a sudden foreboding, and she apologized at once.

"I am sorry," she blurted. "It is this. Intef and Meketra came to the parade ground one morning. I think they were taken aback to see me there. They wanted to add their soldiers to yours, mingle the troops and assume command of the men themselves. Of course they would have had authority over a mere commander and a few captains, and if no one in the house had cared to make sure that the officers were being diligent while you were away, they could have drilled the men as they wished. Their arguments were logical, Kamose. Let us foster co-operation between the fighters of our nomes. Let the soldiers befriend one another to maintain solidity in battle." Now she looked across at him. The tears had gone and the mouth no longer quivered. It was set in a grim line. "Meketra even complained that as he had been left behind to put Khemmenu to rights he had been denied practice in the field and needed the experience of a varied command. I watched your officers as he and Intef were speaking to me. They were afraid that I would allow them to be placed under the Princes' control. I could see no harm in it. After all, the drills and mock battles were simply to keep the troops alert and occupied and why should the soldiers the Princes brought with them be idle? But Intef's insistence that the two of them be placed in authority instead of your commander seemed too urgent. There was something about the whole situation that I did not like. So I refused." She laughed shortly. "They pressed me as far as they dared. I could see the contempt in their eyes before they bowed and withdrew. They had their retainers set up targets and they drew bows until I left the reviewing dais. It was like a challenge." Kamose felt his throat go dry. I am not angry, he thought. Why? The answer came at once. Because anger will only serve to blind me to something I need to be coldly sober in order to examine. "I went to the officers' quarters that evening," Aahmes-nefertari was saying. "They told me that they had been invited several times to drink with the officers who came with the Princes and our own soldiers have been receiving gifts from the men in the Princes' ranks. I do not know what it means, Kamose. Perhaps it is simply the comradeship of a serving army, but I do not think so. Neither did Grandmother and Mother when I told them. Am I being foolish? We have all lived with uneasiness for so long."

They had reached the watersteps and were crossing the stone paving. Glancing to his left along the path to the house, Kamose caught a glimpse of the crowd beyond the thickly leaved trellis and the gleam of sunlight on white canopies. The murmur of many voices came to him clearly. They are waiting for me to arrive so that they can eat, he thought. It is a day of celebration. Six disconcerted Kushites and the nobility of Egypt stood in the temple while I narrated my victories. He touched his sister's shoulder.

"You did well," he said evenly. "I am very proud of you, Aahmes-nefertari. Does Ahmose know of this?" She shook her head.

"We had more important things to do last night," she said a trifle defiantly. "In any case, you are the King. My duty was to tell you first."

"Good. Keep your counsel. I intend to keep mine. Tomorrow I will take them all away, but I will not forget your words. I use them, you know, but I cannot bring myself to like them. What have they done for Egypt in the past but grow fat and complacent on the scraps the Setiu have flung to them?" He could feel the rage beginning to curdle inside, acrid and despairing. "I will certainly warn Ahmose and Hor-Aha, but I do not want to confront Intef and Meketra over something that may mean nothing," he finished with a struggle against the irrational tide of betrayal and offence sweeping through him. "They have grumbled, but so far they have been obedient and trustworthy. I still need them. Let us go and break our fast." And that is the source of the real wound, he admitted to himself as together they passed under the dense curtain of the vine-hung trellis and out again into the sun. I need them, need them desperately, but they do not need me.

He ate and drank, smiled and conversed, received the obeisances and congratulations of the cheerful assembly, while striving to quell his anger and put what his sister had told him into a sane perspective. He had no intention of voicing his displeasure to the Princes, much less his nebulous suspicions regarding their loyalty. To do so would only raise their indignation, perhaps justly. Yet Aahmes-nefertari, as well as the other women, had been alarmed out of all proportion to the event and he himself was left with a tiny but definite pulse of warning when his ire was finally dispelled.

Drowsy and satiated, the guests finally scattered to their couches for the afternoon rest and Kamose also retired to his rooms but he did not attempt to sleep. Sitting in his chair, he went over in his mind what he intended to say to the Princes, what plans he had for this, his third campaigning season. They were few and simple. Egypt was his up to the Delta, therefore he would gather in the army from each nome as he went north, surround Het-Uart, and pull down its walls, brick by brick, if necessary, until the last lesion on the body of his country was healed. He had ascertained that Kush and Teti-En would be no threat. His southern flank was secure. Only Pezedkhu could hamper his drive for complete freedom, and if Pezedkhu ventured forth from the spurious safety of his city, he would be defeated. Kamose discounted Apepa. The struggle would be between himself and the General, straightforward and clean. Apepa's schemes and wiles belonged to the febrile world of negotiation and as such would be useless to him. Physical weapons and good military strategy were all that remained.

In the late afternoon the Princes answered his summons. Kamose, sitting with his brother Ramose and Hor-Aha, watched them file into the room with a cool detachment. Bowing to him, they answered his invitation to be seated. Refreshments had been provided by Akhtoy, but no one made a move towards the dishes and cups. They all look as if they have been drinking for hours, Kamose thought. They are bleary-eyed and sullen. They slump on their chairs like recalcitrant children about to be reprimanded, their hands in their laps, and they will not meet my gaze. Only Ankhmahor smiles at me.

He cleared his throat and rose to his feet. Ipi, cross-legged on the floor beside him, finished smoothing the sheet of papyrus lying on his palette and picked up his pen. "You must serve yourselves if you are hungry or thirsty," Kamose began. "I do not want us interrupted by the movements of servants. What I have to say to you will not take long. There are no intricate plans for our coming march north unless any of you has conceived a way to pierce Het-Uart's defences. Meketra, I do not remember having you summoned here from your responsibilities in Khemmenu. Could it be that you have indeed come up with such a plot and wished to share it with me as soon as possible?" Meketra lifted a pale, expressionless face in his direction but his eyes fixed on a spot just below Kamose's chin.

"No, Majesty," the man said. "Regrettably I have no such

idea. I risked your displeasure in coming to Weset because the harvest around my city was completed and the task of rebuilding continues now without my personal supervision. I was not needed for a time and I wanted to share in your triumph and thanksgiving."

"I am indeed displeased," Kamose retorted tartly. "You are needed where I say you are needed, Meketra. A request to join us here should have come first, with reasons why Khemmenu could have been left in the care of your assistant governor." He wanted to say more, to castigate the man for his base desire to push himself to the forefront as often as possible, but pointing out Meketra's flaws in public could only fuel the obvious resentment the Prince felt at being excluded from the company of his fellows in Weset. "Am I to assume that your presence here together with an unseemly number of your troops indicates a desire to go north with us this spring?" he enquired. Meketra seemed startled and then embarrassed. Kamose did not wait for a reply. He had no intention of including Meketra in his journey and briskly changed the subject. "Tomorrow at dawn you will assemble your men in marching formation," he told them. "The Medjay will take the boats as before. I intend to reach Het-Uart as quickly as possible and stay there as long as possible until, if Amun wills it, the city falls to me. There is no necessity for any detours. Do you have any questions?"

It was as though they had been turned into stone. Every mouth remained closed. Every face went blank and every body became suddenly still. "What is wrong with them?" Ahmose whispered, and at the sound of his voice Intef raised his head. Now indeed his eyes met those of Kamose, filling suddenly with such a flush of hatred that Kamose blinked in shock. But when the Prince spoke it was with an unnatural calm.

"Majesty, we do not wish to go north this year," he said. "We have been conferring with one another and we are not happy.

For two years we have followed you. Our children are growing up without us. Our wives are tired of sleeping alone. We have been forced to delegate our authority to our stewards and our nomes are suffering without our guidance. Harvests and sowings, we have been absent. Give us leave to go home." He waved a deprecating hand. "All Egypt is ours now save a small portion of the Delta. Apepa can do nothing. Let him stew in what juices he has left for another season or two. We are needed elsewhere."

Kamose had listened to Intef's speech with a mounting incredulity that quickened his breath and sent the blood singing through his ears. Now he sought the edge of the table for support and leaned on it, scanning the surly features before him. "You do not wish?" he managed. "You are needed elsewhere? What is this nonsense? Have you not just heard the words I spoke to Meketra? You are needed where I say you are needed, not where you imagine you would like to be! And as for Egypt being yours, who do you think you are, you arrogant Princes? Egypt is mine by right of birth and Ma'at! I have broken my heart to take it back for all of us. How dare you!" His voice had risen until he was shouting. He felt Ahmose's fingers bite into his thigh under the cover of the table top and the pain brought him up short. "I am the King," he finished more quietly. "I will forget this impudence, Intef, providing you do not question my supremacy again. We meet tomorrow morning. You are all dismissed." He sat down and pressed his knees together to quell their trembling, but the Princes made no move to leave. They watched him carefully. Then Mesehti spoke up, his weatherbeaten face creasing into lines of resignation.

"His Majesty is right," he insisted. "We have been selfish, my brothers. Our complaints could be his also, for was he not needed here in Weset? Have his stewards and his women not shouldered as much weight as ours?" He fixed Kamose with his mild stare. "We are not content, Majesty, it is true, but we have forgotten that neither are you. You are our King. Forgive me."

"Traitor," someone muttered, and Mesehti rounded on him. "I told you that this would not work, Iasen!" he shouted. "I told you we were sinning! Kamose deserves better than our mutinous grumblings! If it were not for him, we would still be under the Setiu yoke! I want nothing more to do with such foolishness."

"Fine for you!" Meketra shouted back. "Mesehti of Djawati, living comfortably under the sunshade of the Princes of Weset! No anguish for you! Kamose destroyed Khemmenu and then expected me to raise it to life again!" They had both sprung to their feet and were glaring at each other. Iasen pounded the table.

"We have seen Kamose and his brother reduce Egypt to a shambles!" he cried out. "Two seasons it has taken for the fields to recover, for villagers to rebuild their houses, and does he give us leave to assist them? No! We are made his accomplices and now he demands that yet again we desert our peasants and take the war tracks. Enough! Let us go home!" Now Intef too had left the table, his chair toppling backwards as he kicked it away.

Kamose held himself rigid. Catching Ankhmahor's eye, he nodded once. Ankhmahor made for the door. Hor-Aha had risen and was standing close to Kamose, his hand on the knife at his belt.

"At least with Apepa we enjoyed a balance," Intef spat. "He minded his own business and left us alone to prosper as we saw fit. He did not meddle." His finger shot out, pointing straight at Kamose. "He would not have meddled with you either if your father had not given way to his supreme arrogance! But no, Seqenenra could not accept his place. 'I am a King,' he said, but he did not apply to us, his brothers, for advice or help. He did not need our counsel. He sent to Wawat for that!" The

finger jabbed the air once more, this time at Hor-Aha. "A foreigner, a black tribesman! Your rebellion has gone far enough,
Kamose. Let Apepa have the Delta. We do not care. Why
should you? You have Weset. And what are you anyway? You
are no more than one of us. A Prince. Just a Prince. My grandfather was Sandal Bearer to a King."

"Be silent, Intef!" Makhu of Akhmin urged, tugging at Intef's
kilt. "You are committing sacrilege!"

"Sacrilege?" Iasen shouted back. "Everyone knows that the
Taos have the same black blood in them that runs through the
veins of their Wawat pet! Did not Tetisheri's parents come up
into Egypt from Wawat?" He swung to Kamose. "Send your so-
called General back to where he belongs," he demanded. "We
are tired of kowtowing to him. And let us go home!" With a
curse Hor-Aha lunged across the table, knife drawn, but at that
moment the door crashed open and the Followers streamed
into the room, Ankhmahor at their head. Quickly they isolated
each Prince and the confusion began to subside. Kamose came
deliberately to his feet.

"Sit down, all of you," he commanded. After some hesitation
they did so, Intef breathing roughly, Iasen white to his hennaed
lips, and Meketra attempting a haughty demeanour that could
not hide his distress. When they were settled, Kamose surveyed
them disdainfully. "I knew that you were jealous of Hor-Aha,"
he said, "but I believed that you would come to respect his military acumen and forget about his origins. I was wrong. I was
also wrong in thinking that you were intelligent enough to
understand that your prosperity under Apepa was an illusion
that he could shatter any time he chose to do so." His lip
curled. "You have proven yourselves unworthy of your princely
titles, let alone your birthright as Egyptians. You are Setiu, all
of you. There is no greater insult. As for my claim to kingship,
my ancestors ruled this country and every one of you knows it.

Otherwise you would not have come at my summons two years ago, nor would you have assisted me in my war. I do not cringe at your ridicule, but I am incensed at the aspersions you dare to cast upon my grandmother's roots. The rumours are false. They were started by the Setiu out of fear that one day the rightful rulers of this land might wake to a recognition of their bondage. You know this!" he shouted in disgust, his self-control deserting him at last. "Tetisheri's father, Cenna, was a smer, her mother, Neferu, a nebt-per! Lowly titles but Egyptian names, you ingrates! Why do I defend myself against your accusations? You are not worth a further word. Ankhmahor!" The Captain of his Followers raised a hand. "Khabekhnet should be just outside. Bring him in." When the herald had entered and bowed, Kamose addressed him. "My scribe will prepare a document that you will take to Khemmenu," he ordered. "It is to be delivered to Prince Meketra's assistant governor. The Prince will not be returning to Khemmenu and his assistant is to assume the governorship until another Prince is appointed." Meketra gave an exclamation and Kamose swung to him. "I gave you Khemmenu in return for your service," he ground out. "I restored you to power and favour. Do not speak." With a wave he dismissed the herald and turned back to Ankhmahor. "Arrest Intef, Iasen and Meketra," he went on. "Escort them to the prison and hand them over to Simontu."

"But Majesty," Mesehti protested feebly. "They are noblemen, Princes of the blood, surely you . . ."

"They are treasonous blasphemers," Kamose cut in bluntly. "Take them away, Ankhmahor."

When the three had gone, visibly shaken and surrounded by the impassive guards, the remaining men looked at one another in shock. "What has happened here?" Ahmose said at last. "Gods, Kamose, have we just witnessed a mutiny? Mesehti, what has gone wrong?" Mesehti sighed.

"Letters have flown back and forth between us all for the last five months," he admitted. "We were glad to be settled in our own homes. Some of us simply wanted to stay there. We were tired, Highness. We saw no point in harassing Apepa any further. That, coupled with our growing dislike of you, General," here he nodded at Hor-Aha apologetically, "fanned the embers of the fire that broke out in this room. I expected the protest and your reply. I did not expect such venomous loss of temper."

"That was not just loss of temper," Ahmose contradicted him. "That was an exposure. And as for harassing Apepa, do they not see that as long as a foreigner sits on the Horus Throne, Egypt is shamed? I find it hard to accept that they are stupid enough to put their personal comfort before that awesome truth."

"Majesty, what will you do?" The question came from Makhu. Kamose grimaced. He was finding it difficult to collect his thoughts and his chest ached with the impact of what had taken place. He tried to consider its implications.

"If I execute them, I will be sending a message of disunity to Het-Uart that will inevitably put heart into Apepa," he said. "I do not want to give that viper the satisfaction."

"Execute them?" Ramose echoed in horror. "Kamose, you cannot!"

"Why not?" Kamose demanded. "I executed your father for something similar. Teti carried out his treason. These three had betrayal in their minds. The difference is minimal." He threw up his hands. "But, as I say, I dare not give Apepa any encouragement. Therefore I have little choice. They can stay in prison until I return to Weset before the next Inundation. Hor-Aha, under whose command can I put their divisions? Ramose, pour us some wine. I am parched with thirst." All at once he wanted to put his head down on the table and weep.

For the next hour they discussed their alternatives but all

were suffering from the scene that had spun out of control with such dreadful rapidity and the suggestions made were barely acceptable. In the end it was decided that their departure would be delayed for a week while they thrashed out an alternate strategy. "You could always bestow titles on the division seconds," Ahmose said gloomily as the meeting came to a close. "Create more Princes."

"It is not a light thing to grant hereditary titles," Kamose objected. "Besides, the bloodlines must contain a least some hint of the aristocratic if I am to make Princes."

"You did it for Hor-Aha."

Kamose smiled at him thinly. "So I did, but he was an exception. What sort of Egypt will I rule if its nomes are governed by commoners? I hate them, Ahmose, but I grieve for them also. The fools!"

"There is Sebek-nakht in Mennofer," Ahmose said thoughtfully. "You have an agreement with him and I for one was very impressed by his manner. You might summon him to command a division."

"I do not think so," Kamose responded. "Not yet. He and Ankhmahor are very alike. He certainly seems trustworthy, but Mennofer is very close to the Delta. Too close. I can write to Paheri at Het nefer Apu though and ask what news of the Mennofer Prince there is. Gods what a mess!"

He cancelled the feast his mother had planned as a farewell and refused to see Tetisheri when she came to the door of his apartments in person, demanding to be told what had occurred and why three of Egypt's Princes were languishing in prison. He did, however, confer with Simontu regarding their treatment. "Give them whatever luxuries they need," he ordered. "Let them walk in the compound whenever they choose, under guard of course. Let them pray. Do not forget their station, Simontu."

Behind the security of his doors he forced himself to eat. The food tasted of ashes and the wine was sour, reflecting the anguish within his own spirit. When the servants had removed the remains of his meal, he told Akhtoy not to admit anyone, and placing a cushion on the floor beneath his window he sank onto it, leaning his forearms on the sill and gazing out at the quiet of the garden.

The sun was beginning to set and the light was changing from its hard brilliance to a soft bronze. The shadows under the trees crept slowly across the thick grass of the lawns. Insects danced in the limpid air, themselves transformed into motes of flashing gold as Ra's dying touched them. Kamose's room faced the well-trodden path leading to the watersteps along which two of his Followers were strolling, deep in conversation. Their voices came to him but not the words they were saying and in a moment they disappeared from his sight.

It came to him that in times of similar crisis he had always sought the privacy and solace of the old palace but today he had unconsciously chosen to go to earth in his quarters like a wounded fox. Grief mingled with anger seized him and at last he gave way to it. The rage was safe and familiar, an emotion against which he had struggled ever since Apepa had come and pronounced sentence upon the family, a dark knife aimed first at the Setiu, then at the Princes, sometimes at the gods who had decreed this painful destiny for him. To succumb to its powerful lure was a relief.

But the grief hurt him intolerably, its source a well of loneliness, treachery and spiritual fatigue that spurted scalding from his heart, bringing with it the tears that he had never before permitted himself to shed. Now he did so, laying his head on his arms and crying freely. When he next looked up, eyes swollen, face, neck and chest soaked by his sadness, the sun had gone and twilight was creeping through the garden, warm and dusky.

I would like to be a child again, he thought as he rose. To be six years old, sitting out there under a tree with my tutor, copying hieroglyphs onto pieces of broken clay. I can still see my own hand clutching the pen, feel my tongue caught between my teeth with the effort of learning to write. Amun was supreme in his temple in those days, only a little more omnipotent than Father, who knew everything and could do anything. Life was happy and predictable. Food was placed before me with a regularity I did not question. The river flowed for me alone, to bear my toy boats and to play with me when I threw myself naked into its cool embrace. As unreflective as a little animal, healthy and secure, I lived in the eternal and did not know that time was passing.

Crossing unsteadily to the water jug beside his couch, he dampened a cloth and wiped his face, lit his lamp against the increasing dimness, then took up his copper mirror. His own features stared back at him, distorted by his weeping but still young and handsome, the nose sharp, the mouth full, the eyes, his father's eyes, dark and intelligent. One black curl had fallen onto his brown forehead and he pushed it back with a gesture that reminded him suddenly of his mother's hands, the gentle fingers running through tresses that had always been unruly, the quiet voice exclaiming ruefully, "Kamose dearest, who gave you and Si-Amun this unusual mop?" Who indeed? Kamose wondered, the rich burnished surface of the mirror giving back to him the movement of his lips. Some anonymous denizen of Wawat perhaps? Lies, terrible lies, he thought violently. They all lie. Apepa, Mersu, Si-Amun, Teti, Tani, the Princes, their tongues deceive, their smiles are false. And you, Amun. Do you lie also? Have I wasted my years in running after a mirage?

Shaking his head, he put down the mirror and stood examining himself, the long bones of his legs clothed in firm muscle, the broad chest, the strong arms and supple wrists. He was aware that the events of the day had temporarily unhinged him, inviting a new perception of himself, but he was too drained to fight it, although he sensed its danger. I have lived for Egypt, his thoughts ran on unchecked. I have clung to one ideal like a virgin clinging to her chastity but unlike most virgins I have allowed that ideal to master me. Everything else has been tossed away. Wasted. He watched with intense concentration the play of lamplight on the hills and valleys of his body, his youthful body, his robust body. Pulling off his kilt, he looked down at his genitals, the mat of black fur in which his masculinity nestled, and despair swept over him. I have wasted you as well, he thought. Sacrificed you, sacrificed everything to one word. Freedom. And what may I lay before you in recompense? Two years of bleak struggle, the fruits of which were shattered in one hour. I do not want to pick up the pieces and start again. I do not want to go on. I am heartsick and tired to my very soul.

Chapter
SIXTEEN

Hᴇ sᴛᴏᴏᴅ ᴛʜᴇʀᴇ naked for a long time while the deluge of doubts, fantasies and memories pounded him, pitting the armour of his certitude, piercing the shell of his invulnerability until he could clearly see his ka, now rendered defenceless, peeled and shivering in a sea of nothingness. Not until someone tapped on his door did he come to himself.

"What is it, Akhtoy?" he croaked.

"Your pardon, Majesty, but Senehat is here. She says she must speak to you at once."

"Tell her to go away. I do not want to be disturbed." There was a flurry of whispers, then Senehat's voice came muffled through the wood.

"Forgive me, Majesty, but I have something important to tell you. It cannot wait." Kamose reached down for his kilt. Twice he was unable to pick it up, and when he succeeded in doing so he wrapped it clumsily around his waist.

"Come then," he called. "But it had better be important, Senehat. I am in no mood for frivolities."

The door opened and closed and the girl approached him, bowing as she did so. She was dressed in a plain servant's sheath of white linen bordered in blue. Her feet were bare and a cloud

447

of simple lotus perfume accompanied her. It seemed to smite Kamose with an almost physical force and he had to restrain himself from drawing it in through flared nostrils like a sniffing dog. "Forgive me, Majesty," she repeated. "I have been trying to see you alone since you returned from Wawat." Kamose studied her face but there was no hint of seduction there. Her expression was solemn. A tiny frown formed lines between the wings of her eyebrows. Kamose was conscious of a twinge of disappointment, no more than a weak pang under the smothering blanket of his exhaustion.

"Speak then," he commanded. Her hands came up and gripped each other.

"As you perhaps know, Her Highness Princess Aahmesnefertari asked me to bed with the noble Ramose," she began with surprising frankness. "I agreed to do so. The Princess's reasons for her request seemed pressing to me. I may be only a servant but I am a good Egyptian, Majesty. I have also become a good spy." Kamose smiled at her and with the movement of his mouth came a slight lifting of his mood.

"Sit down, Senehat," he offered, indicating his chair. "Take some wine." She shook her head.

"No. I must not be here long. If the Lady Nefer-Sakharu suspects that I have talked with you in private, she will try to kill me." Kamose's eyes narrowed.

"Kill you? My dear Senehat, if my sister knew you were in so much danger she would have you removed from that woman's influence immediately. Are you not exaggerating?"

"No! Listen to me, Majesty, I beg! I became the Noble Ramose's bedmate some time ago. He is a fine man, kind and appreciative. I learned to care for him very much, but that did not stop me from reporting his words to my mistress. I thank the gods that his conversation has always been blameless. He loves you. He is honest. It is his mother whom you must fear."

She paused, considering what she would say next, and Kamose waited patiently. "By the time you took him south, I had become a member of the Lady Nefer-Sakharu's personal staff," Senehat went on hesitantly. "I wash her in the bath house and do her hair. I wait on her when she eats and I make up her couch. She accepts me because of Ramose but she seldom sees me." The girl flushed. "She is a woman to whom servants are invisible unless as willing hands or ears without the ability to remember or ponder what they hear. She is my better in blood and station but her ka is common." Senehat swallowed and glanced at Kamose with swift apology. "I am an Egyptian servant," she said a trifle defiantly. "I have value under the canopy of Ma'at. Not like the slaves the Setiu tread upon." You are a spirited and clever little witch, Kamose thought. Aahmes-nefertari chose you well.

"I understand," he said aloud. "Go on, Senehat."

"It is no secret amongst your retainers that Nefer-Sakharu hates you for executing her husband and taking possession of her son's affections," she told him frankly. "She hates your family for taking her in and showing her kindness. It is often said that favours breed resentment, is it not?" Kamose nodded. "She showed great courage and dignity on the day her husband died. So say the gossips among your staff. But it was a moment of virtue that soon passed." Moving to the table, she picked up the jug. "May I change my mind, Majesty? Thank you." With practised precision she poured a cup and took a mouthful of wine. "We were all glad when the Princess removed His Highness Ahmose-onkh from her influence, but that only fuelled her hostility."

"I know all this," Kamose prompted her gently. "You still cannot say it, can you, Senehat? Nefer-Sakharu is guilty of treason." She made a distressed face, wiping a drop of purple liquid from the corner of her mouth with the tip of one dainty finger.

"It is no small thing to accuse a noblewoman," she replied. "Even now I shrink from it, although I have been relaying her words to my mistress for a long time. But not this. This is for Your Majesty only. Before you went into Wawat, Nefer-Sakharu did her best to turn the noble Ramose against you. Every day was spent in dripping her venom into his ears. He was upset. At first he tried to argue with her but later he kept silence. She refused to hear him. Some of the things she told him were lies. He questioned me closely regarding the way she was being treated here because her constant assault on him had begun to bear the fruit of doubt. I reassured him and he believed me. All this I reported to Her Highness. Then you went away and the Princes came." She paused to take another sip of wine with a servant's practised economy of movement. "Before they came, Nefer-Sakharu had begun to write to them. Every week she dictated letters. But she was stupid. She used one of the household's scribes and he of course showed what he had taken down to your royal grandmother. I understand that there was no real harm in the scrolls, only an attempt to befriend the Princes. The harm came later." Setting down the cup, she put her hands behind her back and looked at Kamose squarely. "When the Princes arrived, she overwhelmed them at once with invitations, visits, little gifts. She was constantly in their company and I with her to arrange her cushions, set up her canopy, refresh her face paint. All things you in your generosity had made available to her. She told them the strength of your defenders here on the estate and in Weset. She suggested that they might take control of your soldiers and so limit your power. That way you would be forced to listen more closely to their advice and their desires. She reminded them that you had executed an aristocrat, that you had no respect for their station, that their blood would not protect them from your ruthlessness, that you were using them."

"That much is true," Kamose interposed. "I have used them. I continue to use them."

"Yes, but benevolently, and you have promised them great rewards in return for their support. You even gave them the Gold of Valour!" Senehat said emphatically. Kamose allowed himself an inward smile. She was loyal, this little one. "When she saw that they made no objections to her complaints, she became more bold," Senehat continued. " 'Kamose is nothing but a butcher,' she said to them. 'He has murdered innocent Egyptians. He is not to be trusted. Write to Apepa and ask him what he will give you in exchange for Kamose's head.' Then the Prince Intef spoke up. 'I have already done so,' he said. Then Prince Meketra said, 'So have I. Kamose is an upstart and we are tired of his war. We want to return to our holdings and live in peace.' "

I gave Khemmenu back to that man, Kamose thought with a spurt of dull pain. I restored him to his princedom. How can he, how can any man, be so faithless? "What of the others?" he asked faintly. He did not for a moment doubt Senehat's story. It had the dismal ring of a bitter truth about it.

"The Princes Makhu and Mesehti argued violently against them," Senehat told him. "Prince Ankhmahor was not there. I think they deliberately waited until he was busy elsewhere. They knew that he could not be corrupted." She shrugged. "In the end Prince Makhu and Prince Mesehti agreed to make no mention to you of the negotiations that had passed between Apepa and the other two if they would cease such treason at once. In return they agreed to support a request to delay the next campaign for another year. That is all, Majesty. When word flew among the servants that three Princes had been arrested, I knew I had to come to you. I could not come before." She unclasped her hands and spread her fingers before him. "I was not present at every deliberation between the Princes and

Nefer-Sakharu after that. They could have changed their minds, cast off their insanity, and I did not want to accuse without proof. Ipi tells us in the servants' quarters that the proof of their perfidy came out at your meeting."

"But not all of it," Kamose said slowly. "I did not know that they were in contact with Apepa. Oh gods. The poison is so subtle, trickling even into the centre of my security." He felt his belly cramp suddenly, and fought to stay upright. Breathing deeply he waited, and at last the stabbing began to ebb. "I will have to arrest her too," he murmured. "She cannot be allowed to roam free, spreading her malice. Ramose, I am so sorry." He conjured a smile. "Senehat, you have done well. Your memory is excellent and so is your use of language. It is a pity that women do not become scribes. What may I give you in return for your loyalty?" Senehat set the cup carefully back on the table, walked to the window and lowered the rush hangings, then went to stand by the door. Kamose realized that her actions had been largely unconscious as she pondered his offer.

"I would like to leave your service and attach myself to the noble Ramose's household when all the fighting is done," she answered him candidly. "I have been happy in your employ but I will be happier with him." Lucky Ramose, Kamose thought wryly.

"He does not love you," he said softly.

"I know," she responded simply. "But it does not matter."

"Very well. Ipi can write your release and it will be filed until later. I will have Nefer-Sakharu arrested in the morning. Will you be safe until then?"

"I think so," she said gravely.

"Then you are dismissed. Be good to him, Senehat."

"Always, Majesty." In a flutter of ribbon and a swirl of linen she was gone.

He wanted to rush out and arrest Nefer-Sakharu at once,

drag her to the prison, stand her and the perfidious Princes against a wall and have them executed at once, but reason prevailed. Calling Akhtoy, he ordered hot water so that he could be bathed in his own rooms, and when it came he stood with eyes closed while his body servant washed away the tears and sweat and grime of this terrible day. The water had been scented with lotus oil. Inhaling the moist air he smiled with weary resignation. Ramose deserved Senehat and he wished his friend whatever fragile happiness he could seize from the ruin of his life.

Once he was alone, he pulled back the sheet on his couch and lay down, blowing out the lamp and waiting while his sight adjusted to the dimness. Slowly the outline of the covered window emerged, a square of faint greyness filled with the dark striated pattern of the reeds. Light from the torches in the passage outside slid under the door, becoming pale and diffused as it met the blackness of the floor. His ceiling with its spangle of painted stars was all but invisible, the stars themselves no more than indistinct ashy patches that glowed white during the day. I should go at once to Ahmose, he told himself. He and Aahmes-nefertari should be told what Senehat had to say. Nefer-Sakharu and the Princes must be tried in public so that Egypt will not condemn me as a callous butcher when I order their deaths. I no longer care to what conclusions Apepa might jump when he hears of such disunity within our ranks. They must serve as an example to any others whose loyalty might be wavering.

Butcher. He stirred anxiously beneath the sheet. They called me butcher. Is that what I am? Is that how Egypt will remember me, as a wild beast who murdered peasants and burned villages in a long fit of bloodlust? I must have time to expunge those deeds, necessary though they were, he thought. I must mount the Horus Throne. Amun, you must give me time in which to rule with justice, to see my country prosper, to promote good trade, rebuild the temples crumbled through neglect, all the things that could never come to pass without the two years I have spent in ripping apart what was.

The frenzy of his earlier grief had left him with a pounding head and though he was tired, sleep would not come. His thoughts circled the Princes, Nefer-Sakharu, Senehat, Aahmes-nefertari's account on the way back from the temple, and he could not quiet his mind. He considered getting up and making his way to his grandmother's quarters, but he did not want to hear one of her tirades, not tonight. He wanted silence and stillness before the storm he would be forced to unleash in the morning.

Despair filled him. On impulse he left his couch, and kneeling in the darkness before his Amun shrine he began to pray. "I do not want to go on," he whispered to his god. "I have lost the heart for it. My Princes are deserting me. Their contempt stings me to my very bones. All my work and worry, all the sacrifices of my family, the bereavements, the tears, the terror, it has all come to this. I am empty. I can do no more. Release me, mighty Amun. Give me leave to lay it all aside if only for a little while. Your divine hand has been heavy on my shoulder. Lift it I beg, and do not condemn me for my weakness. I have done all a man could do."

After a long while he felt the torrent of his desperate words dry up and as they did so a peace began to steal over him, quieting his mind and soothing away the tensions of his body. You have been praying for your death, a voice inside him mocked him kindly. Is that what you really want, Kamose Tao? To give up and slink into obscurity? What would your father say? "He would commend me for trying," Kamose whispered back. "Be silent now. I think I can sleep." Reaching up, he pulled a pillow onto the floor, and setting his head on it and one hand under it, he closed his eyes. He would go on, he knew, until Egypt was cleansed or the gods took his life. He was a warrior, and there was no alternative.

He woke with a start, his heart already racing, wondering if someone had called his name. His hip and one shoulder ached from lying on a hard surface, and after a moment he got up and tossed his pillow onto the couch, intending to follow it, but in the act of doing so he paused. There was something wrong. Senses straining, he probed the darkness. Dim light still filtered around the edges of the covered window. The silence was absolute. The furnishings of his room were nothing more than vague humps. He could not tell how long he had been asleep but he felt rested and it seemed to him that dawn could not be far away. Frowning, he stood irresolute, the trailing sheet of his bed brushing his thigh. Something wrong. Something small. The silence too deep perhaps. The darkness too dense.

Then he knew. There was no light seeping under his door from the torches kept burning in the passage outside. Nor was there the slightest sound from the Follower who should be stationed there. Cautiously Kamose eased his way forward, and only his outstretched hand prevented him from walking into the edge of a door that was wide open. Someone came into my room while I was asleep on the floor, he thought. Someone who did not see me and left again in such a hurry that they did not close my door. It must have been a servant or even one of the family, otherwise they could not have passed the guard. Then why have the torches been allowed to go out? He stepped carefully into the hall, calling for Behek in a low voice, but no sleepy snuffle answered him from the end of the long corridor.

Instantly he could see better, for the door across whose lintel the dog usually sprawled was left open to admit the cooling night breezes, and he realized at once that the brackets fixed on the walls at regular intervals to hold the torches were empty.

But the floor was not. Just this side of the square that showed him the outline of black palm fronds there was a shapeless huddle and directly opposite him, another. The soldier sat slumped against the wall, legs spread, head drooped on his chest. In two steps Kamose was upon him. "Get up, soldier!" he said harshly. "You will be disciplined for sleeping on duty!" But his foot as he lifted it from the floor was sticky and he had known before he spoke, had not wanted to know, that the man was dead. Squatting beside the corpse, he examined it closely. Blood had pulsed from the gash in the Follower's throat, struck the wall in a thick splash, and spread out under him as he died.

Quickly Kamose retreated to the shadow of his room and paused just inside the door, teeth clenched against the multitude of voices clamouring in his head. How long ago? Who else? How many assassins? Why? Where are they now? He forced himself to think clearly past the shock, past the overwhelming feeling of futility, refusing the vision of a grievously wounded Seqenenra who had himself become a victim of duplicity and deceit. Later, he told himself feverishly. Later I will ponder how the wheel of destiny has turned and turned again to replace my father's face with mine. Now I must move. Weapons. Where are my weapons? Ankhmahor took them to refurbish after Wawat. Is he a part of this? Refusing the invitation to argue his courage away, he glanced swiftly up and down the quiet passage, walked to the body of his Follower, and tugging the man's sword from his scabbard and the knife from his belt, he ran towards his brother's apartments.

He met no one living on the way. He was in too much of a hurry to stop and inspect the corpses lying at regular intervals, but it was obvious that all the household guards had been murdered. Why did they not resist? he wondered fleetingly, and the answer came at once. Because they knew their attackers. And where are the servants? Have they run away? Are they dead on their mats in the servants' quarters? Gods, this silence is un-nerving. Panting, he slowed outside Ahmose's rooms. One man sat with his back against the wall, his sword in his hand. He was wide awake. Coming to his feet, he saluted Kamose who approached him warily. "You are still alive," Kamose blurted breathlessly. The man's eyebrows rose under the rim of his leather helmet.

"Majesty, I was tired but I have never yet fallen asleep on duty, " he answered apologetically, obviously misunderstanding Kamose's cryptic words. "My watch is due to change soon. I am sorry for sitting down." Kamose wanted to shake him.

"Not that, you fool!" he hissed. "Who else has been here?" The soldier's gaze travelled down Kamose and came to rest on his bare feet. Instantly he tensed. Kamose looked down. The result of the carnage was spattered halfway up his calves. "Your fellows are dead," Kamose said curtly. "I have run through their blood. Did anyone ask admittance to my brother's quarters this night?" He dreaded the reply.

"One of your officers with two infantrymen came a little while ago, wanting to speak to the Prince," the Follower said, his struggle to overcome his bewilderment clear on his face. "But the Prince is not within. He left earlier to go fishing. Dawn is not far away, Majesty. They did not ask to see the Princess. They went away again." Kamose felt his bowels loosen in relief.

"Come with me," he ordered, and pushed the door open.

Ahmose and his wife inhabited a suite larger than Kamose's own, a concession to their married status. The small ante-room into which Kamose entered glowed peacefully in the light of one lamp. The two farther doors, one to the nursery and one to the bedchamber, were closed. At the sound of his coming Raa got up from her pallet by the nursery door and Sit-Hathor, Aahmes-nefertari's body servant, peered up at him from hers.

Both women had come to their feet by the time he had closed the door behind himself and the soldier. "Raa, wake your mistress and then dress the children," he commanded. "Sit-Hathor, I want you to go to Ramose's room. He is to arm himself and find Prince Ankhmahor. Do you understand?" She nodded at him, her eyes huge in the yellow light. "There are many bodies in the halls," he went on more gently. "You should put on your sandals. Can you be brave?" Again she nodded. "Tell Ramose we are betrayed and in danger. I will be at the watersteps to intercept my brother. At once, Sit-Hathor!" She had bent and picked up her sandals but had stood staring at him wildly. Now she came to herself and began to quickly tie them on. Raa had disappeared into the bedchamber and as Sit-Hathor let herself out into the passage Aahmes-nefertari emerged, swathed in a sheet and blinking drowsily. Behind her Raa went into the nursery.

"Whatever is the matter, Kamose?" his sister enquired sleepily. Kamose waited, watching her until her features cleared and her gaze became sharp, flicking over him. "You are naked and I think that is blood on your legs," she said. "The Princes have revolted, haven't they? Ahmose went fishing. He said he would take Behek with him. Is he safe?"

"I don't know, but my conclusion is the same as yours. If I hadn't slept on the floor last night I would be dead. They will keep trying, they must know that they have shown their hand, and very soon they will remember that Ahmose-onkh is also a Tao and they will come back here to eliminate him. He must survive, Aahmes-nefertari. Otherwise there will be no King left in Egypt." Beyond the nursery door he could hear the baby begin to cry and Ahmose-onkh protesting over the sound of the nurse's firm, soothing voice. "You must take the children and go out onto the desert," Kamose went on. "This soldier will accompany you. There is no time for argument!" he half-shouted at her as she opened her mouth to object. "I came here straight from my own quarters! I have no clear idea of what is happening anywhere else! Get dressed and do as you are told!" For answer she whirled and vanished into her room and Kamose waited, impatience whipping him. Raa came out carrying Hent-ta-Hent in one arm and grasping Ahmose-onkh's hand with the other. "Hungry," the boy said petulantly. Kamose turned to the soldier.

"Take them straight out through the servants' entrance at the rear," he said. "Pick up any food and drink you find in the kitchens on the way. Go as far into the desert as they can manage, and hide them until night. Then work your way to Amun's temple. Stay with them at all times." You hold the future of Egypt in your hands, he wanted to add. Your life is worth nothing compared to theirs. Can you be trusted? He bit his tongue, knowing that he had no choice but to rely on this man's loyalty and it was pointless to cause him affront. Aahmes-nefertari had slammed her door and was walking towards him, holding out a kilt.

"I am clothed as you ordered," she said. "Put this on, Kamose. It is one of Ahmose's. But I am not going with the children. Ahmose will need me here. So will Mother and Grandmother." He wanted to sweep her up and throw her out into the passage, to rage at her in his haste and fear, but he knew by the glint of obstinacy in her eyes that it would do no good. He did not bother to argue. Laying his weapons aside he wrapped the kilt around himself.

"Highness . . ." Raa put in anxiously. Aahmes-nefertari went to her and firmly pushed her at the door.

"This Follower will look after you," she said. "Just do as he says." Kamose signalled the man.

"Carry the Prince. Keep him out of the blood," he ordered. "Pray as you go. Hurry!" The soldier lifted Ahmose-onkh as though he were a scrap of linen, and the room emptied. Kamose did not wait. He picked up his weapons. "Tell Tetisheri and Aahotep what I know," he said as he headed for the door. "Stay with them. Don't let them wander about. If soldiers come, lie to them." On impulse he paused, and striding back into the room he once more laid aside the sword and knife and enfolded his sister in his arms. "I love you. I am so sorry," he whispered illogically. She held him tightly, fiercely, before letting him go.

"Find Ahmose and fight them, Kamose," she whispered back. "Make them pay. For if you do not, then I shall have to kill them all by myself." It was a poor attempt at humour but it cheered him nonetheless, and he was calmer by the time they stepped into the still-deserted passage and parted.

Keeping to the shadows, Kamose stole through the house, nerves taut, expecting the enemy to step out in front of him at any moment. Swiftly he explored the dusky expanse of the reception hall and found it empty. So were the other public rooms. Not until he came out under the entrance pillars was there life. Two soldiers rose from their stools by the high double doors and reverenced him promptly and with a gush of relief Kamose recognized them as members of his Followers. They were as ignorant of events as the man on Ahmose's door and Kamose wasted no time in questioning them. "Take up your station outside the women's quarters," he ordered them. "Let no one in unless it is the Noble Ramose or your superior, Prince Ankhmahor." He did not wait to see them go. Veering left he set off towards the path leading to the watersteps.

But suddenly he paused and with a groan put his hands on his knees and bent over them. A dilemma had presented itself, diabolical and horrifying in its simplicity. Like the soldiers, Ahmose might not know what had befallen the house. He was out there somewhere on the river, sitting contentedly in his skiff with a fishing line dangling in the water and Behek sniffing the night air beside him. There was a strong possibility that the assassins, whoever they were, had not bothered to look for him. They would wait until he returned. Kamose scanned the sky, already suffused with a hint of the dawn to come. A single bird had begun to pipe its morning salute to Ra's majestic rising and to Kamose's feverish eye the silhouette of the tree trunks around him seemed already clearer.

If he continued on to the Nile, he might be able to intercept his brother. However, if Aahmes-nefertari and his own suspicions were correct and this was a revolt, the Princes would take their officers and make their way straight to the barracks where the local soldiers slept. Before his own officers had rubbed the night from their eyes the army would be under hostile control, all three thousand men, and he would be completely powerless. I might as well stand here and offer my neck meekly to the knife, he thought bitterly. Either I speed to the barracks in the faint hope that I get there before the Princes, thus almost certainly sacrificing Ahmose to the arrows of those who must surely be lying in wait for him but quashing this rebellion, or I try to intercept him, save his life, and lose a kingdom.

But he may already be dead, the voice of self-preservation murmured. You do not know anything, not really. You are making assumptions that could end your life on the chance that Ahmose is not already floating on the surface of the river with his throat cut. At least in heading for the barracks you are attempting to protect the women and restore your supremacy. Go back, circle the house, run for the barracks. Not finding you or Ahmose may have made them hesitate, confused them. They may only now be approaching the parade ground. The gods have given you an opportunity to live and emerge triumphant from this chaos. All you have to do is turn around. After all, Ahmose might stay on the river to toss his throwing stick at a few ducks before he comes home. By then it could all be over.

Amun, help me, Kamose pleaded as he stood frozen and trembling with indecision. I do not know what to do. Either way I choose is a way of death. Do I try to warn Ahmose, a laughably slim chance at best, or do I try to rouse my officers who are probably already under the threat of the Princes' swords? Do not forget Ramose and Ankhmahor. What if Ramose found the Prince and together they had the same thoughts as I? What if they chose to go to the barracks? Ankhmahor is well known to my soldiers. Or perhaps, perhaps they have crossed the river to alert Hor-Aha and the Medjay. That is what I ought to have done with the soldiers at the house entrance. What was I thinking of? You were not thinking at all, he berated himself. Your mind was weak with fears for the safety of your women when only quick and resolute action will suffice.

You have a third option, another voice broke in, softer, more seductive than the other. You could join the children out on the desert, guide them to the temple, claim sanctuary from Amunmose. After all, Ahmose-onkh is a legitimate heir to divinity, is he not? If Ahmose is already dead and your hours are numbered, the boy is all that is left of Tao supremacy. You know for certain that he at least is still alive. For one blinding second everything in Kamose assented to this plan. His spine straightened. His glance took in the rapidly growing grey light that heralded the imminent lifting of the sun above the eastern horizon. But then he began to smile. I may be a fool, he admitted to himself, but I am not a coward. I am my father's son. Our great dream is finished, but others in years to come will remember it and take it up again. Ahmose-onkh perhaps. Who can say? This is all wavering plumes of smoke, Kamose, and you cannot see the fire. Your duty is to ignore it for the sake of your kin, not try to put it out. He took a step towards the river path. It was the hardest thing that he had ever done, but the second was easier. In the strengthening dawn he crept across the grass.

He had expected to find soldiers concealed in the shrubbery close to the watersteps, but though he searched the undergrowth on both sides of the path, and lying prone behind a bush he scanned the placid stone stair lapped slowly by the river, he saw no one. They already have control of the army then, he thought dismally. They can arrest and kill us at their leisure. Retreating, he positioned himself under the vine trellis, pressing himself into the rough, dark grape leaves where he could not be seen from the house, and gave himself up to his wait.

The dawn chorus was now in full spate, a tuneful stridency of bird voices joined, Kamose knew, by the Hymn of Praise even now being sung in the temple. Of course he could not hear it, but he imagined the words and the rich, time-honoured melody with which the priests greeted the birth of Ra. Every morning his rising was sanctified in a burst of gratitude for life, for sanity, for the ordered beauty of Ma'at. Kamose allowed himself a moment of surrender to the scent of the spring flowers beginning to waft to him on the first stirring of the breeze and the grainy kiss of the vine leaves fluttering against his skin. His shadow was beginning to appear on the pebbled path, stretching pale and elongated towards the river. A lizard scuttled over it, tail flicking, its tiny, delicate claws scrabbling inaudibly, and vanished into the unkempt lawn. The light around Kamose flushed suddenly gold and he knew that Ra had lipped the edge of the world.

With a tremor of hope he was beginning to think that Ahmose had indeed decided to stay on the water and hunt ducks, but he heard the sound of oars breaking the water and his brother's voice, loud and cheerful. Someone answered him. Wood creaked and footsteps thudded. Behek barked. Kamose left the shelter of the trellis and broke into a run.

There were two guards with Ahmose. One had jumped onto a submerged waterstep and was tying up the skiff. The other had already gained the stone paving and was glancing about automatically as he had been trained to do. Ahmose himself was clambering after him, a cluster of silver fish threaded on a string clutched in one hand and his sandals in the other. Gaining dry land, he dropped the sandals and began to manœuvre his feet into them, laughing as he did so. All this Kamose saw and noted with a preternatural clarity. The rim of his brother's white kilt had become limp and transparent with water and clung to his brown thighs. The fish glinted wetly, their scales reflecting pink and a delicate blue in the new sunlight. A sodden Behek was eyeing them hungrily. Ahmose had a streak of drying mud on his cheek. He was wearing one plain gold bracelet, thin and loose, that fell against his thumb as he reached down to ease the thong of the sandal between his toes. Both guards were beside him now, one going down on one knee to tie Ahmose's sandals.

Kamose was almost upon them. Then Ahmose looked up and saw him coming. "What are you doing up so early, Kamose?" he called brightly. "Are you taking a swim? See how many fish I caught this morning! I think I will have them fried at once, for I am lamentably hungry!" Lifting the limp bundle he shook it, grinning. Behek's attention, now diverted from the fish, turned to his master. His ears pricked and he began to bark.

At that moment Kamose felt himself struck in the left side. It was as though he had been punched, and he staggered, pitching forward. Regaining his balance, he thought that he had stumbled on, and it was a few seconds before he realized that he was not moving towards Ahmose after all, that he had stumbled and fallen, that his face was pressed to the gritty surface of the path and power had suddenly gone from his limbs. He tried to push against the ground but his palms simply patted the earth. Why is Ahmose shouting? he wondered irritably. Why doesn't one of the guards come and help me up? He felt the vibration of pounding feet and with a great effort he managed to turn his head. Two pairs of feet rushed by him. He heard grunting, a curse and a scream.

Then someone touched him, lifting and settling him, and with the movement pain exploded under his armpit, down his side, along his back. Stifling his own scream, he looked up through eyes blurred with tears of agony. He was cradled across his brother's lap, his neck supported in the crook of Ahmose's arm, his own fingers clinging to Ahmose's other hand. "You have been shot, Kamose. What has happened here? What has happened?" Ahmose's voice cried the words but they came from a far distance for surely he, Kamose, was running and Ahmose was holding up his fish and smiling and it was a bird or perhaps a lizard who had spoken. Kamose could not breathe. There was a lump in his chest. Something was stuck in his throat and when he opened his mouth it slipped out, hot and wet.

"The Princes," he whispered. "Ahmose, the Princes."

"Yes, you are right," he murmured. She. He was mistaken. It was not Ahmose who was holding him it was the woman, and now he knew that he was only dreaming and he would wake to find himself curled up on his floor before his Amun shrine and all would be well.

"Your face," he said wonderingly. "I see your face at last and it is flawless in its perfection. I love you, love you. I have always loved only you."

"I know," she replied. "You have served me with great faithfulness, Kamose Tao, and I love you also. But now it is time for us to part." Bending down she kissed him softly. Her lips tasted of palm wine and her hair, falling about his face, filled his nostrils with the scent of the lotus. When she withdrew he saw that her mouth and teeth were smeared with blood.

"I do not like this dream," he faltered. "Hold me tighter. Do not let me slip." She smiled.

"I will enfold you forever, my dearest brother," she said quietly. "Your flesh will rest deep within my rock, and as long as the waters of my river flow and the wind of my deserts trouble the sand and the fronds of my palm trees drop their fruit, they will sing your worship. Go now. Go. Ma'at awaits you in the Judgement Hall and I promise that your heart will lie so lightly on the scales that her Feather will weigh heavier than gold."

"Please . . ." he choked. "Oh please . . ." his mouth still tingling with her kiss, but it was Ahmose who loomed above him, his mouth dark red, his features contorted.

"Gods, Kamose, don't die!" he begged, but Kamose, looking beyond him to where the sky was darkening and a mighty pylon had begun to take shape, could not answer. Things moved within that gloom, a glimmer of sumptuous metal, a glint of light caught by one kohled eye, but between him and the vision a human shadow loomed. He tried to call to his brother, to warn him, but he was too tired. Half-closing his eyes he saw the shadow shrink, its arm come up, the gloved hand brandishing a wooden club, and then he was standing on the threshold of the Judgement Hall and such small details did not matter any more.

# Chapter ✑✑ SEVENTEEN

AAHMES-NEFERTARI WAS terrified. As she sped through the dim corridors of the house, she tried not to see the things that huddled in the shadows, the dead things, but sometimes they lay spreadeagled across her path and she was forced to jump over them. In a mad attempt to remain uncontaminated by the carnage she lifted the hem of her sheath so that it would not brush the blood-soaked corpses but she could not always avoid the puddles and soon her feet and ankles were sodden. Somehow that did not matter as much as the possibility of soiled linen, the wetness that she would feel as a weight, the stains that could not be washed away.

At the entrance to the women's quarters the two guards lay one on top of the other as though they were embracing. With a shudder the girl rushed past them. The passage beyond was blessedly empty and she felt a quick spurt of relief that the stewards, Uni and Kares, always retired for the night to their own rooms in the servants' lodgings and were probably safe. One torch still burned opposite her mother's door. Aahmes-nefertari fell into Aahotep's bedchamber. Her servant rose immediately and Aahotep sat up. "Mother, get dressed at once and come to Grandmother's rooms," Aahmes-nefertari said.

Not waiting to see if she had been heard she went out, ran the short distance to Tetisheri's apartments, and let herself in.

Tetisheri had a large anteroom in which she gave audience to guests and to which she retired to read or think whenever she needed privacy. It was a large, well-appointed space, purposely daunting in the formality of its furnishings. Many times Aahmes-nefertari had been summoned here to be reprimanded, to recite her lessons, or to receive lectures on how a Princess ought to think and behave. Here her grandmother kept a firm thumb on the organization of the house and here in past months the three women had gathered to discuss the responsibilities Kamose had laid upon them. Those consultations had done much to dispel the inner shrinking Aahmes-nefertari had always felt when the door had swung open to admit her but even now, in a moment of extreme urgency, she experienced a flutter of purely adolescent apprehension. It soon vanished, however, when Isis left her pallet with a polite indignation written on her sleepy face. "I did not hear you knock, Highness," she said. For answer Aahmes-nefertari took up a taper, and lighting it from the one burning lamp she used it to ignite the two larger standing lamps by the far wall.

"Wake my grandmother, tell her I am here, and dress her quickly," she ordered. "Do not question me, Isis. Just hurry." The servant disappeared through the door leading to Tetisheri's inner sanctuary and Aahmes-nefertari, left alone in the deep silence that precedes the dawn, began to shiver. Her feet had left dark brown prints across the spotless floor. Looking down at herself she saw the drying blood encrusted between her toes and girdling her ankles like grotesque jewellery. Repulsed she glanced about for water, but then she paused. They died because of their loyalty, she thought. Their blood does not sully me. To wash it away too soon would be insulting to their sacrifice.

There were sounds outside in the passage and her heart

leaped into her throat but it was only her mother. Aahotep was tying a belt around the waist of her blue sheath as she came. Her movements were as measured and graceful as ever but her eyes darted anxiously over her daughter, coming to rest on the girl's besmirched feet. "That is blood!" she said loudly. "Is it from you? Are you ill? Where are the children? Where is Kamose? Is he here? You have made a mess of the floor, Aahmes-nefertari. You should be washed at once." Aahmes-nefertari did not respond. Her mother would assimilate the shock in a moment, she knew, and indeed Aahotep's clouded face was already clearing. "Gods," she breathed. "What has happened?" Just then Tetisheri emerged into the lamplight, her grey hair awry, her expression fierce.

"I was dreaming of fresh figs and a ring I lost many years ago," she said. "There may be some connection between the two but now I shall never know. What are you doing here?" She stared at her granddaughter's feet for what seemed to be a long time, then she slowly folded her arms. To Aahmes-nefertari the gesture was one of self-protection. "Are you hurt?" she asked. The girl shook her head. "Then speak quickly. Isis, close the door."

"No!" Aahmes-nefertari put out a hand. "No, Grandmother. We need to hear if someone is coming. There has been a revolt, how serious we do not know. All the Followers in the house are dead. Kamose sent Raa out into the desert with the children. He has gone to the watersteps to waylay Ahmose when he returns from fishing. Oh thank the gods he went fishing!" Her voice rose, quivering, and she fought to control it. "Kamose told me to stay here with you. We think it is the Princes."

"How can that be?" Tetisheri demanded. "Intef, Meketra and Iasen are in prison."

"Someone must have let them out," Aahotep said. "Nefer-Sakharu perhaps."

"Simontu and his jailers would never be overpowered by a woman alone," Aahmes-nefertari objected, "and Nefer-Sakharu does not have the authority to order the cells unlocked. Their officers and soldiers have attacked the prison and freed them."

"Then where are they?" Aahotep wondered, and Aahmes-nefertari answered her with a mouth gone suddenly dry.

"They are at the barracks taking command of our troops," she rasped. "They must establish control of our men before we can intervene and that may not be as difficult as we might suppose, seeing that their soldiers have been mingling freely with ours and the officers of the Princes have been giving gifts and regaling our soldiers with feasts. Our forces are superior to the ones they brought with them, but our officers will feel a certain confusion of obligation if faced with direct orders from nobles who have been more than kind to them. I believe that the Princes sent a small contingent here to the house to kill Kamose and Ahmose while they themselves gathered their soldiers and took over the barracks. But Amun decreed that my brothers should be spared." Tetisheri was running a bony hand through her dishevelled hair. She had begun to pace. She seemed calm but Aahmes-nefertari saw her arm trembling.

"For how long?" she said loudly. "The Followers are dead. Ahmose will arrive at the watersteps all unsuspecting, provided that soldiers were not despatched to ambush him on his way home, in which case he is already dead. Kamose is completely undefended. What of Ramose and Ankhmahor? Can we get word to Hor-Aha and the Medjay on the west bank?"

"I don't know," Aahmes-nefertari admitted, and Aahotep gave an exclamation of frustration.

"Isis, go and see if the Lady Nefer-Sakharu is still on her couch," she ordered. "But go quietly. If she is there, do not wake her."

"Majesty, I am scared," the servant said, glancing at her mistress. Tetisheri waved at her.

"It is not far, only along the passage," she retorted. "Hurry up!" Unwillingly the woman left the room and there was a tense silence.

"If what we have surmised is true, Kamose is entirely alone," Aahotep said at last. "There is no one to help him. No one to save him or Ahmose. I cannot believe that everything he has done has come to this!" she burst out passionately. "Nothing but heartache and betrayal year after year and for what? We might as well have gone meekly to the fate Apepa had prepared for us in the first place. I cannot bear the thought that he will win after all!"

"We must do something," Tetisheri urged. "Does Kamose really expect the three of us to cower here until Intef or Meketra comes blustering in to gloat?" Aahotep spread out her hands.

"What can we do?" she protested angrily. "Be reasonable, Tetisheri. Words will not keep my sons alive."

"You speak as though they are already defeated," the old woman snapped back. "But what do we really know? Nothing except that the Followers are dead and Kamose has gone to the watersteps. The rest is supposition. We must ascertain the truth." At that moment Isis returned, visibly pale. "Well?" Tetisheri asked.

"The Lady Nefer-Sakharu is not in her room," the servant told them. "Neither is Senehat."

"Senehat will be in Ramose's quarters," Aahotep said tiredly. "Or would be if all was well. Do you have any suggestions, Tetisheri?"

"I do," Aahmes-nefertari said faintly. She had been listening to the heated exchange between her mother and grandmother with little attention, her own mind racing furiously. There was indeed something to be tried, but everything in her cringed from its audacity. I am only a wife and mother, she said to herself in despair. If I stay here in Grandmother's apartments the Princes will spare me as such, but if I interfere in whatever is going on out there, I will be killed. Then what of my children? I do not have the courage for this. Yet even as she felt her bowels turn to water at the thought, she was giving it voice. "I have spent much time out on the parade ground watching the men go through their paces and talking to the officers," she went on more steadily. "They seem to have a respect for me. Let me put it to the test. I am of the ruling house. If the officers see me, hear me, they will be more inclined to obey me than any of the Princes." She paused and gulped, reaching for the support of a nearby chairback. "If the gods are with me, the soldiers will not know that their King and his brother have been rendered impotent or even killed. They will fear retribution. I can undo any damage the Princes may have done out there if I am swift enough. If I am too late . . ." She shrugged with what she hoped might be seen as indifference. " . . . then the worst they can do is arrest me and drag me back here."

The two other women stared at her, Tetisheri with eyes narrowed in speculation, Aahotep with her usual inscrutable gaze. Then Aahotep sighed.

"If anyone dares this, it should be me," she said. "My authority carries more weight than yours, Aahmes-nefertari." But Tetisheri stepped forward eagerly.

"No, Aahmes-nefertari is right," she said. "The soldiers know her. They are used to seeing her on the dais with Ahmose-onkh. Let her go, Aahotep. It is a good plan." Aahmes-nefertari felt a spasm of violent resentment as she looked into her grandmother's face. You really are a ruthless woman, she thought. Your concern is not for my safety. All you care about is a chance to protect the unique place the family holds in Egypt. If I can do that, it does not matter to you whether I live or die in the trying.

"After all, Grandmother," she could not resist saying aloud, "the Taos do have another son to rule if my husband and Kamose die. That is your only preoccupation, is it not?" She turned to her mother. "Have I your permission to go, Aahotep?" White to the lips, Aahotep nodded.

"I see no alternative and there is no time to come up with one," she said, her voice breaking. "I have no intention of waiting here and going mad either, Aahmes-nefertari. I will go to the watersteps, and if they are not guarded, I will cross the river to Hor-Aha." She opened her arms and her daughter stepped into her embrace. They held each other tightly until Aahotep broke away. "Take weapons with you," she said. Aahmes-nefertari walked to the door and out into the passage beyond. It took all the courage she possessed to turn towards the rear of the house, but breathing a prayer to Amun and keeping her mind full of her husband's genial face, she found it easier than she had imagined.

Aahotep prepared to follow her. "If Nefer-Sakharu is foolish enough to return to her rooms, she must be detained here," she said to her mother-in-law. "Can you do that, Tetisheri?" The older woman pursed her lips.

"Not by the force of this aging carcase," she replied hoarsely. "I can attempt to browbeat her, but if she chooses to leave again I will not be able to stop her. But dawn comes, Aahotep. Uni will have left his couch in the servants' quarters. I can only pray that he is unmolested and will reach the house. He can restrain Nefer-Sakharu." There was nothing else to say. Aahotep hesitated, a dozen conjectures running through her mind. Resisting the urge to discuss them and thus put off the moment when she would have to abandon the illusory safety of the women's wing, she summoned a brief smile and slipped out, closing the door behind her.

The corridor was no longer sunk in darkness. A grey pre-dawn light suffused it, strengthening even as she went swiftly towards the main entrance of the house, bringing the disorderly sprawl of bodies from the realm of nightmare into the dreary focus of reality. A slight chill came with it and Aahotep shivered. She was not afraid of the dead. Nor did she allow her imagination to present her with images of ghosts newly created hovering in the rapidly dissolving shadows. It was terror for her sons that quickened her pulse and kept her gaze high. Anger uncurled in her like some tiny black worm, an emotion that had secretly plagued her from time to time ever since her husband had come home to her in a box full of sand.

She had not gone far when she rounded a corner to be confronted by two soldiers coming towards her. It was too late to hide. Halting, she waited while they approached, her heart tripping in her breast. I should have armed myself, she thought stupidly, but it did not seem to matter, for already they were bowing and the hands holding their swords remained low. "Where are you going?" she demanded.

"His Majesty commanded us to guard the women's quarters," one of them answered. "We are to keep you safe."

"So Kamose is alive!" she breathed, encouraged. "How long ago did you see him? Where was he going?"

"His Majesty came out of the house and we were stationed under the pillars," the same one explained. "He told us nothing other than to guard you. Majesty, what is happening?" Aahotep looked them over, wondering briefly whether or not to send them on to Tetisheri's door before deciding that there they would be wasted. Nor did she want to take the time to explain a situation she herself did not understand, for if she did her nerve might fail her.

"You had better come with me," she ordered. "Be prepared to kill anyone you do not recognize." Bending down, she wrestled a knife from the belt of a corpse lying across the doorway to Seqenenra's office and as she straightened she realized that the shroud of night had lifted altogether. Ra had rimmed the horizon.

At that, she was suddenly filled with a sense of urgency. Hurry, something whispered to her, hurry or you will be too late. She began to run along the passage, past the wide interior entrance to the reception hall, past the small room opposite which held the household shrines, and out under the pillars, the two men panting behind her. The stone beneath her feet struck cold through her sandals and the air was momentarily brisk but the garden beyond was already bathed in sparkling new light and sonorous with birdsong. Warmth struck her skin as she veered towards the path leading to the watersteps but she scarcely noticed it, so compelling was the need to rush on. Part of her consciousness stood back and watched her flight with astonishment. Is this you, Aahotep, moon worshipper, lover of dignity and the exercise of a placid authority, fleeing unpainted and with hair and linen streaming? it asked, and then was engulfed and forgotten in a tide of overwhelming panic, for she heard someone scream.

Tumbling out onto the path she paused, breast heaving, legs shaking with the unaccustomed stress. Beyond the grape trellis a group of men were struggling with each other. A few steps away from her one of them was down and clearly dead, his neck half-severed through. Another lay a little farther away, his limbs spreadeagled on the packed earth. Someone was cradling him, head lowered, his broad back smeared with dust, and with a shriek Aahotep recognized Ahmose. She started forward, dimly aware that the soldiers who had accompanied her had already rushed into a fray where one man wearing the blue-and-white livery of the royal house had been attempting to hold off three others.

Between her and the bowed spine of her younger son another man was running, a wooden club raised in both hands. His intent was clear and with a spurt of sheer despair Aahotep knew that he would reach Ahmose before she could. Her escort, closely engaged, had not seen the danger. She yelled at them as she sped, heard another scream behind her, but now all her attention was fixed on covering the ground. Sweat sprang out over her body, seeping into her eyes, but she hardly felt its sting.

The man with the club had come within striking distance of his victim. Slowing, he swung his weapon. "Ahmose!" Aahotep cried out but her voice was drowned in the shouts and curses of the fighting soldiers and he did not hear her. He went on rocking the body of the man he was holding so tightly. The attacker steadied his stance, feet apart, and it seemed to Aahotep that in the second before he brought his crude weapon thudding against her son's defenceless skull the whole of her world ceased to exist. Time itself became torpid, oozing like thick honey. She was not moving at all and the leaves of the trees to right and left of the path as it wound away into nothingness were trapped into immobility. Silence filled her head. All she could hear was the muffled booming of her own pulse and her own sobbing breath.

Then the club came down. Ahmose collapsed onto his side. But with a fierce shout Aahotep drove the knife into his assassin's back. Pain exploded from her wrist to her shoulder and she knew in a burst of fear that she had merely struck a rib. The man began to turn. It was Prince Meketra, a look of astounded disbelief on his face. Gasping and weeping, Aahotep almost dropped the knife, recovered, and gripping its hilt in both slippery hands she raised it high and drove it into Meketra just beneath his shoulder. This time it sank deep. Meketra fell clumsily to his knees taking her with him, his bewildered glance going to the weapon protruding so incongruously from his flesh. Aahotep placed one foot on his chest and jerked the knife free. Meketra tumbled backwards and Aahotep followed, this time pushing the blade into the hollow of his throat. His eyes widened and he tried to cough.

Aahotep did not see him die. On hands and knees she scrambled at once to Ahmose. He was lying limply with his eyes half-closed, one side of his head a mass of blood, his mouth also smeared. Beside him Kamose rested, an arrow jutting from his side, one hand on his chest and the other outflung as though waiting to receive something that might be placed on his brown palm. He was smiling gently but his gaze was fixed. He was dead.

All at once the world came back. The birds began to pipe again. The trees dipped and quivered in the morning breeze. Sunlight poured onto the path. And Aahotep, crouching dazed between her sons, heard a confusion of noise coming closer from the direction of the watersteps. They will certainly kill me now, she thought dully. The knife. I must get the knife. I must try to defend myself somehow. But she continued to stare in the direction of Meketra's body in a kind of stupor, unable to move.

Orders were called. Heavy feet came pounding up from behind. She hunched her shoulders against the blow she knew must fall but instead she heard Ramose's voice say, "Oh gods, oh gods. Kamose!" and turned her head to see him fall to his knees beside her.

"Majesty?" someone else said. "May I help you? Are you hurt?" Slowly she looked up to see Ankhmahor limned against the brightness of the sky. She nodded wearily, feeling his arms go around her and lift her to her feet.

"Aahmes-nefertari," she managed. "Leave me, Ankhmahor. I do not need you but she does. She has gone to the parade ground to try and bring our troops to heel. The Princes..." She could not finish. Out of the corner of her eye she saw Hor-Aha running, his black face a mask of fury. When his glance fell on Kamose he stopped, stunned. Then he let out a sound, half animal howl, half shriek, that pierced Aahotep's strange lethargy. "How many Medjay have you brought with you, General?" she demanded. He stared at her wildly for a moment, trembling like an agitated horse.

"I swore to my master that I would protect my lord," he blurted. "I have failed in my duty." Aahotep realized with a shock that he was referring to Seqenenra.

"This is not the time, Hor-Aha," she said sharply. "How many?" He came to himself at her tone.

"Five hundred, Majesty," he answered. "They are disembarking now."

"Then get them to the barracks at once," she commanded. "Aahmes-nefertari is trying to stop an insurrection. Put yourself under her. Now, General! And you also, Ankhmahor!" She swung to Ramose who had risen but was staring down at Kamose's corpse, himself pale to the lips. "Ramose, your mother is under arrest," she said in a low voice. "Some of this is her doing. If you find her, do not let her speak to you, I beg. I do not want you responsible for putting her in the prison. Do you understand?" Tears were running down his cheeks but he seemed to be unaware of them. He nodded expressionlessly. "Good," Aahotep went on. "Cull twenty men from the Medjay. I want Kamose carried into the reception hall, but Ahmose must be placed on his own couch. He is still alive. The house is full of . . ." She faltered and swallowed. "It is full of corpses, Ramose. Have them removed to the House of the Dead."

Suddenly she wanted to fall into this young man's arms, to be held and stroked, to sob out the agony that had only just begun, but she knew she could not. Kares was hurrying towards her from the rear of the house with Uni and a dozen servants in an anxious gaggle behind. I cannot collapse, she thought as she turned to deal with them. The physician must be summoned for Ahmose. Kamose must be washed and the sem priests sent for. Kares must have the corridors cleansed. Food must be prepared for Tetisheri. Someone must go and make sure that Ahmose-onkh and the baby arrived safely at the temple. I cannot give way. Not until the Princes are in prison and the army secure. But what if the Princes triumph? Oh, my sons. My beautiful sons. How am I to tell Tetisheri that the light of her life is dead? Stepping over Meketra's prone form with a shudder, she composed herself for her steward.

"Majesty!" he exclaimed as he came up to her. "You have blood all over your hands!"

"That is not blood, Kares," she replied wearily. "It is poison. Give me your arm. I feel very tired and there is much to do this morning."

Aahmes-nefertari's route to the wide parade ground and the barracks that lined it lay past the servants' quarters. She had paused in the house only long enough to relieve a dead Follower of a knife and a small axe, objects that felt entirely foreign to her terrified grasp. As she ran out of the gloom of the house and into a burst of blinding morning light, she bitterly regretted the day when she had wandered beyond the perimeter wall of the estate with an excited Ahmose-onkh by the hand. If I had stayed within the boundaries prescribed for a wife and mother I would not be in this mess, she berated herself. Someone else would be clutching these weapons with a great deal more skill than I, some man with authority and a voice that can shout down any opposition. But who? her thoughts flowed on, even as she swerved towards the larger cells the stewards occupied. I am all that is left. "Uni!" she called as she thrust open his door with the hilt of the axe. "You and Kares are needed in the house at once!" He had already left his couch and was standing naked beside a bowl of water from which steam was rising. His expression of surprise did not last long and she did not wait to see him reach for a gown. She knew that like all good stewards he would respond immediately and with smooth efficiency.

A row of straggling trees grew between the rear of the servants' rooms and the protecting wall of the estate. The gate leading out to a path that ran straight through fields to the desert beyond was usually well guarded, indeed she had hoped to find two strong sword-arms here to accompany her, but today no one challenged her and she pushed through it and turned right, onto the track that would take her to her destination.

Already she could hear the uproar. Men were shouting and a cloud of dust hung over the area. I should have donned a helmet from one of the dead Followers, taken an armband, anything to give an impression of control, she told herself tersely. I feel clumsy and stupid unpainted, my hair undressed, my wrist already aching from the weight of the axe while I try to keep the knife from becoming entangled in my sheath. I am not even wearing a protective amulet. If I die today, will it be as a royal woman with courage or a figure of ludicrous absurdity? She wanted to cry, to sink to the ground and put her head on her knees. She wanted Ahmose to magically appear, take the weapons from her in the gentle way he had, and send her back to her rooms with words of praise for her attempt. The image of her husband's face deepened her despair but it also stiffened her resolve. If I am to die so be it, she told herself firmly. I must not dishonour my heritage. I must not lie down in the mud with Tani.

The parade ground was in sight now, and the back of the dais from which the troops might be reviewed. Perhaps a dozen men were gathered on it, and with a jolt of pure dread Aahmes-nefertari recognized Intef and Iasen among them. The vast arena itself was full of a confusion of jostling soldiers. More were streaming from the barracks themselves. Aahmes-nefertari, slowing to a brisk walk, noted grimly that although many of them were kilted in the white and blue-edged linen of royal possession there were just as many in the various liveries of the Princes. All of them were armed.

Squaring her shoulders and tightening her grip on the knife and the axe, she rounded the corner of the dais, mounted the steps, and with a swift inward prayer to the gods, thrust herself among the small crowd. "Move aside all of you," she said crisply. Out of the corner of her eye she saw the Commander of the Barracks with his hands on his hips, frowning out at the undisciplined mob below. Knowing instinctively that she must keep talking, keep her tone commanding and cold, she gestured to him sharply with the knife. "Amun-nakht, call up a body-guard for me at once and use that horn hanging at your waist. Look at this rabble! Blow until they stop yelling." Amun-nakht's eyes slid uncertainly in the direction of the two Princes, and with her heart in her mouth Aahmes-nefertari took one quick step towards him. "At once, Commander!" she snapped. "You and no one else are responsible to His Majesty for the order and discipline of the troops quartered here. Must I remind you of your duty? How could you allow this mayhem? Have you no pride?"

After a second's hesitation Amun-nakht walked reluctantly to the edge of the dais, beckoning to two Weset soldiers and unhooking the trumpet from his belt. Intef gave a strangled exclamation and began to speak, but Aahmes-nefertari rounded on him. "Neither you nor your troops have any business here, Intef," she said loudly. "Whatever purpose you had in mingling them with my men, you had better separate them before there is bloodshed." The two soldiers Amun-nakht had summoned had climbed onto the dais and were now flanking her, but she sensed their confusion. Amun-nakht had not blown the horn. He was standing with it held loosely in one fist, his whole stance betraying his indecision. I cannot order them to protect me, Aahmes-nefertari thought. I cannot even suggest a weakness or the men here will be on me like a pack of lions.

It was Iasen, not Intef, who challenged her. He had been conferring with a group of officers of mixed allegiance, and when Aahmes-nefertari strode onto the wooden platform, he broke off his conversation but made no other move. He had watched her avidly, eyes narrowed. Now he pushed himself impudently close to her. "I think it is you who have no business here, Highness," he said rudely. "This is a matter for men. Go back to the house. Intef and I are assuming command of the Weset army. Your brothers are no longer considered lords in Egypt. They have forfeited that right by their arrogance and the ruin that has followed their progress during the last two years. If you wish to remain unmolested, go home." It was an outright threat. Aahmes-nefertari felt her temper rise and with the anger her fear evaporated. Thrusting her face into his, she prodded him with the dagger.

"The right to rule Egypt is a matter of blood and precedence," she hissed. "It has nothing to do with the perceptions of traitorous worms like you, Iasen." She pointed the axe rigidly at the furore on the training ground. "Those men belong to Kamose, Ahmose and to me! They are the property of the Taos. Do you hear that, you cowards?"

Turning abruptly from Iasen, painfully aware that she was exposing her back, she stalked to Amun-nakht. "Blow the damn horn," she ordered. "Blow it or I will have you shot for treason instead of just removing your nose for insubordination." Pushing past both Intef and Iasen with as much contempt as she could muster, she confronted the Weset officers and played her greatest bluff. "His Majesty and His Highness are even now putting down the insurrection these Princes have instigated," she told them. "The Medjay are swarming over the estate. If you obey me now, I will do my best to see that your moment of disloyalty is not punished."

"But that is not possible!" Intef burst out. "Meketra assured me . . ."

"Of what?" she asked scornfully without bothering to turn her head. "Of the ease with which he could murder the King? It is not so easy to kill a divinity, Intef." Now she did indeed walk up to both the Princes. "Well?" she went on. "Will you surrender or flee? Make up your minds quickly. The King and my husband will have dealt with your vermin by now and Hor-Aha will be coming to take vengeance upon you."

For what seemed an eternity they met her gaze. Unflinchingly she dared them to call her a liar, to demand why she, a woman, had been sent to restore order among soldiers who would be far more likely to listen to one of their own kind, why Kamose would expose his own sister to extreme danger instead of a group of fully armed Medjay. I hope they see my presence as a crafty ploy on Kamose's part, she thought as she held their scrutiny. They already see him as cruel and ruthless. Any man would pause before running a woman through, particularly a royal one. How long can I afford to let their minds race over every doubt? How stupid are they?

"Arrest them both!" she called harshly to the silently observing officers. "Take them to the prison. Allow no interference!" At that moment the horn blared out, strident and startling. Four times Amun-nakht blew, until the cacophony on the parade ground had died to a discontented mutter and one by one the faces were turned to the dais. Intef and Iasen began to bluster indignantly as they were surrounded but the officers' features were now cleared of any reservation and the Princes were hustled away.

Aahmes-nefertari knew that the battle was not wholly won. The soldiers from the other nomes, seeing their nobles overcome, began to call out in protest, and many of their officers were still on the dais. Aahmes-nefertari hurried to Amun-nakht. "Do the job for which you were trained," she said. "Order them into ranks with our troops at the rear. Weapons on the ground in front of them." Tensely she waited while Amun-nakht bellowed and the men sullenly obeyed. There were still officers belonging to Intef and Iasen on the dais behind her. Aahmes-nefertari was aware that one word from any of them, one shouted order countermanding her own, would result in a riot, but they remained silent.

At last the thousands of soldiers were resolved into formation, their swords and axes lying jumbled at their dusty feet. Aahmes-nefertari, scanning them carefully through the haze, found that she was facing them with her own knife and axe crossed upon her breast like royal regalia. She did not alter her stance. "Now tell them this," she said in answer to the commander's enquiring glance. "They are all to return to their cells together with their officers. The troops belonging to other nomes must remain in the barracks His Majesty assigned to them. There is to be no more mingling with the soldiers of Weset. Any man stepping outside his door will be shot immediately. The weapons will stay where they are." Amun-nakht nodded. While he called out her instructions, she turned to the officers who were watching her warily. "Those of you who owed fealty to His Majesty by way of the Princes are guilty of treason and have earned execution," she said. "However, until I learn His Majesty's pleasure, you will shut yourselves up with your men and perhaps in helping to avert a disaster you will have earned a pardon. As for you officers of Weset..." She paused, forcing each one of them to meet her gaze. "I know each one of you. Have I not spent hours here in your company? Have I not concerned myself with the welfare of the troops? I am ashamed of you." One of them put out a hand.

"Highness, may I speak?" he begged. Aahmes-nefertari nodded brusquely.

"The Princes commanded us to gather here," he explained. "They told us that His Majesty and His Highness were dead and they had assumed control of all Egyptian soldiers. They threatened us with punishment if we refused to oversee the men under us according to their wishes. What could we do?"

"You could have asked to see the bodies," she retorted. "You could have requested verification from General Hor-Aha. You have behaved like witless peasants and are no longer to be trusted. But I will give you a chance to redeem yourselves." Actually I have little choice, she thought to herself. There is no one left to keep order here until the Medjay come. If they come. If this revolt has not extended to them or worse, engulfed them in their sleep. I stand on a knife-edge and I am invisibly bleeding. "I am putting you in charge of enforcing my demands," she went on. "Do not delegate this responsibility to your seconds. You yourselves must set up watches to guard the weapons, arrange for food and drink to be delivered to the soldiers in the cells, and see that no one leaves the barracks until General Hor-Aha himself or a member of the royal family makes new rules. His Majesty appointed you officers. Can you perform these small duties?" Her tone was derisive and the faces staring back at her became grim. "Leave the dais," she concluded. "The men are filing to their cells. See that they go where they should." They saluted her and descended the steps,

going among the crowd at once, but she did not feel encouraged. I have no means of enforcing my brave words, she told
herself gloomily. Anything could still happen.

She rejoined Amun-nakht and for a while they watched the
dispersal of the troops in an awkward silence. Then Aahmes-
nefertari turned to him squarely. "Unless you can be trusted, my
orders to the officers were in vain," she said. "You are Commander of the Barracks. If there is sedition in your heart, I cannot leave this dais. I must bring my couch and camp here." He
glanced at her with swift acumen.

"But surely His Majesty will send a higher grade of officer
than me to take charge," he objected politely. "I am suspect,
Highness. I faltered in my duty. I was swayed by a higher
authority. I am sorry."

"Sorry?" she blurted. "My family was almost murdered, our
estates stolen, His Majesty's war against Apepa brought to
nothing, all those deaths for nothing, and you are sorry? Gods,
Amun-nakht, you and I have taken such pride in these men,
such care of them, and yet when I gave you my first order today
you hesitated to obey!"

"I am thinking that His Majesty would not send his sister to
avert an insurrection if he could come himself," he answered. "I
am thinking that if Your Highness is reduced to camping here
on the dais it is because there is no one else to maintain control
of a very dangerous situation." His gaze returned to her, speculative and yet full of esteem. "I am thinking that the Princes are
stupid not to have arrived at the same conclusions and I am
indeed sorry that I underestimated the power and determination of the House of Tao."

"That does not absolve you."

"Of course not. Tell me if you will, Highness, is His Majesty
still alive?" Aahmes-nefertari drew a deep breath.

"Kamose had a talent for promoting men of intelligence and

insight," she sighed, and made a quick decision to tell Amun-
nakht everything. "I do not know how things stand in the
house. The Followers are almost all dead. Kamose had gone to
the watersteps to warn Ahmose just before I came here. As for
the Medjay . . ." she shrugged fatalistically. "I can only hope
that Ramose or Ankhmahor crossed the river. I pray that my
brothers have already regained mastery over the house but . . .
I know nothing more than I have told you." In a gesture both
impulsive and decisive she handed him the axe. "I could not
allow the army to mutiny," she said simply. "Will you take my
place here, Amun-nakht, or will you arrest me and have my
men free the Princes?" He took the weapon, hefting it easily.

"I was not with His Majesty on any of his campaigns," he
replied frankly. "When the Weset division was quartered here,
I was responsible for keeping order in the barracks. When I was
left with only the household troops, I provided guards for the
house and estate and maintained peace throughout the nome.
I am Weset born and bred. I love my home and the lords who
have done their best to make it safe. I remember when Apepa
came, how humiliating it was for our soldiers to defer to Setiu
officers." He grimaced. "Highness, I did not want to see Weset
come under the yoke of any Prince other than a Tao, but we
were told that the deed was done and what could we say? We
are only soldiers. We have little of our own. We serve whoever
sits at the pinnacle of supremacy."

"But the deed may not in fact be done," Aahmes-nefertari
broke in shrewdly. "And at this moment I sit at the pinnacle of
supremacy. Will you keep me there, Amun-nakht?" He inclined
his head.

"I will so long as I am able," he said gravely. "Send me word
from the house as soon as possible, Highness, and reinforcements from the Medjay. The Princes' officers will not be
happy men."

"Very well." She knew that he had given her the most candid answer she could expect. "You are dismissed, Amun-nakht. I will not bring my couch to the dais just yet." He did not smile at her little joke. Saluting her soberly, he made for the steps, but a dismaying thought struck her and she called after him, "Suppose that all seems lost and I am wrongly optimistic and Prince Ahmose-onkh is the only royal son left. Will you accept my position as King's Regent and Commander of all the Forces of His Majesty, Amun-nakht?"

"Yes, Highness," he called back without breaking his stride.

She stood for a moment watching him cross the empty expanse of the training ground now baking under the mid-morning strength of the sun. I should have asked him about the other Princes, Mesehti and Makhu, she berated herself. And where is Meketra? Nefer-Sakharu? But perhaps if I had plied him with too many questions I would have sounded insecure. Then she laughed out loud and still grasping the knife she left the dais and began to retrace her steps the way she had come. Insecure? Meketra and that bitch may have full control of the house by now. Everyone may be dead. What if I am walking to my doom and everything I have attempted is a puff of wind?

She had reached the gate, and as she let herself through it the trees beyond began to shake. Blinding sunlight beating from the whitewashed walls of the servants' quarters suddenly dissolved into bands of unfocused colour and the path wavered. I am going to faint, she thought distantly. Faltering left, she managed to find a private place behind a cluster of acacia bushes before collapsing with her back against the perimeter wall. With her head lolling between her knees, she waited while her vision cleared and the pricking in her face subsided, then she began to cry. Wracking sobs shook her, the terror of the morning taking their toll. Arms wrapped around herself, rocking to and fro in the acacia's friendly shade, she wept for an action that had taken all her strength of mind and body, for Kamose and his loneliness, for her husband who had slipped from their couch to follow a simple pursuit that had probably taken him away from her forever. When she was spent, she wiped her face on her grimy sheath and came trembling to her feet. The sun still shone. Breezes fluttered through the lawns. A golden dragonfly flickered past, its wings glittering. Aahmes-nefertari made her way back to the path and set off determinedly for the house.

Entering quietly through the servants' access, the knife still held but almost forgotten, she walked a little way along the wide passage and then halted, listening. Low voices came to her and far away someone was crying but there were no sounds of violent encounter. Whatever had happened, for good or ill, it had taken place while she was away. Moving on, she came to the painted doorway that signalled the wider corridors of the main quarters and stepped from beaten earth onto tiling. The floors were usually swept clean of their small accumulation of sand by this hour but now her sandals grated as she went and there was no sign of any servant wielding a broom.

She continued cautiously, aware once more that the knife she raised was really nothing but a show of bravado, until at the place where the passage divided, running ahead to the main entrance and the public rooms, left to the women's apartments, or right to the men's, she came upon four Medjay leaning against the wall and chattering excitedly. Seeing her, they sprang upright and bowed in the quick, perfunctory way they had. "Highness, Highness," they clamoured, and Aahmes-nefertari realized that the house had been saved.

"Where is His Majesty?" she asked. They became very still, regarding her solemnly with their shiny dark eyes. One of them pointed.

"Along there," he said. "In the big room." Thanking them on

a wave of gratitude to the gods, she sped down the central passage. Kamose had been spared. He was in the reception hall with Ahmose and Hor-Aha and the others. Everything was going to be all right. On the way she passed several members of the household staff on hands and knees, scrubbing at the bloodstains where the Followers had fallen. The bodies were gone. Normality has been restored, she thought gladly, and I have done my part and survived. It is over.

But outside the interior doorway she came upon Akhtoy. The steward was sitting on a stool and the face he turned to her as she slowed was wet with tears. Rising awkwardly, he sketched a bow and Aahmes-nefertari's fragile new confidence disintegrated. "What is it, what is it?" she croaked. "Is he wounded? Is Ahmose hurt too?" Akhtoy fought to compose his features before he spoke, and to Aahmes-nefertari his effort to re-establish the anonymously courteous mask of his stewardship was the most alarming thing she had ever seen.

"His Majesty is dead," he said with the barest waver in his voice. "He was shot in the side as he went to the watersteps to warn His Highness." He swallowed, and mesmerized, Aahmes-nefertari found her gaze fixed on the convulsion of his throat. "The Lady Tetisheri sent a soldier to meet you but obviously he did not find you. I am deeply distressed that it is I who have to give you this news. Forgive me, Highness. Your husband, the Prince, has been..." But Aahmes-nefertari did not wait to hear more. Pushing past him she ran into the reception hall.

Kamose's body lay on the huge desk that had been brought from his father's office. One wall of the pillared room was completely open to the garden and although no direct sunlight penetrated, the scene was horribly clear. A dishevelled Amunmose holding a smoking censer swayed at Kamose's feet, chanting quietly. Ramose and Hor-Aha stood together at his mutilated side from which, Aahmes-nefertari saw with horror, the arrow still jutted. Hor-Aha was gripping Behek's collar as the dog whimpered, struggling bewilderedly to jump up to his master, and even as Aahmes-nefertari went forward the General signalled to a servant to take him away. Ankhmahor had his back to them all. He was leaning against a pillar, head bowed, and beyond him on the edge of the garden the servants crowded, some squatting on the grass, some clustered in groups, all silent with grief.

Tetisheri sat at the far end of the hall on the bottom step of the dais where the family and important guests dined when there was feasting. She was motionless, her spine rigid, her knees together under the blue sheath, both gnarled hands gripping her thighs. To a distraught Aahmes-nefertari she seemed already mummified, the puckered and corrugated skin of her face tight and leathery, her thin, lined lips drawn back from yellowing teeth, her eyes sunken beneath pouched lids. She was staring straight ahead and scarcely blinked when her granddaughter bent over her. "Grandmother, where is Ahmose?" Aahmes-nefertari demanded. "Where is my mother?" She laid a hand on the tangled mat of grey hair and Tetisheri stirred.

"They must all die, every one of them," she whispered. Her breath in the girl's face was hot and fetid. "We must hunt them down and slay them like the wild animals they are."

"Where is Ahmose?" Aahmes-nefertari repeated more loudly but the old woman ignored her, and feeling a hand descend on her shoulder she straightened.

"He was badly wounded," Ramose said. "He is on his couch and the physician and your mother are with him. Where have you been, Highness? The sem-priests have been sent for and Kamose must go to the House of the Dead to be beautified. Your mother refused to release his body to them until you returned, but she did not say where you were." Aahmes-nefertari looked full into his face. He too had been weeping. He was pale and his eyes were swollen. "I am partly responsible for this," he said brokenly. "If I had understood the depth of my mother's hatred, if I had reported her to Kamose . . ."

"Not now, Ramose!" Aahmes-nefertari cried out. "There will be time for recriminations later but I cannot bear them now! I must go to my husband."

Nevertheless, in spite of her frantic concern for Ahmose and the guilty relief that was growing because he was still alive, she could not tear herself away from the corpse of her beloved older brother. Approaching the desk through a haze of acrid myrrh, the soft, formal lament of the High Priest piercing her with sadness, she stroked his cheeks, still bloodied and so cold, and pressed his grimed, limp fingers to her face. "Kamose, oh, Kamose," she breathed. "The gods will welcome you, for surely your heart lay lightly against Ma'at's feather, but for us who will not hear your voice again there is only sorrow. I wish that you had lived long enough to know that the rebellion has failed and your great work has not been undone." Gently kissing the slack, blood-encrusted mouth, she turned to the High Priest. "Amun-mose, what of my children?" she asked. The man stopped chanting and bowed to her.

"They are safe in my own cell in the temple, Highness," he assured her huskily, the marks of his own grief clearly visible on his face. "The Lady Nefer-Sakharu is also there. She told me that you had sent her to help Raa with Ahmose-onkh. Raa denied her words, and as I did not know the truth I put the Lady in the care of a temple guard."

"Thank you," Aahmes-nefertari said grimly. "When His Majesty's body is removed and you return to the temple, make sure that Nefer-Sakharu does not escape. She is a liar." Feeling Ramose's agonized glance she refused to meet it.

Beckoning to Hor-Aha, she drew him a short way away and rapidly told him of the events on the parade ground. As she spoke, she saw his expression change from a stony suffering to shock to incredulity. "You did this, Highness?" he exclaimed quietly. "You? Truly the House of Tao has been blessed with hearts of divine courage! Neither Ankhmahor nor I knew of the size of the threat. We believed that the attack on your brothers was limited to the estate."

"Mother and Grandmother and I suspected more," Aahmes-nefertari explained, "and if she did not tell you it was because Kamose's murder drove all else from her mind."

"Your mother stabbed Meketra as he wounded your husband," Hor-Aha said. "You did not know that, Highness? Already she is being hailed as a saviour. His body is still lying out on the path to the watersteps. She commanded that it be left there for all to see."

Aahmes-nefertari stared at him in appalled amazement. Shock had followed upon shock since Kamose had come to her bedchamber and each impact was a fresh blow, unblunted by repetition, but she was not free to fully absorb any of them. Not now, she said to herself silently, as she had exclaimed aloud to Ramose. I will deal with all of it later. "General, you must go to the soldiers' cells to reinforce my orders," she urged. "The Commander of the Barracks, Amun-nakht, is trustworthy I think, but our other officers may already be deciding to disobey me and the troops the Princes brought with them absolutely must be contained. Detail as many Medjay as you can spare and take them with you. Otherwise it is still possible that my brother's death will have been in vain. And send to the prison to make sure that Intef and Iasen are safely guarded. Try to find out where Mesehti and Makhu are." He understood her immediately. Saluting her, he strode towards the garden, and Aahmes-nefertari, with a last lingering look at the husk that only a few brief hours ago had held the soul of Kamose, made her way to the door.

As she was leaving, she encountered the sem-priests. They drew back at her approach, hiding their faces and pulling their robes close to their bodies so that they should not contaminate her, but today she did not care that they were considered unclean. "Beautify him well," she said to them. "Make the cuts with reverence and bind him with respect. He was our King."

And now Ahmose is King. The knowledge struck her like a blow as she hurried to his rooms. Ahmose must take the liberation of Egypt into his hands. Oh gods, I do not know if I am worthy to be a Queen.

Ahmose's door was open, and as she entered her mother rose from her chair beside the couch. She was still wearing the sheath Aahmes-nefertari had seen her in earlier, the front of it now mired with brown splashes of dried blood. The hands she held out to her daughter were also filthy with flecks of blood but Aahmes-nefertari hardly noticed. With a sob she threw herself into Aahotep's embrace and the two women clung together tightly for a long time, rocking and moaning. Then Aahotep pulled away. "You can tell me later what happened out there," she said abruptly. "First you must know that Ahmose was violently clubbed and is unconscious. The physician has just left. He has stitched up the gash on Ahmose's head and applied a mixture of honey, castor oil and rowan wood with a small amount of soil from the peasants' burial ground to prevent infection and dry up any suppuration. His skull was not broken, and for that we must thank Amun. I fancy that the surprise of my advance and Behek's sudden barking helped to weaken the assassin's blow."

"Will he live?"

Aahotep smiled grimly. "The physician thinks that his condition is severe but not fatal. He will regain consciousness in time."

"It is a cold comfort." Aahmes-nefertari sank into the chair her mother had just left and pointed at Aahotep's dress. "And is that . . ." Aahotep laughed harshly, her face falling into ugly lines of exhaustion and scorn. To Aahmes-nefertari the sound held an alarming quality of hysteria.

"Is it Kamose's sweet blood? No, it is not. I struck Meketra twice. It is his life I wear on my sheath and I must confess, Aahmes-nefertari, that I glory in doing so. When his body begins to rot, I will have it carried out onto the desert for the hyenas to devour."

"But the gods will not find him, to judge or to save," Aahmes-nefertari blurted out. "His ka will be lost." Aahotep walked to the doorway.

"Good," she said vehemently. "I do not care one bit. Sit with Ahmose. Talk to him. Pray for him. I am going to fling myself onto my couch and sleep the sleep of the fully justified."

"You saved his life, Mother," Aahmes-nefertari said softly, and saw the other woman's face darken.

"If I and the two soldiers had been by the path just a little sooner, we might have saved Kamose also," she said bitterly. "My husband and my son, both victims of the accursed Setiu. When Ahmose leaves his couch, I will make him swear to bind Apepa and throw him into the fire Het-Uart will become." She lifted both caked hands to her face then let them drop to her sides. "Forgive me, Aahmes-nefertari," she murmured. "I am not myself." The girl heard her step going away down the passage and turned to Ahmose's inert form. When he leaves his couch, she repeated silently, and bending over him she studied him carefully.

The blow had struck him just above the right ear. He was lying on his left side, facing her, breathing lightly and noisily, one limp arm bent over the sheet that had been drawn up to his waist. There was a sheen of sweat on his skin. The oil in the greyish salve the physician had applied had melted a little and run into the stiff mat of his curly hair, and taking a square of damp linen from the bowl on the table Aahmes-nefertari gently wiped it away. He did not stir at her touch. His pallor was alarming. "You must not die, my dearest," she told him in a low voice. "Egypt needs you, but I need you more. If you do not recover, I will be forced to don helmet and gloves and lead the army north myself. Can you imagine a more hopeless and ridiculous sight? Ahmose-onkh has lost one father. Must he lose another? Can you hear me, Ahmose? Do my words echo in your dreams?"

Taking his hand, she began to stroke it and thought that if more tears must come it should be now, but she had emptied herself of such a feminine response to disaster behind the acacia bushes. Something told her that she would not weep again over the things that could not be changed. What was the use? The gods decreed the destinies of men and only by accepting their edicts with the greatest courage, by not turning aside into the fallow and comfortable fields of self-pity and inaction, could those directives be transformed into advantage. Sitting in that quiet room, her eyes on her wounded husband, her mind slowly filling with a new implacability, Aahmes-nefertari shed the last vestige of the diffident, rather timid girl she had been.

# Chapter EIGHTEEN

ALL THAT AFTERNOON and far into the night Aahmes-nefertari sat by her husband's side but there was no change in his condition. Several times the physician had come to wipe away the salve, inspect his stitches, and reapply his mixture and in the end Aahmes-nefertari, completely exhausted, had turned over her watch to Akhtoy and crawled onto her couch. Only when she was certain that the rebellious Princes were safely incarcerated and their troops confined to barracks had she sent to the temple for her children. They had returned to the nursery with an equally tired Raa. Aahmes-nefertari had allowed the nurse to rest and had put Senehat in charge of the two.

Nefer-Sakharu, closely guarded, had been hustled to the prison. She had protested indignantly all the way but Ankhma-hor, coming to Ahmose's bedchamber to enquire after His Highness's progress, told Aahmes-nefertari that a knife had been found concealed in the woman's voluminous sheath and had of course been taken away from her. Nefer-Sakharu had insisted that she had been woken by the sound of scuffles in the passage outside her room and when she had gone to the door she had seen the dead Followers. Frightened, she had snatched up a knife and run from the house, making her way to the

497

temple as the only safe place she could reach on foot. Her story varied from the one she had told Amunmose, that she had been sent by Aahmes-nefertari to help protect the children, and besides, as Aahmes-nefertari pointed out to Ankhmahor, no Follower had fallen near enough to the women's quarters to have woken anyone.

"Is it possible," she had said to the Prince, "that her role in the uprising was to kill Ahmose-onkh? If Kamose and Ahmose had been dealt with, that only left one royal male. The conspirators would know that in order to totally succeed, every male Tao must die." Ankhmahor hesitated.

"It is a serious accusation, Highness," he reminded her carefully. "There is no proof of such a heinous plot."

"We have Senehat's evidence of the woman's hatred," Aahmes-nefertari retorted. "And there is no doubt that she lied regarding her movements last night. I will take no further chances with her, Ankhmahor. She must stand with the Princes to be judged."

"The execution of noblemen will send tremors of insecurity throughout the army as well as the citizenry," he pointed out. "Those men who had been prepared to join the rebellion, whose sense of discernment had been swayed, will fear the same fate. That is bad enough. But to shoot a woman . . ." He spread out his hands. "Such an act will shock Egypt and you will run the risk of losing much support."

"Well, what alternative do we have?" Aahmes-nefertari flared, too tired for diplomacy. "We must show as strongly as possible that we are in control and we intend to remain so. If that means ruthlessness, then we will be ruthless, and sleep all the better at night for knowing that once again the seedling of betrayal has been rooted out. Once again, Ankhmahor." She rose from her stool beside the couch but did not let go of her husband's limp hand. "Ever since my father chose to move against Apepa out of pure desperation, we have fought the invisible tentacles of treachery. Too often the enemy has worn the smiling face of a trusted servant, even a relative. I am so sick of having our kindness rewarded with perfidy, our dream for a liberated Egypt obstructed by men who speak fair but have deceit in their hearts. How do we cling to an ability to trust?" Her shoulders slumped and she ran a shaking hand through her sticky hair. "Look at what trust has done to Kamose, to my husband! If you can propose a solution other than execution for all of them I am willing to hear it."

"You are right," Ankhmahor admitted reluctantly, "and as yet I can think of no alternative. But, Highness, should we not wait until Ahmose recovers before any irretrievable decision is made? What would His Highness want to do?" She gave a strange, twisted smile and sank back onto the stool.

"His Highness has always argued for moderation," she said huskily. "You of all people know this, Ankhmahor. Throughout Kamose's campaigns it has been my husband who pleaded for clemency, for restraint. The anger of a man who offers water to someone who is thirsty, only to be slapped in the face for his kindness will be far greater than that of the man who ignores a beggar's need and is promptly attacked. I promise you that when Ahmose opens his eyes he will want vengeance, and it will begin with extermination. I will consult with my mother and grandmother of course, but you may be assured that they will share my desire for the death of Intef and Iasen. Perhaps for Mesehti and Makhu also. We shall see." He obviously had no answer to that. She could see the truth of her words in his face. Sighing, he asked to be dismissed.

Aahmes-nefertari slept fitfully in spite of her weariness, waking still tired to the following dawn. A bath refreshed her a little and a small meal even more. After opening her shrine and praying for her husband's recovery, she visited the children, sent Senehat back to Ramose's quarters, spoke to the physician, who had nothing new to tell her, and made her way to her grandmother's rooms. As she approached, Uni came to his feet before the closed door and bowed. She greeted him absently. "Highness, please try to persuade my mistress to take some nourishment," he asked her, his brow furrowed with concern. "She has eaten nothing since His Majesty's body was carried into the house but she is drinking too much wine."

"Where is my mother?" Aahmes-nefertari wanted to know, aware of the usual tiny spasm of apprehension at the prospect of confronting Tetisheri.

"I believe she has gone to the prison this morning," he replied. "She wished to speak with the Lady Nefer-Sakharu."

"I see." Even a month ago I would have shrunk from facing Grandmother alone, Aahmes-nefertari thought, but I can do it now. I can do many things now. Uni held the door open for her and she walked through.

Tetisheri's shrine was also open, an incense burner set before it sending out wreaths of bitter grey smoke that filled the shuttered space with a choking haze. Aahmes-nefertari, coughing, went at once to the window hanging and raised it. Plumes of burning myrrh flowed past her as she turned back. Isis had just finished straightening the linen on Tetisheri's couch and Tetisheri herself was sitting beside it, a cup full of wine clenched in both hands and a half-full flagon on the table. A dish of fresh bread, figs and brown cheese lay untouched on the floor. The servant looked harried. "Isis, bring hot water and cloths," Aahmes-nefertari instructed her. "Your mistress needs washing. Hurry up."

With a glance of pure relief Isis left and Aahmes-nefertari went to the old lady, prying the cup from her fingers and tossing its contents out the window. Tetisheri did not protest. She watched her granddaughter with a languid gaze and Aahmes-nefertari realized that Tetisheri was more than a little drunk. Picking up the dish from the floor, she selected a fig and held it out. "Eat, Grandmother," she insisted. "You must have some nourishment." Tetisheri blinked slowly.

"I can smell Meketra," she said with exaggerated care. "I could smell the stink of sedition on him when he was alive and now I inhale the stink of his corruption." Aahmes-nefertari placed the fig on her palm.

"I am going to close your shrine now," she said distinctly, "and empty the incense burner. Put the fig in your mouth, Tetisheri."

"I don't want food," Tetisheri said, wrinkling up her nose like a stubborn child. "I have been praying for Kamose. But praying for Kamose is not as good as praying with him, is it?" Aahmes-nefertari had gone to the shrine and shut its gilded doors. The incense had gone out of its own accord. Turning back, she saw tears dribbling down Tetisheri's lined cheeks and felt a stab of panic. This was the woman with a will that had never been broken. Hers was the rigid backbone against which all of them measured their own strength. If Tetisheri snaps, we will be completely adrift, Mother and I, she thought. I cannot cope with this! Squatting in front of her grandmother, she retrieved the fig and took both gnarled hands in her own.

"Kamose is dead," she said emphatically. "Even at this moment he lies under the knives and hooks of the sem-priests. No amount of wine will bring him back to us, Tetisheri. No prayers will usher him through your door. I loved him also and I grieve for my loss, but Ahmose still lives. Do you not care about him?"

"No," Tetisheri replied tonelessly. "Not now, not today. I am tired of carrying so much weight, Aahmes-nefertari, tired of my own strength. Let me alone."

"Then do you no longer care about Egypt's fate?" Aahmes-nefertari persisted. "Ahmose will be King when the seventy days of mourning for Kamose are over. Does it not matter to you that Egypt still has a King?" Tetisheri took her fingers from Aahmes-nefertari's grip.

"Yes, it matters," she said. "But that King is not Kamose. It should be Kamose. You should have married him, not his brother." Aahmes-nefertari had to stifle a sudden urge to take her by her frail shoulders and shake her viciously.

"There are decisions to be made regarding the fate of the Princes," she said deliberately. "Mother and I need your advice, Tetisheri, we need all your faculties." Tetisheri turned glazed eyes upon her.

"What is there to decide?" she slurred. "Kill them all. Send them to the Judgement Hall and let Sobek crunch their bones." Aahmes-nefertari came to her feet and stood with hands on hips, looking down on her grandmother.

"You will be washed and you will drink some milk and then you will sleep off your drunkenness," she ordered. "I will send the physician to you to see that you have not made yourself ill. We are all suffering, Tetisheri. We should be used to it by now, shouldn't we? But I for one am not." I do not want to be the strong one, she wanted to add. That has always been you. Please come back to us, Tetisheri.

At that moment Uni opened the door to admit Isis and another servant bearing a steaming bowl and towels. Aahmes-nefertari addressed the steward. "If I am needed, I will be at the prison," she told him. "Your mistress is to be washed and given milk and put back to bed. Do not let her argue with you, Uni. Not this time. Isis can fetch the physician. Leave the window uncovered. The air in here is very stale."

I am furious with you, Tetisheri, she thought as she strode through the house. Furious and hurt. Kamose was the one brilliant star in your black sky, so bright to your dazzled, selfish old eye that you could not see the lesser star burning close to it.

Was it a genuine love you felt for him, or a greedy possessiveness that came into full flower when Father died? Perhaps you cannot love. Perhaps Kamose simply fitted the mould of kingship and character you had devised in your own mind, and Ahmose did not. I ache on your behalf, my dearest husband, and my whole soul cries out its loss for you, my Kamose, yet I am denied the indulgence of grief. There is too much to do. I will never forgive Grandmother this self-pitying lapse. Our lives still hang in the balance and breaking the seals on wine jars will not save us. So her mind raced on, churning with the chaos of her emotions, until she came to the outer gate of Kamose's prison, answered the challenge of the guards to either side, and walking through, saw Ramose coming towards her over the hard-packed earth before the door.

He bowed as he came to a halt, his expression strained, and his first words were of concern for Ahmose.

"He is still unconscious," Aahmes-nefertari told him. "There is no change. Have you been to see your mother, Ramose?" He nodded miserably.

"She fumes and accuses and protests her innocence," he said. "She expects me to set her free, as though I have more authority than Simontu. What will happen to her, Highness? Will she be tried?" Aahmes-nefertari considered him warily before replying. He was obviously under great stress but she was in no mood to indulge him.

"You were Kamose's close friend," she said. "Those who plotted against him included Nefer-Sakharu. There is some evidence that she had received orders to kill my son. What would you do with her?"

"She is my mother," he said wretchedly. "How can I answer your question? The gods do not judge benignly those who do not honour their forebears. Yet she has committed treason and connived at my lord's death." His brown eyes were full of anguish as they met hers. "You are going to execute her, aren't you, Aahmes-nefertari?" At his use of her name, Aahmes-nefertari was flooded with memories.

"Whatever is done must be done quickly," she told him. "Egypt must see that retribution is swift, final, there must be no hesitation or the Princes' disaffection may spread. Worse, Apepa may sense a weakness and move to take the country back, particularly with Ahmose wounded and unable to issue any commands." She touched him gently. His skin was hot and she repressed an urge to run her fingers over it, to step closer to him and beg from him a purely masculine reassurance. "Only Mother and I stand between all Kamose achieved and utter disaster," she almost whispered. "I do not think it will be possible to save Nefer-Sakharu." Do not plead with me, Ramose, she spoke to him silently, urgently. Do not beg for a wrong to be twisted until it appears to be a right. Do not ask me to warp the divine decrees of Ma'at for the sake of filial allegiance. Please remember Si-Amun! He smiled sadly.

"I am ashamed," he said. "Of my father, my mother, yet I love them both. I am the most unfortunate man to be living in this troubled age, Highness. I think that peace will always be denied me." Bowing again he stepped around her, and she was left to continue on until she came to the thick wooden doors of the prison.

Simontu's office, to the left of the passage leading to the cells, was large and bare. From his seat behind the desk he rose and greeted her with reverence. Yes, her mother was still within, questioning the Prince Intef. She had been with him for an hour or more. He would tell her Aahmes-nefertari was here.

Taking his chair, Aahmes-nefertari waited. The building was quiet, more than half-empty she knew, and she wondered, not for the first time why Kamose had chosen to restore it. Had he planned to fill it with Setiu offenders once he had taken

Het-Uart? The workings of his mind had always been mysterious and now there would never be an answer.

Her mother came in shortly. Aahmes-nefertari rose respectfully and for a moment the two women regarded one another. Then Aahmes-nefertari said, "Tetisheri was drunk when I went to see her earlier and Ramose is distraught. What shall we do?" Aahotep waved her daughter down and lowered herself into the chair facing the desk. She was wearing blue, the colour of mourning. Her face had been carefully painted. A thin band of gold hung with tiny jasper scarabs encircled her forehead and her plain, shoulder-length wig, and gold glinted on her long fingers.

"My arm aches," she remarked. "I had it massaged but it is still sore. Much strength is required to drive a blade into a man. I had not realized. Still . . ." She gave Aahmes-nefertari a grim smile. "It is a pain I welcome. I have had my soiled sheath folded and put away in a separate box. It is not pride, Aahmes-nefertari. It will serve to remind me of our vulnerability if the time ever comes when we feel ourselves to be invincible." Aahmes-nefertari did not reply and presently Aahotep continued. "I have been here since dawn, questioning Intef and Iasen. I do not think that they have any concept of their own danger even though I killed Meketra. They believe that because we are women and thus to be discounted we will do nothing until Ahmose recovers, and they are confident that he will not only pardon them but understand their dissatisfaction with Kamose. Oh they have not said these things in so many words," she finished as Aahmes-nefertari leaned forward with an outraged protest on her lips, "but their attitude is barely deferential. They have not changed much since Kamose bullied them into action two years ago."

"Did they refer to Mesehti and Makhu?" Aahotep folded her arms and placed them on the table.

"No. We must send someone to Akhmin and Djawati to find them, that is if they have not journeyed straight to the Delta to pledge their loyalty to Apepa."

"They may indeed have gone home, but according to Senehat they argued in favour of Kamose," Aahmes-nefertari pointed out. "If they wanted no part in the plot and yet still felt some loyalty to the other Princes, what choice did they have but to run?"

"They could have warned him!" Aahotep flared. "The cowards!"

There was another hiatus. Aahmes-nefertari watched her mother. Aahotep's jewelled fingers tapped out an absent rhythm on the scored surface of the table. She was breathing deeply, her full breasts rising and falling under the soft blue sheath, her dark brows drawn together in a frown, and all at once Aahmes-nefertari saw her in a different light. It was as though the easy categories into which she had placed her without reflection—mother, wife, mistress of a household—drew back to reveal the true and much more complex facets of her personality. She is indeed my mother, Seqenenra's wife, the arbiter of the house, Aahmes-nefertari reflected with surprise, but I saw all those things in relation to myself. Even when she and Tetisheri and I used to meet to discuss the responsibilities Kamose placed upon us, I saw her as somehow woven into the family, not existing apart from it. Aahotep alone, without those trappings, Aahotep herself, is something detached. "Mother," she ventured at last, slightly awed at her revelation, "Ahmose would not pardon them. Nor would he understand. They have mistaken his mild demeanour for weakness."

"I know." Aahotep sat back. "They must be dealt with quickly before others begin to assume that rebellion carries no punishment. I feel sorrow for their wives and children, but they must be executed immediately."

"And what of Nefer-Sakharu?"

"She is the poison that drips slowly and eventually contaminates all that it touches," Aahotep said gruffly. "What else can we do with her but end her life also? Exile her and her tongue will still wag. We are not safe from her wherever she might go."

"Then I suggest that we send Ramose after Mesehti and Makhu. That way he will not be forced to see his mother finally disgraced or feel compelled to stand with her. I want to mourn for Kamose," Aahmes-nefertari finished, getting up. "I cannot do so until every other consideration is settled." Aahotep stood also.

"Then we are agreed?"

"We are."

"Good. I will tell Hor-Aha to select ten Medjay archers and tomorrow morning the army will assemble on the parade ground to watch the executions. Aahmes-nefertari . . ."

"Yes?" Her mother had paused and was biting her hennaed lip.

"It is a terrible thing that we are doing. Killing Egypt's nobles. Killing a woman. It is as though . . ." She gestured around the thick, naked walls of the chamber. "It is as though I too am in prison, a place where choices are no longer possible." Aahmes-nefertari came around the desk and took her mother's cold hand in both of hers.

"We did not begin this," she said quietly, "but it is our fate to end it. I must go to Ahmose. Come with me, and then we will go to the temple and pray. By the time we return, Grandmother may be awake and sane enough to offer us advice."

"I cannot imagine her proposing a more compassionate alternative," Aahotep retorted. "She will want them dead at any cost." To that there was nothing Aahmes-nefertari could say. Still hand in hand, the two women went out into the blinding midday sunlight.

In the evening they met with Tetisheri. Pallid and enfeebled by her bout of drinking, she had nevertheless regained her lucidity and was vehemently adamant that the Princes should die. "Why should we spare them?" she snapped. "They murdered Kamose without compunction and but for your courage, Aahotep, they would have killed Ahmose too. Sweep them away. They are not fit to call themselves Egyptian."

"Then we are in complete agreement?" Aahmes-nefertari asked. "There must be no doubts, no brooding later." Tetisheri shot her a contemptuous look from the bundle of sheets under which she was resting.

"I do not brood," she said. "And as for you, my little warrior, I rather fancy that your brooding days are over. Ahmose will find himself somewhat short of commanders when he recovers. Perhaps he should offer you a division. The Division of Hathor?" Aahmes-nefertari swallowed past the sudden lump in her throat. Her grandmother's tone had been sardonic but there was no mistaking the sincerity of the compliment. "Now go away, both of you," Tetisheri finished. "If I am to stand with you tomorrow on the dais, I must have the last of the wine massaged away." Outside the room Aahotep turned to her daughter.

"I will leave Ramose to you," she said quietly. "I must summon Hor-Aha. This will sound cruel, Aahmes-nefertari, but I hope that Ahmose remains unconscious until the deed is done. If he opens his eyes before dawn, we will be forced to wait upon his decision. I do not think I could bear the delay." Aahmes-nefertari put a hand to her mother's cheek in silent agreement and they parted.

It was Senehat who opened the door when Aahmes-nefertari knocked. Seeing the Princess, she bowed and stood aside. "I must speak to Ramose in private," Aahmes-nefertari said as she walked past her. "Be pleased to wait in the passage, Senehat." The servant nodded, and at the closing of the door behind her Aahmes-nefertari turned to Ramose.

He and Senehat had been sharing a meal. His table held

cups and a wine jug and several empty dishes. He rose at her approach, reverencing her, and she could see by his expression that he knew what was coming. "I want you to take a herald and a guard and go to Akhmin and Djawati," she said without preamble. "We must know how it is with Mesehti and Makhu. We pray that they simply ran home, but if they headed for the Delta we will have to send troops after them. That is why you need the herald, to send back word as soon as you can. The matter is urgent. We want you to take ship tonight." He looked at her speculatively for a moment, eyes narrowed.

"You have decided to execute my mother," he said softly. "That is why you are sending me north." There is no point in tiptoeing around the truth, Aahmes-nefertari thought, meeting his gaze. Not with Ramose.

"Yes," she admitted. "You have always valued honesty, old friend. We see no alternative that will ensure our safety. Know that we are anguished for your sake but not for hers. She deserves nothing more." He backed up against a chair and sank into it awkwardly.

"Will you at least tell me when it is to be so that I may pray for the journey of her ka? And, Highness, I insist on a proper beautifying for her. I will pay for it myself." Once more Aahmes-nefertari wanted to kneel beside him and take him in her arms, this time for his sake not hers.

"Of course," she replied steadily. "It will be at dawn tomorrow. Ramose, I am so sorry. I do not have the words . . ." He held up a hand.

"No more, Aahmes-nefertari," he begged. "I will do as you have ordered, but now I must be alone. Please tell Senehat to go to her cell. I could not endure her presence either."

Ahmose must compensate him for everything we have taken from him over the years, Aahmes-nefertari vowed feverishly to herself as she made her way through the darkening house. I will personally insist that he is given an estate, a princely title, trade monopolies, anything he wants when Ahmose achieves divinity. But she knew, as she settled herself beside her husband's still form, that nothing could replace the loss of Tani or soothe the wound of his parents' disgrace. Power would not warm his couch. Gold could not erase shame. And promises will not allay the guilt I feel, she sighed inwardly. All of us have become victims to a greater or lesser degree in this struggle, and there is no returning, for us or for Egypt.

She did not sleep that night. In a kind of confused need for expiation she remained with Ahmose, rising occasionally to stretch cramped limbs or trim the lamp but chiefly spending the hours leaning thoughtfully over the couch. Twice the physician came, examined his patient, and with a polite word to her, left again. Akhtoy also slipped in and out of the room with water and fruit for her but she neither ate nor drank. She could judge how time was passing by the quality of the silence both inside the house and outside in the empty garden. Twice she heard the guard change beyond the door and at the second watch she left her husband and went reluctantly to her own quarters. It was time to dress and Ahmose still had not opened his eyes. She did not know whether to be grateful or sorry.

In the chill pre-dawn air she, her mother and her grandmother were escorted to the parade ground by Ankhmahor and the few Followers who had escaped the Princes' purge. The body of Meketra, now swollen and turning black, was carried before them. Aahotep had forbidden it to be wrapped, and Aahmes-nefertari kept her eyes on the helmets of the soldiers so that she would not see the man's lolling, misshapen head. Nevertheless she was sure that she could detect the scent of corruption wafting from the corpse to her nostrils on the first stirrings of the morning breeze. I will not falter, she told herself firmly. I will not shudder or shrink from what I am about to see.

I will remember Kamose and my father. I will think of my ancestors. But most of all I will conjure the face of my son and let my anger be my armour.

The huge expanse of the parade ground was already packed with troops. As the three women mounted the dais, Aahmes-nefertari noted that Hor-Aha had ranked them according to their allegiance, with the Princes' men fronting the one open space. There was hardly a sound. The curious but familiar hiatus that always preceded Ra's rising seemed intensified by the motionless assembly, line upon line of faces turned blankly towards the reviewing stand.

At Aahotep's small gesture Meketra's body was set down where all could see it. A tremor ran through the troops. Amunnakht came forward and bowed, Simontu with him. "Is everything ready?" Aahotep asked the Governor of the Prison. He nodded his assent. "Have the Princes and Nefer-Sakharu completed their prayers?"

"They have, Majesty," Simontu replied. "However, the Lady Nefer-Sakharu is so frantic as to be unmanageable. We have had to bring her here in a closed litter."

"I understand. Amun-nakht, have the prisoners brought forward and tethered, and then I will address the troops."

Aahmes-nefertari restrained an impulse to slap a hand over her heart. It had begun to drum against her ribs almost painfully and she marvelled at her mother's calm. Aahotep's painted features revealed nothing but a certain coldness. Aahmes-nefertari glanced sideways at her grandmother. Tetisheri's face was equally impassive under the many-braided wig. Do I look like that, the girl wondered, or is my agitation betrayed to the whole army? She put her hands behind her back and clenched her fists tightly until she felt her rings digging into her flesh.

A dismal cavalcade was approaching from the direction of Amun-nakht's quarters. At first Aahmes-nefertari could not see the Princes for the crowd of Medjay surrounding them, but as they drew closer and were forced to pass Meketra's obscene remains they came clearly into view. Both Intef and Iasen were naked but for a loincloth. Intef was shivering. Iasen appeared dazed, stumbling with unco-ordinated limbs over the ground. Aahmes-nefertari turned her head from them in shock, only to find her gaze alighting on Nefer-Sakharu. The woman was clad in a billowing unbelted blue sheath. Her feet were bare. She was supported between two Medjay, for it was obvious that terror had rendered her incapable of supporting herself. Behind them Hor-Aha led ten archers.

Three stakes had been erected in the centre of the arena. With a speed and efficiency that Aahmes-nefertari found appalling the three condemned were tied to the wood. Intef stood defiantly, his face to the lightening sky, but Iasen's chin sank onto his chest. Nefer-Sakharu simply sank to the earth until the thongs gripping her wrists would allow her to go no further. Then she began to scream. At a brusque word from Hor-Aha one of the Medjay escorts strode up to her and clamping a hand roughly over her mouth he attempted to muffle the noise, but Nefer-Sakharu would not be silenced. Biting and kicking she struggled, twisting this way and that, until with an oath born of exasperation the Medjay pulled out his knife and cut her throat.

Aahmes-nefertari cried out in horror. The man was wiping his weapon on the woman's sheath while her body still jerked and thrashed. Hor-Aha was at his side in an instant, his leather-clad fist drawn back. The sound of the blow was audible, and Intef began to laugh. "That was murder not execution," he yelled harshly. "Look at the savages on whom you have chosen to rely, Aahotep Tao. They are nothing but wild animals, every one of them, including Kamose's precious General. Two years of military discipline have not turned them into soldiers and wrapping them in kilts has not made them Egyptian. Underneath they will always be black beasts. And you would condemn us to death for refusing to place ourselves under the command of such as those? Kamose made them officers and hung them with gold but he could not make them human."

Aahmes-nefertari could not take her eyes away from the sight of Nefer-Sakharu's blood forming a dark pool. Amun help me, I will never forget this, her mind was clamouring, I will never be free of the horror of it, the brutal suddenness, the memory will stay vivid and soil me for the rest of my life.

Hor-Aha was cutting Nefer-Sakharu's body free of the stake and at his terse word the Medjay who had lost his temper was being picked up from where he had fallen and bound in her place. Whispers and murmurs had begun to run through the ranks of watching men and the tone had an ominous undercurrent of anger. "He is right, of course," Tetisheri said imperturbably. "They are indeed savages. But useful savages. It is a pity that Hor-Aha did not see that coming. It makes us look very bad in front of the army." Aahmes-nefertari stared at her unbelievingly and Aahotep rounded on her at once.

"Keep your conclusions to yourself, Tetisheri!" she demanded. "They are not for the ears of these Followers. You know how soldiers gossip. Now be silent or I will have your tongue removed." She stepped quickly to the edge of the dais, and Aahmes-nefertari saw her take a deep breath. "Men of Weset and all Egypt," she began, her voice ringing out clearly over their mutterings. "The condemned you see before you are about to die. Their crime is not a matter of refusing to serve under the direction of the General who has proved his loyalty to this country and his worth to both my husband and my sons in their fight to rid us all of the Setiu yoke. The validity of their sentence even now lies in the House of the Dead, and if they had succeeded in their treasonous intention there would be two bodies in the hands of the sem-priests. There has been no trial. The proof of their perfidy is in no doubt. I grieve for the disgrace they have brought upon their families but they have left me no choice. His Majesty trusted them and was betrayed and murdered. General, do your duty."

Hor-Aha signalled to his archers, already facing Intef, Iasen and the perverse Medjay. Unslinging their bows, they fitted the one arrow each had brought with them to the string, and in the small pause their actions afforded Aahmes-nefertari dragged her attention away from them to the desert beyond. At once the tightness in her chest let go and she felt her shoulders relax. There was a spurious peace in contemplating the quiet flush of pink along the irregular black line of the wide horizon and an illusion of normality, brief but sweet, in the cool, scentless breath that preceded the fiery birth of the god. It will be over soon, she told herself. Then the stakes will be uprooted and the soldiers dispersed and sand thrown on the blood and I can walk back through the garden to the early morning bustle of the house breathing free, breathing free . . .

Then Intef's voice rang out for the last time, echoing loudly and distinctly as the rim of Ra lifted above the world and his first rays lit the scene, sending long shadows stretching across the tumbled ground. "You will regret this," he called. "You are setting a dangerous precedent, Aahotep Tao. Your blood is no older or purer than ours. We are nobles and Princes of Egypt, and if nobles and Princes can be treated like common criminals, what message are you sending to common men? If we can die like jackals on your whim, they can be trodden underfoot like worms? Kamose was a vengeful murderer. Kamose . . ." Hor-Aha's raised arm came down. The Medjay bent their bows with the effortless skill for which they were famous and almost before Aahmes-nefertari could trace their flight the arrows had sunk into their targets.

A great sigh went up followed by a deep silence. Aahmes-nefertari found herself clutching a handful of her sheath and when she tried to let it go it stuck to her moist palm. Aahotep spoke once more into the warming air. "Some among you were tempted to follow those men into treason and dishonour," she said, and this time Aahmes-nefertari heard a quality of strain in the seemingly confident tones. "You also deserve punishment but it is the nature of soldiers to obey their superiors, therefore I look upon your brief defection with a certain indulgence. I will not do so again. The period of mourning for the King has begun and you are all forbidden to leave Weset until he goes to his tomb. That is all. Hor-Aha, dismiss them."

At once the officers began to bark orders and the ranks of sullen faces broke up. Aahotep beckoned to Amun-nakht. "Nefer-Sakharu is to be taken to the House of the Dead," she said, "but the three Princes must remain where they are until dawn tomorrow, so that the troops may reflect upon their fate. Then they are to be carried out into the desert and buried in the sand. Give the Medjay's corpse to his fellows for whatever funeral rituals they follow. Until the formal mourning for Kamose is over, the men may take exercise here but may not go further than the perimeter. Test the officers. Give them little responsibilities." She hesitated, then sent him away, and turning to the steps she left the dais. "What else can I do?" she murmured to Aahmes-nefertari as the Followers moved to surround them and they set off for the house. "It is all up to Ahmose now."

Nothing more was said until the three women stood together just within the entrance to their quarters. Then Tetisheri thrust herself close to Aahotep. "I will not be spoken to again in that insulting and humiliating manner!" she snarled. "Take care that you do not exceed the bounds of your authority again, Aahotep, for I command a pre-eminence that you will not inherit until I am dead." Aahotep had taken her daughter's arm on the long walk back to the house and several times she had almost stumbled. Aahmes-nefertari had become increasingly aware of the strain the morning's terrible proceedings had put on her mother. Now Aahotep was leaning against the door to her apartment, her face haggard.

"You deserved my reprimand, Tetisheri," she said wearily. "You spoke heedlessly from an arrogance that is not always tempered by wisdom. If we had all retreated into the wine jug as you did, it might have been Ahmose and Ahmose-onkh tied to the stakes out there and your vaunted pre-eminence would even now be dependent upon the doubtful goodwill of a couple of perfidious Princes who would probably have sent us to the river." She had used the euphemism for the dispossessed state of women made homeless by war and Tetisheri had the grace to flinch. "It is Aahmes-nefertari who has become pre-eminent, though you cannot see it yet," Aahotep went on. "I saved the life of her husband but her courage has saved Egypt itself. The power that was yours has passed to her, so be very careful what you say from now on. Go and eat something, both of you. I must rest." The door closed behind her and Aahmes-nefertari and Tetisheri stared at each other warily. Tetisheri drew herself up.

"She is exhausted," she said at last. "I forgive her her disrespectful words." Aahmes-nefertari quelled a sudden urge to burst out laughing. Taking the tiny body in her arms, she hugged her grandmother.

"I love you, Tetisheri," she choked. "You are as stubborn as a donkey and just as noisy when you begin to bray. I am going to the temple later to pray for Kamose. Come with me."

We can begin to mourn for him fully now, she thought as she let herself into Ahmose's room. The horror is behind us. Yet even as she reassured herself, her mind filled with the image of

Nefer-Sakharu sagging against the stake with blood spurting from her neck and the Medjay bending to calmly wipe his blade on her crumpled sheath.

Ahmose's body servant was washing his master and as she came up to the couch he paused to bow. The refreshing scent of mint filled the air and Aahmes-nefertari drew it appreciatively into her lungs before bending to kiss Ahmose's cheek. "The salve has been changed," she remarked. The servant nodded.

"The physician has already been this morning, Highness," he told her. "The wound is healing well and needs only honey on it. Also His Highness has begun to stir and he groans sometimes. The physician is very pleased. He says that His Highness's eyes may open at any moment."

"I will leave you to your ministrations and break my fast with the children," Aahmes-nefertari said. "I will come and sit with him later." She withdrew in relief. Much as she loved her husband, she found herself desperately needing the company of uncomplicated innocence.

She ate without appetite, played with Ahmose-onkh, held her baby, but as yet nothing would blunt the vision that sullied her ka. Only in the temple, standing beside an unrepentant Tetisheri while Amunmose sang for Kamose, did the memory lose some of its sharpness. It returned to pollute her evening meal and sour her wine, and later when she took Ahmose's hand in the way that was becoming a sad little habit, she found it interposed between his tranquil face and the words she wished to say to him. So she watched him silently, trying to pour all her concentration into a contemplation of the curve of his brown cheek, the pleasing fullness of his mouth, the flutter of his black eyelashes as he walked in whatever strange dreams filled his abused head.

Towards midnight, too tired to sleep, she wandered out into the moon-drenched garden and sat in the grass beside the dark mirror of the pool. But there for the first time the fear of the dead crept over her. Surely the shadows under the trees behind her were not empty. Nefer-Sakharu's white, malevolent face was peering out at her and Intef and Iasen were whispering together as they prowled closer to her defenceless spine.

She fought the dread with weapons newly acquired, confidence, courage and strength, and though the fear began to dissolve, she was still sure that she could hear ominous sounds. Faint calls seemed carried on the night air, faint splashes came from the direction of the river, and the undergrowth on the edge of the garden was alive with secret stirrings. I will not run, she said firmly to herself. There are night fishermen on the river, night animals going about their business in the shrubbery, guards pacing, it is the life of the dark hours and nothing more.

But her fragile equanimity deserted her and she scrambled to her feet with a cry as two vague shapes materialized out of the dimness and came inexorably towards her. "Aahmes-nefertari, I have been searching for you everywhere," her mother said breathlessly. "You must go back into the house at once where the Followers can watch over you. There is trouble in the barracks. The soldiers are deserting. They have killed Amunnakht and several others of our officers." The ghosts fled. Aahmes-nefertari looked from her mother to the worried face of Hor-Aha.

"I will go to the parade ground immediately," she said. "What of our own troops, General? Are they running away also?"

"Some of them, Highness," he replied hoarsely. "The Medjay under Prince Anhkmahor are attempting to restore order, but the deserters must not be allowed to get far. Such panic and disaffection will spread to every nome if we do not move at once to stop it."

"Why is this happening?" Aahmes-nefertari felt ready to panic herself.

"They do not trust my words," Aahotep said grimly. "They are afraid that the same fate the Princes met will be meted out to them when I have had time to reconsider the enormity of their blame. The fools! Now they will certainly die."

"What must I do?" Aahmes-nefertari asked, her mind already filling with things she could say to the men remaining, but her mother shook her head.

"Not this time," she said emphatically. "You must stay with your husband. You are not expendable, Aahmes-nefertari. You and Ahmose are Egypt's future. Hor-Aha and I will go together. Send a herald after Ramose. He must be told what is happening. Mesehti and Makhu must be coerced into providing forces to prevent the deserters from spreading north, even from reaching their homes at Qebt and Badari if possible. Hor-Aha will take the loyal soldiers that are left and pursue them from here."

"The herald can go by water," Hor-Aha put in. "The deserters will be disorganized on land and they will not dare to steal boats. I will send Ankhmahor to you with more guards for the house, Highness. Assign them where you see fit." He was obviously anxious to be gone.

"Is there a chance that some of them might attack us here?"

"No, I do not think so," Aahotep assured her, "but it is better to be prepared. Hurry, Aahmes-nefertari. And say nothing to your grandmother. Someone will bring you word later." She did not tarry and Aahmes-nefertari did not wait to see her and the General melt into the darkness. She ran towards the house, her fears forgotten. Reality had provided a far more dangerous threat.

Akhtoy was dozing on his stool outside Ahmose's room. He had insisted on taking up his station there during the night as well as by day while Ahmose remained unconscious and Aahmes-nefertari was never more grateful than when she saw him rise at her abrupt approach. "Akhtoy, go and fetch me a herald as quickly as you can," she ordered. "One that is able to carry a message in his head. There is no time to dictate to Ipi." The steward hurried away and the girl sank onto his stool. Amun, keep my mother safe, she prayed. Do not allow me to be left alone with a sick husband to protect and another rebellion to quash. It is already too much! But probing herself she discovered a steady constancy in her ka and her thoughts were clear.

When Akhtoy returned with a tousled and sleepy herald, she gave her instructions succinctly, and later, facing the twenty soldiers Hor-Aha had sent her, she helped Ankhmahor draw up the hours and positions of their watches without indecision. More than half of them were Medjay and Aahmes-nefertari was glad. She no longer trusted the men of her own nome.

Before settling herself beside Ahmose, she toured the house. All was quiet. The children and Raa slept peacefully and she could hear Tetisheri snoring through her closed door. Reception rooms and offices, bath house and apartments, greeted her intrusion with mute, empty familiarity. Reassured, she made her way back to Ahmose. Akhtoy had resumed his seat, and bidding him not to rise and telling him swiftly what had befallen, she was at last free to walk through the friendly lamplight to her perch beside the couch.

She knew instantly that he was awake. It was in the slight tension of his body, the dawning of a faint intelligence on his face. "Ahmose," she called softly, leaning over him. "Ahmose. You have come back to me. Can you open your eyes?" She saw his cracked lips move. His tongue appeared and his eyelids fluttered. Snatching up a cup of water, she held it to his mouth, lifting his head, but he winced and drew away, so she dipped a piece of clean linen into it and pressed it gently between his teeth. He sucked at it greedily.

"I tried to open them before," he whispered brokenly, "but

the light hurt too much. My head aches intolerably, Aahmes-nefertari. What has happened to me?" He was trying to touch his skull. Aahmes-nefertari caught his hand and pressed it back onto the sheet.

"You have had an accident, dearest," she began, not wanting to tell him the truth for fear the shock might send him back into the shadow world but also admitting to herself that she shrank from the things he must eventually know. He frowned and winced again.

"An accident? I remember holding up my fish for Kamose to see. I remember him running towards me. I saw Meketra, and there were soldiers coming out of the garden." He was becoming agitated. His fingers tightened around hers. "Did I fall, Aahmes-nefertari? Is that it?" She began to stroke his brow, hoping that her hand did not tremble.

"Hush, Ahmose," she soothed him. "You have stitches in your scalp. You must not dislodge them. I am so happy to see you awake, but now you need proper sleep. I want to go to the door and ask Akhtoy to bring the physician. Would that be all right?" He did not reply and she saw that he had lost consciousness. Hurrying out into the passage, she spoke briefly to the steward, then returned in trepidation to the couch. Ahmose was breathing deeply and evenly and he had been cool to her touch. When the physician arrived, he confirmed her conviction that he was now sleeping normally.

"Have him carefully watched, Highness," the man reminded her. "Let him drink water if he needs it, but no food yet. I will make an infusion of poppy for his pain." He smiled. "Now it is simply a matter of time for his healing."

But we may not have time, any of us, she thought as the door closed behind him. Mother has been gone for too long. She said that she would send me word and I cannot leave Ahmose to go to the training ground. Nor do I dare ask

Ankhmahor to go. I need to know that he at least is here, standing between us and the dark.

She was unaware of the dawn until Akhtoy and Ahmose's body servant came in, the latter with hot water. Akhtoy snuffed the lamp and rolled up the window hangings. Pale early light flooded the room, and Ahmose stirred and sighed. "Your mother has just returned," Akhtoy said to Aahmes-nefertari in a low voice. "She met us as we were approaching this door. She is too fatigued to greet you, Highness, but I am to tell you that General Hor-Aha has taken a thousand soldiers after the deserters and the men who are left are burying bodies. There was a skirmish on the parade ground but all is now under control."

"If Hor-Aha has gone, then who is in command out there, Akhtoy?"

"The Lady Aahotep is acting Commander, Highness. I gather that the General has left her in charge." A pang of pure jealousy shook Aahmes-nefertari. Once again I am relegated to the house while greater deeds are accomplished without me, she thought bitterly, then laughed at her pettiness. I am here with Ahmose and he will get better and that is all that matters.

"Put the water down," she instructed the body servant. "I will wash him myself this morning. Akhtoy, have fruit and bread brought to me for I am suddenly starving."

At the first brush of the warm linen against his skin Ahmose opened his eyes. He lay watching her as she lightly and methodically bathed him and when she had finished and offered him water he drank it eagerly. "I was dreaming that I sat by the pool and a dwarf came striding along the path towards me," he said as she laid his head back on the pillow. His voice was thready but stronger. "He was dressed all in military garb, leather and bronze, and I was afraid of him. It is a bad omen, Aahmes-nefertari. It means that half my life will be severed. I would like to speak to Kamose after he has eaten. Or has he gone north without me?" She was saved from answering by a knock on the door. It was Akhtoy with her meal and a small alabaster vial. Setting both on the table, the steward bowed.

"I am very happy to see your Highness has returned to us," he said to Ahmose. "The physician has provided poppy for your Highness's comfort should you need it."

"What are you doing here, Akhtoy?" Ahmose asked sharply. "Why are you not with Kamose? Has he appointed a new steward? How long have I been lying here unconscious?" Akhtoy and Aahmes-nefertari exchanged glances and the steward drew away. "What are you hiding?" Ahmose demanded. His tone had become fretful. "Give me some of the poppy, Aahmes-nefertari. My head hurts abominably. And then you can tell me exactly what has been going on." Aahmes-nefertari gestured and Akhtoy left the room. Pouring a few drops of the milky white liquid into some water, she held it to Ahmose's mouth. He took it all and presently his eyelids began to droop. "Tell me later," he murmured. "The pain is easing and I cannot stay awake." It was with a weak relief that Aahmes-nefertari saw him fall into the sudden sleep of the convalescent.

She had a pallet brought into his room so that he would see her each time he woke, and lying on it she too fell asleep. Akhtoy roused her later and she was amazed to see that she had slept the whole day away. Ra was about to enter the mouth of Nut and his dying light filled the air with a diffused scarlet glow. Ahmose slumbered on. "Your mother is outside," Akhtoy told her. "She wishes to speak with you. I will sit with His Highness."

Aahotep was talking to the guard on the door when Aahmes-nefertari emerged. She turned to her daughter with a smile. "I hear that Ahmose is awake," she said. "That is wonderful news. I wanted to tell you in person, Aahmes-nefertari, that we are safe for the moment. It will be some time before messages arrive from Hor-Aha and Ramose but I believe that the worst is over." Aahmes-nefertari looked at her curiously. Her voice was slightly hoarse. A wide graze ran from below her ear to disappear beneath the neckline of her sheath and the palms of her hands were raw. Seeing her scrutiny, Aahotep's smile grew broader. "I cannot say that they are battle scars," she admitted. "When Hor-Aha and I arrived at the training ground, Ankhmahor was already hotly engaged in the fight that had broken out between the men who were trying to leave and the soldiers whom Ankhmahor had rallied. Hor-Aha ran to take his place. Ankhmahor was attempting to extricate himself so that he could defend me but it took him some time." She lifted her wounded hands ruefully. "I remained standing too close to the conflict. It was brutal and appalling, Aahmes-nefertari, but strangely compelling also. I could not move. Not until it suddenly swung my way and I found myself in the path of a spear. I threw myself to the earth and fell awkwardly, then I rolled beneath the reviewing stand and there I stayed. Not a dignified position for Egyptian royalty. Your father would have been dismayed." She paused to clear her throat, which she did with difficulty. "There was much shouting and cursing," she went on. "I was not aware that I too was yelling until Ankhmahor appeared and pulled me from my hiding place. We stood together and watched the end." She grimaced. "It was an experience I trust I will not be forced to repeat. I think that from now on I will be more grateful for the small tasks a woman is required to perform in her own house." Aahmes-nefertari stared at her.

"But, Mother, I always presumed that you were content," she said. Aahotep shrugged.

"I was. I am. But I have discovered that even a citizen of the city of the moon, if she lives long enough with hot-blooded southerners, will find a little of that fire running through her veins. I am on my way to the temple now. I feel the need to purify myself of Meketra's blood. The rage has gone, Aahmes-nefertari, and sadness for Kamose is taking its place. Give Ahmose my love and tell him that I will visit him tomorrow."

Nothing can surprise me any more, Aahmes-nefertari thought as she returned to Ahmose's room, now filling with evening shadows. I gaze into my copper mirror and no longer recognize the woman who gazes back at me. I meet my mother's eyes and see a stranger. How unpredictable our lives have become! Our very cores have been melted in the heat of suffering and necessity, only to be poured into new moulds whose shapes will define a future that is still hidden from us.

Her reverie was interrupted by Ahmose's voice and she found that she had been standing motionless in front of the uncovered window. "Please light the lamp, Aahmes-nefertari," he said. "My head feels easier. It does not throb as much and my eyes are not paining me any more." She did as he wished, trimming the wick on the pretty alabaster lamp and moving to lower the window hangings.

"Would you like more poppy?" she asked him, half-hoping that he might drink and then sleep again so that she could defer the awful necessity of her news but he waved a hand dismissively and she knew that the time had come.

"No," he said. "I want to see Kamose. Bring him to me if he is still here and if he is not, then I must read his dispatches." Aahmes-nefertari lowered herself onto the stool beside him.

"He cannot come, dearest," she began hesitantly. "He is dead. He was killed as he ran towards you. He was trying to warn you that the Princes had rebelled and your life was in danger but an arrow found him instead. He died in your arms. Can you try to remember that?" He had been lying on his side, his eyes fixed intently on her, and as she spoke she saw his face change. It was as though something inside him was sucking the flesh towards itself, leaving him all pallid skin over jutting bones. The hand that had been resting on his naked chest now crept towards the sheet and clenched it tightly. He rolled onto his back.

"Gods," he whispered. "No. I can feel the string holding the fish. I see him rushing along the path. I see Meketra. I see . . . I see . . ." He was visibly struggling to recall everything and Aahmes-nefertari watched him, numb with misery. "I see, I feel something in my arms, heavy, it is a big fish . . . No, it is too heavy for a fish. I feel stones under me. I am kneeling, yes." His hands came up to cover his face. "I cannot remember, Aahmes-nefertari!"

"It will come back to you," she said urgently. "Do not try to make it come. Your wound was grievous. Meketra clubbed you as you held Kamose. The blow would have killed you if Mother had not managed to deflect it. She stabbed him twice." His fingers had returned to the sheet, kneading it in a slow, intense rhythm.

"Mother? Aahotep? She killed Meketra? With a knife?"

"She did. There is so much more, Ahmose. Try to be calm while I tell you."

Long before she had finished her account of all that had happened he had begun to cry silently, saturating his pillow. She did not interfere with his grief until she too fell silent. Then she wiped his face, took both his hands in hers, and laying her head on his stomach she closed her eyes.

Much later she felt him begin to stroke her hair, and at the sweetly familiar touch she herself came close to tears. "All this while I lay helpless," he said. "Helpless and useless and even now I am unable to sit up for the pain it causes me. Forgive me, my dear one, for leaving you alone to face the army, for causing you to stand against a situation no woman should have to confront."

"Don't be foolish," she chided him. "What choice did you, did any of us, have? I am not just any woman, I am a Tao. So is Mother, by marriage and by her own stubbornness. We did well and we are proud of it. Hor-Aha and Ramose will round up the deserters. It is over, Ahmose. Do not begin to worry or your recovery will be hampered." She sat up, pushing her tangled hair out of her eyes, but he did not release his hold on her.

"You have heard nothing from either of them," he said. "We can presume nothing until we do."

"It is too soon for any dispatches," Aahmes-nefertari reminded him. "But we are safe for the present. Ankhmahor is still here."

"I will want to see him, but not today," he mused. "In a moment I will take more poppy, for my head has begun to pound. Tell me what you think of Mesehti and Makhu. They withdrew their troops and ran. Does it mean that they can still be trusted?"

She answered him in the same vein, aware that in discussing practical matters he was delaying the moment when he must begin to accept his brother's death. The dam of denial was still firmly in place, holding back the flood of grief, guilt and remorse she knew must eventually come, but for now it was necessary for his sanity that they speak of other things and she was thankful.

From then on his recovery was slow but sure. The physician removed his stitches and his hair began to grow back around the scar that he would carry for the rest of his life. He began to take a little nourishment. But Aahmes-nefertari, who had temporarily abandoned all responsibilities that might take her beyond the confines of his room, would often wake to the sound of his crying in the night and lie rigid on her pallet while he wept out his agony. She had Akhtoy bring the children to him and holding Hent-ta-Hent seemed to comfort him.

Aahotep was a frequent visitor. He had thanked her for saving his life in his own simple, straightforward way but he wished for no more details of that day and Aahotep with her usual sensitivity did not supply them. Tetisheri also came, but there were strained silences between them that often stretched into minutes before one or the other of them offered some trite morsel of polite conversation. "She wishes that I were dead instead of Kamose," Ahmose remarked to Aahmes-nefertari, "and she is gracious enough to feel guilty because of it. I pity her." To that, Aahmes-nefertari could make no reply.

Soon he was able to sit for a while beside his couch and then to walk unsteadily about the room. His appetite had returned, and on the morning when he cleared his plate and asked for more Aahmes-nefertari clapped her hands delightedly. "You will soon be out on the river, fishing again," she said, but his face darkened.

"I do not think that I will either catch or eat fish any more," he replied sadly. "I could not do so without missing Kamose. Besides, when we lay him in his tomb I will be King, and Kings are forbidden to eat fish. It is an offence against Hapi."

"I think that while you are still only a Prince, the God of the Nile would be pleased that you so loved his domain," she objected. "And surely Kamose would be saddened if you abandoned something that always brought you so much joy." But he shook his head and did not respond.

At last he was strong enough to be dressed and venture out into the garden, followed by an excited crowd of servants bearing cushions, a sunshade, fly whisk, pastries and his sandal box. He stood outside the main entrance for a while, blinking in the bright sunlight, then he moved slowly over the grass towards the pond. Crossing the path to the watersteps, he paused and glanced down. "This is where I cradled him, and this is where he died," he said quietly. "I have remembered, Aahmes-nefertari. Remembered all of it. May I never forget." Then he lifted his face to the sky, inhaled the perfume from the banks of spring flowers in bloom, and continued on.

They had only been settled a short time by the pool when Aahotep came hurrying towards them, two scrolls in her hand. "Messages from Hor-Aha and Ramose!" she exclaimed. "It is over, all of it! The rebellion is utterly finished. Hor-Aha tells us that although he was forced to execute the officers who betrayed us a second time, he is bringing the soldiers back. There is no fight left in them. Ramose, Mesehti and Makhu will arrive together and together they have been hunting the remnants of the deserters from Intef and Iasen's nomes. Will you pardon their cowardice, Ahmose?" He held out a hand on which his rings once again glinted.

"That depends on how they seem when they stand before me," he replied. "We have learned a hard lesson, Aahotep. Perhaps it is time for reorganization and I think I will begin with the army. I intend to march north as soon as the period of mourning is over, but I will not make the mistakes that drove Kamose to his ruin."

His glance strayed to the pond where a naked Ahmose-onkh sat on the verge kicking up sheets of spray and gurgling with laughter. "It is now the middle of Mekhir. The fields are being sown and I have seeds of my own to strew all over the Delta." He looked speculatively from his mother to his wife. "I have no qualms in leaving Weset to my two warriors," he smiled. "And I swear to both of you that in return for what you have done I will lay a united Egypt at your feet. Give the scrolls to Ipi, Mother, and come in under the sunshade. Today we will talk of nothing but the dragonflies hunting the mosquitoes and the sun on the water."

Aahmes-nefertari found herself studying him curiously. He was the same and yet not the same, her beloved husband, still mild and deliberate in his words and gestures, but the air of vague simplicity that had caused so many to misread him had gone. He has been transmuted like the rest of us, she thought rather sadly. He was struck down a Prince, and he has risen up a King.

# *Select* BIBLIOGRAPHY

## BOOKS

Aldred, Cyril. *Jewels of the Pharaohs: Egyptian Jewelry of the Dynastic Period*. rev. ed. London: Thames and Hudson Ltd. 1978.

Aldred, Cyril. *The Egyptians*. rev. ed. London: Thames and Hudson, 1987.

Baikie, James. *A History of Egypt: From the Earliest Times to the End of the* XVIII *Dynasty*. Vol 1 and 2. Freeport, New York: Books for Libraries Press, 1971.

Baines, John, and Jaromir Malek. *Atlas of Ancient Egypt*. New York: Facts on File, 1987.

Bietak, Manfred. *Avaris, the Capital of the Hyksos: Recent Excavations at Tell el-Daba*. London: British Museum Press, 1996.

Breasted, James H. *A History of Egypt: From the Earliest Times to the Persian Conquest*. New York: Charles Scribner's Sons, 1905.

Breasted, James H. *Ancient Records of Egypt*. Vol. 2 and 4. London: Histories & Mysteries of Man Ltd., 1988.

Bryan, Cyril P. *Ancient Egyptian Medicine: The Papyrus Ebers*. Chicago: Ares Publishers Inc., 1930.

Budge, Wallace E.A. *A History of Egypt: from the End of the Neolithic Period to the Death of Cleopatra* VII. *B.C. 30*. Vol. 3, *Egypt under the Amenemhats and Hyksos*. Oosterhout: Anthropological Publications, 1968.

Budge, Wallace E.A. *An Egyptian Hieroglyphic Dictionary.* Vol 1 and 2. rev. ed. New York: Dover Publications, Inc., 1978.

Budge, Wallace E.A. *Egyptian Magic.* London: Routledge & Kegan Paul, 1986.

Budge, Wallace E.A. *Legends of the Egyptian Gods: Hieroglyphic Texts and Translations.* New York: Dover Publications, Inc., 1994.

Budge, Wallace E.A. *The Mummy: A Handbook of Egyptian Funerary Archaeology.* New York: Dover Publications, Inc., 1989.

Cottrell, Leonard. *The Warrior Pharaohs.* New York: G.P. Putnam's Sons, 1969.

David, Rosalie. *Mysteries of the Mummies: The Story of the Manchester University Investigation.* London: Book Club Associates, 1979.

Davidovits, Joseph, and Margie Morris. *The Pyramids: an Enigma Solved.* New York: Dorset Press, 1988.

Gardiner, Sir Alan. *Egypt of the Pharaohs.* Oxford: Oxford University Press, 1964.

James, T.G.H. *Excavating in Egypt: The Egypt Exploration Society 1882-1982.* London: British Museum Publications Limited, 1982.

Mertz, Barbara. *Temples, Tombs & Hieroglyphs: A Popular History of Ancient Egypt.* rev. ed. New York: Peter Bedrick Books, 1990.

Murnane, William J. *Guide to Ancient Egypt.* New York: Penguin Books, 1983.

Murray, Margaret A. *Egyptian Religious Poetry.* Westport: Greenwood Press Publishers, 1980.

Murray, Margaret A. *The Splendour that was Egypt.* rev. ed. London: Sidgwick & Jackson, 1972.

Nagel's Encyclopedia-Guide. *Egypt.* Geneva: Nagel Publishers, 1985.

Newberry, Percy Edward. *Ancient Egyptian Scarabs: An Introduction to Egyptian Seals and Signet Rings.* Chicago: Ares, 1979.

Newby, Percy Howard. *Warrior Pharaohs: The Rise and Fall of the Egyptian Empire.* London, Boston: Faber and Faber, 1980.

Porter, Bertha, and Rosalind L.B. Moss. *Topographical Bibliography of Ancient Egyptian Hieroglyphic Texts, Reliefs, and Paintings.* Vol. VII,

Nubia, The Deserts and Outside Egypt. Oxford: Griffith Institute Ashmolean Museum, 1995.

Richardson, Dan. Egypt: The Rough Guide. London: Penguin Books, 1996.

Shaw, Ian, and Paul Nicholson. The Dictionary of Ancient Egypt. London: Harry N. Abrams, Inc., 1995.

Spalinger, Anthony J. Aspects of the Military Documents of the Ancient Egyptians. London: Yale University Press, 1982.

Watson, Philip J. Costumes of Ancient Egypt. New York: Chelsea House Publishers, 1987.

Wilson, Ian. The Exodus Enigma. London: Guild Publishing, 1986.

University Museum Handbooks. The Egyptian Mummy Secrets and Science. Pennsylvania: University of Pennsylvania, 1980.

### ATLASES

Oxford Bible Atlas. 2nd ed. London; New York: Oxford University Press, 1974.

The Harper Atlas of the Bible. Edited by James A. Pritchard. Toronto: Fitzhenry and Whiteside, 1987.

The Cambridge Atlas of the Middle East and North Africa. Cambridge, U.K.: Cambridge University Press, 1987.

### JOURNALS

K.M.T. a Modern Journal of Ancient Egypt. San Francisco.
  Volume 5, number 1, Hyksos Symposium at the Metropolitan Museum.
  Volume 5, number 2, Amunhotep I, Last King of the 17th Dynasty?
  Volume 5, number 3, Decline of the Royal Pyramid.
  Volume 6, number 2, Buhen: Blueprint of an Egyptian Fortress.